Praise for *Champion of the World*

"And if you've read as many disappointing books set in sports as I have you would understand my excitement at finding the real thing."
—NPR's *Only a Game*

"A fine, intelligent, and complex novel featuring the unlikely comeback tale of a wrestler named Pepper Van Dean set in the days when wrestling wasn't scripted." —*The Boston Globe* (Best Books of 2016)

"With crisp, muscular prose, this 470-page historical novel illuminates a time of rapid change in America." —*Poets & Writers*

"A terrific debut novel from Chad Dundas, is about professional wrestling in the early 1920s, when the sport wasn't unabashedly fake the way it is today . . . [Dundas] writes exciting action sequences. But his real gift is in making 1920s America and the people who populate it come vibrantly alive. In his hands, *Champion of the World* is an extraordinary trip through time to a culture very different from our own—never does it feel like a dry history textbook."
—*Fort Worth Star-Telegram*

"At first glance, *Champion of the World* is a novel about wrestling in the 1920s. But what's that saying about the tip of the iceberg?"
—*The Oregonian*

"A riveting novel about hardheaded men, tough women, and even tougher times in Prohibition America. It's difficult to believe Chad Dundas's *Champion of the World* is a debut novel—so fluid is its plot movement, so sure the narrative . . . Slyly ambitious . . . One of the most wonderfully controlled displays of storytelling by a new author in recent memory." —*O, The Oprah Magazine*

CHAMPION

of

THE WORLD

Chad Dundas

G. P. PUTNAM'S SONS

NEW YORK

PUTNAM
— EST. 1838 —
G. P. Putnam's Sons
Publishers Since 1838
An imprint of Penguin Random House LLC
penguinrandomhouse.com

First G. P. Putnam's Sons hardcover edition / July 2016
First G. P. Putnam's Sons trade paperback edition / December 2019
G. P. Putnam's Sons trade paperback edition ISBN: 9780399573804

Printed in the United States of America
1   3   5   7   9   10   8   6   4   2

BOOK DESIGN BY AMANDA DEWEY

For Courtney, Bea and Fritz

Part I

★

MASTER OF THE HANGMAN'S DROP

T he clowns came to get him when it was time for the hanging. He met them outside his trailer; a half dozen of them all dressed like cops, looking soiled and road-weary in their baggy blue uniforms, soda siphons hanging from their belts instead of guns and cuffs. No one spoke as they walked him down to the gallows, moving through the narrow alleys between the powerhouse trucks, costume tents and animal cages, heading for the spot on the infield grass where the white tops of the carnival's seven performance pavilions lifted like billowing clouds. With ten minutes left before intermission a few of the candy butchers had already returned their covered pushcarts to the backyard area. They stood leaning against them, smoking cigarettes in orange and white coveralls, bored expressions on their faces. At the back door of the big tent he stopped to bounce a minute on his toes, a light dappling of rain blowing in off the bay, pricking up goose pimples on his bare arms and legs.

One of the clowns made a sour face. "You all right?" His lipstick smile almost touching the corners of his eyes. "You're looking a little chunky."

He ignored it, but the truth was, he was overweight. The night before, the ache in his bad leg had kept him up, and after the two-and-a-half-hour jump from Monterey to San Francisco, he snuck down to the pie car and ate three pickles wrapped in ham. The pickles tasted good but didn't fill him up, so he had a square of apple cobbler for dessert. He shouldn't have done that, and in the morning forced himself to vomit before spending an hour jogging around the backyard area in a heavy overcoat. Now, as he stood there surrounded by the clowns, his belly was empty, and cold fear gripped his heart. He hoped he wasn't about to go out there and break his goddamn neck.

Through a slit in the curtain he could see the horse opera was almost over. For nearly ninety minutes the sparse crowd in the infield bleachers had cheered the evening performance of the Markham & Markham Overland Carnival. They'd seen clowns and contortionists, trapeze artists and tightropers, a hypnotist, a strongman and a guy in a top hat who built a pyramid out of dogs. Now, as the Fabulous Texas Trick Riders of the Loose Deuce Ranch urged their mounts over a series of jumps for the big finale, people squirmed in their seats. Handkerchiefs were pressed to brows, a low murmur of bored chitchat meandering through the stands as fathers pulled out their watches and younger guys passed bottles on the sly.

The carnival's horn players trumpeted the trick riders' closing number and the horses blew past him in a dusty stampede of sequins, silk and fringed buckskin. He closed his eyes against the grit, letting the breeze ripple his cape, savoring the smell of the rain and the clean, lush scent of ball field grass.

Pepper Van Dean had no great love for stick and ball games. During his time as lightweight wrestling champion of the world he'd met his share of ballplayers and found most of them to be soft, shiftless men. Now, as he stood there waiting to go out to be hanged, he suddenly felt a stab of envy, knowing some of those guys made five thousand dollars a year playing a child's game. What a life it must be, he thought, to spend your afternoons chasing a ball around the lawn, consenting to play only if the weather suited you. For years his brand of chewing tobacco had featured a picture of Ty Cobb under the lid. He wondered how much a guy got paid for something like that. Moira would probably know.

"I should've been a ballplayer," he said quietly, his eyes still closed, his toes wiggling inside his soft black boots.

"Shit," the clown spat. "You and me both, asshole."

When he finally looked, the stadium had gone quiet and a pair of stagehands in black executioner's hoods were wheeling the towering gallows frame to the center of the tent. Once it was in place, Boyd Markham himself strolled out and posed in the hot island of a spotlight. Markham was a heavy man with a rolling wave of silver hair, and he wore his signature blood red carnation pinned to the lapel of a slippery tuxedo. Underneath, the silver of his silk brocade vest exactly matched his immaculate bow tie. He pressed his mouth close to a freestanding microphone, filling the tent with a hushed reverence, the audience leaning forward to hear his words over the distant hum of the powerhouse trucks.

"Those of you familiar with physical culture may think you know this next act," he said. "Those of you who are mere neophytes have no doubt still heard rumors of it, as its reputation precedes it throughout the civilized world. Indeed, a version of this daring deed has been attempted by a number of other performers with other, lesser traveling shows, sometimes with disastrous consequences."

A nervous titter moved through the crowd, but the ringmaster silenced it by bringing his voice up a notch. "Martin Burns!" he said, and the name drew some scattered applause. "Rabbit Farnum! You may even recall headlines announcing the tragic death of the strongman Enoch Hughes, who lost his life attempting a similar gambit some years ago. Indeed, this courageous feat of athletic prowess has been tried by other men in other towns. Unfortunately it is my duty to inform you that most of these men are no more than charlatans, and their various renditions of the performance required little more than simple sleight of hand. Tonight, ladies and gentlemen, you will see no gimmicks, no tricks, no illusionist's hoax. Simply put, what you are about to observe here this evening inside this humble cathedral of athletic performance will be the most amazing display of raw strength and boundless endurance that you will see in all your lives. Why? Because we believe you deserve nothing less than the best right here"—a pause—"in the great city of San Francisco!"

He basked for a moment in the cheers, the patient politician waiting out the adoring masses, smiling and nodding while the crowd revved itself up.

"As your humble chaperone this evening it is my duty to inform you that what comes next is not for the weak of stomach or faint of heart. Those who are easily disturbed or have small children in attendance may want to excuse yourselves to the midway, or to our splendid gaming and merchandise pavilions. Those of you who choose to remain will no doubt stand witness to something that will stay with you throughout all your years. I assure you, it has had a similar effect on me."

He shielded his eyes from the spot and peered into the crowd, where no one was making for the exits. "Very well," he said, nodding to someone in the wings. Another spotlight faded up at stage left, revealing the quartet of horn players standing beneath a banner that read "Master of the Hangman's Drop!" in three-foot purple script.

"Enough preamble," the ringmaster said. "Please join me in welcoming the indestructible, unkillable man himself! The former lightweight wrestling champion of the world! Ladies and gentlemen, clap your hands for the master of the hangman's drop! The immortal Pepper Van Dean!"

The horn players blasted out a *Ta-da!* as the clowns pulled back the curtain. They all walked out together, blinded for a moment by the heat and light. The polite applause turned to cheers as Pepper suddenly burst free of the clowns, sending them toppling in a heap, and jogged around the ring, raising a hand to wave at everyone and no one. As he came to the front he whipped off his cape and gave them all a good look at him in just his boots and wrestling tights.

He was a small man, all bone and gristle, his legs a little too short, his arms a little too long. His neck was so thick and powerful that it seemed to swallow up his shoulders. Cords of muscle rippled in it as he turned his head one way, then the other. Without warning, he spun and bent backward, balancing like a crab on the crown of his head, rolling and stretching his neck from side to side before kipping up to his feet.

One of the stagehands came forward with a pair of handcuffs, holding them up for all to see, drawing the appropriate oohs and aahs as he jerked Pepper's arms behind his back and led him around to the gallows. Once they'd climbed the steps to the platform, Boyd Markham strolled over, silver hair and dark suit shining, microphone now cupped in his hand. "Mr. Van Dean," he said. "Any final words?"

"Well," Pepper said, voice cracking so badly he had to clear his throat and begin again. "Well, I'd just like to say"—taking some time to think it over—"God bless America. I hope everyone had a great Fourth of July, and if I don't see you, have a good Thanksgiving, a merry Christmas and a happy New Year, too."

Some chuckles from the crowd.

"Is that *all*?" Markham asked, a tease in his voice.

Pepper swallowed hard. "Anybody got a drink?"

It was late August 1921, and Prohibition jokes killed. One of the stagehands produced another black hood from his pocket and tugged it over Pepper's head—his world suddenly flushed into darkness—before dragging him back a few steps to the middle of the platform. His feet stumbling and scraping across the wood. Inside the hood, it smelled like mildew and old sweat. Though he couldn't see, he knew by heart what happened next. The stagehands stood him on his mark and slipped the noose, fat and deadly, over his head. Two more men in executioner's hoods brought torches out from the back and planted them in the dirt on either side of the gallows. The spotlights dimmed and the torches bathed them all in a pale glow.

"Enough pretense," Markham announced. "Shall we put this man out of his misery?" The crowd cheered. "Okay, boys," he said to the stagehands. "Let's do it."

Pepper sucked in a gulp of air and held it, pinching his eyes shut. He couldn't hear the crowd or the rumble of the powerhouse trucks or the crackle of the torches. Just his own breathing inside the hood. Footsteps moved across the platform as the stagehands approached a large red lever at one side of the gallows. He drew himself up as straight as he could, locking the muscles in his neck, back and shoulders, imagining Markham raising a hand to shoulder level, holding the crowd's attention like Caesar deciding the fate of a defeated gladiator. Long moments now, and he cleared his mind, thinking only, as he always did, of Moira's face just as Markham chopped his hand downward with a dramatic twist.

The stagehands pulled the lever and the trapdoor fell out from under him. He dropped like a shot, three feet, and jerked stiff, the tent quiet except for the clatter of the trapdoor and snap of the rope. The horn players blasted another triumphant *Ta-da!* but Pepper didn't move. A few moments of murmured confusion passed, and then the players tooted it again. *Ta-da!* Nothing. His body just hung there, still.

Whispers spread through the audience as the stagehands ran down the steps and under the platform. Markham jogged over. "What the hell is going on?" he demanded.

Another group of stagehands sprinted out carrying a stretcher, trailed by a man in a white doctor's coat, a black bag in his hand. Markham leapt up and tore off Pepper's hood, revealing his pallid, frozen face. A horrified gasp echoed through the stadium. Parents covered their children's eyes. Men grumbled to each other, not sure if they should get up and leave. Then the stage lights winked out, leaving only the rippling torches.

Somewhere far off, an elephant trumpeted.

In the dark, a woman screamed.

The longshoreman was dressed for an evening on the town, in a leather vest emblazoned with the seal of his union chapter and a silver bear claw belt buckle holding up herringbone slacks. His red hair hung loose to his shoulders, and the single gold tooth in his mouth glinted under the lights each time he won a hand of five-card poker. With the big clock in the gaming pavilion creeping up on half past seven, Moira Van Dean folded a pair of kings and let him take down a lukewarm pot with the tens she knew he had hidden. As he raked another stack of chips into his lap, the longshoreman blew her a kiss.

Some men just didn't know how to win without making a spectacle of themselves.

For the first half of her shift, she had managed to make nice, letting the longshoreman win hand after hand without so much as a knowing laugh or an *Oh, I do declare*. This, though, was too much. As the next hand began, she showed him the honest, square-john grin she knew was best for taking people's money, and he looked back like he wanted to sink his teeth into her.

"Now the little lady is ready to play cards," he announced, as if they were all about to watch a monkey try to tie its shoes.

The rest of the sleepy-eyed drunks slouching around the table chuckled along with him, each of them watching her with the usual mix of boredom and animal lust. She wasn't fooling anyone. In her apricot evening gown and beaded amber necklace, they knew she was the carnival shill. They all thought she was there to keep them company and to see that the carnival got its five percent rake out of every pot. In truth, her job was more about making sure the action at the table didn't lag, that chips moved from one side of the table to the other at a brisk pace, and that they all continued ordering the watered-down highballs the carnival sold in paper soft drink cups for fifty cents apiece.

Any money she collected went back to the carnival's kitty, so her job was also to win a few hands from time to time—just not so many that it disrupted the game or the men gave up. In addition, she was there to cut any company losses, to make sure nobody won too much money. If one of these dockworkers and two-bit grinders proved sharp enough to put together a big stack of chips, Moira was tasked with winning some of it back. It was not challenging work. Once the evening performance got under way across the carnival lot, only the worst men remained inside the gaming pavilion. It would take a team of plow horses to drag any of them away before all their money was gone.

Gaming pavilion was what employees of the Markham & Markham Overland Carnival were required to call it, though it was really just a weathered twenty-by-twenty canvas tent battened by yellowing sidewalls and domed in the middle with a thick wooden stake. It smelled of damp wool and trampled grass, the ground cold under her open-toed shoes. Electric lights were set up on poles in all four corners, and under the clamor of the men drinking and writhing and giving away their savings, you could hear them buzzing.

The game was standard stud poker. Each player got five cards—

three up, two down—with a series of betting rounds between. By the time the dealer got three cards into the next hand, most of the men at the table had folded, leaving just Moira and the longshoreman to play heads-up. The dealer flopped the longshoreman a jack of clubs as his fourth card, and when he bet on it like a bull charging for a matador's cape, Moira fought down a smirk. One look at the longshoreman's drunken, bloodshot eyes told her he had a hand he liked. She signaled the dealer by putting both her elbows on the table and the dealer gave her the high sign to fold, idly touching the knot of his necktie with the tips of his fingers. Before she made a move, she chewed a fingernail and let her eyes stray nervously around the table, wanting the men to think she was uncertain. Finally, painfully, with her head tipped slightly to one side and her mouth pinched in a regretful scowl, she pushed in her cards.

"Fold," she said.

The longshoreman made a clucking sound with his tongue and swept up another meager pot. "Cowardly," he said.

She bit her lip. She wanted to tell him she knew he was holding at least one more jack, that he had her pair of fours beat all to hell, but instead she just frowned into her lap. The longshoreman flipped his cards to show off three of a kind, and she clamped her hand over her mouth, wide-eyed, hamming it up. The men shifted in their seats, embarrassed for her, and as the dealer began to shuffle again they busied themselves counting their chips, congratulating the longshoreman with the looks of men who believed it should have been them.

"For your trouble," the longshoreman said, plucking a twenty-five-cent chip from his stack and flicking it across the felt at her.

When she explained to him she was not allowed to take tips from players, the longshoreman sneered. "Take it as a loan," he said, letting the chip lie. "When I bust you, maybe we can work out some form of repayment."

Right then, she should've taken her chips and walked away. She could've let one of the other girls take over the poker table and switched to dice or even blackjack. It would've been the smart move, but sometimes the card player in her got the better of her good sense.

She won the next three hands without looking up from her cards, ignoring the dealer when he touched his tie knot. Grumbling, a couple of the other men decided to take their chips to a different table, and underneath the skirt of the tablecloth the dealer kicked her in the shin. She promised herself she would fold the next hand, but when her first two cards were a pair of queens, she felt the stir of good fortune in her belly. She couldn't fold two queens. Again she blew through the dealer's fold sign, playing her hand slow and careful, trapping the longshoreman into making a big bet on the final round.

"Let's see what you've got, girlie," he said, fingers playing idly at his belt buckle.

Just for show, she checked her hole cards one last time. "My, my," she said. "What's a nice girl like me doing with a hand like this?"

When the longshoreman saw her queens, black hatred spread over his face. From a shoulder sling under his vest he pulled out a short, bone-handled dagger and began using it to clean his fingernails. The sight of the blade twisted her stomach, and the snub-nosed pistol she had strapped over her ankle suddenly felt as hot as a lump of coal. She tried to catch the dealer's eye, but now he was steadfastly avoiding her gaze. She crossed her legs and eased the gun out of its holster.

When there was trouble at the tables, it reassured her to think of her father bellied-up and dealing a card game in his pin-striped shirt with garters around the elbows. By the time Moira came along, her father had already ditched the pinched nasal accent of his Pennsylvania upbringing in favor of the soft drawl of a riverboat card dealer.

Even as a little girl she understood he was the sort of man women adored. Casino cocktail girls made sure his drink was always full. Men liked him, too, drawn to his easy manner and dry wit. Most of the time he could cool out a sore loser or broke drunkard armed with just his smile and a handful of complimentary chips.

"I'm just the middleman," he told her on the first night she worked running ice in the casino ballroom, age twelve. "My job is to make it as painless as possible for people while I empty their pockets."

Now she tried to put some of that faux Southern hospitality into her voice as she batted her eyes at the longshoreman and said, "Surely there's no need for that. Stow that thing away and let us refill your drink on the house."

He ignored her, puckering up to blow a speck of grime off the tip of his knife. She looked around for a roustabout or a pit boss, but all the men had gone out to the big tent to help with the show. There was nothing to do but play the next hand, and by the time four more cards had been dealt, the other men got out of their way and it was just the two of them again.

"I fold," Moira said, without even bothering to look at her hole cards.

"You got the best hand," the longshoreman protested. "You don't fold the best hand."

She eyed his cards across the table and then sighed at him, this stupid man. "You're chasing a straight," she said, "but you're not going to get it."

"Now, see," the longshoreman said. "How could you possibly know a thing like that?"

A strange barking laugh escaped her lips, and it seemed to stoke his anger even more. He leaned forward in his chair and ground the tip of his dagger into the table's wooden rail. He said, "You think I haven't noticed the two of you signaling each other all night long?

Your carnival shams might fool these other mugs, but it hasn't worked on me, has it? I'm too skilled a player for you—for any of you—even in a rigged game. Now, play on."

Her knees felt watery and she thought of telling him the truth: the only way this game was fixed was to keep Moira from cleaning him out in minutes. She didn't need to cheat. She could explain the numbers of this hand to him, why following after an inside straight was a sucker's bet, but the odds would mean nothing to him. Plus, she was not a card counter. Her own game was more guts and instinct than any kind of science. She could read the lay of a gambling table like a boat captain saw the rolls and draws of a current. With the slightest move, a quiver in the corner of an eye, a crossed or uncrossed leg, another player could tell her what they were about to do, the same way an outfielder could tell where a batter was going to hit the ball by the position of his feet and the angle of the bat. But why try to explain that to a man as obviously bad at cards as the longshoreman? Why think he might understand when she didn't fully understand it herself?

"Fine," she said, giving him the full benefit of her eyes. "I bet all."

The longshoreman measured her stacks with a wide skeleton's grin. She had a little more than half his own holdings left. A smart player would have at least taken some time to think it over, but the longshoreman called the bet immediately. She turned slightly in her seat, aiming the gun at him under the table, curling her finger lightly on the trigger.

Don't make me, she said to him in her head, trying to breathe and hold the thing steady.

Just as the dealer sent their last cards around facedown, the flap on the tent's door rustled and over the longshoreman's shoulder she saw Pepper come into the gaming pavilion. He was still in his purple cape and wrestling tights, his fingers massaging the groove in his throat where the noose had caught him. After pausing to give his eyes a chance to adjust to the glare of the lights, he gave her his funny, crooked smile. It felt like someone had set a flock of doves loose in her chest.

She didn't even bother checking her last card. She knew her ace high would carry the day, so she flipped them over to show the table and waited for the longshoreman to realize he'd lost. His eyes danced back and forth between his cards and hers. She watched it register in his face as he tried all the possibilities in his head. When he saw there was no way he could win, a low growl came from deep in his throat and he lashed out with one arm, scattering chips like a cloud of flies. His chair toppled backward as he stood, dagger clutched in one fist. Before he could move, Pepper was standing by his side, laying a hand casually on his shoulder.

"What's all this?" he said, like they were all in on some kind of joke together.

The longshoreman jerked away, wheeling and slashing with his dagger, but then he was down on one knee and Pepper was bending his knife hand back toward his elbow at a sickening angle. The longshoreman cried out and the knife dropped to the ground. With a quick twist, Pepper forced him down onto his belly and put a knee between his shoulder blades. The longshoreman cursed and thrashed, but Pepper's expression was as flat as glass as he scooped up the knife and set it on the table. A couple of roustabouts showed up then, too late as usual, and hauled the man to his feet.

"Cash this fellow out," Pepper said, stuffing chips into the longshoreman's pockets. "Make sure he knows not to come back."

As they dragged him away, the heels of his boots skittering in the grass, the longshoreman yelled something at them. Moira couldn't make it out, but in his voice she recognized a lifetime of anguish and misfortune, a man foundering with no end in sight. Her throat felt dry and she realized she still had the gun pointed at his upturned chair. Slowly she lowered the barrel into her lap and turned to the dealer.

"Aren't you just about the most useless man?" she said.

Pepper touched her lightly on the arm. "Easy," he said, and bent to pick up the longshoreman's chair. "It's taken care of now."

They left through the tent's rear exit, walking into the carnival's backyard area, where a couple of Wild West trick shots stood in fringed jackets, balancing the butts of their rifles in the grass like walking sticks. When he saw how badly her hands were trembling, Pepper took her lighter and lit her cigarette. She took a greedy first puff, the smoke scorching her lungs and easing her nerves.

His smile dried up when he saw the pistol in her fist. He took it from her and tucked it under his cape. "Jesus, Moira, that's really stupid," he said quietly. "What were you thinking?"

"I was thinking I might have to shoot that longshoreman," she said. "He came at me with a knife, in case you didn't notice, so I could really do without the scolding."

They moved through the alley between the backyard fence and the trailers, the names of the carnival's various acts painted on them in big bright letters. *Hedgweg the Great Colossus! Wayne Munro & His Congress of Performing Hounds!* Beneath the words were full-color portraits of the performers: the Human Projectile streaking across a blue sky; the aerialist Starr DeBelle, her dark hair flying as she turned a flip; and Jupiter, the carnival's sickly old elephant, rearing up on hind legs. When they got clear of the trailers Pepper slipped his arm around her waist.

"Can you imagine the hell Boyd would raise if assholes started getting shot at the gaming tables?" he said.

In spite of herself, she smiled at him. They wound their way past the animal trucks, where a roustabout rolled two big, claw-marked balance balls out of a prop box while a couple of other men struggled to fit a bear with roller skates and a tiny top hat. Drugged up on something powerful, the bear's eyes tracked them lazily. A few feet away, the animal trainer sat oiling his whip. By the time they got to the outfield wall, a twelve-foot green barrier covered in peeling billboards for cigarettes and safety razors, she was starting to calm down. Her hands were steady as she pitched the butt of her smoke onto the ground.

"How was the drop?" she finally asked him, ready for a new subject.

He tried to hide the tightness in his face. "Fine," he said.

She stepped back and gave him the once-over. "How's your weight?"

He rolled his eyes, shrugging like a kid forced to model his new Sunday school clothes. "My weight's good, Moira," he said. It was a lie. He swung his arms at his sides as if trying to get the feeling back in them.

"If you were overweight," she said, "you'd tell your loving wife the truth about it, wouldn't you?"

"It's just a couple of pounds," he said.

She shook her head. "But you went ahead and did the act anyway. I suppose this is the part where I ask you what *you* were thinking."

"It's just a couple of pounds," he said again. "It's not a big deal."

His eyes danced up over her shoulder, where a group of clowns had come out of a dressing tent and stood passing a hand-rolled cigarette around in a tight circle. The confrontation with the longshoreman had drained her energy, and now she felt suddenly exhausted. She didn't want to play the nagging wife just then.

"It's fine," she said. "You'll skip dinner and lose it overnight while we make the jump up the coast."

"I'm hungry, Moira," he said, "and I'm tired. I'm going to put this gun back where it belongs. Then I'm going to the pie car and I'm going to buy some hemp from those clowns. Come and get me when it's time."

She heard the whine in his voice and could barely blame him. They'd been on the road all summer, trouping down the Atlantic coast from the carnival's winter quarters in New York and then cutting a jagged path through the South all the way to the Pacific before marking a course north. From here they would head all the way to the Canadian border before making for home, through either the American Rockies or even Canada if Boyd could get the work permits. It had been a tough trip for Pepper already, starving himself to keep his weight under 155 pounds in order to do the hangman's drop while taking on all comers in nickel challenge matches during the carnival's athletic show. They still had a long way to go.

"Of course," she said, trying to soothe him. "Where will you be?"

He nodded toward the wall. "Across the street," he said. "Where it's quiet."

"Where it's morbid," she said. She was wearing heels, so she had to lean down to peck him on the cheek. "Thank you for saving me from the bad man."

His response was to raise a victorious fist above his head as he turned and went.

It surprised her sometimes how attracted to him she still was after all these years. She liked the sharp blade of his wrestler's body and the look he always carried around in his hard walnut eyes, indifferent and challenging at the same time. Like he was daring the world to give him a reason. Other men feared him, and she'd admitted to herself a long time ago that she liked that, too. Still, at times his bullheadedness was a burden. She tried not to be so hard on him, knowing that the way he worked he deserved to treat himself now and again; but she also knew he was the kind of man who didn't think about the landing until after he'd jumped. The kind of man who'd rather run through a wall than try to find a way over. When the reaper finally came for him, which she hoped with all her might was years from now, she knew Pepper Van Dean would ask him if he wanted to wrestle for it.

A racehorse, her father told her once, would run itself to death if the jockey let it. This was on one of their first Sunday trips to Jefferson Park in New Orleans. The riverboat was docked on Sundays and Mondays so the crew could go ashore. For her father that meant the racetrack, a cardroom, or a dark saloon with a chalkboard giving odds on the ball games. She had just started helping out in the boat's gambling hall when he began inviting her along, figuring if she was old enough to hold down a job she was old enough to learn how to be good at it. That first day, wearing her best dress in the magnificent, pillared grandstand at Jeff Park, she was thrilled by the teeming crowd and how, atop every gleaming, whitewashed turret and gazebo, flags rippled and popped in the breeze. Eighteen, she'd counted by the time they took their seats.

Before the first race a horse with emerald green diamonds on its hood had panicked in the blocks and thrown its rider. It scared her, and she asked her father if the men were hurting the horses by forcing them to race each other.

"No, honey," he said to her. That smile, that voice. "It's the thing they love most in the world. It's what they were born to do."

That day they blew their whole bankroll on doomed bets, but it didn't matter. Her father saved out a dime and bought them both ice creams on their way back to the boat. For years after that the two of them were inseparable during their time off, always seeking out the track or a card game. They earned a reputation as a team, a father-daughter tandem that could empty your pockets as fast as any stickup artist. She learned to navigate the world the way only a gambler's daughter could. She loved her father. He was the smartest, most put-together man she ever knew. Then, on an overnight trip during the summer Moira turned sixteen, he left their family's cramped stateroom for a late shift in the riverboat's cardroom and fell into the water, or was thrown.

3

Inside the right-field scoreboard was a narrow passageway that smelled of dust and oiled leather. It ran the length of the stadium in either direction, and on the far wall, rows of numbered scorecards dangled from metal hangers. A line of overhead bulbs squatted dead in their sockets, but enough light seeped in through the seams in the wall that Pepper could make out where someone had scrawled *To Hell with You Jimmy Claxton!* in smart little pencil writing next to the door to the street.

The rain stung the back of his neck as he jogged across the cobblestones and vaulted the low fence into the cemetery. Night was coming on moonless and cold and he felt the chill through the seat of his tights as he hoisted himself up and sat on a high headstone. Dangling his boots six inches above the grass, he fired up the hemp cigarette and filled his lungs. His shoulders throbbed from the hangman's drop, but as he blew his first cloud of green-gray smoke up into the tree branches, a calm settled over him. Taking his chin in his palm, he turned his head one way, then the other, until a series of cracks raced down his back. The adrenaline from the performance and then the trouble in the gaming pavilion was starting to ebb, leaving him with a shaky, empty feeling. His belly rumbled and he pulled out the two pickles he'd gotten from the pie car. The pickles were wrapped in paper and he peeled them like bananas as he ate.

He didn't have high hopes for the athletic show. In his four and a half years wrestling openweight challenge matches for the carnival, this summer's crowds were the worst he'd seen. Tonight, after the evening performance in a city big enough for people to have other things to do, he'd be lucky if a dozen guys stuck around to try their luck against him. He wouldn't argue with making an easy time of it, but it also meant another boring night on a tour full of them. He hoped things would get better as they moved up the coast, especially once they reached the timber camps in the hills of Northern California and Oregon. There would be some tough guys up there, he told himself. He was looking forward to it.

His father had worked as a lumberjack for a short while. At one time or another his father was also a miner, a horse jockey and a barroom bouncer, and had failed at all of them. The summer Pepper turned nine years old, the old man lost his job at a feed store outside Salina, Kansas, and moved their family west to Boise, Idaho, where he'd heard a bunch of big tree-cutting operations were starting up. Of course, the lead was a dead end and by fall he was working early mornings sweeping out neighborhood stores before the shopkeepers opened and nights guarding the door at a local tavern.

The bouncing at least seemed to agree with him, despite his small stature and the fact he spoke almost no English. He was proud of the cuts and bruises he sometimes brought home, stooping down so Pepper could poke and prod the spots with tentative fingers until his father winced and pulled away laughing. Later that same year his mother developed facial tics and a tremor in her hands. It got so bad that she had to quit her job as a seamstress for one of the town's big mining companies. A doctor in Pocatello confirmed a lesion on her spine and said there was nothing to be done.

His father grew more unruly as she withered away. His fights with Pepper got worse and more common. Then early one morning during the fall of 1898, Pepper woke to find his father crouching over him, pressing a gun to his mouth. His father's clothes stank of the barroom, the barrel of the pistol cutting into Pepper's lips.

"You think you're something," he slurred in their old language, burrowing the gun in past his teeth. "You're not something."

Then he was gone, clattering things onto the floor in their tiny kitchen before finally tumbling off to bed. Pepper stayed still until he heard the slow, choked sounds of his father's snores before he slipped out from under his blanket, gathered a few things into a knapsack and snuck out the back door. Their shotgun house was built into an embankment downhill from the railroad tracks, so he didn't have far to go before he found a place where the trains slowed around a wide bend. He sat for what seemed like hours in the cold, an old shirt pressed against his lips to stop the bleeding. It was nearly dawn by the time he mustered the courage to race down the small hill of frozen sand and hop into the half-open door of a rickety box-car as it passed.

It was cold on that train. The kind of cold that cut through his pants and heavy shirt as if he were naked. It froze the hairs of his nose and crept up into the soles of his boots. He was so miserable when the train finally lumbered to a stop the following afternoon that he might've snuck into town to find a way home if a rail yard cop hadn't caught him shimmying out of the car. The guy saw his split lips and the blood all over his shirt and went easy working him over.

Pepper went to jail, where they gave him warm clothes and food. It turned out he was still in Idaho, in a small town in Handsome County near the Canadian border. He refused to tell anyone his name for fear they would send him home, and it quickly became clear that no one knew exactly what to do with him. For three weeks he stayed with the sheriff and his wife, kindly people who fed him pie and let him sleep in the room they'd kept for a son who'd either died or never been born at all. For a while he dreamed the sheriff would adopt him, but soon people got tired of asking him questions he wouldn't answer, and a watery-eyed judge with blossoms of broken blood vessels in his nose ordered him sent north to the Handsome Academy for Boys. He spent the next five years there.

As he tipped his head back to take a second pull on the marijuana, he could still feel the warm blood and the bits of broken teeth in his mouth from the gun. He could taste the cold, oily metal and picture the sad, desperate look in his father's face. As he exhaled, he opened his eyes and saw a shadow detach itself from the outer wall of the stadium, just beyond the reach of a streetlamp at the end of the block. He let the smoke trail slowly out of his lungs, a quiver of curiosity stirring as the hulking shape of a man made its way toward him. The figure moved slowly along the sidewalk, pausing once to look back as if he wasn't sure he knew the way. Hidden in the gloom of the cemetery, Pepper thought the man would pass by without noticing him, but once the dark figure got within twenty-five yards it veered off the concrete and hopped the fence. In order to free both hands, Pepper clamped the rolled smoke in the corner of his mouth, hoping for a mugger, hoping for something more interesting than a beat cop out hassling drunks.

As the figure got nearer he recognized the tilt of the bowler hat, the barrel chest and the curlicue mustache.

"Before you come any closer," he called out in the dark, "tell me how worried I need to be."

Fritz Mundt's laugh was like gravel rattling in a tin can. The big man closed the distance between them in a few long steps, looking as nimble as ever on his feet. "Relax," he said. "I'm not here to bust anybody up."

"Lucky," Pepper said. "I don't think I could carry your big ass all the way to the hospital if you tried."

Fritz grinned at him and pulled him down from his perch into an awkward, backslapping hug. They hadn't seen each other in five years, since the night in Pittsburgh when Pepper lost the world's lightweight title to a bum named Whip Windham. Before that, they'd been friends and training partners, working as regulars in Abe Blomfeld's midwestern wrestling operation, forging the bond men shared through killing themselves in the cramped gym the old man kept above his butcher shop on the North Side.

In the ring, Fritz was a hardworking heavyweight—good, not great. Better with a blackjack or a length of pipe, at least in those early days when he padded his pockets collecting Blomfeld's debts. He was smart, too, the way a bear could be smart once it had you up a tree. The only time the two of them had ever wrestled each other for real was in an openweight match for five hundred people at a Grange Hall outside of Dayton. How long ago had that been, Pepper wondered, nineteen thirteen? They'd gone ninety hard minutes before Pepper finally took the bigger man's back and rendered him unconscious with a stranglebar choke. Even back then Fritz outweighed him by seventy-five pounds, and from the size of the gut he was carrying around now, it looked like more. The big guy had gone soft, Pepper thought, but he held his tongue about it for now. He decided it was best to wait and see what he wanted. It used to be when Fritz Mundt came to see you, it wasn't good news.

"I knew I'd find you out here," Fritz said, holding out two fingers for the hemp. "Give it here."

"Old habits," Pepper said.

Fritz produced a flask from the inside pocket of his jacket and they traded. "I've been tracking you for a week," he said. "Just missed you in Bisbee. From there I thought you'd jump to Phoenix, then Los Angeles, but if you did I missed you there, too."

"Swung down through Mexico," Pepper said. "Boyd Markham can be a wildcatting son of a bitch when he gets a taste for it."

Fritz leaned back and squinted at him. "How's your weight?" he said. "You're looking a little loose in the cage, you don't mind me saying."

"Pot meet kettle," Pepper said. He smelled the pungent fumes of back alley rotgut before he tipped the flask to his lips. The whiskey burned like acid going down, but he didn't take his eyes off Fritz, trying to get a read on him. The big man seemed oblivious, sucking on the marijuana with his eyes fixed on its glowing cherry.

"Blomfeld's dead," he said finally, holding in a lungful.

"I should hope so," Pepper said. "What would he be now, a hundred and five?"

Fritz exhaled with a hiss. "I've been looking after the gym since he passed. What's left of it. Tried my hand at booking for a while but had to shut things down. Not enough happening at the box office, as I'm sure you've heard."

"Maybe you don't have the mind for it," Pepper said.

He knew it had been hard times in the wrestling business since Frank Gotch retired and kicked the bucket at his farm back in Iowa. Crowds had been getting smaller and the ink in the big city papers harder to come by, but he figured it was just a matter of time before promoters found some new star to prop up in Gotch's place.

Fritz passed the smoke back. "It got so bad I thought I might have to close down entirely, but guess who showed up out of the blue last winter talking about a comeback?"

Pepper didn't like to guess and said he couldn't possibly. Fritz took the flask and killed it, screwing the top on tight before stowing it inside his coat. "Garfield Taft," he said, spreading his hands like he'd just pulled off an impressive magic trick.

Pepper groaned. "Speaking of the dead and buried. I thought pimping out white girls could get you lynched in Ohio."

"I assure you Mr. Taft is very much alive, and his comeback is real," Fritz said, swallowing a frown. "It may interest you to know that

I've even been talking to certain parties about a shot at the world's heavyweight title."

Pepper had to laugh at that. "Bullshit," he said. "I highly doubt that Billy Stettler and Stanislaw Lesko would give a black man the chance to win the world's title. Let alone an ex-con. The press would murder them for it."

"Things have changed more than you know," Fritz said, muscles in his jaw flaring. "Point of fact, I've already got a tune-up match arranged ten days from now. If Taft wins, Stettler and Strangler Lesko are willing to sign on for a championship bout at Christmastime."

"Sounds like you've got it all figured out, then," Pepper said, thinking every word of it had to be a lie. "What does any of it have to do with me?"

Fritz rearranged his feet in the soft earth. "Actually," he said, "I hoped you might consider joining up with us. What would you say to becoming Taft's trainer?"

That got his attention. He'd given up on the idea of ever getting back into the wrestling business, and now he laughed to cover the bloom of hope he felt in his chest. The serious look in the big man's eyes didn't change.

"Jesus," Pepper said. "You're not joking."

When Fritz spoke again, there was an added weight to his voice. "Do you think it's accurate to say we know things about each other that no one else on this earth knows?"

Pepper glanced across the street at the ballpark. "I know I never said anything," he said. "I can't speak for you."

Fritz nodded. "Then you might believe me when I tell you this," he said. "When we get our title match—and we will get it—we're going to need a hell of a scientific wrestler to get Taft ready for Lesko. Given the situation, there's only one name on my list. If there's a man alive who knows his way around the catch-as-catch-can style better than you, I never met him."

"You got that right, anyway," Pepper said. "Consider me interested. Now tell me the part you're not telling me."

"Taft is married to a white woman," Fritz said. "It caused no end of trouble in Chicago. We've had to move our operation out west. Where we are now, it's not as if people are falling all over themselves to sign on to train him."

Pepper let out a low whistle at hearing this news. "Where?"

"Join up with us and I'll draw you a map," Fritz said. "Until then, you'll forgive me if I keep the particulars to myself."

He held up a hand, rubbing the thumb against his index finger. "What are we talking?"

"A hundred and fifty dollars a week," Fritz said. "Meals, lodging, everything included. Plus, if we get Lesko to sign on, ten percent of the purse."

"Plus five of the gate?"

Fritz smiled at him. It was not a nice smile. "Let me tell you something," he said. "The fact that you allowed a snake like Boyd Markham to turn you into a circus performer is one of the great tragedies in our business, but I'm not here offering to grab my ankles. You want to go on taking the hangman's drop every night, twice on Sunday, for twenty-five dollars a week? Making every rinky-dink town, wrestling every cattleman and miner who has a nickel to spare? Fine. I'm offering you a chance at something different, that's all."

Across the street, the door in the stadium wall opened and Moira appeared. In the night mist and the electric buzz of the streetlamps she was stunning: tall and slender, walking with easy grace, her blonde hair bobbed around the ears. Bunching a handful of cloth so the hem of her dress wouldn't drag on the cobblestones, she picked her way across to the graveyard fence. When she saw Fritz Mundt standing with Pepper, her face dropped and her voice was cold.

"It's time," she said.

Fritz doffed his hat. "Moira."

"Hello, Freddy," she said. "Please don't talk to me." Then to Pepper: "It's time." She gestured toward the stadium in a way that said she would only stand out there as long as he made her.

He pinched out the hemp and tucked it away. As they shook hands, Fritz passed him a folded scrap of paper with a phone number scribbled across the bottom.

"I'm at the New Palace Hotel for another week or so," he said. "Come with me to see Taft in that challenge match I mentioned. No strings."

"Whatever it is, we're not in the market," Moira said. "If Boyd Markham catches you out here trying to shanghai one of his top drawing cards, he'll cut your throat with that little pigsticker he always has on him."

Fritz dug a cigar out from inside his suit. "Only to be saved by the grace of God and my own catlike reflexes," he said.

Pepper vaulted back over the fence and stood waiting for Moira, who suddenly seemed like she wasn't ready to go. He could feel tension radiating off her, her spine straight, shoulders back, with one hand still on the top rung. "Box office is around front," she said to Fritz. "You want to see us again, buy a ticket."

The flame of Fritz's lighter flashed across his face. "Funny thing about the hangman's drop," he said. "I've never known anyone to survive it so long. We all know you're tough—don't get me wrong—but a man can only press his luck so far before—" He dragged a thumb across his throat.

Pepper had to catch her by the wrist to keep her from going over the fence. "C'mon," he said. "He's just messing with you."

Reluctantly she came away. He fit his palm into the small of her back and guided her off the curb, the clicking of her heels on the stones echoing in the deserted street.

4

A week later, when the carnival arrived in New Vermillion, Oregon, the scale in the Guess Your Weight tent said Pepper weighed 161 pounds in his socks and tights. The scale was a seven-foot Toledo with a peeling candy-cane paint job and a sturdy red arrow mounted inside an oval viewing window. Black embossed lettering around the inside said: *No Springs! Honest Weight!* and there were two giant footprints on the platform to show you where to stand. Twice he climbed off and back on, just to be sure. After the third time, he spat into the dirt and cursed, slapping his palm hard against the glass. The arrow quivered but didn't budge.

He hopped down and bent to stretch, listening to his back pop and whimper as he reached for his toes. Between his legs and out the open mouth of the tent he could see the roustabouts making their final preparations for the evening show. Two of them were unrolling a giant spool of cable from the powerhouse trucks, while behind them a team checked and rechecked the support wires on the big tent. A man in overalls with a flaming-red beard trucked by with a long-handled maul over his shoulder, running like whatever he had to do needed to be done five minutes ago. Close on his heels a seamstress in a denim apron trundled along carrying a studded leather saddle.

When he was sure no one was watching, Pepper peeled out of his tights and tossed them in a pile on top of his discarded boots. He closed his eyes, tipping his face back, lifted his arms above his head, and huffed all the air out of his lungs. *Please,* he thought. *Please, please, please.* He stepped slowly back onto the scale, rubbed his hands over the prickly stubble on his cheeks and opened one eye.

One sixty-one.

He found Moira in the trailer shimmying into a silver dress. Her face was done up, a little too much mascara clumping in her lashes as she watched him in the mirror. The trailer was a teardrop-shaped single-axle, decorated on the outside with a picture of Pepper dangling from a rope, a wide smile on his face, the words *Master of the Hangman's Drop!* arching over his head. Even for a short guy there was barely enough room inside to stand up straight. He turned to look at himself in the glass next to her, letting the shoulders of his tights fall loose around his waist.

His chest was flat and ashen, knotted with yellowing bruises, his ribs like xylophones up and down his sides. A crescent-shaped scar zagged over one nipple and another stitched out from a hip, inching its way toward his belly button. Just below his sternum a hard, bony knob jutted out where something had broken years ago and hadn't healed right. His cheeks were so sunken that when he smiled he could see the bones in his face. He tried to fix the mirror with a tough-guy stare and didn't like the way it looked.

Moira patted her lipstick with the tip of a finger. "Say the word if you want me to leave you two alone," she said.

"You might want to think about sleeves," he said. "A bunch of these towners are already barking drunk."

She leaned over and kissed him. "Wish me luck," she said. "I'm off to bread-and-butter the natives." As she turned around she saw him from a distance for the first time and stopped short.

"You're still overweight," she said.

"No," he said. "I'm fine."

He tried to turn away from her, but she caught him and pushed him back in front of the mirror. Standing behind him, she ran her fingertips down his chest, feeling the way the skin slipped easy over his stomach muscles. You couldn't lie to Moira.

"You're fat," she said. "You're one sixty if you're a pound."

"It's going to be fine, I said."

She bit a lip. "You should run," she said. "You want me to get your coat?"

He turned around, bracing his hands on her shoulders. "Stop it," he said. "Just cut it out, what you're doing."

"You should spit in a cup," she said, starting to paw around in her tiny purse for her cigarettes. "Anything."

"It wouldn't do any good," he said. "I'm all sucked up."

Something in his voice must have given him away. "What did you eat?" she said.

"Nothing," he said. "Just water since yesterday afternoon."

He fumbled his tights back up. That morning the gals at the pie car had fixed him a meat loaf sandwich and a side of leftover slaw. He didn't regret it, but four pounds? Definitely he hadn't eaten four pounds.

"How far over?" she asked.

"Just a few."

"You said a *couple* just a minute ago," she said. "How far?"

He sighed. "One sixty one."

The look on her face scared even him. "That's crazy," she said. "You can't go on like that. You have to talk to Markham."

"What's he going to do," he said, "besides get angry over nothing?"

She squinted at him, a probing look he didn't care for. "How long do you think we can keep this up?" she said.

"What?" he said.

"Letting Boyd Markham drag us all over hell and back every

summer," she said. "You risking your life every night. We used to be on our own. We used to have fifteen rooms. Now we're just counting down the days until they have to take you out on a stretcher for real."

He was trying to put together a response to that when somewhere outside a crier yelled, "Doors!"

It was time for her to go.

"Fine," he said. "I'll go see Boyd. I'll throw myself at his feet and grovel for forgiveness."

That seemed to satisfy her. Her face softened a bit and she kissed him hard on the mouth. "You want the gun?" she said.

He thought about the snub-nosed .38, still where he'd stashed it under a stack of blankets in their steamer trunk. "Nah," he said. "If the fat bastard tries anything I'll just strangle him."

O utside the trailer it was almost full dark and he had to wait while a traction engine crawled by dragging a load of logs. New Vermillion wasn't much more than a shotgun blast of rough weatherboard shacks lost in the hills fifty miles from anywhere. To the east, thick stands of fir and pine crowded up against the banks of a muddy, stagnant river. To the west somewhere was the ocean, though he couldn't smell it on the evening breeze. All he could smell was tree sap, a tingle of sawdust, and the faint taste of motor oil greasy on his tongue. The mill sat on a rise at the edge of town, the saw house towering above everything else, dirty smoke drooling from a series of stacks. A run of smaller iron-roofed buildings trailed behind, and from them a spiderweb of narrow dirt roads bled out into uneven rows of houses and shops, all built from the same blonde wood they were cutting out of the hills.

The three dozen trucks and trailers of the Markham & Markham Overland Carnival had arrived after midnight the night before, coming up from Ashland in the rainy dark, running late because one of the trailers blew a tire. They set up the yard at the south end of the valley, circling up to give the towers a good look at the colorful trucks. Markham liked to brag he ran the fastest, most agile carnival in North America. While most of the other big operators like Ringling and Sells-Floto were still tied to the rails, he'd switched to gasoline years ago. Hence the word *Overland* and the slogan printed over the wheels of every truck in his fleet: *World's Largest Motorized Circus!* The trucks allowed the carnival to go places the bigger shows couldn't touch, places deep in the woods and swamps. Markham's game was to target the small towns, mining camps, and timber ventures, where they drew crowds of rough men and women who came out looking for dice games, peep shows and the occasional fight.

As Pepper stood waiting, a shift whistle blew and a group of guys in wood-flecked overalls came down from the mill to join the crowd drifting into the evening performance, a bunch of them with their lunch buckets still swinging in their hands. The roustabouts had just opened the main gate and were doing their best to scout for weapons and liquor as the towners streamed under the twenty-foot banner blaring the Markham & Markham name in bright red letters. Smaller flags lined the path to the big tent, waving with the names of featured acts and promising *Spectacular Performance! Games! Menagerie! Athletic & Side Show!* One of them was his: *The Immortal Pepper Van Dean! Master of the Hangman's Drop! Meeting All Comers in Timed Challenge Bouts!*

The townsmen were mostly hatless, dressed in what passed for evening wear in these hills: plaid and checkered shirts tucked into denim or old wool. The few that wore jackets and ties did a poor job matching them. Overcoats were old and shiny, and most everyone wore work boots or cracked brogans. A couple of big sawyers had pulled off their boots and now walked barefoot in the damp, their feet oozing from ugly blisters. The women were hard and bright as stones, their dresses home-stitched and fraying, their children running wild, whooping at the prospect of something to do. He saw a couple of toddlers rumbling along in the nude as the hot, stinking mass of them moved across the midway toward the tent.

None of them paid him any mind as he crossed the road behind them and knocked on the door of Boyd Markham's double-sized trailer. Receiving only a low grunt in response, he clicked the latch and stepped inside, where the smell of man was thick in the air. Clothes were everywhere, thrown over chairs and piled high atop a matching pair of Saratoga trunks. The only light came from a small wall-mounted sconce, but in the gloom he saw that a Chinese girl stood in the middle of the room, naked except for a pair of black slippers. She had a solemn, pretty face and spared him only the quickest glance as he came in. The girl was balanced on top of Boyd Markham, who lay on his belly wearing a light-colored vest, matching pants, and thin brown socks. Pepper couldn't see his face, only the pink roll of his neck beneath his razor-cropped mane of silver hair, but he could hear him fat-man breathing into the carpet. Putting her feet between his shoulder blades, the girl wiggled from side to side, doing a little dance. Markham groaned. She turned and toe-crawled back down to his waist, repeating the dance. Markham groaned again.

Pepper cleared his throat. He said, "If you want me to come back . . ."

The carnival barker sighed and lifted both his hands off the floor as if to say, *You're here now.* The girl jumped down, slipping wordlessly into her robe. As she went past he caught a whiff of her, some flowery scent tickling his nose. When the trailer door banged shut behind her he waited while Markham hefted himself up off the floor, feeling a twinge of disgust at the sight of the enormous, soft ball of him.

"We are in the high grass now," Markham said, peering briefly out a window. "It feels like a whiskey kind of night. I'd offer you one, but I know you're trying to watch your figure." He gave Pepper a squint-eyed grin, then seemed to notice something was wrong. "What is it, son?"

Markham poured himself a rye and sat heavily in one of the chairs. The other chair was full of laundry, so Pepper couldn't join him.

"I got on the scale today," he said.

"As I'm sure you do every day," Markham said, like he already knew what was coming.

Pepper folded his arms. It had only been a few minutes since he'd weighed himself. Markham was as wily as any carnival man alive, with eyes and ears everywhere inside his own troupe, but not even he could have gotten word that Pepper was overweight. Not this fast.

"I'm one sixty-one," he said.

Markham grinned at the amber slosh in his glass. "I know that can't be true," he said. "One hundred sixty-one pounds would put you a full six pounds over the limit for performing the hangman's drop trick. You would be in violation of your contractual agreement with the Markham & Markham Overland Carnival. A contractual agreement that in no uncertain terms dictates that you, as the humble servant of your employer, and the dumb-as-dirt redneck grappler who signed it in the first damn place, shall perform the hangman's drop trick while weighing no more than one hundred *fifty-five* pounds."

Pepper's ears felt very hot. This world never made sense to him—contracts, figures in a ledger. He couldn't make the numbers talk to him the way Moira could. "I know what the contract says," he said. "But I'm one sixty-one, so there we are."

"And as I previously iterated," Markham replied, "you must be mistaken. Being in violation of your performance contract would not be good for you, Mr. Van Dean. It would not be good for Moira. Such a sad state of affairs would entitle your employer to seek restitution in the form of garnished wages for any amount he felt such a violation would cost the reputation and overall well-being of the world's largest motorized circus."

Pepper worked his jaw back and forth. "You really going to play hardball with me on this?" he said.

"What other course of redress do I have?" Markham asked sadly. "If you have some bright idea you have yet to elucidate, by all means, please enlighten me."

"It's your call, boss," he said. "If you want to scratch the hangman act for tonight, that's all right."

In a burst of speed surprising for a man of his size, Markham threw his whiskey glass against the sidewall of the trailer. It shattered and the shards flew back at them, forcing Pepper to shield his eyes as glass whipped over his skin like raindrops.

"I know whose call it is," Markham shouted, "and it is *not* all right! It is not all right, you insipid little dwarf, for one of my most popular attractions to suddenly pull up lame like a goddamn show pony when I've got a packed house sitting out there, I've got two weeks of advance advertising on the books, I've got fliers nailed to every freestanding structure in this awful town. We marched a goddamn *parade* through the streets, for Christ's sake, and now what? I'm supposed to go out there and tell them the master of the hangman's drop is too fat to go on?"

Pepper held up his hands, but a fire was burning in his gut. "Wait a minute, Boyd."

"What should I do about the people who want refunds?" Markham said. "I'll have no choice but to take that out of your pay as well."

Pepper took a step forward. "Listen," he said, but stopped when Markham crossed his legs to show the knife he had strapped over one boot.

"Please," the carnival barker said, cool as could be again. "I implore you to see things from my perspective. You remember where you were when I found you? When I *discovered* you?"

Pepper remembered.

"Given the circumstances," Markham said, "you can't blame me that I feel a certain pride of ownership over you, over your act."

Pepper nodded, something alive and crawling around in his neck and shoulders. He fidgeted, scratching at the side of his head. "I suppose I might," he said.

"Then hear me when I say this," Markham said, his voice taking on its ringmaster boom, that bass tremolo that sounded so good when shouted into a microphone. "You are the most gifted goddamn showman I ever saw in my life and I swear on the lives of my children that I would never do anything to cross you up or put you in unnecessary danger. You understand what I'm saying? The lives of my children. Their very souls. But the simple fact is, we've got people out there who've paid to see a show."

"I hear you," Pepper said.

"People," Markham repeated, "who paid to see a show."

"I said I heard you."

"With that in mind," Markham said. "It occurs to me that perhaps I misunderstood you. Why, I'm sure your weight is just fine. I'm sure you're in the kind of tip-top shape we at the Markham & Markham Overland Carnival have come to depend on from the former world's lightweight champion. If nothing else, perhaps we both merely misinterpreted the parameters of our previous discussion. Yes?"

"Yes," Pepper said, his tongue dry and stiff in his mouth. "I think we both may have misinterpreted the parameters of our discussion. If I was not clear right off, I apologize. I came here tonight only to confirm with you that my act goes on as scheduled and to release the Markham & Markham outfit of any liability in the unlikely event of a mishap."

"A mishap," Markham said, "like you break your fucking neck."

"Like I break my fucking neck," Pepper said.

Markham slapped his knees like he'd just wrapped up a tidy little piece of business. They shook on it, and Pepper had one hand on the latch of the door when Markham spoke again.

"I'm told our mutual acquaintance Fritz Mundt came to see you recently," the carnival barker said.

Pepper turned. "That's right."

"What did that washed-up meat tosser think he was doing tampering with one of my top draws?" Markham said.

"Nothing," Pepper said. "Not much. No tampering. He only came by to shoot the breeze."

Markham looked at him with the eye of a stockman appraising a side of beef. "That's good," he said. "I'm sure you understand it would be a violation of your exclusive performance contract for you to be consorting with another promoter, in this industry or any other."

"I do, Boyd," Pepper said, trying to use his tone to let the carnival barker know exactly how much he hated him at that moment. "I do understand that."

"Good," Markham said, a grandfatherly grin spreading across his fat cheeks. "Now, skedaddle on out of here, son. I need to get myself equipped. I'd tell you break a leg, but I understand Mr. Mundt took care of that for you some years ago."

5

They packed a good house. The grandstand under the big tent was filled to capacity by the time Markham stepped out from behind the curtain, a small grin playing on his lips. The townspeople were rolling drunk, clapping and catcalling as he strolled to the center of the performance ring and took a low bow. "Timber!" someone shouted from the back. It got a few laughs, but the noise died quickly as he approached the microphone, letting the moment stretch before he dabbed the sweat away from his face with a folded handkerchief and said: "Welcome."

Moira had her eye pressed to the rear wall of the tent. She'd paid another girl a dime to cover her spot at the poker table so she could sneak away from the gaming pavilion to watch. If Pepper was going to go out and kill himself doing the hangman's drop, she wasn't about to sit idly by at the tables only to hear about it later from some roustabout. She was still fuming over Markham's insistence that he go on with the show, imagining the feeling of getting her fingers around the ringmaster's thick neck, but now she had to hand it to him. He might've been a snake and a tyrant, but he was the best she'd ever seen at working an audience. He could grind on a set patter, but was also quick with ad libs and improvisation, a master of reading a room and then taking a crowd wherever he wanted to go. As he started in on his standard opening for the show, he had the entire population of New Vermillion rapt.

"Skilled performers who have thrilled crowds as far away as New York City!" he said, the mention of New York eliciting some murmured boos. "Chicago!" he cried, and the boos picked up speed. "San Francisco!" The grandstand trembled as the people crowed, starting to feel they were in on some kind of joke. "Even," he announced with a mischievous glint in his eye, "the lush green hills of Oregon!"

The place went crazy.

In the backyard area, a half dozen horn players loafed around with their instruments propped on their shoulders. They all wore maroon jackets with matching stovepipe hats, and one man in their group stood holding hands with a monkey. The monkey didn't wear a jacket but had a hat to match the rest and waved a toy trombone in his free hand. Just as Markham was reaching the crescendo of his speech, the horn players suddenly struck up a warbling tune, stumbling through the curtain into the performance ring.

Their melody was scattered and messy at first, but came together as they neared the center, their clumsy walk turning into a kind of haphazard choreographed dance. Markham stepped back from the microphone and stared. The crowd was caught off guard, too, the music snapping them out of the spell he'd been building. The lead musician waggled his hat in one hand and turned a little pirouette as they strutted across the ring. Markham stomped over, hands on his wide, womanly hips, and caught the bandleader by the collar. The two of them started a pantomimed argument while the other musicians stood shrugging, holding their hats and horns in their hands. Markham turned a deep shade of purple as he and the lead horn player got in each other's faces. When their row reached its fever pitch, one of the roustabouts ducked his head into the tent and yelled: "Let them play!"

The crowd picked up on it. "Yeah, let 'em play!" someone called out.

Hearing that, Markham reared back and bumped the bandleader with his enormous belly, sending him tumbling into the sawdust. The townspeople, suddenly realizing this was all part of the show, erupted in laughter. Wood chips flew as the bandleader hopped up and gave chase, followed by the rest of the horn players all tooting an angry fugue. Markham ran a long circle around the ring, making sure every section of the grandstand got a front-row view of the pursuit. As he came back through the center of the tent he stopped and shouted into the microphone: "We've got a great show for you tonight! First up, the aerialist Star DeBelle and her team of lady acrobats! Give them a hand!" Then he sprinted for the exit with the horn players still on his tail. The crowd roared as he left the tent and the lady acrobats tumbled in, a few of them turning handsprings while the rest waved a rippling rainbow of five-foot flags.

Moira pulled her eye away from the sidewall and she saw Pepper ambling down from the trailer in his cape and tights, flanked by his escort of clowns. From the look on his face, you'd never guess there was anything the matter with him. He kept his eyes straight ahead, his shoulders back, his walk steady. He looked confused for a moment when their eyes met, not expecting to see her there, and then he smiled as if he understood. The smile was cocky and dangerous and filled her to the point of bursting with love for him. He had smiled at her just that way the first time they'd met, years ago now, before either of them had ever heard of Boyd Markham, his traveling carnival, or the hangman's drop.

The first wrestler to show up at The Green Sheet that night in 1912 was Aldous Hawthorne, a strutting fireplug with a sandy mustache who wore no jacket over a blazing pink shirt with white French cuffs. Moira didn't know he was the world's lightweight champion until one of the waitresses told her, but from the way he breezed into the club without paying the cover charge—two toadies following him like they were sewn to his elbows—she knew he was somebody.

Being somebody didn't necessarily distinguish Aldous Hawthorne from the rest of the clientele at The Green Sheet. The club belonged to Jellyroll Hogan, a St. Louis alderman and part-time gangster, and everyone who drank, gambled and danced there did so with an unqualified belief in their own specialness. On a Saturday night, it was typical for ballplayers and tycoons to rub elbows with politicians and hoodlums. If a man didn't at least bring a stage actress as his date, he could count on being mocked behind his back, all of them competing at an unspoken game of who was most important, who was most dapper, who would live forever and never grow old.

This night the staff had been warned of a wrestling program at the Coliseum downtown and expected most of the mat men to drop by for a party afterward. Hawthorne had only been at his table near the dance floor for fifteen minutes before he dismissed his waitress and asked for Moira to be sent over. She was the floor manager of the club's casino room, not a waitress, and told him as much as she stood over his table with a clipboard in her arms and pencil tucked behind her ear. Hawthorne sat and listened with his thumbs hooked in his belt loops. When she was finished he said he'd been watching her and thought she might like to have a drink with him. Up close she could see he had gray hairs around his temples and in his mustache. His British accent was thick and briny, his frankness disarming. His eyes said he knew what he wanted and saw no reason to hide it. In a room full of people acting out vaudeville parts, she thought he might be the only one just being himself, and she liked him for it immediately. Later, she would come to associate these qualities with wrestlers in general, but at the time she was just a few years off the riverboat and The Green Sheet was her first real job. She accepted his offer and sat at his table.

Hawthorne said he'd had an easy night of work, taking two straight falls off some local boy in under forty-five minutes. He'd barely got a sweat going and now he couldn't recall the kid's name.

"Riffraff, mostly," he said when she asked which of the other wrestlers might turn up at the club. He mentioned again that he was the lightweight champion, and when she didn't seem impressed enough for his liking, he sipped his scotch and added: "That means I'm the best in the world."

"I gathered that from context," she said.

He told her that in his younger days he'd traveled around England taking on all comers. The place he was from was called Lancashire, and from the way he talked about it, it seemed all the men there were wrestlers. At first his stories thrilled her, but after an hour of listening she started to wonder if he enjoyed the sound of his own voice more than she did. Still, she couldn't stop herself from feeling envious of the life he described: staying in the finest hotels and moving from one town to the next in expensive private train cars. From what she could tell, it sounded as though Hawthorne spent less than an hour in the wrestling ring each night and the rest of his time carousing. When she said so, he scoffed.

"There's a good deal more to it than that," he said.

When the other wrestlers began to show up, her first thought was that they all looked like slightly different versions of the same man. They all stood a little bowlegged, with wide, flat chests, heavy brows, and the impassive, deep-set eyes of apes. They didn't have the show-off muscles of strongmen or body sculptors, but they had big shoulders and blunt, scarred hands like fieldworkers. The club regulars gave them a wide berth, which only made it easier for the shills, cocktail girls, and prostitutes to get to them. The wrestlers didn't seem to mind.

Moira could tell Hawthorne was warming up to ask her back to his hotel, when another wrestler in a floppy newsboy cap appeared at their table. At first she didn't notice anything special about him, just a guy with the same face as the others, one pounded flat and rubbed smooth by the wrestling mat. His nose was still mostly straight, which made him look younger than some of the others, and his suit didn't fit him, his shirt collar left open around a tree-trunk neck. It was his ears that set him apart. Shriveled and misshapen, they stuck out from the sides of his head like clenched fists: the left one just a bubble of scar tissue with no discernible hole or lobe, the right a dying flower, wilting in on itself.

She felt an itching at the back of her neck and turned her head just enough to see that the wrestlers crowded around the bar had stopped what they were doing and were watching them.

"Mr. Hawthorne?" the young man said.

"In the flesh, my boy," Hawthorne said, giving Moira an amused wink. "What can I do for you?"

The young man stuck out his hand and Hawthorne shook it lustily. "I knew it was you," the guy said, grinning. "I saw you backstage at the Coliseum, but you cut out before I could catch you."

"Sounds like you've been hot on my tail," Hawthorne said, enjoying the chance to parade his fame in front of her.

"Yes, sir," the guy said. "I wanted to introduce myself and give you the chance to meet the man who is going to take your title."

Hawthorne's smile turned to tin on his face. "I beg your pardon?" he said. His two toadies, who'd been sulking at a nearby table since Moira sat down, caught the scent of trouble and scooted closer.

"It's nothing to get hot about," the young man said. "I've seen you wrestle a hundred times. You're a fine champion, sir, but you're just not me."

In an instant Hawthorne was up out of his seat, his face flushed, a sheen of sweat on his brow. Moira felt a tightness building in her chest and flashed a signal to the bouncers standing in the doorway to the casino. They frowned back at her, clearly in no hurry to get involved. Some of the wrestlers hooted at them from the bar.

"I'll not sit here and be disrespected by the likes of you," Hawthorne said. He was taller than the new man and used his bulk to brush him back.

"You've got the wrong idea," the guy said. "I didn't come over to make threats. I thought I might buy you and your lovely wife a drink. A kind of passing of the torch, if you will."

Hawthorne sucked his chin deep into his chest. "You strike me as a crazy person," he said. "I assure you that you are no threat to me. As for this whore, I've only just met her."

Moira saw disgust flutter across Hawthorne's face and was immediately angry with herself for sitting with him for so long. She lit a cigarette and said to the guy: "If you're buying, I'll have a gin rickey."

The guy smiled but didn't look at her. "You haven't even got my name yet," he said to Hawthorne.

"Nor do I care to," the champion said. He shoved the man, and suddenly they were all in a tangle on the dance floor—Hawthorne's toadies and the bouncers and even a few of the wrestlers who'd hopped the rail from the bar. Everyone pulling and swearing and knocking over tables. It took the bouncers a few minutes to pry them all loose while Moira retreated to the safety of the bar. The wrestlers looked amused at the efforts of the bouncers, but they backed off, some of them holding up their hands like they were being held at gunpoint. The last man off the floor was Aldous Hawthorne, yanked up and hanging from where the bouncers had him by the shoulders. Blood was running down his chin, his pink shirt dotted with it.

"This is outrageous," he said.

The bouncers paid him no mind. They looked to Moira, who stood with her hands on the bar and her heart flapping like a bird against her rib cage. She gave a quick sideways nod at the door, and even as a team of bouncers hustled him off with his toadies, the lightweight champion of the world was trying to explain to them who he was.

"What about 'Tiny' here?" another bouncer asked Moira.

It took her a moment to realize he meant the young guy, who had somehow avoided the worst of the fracas and was scouting around underneath the tables for his cap. His hair was a deep brown brush cut, which made him look even more like a schoolboy. "Say that again," he said to the bouncer as he located his hat beneath a chair and reset it on his head, aiming for a little tilt. "I'll pull your tongue out and step on it."

The bouncer simmered, but Moira sent him away with a slight shake of her head. His lips twisted in a way that said letting the kid stay was a mistake, but a moment later he moved back to his spot at the door to the casino room. The wrestlers retreated to the bar, and music filled the air as the band struck up again. Maybe they'd never stopped playing; Moira didn't know.

For the record, she told the guy as he took a stool across from her, she wasn't a whore. Secondly, the club had a two-drink minimum, so he'd have to order something if he wanted to stay. The guy looked around and then asked what Aldous Hawthorne had been drinking. Moira brought him a scotch and soda and told the bar manager to put it on her tab.

"He got the message," the guy said, staring at the closed back door through which the bouncers had deposited the Englishman, "but I'd say the meaning was lost on him."

Moira hid her grin. "A man takes off his hat when he speaks to a lady," she said.

He stared at her a long time before pulling off his cap. "Sorry for queering your evening," he said, leaning forward to offer her a warm, dry handshake across the bar. "I'm Pepper Van Dean."

That night she took a bottle of red from the club's back room and they stayed up late sitting on a bench, watching the river, sipping out of paper cups. She was delighted to find he couldn't hold his liquor. After just a few drinks he told her about running away from home when he was twelve years old, winding up at a religious school for boys in the Idaho mountains. The older boys there made things tough on him, he said, until one of the brothers saved his life by forcing him to join the wrestling team. She left him with a handshake as dawn broke over the city, knowing she would see him again. Sure enough, a month later he was back, and then every few months after that, as part of Abe Blomfeld's stable of wrestlers, which toured the midwest in an endless loop. They went on two proper dates and then he started showing up at The Green Sheet unannounced, confessing he had no match in town, that he'd taken the train down from Chicago just to see her.

The night he proposed, they went to dinner at the Cottage and then roller-skating through Jackson Park. At the steps in front of the Palace of Fine Arts building, he got down on one knee and presented her with a ring so big and tacky, she had to ask if he had stolen it. He laughed but stayed down there, looking at her with those confident eyes of his. Like he already knew the answer. She said she wasn't going to marry him until he told her his real name.

That set him back. "How did you know?" he said.

"Please," she said. "Nobody's named Pepper Van Dean. It makes you sound like a comic-strip character."

He still had the ring in his hand. Shifting from side to side on one knee. "Zdravko Milenkovic," he said after a bit, looking as sheepish as she'd ever seen him. "There. Nobody else knows that."

She whistled, the sound of it echoing off the stone front of the building. "Let's just stick with Van Dean when we go see the judge."

A year and a half later, she sat ringside at Convention Hall in Kansas City as a crowd of three thousand people watched him take the lightweight title from Aldous Hawthorne in straight falls. For months the two men feuded in the press, and by the time Pepper stood in the ring while Blomfeld strapped the title belt around his waist, he was maybe the most famous wrestler in the world not named Frank Gotch. For almost a full minute after he'd been beaten, Hawthorne slumped in a corner with his forearms braced on the top rope and his face pressed into the turnbuckle. When he'd finally collected himself, just a glint of tears in his eyes, he limped out and shook Pepper's hand. She had to give him credit for that much.

Even now, she couldn't make sense of the giddiness she felt seeing Pepper win the championship. Perhaps the biggest surprise to her had been the sudden realization that he might actually be as great as he said he was. Before winning the title, he'd been a darling of the press for his quick wit and sharp tongue, but she'd always assumed it was mostly puffery. Sure, he was tough and clever, but the best in the world? It seemed too much to hope for by half.

After he became champion, they moved out of their cramped rear-facing room on Chicago's South Side to a sprawling two-story house outside the city. The backyard, with its stone patio and enough grass for a ball field, was perfect for entertaining. Nearly every weekend they hosted the wrestlers of Blomfeld's troupe, along with any other sporting types who happened to be passing through town.

The wrestlers were odd men, as different from each other as they were the same. A surprising number of them had done at least some college and could talk about art, books and food in ways she'd never heard before. Others were nothing more than street toughs, with scars like fat earthworms burrowed in their eyebrows and under their chins. Some were gifted scientific wrestlers, with encyclopedic knowledge of holds and escapes and a hard-won understanding of angles and leverage. Others were just mean. Some, like her new husband, were both.

Moira suspected they imagined themselves to be immortal. None of them spared a thought for tomorrow, spending money without counting it, unable to conceive of a day when they might wish they'd stashed it away. The longer they all wrestled, the more they looked alike as their faces grew shiny with scar tissue, their ears calcified hard, and the corners of their eyes drooped from nerve damage.

One of their backyard parties was where she first encountered Fritz Mundt, a rookie wrestler who seemed to have a new girlfriend every week and was always talking about how life would be after he became heavyweight champion. In those early days Fritz was one of her favorites, a fact that now burned especially badly. He had a funny way of pretending to be dumber than he really was, when in truth he was always playing some angle.

It took her a little while to get used to being rich and having friends. As soon as they moved out of their apartment, Pepper insisted she stop working, and even though it gave her an uneasy feeling, she agreed. She was not a person who dealt well with spare time, and after a month of sitting around the house, trying to plan dinners and hovering over the cleaning lady, she asked him what he would have her do. He just handed her a wad of bills and told her to go find out what she loved.

First she tried shopping, following the women who were now her peers around the streets, watching them get gooey at the sight of sale signs in shop windows. The new house had closets bigger than the riverboat stateroom she'd grown up in, and she did her best to fill them with hats and shoes and dresses. When she discovered that buying wasn't her talent, she tried joining. She went to meetings of the Women's Peace Party, the Women's League for Peace and Freedom, the Daughters of the American Revolution and the Women's Auxiliary to the Republican Party. She met suffragists, patriots, pacifists, Bolsheviks and anarchists. She had tea with women who were outraged at the expansion of what they called the *"American Empire,"* women who seemed to care more about the Philippines and Latin America than their own children. She met women who decried alcohol as a tool of Satan, the ruination of the modern family; rich women who buried themselves in orphans, and wet-eyed, earnest women who filled their mansions with stray dogs and cats. Then there were women who just wanted her to read *Frankenstein* so they would have someone to talk with about it. They had petitions for her to sign, newsletter subscriptions to push, donation plates to pass after the coffee was served. Nine times out of ten there was a sales pitch hidden somewhere in the slogans, the hymns and all the sisterhood.

These women embarrassed her, and she sensed the feeling was mutual. Her membership in groups quickly assumed a recognizable pattern. She would go to a few luncheons or sewing circles and at one of them she would drink too much or whisper too many jokes to the lady next to her and would not be invited back. That was fine with her, she told herself, and it was this acceptance of herself as a loner that eventually led her to admit there was nowhere she felt more at home than at a gambling table.

She began scouting out every racetrack, gaming hall, and card game in the city. Thinking back on it, the memory of those carefree days filled her with longing but also a sense of dread. It had been the best time of her life, but now it seemed like she'd known all along that something was lacking. It was undeniably less exhilarating to bet on the ponies or the ball game when there was no risk involved. If she dropped five or ten dollars on a race or a boxing fight one week and then won it back the next, it didn't really matter. The triumphant lift she felt from winning and the stab of regret she got from losing were both dulled. They had so much money, the money became meaningless. To compensate, she bet bigger and bigger, but it still didn't give her the same thrill as the nickel and dime bets she'd made with her father as a girl, when every penny seemed like a fortune. She typically won more than she lost, but the times she went back to Pepper needing more, he always had it for her.

Toward the end, something changed. During what turned out to be the last six months of his title reign, Pepper was withdrawn and quiet. With newspaper reporters or in public he was boisterous, full of jokes and brags. At home she could hardly squeeze a word out of him. At first she assumed Blomfeld was having trouble finding worthy opponents for him. The general consensus in the press was that Pepper had already bested every lightweight worth his salt and now promoters were resorting to booking him opposite bigger and bigger men or against two-bit bums on the undercard of more important bouts. She knew his reputation as a drawing card and his salary were suffering because of it. Over time she realized something deeper was troubling him. She asked him over and over what was the matter, but he refused to say.

When they booked him to face Whip Windham in Pittsburgh during the fall of 1916, everything fell apart on them. To prepare for the match, Pepper spent days and sometimes nights in the private gym above Blomfeld's butcher shop. He became choosy about who he allowed around him, training only with his closest, most trusted friends. A week before the match, he called her late at night from the hospital to say his leg had been broken by Fritz Mundt during one of their regular grappling sessions. Everyone swore up and down it was an accident, but Moira felt Fritz must have betrayed them. Nothing like it had happened before, and the only way she could make sense of it was to assume someone had gotten into the big man's ear, and into his pocketbook.

She begged Pepper to pull out of the match, but he wouldn't hear of it. He said there wouldn't be enough time for Blomfeld to find a replacement—that he'd have to cancel the whole show, which would only mean hard times and lost money for everybody, including the undercard wrestlers who were counting on making a payday. Real men and champions didn't pull out of matches, he said, and that was that.

He could barely walk from the dressing room to the ring on the night of the match, but he climbed up the stairs, limped through the ropes, and lasted nearly an hour before Windham pinned him in straight falls. The whole thing stunk to high heaven, but he wouldn't tell her what it meant or why it happened. Not then, not now, not ever; he just kept giving her the same sad smile and telling her that Fritz hadn't intended to do it. It had been a mix-up, that's all.

It was an obvious lie, and she became more convinced of it after the bout when Blomfeld refused to let Windham wait for Pepper to recover so they could have an immediate rematch. Instead, he sent the new champion on the road. A few months later, when Windham had already lost the title to someone else and it was clear Pepper's leg wasn't healing as fast as they'd hoped, Blomfeld released him from his contract. Moira was sure some other promoter would snap them up, but none did. Month after month they waited for a new contract offer, a comeback match. By the time they realized it wasn't coming, it was too late. Too many bills and mortgage payments had piled up around them. To pay off their creditors, they sold the house and the car and, eventually, everything else. The day the new owners turned them out of the house was one of the saddest of her life, yet she'd still had no idea how much she'd grow to miss it all.

When they got to the end of the long driveway carrying their suitcases in their hands, they found Boyd Markham chewing on a cigar, one shoe propped up on the bumper of a Model T Ford. The carnival barker put them up in a swanky downtown hotel for two nights while he wooed them and, once Pepper's contract with the circus was signed, loaded them on a train back east. The finality of it didn't hit her until she saw their new apartment at the Hotel St. Agnes in Brooklyn. It was a shabby, small space with cracking plaster walls and grit-streaked windows—the kind of place where even on the brightest summer day it was impossible to get enough light inside. The upside was, they were barely there. Even after she got used to the greasy snow-blind feeling of the road, she never forgot the view from the bay window in their big house in Chicago. She never forgot what it was like to slip under the covers of their king-sized bed and feel every muscle and joint in her body relax.

She even missed the boredom and the awkwardness of trying to fit in with people who ultimately wanted no part of her. At the time, she'd felt belittled by it—and disturbed by the fact her gambling no longer seemed to satisfy her in the same way—but now she knew it was just the feeling of security, strange and distressing to her because she'd never felt it before. Now she understood that if trying to make friends with rich women and betting against the Cubs was what passed for trouble in your life, you had no troubles at all.

She wanted it back. She wanted all of it back.

Pepper went on just before intermission, the stagehands wheeling the rigging for the gallows frame out into the main ring. She watched him stand with the clowns in the dark, his chin tucked and his chest heaving as he took a few deep breaths, hands groping his stomach underneath the furls of fabric. A scratchy anticipation crept under her skin, putting a watery creak in her knees. Still, she willed herself not to look away. Maybe she imagined that simply by being there, just by watching, she could will him to survive the cruel physics of the trick, which said he was supposed to break his neck if he tried to do the drop weighing as much as he did.

The stagehands brought out the torches and planted them in the dirt on either side of the gallows, a somber silence filling the tent as people saw the noose. She was vaguely aware of Markham going through his normal spiel, but didn't catch the words. When the ringmaster reached his cue, Pepper and the clowns shuffled through the curtain, blinking out of the darkness as the band blasted out his entrance music. He threw up his arms and the clowns all did their pratfalls. Smiling as he came to the center of the ring, he whipped off his robe and did a slow turn. A couple of the women in the audience whistled at him as the stagehands came out and cuffed his hands behind his back.

"Make a run for it!" somebody yelled, and Pepper shrugged in the direction of the man's voice, as if to say, *You're telling me!* They hustled him up the steps to the gallows and stood him on his mark as Markham appeared underneath.

"Mr. Van Dean, any final words?"

"Well," Pepper said, voice cracking. He cleared his throat. "Well, I'd just like to say"—taking some time to think it over—"I'd like to thank the people of the great state of Oregon for their hospitality. If by the end of tonight I somehow find myself having an audience with the man upstairs, you know, I'll be sure to put in a good word. See if I can do something about all that rain."

"Is that all?" Markham asked through the crowd's guffaws.

Pepper swallowed hard. "Anybody got a drink?"

Then the stagehands put the hood on him. Moira made fists, willing herself not to look away.

"Well, folks," Markham announced. "Shall we put this man out of his misery?"

The platform creaked as the stagehands approached the lever. She held her breath, then felt the lurch in her chest as the trapdoor opened and his body took the sickening plunge, the crack of the rope as loud as a gunshot when it yanked him up short.

They stretched it out as long as they could, and Pepper started to worry that Markham might let him strangle just to teach him a lesson. Finally, he felt the cold metal of the doctor's stethoscope as the stagehand they dressed up in a white smock made a show of checking his chest. He could hear the audience grumbling with impatience, few of them seeming overly concerned for him. "On with the show!" somebody called from the bleachers as Markham yanked the hood off his head. Pepper waited and waited, neck muscles cramping, breathing as shallowly as he could, trying to make subtle changes in the positioning of his body as the rope twisted and groaned. Each time it felt like the rope was on the verge of completely cutting off the blood to his brain, he would shift into the pressure, find a little space and survive. It seemed like hours, it seemed like forever, but finally the "doctor" gave him the high sign: a short, stiff pull on one heel that the audience wouldn't notice in all the fuss.

Pepper's head snapped up, eyes wide and bright, grinning out at the crowd. Everyone else did another round of pratfalls, and the uncertain silence was broken by laughter and applause.

"Ladies and gentlemen . . ." he announced, but stopped, his voice weak. Using one finger, he pulled at the rope like a man feeling hot under the collar. The crowd chuckled, going with it now.

"Ladies and gentlemen . . ." and again he stopped. He cleared his throat and, as the horn players tooted another fanfare, climbed hand over hand up the rope. He pulled himself back through the hatch in the floor of the gallows frame and sat with his legs hanging over the edge of the platform. As he slipped off the noose, giving the rope a good snap so the crowd could see it was the real deal, he could make out a couple of guys in the front row smiling at each other, embarrassed at being suckered. He winked at them like they'd all been in on the joke the whole time.

"That's better," he said, rubbing his neck a bit. "Ladies and gentlemen, we'll now enjoy a short intermission, during which we invite you to sample the offerings in our refreshment pavilion. Who knows, maybe a game of chance or one of our tremendous prizes will catch your eye? But don't forget, be back in your seats in thirty minutes, as the second half of our show includes such acts as the human projectile, Hedgeweg the Colossus and Jupiter the Educated Elephant. You won't want to miss it."

Two hours later the performance in the big tent ended with the elephant dancing on its hind legs to "America, I Love You" as the roustabouts pulled open the rear exit to let the crowd spill onto the midway. Suddenly free of the cramped bleachers and out in the open air, the people buzzed with giddy energy. Part of the crowd veered right, heading for the gaming pavilion and midway. The rest went left, padding across a short stretch of dead grass into a tent draped with the streaming banners of the athletic show.

All New Featured Performers! the largest one said. *The Best of Everything and Nothing but the Best!* A run of smaller signs bore the names of the performers: *Pepper Van Dean! Hedgeweg the Colossus! Gun Boat Walters!* and below that a wide banner that proclaimed: *Masters of Physical Culture!*

In this tent there were no seats. People gathered around a small riser where the massive strongman Phineas Hedgeweg hooked them with a simple patter and fifteen minutes of bar bending and keg hoisting. Pepper waited behind the tent, standing in the weeds beside Gun Boat Walters, a giant black prizefighter whose promising career had been cut short after he went blind in one eye. They didn't talk but did jumping jacks, deep knee bends and pummeling drills to keep warm as the stars winked above them.

When the strongman was done with his show, the horn players blew a short tune to draw attention to the opposite end of the tent, where a sagging boxing ring stood under a circle of lights. Pepper spit out his plug of tobacco as he and Gun Boat Walters climbed up the steps. They leaned in opposite corners, the prizefighter strapping thin gloves over his massive fists. A roustabout dressed in white pants and a referee's shirt stood behind the ring, resting his forearms on the apron. As the spectators drifted over, Markham appeared from a side entrance and riffed a bit about both fighters, going on about their physical gifts, their mental acumen and their boundless heart. Pepper could feel eyes moving over his body, sizing him up. On their cue, he and Gun Boat began to work through some demonstrations. He caught a series of the boxer's crushing blows with handheld pads, each punch pushing him back, the impact strumming through his arms and shoulders. The crowd gasped and shrunk back a couple of steps. People were always afraid of Gun Boat, because for his size and power he was very fast. It helped that he smiled a lot and called out friendly things like "Watch me now!" and "Look here!" as he cracked his fists against the pads.

They switched places and Pepper performed a short routine of tackles and throws. The crowd loved this part, enthralled with the way he tossed Gun Boat around, shooting a quick single leg, flopping him over with a fireman's carry or hoisting him high in the air for a belly-to-back slam. After every throw, Pepper stopped to pose for a splatter of applause. He flexed and stretched while the boxer, still grinning, picked himself up off the old, stained mat.

Behind them were two large banners announcing the rules for the nickel challenge matches. The boxing rules were simple: Any man who survived three minutes in the ring with Gun Boat without being knocked out or quitting won fifty cents. Things were a little more complicated for the scientific wrestling bouts. Pepper's banner was painted in the same garish script as the sign bearing his name on the outside of the tent. Across the top it said: *Wrestle the Unbeatable Pepper Van Dean! Former World's Lightweight Champion!* and underneath: *Catch-as-Catch-Can Bouts! Many Ways to Win!*

Any man who battled him to a ten-minute draw without being thrown, pinned or submitted got his nickel back. If a local boy managed to throw Pepper, he would win a quarter. A concession was worth a dollar. At the bottom, written in gold script, it said: *Pinfall Victory Worth $10.00!* This had never happened. In his nearly five years working for Markham & Markham, the only money paid out from Pepper's matches was for time-limit draws, and those were few and far between. Near the side of the ring was a large caged gymnasium clock so the crowd could keep track of the time during each match.

Just as Markham stepped forward to announce that the great Gun Boat Walters and the unbeatable Pepper Van Dean would be taking on all comers, he saw Moira step through the door at the back of the tent. She smiled at him a little, the look saying she was happy he was alive but maybe wasn't fully done being mad at him yet.

It took a few minutes for the first man to get the proper courage to challenge one of them. While they waited, Pepper busied himself doing stretches inside the ring—bending over to touch his toes, then reaching toward the ceiling and side to side. He jogged in place a bit to work out the kinks in his legs and lower back. He didn't need to do this, but knew the crowd liked to see him warm up. Any man who worried about cramps and muscle pulls couldn't be as unbeatable as the carnival barker claimed.

The first contestant to drop a nickel in the pot and climb into the ring got a nice ovation from his friends. He was a big redheaded sawyer with sweat rings on his overalls and nine toes on his bare feet. Pepper could smell the sap and dust in his clothes as they shook hands and the timekeeper tolled the bell. The man looked strong, but from the way he lumbered around the ring, Pepper could see there was no science to it. Soon after they began circling each other the guy tried to grab him for a tie-up and Pepper dropped low into a double leg tackle. The speed of it caught the sawyer by surprise. Locking his hands behind the man's hips, he turned like the rudder on a boat and drove forward. The sawyer grunted as they hit the rough canvas, his eyes wide. He tried to pull himself back to his feet, but Pepper latched onto his legs and yanked him down. From there it was simple. He hopped forward, caught the sawyer in a cradle and leveraged his shoulders down. The referee slapped the mat once and Pepper jumped back to his feet, jogging in place to keep his blood up.

The sawyer sat up, red-faced and blinking, unable to believe it. The match had taken less than thirty seconds. Pepper didn't look at him, acting like the man wasn't even there as the sawyer shuffled out of the ring and down the steps, past where several others were now lining up with nickels in their fists.

The second man was slight and wiry, quicker than the sawyer, but just as green. His balance was all over the place. Right off, Pepper clinched with him, slipped his grip under the man's armpits and sent him flying ass over everything with a lateral drop. It was a good throw, clean and true, and the referee stepped in to wave things off as the man tumbled across the ring. That was that. It had taken five seconds.

As the night went on he beat more and more men, for a time forgetting about his anger at Boyd Markham and his worries about his weight. This was the thing he lived for, the thing that drove him night after night. When done right, there was beauty in it, a clean triumph in each victory. He loved the focus it demanded, the particular single-mindedness, the ability to block out the things that had happened that day and the things that might happen tomorrow. When he was having a match, everything beside himself and the man across from him faded away, as if they were the only two people in the world. The one thing that mattered, the entire point of life, was to win. The moment his opponent's shoulders touched down and the referee's hand slapped the rough canvas, it was as if he'd emerged from a tunnel on a speeding train. The world would burst wide-open around him, sounds and smells now brighter than before, the rush of winning jittery in his arms and legs.

That was good. That never got old.

The trick to the nickel challenge matches was to win as fast as possible while using the least amount of energy. In certain matches, though, he couldn't help himself. As a small man, one of his strengths as a wrestler was his wind. He got better the longer things went on and liked drawn-out matches best. He loved letting his opponent have the upper hand, allowing the man to believe he had a chance, before battling back to win. This technique was particularly useful if he felt the audience's attention starting to wane. He might let a guy take him down, force a near fall or climb on his back. Once he heard the cheers start to build for the local boy and was sure the crowd was caught up again in the action, he would take control and fight his way back for the win.

His favorite part was the moment he felt other men break—the instant men who'd climbed into the ring feeling tough and ready realized that they were beaten. He could feel their spirits collapse as the matches went on, first little by little, then all at once, like a dam giving way. Their own foolishness always seemed to shock them, but when they finally realized it, the men would let themselves be thrown or pinned or tap the mat in concession to save themselves a broken arm or leg, or the indignity of being choked unconscious in front of their family, friends and the people they had to go to work with the next day.

It fascinated him to think of a man's will as a physical thing, to know that determination and the desire to win were not unlimited. Even a man who believed he was fighting for his life didn't fight forever. Eventually his muscles cramped and his wind gave out. Pepper remembered that feeling from a long time ago, the knowledge that your own courage was rapidly draining from your body. There was something animal in it, a message passed between the two wrestlers. He would feel it moving in his body like blood. Better than the actual winning. Better than any feeling he knew.

That night in New Vermillion, he had to wrestle half a dozen guys before he found one with any skills. When Pepper saw the ears on the man in the checkered lumberjack shirt and tattered work pants, he knew he had a match on his hands. The man was bigger than Pepper and stripped off his shirt to show a long, jagged scar across his shoulder. When the referee called for the bell he came immediately to center in a decent crouch and Pepper mirrored him. For the first minute all they did was hand fight, stalemating each other with slaps and feints. After another thirty seconds he knew the lumberjack was trying to stall him, hoping for a time-limit draw, trying to get his nickel back so he could brag to his friends in the saloon later. Or maybe he thought Pepper would get tired and give him an opening to attack. As the timekeeper called two minutes gone Pepper tried a double leg shot, but the man sprawled out of it and shoved him away. The crowd oohed and Pepper came up grinning.

"Nice," he said, meaning it. "Good."

For another minute they circled, with Pepper trying to bait the man into trying an offensive move. Each time he came forward, the lumberjack slipped away from him. He was aware of the big clock crawling past the halfway point of the match and a few cheers floated up from the crowd. The timekeeper called out five minutes, and just for an instant it distracted the lumberjack. He snuck a glance at the clock, and it gave Pepper the opening he needed to step in and trap him in a corner, stomping hard on the man's foot so he couldn't get away. The lumberjack's mouth quivered with pain and surprise as Pepper tied him up with a collar-and-elbow hold and dragged him down to the mat. The man had good balance and almost managed to reverse him, but at the last moment Pepper bucked his hips and leveraged him onto his side. He seized one of his arms in a hammerlock and bent it behind his back. The lumberjack grimaced, a rope of spit caught on his lip, but he refused to roll over and give up the pin.

"Don't be a hero," Pepper said to him. "You're finished."

The lumberjack's eyes flooded with agony, but he didn't budge.

"C'mon," Pepper said. "We're done here."

He wrenched the arm back further and felt a little tremor go through the man's body as something popped and came apart in his shoulder. It felt like tearing loose a piece of chicken at the dinner table. The lumberjack groaned and quietly said uncle. Pepper jerked the arm back a little farther and told the man to say it again, loud enough for everyone to hear. He did and Pepper turned him loose, feeling the air drain out of the tent as the lumberjack curled up in the middle of the ring, clutching his arm to his chest. The crowd booed and a few guys made their way toward the exit. Markham saw it and stepped forward to announce for the next ten minutes it was half price to take on Gun Boat Walters in a prizefight. That was enough for a few more towners to come forward and put their money in the jar.

Gun Boat Walters didn't like to hit guys in the face if he could help it, so he sent his first two opponents hobbling out of the ring, clutching their sides, their faces green with sickness. The last man was rangy, his chest corded with lean muscle, and he clipped Gun Boat across the eyebrow with a right hand as the referee broke them out of an early clinch. The crowd went crazy, but Gun Boat just stepped back and touched one glove to his forehead to check for blood. Cocky from his one punch, the rangy man sprang forward and put his whole body into a wide, looping hook that Gun Boat ducked easily. He planted his feet and threw a ripping uppercut that sounded like someone swinging a hatchet into a tree when it landed on the rangy man's jaw. For the next few minutes the only sound in the tent was the man's snoring as the referee and Gun Boat Walters slapped his face trying to bring him around. Nobody wanted to fight Gun Boat after that.

"Time for one more," Markham kept saying. "Time for one more bout if any local boy thinks he has the sand to give either of these mighty fellows a go."

The crowd shifted, unsure, until a garbled, drunk voice cut through the hubbub. At first Pepper couldn't make out the words, but he noticed a tide rising in the people. They began whispering a funny name, one that sounded like a joke.

"How about Greenchain Charlie?" they said.

A man standing at the rear of the tent looked up at the sound of his name. Soon he came forward, hesitant, into the light and Pepper saw the one called Greenchain Charlie was a hulking giant of a man. He wore a soiled red work shirt and denim pants. His blond beard was as thick as the hair on top of his head and his brow sloped back above wide bug eyes. Kicking off his untied boots, he stepped up onto the ring apron without using the stairs. Markham recognized the hush that had fallen over the crowd and hopped into the ring to announce that for this one match only the carnival would cover side wagers from all takers, giving two-to-one odds.

As bets were counted and guaranteed, Pepper leaned back against the turnbuckle, studying the fellow who now stood opposite him. Greenchain Charlie's clothes were damp and tight on his body, and from across the ring he smelled of dirt and whiskey. His eyes were a hard green, too dull-looking to show any fear. Pepper guessed that the top of his own head would come to the guy's armpits and hoped like hell he didn't know how to wrestle.

When they were set to go, Greenchain Charlie shrugged out of his shirt to show a body as smooth and hairless as a toddler's. The referee clapped his hands, the clock started winding, and it took a few seconds for either man to decide on a first move. Pepper took the center but misjudged the length of Greenchain Charlie's arms and immediately the bigger man grabbed him around the shoulders and lifted him off his feet. He might've been thrown, but he hooked a foot into the inside of Greenchain Charlie's knee to block it. The man had to set him down, but as he did he kicked one of Pepper's ankles out from under him, sending him tumbling to the mat. Greenchain Charlie collapsed on top of him and the crowd hollered with glee. It felt like a five-hundred-pound sack of coal had fallen onto him, and Pepper shifted up onto one hip to avoid being pinned. Burying his head in the big man's chest, he locked his hands behind Greenchain Charlie's back and hung on. For a few seconds Greenchain Charlie didn't seem to know what to do. Frustrated, he threw a couple of pawing punches at Pepper's ribs and Markham called out: "Easy, boys! Take it easy!"

After a moment to think about it, Greenchain Charlie reared up off the mat and slammed down, belly-flopping onto the canvas with Pepper underneath him. Once, twice, three times, crushing the air out of his lungs, until he let go. There were still five minutes left on the clock and the crowd moved closer to the ring, clapping in unison to its own beat. Pepper managed to get his knees up to make a little space, but he was still trapped and wasn't sure how much longer he could avoid a pinfall.

Throwing his legs up over Greenchain Charlie's shoulders, Pepper caught him in a jujitsu stranglehold, something he would not have done unless he felt it was absolutely necessary. It was a simple move to avoid if you knew it, but he hoped no one in these hills had seen it before. He pulled down on the man's head with both arms and squeezed his legs with all the strength he had left.

Greenchain Charlie knew immediately that he was in trouble, though the crowd hadn't realized it. Everyone was still clapping and screaming for him even as he began to panic and flail his arms. He got up to his feet, bent awkwardly at the waist with Pepper locked around his neck, and tried to shake himself loose. The effort used up the last of his air and he fell backward onto his ass. For the first time the crowd sensed something was wrong, but before the mob could fully grasp it the big man went limp. Pepper let go of the hold and Greenchain Charlie's body tumbled over on the mat like a pile of dirty laundry. The referee came forward waving his arms, and Markham hopped up into the ring to stretch the man out in the center of the mat. Markham lifted Greenchain Charlie's legs to let the blood flow back into his head while Pepper rubbed his neck and shoulders, trying to bring him around.

"Jesus," Markham said under his breath. "That was a close one."

"Nah," Pepper said. "He never had me."

Boos came from the crowd. A couple of locals came up to collect Greenchain Charlie just as he lurched awake with a snort. He looked at them with the wild-eyed stare of a man who had no idea what had just happened. They all climbed slowly out of the ring, moving like some great wounded animal, and Markham stood up to announce the end of the athletic show. The crowd was surly, seeming much drunker now, cussing the performers and the carnival itself as they filtered toward the exits. Pepper ignored them, leaning against the ropes, getting his breath back and going over his body, looking for injuries, pleased with having defeated the big man and relishing the idea that after tonight he would never see this place again.

7

The saloon had no windows and no name, but was easy to find in the dark from the buzz of voices and clatter of music spilling out the open doorway into the street. As Pepper and Moira walked down from the circus lot, Markham came out of his trailer and fell in beside them, mouth curling around a hog leg cigar. He had changed out of his ringmaster costume into a canary yellow shirt with a flowery blue ascot. His gold nugget fob chain clattered in the dark as he clapped Pepper on the shoulder.

"Never a doubt in the world, my boy," the carnival barker said, making him unsure if he should laugh or deck the fat bastard.

The men inside the saloon turned to look at them as they came in, veils of smoke swirling around dull faces. They filled the room to overflowing, standing elbow to elbow at the long bar and huddling around a scatter of rough-hewn tables. In a far corner a trio of musicians hacked through a rendition of "Old Black Joe." The heat was stifling, and as Pepper scanned the crowd, he saw Moira was the only woman.

The saloon and almost everything in it were built from the same straw-colored wood as the rest of the town. The bar itself was conspicuous for its buttery-brown mahogany, shining at a high gloss and running the length of the room. Whoever built this place was a kind of carnival huckster himself, Pepper thought, having no doubt that once the mill had exhausted its tract, the owner would pack the bar with him and move on to the next boomtown.

"I take it they don't spare much thought to the wishes of the federal government in these parts," Markham said.

Pepper said, "Get a load of that nude."

On the wall behind the bar a naked mermaid lounged across a wide white shore. Her scaled tail curled around her, hair swirling like fire around pink breasts as she watched a clipper ship cutting through the bottle-blue sea. Something about the painting's point of view wasn't quite right—the ship a little too big, the mermaid's face a little too narrow. Like the wood of the bar, the old mural was an obvious import, stained with water spots and smoke. It made Pepper feel dizzy to look at it and for a moment he wondered if he ought to have stayed in the trailer. But tomorrow was an off day while the carnival made the haul north to Seattle, and Moira had insisted they find a card game. He looked around the saloon now and didn't see one.

There was space at the end of the bar, and as they stood waiting for the bartender, Pepper felt the towners watching him. The bartender took a long time fiddling with things behind the counter before making his way over. When he finally did he scowled like he might say something about Moira being there, but decided against it.

They ordered schooners of beer, drained them and ordered seconds before the bartender could make change. "If that's as big as they get," Pepper told him, "you better bring reinforcements."

The next time the bartender brought them two mugs apiece and a couple of whiskey shots he said were on the house. He poured himself one and showed them how to knock the bottoms of their glasses against the bar before firing them down.

"Making friends," Pepper said when the man drifted away.

"Story of our lives," Moira said. They sipped their beers and then she asked: "How many guys you beat tonight?"

He had to think about it. "Fourteen," he said. "Fifteen."

"It seemed like more," Markham said.

"Maybe."

They'd worked their way into their backup drinks before a group of men surrounded them. Pepper recognized one as the lumberjack with the checkered shirt, the man whose shoulder he'd popped during one of that night's tougher challenge matches. The man carried the arm in a sling made from a torn bed sheet.

"Company doctor tells me I'm fired," he said, a hint of some old country accent in his voice. "Says I might need to go to the city to see a specialist."

Moira stepped forward, blocking Pepper with her body, and gave the lumberjacks a friendly grin. "That's a sad story," she said. "Can we buy you a drink?"

"We got drinks," one of the other lumberjacks said. They were passing around a bottle of homemade liquor, a brownish swill with little black plums floating in it.

"We owe you men nothing," Pepper said over her shoulder. "You pay your nickel and take your chances like anyone else."

"Legally speaking," Markham said, "the Markham & Markham Overland Carnival assumes no responsibility for personal injury."

The men in the group ignored the carnival barker. "That's adorable," one said. "He hides behind a woman."

"You hide behind your mob," Moira said. "Who's to say which is worse?"

The lumberjacks looked as though they hadn't bargained on sass from a lady. It took some of the steam out of them. "You don't know a thing about us," one of them said, sounding like he was tired of saying that to people.

"I know when men come to fight, they don't stand around talking about it first," Moira said, "so tell us what you want or leave us be."

The man with the checkered shirt rolled his shoulder as if trying to reset his arm in its sling. "That move you used on me," he said to Pepper. "I wrestled my whole life and never saw a move like that."

"That's probably why it worked on you," Pepper said. "No shame in that."

The lumberjack took his time trying to gauge whether Pepper was mocking him. Then a bloodless grin broke across his face. "We came over to say no hard feelings, is all," he said, offering an awkward left-handed shake. "We'll take you up on those drinks, if the offer stands."

They ordered up a fresh round of beers. The lumberjacks emptied their schooners and chased them with nips from their bottle, making no effort to hide it from the bartender.

"Slivovitz," one of them said to Pepper, passing it over.

The liquor was syrupy fire in his mouth—a foul plum brandy that made him cough and choke enough that the lumberjacks laughed and slapped him hard on the back. While the men drank, Moira searched through her purse for three small red dice, giving Pepper an innocent shrug when he saw them in her hand. She gave the dice a few rolls across the bar as if she was just passing time and then asked the man with the sling if he was interested in a chance to win his nickel back.

"I know better than to play with a lady who keeps dice in her handbag," he said, but offered her the bottle all the same.

Moira drank and grimaced at the taste. "Here," she said, sliding the dice across the bar to him. "If you're worried about loads or tricks you can check them yourself."

He scooped the dice in one big fist and shouted for the bartender to bring them another round. "Fair enough," he said. "What sort of contest did you have in mind?"

"That depends," she said. "Have you got five friends?"

The lumberjack roared with laughter. "Five? Little lady, today was payday. I have a room full of friends."

Once he'd gathered a group, she explained the game to them. "Pay attention," she said, emptying a handful of coins from her purse. "I don't like repeating myself."

Pepper tried to catch her eye, making a slashing motion in front of his throat, but she ignored him. She had each man pick a number between one and six. On every roll of the three dice they would all bet a dime, she told them. If a man's number came up she would pay him even money. If someone rolled doubles, the man who'd picked that number would get paid twenty cents. In the event three of a kind came up, well, the lucky fellow holding that number would get paid three to one.

"What if our number don't come up?" asked the lumberjack Pepper had wrestled.

"In that case, you pay the house," Moira said.

"What's the house?" said a dull-looking guy too small for his clothes.

"I am," she said, "but the important thing for you boys to remember is that at least one of you wins money on every turn."

They agreed that sounded good enough. The first man scooped up the dice and clattered them onto the bar, coming up with one-four-six. Moira nodded approvingly and gave a dime to each of the three men who'd picked those numbers. From the other three, she collected their dimes and added them to her pile of change. The next man rolled three-three-four, so she paid out the two winners—the man who'd picked three pounding his fist on the bar in excitement—and took dimes from the four losers. Two rolls later, the dice turned up all fives, eliciting another hoot of enthusiasm from the men. Moira gave thirty cents to the one who held number five and collected five dimes back from the others.

"Chuck-a-luck," Pepper whispered to Markham. "I wonder how long it'll take them to figure it out."

Markham sighed. "From the look of the beasts," he said, "it could be a while."

———•——•———

Around midnight, an old man with a dented star pinned to his work shirt came through to clear out men who had morning shifts. Those that remained organized arm wrestling bouts and chugging contests, and at some point a guy got up on a chair and sang an off-key version of "Dear Old Lady" at the top of his lungs. Pepper could feel the room warm to them, and soon he was slapping backs and borrowing money out of Moira's winnings to buy drinks for anyone near him. With the clock above the door creeping up on two o'clock, he was making a run to the bar when he found Greenchain Charlie leaning there, watching him with heavy, drunken eyes. When he tried to wedge past him, the big man blocked his way.

"You cheated me," Greenchain Charlie said in a voice so surprisingly high that Pepper nearly laughed. "You used a stranglehold. I didn't know you could do that."

"I could probably fill a book with the stuff you don't know," Pepper said.

"I'll tell you what," Greenchain Charlie said. "I'll fight you again. A real fight this time, not some bullshit rigged wrestling match."

Pepper rolled his eyes in a way he hoped showed how stupid that was. He tried again to get past to the bar, but Greenchain Charlie grabbed him by the shoulder. As he twisted out of the grip, his shirt tore.

"You don't get it," Pepper said, his face getting hot. "I'm a professional. That means I don't fight for free. I don't fight yokels in bars because they get sore after I whip their ass."

"I'll fight you for a hundred dollars," Greenchain Charlie said. "Dog-eat-dog rules. If you back down, you're a coward. If you propose a counter bet, you're a coward."

Pepper slapped his hand against the bar, rattling glasses. Now even the men who were playing Moira's dice game looked. He peered up into Greenchain Charlie's face. The man looked very calm. "If you've got that kind of money," he said, "put it on the bar."

He found Markham holding court under the mural. "I'm supposed to back you in this foolishness?" the carnival barker said. "This is small-minded."

"Easiest score you ever made in your life," Pepper said. "Head back to the pie car if you don't want to watch. Order me a couple eggs and I'll beat this kid before they can cook them. I just need the hundred to put up for the bet."

Moira was pulling at his elbow. "Don't do this," she said. "It's not worth it."

He could tell from the look in her red eyes that they were both very drunk, but it was too late to back down now. He pulled free of her and put his hand on the wall next to Markham's head, leaning closer. "It's only money," he said, hoping the feeling would pass between them that Markham owed him after he'd risked his life in the hangman's drop. "Not anything that really matters."

"Call it a limited partnership, then," Markham said. "What kind of split do you propose?"

Pepper told him fifty-fifty and Markham frowned like he might ply him for sixty-forty, but just sighed and dug into the pocket of his slacks. "This means your ass," he said, waving a long leather wallet at him like a scolding finger.

They fought in a circle of men holding schooners and waving dollar bills. Both Pepper and Greenchain Charlie stripped off their shirts and hung them on barstools, the bigger man already glistening with sweat. As he stared across the circle at him pacing back and forth, Pepper's throat felt so dry it was hard to swallow. He took a swig of beer, but it only made his mouth feel gummy and hot. He bounced on his toes trying to get his blood moving. A man with just stumps for his two middle fingers was trying to find a taker on a bet for a plug of Peerless chewing tobacco.

"I'll take that bet," Pepper told him. They shook on it, the guy's two mutilated fingers as hard as hickory sticks in his hand.

The noise reached a crescendo as one of the lumbermen came to the center of the circle with his handkerchief raised and called out, "Fight!"

Pepper thought Greenchain Charlie might storm out wild and start swinging, but instead the big man stalked from side to side, looking unexpectedly light on his feet. Pepper knew enough about boxing to flick out some jabs to gauge the distance, popping Greenchain Charlie's head back with a couple of them. In response, the big man just smiled at him. They circled for another minute before the crowd started to razz them, calling out that they wanted a fight, not a staring competition.

A couple of times the big man came forward with lunging punches and Pepper slipped them by feinting his head to one side or the other. As each blow missed, he could see Greenchain Charlie's brow knot tighter with frustration. The big man pushed forward, closing off the space, trying to trap Pepper with his bulk; but he just took a half step back and slithered out of the way again, hoping he was making it look casual and effortless to the men watching.

Finally, after finding only empty space in front of him again and again, Greenchain Charlie got fed up and tried to take Pepper's head off with one massive, wild swing.

As soon as Pepper saw him plant his feet to throw it, he ducked under for a double leg tackle. It was a clean shot, beautiful and pure and lightning quick, and even as he moved he heard the crowd hush, the breath caught in its throat. He almost grinned at how easily he got inside on the big man, ducking his head to one side and locking his hands behind the hips. It wasn't until he pivoted on his back foot and tried to drive his weight forward that he realized Greenchain Charlie had greased his body with lard.

The raw animal stink filled his nostrils, a fatty daub smearing across his cheek as his grip slipped. Greenchain Charlie threw a ripping uppercut into his throat and he stumbled back, choking. The big man was on him before he could recover, backing him through the circle of men and against the wall with a series of hard jabs and a wide hook to the body that felt like it had caved in his rib cage. Greenchain Charlie pinned him against the wall, grinding one massive forearm into his face until it broke his nose.

Pain flashed white behind his eyes as warm blood spilled down his throat. He staggered, trying to throw a last, blind punch that missed everything as he went down on his hands and knees. The whole room went sideways, the heat of it suddenly suffocating. His blood poured into the sawdust between his hands. The crowd turned loose a thunderous roar and he saw the group of lumberjacks he'd been drinking with just a few minutes earlier celebrating and hugging each other. The man with one arm in a sling was up on a chair, laughing and waving a fistful of dollar bills in his good hand. He saw Moira screaming, trying to get to him as another man held her back. A fiery hatred bloomed in his chest. He tried to stand, but his legs were rubber and wouldn't take his weight.

He went down again and there was an awkward moment where

no one knew what to do. They hadn't talked about how it would end. The uncertainty lasted just a heartbeat before Greenchain Charlie rushed forward and kicked him in the side, the force of it flipping him onto his back. The big man pinned a knee across his chest, crushing the air out of his lungs. The first punch was a thunderbolt that landed on his left cheekbone, knocking the back of his skull against the floor. The second punch turned everything black. The third punch he didn't feel at all.

H e woke up to rain on his face and for a second made the mistake of believing he was okay. The sky was cool gray and the ground was freezing, his arms and legs trembling. The pain didn't hit him until he tried to move, poison and sickness wracking his body, his stomach clenching like a fist as he sat up and dry heaved into the dirt. Bile burned raw in the back of his throat, the taste of rotten beer sticky on his tongue.

"Oh, what dog," he laughed, and then trailed off, leaving the *shit in my mouth* part unsaid when he saw he was sitting in a patch of wet black earth in an otherwise deserted field.

He pushed himself to his feet, pain lancing his ribs, the beating he'd taken the night before returning to him in a dim flash. When he ran his hands through his hair they came back flaked with bloody sawdust and he wiped them on his pants. From the tire tracks and trampled weeds he knew that yesterday this place had been the circus lot. Now the wind moved across it, whipping the grass, rustling trees on the opposite end of the clearing.

Empty.

His swollen face beat a dull pulse, the gears in his brain finding purchase, and he knew: They'd left him.

Something yellow and sickly-looking scrambled across the

ground near his feet. It was his shirt collar, dirty and misshapen, and he bent to pick it up, the dizzy feeling welling up in him all over again. He'd heard of this happening to men in other troupes, guys who'd royally screwed up getting let off at the side of some lonely country road, or ditched while they ducked in to use the washroom at a filling station. But not him. He thought of Moira, half hoping to see her walk down the hill from town carrying mugs of coffee and breakfast plates. Would she have just left him along with the rest? After all this time?

He turned and saw their steamer trunk sitting in the dirt like a tiny silver coffin. The sight of it loosed another memory from the depths: Hedgeweg the Colossus carrying it out of the trailer, dropping it on the ground in this very spot while Moira cried and begged him not to do it. He couldn't remember the strongman's face or if he'd said anything. He didn't know if Markham had read him the riot act. Maybe not. The carnival barker wouldn't have had to say a word after Pepper pissed away a hundred dollars of his money.

He found he could walk so long he kept a palm braced on his ribs. At least one was definitely broken. He'd have to try not to breathe too much. The lock on the trunk was broken, so he used the toe of his boot to lift the lid. Markham had certainly rifled through it in search of any valuables he could find to offset his loss. Their good wool blanket was gone. Inside were a few of his shirts and the cigar box where he'd stashed the pistol. As he picked it up he could tell from the weight that the gun was gone, too. Cursing, he kicked the side of the trunk and immediately regretted it. He slammed the lid shut and sat down on top of it to let the pain pass, smelling the stomach-turning stench of alcohol, smoke and sweat on his skin. He was about to lie back on the trunk when his wounded brain clicked into place again. *The lock was broken.* That meant Moira refused to open it for Markham. He picked his head up, scanning the horizon—hoping, hoping—and his heart nearly stopped when she stepped out of the tree line fifty yards off. She was wrapped in the wool blanket, and as she got closer he saw she had the pistol in her hand.

"They marooned us," he said.

"Look at you," she said. "Just back from the dead and already stating facts."

"Give me that gun."

"Demands, too," she said, handing it over. "Here you are, my love, just shoot us both and save us the indignity."

He sat back down on the hard metal and rested the gun in his lap. After a moment he lay back across the trunk. The coolness felt good on his ribs. He tested his face with his fingertips, finding the sore, swollen spots and pushing hard enough to know nothing was broken. Moira sat, too, holding his mashed face in her hands as he stared up at the smooth, mother-of-pearl clouds. He could feel the anger in her like hot straight wire.

"You're the dumbest man I ever married," she said, stroking his hair. "You know that?"

◆—————◆

The mill manager had a nervous laugh. Every time Pepper started in on what he was going to do to Boyd Markham when they caught up to him, it escaped his lips in girlish little puffs. The mill manager wore wire-rimmed glasses that he kept adjusting with his fingertips, a nervous tic that reminded Pepper of the marionettes the circus puppeteers carved out of wood. They were in his office on the second floor of the mill's administration building, and out the window they could see the looming hulk of the saw house. About a half hour after Pepper had woken up, a couple of mill workers had found them in the field and brought them there. Now he and Moira sat in a matching set of small, creaky metal chairs while the mill manager peered over his big battleship desk at them, laughing and touching his spectacles. It made Pepper think of the orphanage, the way some of the brothers there were barely older than the kids themselves. A few of them couldn't hide how thrilled and terrified they were by their own power. They would stand up in front of a classroom and fiddle as they lectured on history or arithmetic or some other nonsense, touching things, arranging and rearranging the items on the lectern. The mill manager was a big, handsome man, but soft, precious in his gestures, with his free hand tap, tap, tapping the butt of a pencil on his ink blotter.

"Could you sue?" he asked them. "Breach of contract, something like that?"

Pepper grimaced. "Are you serious?" he said.

Moira rested a hand on his knee.

"I see." The mill manager took off his glasses and polished the lenses on the folds of his white linen shirt.

Pepper fought back the urge to rip the glasses from his hands and stomp on them. His eyes shifted to the big bay windows, where two men in overalls were at work stacking a pile of freshly cut planks in the yard below, their caps battened tight against the rain. He watched as one said something to the other and jerked his thumb toward the window. They both turned, eyes peering up to the mill manager's office, and then laughed. He reminded himself how decent the mill manager had been so far, bringing them in and getting his office girl to bring them hot coffee and slices of buttered bread. The chill of the morning was just now draining out of his bones.

"Would you even know where to look?" the mill manager said. "To find them, I mean?"

"They'll make the jump up to Seattle," Moira said. "Maybe hold over for another night if Boyd can find a venue and thinks he can squeeze an extra dime out of it. Then they'll load everyone back on the trucks and haul the whole kit and caboodle back to New York for winter quarters."

"But as you yourself have explained," the mill manager said, "is there even any use in chasing them down if they don't want you?"

"We've got to head that way anyway," she said. "That, or south to Portland. Someplace we can catch a train. If we could find them before they go back east, there's a chance we could make amends."

"And what?" Pepper said, shifting in his seat to try to ease the ache in his ribs. "Beg forgiveness?"

"What's your plan?" she said. "Scout the want ads? See if anybody's advertising for a thirty-five-year-old carnival wrestler with a busted face and a bad attitude?"

"There are options," he said. "We have options."

"We don't, my dear," she said. "We have no money and no plan and no prospects."

"You know we do," Pepper said. The truth was, the idea of it had been picking up speed in his mind ever since Fritz Mundt had shown up in San Francisco.

"You will not," she said. "You will not call that man."

"Suppose you recovered the money you lost," the mill manager cut in. "Would that help?"

"From the asshole who cheated me?" Pepper said. "Did I tell you he was greased up?"

"You mentioned that," the mill manager said.

Pepper nodded. "Like a well-buttered eel," he said, almost to himself.

"If you like, I'll have him brought here," the mill manager said. "He might've drunk away some of the money by now, but a good bit of it is still most likely on his person."

"It might help," Moira said.

"No," Pepper said. "I got no beef with him. He beat me. It was my job not to let that happen, no matter what."

Their bickering made the mill manager look uncomfortable. He shifted in his seat. "Suppose I could put you on here," he said.

That was a surprise. Even from across the yard, Pepper could feel the whir of the saw house vibrating the floorboards under their feet, hear the occasional screech of metal and thump of wood. He thought of the men he'd seen in town. Their overalls damp and cracked, scarred hands and missing fingers, chunks of skin torn from arms and necks. The idea of slaving and sweating all day inside the steel walls of the mill, or even somewhere outside, deep in the forest with a saw on his hip, living for a drink in the saloon after his shift, only turned up the heat on his hangover.

"The only thing I've ever done is wrestle," he said.

"This isn't exactly intricate work we're talking about," the mill manager said.

"We appreciate the offer," Moira said. "But we couldn't do it."

The mill manager pulled open a desk drawer and took out a long leather book. He flipped it open on the blotter and scribbled, then ripped out a thin sheet and passed it across the desk. It was twenty-five dollars. Pepper looked at it and handed it to Moira, who smiled in a way that broke his heart.

"What are we going to do with a check?" she asked.

The mill manager sighed. Pepper wondered if the man had a wife here, or children. There was a hint of East Coast schooling in his voice, his manners too refined for a guy who managed a rough-and-tumble timber camp in the middle of nowhere. It struck him that perhaps this wasn't what the mill manager had imagined for himself as a younger man. Maybe he understood how things happened, how choices were made and things changed slowly over time, until one day you realized you'd started out heading for one place and wound up somewhere completely different.

"What will you do, then?" the mill manager said. "Where's home for you?"

Pepper put his hand on Moira's. "Back to New York, I suppose," he said.

It was a lie. The first thing Markham would do was wire Brooklyn to cancel their room at the Hotel St. Agnes, maybe have their things thrown out in the street. His eyes moved up to her face. She knew there was no place for them back there. Not anymore.

"You've had this idea now and you're not going to let go of it," she said. "Are you?"

"It's the only way," he said. "It's all we've got."

Her shoulders slumped and she worked her jaw from side to side, staring at something in the middle of the floor. "Fine," she said. "But when it all comes out in the wash, I want it noted for the permanent record what a stupid idea I said this was."

He turned back to the mill manager. "Is there a telephone in this place?"

The mill manager said his office girl would show him. As Pepper let the door to the office swing shut behind him he heard Moira say: "This isn't normal for us."

"I'm sure," the mill manager said. Pepper could almost see him fingering his glasses.

The office girl was a curvy brunette with thick ankles underneath a navy-blue skirt and white blouse. She took him through a cramped hallway and down a creaking flight of stairs to an out-of-the-way room on the building's first floor. Inside, an old man with a two-day beard stooped over floor-to-ceiling shelves crammed with dusty ledgers and invoice stacks. With fingers dotted in ink he showed Pepper the telephone.

"Only one for twenty-five miles," he said, like Pepper had come down there just to look.

Fritz Mundt's card was the only thing left in his wallet. He did his best not to think about that part as he unfolded the card and held it up to the light to make out the numbers. The operator was in Portland and it took some time for her to make the connection. The phone rang for a long time and Pepper was about to tell her to forget it when he heard a click and then that unmistakable voice echoing somewhere out in all that static. It took a moment for Fritz to figure out who was calling and for them both to be sure they could hear each other.

"Listen," Pepper said when there was nothing else left to say. "You still need someone to train your darkie?"

Part II

★

CINCINNATI SMOKE

He left the lodge at sunup, waiting until he was out on the porch to sit down and put on his shoes because he didn't want to wake Carol Jean. The railing creaked as he hoisted himself up, taking a few experimental steps into the sparse grass to test his balance. He was pleased to find his head unmuddled and free from the pressure that walled up behind his eyes so often now. He felt no dizziness, no flashes of pain. As he made his way down the hill, working the stiffness out of his neck and back, Garfield Taft hoped today would be one of his good days.

Fitch and Prichard waited for him by the row of tiny cottages. Two chubby white boys looking pale and unshaven, a couple of 175-pound guys trapped in sloppy 200-pound bodies.

"All the way down today, champ?" Fitch said, hopeful smiles spreading across their heavy pie faces.

Taft walked past and propped one leg on top of the rail fence, reaching to grab his toe. Summer was still hanging on, but he could feel the mornings getting colder, the deadness of sleep lurking in his body longer and longer.

"Maybe we take it easy today," said Prichard. "Not shoot our load before Jack Sherry."

The way Taft curled his lip made the other white boy laugh.

"Don't be such a milksop, Prichard," Fitch said. He glanced at Taft like *Am I right?*

Taft turned and began to run, following the fence to where the main gate of the hunting camp loomed some twenty feet above the road. The gate was an arch fashioned from three huge trees, two of them cut into Y-shaped supports and the third laid across the top, polished and lacquered to a high shine. You could tell the hunting camp had been something once, though the big lodge remained unfinished and the four smaller cottages below had fallen into disrepair. Up the hill from the lodge was an empty barn that once must've housed pack animals, and set off to one side was the automobile garage Fritz Mundt had cleared out and turned into a gym. All of it so grand and proud in spite of being way out here in the middle of nowhere. For Mundt to be able to afford this place, Taft guessed something very bad had happened to the men who built it.

Fitch and Prichard fell in step behind him, the three of them trotting in silence under the archway. In this direction the road twisted six miles down the mountain through deep forest all the way to the outskirts of town. Where it went the opposite way, Taft didn't know. Canada maybe. Alaska. Santa's workshop. He didn't care.

After less than a minute of running, the tightness in his legs and lower back began to bother him. In another five the chill had been run out of him and the sun felt hot on his neck and shoulders. He started sweating, trying to ignore the dull ache in his bad ankle. The hard-packed gravel inflamed his shins so that after the first mile or so his only thought was *Goddamn it, goddamn it, goddamn it,* pounding along with each step.

Putting his chin into his shoulder, he asked what day it was.

"Friday," one of the white boys said.

"Friday," he repeated, and from the stupid way they grinned back at him he must have been smiling.

"Tomorrow's the day, champ," the other one said. "Sherry don't know what's coming for him."

"Hush, now," Taft said.

Friday meant the schoolboys would be waiting for him. It was time to lose the chaperones. He picked up the pace as he rounded a bend and started up a rise, his long legs tugging at the ground, and immediately began to pull away. The shorter, dumpier men tried to match him but couldn't keep up. Soon their huffing and puffing faded from his ears, his thighs pounding and arms pumping as he drove up the grade. Gravel went in his shoe and blistered his heel, but he kept running. At the top of the hill he looked back and saw the white boys struggling, barely halfway. After one more switch-back, he left the main road, snaking onto an old game trail partially hidden in the brush. He kept his pace up a bit longer, but as soon as he was sure he was far enough into the trees that they wouldn't see him, he stopped to walk.

This place was near the continental divide, Mundt had told him once, and the country out here was strange to him. At times the forest could be so densely packed with needle trees that you couldn't see more than fifty feet. Then, suddenly, it would open up into weed-clustered hollows where deer, foxes and chipmunks darted around boulders as big as cars. Other times the woods would come up short at treacherous, rocky cliffs only mountain goats could climb. It gave him the feeling that this whole place was perched out on the edge of the world.

This is no country for you, he told himself as he stepped over rocks that sat waiting to break a toe, loose patches of dirt that could twist an ankle if he put his weight down in one. These were not the lush, mossy woods of central Ohio, where they'd sent him to serve his three years at Foxwood, nor was it the high desert of Utah, where he'd met Judith, his first wife, while on a wrestling junket. It certainly wasn't Cincinnati, with its rolling hills and streets lined with trees that turned golden-apple red this time of year.

It made him feel foolish, how much he missed that town. When they let him out of Foxwood, the first thing he and Carol Jean did was get the Rolls out of storage and drive back to Cincinnati so he could buy ten loaves of his favorite bread from Winton Hill Bakery. She pitched a fuss over it, of course, saying she'd rather celebrate with steak or lobster, pointing out their room at the Hotel Gibson was just a few blocks in any direction from some of the city's best restaurants. He told her to just pack her shit and get in the damn car, and when they got there and filled the Rolls with the smell of fresh bread and drove down to a spot he knew on the banks of the Mississippi to share a piece slathered in soft butter, she didn't have many negative things to say.

On the way home he told her they couldn't stay at the Gibson anymore. At first she thought he was pulling her leg, but he saw a cloud fall over her face as he explained that after paying the trial lawyers, appeals lawyers, tax lawyers and divorce lawyers, the Rolls was about all they had left. After that he thought one morning he'd wake up and find her gone, yet somehow she was still here, still with him. He had to hand it to her for that.

The thought of Carol Jean pushed him to start running again. He kept it up as long as he could but stopped after a few minutes, this time leaning a hand against a tree trunk while he caught his breath. That was the funny thing about quitting. Once you stopped to walk once, it was easier to do it the next time. The trick was to push through the whole run with no breaks, to not even unlock the part of your mind that let you give up. Once you did, you might as well just head back to the lodge.

He thought about Jack Sherry, hoping it would get him mad, but the only thing he felt for Sherry was a vague sort of pity. That old boy must've been pretty desperate to sign up for this shit, riding all the way out from Reno to Washington State just to take a beating. It was hard to believe Sherry thought he might win—even if their match would be just a single fall—but some men insisted on learning things the hard way. Maybe Sherry was one of those.

The trail was steep and slow going, cutting straight down the grade to the base of the mountain. Even at his crawling pace he reached the bottom well before Fitch and Prichard. As he got close to the spot where the trail met up with the main road, he scooped up a handful of pebbles and dropped into a crouch, waddling along quick and quiet through the weeds. Soon he could see the boys up on the road, four of them straddling bicycles, staring up into the hills, waiting. This gang had been showing up every Friday all summer, getting up long before dawn in order to pedal all the way out here to see him come running down the mountain. How strange he must seem to them, Taft thought, shirtless and dripping sweat, thundering down the hill, grimacing from the pain. Maybe they imagined he was some kind of ghoul or monster. Or maybe, if they were old enough, the boys would know him from the papers and might think of him by the awful names the sportswriters had for him: the Dinge or the Great Ape Man or Cincinnati Smoke. Taft had no children of his own, so he was no good at telling their ages.

After creeping as close as he dared to the road, he sat on his haunches to watch. One of the boys already looked antsy, rocking the wheels of his bicycle back and forth like a jockey trying to keep his horse from busting through the starting gate. Taft sifted through the pebbles until he found a good one and tossed it, pinging it off the front fender of the boy's bicycle. At once they all stopped fidgeting and looked around. When he was sure they still couldn't see him, Taft tossed half a handful up into the sky, sending a shower of rocks skittering around their wheels. It spooked them, and just as they spun around he leapt from the weeds, flailing his arms in the air and howling like a rabid dog.

The boys screamed, fumbling to get their bikes turned around as their feet scrambled for the pedals. They darted off, spraying dirt, squealing with terror and delight as they raced away, little legs pumping like pistons. Taft chased them a few steps and then stopped in the middle of the road to prop his hands on his knees and laugh.

⊷————⊶

He'd gone half a mile back up the old game trail when the pressure started to build at the front of his skull and the ground lurched under his feet. He had to stop to brace himself against the side of a huge boulder, his breath coming in short, shallow huffs and his vision pinching in at the corners. The trees seemed to press down on him, bending from all sides to scold him with long, spindly branches. He doubled over, a flash of pain piercing his head. When he straightened up again he wasn't sure which way he was supposed to be heading. He closed his eyes and tried to steady himself. *Not here*, he thought, *not out here all alone*.

As he always did at times like this, he thought of Fleetwood Wallace. Tipping his head back against the rough surface of the boulder, he forced himself to picture the little man's long, wiry arms and his friendly face shaped like an upside-down teardrop. Fleet, as he insisted on being called, was a lifelong con and petty thief who'd been Taft's cellmate for all but the last year of his stay at Foxwood. He claimed to have spent more of his years on earth inside a prison cell than out. He could be surly and sulky and utterly ruthless, and without him Taft wouldn't have survived even the first month in that place. He remembered the moment they met, after two big jailers marched him past what seemed like an endless row of cells before suddenly herding him into an open doorway with the jab of a nightstick. Fleet was sitting on top of the cell's tiny table, smoking a cigarette with his feet resting on a chair. When he saw Taft, he patted his poof of hair with his free hand and flashed a gold-toothed grin.

"Well, hey," he said, standing up, his voice lilting and high like one of those jazz singers. "Hey."

The guards left him without a word and Taft stood in the doorway, a folded stack of bedding and a change of clothes piled in his arms like he was bringing in a birthday cake. The cell was narrow and not too deep, with just enough room for a pair of bunks and a tiny writing table that bolted to the wall. In back, the toilet and sink were set so close you could wash your hands while sitting on the pot. Taft didn't yet fully understand prison—the suffocating loneliness, the inability to ever get comfortable, the terror—but thinking back on it he knew his first look at that cell put the initial crack in the wall he'd built up inside himself. The rest would come with time. In that moment, though, all he saw was a skinny little guy with a home-done haircut standing in the middle of the cell like he didn't know what to do with his hands. Finally, Fleetwood Wallace got up the nerve to offer him one.

"I know who you are," he said before Taft could tell him.

Taft stooped to set his belongings on the table. "Course you do," he said.

Fleet's things were spread out on the bottom bunk, a ratty blanket pulled tight over the meager lump of mattress. Taft made a show of inspecting it all. "I'm too damn big for this top bunk," he said, giving his new roommate a sharp sweep of the eyes. "How about we switch?"

"I'm accustomed to the bottom," Fleet said.

Taft put his hands on his hips in a way that swelled his chest a little bit. "Look at me," he said. "No way will this take my weight. I'll crash straight through and crush your skinny behind while you sleep."

Fleet fidgeted, his mouth clicking to the side a few times. "Ah, hell," he finally said. "You can have it."

"I thank you kindly," Taft said, stepping back while the smaller man stripped the low bunk and stood on the second rung to fix up his new spot.

Taft sat down, the bed hard as a sack of stones, and fixed his gaze on the chipped, slate-colored wall.

"If you're trying to stare a hole in it," Fleet said, resuming his position on top of the writing table. "I tried that already."

With a quick flick of the wrist, he tossed something at him, and Taft snatched it out of the air. A tobacco pouch with a packet of rolling papers tied to it with a piece of string.

"If you ain't a smoking man," he said, "you best become one."

That's how it began. "See the whole scene," Fleet told him during one of their first days on the yard together, making his eyes wide and sweeping one hand in front of him. "That's the best thing I can tell you. See the whole scene, then double-check to make sure you *seen* it right."

It took a while for Taft to understand what that meant. He had never been what you might call a curious man, but soon enough he began to discover how much you could learn about a place by watching. In time, he could tell which prisoners were hiding blades up their sleeves from the way they held their arms close to their sides. He could pick out which handshakes passed rolls of cash and tiny envelopes of dope. Fleet taught him which men on the yard could be trusted, which couldn't, and which ones to stay away from altogether.

Now Taft opened his eyes. He rolled his back across the face of the boulder a few times to loosen it. "See the whole scene," he said to himself, blinking and taking big, slow breaths until the trees went back to normal.

Then he remembered: the boys on bicycles. Of course. If he just followed the game trail up the hill he would hit the main road and eventually the hunting camp. Carol Jean was there waiting for him. He stood still a few minutes longer, making sure his wind was sturdy despite the thudding pain in his head, and then started to walk again. After a while he jogged some more.

Just as they had been before, Fitch and Prichard were standing by the main gate. The two white boys leaned against the fence, red-faced and sweaty after chasing him down and up the mountain without ever finding him.

"You all are some lollygaggers," Taft said, clapping Prichard on the shoulder as he walked past.

He kept a bottle of Dr. Paulson's All-Purpose Pain Remedy stashed in the weeds behind the outhouse. The thick, dark syrup coated his insides as he chugged it down, and by the time he relieved himself and began carrying buckets of water up from the well, the pain in his head had mellowed and he was feeling good again. There was an old trash bin he'd hauled down from the garage and spent a couple days scrubbing out. It took half a dozen trips up from the well with buckets in each hand to fill it, but it was worth the work. The mountain water was frosty cold and felt like a million tiny pinpricks on his skin as he dunked himself to the armpits. Water sloshed onto the ground and he rested the back of his head against the metal lip of the bin, the freezing, burning pain alerting him to every sore joint, every swollen knot, places he didn't even know hurt until just now. It wasn't as good as the ice baths and rubdowns he used to get at the Chancery Athletic Club in Cincinnati, but it was close.

As he rested there, Carol Jean came out onto the porch in her nightgown. She had a coffee cup pressed in both hands, and her auburn hair fell over her shoulders in a mussed-from-sleep kind of way he liked. He hoped it was coffee in that cup. He hoped she wasn't in one of her moods.

"How you feeling, big smoke?" she said, a little smile telling him she was good.

"Lazy," he said. "Shiftless. With a yellow streak up my back like a Chinese."

He stood as she came down the steps and planted a kiss on his neck, leaning into him so he wouldn't drip on her gown. Looking fragile in her bare feet in the middle of all this wilderness.

"Goodness," he said, sinking back into the water. "That's the best thing to happen to me in at least two hours. Maybe ever."

"Wait till you taste the bacon," she said.

She went back up the stairs, putting a little wiggle in her walk for his benefit. "What time's your train?" she said when she had her hand on the doorknob.

"Evening time," he said.

She scrunched her face into a pout. "I wish you'd let me be there," she said. "I want to see you whip Jack Sherry like a stagecoach horse."

He snorted, flicking some water out of the tub to show his patience was running out. "We talked about this," he said. "I can't afford to have my attentions divided, not right now."

"But when you wrestle Strangler Lesko?" she said. "When you win the world's heavyweight championship?"

He tried to smile. "They'd have to lock me up again to keep me from taking you to that one."

He held his breath and plunged his head under the water, a frozen rush across his cheeks and over his scalp, the cold buzzing against the base of his skull. It hurt, but he stayed under as long as he could, a school of bubbles slowly trickling from his nose and mouth. He reminded himself to tell Carol Jean about the schoolboys, betting she would get a kick out of it; but when he came up for air, she was already gone.

The mill manager took a cash draw of twenty-five dollars from the safe in his office and sent them out of New Vermillion on a pump trolley hauling a skiff of freshly cut boards. Their pilots were two sour-smelling men in the wide, soft hats of hill people who spat at each other in some coarse language Moira didn't know. There were no seats on the pump trolley, so she and Pepper hunkered down on the floor of the car, trying to keep out of the wind and sun and rain until the men let them off at a lonely station in the middle of the forest. The first train to arrive was headed south to Portland, so they bought tickets from the conductor and fell instantly to sleep in the deserted passenger car, waking only to change trains for a daylong trip in the opposite direction to Bellingham, Washington. They arrived at dusk, Pepper telephoned Fritz Mundt from the station and he showed up five minutes later to collect them, making little effort to hide a self-satisfied smile.

"Sakes alive," Fritz said, fanning himself with his hat. "You smell like a carload of railroad tramps."

It curdled her guts to see him again. He was thicker around the middle than the young man she remembered knowing in Chicago, and with his hat in his hand she noticed he'd gone bald on top of his head. He was probably barely into his thirties, but the years had put deep creases in his forehead and turned his mouth into a hard little line. When he clapped Pepper on the back and offered to carry their trunk, she felt a twinge of guilt for hating him so much.

As they left the train yard, Pepper remarked he was anxious to meet Garfield Taft, but Fritz said Taft wouldn't arrive until the following day, just a few hours before his match against Alaskan Jack Sherry.

"Wait until you lay eyes on him," he said to Pepper, the two of them walking along like grammar school friends who'd never shared an unfriendly word. "I have no doubt you'll see exactly what I see."

"A meal ticket?" Moira asked, and they both looked at her.

"Quite possibly the most naturally skilled mat man I've ever seen," Fritz said. "And if you don't mind my saying, Moira, the only meal ticket I know of in this scenario is me."

"I'm sorry to be the fly in your soup, Freddy," she sneered back at him. "My feelings are just a little tender at the moment."

Fritz put them up at a hotel downtown, small but nice. The only thing Moira wanted to do was have a bath, and when a crusty old railroad worker at first refused to give up the tub at the end of the hall, she sent Pepper down there to run him off. Afterward, she locked the bathroom door and sat in the water until it turned ice-cold, ignoring a series of knocks at the door as she scrubbed and soaked. It felt like rubbing off an extra layer of skin. They sent their clothes down to be laundered and found them already delivered the following day, hanging on hooks outside their door.

They'd slept through breakfast service, but it felt like a great luxury to put on clean clothes and wander around the corner to a diner for lunch. She ate bacon, lettuce and tomato while Pepper ordered two entrées: a cheeseburger and a baked ham and Swiss sandwich on rye bread. His smile was alive with mischief at the idea he could eat whatever he wanted without worrying about his weight. She felt a little sorry for him, sitting there with his face still swollen and discolored from losing his fight to the huge mill worker. But his mood had lifted so much—even pointing out a couple of amusing entries from the local paper's police blotter—that for the moment she kept her feelings about seeing Fritz Mundt to herself. They both drank cups of strong coffee and her sandwich really was pretty good.

That evening Fritz came to collect them for the match and the three of them walked down to the water, where she could see the town curling around the bay like the jaws of a serpent. A mist hung over the breaks, so thick she couldn't make out the ends of the long docks that thrust out from the shore. They had visited so many towns during their time with the carnival that it was difficult for Moira to tell how any of them were special, but as night came on she could feel Bellingham pulsing with the raw energy of the west. These were places built on rushes for gold, timber and coal, and even as they grew from tent camps into brick-and-mortar cities, they never lost their wildness. There was a time when a place like this would've made her feel homesick for the sweaty, electric buzz of a steamboat cardroom. Now the only thing it stirred in her was a kind of thirst. This town itself had once been just a gamble. She liked to think the men who built it were of her feather.

As they turned in to the center of town, she listened to Pepper and Fritz going on about Garfield Taft. It was a name she'd heard a great deal during the past forty-eight hours, but she didn't recall if she'd ever met the man during Pepper's wrestling days. On the pump trolley out of New Vermillion, he had told her that Taft was once the most famous black grappler in the world. A heavyweight, an undefeated one, and after he'd beaten the rest of the best black wrestlers in the country he'd campaigned in the press for a shot at the world's championship. Frank Gotch had retired by the time Taft came into his own, but new champion Joe Stecher was holding firm to wrestling's color bar. Taft publicly called him a coward for it, even following Stecher on a tour of Australia during the summer of 1916.

He sat in the front row of all the champion's matches and openly mocked him as Stecher easily defeated a string of lesser talent.

The papers murdered Taft for his insolence, writing that he was an affront to the sport, yet another sign of our unraveling culture. Still, they gleefully printed all of his taunts about the champion, writing that the audacity of the modern Negro was without limit. By the following fall, Stecher's resolve never to grant a black man a chance at his title might've been crumbling. He told his friends and training partners that, if the money was right, he might not mind giving Taft the whipping he deserved. Before the two could arrange a match, however, Taft was arrested and sent to prison for operating a whorehouse out of a property he owned in Cincinnati. Nobody had heard from him since.

At the top of a small hill they made a right and approached a stone building with the bulbous flared corners and narrow vaulted windows of a castle. The Bellingham National Guard Armory loomed dark and sturdy over the intersection, where a bored-looking traffic cop stood waiting for traffic. His eyes tracked them as they crossed the street. She smiled and the cop looked away, waving a lonely Studebaker through on a left-hand turn. Inside the armory an old woman sat at a table with her waxy purple hands folded on top of a metal cashbox. The woman nodded at Fritz, looking impressed with herself for remembering him, and allowed them to push through the double doors behind her without paying the cover charge.

Moira was surprised to find the armory's gymnasium less than half full. Most of the audience sat in rows of folding chairs set up on the floor, while the bleachers that had been pulled out from the walls stood all but empty. The majority of the men were white and looked like slightly more citified versions of the loggers and mill workers they'd encountered in New Vermillion, in sagging overalls and sweat-ringed caps. There were a few blacks clustered around the back row of chairs and she saw one group of Indians, whose braids hung past the shoulders of their denim shirts. Fritz led them up an aisle and picked out seats in the center of the bleachers. She estimated there couldn't be more than two hundred people in all.

When Pepper had told her they were going to a wrestling match, she imagined it would be held in the town's best theater—men in suits and silk hats, girls going around serving refreshments—but the armory gym was dusty and dank. Threadbare tapestries hung from the walls, boasting of the achievements of the local National Guard reserves and the young officer training corps. The closest thing to a concession stand was an old man in short sleeves selling popcorn from a pushcart.

"This is a paltry affair," she said as they settled into their places.

"It's a decent little crowd for a bout like this," Fritz said. "Between you and me, we were lucky to find a recognizable opponent for Taft in this area. Alaskan Jack was already out in Reno to face Chris Sorensen when we contacted him."

The timekeeper tolled the bell to quiet the crowd. The ring announcer, a man with a shaggy beard and an ill-fitting blazer, held up a paper megaphone emblazoned with the blue and gray logo of the Washington State Normal School and reminded the crowd that the evening's main bout would be one fall to a finish.

"Only one fall?" Pepper said.

"It's all we could get Sherry to do," Fritz said. "I wager he thinks he can walk out of here with a fluke win."

Alaskan Jack Sherry was announced as weighing 210 pounds and wrestling out of the central fire station in Oklahoma City, Oklahoma. He appeared to little fanfare, coming out of one of the locker rooms on the far side of the gymnasium. He was a weather-beaten man with jet-black whiskers and a thick crop of hair that hung almost to his ears. He wore a pair of knee-length wrestling tights; short socks rolled down to the tops of his black boots; and a towel that may once have been white slung over his shoulder. He kept his eyes on his feet as he strolled to the ring, not acknowledging the smattering of applause, his jaw fixed, his expression flat. *Steadfast*, Moira decided was the word for him.

"If no white man will wrestle Taft," she said to Pepper as Alaskan Jack ducked through the ropes and into the ring, "then why is Sherry game?"

"Sherry's a half-breed," Fritz said, leaning around to look at her, "and he'd like to earn a shot at Strangler Lesko himself. A win here lifts either man's standing."

"Theoretically," Pepper said.

When Garfield Taft stepped out of his locker room and into the light, it felt as though every man in the room stopped talking at once. Even Fritz forgot what he'd been saying, trailing off in midsentence. Taft wore a crimson robe with a towel rolled underneath the collar. He was tall, his bald head nearly reaching the top of the locker room doorway, and his body lacked the stocky bulk carried by some heavyweights. Instead he was built straight up and down, with impossibly broad shoulders, long limbs and calves thick with muscle. He was announced at 240 pounds and hailing from Cincinnati, Ohio. As he walked to the ring he surveyed the crowd, a small smile on his round face. He paused to wipe the soles of his boots on the ring apron before stepping over the ropes and into a corner opposite Sherry. The audience sat transfixed as he shrugged out of his robe and began to loosen up, swinging his arms lazily over his head and across his chest. A natural showman, Moira thought. She'd seen very few men who could hold a room by just standing in the ring. Pepper was one. Frank Gotch was another, the one time she'd seen him wrestle in front of a packed arena in Indianapolis.

The crowd came out of its spell when Taft stepped forward to shake Sherry's hand, and a man in the front row who held a pair of spectacles in a tight fist yelled: "Kill that nigger!"

Taft's smile only gleamed wider in response. He wore a black singlet, the trunks tied with a sash matching the color of his robe. When he turned to hand his towel to a ring attendant, Moira caught sight of a scattering of pockmarked scars bubbling pink across his back.

Pepper saw them, too. "What's that about?"

Fritz shrugged. "Negroes have scars," he said. "All the boys have scars."

The referee gave them their final instructions, and Moira noticed one of Pepper's legs was jittering. She put her hand on his knee to stop it. Men in the front rows were cupping their hands around their mouths to shout things at Taft, but their voices were lost to the din in the room. A scuffle broke out, two Indians clawing at each other's faces as they tumbled to the floor, knocking over a row of chairs. Their friends pulled them apart, both men coming up bloody and winded, and Moira noticed for the first time that there wasn't any security here. The men just went back to their seats still grumbling and glaring at each other.

The referee stood in the center of the ring clapping his hands to begin the match, and Sherry came out of his corner in a low crouch. Taft strolled around the edge of the ring, casually trailing a hand along the top rope. Sherry's face remained blank as he followed him with his eyes, but neither man was in a rush to engage with the other.

"Get on with it!" a man shouted from the front row before a full minute had passed.

It was loud enough that Taft stopped to glare down at him, and Sherry took that as his cue, gliding forward to shoot in for a tackle. Taft turned as if noticing Sherry for the first time and, putting one hand on the back of his neck, pushed him down onto the mat face-first. Stepping out of his grasp, Taft walked away, giving his opponent a full view of his back as he crossed the ring. The arrogance of it rankled the crowd even more, and a man moved the ringside barrier a foot forward as he sprang out of his seat to jeer at him.

"They don't seem to mind that Sherry attacked him while he wasn't looking," Moira said. "Do they?"

Pepper and Fritz were transfixed by the show in the ring. They didn't answer her as Taft walked back to his corner and leaned against it, looking at Sherry like he'd just told a very old joke. Sherry got up from his knees and shook his arms out, working his neck back and forth a few times before coming forward again. This time Taft met him in the center, using one long arm to brace against Sherry's forehead while the other dipped low and plucked his nearest ankle off the mat. The ease of it was startling, and as Sherry toppled over onto his backside, Moira saw Pepper look over at Fritz with his mouth in a silent *Oh.*

Sherry tried to scoot away, but Taft held firm, keeping him cradled on his side by pressing his weight down on top of him. For a moment it appeared they were both stuck. As long as Sherry didn't move, Taft couldn't pin him, and Taft couldn't risk letting go long enough to improve his own position.

"He should be trying to snatch that arm," Pepper said. "Sherry's practically giving it away."

The two wrestlers stayed like that, neither looking like he knew what to do, until Sherry began to writhe and stretch, eventually jiggling one of his legs free. When Taft moved to try to recapture it, Sherry sprang backward, coming to his feet as the crowd crowed its approval. Taft was slow getting up, and when he did, Moira saw he was slick with sweat, the smile gone from his face. Suddenly Sherry seemed to be the fresher man. He started to muscle Taft around the ring in a collar-and-elbow tie-up.

Fritz shifted in his seat, the bleacher muttering under his weight. Pepper leaned forward, bracing his elbows on his knees. Moira realized she was holding her breath and inhaled deeply as Sherry backed Taft into a corner. It was clear that Taft's size was giving him trouble. Try as he might, Sherry couldn't get enough leverage to trip the big man and couldn't get close enough to his body to grab for another tackle. The frustration and exhaustion were plain in both their faces. They might fight to a draw, Moira thought, just before Sherry reared back and thumbed Taft in the eye.

It was a quick, stabbing blow, but still simple enough to make out from their seats in the bleachers. Taft grunted and turned his head to the side, a trickle of blood and a welt already appearing beneath his eyebrow. When the crowd saw him in pain, it only cheered louder.

The referee did nothing, pretending he hadn't seen, and anger rose in Taft's face. A curtain dropped behind his eyes. With one quick step, he ducked out of the corner and got behind Sherry, sweeping his legs out from under him with a vicious kick. Sherry fell onto his belly and Taft followed him down. Locking his grip tight around the other man's waist, Taft laid his head in the middle of Sherry's back and rolled. Throwing his hips over to the side, he bridged, forcing Sherry's shoulders to the mat while his legs flailed impotently in the air. The referee went to his knees, pressing his cheek to the canvas to check the pin, and then slapped the mat with an open palm.

Moira thought a riot might break out. As Taft came to one knee, a hailstorm of crumpled programs and popcorn boxes roared down around him. An old man near the front had taken his false teeth out and was trying to decide whether to throw them. Taft used the top rope to pull himself to his feet and prodded at the swelling around his eyes with the tips of his fingers. He gave no indication at all that he noticed the bedlam in the stands. After ducking through the ropes and descending to the floor, his gaze locked on the place where Fritz, Pepper and Moira were sitting, and for a moment she felt glued to her spot. In an instant he looked right through her without seeming to see and then turned to stride down the aisle to the locker room. Not giving anyone in the crowd another glance.

It took close to fifteen minutes for the audience to filter out of the armory into the street, many of them still jostling and shoving each other in a way that made Moira feel sorry for the town's speak-easies. By the time she, Pepper, and Fritz were able to work their way down off the bleachers and to the locker room door, a man sweeping the floor in a pair of coveralls told them Taft had already left.

"Left?" Fritz said, like it might be a put-on.

"Had me order him a cab before the match even started, sir," the janitor said. "Told me it wasn't going to take long."

"I can't say I blame him for not wanting to stick around," Moira said, watching the last and drunkest of the crowd getting shepherded out a side exit by the old woman they'd seen manning the cashbox.

"Mr. Taft shares quite a bond with his new wife," Fritz said, re-covering. "I'm sure he left as soon as possible because he couldn't stand the thought of being without her any longer." He clapped his hands as if signaling the close of business and then offered to buy Moira and Pepper a late dinner.

The restaurant was not far from the armory. Nothing in Belling-ham was far, it seemed, as most of the downtown area was clustered in the same three or four blocks. The place's dining room was dimly lit and featured wildlife stuffed and mounted on all four walls. Their table was directly under a scene showing a mountain lion leaping down to sink its teeth into the neck of a deer, and Moira was proud of herself for not bringing up how apropos that seemed. Fritz ordered roast capon and lima bean salad while Moira chose the broiled impe-rial squab. Pepper asked for top sirloin steak served bloody under bordelaise sauce.

"What do you make of Taft?" he asked her when Fritz excused himself to go to the restroom. "Him running out like that."

"I think we ought to follow his lead," she said, and he scowled at her.

Once Fritz returned, the wrestling match dominated the dinner conversation. Moira said very little, watching Pepper stuff himself while Fritz picked around the edges of his cooked bird. She searched his face for some glimmer of the man who had betrayed them years ago but didn't see it. All she saw was a guy who looked happy to be back in the company of his old friend.

"Well?" Fritz said once the plates had been cleared and he'd pulled a clay-colored cigar and gold hinge-top lighter out of his jacket pocket. "You think he looked up to scratch?"

Pepper sat back in his chair, hands folded over his belly. He looked a little green around the gills from overeating. Finally he said: "Eh."

"'Eh'?" Fritz said, and then laughed. "No, you must've seen the way Taft captivated the crowd."

Now Moira spoke up. "They really hated his guts," she said.

Fritz passed the cigar under his nose before firing up his lighter. "I know," he said. "Wasn't it fantastic?"

"If you say so," she said.

Fritz repositioned himself in the chair, pointing the cigar at her like it was one of his fingers. "I get the darnedest feeling you have something you want to say to me, Moira," he said.

She steadied herself a bit. "I just find it curious that you would come back for us after all this time, Freddy," she said. "Especially since I know the last time we were all together someone paid you five thousand dollars to break my husband's leg during training before he lost the title."

"Moira," Pepper said.

Fritz stared at her like she'd accused him of murdering a child. "Now, wait just a minute," he said.

"Whoever paid you must've known there was no way a rummy like Whip Windham could beat Pepper so long as he had two good legs under him," she said. "I think it's past time we had the truth."

"I'm not sure which makes you dumber," Fritz said, "that you feel you're on stable enough ground to make these accusations in the first place, or that you expect me to sit here and listen to them."

Pepper stood up, the legs of his chair squeaking across the parquet floor. "Hey, now," he said.

The two men glared at each other. It might've turned into something if their waiter—a scarecrow wearing thin suspenders—hadn't come to see if there was anything else he could bring them. He slowed when he saw Pepper on his feet and Fritz gripping the edge of the table like he meant to snap it in half.

"I apologize," Moira said, a little too loudly. "Obviously, I've gotten the wrong impression somehow."

Pepper sat down, but Fritz wasn't ready to let it drop. "I'll not suffer these accusations against my character," he said. "As a promoter, my reputation is all I have in this world."

"In fairness," Pepper said, "you haven't promoted shit yet."

The waiter laughed at that—a sudden bubble of a laugh—and they all looked up at him, reminded that he was still standing there. An embarrassed look passed over his face and he asked if they were interested in a nightcap. Pepper said they were. By the time they'd all ordered drinks and sent the waiter on his way, the tension had eased a bit.

"I apologize for my tone just now," Fritz said, not looking all that sorry. "Surely the thrill of tonight's action is still in all our blood."

"I'm certain that's it," Moira said, trying to make it sound genuine.

Fritz said he understood if they were on edge. They hadn't had an easy couple of days. He said they should drink their drinks and call it a night, that they had an early train in the morning. He said he was sure their moods would improve once they all got to where they were going.

"It's the most picturesque little spot," he said. "What's the word? *Bucolic.*"

Moira didn't like the way the word sounded on his tongue, like the name of a disease or an ingredient in some chemical formula.

She was done making an issue of things for one night, though, so she just smiled and hoisted a glass when the waiter brought it.

"You've been awfully coy about all this," Pepper said to Fritz. "You said you had to get Taft out of Chicago. Where are you head-quartered now? St. Louis? Louisville?"

Fritz grinned. "Louisville," he said, like it was the punch line to a joke. "No, no. At the moment, home is much closer than that."

They caught an eastbound train out of Bellingham before sunrise. Fritz reserved a private sleeper car for them, saying that even after a couple of nights in hotel beds they looked like they could use the rest. Pepper didn't argue. With his busted ribs, the idea of riding crammed into one of the open passenger cars made him feel hungover and sick all over again. There was just a small crowd waiting for the first ride out of town on Sunday morning, most of them too polite to stare much at his black eye and puffy cheek. While Fritz went off to send a telegram, Pepper and Moira used the last of the mill manager's money to buy a soda pop from the station's refreshment window and shared it while sitting on one of the platform's narrow benches. As soon as they got on the train, Moira started pocketing things.

"Can you bring us something?" she asked the steward as he punched their tickets and unlocked the door to the sleeper. "Some chewing gum or hand towels?"

There were mints in a dish and she emptied them into her purse before she started digging around under the washtub for extra soaps. "We're not going to prison," Pepper said. "Do you have to act like a pack rat building a nest?"

She didn't look up from what she was doing. "After the past few days," she said, "I think you'd be best off to suffer through a few of my peculiarities in silence."

They washed up in the tub, Moira leaning over to cover his eyes with an outstretched hand when she ran a washcloth between her legs. "I do so love a whore's bath," she said. The clothes they'd gotten cleaned in Bellingham were all they had, so they hung them in the sleeper's tiny closet to air out and sat together at the window seat in their underwear. They watched the close quarters of the city empty into the flat green farmland of central Washington. Eventually she put her head on his shoulder and closed her eyes.

"Montana," she said. "You don't think *that* seems a little odd?"

"I wasn't about to start asking questions about it," he said. "I practically had to beg him for the job in the first place."

Moira sighed. "Now that we've watched each other scrub our privates, though, maybe it's time for a frank assessment of the facts," she said. "None of this adds up."

She recounted it all for him in slow, painstaking detail as if he didn't remember: Fritz showing up in San Francisco, Taft's match against Sherry in a crummy little venue still only half full, Fritz paying for dinner, for a hotel, for the train, promising to take them shopping when they got to where they were going. That was the other thing: where they were going. Not Chicago or even some farm out in Wisconsin, Iowa or Indiana, or anywhere inside the territory Fritz took over from Abe Blomfeld. Middle-of-nowhere Montana. More than anything, that didn't track.

"Everybody says it's hard times in the wrestling business," she said. "Yet Freddy is spending cash like he's got a printing press stashed somewhere."

"What's that saying about a gift horse?" Pepper said. "Don't kick him in the balls while he's handing out candy? Something like that."

She opened her eyes. "Why are he and Taft hiding out like a

couple of Wild West outlaws?" she said. "Why isn't Taft traveling with us? You act like you haven't considered any of this."

"I told you," Pepper said. "Fritz needed a place where Taft could have his white woman and not make a scene. This is the first lucky break we've caught in God knows how long, Moira, so I'm inclined to take it at face value for the moment."

"I don't believe in luck," she said. "Luck is for suckers."

"You believe in it just fine when it suits you," he said.

They dozed, but Pepper couldn't get all the way to sleep. He knew she had a point. He was shocked when Fritz said they were bound for Butte, Montana, on the Milwaukee Road Line. It didn't exactly seem like the most convenient place to have a training camp. Even if Fritz had to get Taft and his wife out of Chicago, why not set them up somewhere closer? Someplace where it would be easy to find gym space and training partners. Pepper had never spent any time in Montana, but it was near enough to Idaho and the orphanage to remind him of the old creeping fear.

Close to midnight they began the long, slow climb into the Rockies. As they passed through Coeur d'Alene, he crooked his neck against the glass to see the tops of the mountains, the moonlight shimmering off the surface of the lake. He imagined if he got off the train and drove almost a full day south he'd arrive in Boise and could look up his old man. Surely his father would be dead by now, he thought, if not knifed by some barroom drunk then from the rotgut he drank. He wondered if there would be a grave somewhere. At some point he must've drifted off to sleep, because the next thing he knew the sun was coming up. They rolled through a couple of mining camps, blowing the horn as the miners went about their business without looking up. He and Moira ate breakfast in their compartment and then sat smoking cigarettes on the divan as the train rattled over trestles and through little towns whose names they'd never know.

The ride didn't last as long as Pepper wanted. He would've liked to sit by the window watching the world glide by for days, weeks, the rest of his life, but a little after two o'clock that afternoon they clicked and chugged up one final hill and emerged on the high, flat tabletop of land he guessed gave Butte, Montana, its name. The town sat out there like a coiled snake sunning itself on a rock, a murky industrial haze scuffing up the sky.

The air struck him as they shuffled off the train. He knew they'd climbed almost six thousand feet into the mountains, and the breeze sang with prickly, sulfurous smells. They met Fritz on the platform and he led them out to the street, where lines of cars hogged the curb and the sidewalks were flush with people. Their car was a brand-new Oldsmobile sedan parked half a block down, easy to spot by the dumpy, potato-faced wrestler leaning against it. There was no mistaking the heavy brow and the cauliflower ears, though the man also had red-rimmed eyes and a roll of flab hanging over his belt. He lit up when he saw Fritz and Pepper, grinning as he helped them get their trunks loaded into the car. As he opened the door for them, the guy stuck out a fleshy hand.

"Steve Prichard," he said. "You remember me?"

"Sure," Pepper said, though he didn't think they'd met before. "Of course."

He let Moira take the front seat and scrambled onto the back bench beside Fritz. Prichard wheeled them out into traffic, half watching where they were going while telling them his life story over one shoulder. It seemed like a tale he was used to telling and he looked excited to have a new audience for it. Pepper listened long enough to hear the parts about a promising wrestling career derailed by injury and Prichard joining the army, and then tuned the guy out. He wanted a look at this place.

The roads of Butte were a wide jumble of odd corners and sudden slopes, built wide but never quite flat. Even in the light of day, storefronts and rooming houses glowed with electric lights. There were so many mines—some of them built square in the middle of neighborhoods—that tailings bled out into the streets, giving the town itself the look of being dug into the earth. On the bald hill north of the city, he could see the surface works of bigger digging operations, the spider shapes of a thousand steel headframes standing out black against the horizon. A jumbled network of dirt tracks connected them, and trucks huffed and puffed as they crawled along between sagging wooden buildings. Smokestacks smoked and lifts went down and up, dropping the men miles into the ground and pulling up ore to be shipped off to the smelters. They passed a streetcar stop where a group of miners stood waiting for the train to take them up to work. They were unshaven, several of them still dirty from the previous shift. Their eyes followed the car as it rolled by, Moira's blonde hair trailing in the breeze and Pepper sitting behind her with his arm hanging out the window.

"We're making one stop," Fritz said. "Get you gypsies some presentable clothes."

Their destination turned out to be a department store on the ground floor of a huge redbrick building with copper arches over every doorway. Inside there were high vaulted ceilings and deep carpets, the trim on the walls and the fixtures of the water fountains done in the same copper metalwork as outside. Fritz bought three new suits for Pepper and three dresses for Moira, slapping down his checkbook and scrawling out a note for a hundred dollars without blinking, then breezing them out as quickly as they'd gone in.

At first Pepper thought they might be headed for one of the big hotels he could see on the outskirts of downtown, but a couple blocks after leaving the department store Prichard steered them off the paved road onto a dirt track as rough as an old wagon trail. The car tipped and dipped on its axles as it blew through a neighborhood of tightly packed shacks where children chased balls on dead lawns and men sat shirtless on wooden steps. A woman in a ragged housedress burned trash in a can at the curb. The last they saw of the city was its immense brick slaughterhouse, where they had to stop while a couple of boys urged a crowd of fat hogs across the road.

While they waited, Prichard said: "I was at Fort Omaha when I read about you losing the title to that fellow Windham."

"Were you," Pepper said. He thought he saw the muscles in Fritz's neck stiffen.

Prichard's big pumpkin head bobbed up and down. "Mother mailed me the press clipping," he said, then whistled low. "Whip Windham. No one saw that one coming, am I right?"

He said it like it was supposed to be some great compliment. Pepper leaned forward and rested his forearms on the seatback. "I wrestled that match with a broken leg," he said. "Did you know that? Did Mother write that in her letter?"

The corners of Prichard's lips turned down. "The newspaper account focused mostly on the winner," he said. "There was a war going on overseas and we were worried we were headed for it. Nobody wanted to read a guy's excuses."

Pepper started going over things he might say to that as they rounded a tight bend in the road, but Prichard pushed down on the accelerator, shooting them through a stand of trees and filling the car with the growl of the engine. The momentum sent him rocking back in his seat, clutching his side, cradling his injured ribs.

Fifteen minutes later they were crawling along the washboard switchbacks, going up and up into the craggy mountains, where the breeze was sweet on his bruised face. Finally they drove under an enormous wooden gate and onto a tight gravel drive where a run of small cabins sat at the fringe of the tree line. Pepper's gaze followed the road up a low hill to where a large hunting lodge loomed. To one side sat a low-slung but sizable building that might have been a garage, and up the hill a big red barn was melting into the earth. He could see that the lodge stood unfinished, half of the upper floor just framing studs.

As they crept farther up the road they came upon a dark-colored car parked at the edge of the woods. From the drab brown uniform and mulish build of the man who stood by the back bumper, Pepper could tell it was the police. Prichard stopped and the cop came and stuck his head in the driver's-side window. He had white-blond hair and a lantern jaw, and his cap was pushed back on his head in a way that made him look like a simpleton.

"Who among you is Fredrick Raymond Mundt?" the cop said, reading the name off a folded piece of paper he had in his fist.

"What's it to you?" Pepper said.

"I'm Fritz Mundt," Fritz Mundt said.

The cop gave Pepper a long, disinterested frown. "Captain wants to see you," he said to Fritz.

They all piled out of the car and Fritz followed the hulking cop up the gravel drive toward the lodge. Pepper, Moira and Prichard waited in front of the row of smaller cabins.

"Who *among* us," Pepper said, shaking his head and spitting a string of tobacco.

Up the hill, a hawk-faced man with a push-broom mustache had come out of the lodge. He was slimmer than his underling and wore a dark suit under his smoke-colored overcoat. He shook hands with Fritz and then the two of them walked off in the direction of the outbuildings. The uniformed cop was left alone and stood in the grass, looking down at the cabins with his hands in his pockets.

"What manner of beast is this?" Moira said.

At first Pepper thought she meant the cop, but then he noticed that a small creature was creeping out from the trees. It was a plump ball of orange fur, and as it got closer he saw that it was an old, limping tomcat. It slid along toward them with its ears flat and its nose close to the ground. One of the cat's eyes was missing, its tail just a hairless stump. Its fur was matted and crosshatched with scars, but when Moira knelt it trotted over and presented its back to her.

"Brave little fellow," she said. "How do you think he gets by out here?"

"I'd be careful around that thing if I were you," Prichard said. "No telling where it's been."

"She shook hands with *you*, didn't she?" Pepper said.

The cat snuffled at Moira's fingers and rubbed against her knee, but when it was satisfied she had no food to give, it slunk away, disappearing into the trees on the opposite side of the road. Pepper looked up the hill and saw the policeman in the suit putting something in his jacket as he and Fritz walked back toward the cars.

"We're through here," the one called the captain yelled to the blond cop, pointing an emperor's finger at the waiting sedan.

After the policemen left them in a bluster of dust and whipping gravel, Fritz unlocked the door to one of the cabins, revealing a single room with a brass bed, a little potbellied stove and a small kitchen setup. He pointed out the window to the outhouse and the pump where they could draw water from the well.

"Through with what?" Moira asked after Pepper carried in their trunk and set it at the foot of the bed.

"Those men? The police?" Fritz said, pointing down the road like she could have meant someone else. "Just indulging their curiosity, I suppose. Small-town stuff. It's not every day an odd bunch like us moves into a place like this."

Dinner would be at seven, he added, and then he and Prichard left them to get situated. Moira cracked a window, letting the smell of pine trickle in, and sat on the bed. "And now Fredrick Raymond Mundt has bribed a police officer," she said. "You still think this plan is the bee's knees?"

Pepper watched Fritz and the big mutt Prichard motoring the car up the hill toward the lodge. Nothing stirred up there. No sign of Taft or anything else. Deep in his gut he felt the kind of plummeting feeling that would jolt a man from sleep in the night or make him clutch the sides of his chair when the train he was on flew over a hill or took an unexpected corner.

They were both too tense to rest any longer, and when Pepper got down on the floor and started on a regimen of sit-ups and push-ups, Moira announced she was going for a walk. The sun was folding itself into the mountains in the west as she left the cabin. The growling in her stomach told her they wouldn't have long to wait before dinner. She strolled down the dirt road back to the main gate, watching chipmunks chase each other's little exclamation point tails at the fringe of the woods. When she reached the giant wooden arbor she lit a cigarette and turned to look at all of it, this big, strange place. The lodge loomed at the top of the hill, grand but shabby, as if it had been a long time since anyone had properly cared for it. Its windows were dark, its curtains pulled tight. The only sign the place wasn't abandoned was the thin finger of smoke rising from a rear chimney.

She could tell it was going to get cold overnight. Back in the strange little city where they'd gotten off the train, it was warm enough to convince you that summer was still on. They were at an even higher elevation now, though, and up here fall was already closing its grip. The lodge and little cabins might be a cozy spot, she thought, if everything about them didn't give her the shivers. What was the angle here, she wondered, and what was their part in it?

Were they conspirators or marks? What could they have that Fritz wanted, when nearly everything had been taken from them already?

She tried to work it out as she wandered back to the cabin and was standing on the narrow front porch when the door to the lodge opened and the large shadow of a man appeared in the doorway. Backlit from an overhead light in the foyer, she couldn't make out his features, but she knew him at once. His shoulders were as broad as one of the boulders that sat at the edge of the clearing, and even in silhouette she recognized the long, muscled arms and the dome of his bald head.

A hundred yards apart they eyed each other like gunfighters, and then the figure in the doorway crossed its arms and leaned a shoulder against the jamb in a way that mimicked her own posture. When she tipped her head back to take the final drag on her cigarette, the figure did the same. When she dropped the butt and ground it out with her toe, he copied her, doing an exaggerated shimmy, swiveling his hips and pumping his arms like crazy. She couldn't make out a face or the look in the big dark eyes, but she smiled, and hoped he was smiling back. There was movement in the lodge and the figure retreated, closing the door just as the sleeve of a woman's gown appeared in the light of the foyer. Moira watched the house a bit longer, but when she saw no more signs of life she kicked dirt over her cigarette and went back inside.

No one came for them when the bedside clock said seven. They had no choice but to trust it, since Markham had taken both their watches when he rifled through their things looking for valuables, so they dressed in their new clothes and walked up by themselves. Fritz must've seen them coming, because he came out to greet them wearing the same confident grin he'd been sporting since San Francisco, leading them into a towering entryway paneled in old, dark wood. A crystal chandelier dangled like a giant, glittering spider in the middle of the room, making her feel as though they'd stepped out of the woods into some upper-crust neighborhood of Chicago or St. Louis. They followed Fritz up the wide staircase and down an equally mammoth hallway to where a pair of double doors stood open, the voices of men spilling out.

Inside, he'd set up an office in a parlor room that might once have been used for billiards or cards. The carpet was deep and green, and to one side was a small sitting area with two couches and a coffee table. On the other, a big, sturdy desk stood guarded by a pair of occasional chairs. Prichard was there, along with another of Taft's training partners—a jowly fellow with a red nose that looked like it had been broken a hundred times. A third man, slim in a blue suit, sat on a corner of the desk holding a handkerchief over his mouth.

Fritz spun a dramatic, sweeping turn as they came in, like a shopgirl showing off a sales display. "What do you think?" he said.

"I think it's just about the weirdest goddamned place I've ever been," Pepper said. "What is it?"

"A hunting camp built by copper speculators," Fritz said, like that was the most natural thing in the world. "Men who thought they were going to get richer than they did, I suppose. Turns out they didn't have as much time for hunting as they planned."

"Isn't that always the way?" said the man in blue. He'd come away from the desk to meet them in the middle of the room.

Fritz cleared his throat. "Of course, you remember James Eddy from Chicago," he said.

"How could I forget?" Pepper said as the two shook hands, a flaring muscle in his jaw telling Moira they didn't like this man.

"Mrs. Van Dean and I have never had the pleasure," said Eddy, stepping forward to plant a dry kiss on the back of her wrist. As he straightened up he dabbed his lips with his handkerchief, as if he'd just had a drink from a particularly dodgy public fountain.

Moira had seen the inside of enough smoky gambling halls and rancid wrestling gyms to know every kind of man on the make, and as soon as she laid eyes on James Eddy, she knew he was one of them. Up close his suit looked pricey and new, but he was uncomfortable in it. The jacket seemed to swallow him and the trousers hung awkwardly on his narrow hips. His wolfish smile revealed the sort of pockmarked skin a man couldn't hide no matter how much he paid for his coat and tie. As they all moved across to the sitting area he watched her with the wide, vacant eyes of an infant, detached from the smile on his face, like the only reason he was grinning and nodding was that he saw everyone else doing it.

"It's been my experience that once a person gets a little money in his pocket, he starts to believe it will always be that way," Eddy said. "When the cash flow finally gets shut off, so to speak, it can come as quite a shock."

Pepper nudged her. "When he says 'experience,'" he said, "he means as the guy who turns the wrench."

She smiled and nodded, though she didn't really know what that meant. They sat on one of the small couches while Fritz lowered himself into an armchair and Eddy perched, birdlike, on the armrest of the other. He was still looking at her with those unsettling eyes as if he hadn't heard Pepper's jab at him. Fritz asked the wrestlers to fix some drinks, reintroducing Prichard and saying the other man was Dave Fitch of Waterloo, Iowa, as if that was supposed to mean something to them.

"What are we?" Prichard said. "The help?"

"Fix yourselves one, too," Fritz said without looking at them.

Moira said she'd like a vodka and soda, but Prichard and Fitch brought them all whiskeys in matching tumblers. She smelled the sweet and peaty scent of it as she lifted her glass to her lips and took a small sip. She wanted to ask Fritz more about this place, this Peter Pan camp with only one kind of drink and all these odd men lurking around, but he was already scooting forward and hoisting his glass in a toast.

"To a successful camp," he said, "and a chance at redemption for all involved."

"What do we need redeeming for?" Pepper asked, a small smile playing on his face as he touched the side of his glass to Fritz's tumbler.

"This is a good opportunity for you, too," Prichard said. "A chance to change the sporting public's lasting memory of you as the guy who lost his title to Whip Windham."

Pepper looked at Fritz. "Is this guy lecturing me?" he said. "*This* guy?"

"Will Mr. and Mrs. Taft be joining us for dinner?" Moira asked.

Fritz checked his watch. "I have no idea," he said. "Mr. Taft doesn't concern himself with the schedules of others."

"That's about to change," Pepper said.

"I saw him a bit ago," Moira said. "From afar. I was smoking near the cabins and he came onto the porch to watch me."

"The glowering Negro," Prichard said, pronouncing the words like a phrase from a story he'd read.

"It wasn't like that," Moira said. "He was, I don't know, funny."

Fritz laughed. "'Funny' is not the word I'd use to describe Taft," he said.

"What word would you use?" Moira said. "'Glowering'?"

"'Gifted,'" Fritz said. "Mr. Taft is perhaps the most gifted athlete I've ever seen, and I've seen a lot. There's no doubt in my mind that, with the proper instruction and training, he could be champion one day."

"'Pain in the ass' is how I'd describe him," Eddy said.

"'Willful,'" said Fitch, nodding.

They all had another round of drinks and were about to move down to dinner when the door to the parlor room opened and Garfield Taft strode in, followed by his wife. Their sudden appearance caused everyone to turn and look, and Moira knew it was the kind of entrance they were used to making.

Mrs. Taft was tall and beautiful, wide through the hips and shoulders, with a shock of hair the color of pumpkin pie pinned up in an elaborate manner Moira couldn't duplicate if she had all day to work on it. Carol Jean Waverly Taft—as Fritz said her name was—shook Moira's hand without really seeming to touch her. Her eyes matched the dark bottle green of her cocktail dress and they held her in their clutches for a moment before moving on to the rest. There was something clipped in the way she moved, a tightness that might have been nerves but reminded Moira of the way a noontime drunk straightened up when he saw a beat cop round the corner.

Mr. Taft was resplendent in midnight blue, his maroon kerchief crisply tied and white shirt freshly starched. He towered over all of them, one of his eyes still pinched almost shut from where Jack Sherry had thumbed him. He smiled and doted on each person with an expression both bold and precious, as if he were some minor duke coming down to visit the servants' quarters. When Pepper had first told her that Taft had a white wife, she remembered wondering how that was possible. Now, in a glance, she understood.

"I believe you could loan me a cigarette," Taft said to her as they were introduced.

She dug through her purse to find one, and Pepper stepped up to offer his hand. They shook, and Taft made a show of admiring the way the smaller man's neck strained against the collar of his shirt.

"Heavens," he said. "At least we know that head isn't going anywhere."

All the men laughed and Pepper tried to grin along with them as he stuck his hands in the pockets of his slacks and rocked back on his heels. Taft turned and explained to his wife who Pepper was, and her face lit up as if remembering some old private joke.

"Of course—the carnival wrestler!" she said, clapping her hands lightly. "You must tell us some tales from your dusty circus days. I do love a bawdy story."

"I doubt I could tell you any you don't already know," Pepper said.

The remark floated up like a balloon waiting for someone to pop it. Taft opened his mouth to make an issue of it, but Fritz put one hand on each of their shoulders and stood between them.

"Who's hungry?" he said. "The hired girl slaved all day to make us a feast."

The dining room took up one half of the lodge's ground floor, a long and airy space with copper wall sconces and built-in bookcases standing empty around a long banquet table. Fritz's hired girl was a sallow, frail-looking creature who served lamb stew with broiled mushrooms and celery doused in cream without a second glance for any of them. As the girl set a bowl in front of Moira, the smell of the meat and thick broth made her squeeze her spoon a little tighter. She took her first bites greedily, still starving despite their lavish meals in Bellingham and the snacks they'd had on the train. The stew filled her belly, and she liked to think it fortified her for whatever lay ahead.

Eddy had excused himself to wash up before eating, and when he returned he took a seat next to Fritz at the far end of the table. Prichard and Fitch sat in the middle, with Pepper and Moira across from the Tafts at the opposite end. The table was built to seat a larger crowd, so even though they were now eight, they spoke loudly to fill the space. For most of the meal, the men all sat telling stories about the best wrestling matches they'd ever seen. Garfield Taft ate quietly, now and then exchanging glances with his wife, but otherwise not contributing much to the conversation unless someone spoke to him directly. When the entrées were finished and their bowls cleared, Pepper turned and pointed his spoon across the table at him.

"We were in Bellingham to see you take on Alaskan Jack Sherry," he said. "I'm keen to get to work. I feel I've got a lot to show you."

Taft looked amused again, his one good eye crinkling. "I'm afraid I don't need anyone to show me how to wrestle, Mr. Van Dean," he said. "If you made it out to Washington, you already saw I'm the genuine article."

"I saw a guy who nearly got whipped by a walking corpse like Jack Sherry," Pepper said. "You're big and quick, and maybe you're talented like everyone says, but Strangler Lesko is all that and something a lot more dangerous: he's mean. You go out to wrestle him in the same shape I saw in Bellingham and all we'll get back is a box of your bones."

Taft set his glass on the table and turned it just so. "I've had a lot of trainers like you," he said, "coming in with big ideas about how to change my routine. Thinking they've got all the answers. None of them found me to be the receptive type."

"Fritz warned me that might be the case," Pepper said. "There's one thing about it I can't figure, though. If I were a fellow with as much baggage as you, I think I'd recognize my last good chance to make something of myself when it was staring me in the face. Makes me wonder if you're not just allergic to hard work."

"A month from now no one will even remember you were here," Taft said, pleasant as could be.

"Baggage," Carol Jean said, like it was a dirty word. It was the first time she'd spoken to the group since they'd taken their seats. "I'll have you know those newspaper stories were dead wrong. Garfield had nothing to do with all that ugliness in Cincinnati. Not like they wrote he did."

She looked like she would go on, but Taft silenced her with a raised hand.

"If I were *you*, sir," he said to Pepper. "I'd be happy I wasn't working a tandem saw in the woods somewhere."

A couple of times as they had sat drinking in the parlor room, Moira caught James Eddy staring at her in a way that sent a frightened tickle down the back of her neck. Now she watched as his eyes darted back and forth across the table like a spectator at a tennis match.

Fritz planted his hands on the table. "Enough of this kind of talk," he said. "Let's not ruin our first night together by quarreling."

"No," Pepper said. "I want to know what kind of man I'm working with. Is Mrs. Taft saying the police, the papers, the judges and all those lawyers were mistaken when they threw you in prison those years ago?"

"I have nothing to explain to you," Taft said. "Even if my wife speaks the gospel truth, I doubt I could convince any of you. Not if I sat here all night swearing up and down."

"You might," Pepper said. "But somebody told me recently that nobody wants to hear a guy's excuses. If there's a different story to why you got locked up than the one we all read about, I'd insist on hearing it straight."

Taft showed an evil grin. "Maybe it was something I said," he deadpanned. "Maybe a bunch of white folks got together and decided I was too big for my britches. Maybe I refused to lie down for Joe Stecher and it aggravated the wrong men. Maybe those cops and judges and lawyers you talked about were just angry they couldn't get Jack Johnson, so they got me instead."

"I doubt that very much," Pepper said.

Moira remembered reading newspaper stories about Johnson, the black boxer, being released from prison a few months earlier. "They did get Mr. Johnson," she said to the table. "Eventually."

Taft nodded slowly. "Now old Jack's ruined," he said. "He's just a tired vaudeville act. Dempsey will never fight him. Nobody of any merit will fight him. I promise you I won't wind up like that."

Eddy made a clucking sound with his tongue. "I thought the

Negro was supposed to stick together these days," he said. "Universal improvement and all that."

"Garfield's not political," Carol Jean said. "Are you, honey?"

"I hope the best for my people and nothing else," he said. "But trying to go raise civilization out of the dirt somewhere across the sea? No, I'm not interested in that."

"What *are* you interested in?" Moira asked, very aware of her own voice in the enormous room.

"I just want what they took from me," Taft said. "I want to be rich again and the chance to be champion. What else?"

"That's quite a dream," Pepper said, "considering you don't want to work for it."

Taft smirked into the tablecloth, a round divot there where his bowl had been. "I do believe we'll say good night now," he said. "But not before we thank you all for a lovely evening."

The two of them got up from the table and breezed from the room like people who were used to being asked to leave. When Pepper told Taft he was looking forward to seeing him in the morning, the big man didn't respond.

"Now you see what I've been trying to tell you," Fritz said when they were gone. "Taft is a man who doesn't know his place."

Pepper seemed to weigh it in his mind for a moment. "I've met friendlier," he said, "but there are worse things to be in our line of work. Give me an asshole over an ass-kisser any day. You think Lesko and Stettler will really agree to meet him in the ring? It's hard to believe."

"Desperate times," said Prichard, shrugging, and Pepper looked at him like nobody had asked him.

Fritz sat back, chair groaning under his weight. "I do hope the two of you can come to an arrangement," he said. "I'm starting to think you might be our last hope. Until now, we've tried to do things his way. Trainers who wouldn't push him too hard, wouldn't offend his delicate sensibilities." There were a few guffaws around the table at that. "As a result, I'm afraid we're nowhere near where we should be."

"Why do you think I'll be any different?" Pepper said.

Fritz said they needed a hard man for this job, as well as someone who could give Taft a crash course in the catch-as-catch-can wrestling style that Lesko would bring to their bout. Taft was a solid all-around wrestler, but he knew little about the concession holds and chokes that Lesko would insist on being allowed. On top of that, they needed someone who could improve Taft's wind, really make him work, a trainer skilled enough to compete with him on the mat and bullheaded enough to put up with him off of it.

"When we talked about it," Fritz said, "we thought it sounded like you all over."

"I understand," Pepper said, and Moira could see he was pleased.

"Besides," Eddy said, "it's not like you can quit. You've got nowhere else to go."

Fritz, Eddy and the two wrestlers all laughed at that.

"When Stettler and Lesko come calling, I want you to go to Chicago with me to meet with them," Fritz told Pepper. "They'll respect a former world's champion's opinion over mine. If you think Taft can sell tickets and make a good opponent for Lesko, it'll mean more coming from a guy who used to wear the gold."

"Will we get a cut of the promoter's fees, then?" Moira said. "If this match actually does take place?"

Fritz scoffed. "You're fortunate just to have the coaching job," he said.

"It sounds like we're here for more than just coaching," she said. "Which frankly isn't surprising—that you'd change the deal on us now that we've arrived."

The swinging door at one end of the dining room banged open

and the hired girl came through hauling a tray. "Bread pudding," she said, "with confectioners' sugar."

She came around with another round of little glass bowls, Prichard and Fitch offering to take the extras she'd made up for the Tafts. Fritz looked like there was more he wanted to say to Moira, but he let it pass. They drank more drinks and the evening went late. They all got a little drunker than they intended. Eventually Fitch and Prichard excused themselves, saying they wanted to get some sleep before their first day training with the new boss. As they stood by the coatracks, shrugging into their jackets, Pepper went and shook Prichard's hand one more time.

"Fifty-two and one as a professional," he said. "How's that for an excuse?"

"I'm sorry?" Prichard said.

"Earlier," he said. "What you said in the car."

Prichard looked befuddled for a moment. "Well," he said, "it sounded like a hell of a match, was all I was trying to say."

Moira put her hand on Pepper's arm and announced that she, too, was bushed. Pepper conferred a moment with Fritz, who was sitting with Eddy, both of them still working on half-full drinks.

"Give her some time to get used to the situation," Moira heard him say. "You know she can't help herself."

She felt her face flush and her hands make sweaty fists at her side. As they walked across the lawn and down the hill to their tiny cabin Pepper tried to take her hand, but she drifted out of his reach. They undressed just inside the door and fell into bed. In minutes he was snoring softly while she stared up into the blackness of the ceiling.

"Who can't help herself?" she said finally.

He didn't stir. Just his breathing in the dark. She elbowed him.

"Wake up," she said. "*Who* can't help herself? And who is James Eddy?"

When he answered, his voice was thick with sleep. "Who?"

"That man Eddy," she said again. "He's up to something. Everybody in this godforsaken place is up to something. Who is he?"

"Nobody," Pepper said, turning over to put his face in the pillow. "He's just some gangster, that's all."

13

Taft had to guard his swollen eye with one hand as he pressed his ear to the keyhole of the bedroom door. From what he could tell, it sounded like a pretty good party broke out after he and Carol Jean had gone up. A few minutes earlier he'd watched through the window as the Van Deans left the lodge and headed for the cabins, the two of them weaving on uncertain legs as they made their way down the hill. Fritz Mundt and James Eddy were still downstairs, pouring one last drink and talking in voices too low to make out. Behind him on the bed, Carol Jean was pretending to read her book.

"What do you suppose they're talking about down there?" he said.

"What do you think?"

He nodded, touching his forehead to the cool brass of the doorknob. "How'd you like Van Dean trying to tell me how it's going to be?" he said. "Like he's the boss of anybody."

"It's the wife we ought to worry about," Carol Jean said. "She's a meddler if I ever saw one."

Taft said nothing to that. He half remembered Van Dean from the old days, though he'd lost the lightweight title and disappeared from the sport before Taft really came into his own. There had been whispers his match against Whip Windham had been fixed, but

Taft didn't put much thought into it. Now he reckoned Van Dean was about what he'd expected. A tough little guy, cocky and reckless the way small men were. Taft had enjoyed sparring with him over dinner and seeing the look on Van Dean's face when he realized Taft wasn't just going to kneel down and kiss his ring. Taft had already done his part, going out to the coast to wear Sherry around the ring like a hat. Now it was Fritz Mundt's turn to prove there was more going on here than just promises. Until that happened, Taft felt disinclined to give anyone the satisfaction.

Mundt had been making grand plans for almost a year now, ever since the freezing day a couple weeks before the previous Christmas when Taft had gone to Chicago looking for Abe Blomfeld. He and Carol Jean had been staying in a little kitchenette apartment on the crumbling edge of Cincinnati, and Taft had to scrounge up money for bus fare in order to make the trip. The man who owned the kitchenette had once been a bartender at Taft's favorite nightclub. He'd made a lot of money betting on Taft's matches and so he qualified as one of the only people left in the world who felt like he owed the wrestler a favor. Taft had sold the Rolls in order to put down the deposit, make rent and have enough money to live on for a few months. Just as that money was about to run out, the bartender turned landlord showed up to announce his sister was moving up from Birmingham—that she would need a place to live when she arrived and that Taft and Carol Jean would have to clear out.

Blomfeld's gym was situated above a fancy butcher shop on the north side of town. That day Taft lingered a moment under the bright lights of the place, the white tile floor polished so recently he could see his faint reflection as he stooped to inspect a tray of ground sausage that had been sculpted into the shape of a hog's head. There were bins full of pre-marinated chicken breasts, neat rows of steaks stacked on strips of wax paper, pork chops stuffed fat with apples and bread crumbs. He stopped in front of a case of rib chops soaking in red-orange mesquite barbecue sauce, the raw smell of the shop an insult to his empty stomach. He'd just begun to wonder how much of this stuff they would end up throwing out when a man in a spattered apron approached to ask, not necessarily in a nice way, if he could help him. Taft had taken off his hat and flapped it silently in the direction of the back steps. After a long moment of thinking, the man let him go.

Upstairs, the gym was empty and dark, and the loneliness of it gave him pause as the door clicked shut behind him. The last time he'd been here, the wrestling room was full of the rumbling of men and he remembered now that even downstairs you used to be able to hear the faint bumps and bangs of their training. A moment ago Taft had been so distracted by hunger that he hadn't noticed how quiet it was. It was the first time since prison that he'd been inside a real gym. The feeling of it put a tingle in his fingertips. He'd wandered all the way across the mats and was eyeing a high pull-up bar when he noticed Fritz Mundt leaning in the lighted doorway to Blomfeld's office.

"Where is everybody?" Taft said—the first words to pass between them.

Mundt had a thumb looped into the small pocket of his vest. "If you are who I think you are," he said, "you've got an awful lot of nerve."

The tone of his voice implied that wasn't the worst thing in the world. Mundt stepped forward to introduce himself—Taft striving to remember him—and they went into the office to talk. He asked again about the gym and Mundt laughed it off, saying it was early in the day yet. But Taft had seen cobwebs along the ceiling and a fine layer of dust collecting on the rubdown table. When Mundt explained that Blomfeld had passed, Taft stood up to leave, shaking his head at another dead end. He was thanking Mundt for his time, his hand reaching for the door, when the man showed him a friendly grin and said he was just about to send out for meat loaf sandwiches from a little diner around the corner. Wouldn't Mr. Taft like to stay?

Forty-five minutes later, Mundt's desk was cluttered with grease-spotted wrapping paper and wadded napkins. Taft had drunk a bottle of Coca-Cola while he told Mundt his story and what he wanted. He half expected Mundt to laugh in his face, but when he was finished the man merely balanced his own soda on a stack of papers and asked how many promoters he had already been to see.

"Every one that would take my call," Taft said, and they shared small, rueful smiles. "Given my particular brand of notoriety, they agreed to a man that nobody would draw more money opposite Stanislaw Lesko than I would. Then they all shook my hand and sent me on my way."

"I can't blame them," Mundt said. "A Negro getting a chance at the world's heavyweight title? Who would want to put their name on *that*?"

The office was papered with old wrestling flyers and Taft reached out to inspect one of them. He let his eyes drift over Mundt's head, taking in the rest of the dilapidated, musty little room, hoping to give his next words more gravity. "I suppose I'll have to find someone who needs a lucky break as badly as I do."

Mundt had a cigarette burning on the lip of a blown-glass ashtray. He picked it up and examined it, knocking off the ashes. "I understand what this looks like," he said. "The gym empty, things practically boarded up. But I assure you it's not as bad as all that. You didn't waste your time coming here today."

"Let me be clear that what I demand is an on-the-level match," Taft said. "No funny business." Mundt scowled at the word *demand* but didn't protest, and Taft went on: "I expect you know the story about me and Joe Stecher."

Mundt said he'd heard the rumors, but they both knew what rumors were worth in the wrestling business. So Taft told him the whole truth: that after chasing Stecher all over the world for more than a year, the champion had finally sent word that he would agree to a match. At first Taft thought things were finally starting to break his way. Then a man he had never seen before showed up at his hotel room to let him know exactly what would be asked of him.

The champion just needed a couple hours of good work in the ring, the man said, his meaning as plain as if it sat there in the room with them. There was more money in it for Taft if he went along without making a fuss, maybe even save himself an ass kicking, the guy said, setting a brown paper envelope on the hotel room's small table. The envelope was the size of a stack of bills. Taft told the man if he didn't put the envelope back in his pocket and leave the room that instant, the wrestler would pin him down on the carpet and break each one of his fingers. That hadn't gone over well, but the man had done as he was told. After he was gone, Taft assumed the promoters would call off the match, but that wasn't what happened at all.

"I wouldn't do business for Stecher," Taft said, "but if they meant to show me the error of my ways, I'm afraid they came up short. A fair match for an honest wage is all I'll accept. Nothing less."

Mundt shrugged with just one shoulder. "Stanislaw Lesko isn't Joe Stecher," he said. "His manager and I go back. Maybe I could make it happen."

Mundt had a round face and thin, bloodless lips, but when Taft looked into his eyes he saw hopelessness lurking behind all the big talk. It made him want to laugh and tell the man he knew the feeling. Instead he let the silence spread out between them. There was no reason for Taft to think he could trust this man except that he was out of money and down to his last bus trip. He was at the end of his patience for going to see white men with his hat in his hand. The thing Taft was asking for, it was not a small thing, but Mundt seemed sincere in his belief that he could deliver. Maybe it was only because Taft couldn't stomach the thought of the alternative, but in that moment he decided he believed the things Mundt said.

"I'll need a place to live," Taft said. "My wife and I. I'm sorry to say, Cincinnati is plumb wrung out for us."

Mundt said that was fine, he could accommodate that as well. They shook hands and then Mundt stood up, unclasping his cuffs and pulling at his tie. Taft, who was still in his chair, asked him what he was doing, and Mundt grinned down at him, the desperation suddenly gone from his face.

"I don't see anyone else here, do you?" he said. "How else am I supposed to find out what I just bought?"

Taft chuckled now to think of it. Behind him, the bedsprings groaned as Carol Jean put her book on the nightstand and got up. It was strange, staying in this big, empty place. The lodge was so large you'd think it would swallow up every sound, but instead it seemed to magnify them in its vast, hollow space. In the day, floorboards creaked and croaked like the deck of a swaying ship. Chairs scraped on tiles. Oven and furnace doors slammed shut like gunshots. Now he heard every step as she padded over and stood behind his chair.

"You shouldn't have shushed me during dinner," she said. "We should tell them the truth."

"Tell who what?" he said.

"You might not mind being the Great Ape Man," she said, "but it hurts me to read all the vile things they write about you."

"I got news for you, Carol Jean," he said. "Strangler Lesko isn't thinking about giving me a shot at the title because I'm a credit to my race. Right now the fact that a hundred million white people want to see me lynched is one of the few things we've got going for us."

"I just wish they knew who you were really," she said.

She bent forward, her hands parting his bathrobe and sliding down his chest. When she got to the waist of his pajama pants, he took her hands in his and stood up. "Baby," he said, "I'm still licked from Jack Sherry."

"You're impossible," she said. "If you can't do it before a big match and you can't after, then when can you?"

He tried to be easy with her. These days he had to keep reminding himself that it wasn't all about his pride anymore. "Hey," he said, wrapping his arms around her. "You remember that time we took the Rolls all the way out to Atlantic City? Remember that?"

"It rained," she said to his shoulder, sounding pitiful, but he could tell she was smiling.

"You're goddamned right it did," he said. "They stared at us like we were a couple of wet dogs dripping all over the lobby of the Traymore."

She pulled her head back and gave him her eyes. Now he had her. "They were staring at us because you were the only black man in the Traymore not carrying someone's bag," she said.

"That too," he said. "But they let us stay, didn't they? Let us have the biggest suite in the east tower."

"They did," she said. "And we wore that room out."

"Our time's coming again, Carol Jean," he said. "We've just got to hold the line until it does."

She smiled wider. He felt the warmth of it in his chest. "Come on to bed, baby," she said. "I can't sleep in this big bed by myself."

Hours later he lay awake, his mind twisting itself in circles. Carol Jean was curled up next to him chasing ghosts in her sleep, the warmth of her rump pressed against his hip. A feeling of helplessness had dogged him since that morning in the woods, before he'd gone to Washington. It was nothing, he told himself; he was just tired. He shut his eyes and was almost asleep when the sound of tree branches scraping against a bedroom window jarred him awake. The rustle of the wind and the tiny *creech-creech* of wood dragging across glass.

At first it sounded soft and far away, but as he listened it grew louder. Soon it felt like a loudspeaker blaring in his ear, the sound tinny and crackling when each new gust whistled through the trees. *Creech-creech, creech-creech.* A sudden storm rolling through the valley, though the afternoon had been sunny and still. He turned onto his side and covered one ear with his arm, but it made no difference. He tried putting a pillow over his head but didn't like the way it smothered his breathing and took it off again. The sound still was there, almost all his mind could focus on.

What are you, he thought, *the princess and the pea?* It was one of the old stories his mother used to teach him to read, back in their tiny little place in Madisonville. He could remember his mother sitting with him in the rocking chair his father had built, spreading the book across his lap, helping him with his letters. Even back then he'd known he was special, as none of the other kids in his neighborhood could read and few of them cared enough to try. It still made him proud to think of it and he tried to hold on to that memory even as he could feel it fading.

Creech-creech, creech-creech.

"How can you sleep with that racket?" he said, his voice loud in the dark.

Carol Jean barely stirred. "I don't hear," she said. Words she wouldn't remember in the morning.

Annoyed, he sat up, his feet searching out his slippers on the cold floor, the feeling of the freezing wood reminding him of prison. It was funny to him now how the judges and lawyers and normal folks talked about jail, none of them having ever been there for more than a visit. He remembered how, at the end of his five-day trial, after the bullshit jury had found him guilty and the judge handed down the sentence, his lawyer—who'd made a fortune off Taft, then barely put up a fight on his behalf—looked at him and smiled like three years in Foxwood was some kind of victory. "Could have been a lot worse," the lawyer had said, loading up his briefcase in the little room off the main court area before going home to his wife and family and his own bed. "You'll still be young," he said, "you can still have a life." Then the guards came in and fit him with leg irons that were too small. One of them held him while the other leaned his weight down until the cuffs mashed against his skin and pinched bone enough for the locks to click shut.

A life. Yeah.

Taft pulled his robe on in the dark and crept to the bedroom window, not knowing exactly what he planned to do when he found the offending tree branch. Throw open the window and break it off with his bare hands? Shake his fist and cuss the wind? He cocked his one good eye and peered out, seeing nothing but darkness. Their room looked out on the grassy courtyard between the lodge, the cabins and the wrestling gym they'd built for him. There were no trees growing on this side of the building and the grass of the clearing stood calm and still. There was no storm. The noise must have been coming from somewhere else.

He crept to the door and stuck his head into the hallway. *Creech-creech.* This time the sound seemed like it was coming from the other side of the house. Slipping out, he padded a few feet down the hallway and lit an old oil lamp that sat on the table there. This made him feel more foolish than ever, a big man in his pajamas carrying a lamp through the house to search out mysterious sounds. He might as well be wearing a pointed nightcap. He got to the top of the stairs and balanced himself by resting one hand on the fancy decorative globe that sat atop the banister. He could smell kerosene burning in the lamp, and the shadows cast by its glow made him feel disoriented.

Not again, he thought, shaking his head to clear it. He was about to put one foot down on the top step, when he paused. Again he shook his head from side to side, then slowly turned it from right to left and back again. Nothing changed, he realized. It didn't matter which way he turned his head, which way he cocked his ears, the *creech-creech* sound was the same. Same volume, same fullness as when he'd been in bed. It didn't seem to be coming from any one direction.

Taft sat down at the top of the stairs and set the lamp to one side, the chill of the floorboards creeping up his back. He took two fingers and stuck them in his ears, feeling the hole in the pit of his stomach deepen when the sound did not change. *Creech-creech, creech-creech.* He turned his head from side to side again. Still no change. The sound was still there. He cursed under his breath. Was it already happening? Was he going crazy? Reaching over to turn off the lamp, he rested the side of his head against the banister and closed his eyes. The sound couldn't go on like this in his head forever. Eventually it would fade.

He would wait this out. That's what he would do.

14

After Fritz Mundt had finally gone off to bed, James Eddy took the whiskey bottle by the neck and carried it to his room on the second floor of the lodge. His door was at the end of the hallway, past Mundt's bedroom and the room Garfield Taft shared with his whore wife. Inside was a small desk with two chairs, a cot and a long wooden credenza with a washtub, lamp and bar setup. His rifle stood loaded in the corner, half hidden behind a freestanding coat-rack. When he'd first arrived at the hunting camp there had been a big, gilt-framed mirror hanging over the sideboard, but Eddy had removed it. Now the room was a cold, practical space, and it re-minded him of his days coming up with the Market Street Gang, when the rule was: Don't own anything you can't carry with you if you have to leave in a hurry.

He washed his hands in the tub and then, after inspecting them for specks of grime, washed them again. When he was done the water was a soapy froth, and he thought he saw bits of filth floating in it. He'd have to have the hired girl bring up a new bucket first thing in the morning. She would probably roll her eyes and he'd have to be stern with her. Getting the clean water was something that would be in his thoughts until it was done.

There were eight tumblers on his bar setup and he gave each of them a half counterclockwise turn with the tips of his fingers before deciding he'd stick with the bottle. Tipping it to his lips, he went out to have the day's last smoke, going through a second interior door, which led out to the unfinished part of the lodge. The room he entered was probably meant to be a rear-facing parlor, but was left undone when the lodge's original owners were forced to abandon it. Now it was just a skeleton of studs, vaulted rafters and open air.

Back in Chicago, Eddy had allowed himself no more than two whiskeys in a night, but Montana drove him to drink. The months before he'd traveled west had been some of the lowest of his life and he'd hoped the change might do him good, give him some peace and quiet to help him collect his thoughts. Instead, the desolation of the place felt like a weight on his chest. Its wide swaths of empty land tightened his throat, the endless skies bearing down on him as if he were an ant waiting to be crushed. It made him long for the close quarters of the city and he wondered if this was how sailors felt when, day after day, they woke to nothing but the boundless black sea churning all around them.

It had been five years since he'd last seen Pepper Van Dean, and when the wrestler appeared at dinner that night with his pretty wife, it took Eddy's thoughts back to when things had been good for him. He first met Van Dean on a chilly late-summer afternoon in 1916 when Eddy and a couple guys went to Abe Blomfeld's gym to convince him he really ought to lose the world's lightweight title to Whip Windham. Eddy had leverage on Van Dean—he knew about the money he owed all over town—but no matter how many times or how many ways he outlined it, Van Dean would listen to everything he said, nod along like he saw his points and then tell him to go fuck himself. Just like that.

Eddy had brought along some big guys, knuckle draggers who looked mean just getting off the bus, but Van Dean was oblivious. They had him surrounded, sitting in a chair against the wall in

Blomfeld's office, towering over him, and from the look on his face you might think they were out for a Sunday drive. Then one of the big fellows put a hand on him and Van Dean broke the guy's wrist without even getting out of his seat, just grabbed it and twisted and the guy dropped like a sack of sugar.

Right there they should've put a beating on him, but through the small, greasy window into the gym Eddy saw some of the other wrestlers stop to stare when they heard the big guy's screams. He was worried one of them would call the cops. Anyway, the dead air inside the gym and the feeling of all the wrestlers rolling and bleeding and dripping all over everything made his skin crawl. He needed to get out of there.

For a day or two maybe Van Dean thought he'd gotten away with it, but then Dion O'Shea decided they just ought to murder the hardheaded little mug. For three days and nights Eddy tailed Van Dean around the city, studying his routine, quickly and glumly realizing the wrestler would be easy to kill. Just pull up next to him on a deserted street while he was out on his early-morning run, poke a 12-gauge out the window—*kaboom!*—and drive off. The thought gave him no satisfaction at all. The more he saw of Van Dean, the more Eddy was convinced asking him to kill a man as proud and careless as this was like asking Henry Ford to build your kid a wagon.

Still, there was something fascinating about the guy. Van Dean seemed to power through life with a special kind of thoughtlessness, a blithe confidence that Eddy couldn't fathom. His own mind never gave him a break, constantly spinning, picking things apart. To navigate the world the way Van Dean managed it seemed like an impossible luxury. Was Van Dean really too stupid to be scared of them? Or did he just not give a damn?

In the end O'Shea decided to give the wrestler one more chance. He went along with Eddy on a second visit to the gym and explained to Van Dean what would happen to his wife if he didn't play ball.

Van Dean heard them out, an expression on his face that would melt the paint off a house, but this time he didn't tell them to go fuck themselves. A few weeks later Windham won the title and everybody made a nice payday on it.

Those years just before the war had been lean times for Eddy and O'Shea. There was a lot that needed doing. They had just begun slugging it out with the Italians for control of the city. A month after the job with Van Dean, Eddy intimidated the head of a large machinist's union into dropping a grievance against one of O'Shea's trucking companies. A few weeks after that he murdered a low-level soldier named John Duffy, who they suspected was double-crossing them with Jim Colosimo and John Torrio. After that there was a North Side club owner who wouldn't pay tribute, a couple of unruly stickup artists down in Cragin and a showgirl who kept bothering O'Shea about paying for an abortion. He'd gone right along living his life without thinking much at all about the business with the wrestlers until much later, after Eddy ended up doing the killing that spoiled everything for him.

•────•

It started with a haircut.

This was a year or so after the job with Van Dean, and President Wilson had just gone back on his promise to keep America out of the war. On the scheduled day and time of his monthly haircut appointment, Eddy walked up to his regular barbershop on North Kedzie Street to find it shuttered and a sign on the door saying the barber had shipped out with his naval reserve unit. *DATE OF RETURN UNKNOWN*, it said across the bottom in hasty block letters.

Eddy didn't like that one bit. He'd been using the same barber for nearly three years and the thought of trying to find a new one sent ants creeping down the collar of his shirt. Haircuts were particularly tough for him. He hated being forced to sit still in the muck of the barbershop while a stranger smeared him with oils and made small talk. It had taken a few disastrous trials before he finally settled on a regular barber, a man who kept his shop impeccably clean, was quick and capable at his work and above all else did not talk. Now the man was gone and the words *RETURN UNKNOWN* jangled in Eddy's head.

He hurried back to the apartment he shared with O'Shea and refused to come out of his room for almost two days. Finally he went and sat in front of the mirror in the bathroom, imagining he could see his hair growing by the minute. Clicking open an old folding knife he sometimes stuffed into one boot, he began hacking. Clumps fell heavy on the tiles, and when he got the nerve to show himself the finished product, he almost screamed. His hair was sawed and gutted as if a child had done it, in some places sticking out straight from his head, piling in on itself like a bird's nest. He ripped the bathroom mirror from the wall and in his haste he dropped it on the floor. After taking some time to bandage the cuts he got cleaning it up, he found O'Shea studying a racing form in the front room.

"Calm down," O'Shea said, tucking a pencil behind his ear. He was an easygoing man and had a way of making everything a joke— until suddenly it wasn't. "It doesn't look that bad. Listen, I'll get you an appointment with my own man. He'll fix you right up. This fellow is a tonsorial master artist."

O'Shea called around for someone to drive him, and by the time the car showed up Eddy felt like a hideous ape. Luckily, the guy behind the wheel barely glanced at him as he huddled in the backseat with his hat pulled low. The barbershop was an upscale place with a view of the water, but as soon as he walked in, Eddy knew it was all wrong. It just didn't feel the same as his normal place. The air was too cool, the lights too bright. He saw scraps of hair on the floor as O'Shea's barber, a husky man with a waxed mustache and a beard that pointed neatly from his chin, walked him back and sat him in the chair.

The apron he threw over him smelled faintly of body odor, but at least it kept the man from seeing Eddy's knuckles go white as he gripped the armrests. The barber curled his lips when he pulled off the hat, like it physically pained him to look at the ruin Eddy had made of himself. He asked what he was supposed to do with this, his voice full of some accent Eddy couldn't place. Eddy managed to say he just needed it nice and short, nothing fancy. He told the barber to crop the sides close above the ears and to bring the top into respectable shape so he didn't look like some heathen. He watched the man's eyes in the mirror as he talked and thought he saw contempt lurking there.

"Could we maybe do without the mirror?" Eddy asked. "Is that possible?"

The barber spun him around so he couldn't see himself and went to work. Perhaps O'Shea had called ahead, because the man didn't say a word, just whistled some tuneless song that made Eddy dig his fingernails into his own thighs to distract himself. The whole process probably took only a few minutes, but to Eddy it felt like hours, and when the barber finally set his tools down and spun him around to see his handiwork, he blinked at his own reflection.

"It looks the same," he said. "It doesn't look any different."

"Sir," the barber said, "I do exactly what you say. I take off half an inch."

Eddy looked again at the mirror, squinting. He still looked shaggy, his wet hair drooping around his face, and when he tried out a smile it came off as a frightening grimace. "Shorter," he said.

The barber folded his arms over his chest, his white jacket puffing at the shoulders, his face slack with the smug look of a craftsman who knows his trade. "I refuse," he said. "This cut, you have all the women in the neighborhood after you. You'll see."

Eddy gave him a look in the glass. Though he didn't consider himself an intimidating person, he had an expression he could put on when he needed to do it, flat and menacing. The barber stared at it for a few moments and then sighed, reaching for his scissors and a straight black comb. Again he went to work, still whistling, and when he was done Eddy still saw no change in the mirror. He demanded the man go back and cut it shorter still, and this time the barber turned a deep shade of red. His fingers seemed to move with more purpose now, each snip like an angry shout in Eddy's ears. Again he turned to face the mirror and again he shook his head.

"No," Eddy said. "Start again."

"You are almost bald," the barber said.

"Shorter," he said, trying to keep the quaver out of his voice. "You don't understand. We have to go shorter."

The man reached for a hand mirror as if to show him the back, but Eddy grabbed it from him with such ferocity that the barber jumped back, a few strands of his mustache hanging loose.

"You get out," the barber said, pointing. "I'm going to tell Mr. O'Shea about this."

Eddy set the mirror in the seat of the chair as he turned to go, the barber stooping with a short broom and dustpan to begin sweeping piles of hair from the floor. He'd taken a few steps toward the door before the desperation that lurked in his chest turned to rage. He spun back around and was suddenly standing very close to the barber when he said, "Now you listen—"

It was as far as he ever got. Later he realized that maybe he had startled the barber by turning on him like that. Or maybe he'd just pushed the guy too far. Whatever the reason, the barber jerked his arm up and threw the dustpan full of hair in his face. Eddy was in the middle of saying something when it happened and hair went into his mouth and down the front of his shirt. It clung at the corners of his eyebrows and tickled the inside of his nose as he drew back, the nervous feeling of being covered in spiderwebs. He gagged, and then his pistol was in his hand.

This should've scared the barber more, but instead the man pulled his scissors from the skinny breast pocket of his smock and lunged at him, stabbing into the flesh of his upper arm. Eddy shot him. The sound of it shook all the glass in the shop, the mirrors and metal-topped jars full of tonics and even the front windows trembling.

The barber's head opened up like a pumpkin as he flipped backward onto the floor, landing in a spreading pool of blood and hair. As soon as the roar of the pistol faded from his ears, Eddy knew he'd made a colossal blunder. He moved quickly, emptying the cash register and using the butt of his gun to smash the keys, doing his best to make it look like an amateur job. He used a hot towel to wipe the hair off his face and shirt before grabbing his jacket off the coatrack and locking the door behind him as he left. They'd already driven a few blocks back toward the apartment before his driver turned, pointing a tentative finger at him, and Eddy realized the barber's scissors were still sticking out of his arm.

It was the worst murder he'd ever done, a spur-of-the-moment hack job, and O'Shea had been cold and deadly when he found out, his pale pie face betraying nothing as he sat Eddy down in their apartment's one armchair. Eddy thought of trying to deny he'd done it, but he knew the driver had heard the shot and would snitch on him for having the barber's scissors stabbed in his shoulder. He knew O'Shea would only be angrier if he heard it from someone else.

"He shouldn't have disrespected me that way," Eddy said, trying not to make it sound as desperate as he felt.

O'Shea just leaned against the far wall with his chin resting on his chest. "Jesus, Jimmy," he said. "Jesus."

For a few days, Eddy walked around half expecting one of their mop-up guys to pop out of an alley and put him out of his misery.

Instead, it was the police who came for him. They'd found his name written in the barber's appointment book. They knew he'd been the last person to see him alive. When Eddy heard that, it made him want to kill the barber all over again. He couldn't believe the man would be so stupid, but the cops dropped the book on the table in front of him and he read it for himself. The barber had spelled his name wrong.

They chained him to the table in a room that was hot and small, everything in it rubbed smooth by worrying hands. It smelled like fear and the stale breath of cops, and at first he thought he'd suffocate in there. After he got some time to relax and breathe, though, he realized the barber's appointment book was all they had. They knew he'd been there and they knew his past, that he was a killer they had never been able to catch. Once he realized they didn't have enough to book him, he hung on through three days of questions and punches to his ribs, saps on his ankles and kicks to his kidneys until they finally dumped him out a rear door into the alley behind the station.

He felt giddy at being free, at the prospect of dragging himself home to take a long hot bath. The panic returned, though, when he didn't see or hear from O'Shea for almost a week. It got to the point that Eddy actually started wondering if something had happened to his friend. The two of them had lived in the apartment together since they first caught on with Market Street, and unless he was on a job or taking in a sporting event, O'Shea was almost always around. Finally a car showed up—the same guy who'd driven Eddy to the barbershop telling him to get in again and then watching him in the mirror like he was a chimp in a zoo cage.

They drove all the way out to Evanston before the guy pulled over. O'Shea was there, sitting by himself at a picnic table in a small roadside park. Eddy got out slowly, one foot at a time, scanning around for the likeliest places to hide an ambush. He nearly jumped out of his skin when the car roared off behind him, the driver making a U-turn and heading back toward the city. That didn't seem like a good sign. O'Shea sat stock-still as they eyed each other with their hands shoved in their pockets. One of Eddy's fists closed around the butt of his pistol, and then O'Shea said: "Sit down, Jimmy."

Of course O'Shea knew about the cops and about the appointment book and went over it all again at a slow, easy pace, just to make sure everything he'd heard was right. Eddy sat there nodding, feeling every knot and bruise on his body from his beatings at the station. The cops had never been this close before, O'Shea said. It was making a lot of people nervous.

"I know I messed up," Eddy said, feeling the desperation settling at the base of his neck, "but they don't have a thing on me, Dion."

O'Shea said Eddy didn't need to worry about that. He was going to take care of it. As they talked, a bus appeared in the distance, coming down the road from the city. O'Shea stood up. Eddy put his hands in his pockets again and O'Shea shook his head.

"Give me the gun, Jimmy," he said.

Every fiber of Eddy's being told him not to give up that pistol, but he took it out of his jacket and set it on the table. O'Shea snatched it up and hid it away. Together they walked out to the curb, Eddy feeling confused but blank now, as if this were all happening to someone else.

He expected the bus to drive right by, but it didn't. It slowed to a stop in front of them and Eddy saw men inside. Guys about his age and younger, wearing regular clothes and looking like they were as confused as he was about stopping way out here. The bus was dull green and had no markings on it at all, so Eddy didn't fully understand what was happening until the side door opened and a guy in a brown army coat stepped off.

Eddy took a step back, but O'Shea had a hand on his elbow.

"Are you crazy?" Eddy said.

The guy in the uniform was skinny, with a thin mustache that ended abruptly at the corners of his lips. O'Shea introduced him as Sergeant So-and-so from the National Guard. The sergeant had a clipboard tucked under his arm that had already been filled in and marked with *X*'s to indicate the places Eddy needed to sign. As he took it he looked over his shoulder, scanning the bushes for shooters again. He felt panicked—thought of making a break for it—but O'Shea was still standing there, holding his arm. Not squeezing, exactly, but putting enough pressure on it that he knew nobody was asking for his opinion.

In a low voice he explained that this was what Eddy needed to do to save all their asses. They both knew that the cops weren't going to give up on him, he said, not on the out-of-the-blue murder of an honest citizen. They would come back and keep hammering him, keep poking their beaks in until they found something they could use. O'Shea said they couldn't take that chance.

Besides, he said, this wasn't forever. Eddy just needed to get out of town for a little while, and when the heat died down he would come back and everything would be like it was before. Eddy wanted to scream, but he kept it together and reminded the two of them, as calmly as he could, that there was a war on. O'Shea said he fully understood that. Eddy looked into his eyes and knew he would be dead by the end of the week if he said no. Probably he should have said no anyway, but at that moment he was so sore and tired from the beatings and the worry and the shame that he just nodded and held a hand out for the sergeant's pen.

***

N ow, as he slipped his jacket on over his shoulder holster and set out on his nightly rounds of the hunting camp, he could feel the old scar from the barber's scissors itching. He took the bottle with him, noting the finger of light still showing under Garfield Taft's bedroom door. Eddy reminded himself to talk to the druggist about getting Taft a few more bottles of his pain remedy the next time he went into town. The stuff was the doctor's own concoction and hard to get. Last time he hadn't bought enough and then had to spend the better part of two weeks listening to Taft toss and turn and complain about the pain in his back and head.

Eddy was no expert on physical culture, but it had been a long time since he'd met a man he considered worse suited for his job than Taft. The big baby was always griping about something, and the way he'd approached Eddy about the medicine was pathetic. Taft had shrugged and said, "These old joints ain't what they used to be," like he wasn't even embarrassed about admitting it. Eddy suggested they have the hired girl add the tonic to the camp's regular grocery orders, since she came and went from town every day, but Taft said he wanted to keep the arrangement between the two of them. Eddy thought it over—considered the responsibility he had to keep Mundt and O'Shea informed but in the end figured *What the hell* and told Taft how much it would cost him. After that, Eddy was picking up Taft's special orders on his regular trips to town every couple of weeks.

The smell of frost greeted him as he exited the lodge's front door. They'd be lucky if they didn't all get snowed in up here, he thought, icy roads cutting them off from the hired girl's supply runs. Eddy unable to get to town for his regular telephone conversations with O'Shea. Their weird little group stranded, fending for themselves. Eddy didn't know much of what to expect from winter in this part of the country, aside from the fact there would be snow and the vague notion that high in the mountains was not the place to be when it started. He wondered if it would be as cold as winter in Chicago, where the freezing air hung on you like an extra set of clothes, the roads and sidewalks treacherous with ice.

Even in the dark he had the camp's nighttime routine down by heart, trudging up the hill to check the locks on the doors to the horse barn before walking the perimeter fence down to the main gate, making sure that was locked, too. He crept along behind the dark row of cabins, seeing nothing except trees and hills, hearing nothing but wind and the occasional grunt of an owl. As he stepped carefully through the weeds he wondered for the thousandth time exactly what he was supposed to be looking and listening for out here. A campfire in the woods? The sound of a motor? A secret camp of federal agents ready to storm out and take them in a rush of fire and brimstone? There was none of that. Nothing was amiss. No one was coming to get them.

By shipping him out to Montana, Eddy knew O'Shea was delivering a message. He'd fucked up when he killed the barber and now, as if sending him to war hadn't been enough, he was serving out more time. Like a kid who'd been put to bed without supper, O'Shea wanted him to march around in the dark like a fool, thinking about how sorry he was for what he'd done. He'd be lucky if he didn't fall and break his neck. Or maybe luckier if he did; he honestly couldn't decide.

Of course, hidden inside O'Shea's message was another one: *Don't fuck this up.* If Eddy ever wanted to be welcomed back into the fold—if he ever wanted things between him and O'Shea to go back to how they'd been before the war—he needed to impress Dion with how he handled this Montana assignment even if it tasted like a shit sandwich. For that reason he was doing his best to take his job as glorified night watchman seriously.

Before he started back up the hill toward the lodge, he stopped for a moment to survey the camp, looking for the weakest places in the perimeter, searching out the blind spots. On either side of the fence, steep tree-covered hills sprinted upward into the darkness. Eddy grinned at the notion that—if somebody really did mean to do them harm—it wouldn't be too difficult to find a secluded spot and sit up there with a rifle and telescope. Pick them all off without breaking a sweat. He put the likelihood of that happening at approximately seventy million to one but thought maybe the next morning he'd go on a little hike around the camp, look for signs that anybody had been poking around.

As he got to the crest of the hill he reared back and threw the empty whiskey bottle into the woods, hoping to hear it shatter against a tree trunk. He missed his mark and instead watched as the bottle sailed wide between the branches. When it hit somewhere out in the dark, it didn't make a sound. He turned and looked out at the surrounding valley, surprisingly bright in the moonlight. Not a man-made structure to be seen. Not an electric glow. So big and empty. A man could get away with anything out here, Eddy thought, if only he could find something worth getting away with.

15

The next morning, Pepper arrived thirty minutes early for his first training session with Garfield Taft. He'd set the bedside clock for five-thirty, but switched off the alarm and slipped out of bed with ten minutes to spare. *First to show, last to leave,* he repeated to himself as he trotted up the road in the dark, the impact of every step throbbing through his rib cage. It would be important to set a proper tone for the new camp, not just so Taft would know who was in charge, but for Fritz and the training partners, too. Let them all know that playtime was over.

The lodge was dark as he jogged by, and that made him smile. Banking left at the fork in the road, he followed the rocky path up to the old automobile garage that had been converted into a gym. The opposite fork led to the horse barn, where they'd seen Fritz take the police captain when they arrived, but Pepper barely glanced at it as he passed. He was trying not to speculate about James Eddy, whose presence made him choke on his own spit when they saw him at dinner. Eddy skulking around wasn't good, but Pepper tried to tell himself he didn't care why the man was there, so long as it didn't interfere with his own efforts to get Taft ready to wrestle Strangler Lesko. He imagined what they'd say when the other men showed up to find him already there, standing with his arms folded, maybe with one foot up on a bench and his lips set in a hard, unreadable frown. It would send a message.

Compared to the lushness of the lodge, the garage was out of place in its straightforwardness: just a windowless heap of drooping clapboard built at the edge of the tree line. Inside it was surprisingly roomy—quiet and cold enough to make him wish he'd brought a jacket. On the side nearest the main entrance a small wooden bleacher stood on the gravel floor overlooking a spread of brown canvas wrestling mat. The other half of the garage held racks of cannonball dumbbells and a couple of low wooden benches. A thick climbing rope sank from the ceiling. Along one wall he found artifacts from when the building was a working garage: a gas can with a few drops still sloshing around inside, a large metal funnel that smelled like motor oil, a toolbox full of greasy wrenches.

For nearly twenty minutes he stood and stared at the open doorway. Eventually he dragged one of the benches over and straddled it. He was only in shirtsleeves and after another ten minutes began to tremble. The bench turned to ice under his behind and he stood up. A shaft of sunlight played in the dirt near the door, and he knew it must be after six. Where were they? The wind picked up, rattling the clapboard siding on its studs. Finally he couldn't take it anymore and jogged down to the cabin to get his coat. By the time he got back, Prichard and Fitch were there, limbering up against the garage's far wall.

"About time," said Fitch.

"After we get our cut of the show money," Prichard said, "I'm buying everybody in this camp a watch."

Pepper asked if Taft had arrived.

"I'm sure he'll be along," Fitch said.

"Are you it?" Pepper said, miffed that his plan had been spoiled, but glad he'd got back before Taft showed up. "There are no other training partners?"

Prichard and Fitch said they guessed they were and he nodded slowly in a way he hoped both found meaningful.

"Fine, just fine," he said. "I'll leave you to it, then."

He saw confusion on their faces as he stepped away, walking down to a pair of big barn doors at the far end of the building. He threw up the wooden crossbar and pushed out into the low brush beyond, finding some of it still rutted with old tire tracks. This part of the grounds looked out over a slope of trees and down into a wide, empty valley. On the horizon a line of mountain peaks muscled out of the earth.

The landscape reminded him of Idaho and the Handsome Academy, which also sat nestled in a valley, hidden from the world except to the woodsmen who might stop on one of the surrounding peaks to look down on it while they ate lunch. A hulking three-story dormitory and schoolhouse built of weathered gray brick dominated the orphanage grounds. Behind it, a group of smaller wooden buildings trailed behind like baby ducks waddling after their mother. The sheriff drove him up there in a buckboard wagon, and the first time he saw the school a coldness crept into Pepper's chest. All these years later he could still feel it if he closed his eyes and remembered hard enough.

One of the first things he noticed about the orphanage was the mud: fields of it, yellow and thick as mustard; it sucked at his boots as he stepped down from the wagon and followed the sheriff across the lot toward the brick building. He didn't know yet that the mud would soon be part of him. Like sand in the desert, water in the ocean, it was an ever-present part of life in the orphanage, especially when the seasons changed. It clogged the treads of his shoes and clumped on the cuffs of his pants, weighing him down. It got into everything, so that after a while his clothes weren't really even considered dirty if all they had on them was mud.

The sheriff left him with a firm handshake and a punch on the shoulder for luck. Pepper went to the window of the admittance office and watched the man climb the hill again in his wagon, growing smaller and smaller until he was out of sight. Another kid brought him a pair of sand-colored denim pants and a matching shirt and showed him his cot in the big, open sleeping quarters.

Early on, because he was small, the other boys tried to test him. This was something he expected. It almost made him glad of his father, to know that he could handle himself in a fight. Still, he spent a lot of that first year limping, easing around trying to hide the sore spots as the brothers herded them from their beds to the classrooms in the mornings, then to the surrounding fields in the afternoons. The boys were responsible for the orphanage's annual crops of potatoes and sugar beets. They kept small herb gardens and a few rows of plum trees. Sometimes he spent entire days lying on his cot with a broken nose or swollen ankle while the other boys were out working or attending the school's simple trade classes.

He was by himself in the dormitory hall, resting a set of broken ribs, the first time Willem Van Dien came to see him. Van Dien ran the academy's wrestling team and he was one of the older brothers, into his early fifties by the time Pepper arrived—ancient in the eyes of a twelve-year-old. The boys all called him "Professor," though Van Dien freely admitted never graduating past grammar school in his native Denmark. Later, when they became better acquainted, Pepper discovered Van Dien had been arrested at age nineteen for stealing a pair of women's shoes from a fashionable shop in Copenhagen. Somehow, instead of jail, he wound up on a boat to America, where he enlisted in the Union army to win his citizenship. It was in the army camps of the Civil War that Van Dien learned the brutal style of catch-as-catch-can wrestling he would eventually teach the boys at the orphanage. That day, though, Pepper didn't know a thing about him as he squatted next to him and talked to Pepper in a low, kindly voice.

"Do you know why you bit that boy?" Van Dien asked him, and Pepper twisted on his cot. He was nervous in the presence of this man, with his cool blue eyes and stale coffee breath. "No?" Van Dien said when Pepper didn't answer him. "Well, I do. You wanted him to remember you. Even though you lost that fight, you wanted to leave your mark on him."

"How's that, sir?" Pepper said. Had this man come there to punish him?

"You took a piece out of him. There's no shame in admitting it," he said. "You wanted those boys to think twice the next time."

"It was a mistake, sir."

"Maybe," he said. "But it showed me you'll do what it takes to survive. Have you ever thought about wrestling?"

The gym Van Dien had constructed was a simple rectangular room that smelled of varnished pine. There were no mats, and the boys wrestled on the bare wooden planks. The room's only decoration was a large canvas mural depicting a yellow sun rising over a dark mountain, and underneath in unpretentious script, a quote from Ephesians: *Wherefore take unto you the whole armour of God, that ye may be able to withstand in the evil day, and having done all, to stand.*

Professor Van Dien became the first and only real wrestling coach Pepper ever had. As he stood in the weeds outside the hunting camp's garage, he decided that if he could muster half the old man's knowledge and poise, things would be all right with Taft. The air was sharp and fresh, and for the first time since the big sawmiller had knocked him out on the floor of that barroom back in Oregon, he felt a rush of hope.

After a few minutes he began to hear the slapping and grunting noises of Fitch and Prichard warming up. He walked back inside, finding the two men pushing each other around the mat in a collar-and-elbow tie.

"Easy, boys," he called out to them. "Don't spend it all in one place."

Fritz showed up an hour later, looking pale and tired in just a pair of light slacks and an undershirt beneath his jacket. He didn't seem surprised to find training not yet under way for the day—that it was just Pepper sitting on one of the benches, watching Fitch and Prichard take turns trying to climb the rope.

"All these weights," Pepper said as he came over and sat down. "You'd think we were getting ready for a beauty contest."

"Don't start," Fritz said. "I drank too much and now I'm going to die."

"No Taft yet," Pepper said.

"He'll be along," Fritz nodded. "Taft's all right. He's one of the boys, just like you and me."

"I'm not sure he would see that as a favorable comparison," Pepper said. "So far he doesn't seem particularly taken with me."

"He isn't accustomed to being pushed," Fritz said. "He likes getting his way."

"Don't we all," Pepper said.

On the other side of the room, Fitch had managed to get himself halfway up the rope before he let go and crashed back to his feet, shaking his hands like the thing had bit him.

"You think we need to have a talk here?" Pepper said. "Me and you?"

"A talk about what?"

"You know what. About last night."

"About your wife trying to bilk me out of a cut of the promoter fees, you mean?"

"Not that," he said.

Fritz sighed the sigh of the terribly hungover and pinched the bridge of his nose with two sausage fingers. "I know everybody wants it to be a perfect world," he said. "Like big-money wrestling matches just fall out of the sky and we all get rich. But you know it doesn't work like that."

"If you're getting into hock with people like James Eddy, I just hope you know what you're doing."

"I should take advice from you?" Fritz said. "Because you handled that part of your life so well when you had the chance?"

He was trying to think of something smart to say to that when Prichard—himself now nearing the top of the rope—cried out and fell, landing flat on his back in a puff of dirt a few feet from the weight racks. He groaned and rolled onto his side and lay there wheezing while Fitch came and stood over him.

"Ker-clunk," Fitch said.

Pepper grimaced. "You got an extra set of tights lying around?" he said to Fritz. "I might need you here."

That made Fritz laugh. "Not me," he said. "Not today."

They had just gotten Prichard up onto one of the benches and sitting with a towel draped over his head when Taft came in wearing a long winter overcoat with fur on the lapels. Pepper and Fritz both stood up, but, instead of coming over to them, Taft walked to the other side of the gym and shrugged out of the coat, taking care to lay it flat across a row of bleachers.

If he stood shy of six and a half feet, it was only by an inch or so, and his shoulders were piled high with muscle. He easily slung one leg up onto the top step of the bleachers and reached to grab his toe, pressing his great bald head close to his knee. His only obvious weaknesses were his long, skinny limbs and the slight pooch of gut that hung over the waist of his trunks. As he straightened up he turned, and Pepper saw the scars again, the mottled pink mass that made it look like his back was boiling.

Taft took his sweet time limbering up, and when he finally made his way over to Fritz and Pepper, he seemed to gaze over the tops of their heads out the open end of the garage.

"Here's how this'll work," he said. "Tuesday and Thursday are my grappling days. I roll for an hour in the morning and an hour in the afternoon, with an hour break between for lunch. Monday and Wednesday are for my strength and wind training. Mornings we do roadwork, down the hill to the edge of town and back. Then we break for lunch. Afternoons or evenings I lift weights and do drills if I choose. I don't do squat thrusts on account of my knees and I don't do pull-ups after one of these"—he pointed out Fitch and Prichard like there was no word for them—"messed up my shoulder. Fridays, I run and then drive into town to get my rubdown at the Chinaman place. If we have to meet at all that day for business, what have you, it'll be after I return. Saturdays and Sundays I reserve for my wife. That's our private time together and I won't be disturbed. Monday morning we go again with weights and wind, see? It's a good schedule, and if we can stick to it, we won't have any troubles."

His voice was a sweet baritone, a hint of book learning and good manners making it sound friendlier than it should have. He showed an easy grin, and when he finally looked Pepper in the eye, it was plain and unchallenging. The look you give a steward when you ask if he could bring your bags up from the lobby. Fritz turned to Pepper like he should say something.

Pepper chewed on his bottom lip, weighing different ways to play it. Finally he said: "What day is it today?"

Fritz patted the pockets of his pants like he might pull out his watch and then said it was Tuesday.

"Very good," Pepper said. He clapped his hands and swept an arm out to the side like a theater usher, inviting Taft out onto the mat with Fitch. Prichard was still getting his breath back from his fall, towel hanging around his shoulders, watching.

As Taft shook out his arms and strolled onto the mat, he gave Pepper a look out the corner of his eyes, as if to let him know he understood he was being tested. Fitch came at him in a crouch and they'd barely touched hands before Taft went under him with a tackle so fast, it made Pepper smile to himself. Sprawling his legs backward, Taft walked a full circle around Fitch's prone body before shoving him away and letting him get back to his feet. It was a pure show-off move, and Fitch had barely gotten up before Taft swooped in and took him down again. This time he leveraged him onto his side, snared his arm in a hammerlock, and used it to roll him to his back. Fitch was helpless, kicking his feet in the air like a dog in its owner's arms. Taft pinned him and slapped his own hand on the mat.

"Fall," he announced, voice booming in the rafters.

They stood once more and Taft called out for the Cumberland style. The two men began again with chests pressed together, chins resting on each other's shoulders. It seemed for a moment that Fitch might be able to overpower Taft, but Taft was just playing possum, letting the smaller man back him up before he suddenly twisted his hips for an easy throw. Fitch bounced completely off the mat and into the dirt, coming to rest near the same spot where Prichard had fallen off the rope. He was bleeding from one elbow but smiled and punched Taft lightly on the arm to tell him good job as they passed. Taft patted Fitch on the belly.

They went once more in the Irish style, starting from a collar and elbow. It lasted barely ten seconds before Taft simply whipped him off his feet. Both guys had a light sweat going, and as Fitch collected himself Taft put up a hand to call for a five-minute break. Fitch went back to the side of the garage where Prichard was up and stretching and Taft walked back to the bleachers, where he rested his elbows on his knees and sat dripping sweat into the dirt.

"What do you think?" Fritz said, a sly smile creeping across his wide face.

Pepper thought it was a joy to watch Taft move. There was a smoothness to everything he did, a glide in his step, a thoughtless grace in how he floated around the mat with the speed of a much smaller man. He was like an enormous greyhound, sleek and quick, albeit a few years past his prime. The spectator in him wanted nothing more than to sit and enjoy the show, yet in the same instant the wrestler in him was already cataloging Taft's weaknesses. He saw at once that his greatest strength was also his biggest fault: Things were too easy for him. In his effortlessness, Pepper saw holes. Taft misplaced his feet on certain throws, leaving himself open for easy counters, his moves unguarded, as if he was so sure of his own success that he didn't see the point in being cautious.

"I think Lesko will wipe the floor with him," Pepper said, and watched Fritz's smile falter a bit. "Let's see how he does here."

This time Taft worked against Prichard, who was bigger, younger and more mobile than Fitch. They ran a few drills first, moving through tackles and defensive positions at half speed, going light. Then Taft called out for the catch-as-catch-can style and the intensity picked up. Prichard came out of his corner aggressively during their first go, backing Taft up against the edge of the mat. The bigger man went with it, letting the momentum build until he suddenly dropped into a fireman's carry, tossing Prichard over his shoulders like a farm boy bucking bales. As soon as he hit the ground, Prichard tried to scramble to his feet, but Taft threw himself with surprising elegance across his opponent's back.

Prichard's hands went to his throat as Taft roped a massive arm around it in search of a stranglehold, a sly smile creeping across his face. They started hand fighting, huffing and puffing, and at first it looked like it would be only a matter of time before Prichard conceded. He was a veteran, though, and didn't panic, finally making some space for himself to breathe. All at once he sat out and hit a switch, kicking his hips out of Taft's grasp and stepping around to reverse the position. The move elicited a whoop of excitement from Fitch, who was sitting cross-legged just off the edge of the mat.

Pepper could see from the pained looked in Taft's eyes and the grunting sounds coming from both men that, maybe for the first time all morning, he was in trouble. Though he now found himself in a defensive position, Taft was still too strong to allow Prichard to get his arm around his neck.

All at once, Prichard seemed to give up on the idea of a choke, ducking low to seize one of Taft's ankles. Taft grunted in surprise but couldn't pull his leg free as Prichard tried to use the hold to turn him over to his back. Prichard went for a toehold, the kind of move that could easily tear a knee or coil up an ankle if done in real competition. Usually the man stuck in it had no choice but to save himself by conceding, or offering up an easy pin. Prichard almost had the lock closed and Pepper could see Taft grimacing in pain as he fought against it. Fritz had opened his mouth as though he might say something, when suddenly Taft flipped himself into a kind of belly-down somersault and wrenched his foot free.

It was a beautiful escape and before they knew it, Taft had completely swallowed one of Prichard's legs, wrapping his arms around the calf and folding his legs around a thigh. For a moment Taft was upside down, but the force of the move sent Prichard toppling to the mat. He was done and knew it, unable to free the leg against the force of Taft's body. Putting Prichard's ankle under his armpit, Taft barred his knee in a way that would hyperextend it if Prichard didn't quit. He cried out and then slapped the mat to concede, his face showing the pain and frustration.

Taft turned him loose and they both rolled to their knees, facing opposite directions, their chests heaving and eyes blinking. Fitch clapped once in appreciation. It was a good round. Pepper sat back, pressing his back against the side of the garage, realizing he was sweating.

"That's it," Taft said, waving one hand dismissively. "I'm done for today."

They hadn't been at it much longer than an hour. Pepper looked up but couldn't catch Fritz's eye as he crossed the room to where Fitch and Prichard were toweling off, collecting their belongings as if this were the normal state of things. Fritz clapped both men on the back, chattering to them as he began peeling bills off a roll of cash he'd pulled from his pocket. Taft stayed on his knees for a bit longer, then slowly hoisted himself upright. He tipped his head back, eyes closed, and paced a circle around the mat before turning toward the bleachers. From the look of him, you'd think he'd just returned from the war. Pepper snorted and was about to say something about what a meager practice it had been when Taft stumbled and his legs gave out. He put out a hand as if to catch himself, but his knees buckled and he crashed down onto the floor of the garage.

"Christ," said Fritz, dropping his bankroll on the ground as he raced over.

Pepper got there at the same moment and together they rolled Taft onto his back, like turning a great log. He flopped over, his eyes shut, one half of his face sticky with blood and dirt. Fritz brushed at it with a handkerchief and tried to bring Taft around with a few light slaps on the cheek.

"It must be exhaustion," Fritz said, pressing the cloth to a cut under Taft's chin.

"It goddamn well better not be," Pepper said, pulling the man's impossibly long legs out from his body and hoisting them up to try to force the blood back toward his head.

Pepper asked if there were any smelling salts and Fritz just shrugged helplessly. Prichard and Fitch loomed over them, murmuring to each other until Pepper yelled at them to give him air. As they stepped back Taft stirred, his eyes fluttering open as if waking from a nightmare, one hand coming up to his face, smearing the blood.

"What happened?" he asked, voice thick.

"You swooned, beautiful," Pepper said. "Fainted dead away."

Taft yanked his feet free and stood, shaking his head from side to side to clear the cobwebs.

"Easy," Fritz said. "Easy. Not too fast."

Taft ignored him, patting his face with a towel before draping it across his shoulders. He turned, realizing they were all still staring at him, and a menacing look flickered across his face.

"I didn't eat breakfast," he said. "That's all."

He folded his heavy coat over one arm in a way that reminded Pepper of a man returning from the opera. It was slow going, still a little unsteady on his feet, but he spun on a heel and walked out of the garage, his head high and his shoulders back, disappearing into the shaft of bright sunlight that filled the doorway.

The big orange tomcat sat on the porch while Moira split wood. The axe she found buried in a stump behind the cabin was rusted but sharp, so she went along slow and careful as she chopped a few logs into kindling, trying not to imagine the sorts of infections she might get if she cut herself. When she had enough to fill the little box beside the stove, she walked up to pump water from the well, filled a glass for herself, and put a little saucer down for the cat.

"Here's to pioneer days," she said as they both drank. It had been hard work and the water tasted icy and sweet.

She left the front door open while she lit a fire and filled a cast-iron teakettle with the rest of the water. When it boiled, the shriek from the kettle sent the cat racing off across the road and back into the woods. Moira brewed a batch of tea from a jar of loose leaf she found above the sink and carried it across the lawn on a wooden tray with two cups and a sugar dish, a spoon but no sugar.

Fritz's hired girl answered the door to the lodge in a yellowing dress, telling her to wait while she fetched Mrs. Taft. Moira set the tray on the porch's small sun table. From the amount of time she had to stand there, she knew Mrs. Taft was still asleep.

When the woman of the house finally appeared, it was with the special flare common among show people, sweeping onto the porch with a slight curtsy while holding a pinch of her dress away from her legs. In the light of day and free of makeup, Carol Jean Taft was pale and freckled and wore her wild tangle of hair pulled back from her face with a simple gold ribbon.

"I was afraid we all got off on the wrong foot at dinner last night," Moira said as they sat. She pointed to the tea, saying she'd have to borrow some sugar.

Carol Jean took the top off the teapot and looked inside before telling the hired girl to bring out a pot of coffee and a plate of cookies. "Sugar, too," she said, giving Moira a quick wink. "Or something stiffer, if that's more your speed."

"A bit early for me yet," Moira said, putting a mental checkmark in Carol Jean's column for the ease with which she'd parried her meager peace offering. It told her this woman was a more capable and observant player than she'd seemed at the dinner table.

"It's the one upside of this god-awful place," Carol Jean said, crossing her legs with an extravagant little kick. "We're too far away from anywhere for anyone to care what we do or what we drink."

"The police were here, though," Moira said. "Yesterday when we arrived they had a look around."

"The two buffoons in the car?" Carol Jean said. "I'm certain Mr. Mundt and Mr. Eddy can keep a lid on them."

The hired girl, whom Carol Jean introduced as Eleanor, brought a tray with coffee, cookies, and a smaller version of the glass whiskey snifter Fritz had in his office. Moira guessed the girl and Carol Jean were friends, and made a point of smiling at her and touching her lightly on the elbow as she thanked her.

"Yes, Mr. Eddy," Moira said as Carol Jean poured coffee and then added slugs of whiskey and spoonfuls of sugar. "What sort of character is he, do you suppose?"

"A peculiar little fellow," Carol Jean said. "But I don't pay him any mind."

"What do you think?" Moira asked the hired girl as she cleared the tea things off the table.

The hired girl blushed, looking like she was embarrassed to say, but was emboldened when Carol Jean gave her a small, encouraging nod. "I think he's a troublesome man," she said, the bitterness surprising Moira a bit. "Always looking over my shoulder, telling me I haven't scrubbed the dishes well enough or I missed a spot on the dining room floor. I've never seen a man as interested in cooking and cleaning as that one."

Moira smiled at her again, and as the hired girl drifted back into the house, Carol Jean offered a toast.

"Aren't we a couple of hot toddies?" she said. "If there were any gentlemen to pass by, I'm sure we'd turn their heads."

They touched mugs, and Moira studied her as they took their first sips of coffee—strong and hot and really a lot better than anything she might've lugged up from the cabin. From the practiced way she sat with an elbow resting on one knee, holding her mug in the air in front of her, Moira guessed Carol Jean had either been a singer or an actress once. She was beautiful, and there was something desperate in her eyes that made it hard not to look at her.

"You were saying?" Carol Jean said. "About dinner?"

"That my husband and I have only just arrived," Moira said. "I wanted to assure you we don't mean to cause any trouble."

Carol Jean smiled at that. "Sure you do, honey," she said. "Every person Garfield and I ever met meant us some kind of trouble."

"What I meant to say is, we're still getting the lay of things and I hope Pepper's enthusiasm about training with Mr. Taft didn't put you off."

"It was nothing," Carol Jean said. "At this point it takes more than one little man with poor table manners to get past our defenses."

Moira didn't let the insult register on her face. Walking up from the cabin, she'd gambled that if anyone knew what was really going on in this place and would talk about it, it was this woman. Now she made Carol Jean for what her father would've called a runner: a person who had a story to tell and came to the gaming table with the express interest of telling it. Maybe they'd had too much to drink, or the game put them on edge. Maybe they were just lonely. It didn't matter. The only thing to know about a runner, Moira's father said, was to let them run.

"I was hoping you could help me find my depth," Moira said. "You know, woman to woman."

"Oh, honey," Carol Jean said. "I think you'll find that out here even the deep end of the pool isn't terribly deep."

"Meaning what?"

Carol Jean sighed as if already growing tired of her. "When I met Garfield Taft," she said, "I was working as a taxi dancer at the Olympia Ballroom in Cincinnati. My first day on the job I showed up and discovered there wasn't a single dress in the storeroom that would fit me. All the other girls were just these flea-bitten little things, you see. One of the girls brought me up to see the owner, Mr. Herman Cohn, this Jew who'd been in the business heaven knows how long, and he looks at me, kind of squinting, you see, and tells me: 'Come back when you lose fifteen pounds.'"

She refilled her coffee and Moira gave her an encouraging nod. "Well," Carol Jean said. "Me, I'm all of twenty-one, twenty-two years old at the time. I guess I had a pretty high opinion of myself, the way young girls have, and going home and losing fifteen pounds wasn't on my to-do list. I needed money right away, you see. So instead I just walked out of that office, straight down the stairs, and out onto the dance floor and started working. Started working in whatever old thing I had on at the time. At first it was slow and I was nervous, of course, but soon I learned a very strange thing. Those men out there on that dance floor? They loved me. I was the only redhead working in the place, for starters, and the only girl with any meat on her bones. That first night they danced me until I thought my feet would wear down to the ankles. Five hours, no breaks, and when it was over, why, I marched back up to Mr. Cohn's office and dropped a purse full of dance tickets on his desk and said, 'Should I take all these with me when I go home to lose that fifteen pounds? Or should I take them up the street to the Barbary Coast and try my luck there?' I tell you, that little bastard's eyes just about popped through the panes of his spectacles. Right then and there he gave me all the hours I could ever want. More hours than one girl could ever dance in her lifetime. And the moral of the story is, four months later? They were tailoring dresses for *me*, not the other way around."

"I see," Moira said, though she didn't at all. "And the Olympia was where you met Mr. Taft?"

"Mr. Taft?" Carol Jean said. "Six months later Garfield Taft pulled up to the Olympia with his Rolls-Royce and his fur coat and his pocket full of hundred-dollar bills and I never danced another night in my life. Meeting Mr. Taft's not the point of the story, honey. The point of the story is this place. Fritz Mundt's little business venture? This training camp? You, me, your husband and all the others? We're just window dressing. This place is all about my Garfield. He's the big-titty redhead everybody wants a piece of, and that, in terms of finding your depth, is all you really need to know."

They sat for a moment watching the grass ripple in the breeze. On the opposite side of the clearing, a deer picked its way through the trees on dainty hooves. Halfway across it stopped and looked at them, big ears standing out like gramophone horns. Then, without them moving or saying a word, it turned and bounded into the woods.

"Now," Carol Jean said, "why don't you ask what you really came to ask?"

"I wasn't aware I had ulterior motives."

"You want to know what it's like," she said.

Moira said she didn't follow, and Carol Jean rolled her eyes. "Being married to a Negro?" she said. "Being, what would they call it? In his thrall? Please, honey. I've been around the block enough times to understand the first things other girls want to hear from me."

"Is that so?" Thinking: *Let her run.*

"In a lot of ways I expect it's no different than being married to any of them," Carol Jean said. She waved a hand to indicate the men in the garage. "They're all still children, really, but I don't have to tell you that. The boys, they all call each other, which is just the funniest thing when you think about it."

"They have their moments," Moira said.

She blushed a bit when she said it, thinking of Pepper, but Carol Jean cut her a glance that said she'd taken it a different way. "Believe me, honey, you wouldn't want the trouble," she said. "People say the most awful things. Everyone assumes I must be some kind of sex fiend, but it's not like that at all. Maybe at first. But to stick it out through the things we've endured, him and I? It's more than just the way we are in the bedroom. No, I love Garfield Taft because he's a wonderful man. A wonderful, sweet man who's already shouldered more than any one person should be expected to bear. At this point, I can't imagine anything that could pull us apart."

"I heard you had trouble in Chicago."

"Oh?" Carol Jean said. "I quite enjoy the big city, myself. I'm sort of a metropolitan girl, I suppose. But then one day Fritz Mundt calls up and says, 'Go west, young man.' Not exactly my idea of a fun vacation, but I'd live in an igloo in Antarctica if that's what it took to be with my husband."

"You seem very happy," Moira said, even though it wasn't true.

"I'd better be," Carol Jean said. "I gave up everything I had for that man."

"Do you think they'll let him win?" Moira said. "If Fritz lands a match with Strangler Lesko, do you believe they'll really give Mr. Taft a fair shake?"

"Mr. Mundt says so," Carol Jean said, "and Garfield believes him."

"Do you?" Moira said.

"I'll tell you a secret," Carol Jean said, though she made no effort to lower her voice. "Despite what your husband might think, my Garfield will tear this man Lesko limb from limb if they let them in the same wrestling ring. Once he's heavyweight champion, well, we'll just sit back and let the world come to us."

There was something hollow about her words, and Moira realized they sounded very much like what she'd been telling herself the past five years while they were trouping around the country with Boyd Markham's carnival. Now hearing them from the opposite side of the conversation, she realized how foolish they sounded.

"I admire your confidence," she said, before her mind could wander too far down that path. "If there's one thing Pepper knows, though, it's wrestling. As nothing more than an interested observer, my advice would be that Mr. Taft heeds what he has to say. There could be no harm in it."

Carol Jean gave her another icy glance. "We're lucky, then," she said, "that nobody asked for your advice."

Moira set her coffee cup down and was about to say her good-byes when Garfield Taft emerged from the darkness of the garage a couple hundred yards up the hill. He walked unsteadily, wearing wrestling trunks and carrying a jacket under his arm, making his way down the hill and across the grass toward them. He was stoop-shouldered and stiff-legged, his head bowed as if he'd just suffered a great hardship. When he got close enough, they saw that someone had done a poor job wiping a mess of blood and dirt off his face. Carol Jean dropped her cup on the table and ran out to meet him. Moira stood up, watching as Carol Jean fit herself underneath Taft's arm and brought him up the steps. His eyes were bloodshot and his teeth clenched against the effort, but when they got to the top, he turned his head and nodded to Moira.

"Ma'am," he said.

Carol Jean's surprise turned to anger as she helped Taft limp across the wide porch. "No harm?" she said over her shoulder. "Is this what no harm looks like to you?"

Then the two of them went through the door into the lodge, closing it behind them, not quite a slam. Moira picked up the tea tray and carried it across the grass to the little cabin where, feeling day drunk and unsure what to do with herself, she lay down on the bed and closed her eyes. Fifteen minutes later she woke with a start to the sound of the orange cat clawing at the closed door. The beast wouldn't stop until she got up and let him inside.

17

The morning air smelled of pine needles and sang against Taft's black eye as he made his way down toward the main gate. He was sporting a fresh gash in his chin from the fall he'd taken the previous day, and the way it seemed to buzz in the chill made him think winter was nearly upon them. He had not slept well, and about halfway down the trail he stopped suddenly in his tracks as he became aware of a distant banging sound. More phantom noises, he thought, closing his eyes, whispering a silent prayer he hoped would banish this new racket from his mind. When he opened them, the sound was still there, mirroring the shame and terror that were thudding along in the darkest parts of his heart.

As if God is going to help you, he thought. *You don't think God reads the papers?*

He knew this was Foxwood coming home to roost, and it made him feel as scared and vulnerable as a child standing there in the middle of the trail. He hoped a morning jog would take his mind off things. Maybe the phantom sounds would fade if he could distract himself with some hard work. Perhaps he could run his mind into shape the same way he could his body.

When he got to the gate, Fitch and Prichard weren't there. He kicked dirt and waited a couple of minutes, but the quiet, deserted feeling told him that they weren't going to show. As he bent to stretch he noticed that the hammering sound had changed: it seemed closer now. He followed the noise up a short rise through a stand of trees to the garage. Pepper Van Dean was up there, nailing heavy boards across the building's side door. As Taft came up out of the trees, Van Dean stopped hammering and smiled at him like a cat that had a secret.

Taft was used to being despised by white men. Before he was even a teenager, grown adults began looking at him with loathing and fear. Quick to threaten him, put their hands on him, tell him to know his place. As he got bigger, they stopped touching him, but the sidelong glances grew more murderous. Their mouths pressed into hard frowns, eyes shining with something more than rage. At the height of his fame as a wrestler, he knew very well his lifestyle was a thumb in the eye of so-called good, decent folks. He lived that way on purpose, with his fast cars and white mistresses. It only got worse when they put him in the papers as a whoremonger. Worse even than that when he married Carol Jean.

The way Van Dean looked at him was different, though. There wasn't a scrap of worry or nervousness in his eyes. Taft could tell right away Van Dean didn't hate him out of dumb cowardice. The little man was not afraid. This was something else.

He walked to the end of the garage and looked around the corner, where the big doors had also been shackled with a hefty chain. Heat rose in his face and he spun around, asking just what the hell Van Dean thought he was doing.

"Day one stuff," Van Dean said through tight lips. He was holding a nail between his teeth. The bruises on his face were yellowing as they healed. "You can't be the boss of your own training camp. In fifteen years, I've never seen that work out. Not once."

Taft's head was still buzzing, and just as Van Dean began to speak, he experienced a moment of vertigo. He took a step back, bracing one arm against the garage.

"This is Wednesday," he said, sounding shaken and weak even to himself. "Wednesday is for my roadwork and weights."

"Not anymore," Van Dean said, taking the nail out of his mouth and plunking it into a coffee can he had sitting next to his toolbox. The hammer swung loosely in his hand. He didn't seem to be sweating or struggling with the work he'd been doing. "As head coach, I'll be implementing a new training regimen of my own design. You're a wrestler, not a strongman, and you're carrying around too much muscle as it is. All that bulk takes blood and wind to make it run, and after your little display yesterday, wind looks to be in pretty short supply around here. We aim to lose pounds, not pack them on. As a result, no more weights."

"You don't understand," Taft said, finding his legs now, feeling steadier. "My agreement with Mr. Mundt gives me final authority over my own person and workouts."

"Right," Van Dean said, "and that's why you look like a baked potato with muscleman arms."

Taft swallowed the urge to knock the little guy's teeth out. He cleared his throat. "Where are Fitch and Prich?" he said. "Where's Mr. Mundt?"

"I fired those two ham-and-eggers," Van Dean said. "As for Fritzie, I figure he's asleep. It's still pretty early in the morning."

Taft did not like the way Van Dean had of pointing out the obvious, as if everyone around him was stupid. He told him this and informed him that he was not stupid.

"Now," Taft said, trying to get it under control. Trying not to sound hysterical. "Maybe you mean to tell me how I'm supposed to train with no training partners? How I'm supposed to train at all with my wrestling gym all boarded up?"

"That's the other thing," Van Dean said. "No more wrestling. Not until you build up a constitution that can handle it without, you know, further episodes."

Taft's jaw felt as tight as if he'd spent the last week chewing tire rubber. He put his hands on his hips, then behind his back. "This won't do," he said.

Van Dean seemed to only be getting calmer. "Are you really that simple?" he asked. "Are you really dumb enough to believe you can go on curling your little dumbbells and rolling with your chubby training pals and it'll get you anywhere besides having Stanislaw Lesko whip your ass in front of ten thousand people? Ten thousand *white* people who all paid their money for the *express purpose* of seeing you get your big black ass whipped? Would you like that? Is that the end result we're aiming for here?"

"We don't even know if Strangler Lesko will agree to wrestle me," Taft said. "We've got no contracts, no bout agreements, nothing we're even working toward."

"Well, that's a fantastic way of looking at things," Van Dean said. "If that's the case, then I suppose we all might as well just go on being unbelievable fat-asses."

This time Taft did swing at him, a right hand aimed for the bridge of the shorter man's nose. Except, when the punch got there, Van Dean was gone and Taft's fist collided with the rough wood of the door. A sharp jab of pain bolted up to his elbow as he drew it back. He turned to where Van Dean had slipped a step to the side, still not breathing hard, still not sweating, still holding the hammer.

"To hell with you," Taft said, shaking the pain out of his hand. "I quit."

Van Dean gave him that small man's smirk of his. "Quit what?" he said. "You quit not working hard? You quit taking handouts from Fritz Mundt for a match even you say might not happen? You quit having every physical advantage and none of the heart to make it worth a damn?"

Taft shoved him, sending him skittering backward, his shoulders bouncing off the side of the garage and the hammer clattering to the ground. The surprise that bloomed in Van Dean's eyes boiled quickly into anger and he took a long, deliberate step forward. He was so short, Taft almost smiled. They stood there staring into each other's faces, each daring the other to do something until the sound of a door slamming echoed across the hunting camp lawn. The hired girl came out onto the back porch of the lodge and began beating a hallway runner with a long wooden spoon, watching them with the bored eyes of a housewife keeping tabs on the neighborhood. Taft took a step back and Van Dean reset his shoulders, smoothing the front of his shirt with his hands. He gave Taft a long look, ferocious hatred plain on his face, before he stooped to retrieve the hammer.

Ten minutes later they both walked into Fritz Mundt's office and found him sitting behind his desk, wearing a bathrobe. He rubbed a palm across his face as if still trying to wipe away the sleep and pulled the bell to call for coffee. The toes of his slippers stuck out underneath the front of the desk, playing a quiet drumbeat against the carpet. James Eddy perched in the room's sitting area looking as put-together as ever, as if he had been up primping since four that morning. Taft and Van Dean took chairs facing them.

"This is a first," Fritz said. "This is a new one on me."

"You brought me in," Van Dean said. "This is my way."

"We brought you in to train our wrestler," Fritz said. "Not shut down training camp on your first day."

"Second day," Van Dean said. "The first day was the day your *wrestler* fainted after one of the lighter workouts I've ever seen. And I've seen some light ones."

The way Van Dean twisted his mouth around the word *wrestler* needled Taft's gut. "Did you ever think," he said, turning slightly in his seat, "that you were only hired because nobody else would agree to move out here to play Daniel Boone?"

"Far as I know," Van Dean said, "they brought me in because I'm one of the best scientific wrestlers in the world, pound for pound, and your technique—even when you're not unconscious—is lousy."

Taft appealed to Fritz. "Look," he said. "You told me to move into the boonies. I did it. You told me to ride out to Washington and whip Jack Sherry. I did it. Now, if you can get me a shot at Strangler Lesko, make it happen. Show me something on paper and I promise you I'll work as hard as anyone to get ready."

"Right," Van Dean said. "Every heavyweight I ever knew was just *about* to start training hard."

"So long as our wrestling room is boarded up, no one is working hard," Fritz said, scowling. "Frankly, I'm as stumped as Mr. Taft. What are you proposing we do here if we're not wrestling and we're not working out?"

"I propose we run," Van Dean said. "I propose we run and run and run and run."

Taft snorted. "Show me contracts," he said again. "Until then, I don't see the point of killing myself chasing the great white whale."

"I see some logic in it."

This was Eddy, out of his chair and strolling over to join the group. He lit a cigarette, leaning one hip against the side of Fritz's desk, a white swirl of smoke curling up into the air around him.

"You're never going to out-muscle Lesko," he said, "so you better outwork him, isn't that it?"

Van Dean nodded, though his face said the last thing he wanted to do was agree with Eddy.

"Be that as it may," Fritz said, going along deliberately as if he was annoyed with the interruption. "I'm not sure how comfortable I feel committing the daily operating funds to a training camp that's not operating daily."

"He's not ready," Van Dean said. "You put him on the mat with me or anybody else worth spit, it'll be a lot uglier than things got yesterday. It'll be a lot uglier than Jack Sherry."

Taft raised his arms to Fritz as if to show the size of his headache.

"Pepper," Fritz said, straining for a sensible tone. "Is there anything we can do here?"

Van Dean smiled again. The same smile Taft saw outside the garage that morning. The same look in his eye, contemptuous and chiding. A deeper hurt lurking in there, too, and for the first time he started to wonder if testing wills with this man was an unwise thing to do.

"I'll make you a deal," Van Dean said. "I'll strip those boards off that garage and we can go back to work on wrestling the day the illustrious and celebrated *Mister* Garfield Taft beats me in a footrace."

Fritz and Taft both scoffed and Eddy clapped his hands. Van Dean just went on, laying it out. Same as the old routine, he said: they would run from the camp down the road to town and back. If Taft made it back to camp before Van Dean did, he would open up the wrestling room. If not, he said, they do it all over the next day and the day after and the day after, until Taft beat him.

When he was finished, no one spoke. Taft nodded once, definitively, and stood up.

"Fine," he said. "I've already got my gear on."

"What?" Fritz said. "Now?"

"You sure about that?" Van Dean said. A muscle in his face quivering as it had the moment Taft had shoved him against the garage. It pleased him each time he could do something to knock him off track a bit, and he reminded himself to try it more often.

"Sooner we get this foolishness over with, the sooner we can get back to real business," he said.

Van Dean stood. Eddy smiled like a man attending a play that turned out to be much funnier than he'd expected.

"All right," Van Dean said. "Let's get to it, though please allow me to assure you, Mr. Taft, the day you beat me will not be today."

"I had a dog like you once," Taft said. "You remind me a lot of him."

Fritz pulled the bell again, and when the hired girl showed up apologizing for being late with the coffee, he snapped at her to forget about it. Instead, he asked her to lay him out some proper clothes.

•————•

The race began with Eddy standing at the hunting camp's main gate, shouting, "Mark . . . set . . . go!" and waving a handkerchief. Taft started out at a normal speed, plodding down the dirt road into the trees. He looked back once to see Van Dean clipping at his heels and, behind that, Fritz hurrying down the front steps of the lodge, pulling on a jacket.

During the first hundred yards, Taft was surprised to find that Van Dean kept pace with him, not lagging behind like Fitch and Prichard and not racing ahead like he imagined he might try to do. Van Dean just ran alongside him, talking. This was maybe the biggest shock, since Taft had begun to think of Van Dean as the kind of guy who kept quiet until he had something snide to say. Now he wouldn't shut up, lecturing Taft about the land around them, about the trees and the animals they saw as they ran. Taft realized he knew nothing about Van Dean aside from the fact he'd won the world's lightweight title while Taft was working his way to contender status among the heavies. He glanced over at the little man, running, smiling at nothing.

"Shut up," Taft said to him, his voice already sounding a little strained. "Shut up."

Van Dean didn't acknowledge him in any way, just kept prattling on about crops that might grow up there. Sugar beets, Van Dean said, would thrive. Taft tucked his chin into his chest and willed himself to go faster.

It was shaping into one of those tricky fall days when mornings went from chilly to uncomfortably hot as soon as the sun had a chance to warm the ground. They were barely out of sight of the hunting camp when sweat popped out on Taft's arms and forehead and a burning sensation spread through his lungs. Maybe Van Dean was pushing the pace after all, tricking him into running a little bit faster than normal. As an experiment, he slowed a bit and noticed that Van Dean deliberately stayed alongside him, saying something else about beets, sounding like a grammar school lesson book.

Soon Taft started to feel woozy and heavy, a kind of drunken dizziness spinning behind his eyes. He tried not to think about sounds that were not there or about fainting spells or the cold, dark hallways of Foxwood Prison, where the night after his arrival the guards hauled him down to a small exercise room and locked him in with five other prisoners. He knocked two of them down before their numbers overwhelmed him, with the guards watching from a catwalk above the room. He struggled to keep his mind in the moment, concentrating on the ground in front of him, making sure to step over the chunky, jagged rocks that scattered across the road.

He planned to lose Van Dean at the hill. If it was wind he wanted to see, Taft would show him he had it pretty good for a big guy. When the grade of the road began to increase, he lengthened his stride and dug in, pumping his arms, feeling the pressure in his ankles and shins as he picked up the pace. A funny, metallic taste rose in the back of his throat, and whereas before his legs had felt leaden and stiff, they now turned rubbery and unresponsive. Van Dean acted like he hadn't noticed. He just ran and talked, not sounding the slightest bit out of breath. These bushes might sprout edible berries come spring, he said. Those trees would smell like vanilla if you pressed your nose close to the bark.

When he started in about snow—about different kinds of snow—Taft felt like shouting at him to leave him alone. But he could not shout: He was out of breath from the charge up the hill, nearing the top now with Van Dean asking him if he'd ever been skiing or snowshoeing.

"I highly doubt that you have," he was saying, voice pleasant. "I know your people aren't much for cold weather, but the winter sports are some of the best for strengthening the lungs. Good for the blood, too. Why, after we get a couple months training at this altitude in some good, cold weather, Strangler Lesko won't be able to keep pace with you for more than five or ten minutes."

That's when Taft stopped running. He doubled over, hands on hips. "Enough," he said, wiping away a string of spit. "Goddamn it. Enough."

He felt like he could barely keep his feet. Bracing the fingertips of one hand on the ground, he steadied himself and tried to breathe. Van Dean turned around and walked over, squatting in the dirt next to him, putting a hand on his shoulder. Taft wanted to shake him off—he wanted to slug him again—but he didn't have the energy.

"You want to know why we're really doing this?" Van Dean said. "Why we're going to keep doing this until you're ready to start real training? Because what I saw in that wrestling room yesterday was offensive to me. I don't care if you want to walk around like some kind of nightclub star with your white wife and your fancy outfits, thinking the world has a blank check waiting for you because you used to be somebody, because at one time in your life sharpies and the after-hours crowd found you amusing. If that's how you want to play this, I couldn't care less. But let me tell you something. There's a million guys who would kill their own mothers to be in your position right now. For you to get out of prison, Johnny-come-lately, and luck your way into a shot at the world's heavyweight title? You took somebody's spot, Mr. Taft. There's a guy in Iowa or Pennsylvania or Ohio right now murdering himself in some wrestling gym, trying to get where you are, and you spend your time lollygagging? Like you don't give a shit? That's sickening to me. You're standing on somebody's dream. You stole it and you don't even care enough to try hard. That makes you about the lowest son of a bitch I've ever met. I won't stand for it."

Taft blinked at the ground. When Van Dean finally stopped talking, all he could hear was his own breathing. "A million guys," he said. "You mean guys like you?"

Van Dean didn't answer him, and now it was Taft's turn to smile. Lifting his hands out of the dirt, putting them on his hips. "News flash, asshole," he said. "Those million guys? They aren't here, and they'll never be. Just one. Just me. Just me, because I deserve it. You hear me?"

Again Van Dean didn't answer, and when he turned around, the little man wasn't there. He was fifty yards down the trail, still running, facing straight ahead, his arms and legs driving away.

18

For the next two weeks Taft didn't show up for their runs. In fact, Pepper didn't see him at all. Part of him was glad for it, since the break gave the swelling in his face a chance to go down and his ribs the opportunity to rest to the point where he didn't have to think about them every time he took a deep breath. The first couple of mornings that Taft didn't meet him at the gate, he'd gone up to the lodge and pounded on the door until Taft's wife—the big-bosomed redhead whose name he couldn't remember—came to the door and said the mister wasn't feeling well. Used those words, like Taft was the lord of the manor. Both days the woman ended the conversations by reminding him to say hello to Moira for her, a hopeful tone in her voice that put him off his guard. It offset his annoyance with a pang of sympathy for her, so he just nodded and said yes, ma'am, he'd be sure to do that.

The tenth night he sat up by the cabin window, watching lights go on and off in the lodge. The unfinished part of the house was spooky in the moonlight, the open rooms and bare studs sticking out in a way that made it look like a decaying corpse. A couple of times he saw a shadow too big to be anybody but Taft moving behind the shades. Moira eventually dragged him away from his perch and they played cards by candlelight at the enamel-topped table. The mangy old cat she was intent on adopting resting on the windowsill, pressing its nose against the glass, looking for ghouls in the dark. They played two-handed poker and she won every time. Then they played go fish and she won every time. When she suggested they start in on rummy, he went to find his tobacco pouch.

"Are we a threesome now?" he said, leaning against the sink, jutting his chin at the cat.

"It's just a cat," she said. "He comes and goes as he pleases. Wouldn't that be nice?"

"I need you to go up to the lodge tomorrow and find out what he's doing over there," he said.

She dealt another hand to his empty chair. "Who do I look like?" she said. "The Scarlet Pimpernel?"

He had no idea what that meant. "If I could just put my brain in that body, we might have the greatest scientific wrestler the world has ever known," he said.

"Isn't that the idea?"

"The woman likes you," he said. "She'll talk to you."

They played, and Moira made gin while Pepper was trying to decide between hearts and spades. He grinned at her and said she must be just about the smartest woman alive. She didn't fall for that. She told him what was going on up at the lodge was none of their business, and besides, she felt too sorry for that woman to use her like that.

"If I'm being honest, she reminds me a little of myself."

"Look who's sprouted a conscience all the sudden," he said. "I'll have you know it *is* my business so long as I'm in charge around here."

"You know exactly what's going on," she said. "Taft gets out of jail and he and Carol Jean need money, just like another man-and-wife team I could mention. They find Fritz Mundt and James Eddy, and for a while the setup probably seems pretty sweet. Then along comes you, Mr. Hard-Charger, and in the very first two days you run him damn near to death. I might stay in the house, too, if that's what happened to me when I went to work."

"Work," he said. "That's what it's supposed to be. I'm getting paid to do a job, and it's not to traipse around picking wildflowers."

"As far as I've heard, the getting paid part is still theoretical," she said. "As is the match you're supposed to be training for."

"You taking his side on this?"

"I'm just saying, try to see it from their shoes. It must be quite a shock," she said, reaching across the table to squeeze his hand. "Now, tell me what else is bothering you."

He sighed, tossing his cards in, and told her about Taft collapsing in the garage that first day. Pepper had been in a million wrestling gyms. He'd seen a million bad things happen. He'd seen guys grind off the bottoms of their feet on horsehair mats. He saw a guy lose an eye after taking a thumb during tie-up drills. Once he even saw a guy break his own neck on a takedown gone wrong. He'd seen guys pass out from exhaustion, and what happened to Taft in the garage didn't look anything like that. It looked like something else. He just didn't know what.

"I tried to ask her about the trouble in Chicago," Moira said. "She acted like she didn't know what I meant. You think there's something else going on with them?"

"I don't know," he said. "All I know is, if I keep letting Taft do the old soft-shoe around the gym with his yes-men, he'll get himself murdered by Strangler Lesko. Then we'll all look like laughing-stocks."

"As opposed to what?" she said. "Our current sterling reputations?"

"This could be our chance, Moira," he said. "I don't even need Taft to beat Lesko to come out of this thing smelling like a rose as a trainer. I just need him to look good. Decent, passable, anything to have a chance that some other promoter will want to take me on full-time."

"You sound like Mrs. Taft," she said.

"Isn't this what you want?" he said. "Isn't this all you talked about while Boyd Markham was dragging us all over hell and back?"

"That's just it," she said. "We sat around for five years waiting for someone to scoop us off the bottom of the sea. What's changed now to make them interested in us again?"

"You heard them," he said. "They're desperate. Gate receipts are down across the board. Stettler, Lesko, Fritz—all of them must be in a panic. That's why they'd even consider Taft as an opponent for Lesko in the first place. But it's going to come back, Moira, the people will come back. The money will come back. It always does. When it happens, it'd be nice to be along for the ride."

She looked at him in a way he didn't like. "Did I ever tell you about the first thing Abe Blomfeld ever said to me?"

"No," he said. "What?"

"It was right after you won the title," she said. "That party we had for Roughhouse Rawlins."

"Good old Roughhouse," he said.

Roughhouse Rawlins was a hardworking heavyweight who retired when he was twenty-nine years old to marry a local girl and take over his father's plumbing business in Naperville. Pepper and Moira, eager to show off their new house, hosted a combination retirement and engagement party for them. Everybody turned out because everybody liked and respected Roughhouse Rawlins. He was a solid man and a handful on the mat for anyone alive. He was just never going to be champion. He was a step too slow, a shade too predictable. The sort of guy who would always have a little gut on him no matter how hard he tried to lose it.

In the early evening, the party spilled out onto the back lawn, some of the boys throwing a baseball around while the rest stood sipping drinks and arguing about wrestling. Roughhouse Rawlins floated from conversation to conversation, shaking hands and slapping backs, promising everyone they wouldn't lose touch. He would come to all their matches. He was still a student of the sport, he said; it was in his blood. He would never quite shake it.

Moira was in the kitchen, standing at the back window, when Blomfeld came in to use the restroom. Even then he was ancient, a tall beanpole of a man who sometimes wore dark lenses in his glasses to protect his eyes from the sun. He saw her there and came over to see what she was watching. It was Rawlins, of course, hovering around the fringes of the men, never staying in one place too long, moving around like he wasn't sure where to stand. The others were nervous around him, not knowing how to deal with the idea that he was trading it all in for a set of pipe wrenches and a rubber plunger.

"They've already forgotten him," Moira had said. "It's like he's vanishing bit by bit in front of our very eyes."

Blomfeld only smiled and pressed his face close to the glass. "He's the luckiest one of the bunch," he said.

Moira leaned a shoulder against the wall. "Why do you say that?"

"Because he knows it's time to go," Blomfeld replied. "Rawlins could never be more than a curtain jerker, wrestling for peanuts in preliminary matches that end while fans are still finding their seats. The lucky ones figure that out early. Some of them never do."

"I thought the lucky ones become champions," she said.

Blomfeld chuckled. "That's got nothing to do with luck," he said. "Even the best of them will be done before they're forty. This sport isn't much of a career, Mrs. Van Dean, more like a bridge to the next thing. Get in, make as much money as you can and get the hell out. That's the only way to win this game."

When she finished telling the story, she sat looking at him in a way that made Pepper feel like she could see straight through to the back of his head. "Hell," he said, "if I thought like that, I don't know how I'd get out of bed in the morning."

"It's worth considering, though," she said, "whether we're running to catch a train that's already left."

Just then the cat jumped down from the window and scurried, mewling, to the front door. It scratched at the wood and they heard the sounds of someone coming up the walk. Pepper stood and peered out in time to see Fritz step onto the porch in a pressed suit, his head scrubbed pink and shining like glass in the porch light. Pepper pulled the door open just before he knocked and Fritz showed him the delighted grin of a lottery winner. "You'd be wise to pack some things," he said, passing him a thin, cheap piece of yellow paper.

It was a telegram. Pepper read the few words printed there. "That's about as vague as it gets," he said.

"If they're sending for us, it means we're in," Fritz said. "If we weren't, they'd just let us twist."

Pepper glanced at Moira, then back out the window toward the lodge. "You seeing much of Taft these days?"

Fritz snatched the telegram back and stuck it in his pocket. "You're not jumping for joy the way I thought you might," he said.

"He needs time," Pepper said. "That's why you brought me here, right? To train him? Too soon and he won't be ready."

A scowl broke across Fritz's face. "Once we bring him the match, he'll make the effort just like he told us," he said. "Besides, that's sort of your area, isn't it?"

Moira pushed her chair back from the table and followed the cat out into the night. She left the front door open, so they could see her out there lighting a cigarette as she shrugged into the men's hunting jacket she'd taken to wearing around the grounds. Pepper watched her and thought about what she'd said. If Fritz was right, then maybe that changed things.

"So Stettler and Lesko want to meet," Pepper said. "You really think this is it?"

"I've already bought our tickets," Fritz said, as if that was all the explanation he needed. "We leave tomorrow after lunch."

19

Eddy dropped Mundt and Van Dean at the train station and then stopped at a café on Park Street to buy a copy of the local paper. That morning he'd had another run-in with the camp's hired girl—the woman always needed to be told what to do two or three times before she got it right—and wanted a coffee and some time by himself to settle his mind. The owner of the café was a fastidious Irishman straight off the boat from County Cork, and he protested at first when Eddy tried to buy the paper, saying they had complementary copies for customers. Eddy smiled and said he knew that but that he'd rather have a copy of his own, in case he wanted to take it with him. They had this conversation every time he came to the café. It had become something of a friendly game between them.

He took his customary table in the back, facing the door, and in a few minutes the owner brought out his coffee, shaking his head at the idea of Eddy wasting his two pennies buying a paper. Eddy liked the man—so much like the old guys who hung around the cafés and bakeries back home—and he liked the sumptuous, inky coffee he served in sturdy white mugs. Today, though, Eddy was in a poor mood, and though he tried to smile and play along with the café owner's gags, he felt like a fog was following him.

He was jealous of Mundt and Van Dean for shipping off to

Chicago. He didn't like to admit that to himself, but it was true. Mundt had spent the entire drive into town bubbling about this and that while Van Dean sat in the rear seat not saying a word, burning a hole in the back of Eddy's head with his gaze. The little guy still hated his guts and Eddy didn't blame him for it. Now, though, he couldn't shake the idea of Mundt and Van Dean sleeping in soft hotel beds, eating at all his favorite places.

He'd come to believe there was something about the city, with its mighty steel buildings and twisting narrow avenues, that kept his mind moored. Out here in the wide-open country his thoughts just wandered in circles until he could no longer keep them straight. If there was anything he could take solace in, it was the idea that Mundt intended to return with a match signed for Taft and—hopefully—a definite expiration date for their time in Montana.

Eddy was trying to focus on that, burying his thoughts in the paper. It was just a couple of pages, paltry compared to the *Tribune* or *Daily News*, but he had begun to relish his time reading it. Aside from the gossip the hired girl brought with her from town, his telephone talks with O'Shea and the occasional underwhelming conversation with Mundt and the Tafts, it was his only contact with the outside world.

On this day there was not much to report, but at the bottom of one of the back pages he found a small display advertisement that caught his interest. The sketch showed a Craftsman house, neat and new, with a car in its own drive and a couple of small fruit trees growing in the front yard. The owner sat on a wide porch, his legs folded contentedly and a squiggle of smoke trailing from his pipe. Across the top, written in bubbling script, were the words *Beautiful Inglewood*. Underneath in block letters it said SUBURBAN ESTATE LIVING WITH EVERY MODERN CONVENIENCE. He noted the price—$7,500— and twice read through the paragraph of small print advertising "a rare investment opportunity and orchard views, 10 miles from downtown Los Angeles," before turning back to the front page.

The words *rare investment opportunity* made him think of the night the previous winter when he'd run into Mundt at a speakeasy on Grand Avenue. As Eddy thought through the series of conversations that eventually led to his exile in Montana, that one always stood out as the most important to him. Maybe because it was the only one during which he felt like he had any say.

When he first saw the big man blunder through the speakeasy's rear door, shaking snow off his hat like a moose clearing its antlers, he thought it was just coincidence. Now he knew better. He knew Mundt must have contrived to meet him there, must have followed him and watched him until he'd learned his routine, planning the perfect place to get to him, just as Eddy himself had done to countless other men. He kicked himself for not picking up on it at the time.

Mundt had made a good show of it, looking surprised and even a little bit scared to find Eddy sitting at the bar. After a moment, though, he made his way over and bought him a drink, even though Eddy told him he was already at his limit. Mundt obviously wasn't doing well, his suit tatty and tight across his wide back, his hands shaking as he produced his wallet from an inside pocket. Why had Eddy accepted that drink? Why hadn't he slipped off his stool and wandered back out into the night? Maybe he felt sorry for Mundt, or maybe—sitting there hunkered over his drink like it was a potbellied stove—he needed the company.

Things had changed in Eddy's life since he returned from the war. O'Shea was boss now and he was just an underling. On the south side, Big Jim Colosimo was out and Dion was running neck and neck with John Torrio. Without warning, O'Shea had moved out of their little apartment and set up an office above a tailor's shop he owned in River North. He was no longer consulting Eddy on big decisions, instead sending him on outings fit for an errand boy, small-time stuff, barely saying two words to him when they had to be in the same room together.

So maybe Eddy thought he and Mundt could spend a few minutes swapping stories. They remembered each other from that old business with Van Dean, and Mundt was known in the city as the chief enforcer for the promoter Abe Blomfeld. Perhaps he wanted to share a drink with him so they could complain about their bosses. Or perhaps he just thought having one drink with the guy and hearing his sob story would be the easiest way to get rid of him. Either way, he'd been wrong.

Mundt told him Blomfeld was dead and the wrestling operation the old fellow spent his life building had followed him to the grave. Mundt said the culture of sport was changing. Nobody wanted to spend his Saturday night sitting in a smoky theater, watching two men wrestle a two-hour match. They hungered for the blood of the prizefight or to spend long, relaxing afternoons basking in the sun of a ball game. Some of the young people were even going in for football. Eddy had never been much of a sports fanatic—that was O'Shea—and while Mundt talked, he stared at his whiskey, watching the ice floating in the amber, imagining he could see it getting smaller, layer by layer.

It was a sad story, Eddy said when Mundt was finished, but what could you do? "It's hard times all over," he said, which was his way of telling the big man to put a cork in it.

Instead of taking the hint, Mundt peeked over both shoulders and then slid along the bar until they were conspiratorially close. Alarm bells went off in Eddy's head. He could smell Mundt's cheap cologne, the booze on his breath.

"Say," Mundt said, his voice a comical stage whisper. Being so obvious about it that the bartender set down the rack of glasses he was preparing to wash and walked all the way to the other end of the room. "Do you think you could broker me a meeting with Billy Stettler and Dion O'Shea?"

Investment opportunity was exactly the phrase Mundt had used that night, and now it made Eddy flip the paper back to the advertisement. He studied the picture again: the detail of the roof, the line of windows that ran across the front of the house, the satisfied twist on the mouth of the man with the pipe. It was a very realistic rendering. At the bottom of the display was the name of a real estate company, Frank & Livermore, Los Angeles, California, but to one side of that was a note instructing interested parties to inquire at a local address.

When Eddy finished his coffee, he set the cup at the far edge of the table where it wouldn't leave a ring on his paper as he read. The café owner swooped back around the counter to refill it from his carafe, looking crestfallen when Eddy put his palm over the mouth of the mug. The café owner offered to fix him a plate of steak and eggs, but Eddy declined and counted out a decent tip. He said he really ought to get back to work. This wasn't true. He knew he still had a couple of hours to kill before he was needed back at the hunting camp.

◆━━◆

As he came out into the evening air, Eddy felt like walking. He decided to stroll a few blocks up the street and have a look at the address listed in the real estate advertisement. Why not? He imagined he might peek in the storefront windows, see if the office had any handbills with more information about houses in California. When he got there, though, it turned out it wasn't an office at all, but a rooming house three blocks up the hill from the center of town, too nice for transient workers but a step below a hotel suite or steady apartment. A man was sitting on the rooming house's front porch, the heels of his western boots propped up on the rail.

"I thought you might be the cabdriver," he said when he saw Eddy approaching. "I was about to congratulate you on being early."

The man introduced himself as Howard Livermore and he was shaking Eddy's hand and ushering him inside when he doubled over in a coughing fit. The door had shut behind them with a loud *click-clack*, and Eddy turned to give it a long look. His palm had come back from their handshake feeling clammy and soiled, and while Livermore collected himself, he dried it with his handkerchief, wondering what exactly he was doing there. His plan had been merely to look, but somehow he'd followed this strange, sickly man all the way inside without so much as a second thought. If he caught his death in there, he decided, he deserved it.

"My God, man," Livermore said when he was recovered, his voice all casual manners and the droll good humor of the west. "You look petrified. I assure you, the doctors say I'm no longer contagious."

He said it as if it was supposed to be reassuring, but Eddy found it hard to get around words like *doctors* and *contagious*. All the while, Livermore stood there grinning at him. He had a wide, fleshy face and a great mane of blond, pomaded hair. His skin looked stretched, so tanned it was nearly orange. He wore a clay-colored vest with a string tie and stood a little bowlegged in his cowboy boots as if at any moment he might be asked to milk a cow.

"I hope I haven't disturbed you," Eddy said. "Is it something dreadful?"

Livermore laughed. "Just the common cold. You're not scared of a little bit of sniffles, are you? These frigid climes don't agree with me, is all."

Eddy waved around at the luggage scattered across the floor. "If I've caught you at a bad time—"

"Not at all," Livermore said. "I was just waiting for my ride to the station. Afraid it's my last day here. Better now than never, though, I suppose. I've got some time. What can I do you for?"

Livermore escorted him through an open doorway into a large sitting area and sat him in a leather armchair. The rooms were nicer than Eddy first thought and it made him reconsider his opinion of the man, whose clothes were clean and new and whose easy bearing told him he was used to chatting with people he'd just met.

"I saw your advertisement," Eddy said. Then: "Last day?"

"Happily, yes, I'm off to"—Livermore consulted a train ticket before stuffing it back in his hip pocket—"Billings. Then on to Fargo, then Minneapolis, then God only knows where. Someplace warmer, I hope."

"So you're not based here."

"God, no." Livermore hadn't sat down. He was moving effortlessly around the room, hauling a couple of collapsible easels out of his bags. "Came in a few weeks back to give an investment presentation to a few of the local craft unions. I'm a California man, myself. Well, Colorado originally, but I've been out on the coast for, my word, almost ten years now."

"I'm not sure I've ever heard of a traveling real estate salesman before," Eddy said.

Livermore shrugged. "You got to go where the buyer is," he said. "Did you know that, aside from Florida, California is the fastest-growing region in the United States? I have projections showing that one hundred thousand people a year will be moving into the Los Angeles area by 1925. My job is simply to make sure as many of them as possible do it in a Frank & Livermore."

"Now it sounds like you're getting into your sales pitch," Eddy said.

"That's what you came for, isn't it?"

"I suppose it is," he said. He was enjoying the back-and-forth between them. He could tell Livermore was a capable salesman who could rattle off a set speech and make it sound like something he was making up on the fly—the kind of guy who made you think he believed his own sales pitch, maybe because *he* actually did.

Livermore asked what Eddy did for a living, and Eddy described the hunting camp for him in the broadest possible terms. An athletic training center, a property owned by interests from out of state.

"Sounds interesting," Livermore said. "I was a bit of a sportsman myself in my day. What is your position there?"

"I'm the manager," Eddy said. "I don't own it, but I'm the man in charge."

Livermore nodded absentmindedly as he set a stack of placards on each easel. The first was a reproduction of the advertisement Eddy had seen in the newspaper, only this one was larger and in color. He stared for a moment at the rolling green grass of the lawn, the warm blue of the sky. The other card was just a list of numbers printed out in sturdy rows. Across the top were four figures, starting on the left at $5,000 and going up to $8,000 by the time it got to the opposite side. There were other numbers beneath, but they were too small for Eddy to see from where he was sitting.

Livermore asked him why he thought he wanted to move to California, and Eddy said he wasn't sure if he did. He was just a man who was always looking for investments, he said. This was a lie: Eddy didn't want to move to California at all, and had no investments to speak of, but something about the advertisement in the newspaper had driven him to come there. As he sat there listening to the cheerful boom of Livermore's voice, their meeting had a dreamlike quality. He'd never thought of owning a home and had no intention of buying one today. He'd rarely thought of having a life outside Chicago. Somehow, being here gave him a strange buzzing sensation in his chest. He realized it was the thrill of having a secret, knowing that they were the only two people on earth who knew this meeting was happening. No, Eddy wouldn't end up buying a plot of land in a state he'd never visited, but the feeling made him want to sit there a bit longer. Even if it was just fantasy, these few minutes were only for him, and he would play them to the hilt.

Livermore's coughing brought him back, and Eddy covered his own mouth with his fist, trying not to breathe. Maybe he wouldn't stay there much longer after all. Livermore had dragged a chair over from the dining area and positioned it in the middle of the room, facing Eddy. "Unless I miss my guess," he said as he sat, "you're a serviceman. Is that right?"

Eddy nodded and Livermore made a solemn face. "I was over there with the 117th Engineering Regiment," he said. "What an awful business."

"National Guard, 132nd Infantry," Eddy said. "Later attached to the British Third Army as a sharpshooter."

He did his best to match Livermore's thin-lipped, serious look as he said it, though the truth was the war hadn't been all bad for him—rather, the most complicated but exhilarating time of his life. He'd hated O'Shea at first for signing him up, but learned quickly that the structure of army life suited him. There was a calmness there, hidden beneath all the shouting and running around. In many ways he was a model soldier, though early on the close quarters and forced camaraderie of training at Fort Sheridan threatened to drive him mad. He enjoyed mastering the techniques and tactics by day, but sleeping in a barracks with a hundred other men, smelling their stink, listening to their snores, the blats of their farts, the droning of their terrible conversations, seemed like a nightly death.

The front, of course, was a disgusting mess when they got to it. The mud and disease, the yellow, buggy water and moldy food, launched Eddy into a full-throttle panic during the first week. He thought of deserting, or of trying to get himself wounded on purpose, before a first sergeant he barely knew ordered him to the rear and told the colonel there that Eddy was one of the best natural riflemen he'd ever seen. A few days later they sent him to a village in the north of France for special instruction in becoming a sharp-shooter.

He was not sorry to leave his fellow guardsmen behind, and this was the assignment that changed his life. It was perhaps the first lucky break that Eddy had ever known. He excelled at his new post. On the first day of school he was able to recite from memory the names of fifteen objects the men were allowed to study for just one minute before being removed from the room. Those rigorous days he spent learning the arts of scouting, reconnaissance and careful, stealthy killing were among his best. As a sharpshooter, he was largely on his own and quickly realized that's how things should've been for him all along. He studied camouflage, how to find proper cover and how to glass a battlefield through a telescope without the glint of the lens giving away his position.

By the time he got back to the front, the war was all but over. The trench combat had broken up and he spent the rest of his time in France chasing Germans through the countryside with his rifle, a barometer and a small gauge he used to measure wind speed. It was bold, terrifying work, and if the fighting had gone on forever he might not have complained. The only things he didn't like about it were the dirt and the fact the army always made them travel in pairs. He killed seventeen men at the battle of Amiens and was awarded a distinguished conduct medal by the British Army. He liked to think he would've killed many more if he hadn't gotten back to the front too late.

Now, from the way Livermore's face twisted as he said the word *sharpshooter*, Eddy could tell he didn't think much of the profession. Because he felt like Livermore was waiting for it, he also tried for a sour expression, ducking his head gravely as he said, "Awful business indeed."

"On the bright side," Livermore said, "I'm able to knock five hundred dollars off the asking price for veterans."

He got up and stood between his easels. As he began lecturing he used one meaty hand to point out various figures printed on the placards. He said the Frank & Livermore Company had recently acquired a large tract of land in the Centinela Valley, just miles from downtown Los Angeles, which, as he'd said earlier, was among the fastest-growing communities in America. They were in the process of developing a number of homes there.

"I'm not talking about shoddy old row houses or cramped apartments," Livermore said. "We're talking single-family stuff. All brand-new. The comforts of country estate living with the convenience of the city."

With a flourish he removed the display ad Eddy had seen in the paper and tucked it into the back of his stack. The card behind it showed the schematic floor plan of a house and surrounding yard. Eddy stood so he could get a better look, nodding along as Livermore pointed out the features. Three bedrooms, including a nice-sized master suite. Nice-sized parlor. Nice-sized front lawn. A driveway and full garage that could be turned into a workshop, if that was more his style. While Livermore talked, Eddy imagined the cool, dry air of an early-summer afternoon on his skin as he parked in the drive and walked across the lawn into the house. The scent of fruit trees tickling his nose. The warmth of sunlight streaming into the front windows. The gleam of brand-new hardwood floors. A life he would never have, but which at that moment seemed real enough to him that he could hear the chirping of birds and feel the heavy, satisfying click of tumblers falling as he unlocked the front door.

"Plenty of room for the kiddos to roam," Livermore was saying, pointing out the dimensions of a hedged backyard. "Are you married, Mr. Eddy?"

He shifted on his feet—a twinge of embarrassment as he considered manufacturing a make-believe family to tell Livermore about. Finally he shook his head.

Livermore waved the idea away as if he felt silly for even bringing it up. "Plenty of time for all that," he said. "California is for new beginnings. The start of a new chapter. Believe me, because I speak from experience."

Eddy reminded him that they hadn't talked about money, and Livermore nodded like he'd asked him if he believed in God. Slowly he took Eddy through the four different tiers of available properties. The floor plan they'd been looking at was for the top available model, called the Presidential Line. It ran eight thousand dollars. Eddy had several hundred dollars in his pocket, but not that kind of money—not at his fingertips, anyway, even if Livermore gave him the dough-boy discount.

"Interest rates have never been lower," the real estate agent said. "I don't want to pressure you, but my train leaves in two hours and if you can muster a down payment today, I could save you some money and lock you in at 4.66 percent."

It felt like a shove, jogging Eddy from his fantasy. He gave Livermore his driest smile. "I assure you, sir," he said. "You won't pressure me."

Livermore's friendly stare flickered and came back to life. "Wouldn't dream of it," he said. "I just figured, why lay out all that dough at once if you don't have to? For a big shot such as yourself, seventy-eight dollars a month on a fixed ten-year plan? That'd be a steal on a cherry spot like this. Why, if investment is what you're after, these places are practically guaranteed to double in value before your term is up."

"Sight unseen?" Eddy said. "If I didn't know better, Mr. Livermore, I'd think you were trying to scam me."

The color in Livermore's face darkened—something Eddy might

not have thought possible—and he made a show of pulling his watch out of the small front pocket of his vest. He studied it, snapping it shut with an audible click. "This is my name," he said, reaching out to tap the bottom of a placard, where the Frank & Livermore crest and address were printed. "My name, sir. It's everything I am and everything I stand for, and I assure you what I've told you here today is very much on the level. Now, if you'll excuse me, I have a very limited window of time here."

He began taking down the placards and stacking them against a wall near one of his suitcases. Eddy blushed. There was still something about the picture of the house, about the floor plan, that moved him. He realized he'd like to see the place in person. Surely, once his business in Montana was completed, O'Shea would owe him some time off. He'd never taken a vacation in his life, and this time he would have earned one. The idea of California—a place so warm the sunshine could turn you the color of old leather—had been growing inside him since he first saw the advertisement. If he went there and it was half as good as Livermore said it was, maybe it could be something all for himself. A place for his golden years, if he lived that long, or a place to start over if things ever finally bottomed out with O'Shea.

"I'd like to see it," he said. "That's all I meant. If I've offended you, I apologize."

Livermore was wrapping the placards in white cloth, but he glanced up, still not looking all the way convinced. "Nobody's saying you have to buy right now," he said. "If you put down a five percent deposit of earnest money, I could have the home office save you a plot until you can get down there on an investor's trip. Take a look around. Make sure I'm not just peddling snake oil. The only catch is, if we go that route, I can't lock you in at these rates. All I can give you is a good-faith estimate."

"Good faith," Eddy said.

"Sure," Livermore said. "We can both sign some paperwork saying this is the deal I've offered you. If you go down to California and like what you see—and, believe me, everybody likes it—the people in the office down there will do their level best to give you the same rates."

"But it's not guaranteed," Eddy said.

"No, sir, it's not," Livermore said. "But it's as close as we can get if you're not prepared to go all in today."

Eddy thought it over. Five percent was three hundred and seventy-five dollars. Still a chunk of change, but he could cover it. What did it matter in the long run? he figured. Even if he decided this had all been a gag, he wouldn't really miss the money. He could earn that much in a week back in Chicago when O'Shea finally let him come home. Until then, the monthly wire transfers he received to keep the hunting camp up and running were paying his way. He looked at Livermore, standing there now with his hands in the pockets of his slacks, and decided the man was giving it to him square. If he wasn't, that was something he could deal with at a later date. If the real estate agent was traveling around, checking into hotels under his real name, he'd be easy to find. Eddy also still had the Frank & Livermore advertisement in his pocket. The address printed there would at least give him a place to start looking.

He consulted his own watch and discovered he'd already stayed in town longer than he had meant to. No bother. If he hurried back he would still have time for a quick supper before he had to meet the men who were coming to the hunting camp.

"Is it a lengthy process?" he asked. "Doing this paperwork?"

It turned out Livermore already had the papers mostly filled out, and kept them all in the small side compartment of his soft briefcase. They completed the forms in duplicate at the table in the room's dining nook, and if Livermore found it strange when Eddy counted out the five percent deposit from a riffle of cash he kept in his pocket, the man's face didn't show it. When it was all completed they shook hands again, Eddy holding his breath and then wiping his hand on the leg of his trousers. As Livermore bent over the table to stack the papers, he was seized by another coughing fit, this one worse than the first. Eddy took a step back, dismayed, imagining Livermore blowing tiny chunks of spittle all over everything.

The fit lasted only a few seconds and then the real estate agent adjusted his vest and kept stacking. When he had it all together, he turned, wordlessly offering Eddy his copies in one outstretched hand. Eddy looked at the papers, suddenly feeling as if a thin layer of grime was covering his skin. He could see damp spots on the top page, but Livermore just stood there, offering it to him with a smile.

"For your records," he said, urging him to take the stack.

Eddy nodded and made Livermore wait while he pulled on his driving gloves.

20

The trucks came at night, waking Moira from a dream about her father. In the dream the two of them were standing in a room she couldn't quite see, but from the way the floor listed under her feet, she knew they were on the riverboat. Her father wore his gold vest with blue starbursts spangling the back. His hair was full and pomaded, a younger version of himself than she had known in life. He smiled at her, saying something she couldn't hear, and as she reached for him he vanished, leaving her alone in a cold mountain cabin a thousand miles from home. When she opened her eyes, she could hear the low growl of engines and the sound of gravel crunching under slow-rolling wheels. It was so warm in the bed and so cold out of it that she almost drifted back to sleep, but then a car door slammed and another and another, and she sat up. What in the world . . . ?

Wrapping the quilted hunting jacket over her nightdress, she went out to have a look. On the road near the old horse barn she could see lights and a cloud of dust pluming into the sky. At first her groggy mind thought stupidly it must be the carnival, but the commotion wasn't nearly big enough. There was only one truck parked in the shadows of the barn, with a single sedan idling nearby. The shapes of men darted in and out of the headlamps, and even from this distance she recognized James Eddy up there directing traffic. The other men were strangers. Pulling on her shoes, she hiked up the hill to see what was happening, but only got as far as the lodge before she found Carol Jean leaning against the steps, smoking a cigarette. Ten minutes later they were sitting at the table in the parlor, cups of steaming coffee pressed between their palms.

"Who are they?" Moira said.

"Who's to say?" Carol Jean said. "And really, who are we to ask?" As she spoke she swirled her drink to confirm what Moira had already guessed. The trucks were hauling booze.

"Oh, honey, you should see your face," Carol Jean went on. "Like someone rode in and told you there is no Santa Claus."

Moira took a drink of coffee; bitter, maybe a day old. "How often does this happen?" she asked.

"Honestly, I thought you would've figured things out ages ago," Carol Jean said. "Smart girl like you. Maybe you don't see as many of the angles as you thought, hey?"

"And the rest of it," Moira said. "Me, you, our husbands, Fritz Mundt, the supposed wrestling camp—what are we? A front? Some gangster's cover story?"

"Don't be dramatic," Carol Jean said. "You're here, aren't you? It costs a lot of money to keep those boys in tights and boots. What would be the point if it were all just a put-on? No, honey, I assure you, Mr. Mundt's belief in my husband as a drawing card is very real."

Moira filled in the rest, trying to put herself in Fritz's shoes. Abe Blomfeld died and left him the gym, but the wrestling business was in the tank and Fritz didn't know the first thing about being a promoter. It took all of six months for the operation to go belly-up. He must've been desperate by the time Garfield Taft showed up on his doorstep, claiming he was ready for his big comeback. Fritz would have to be down to his last dime to bet on a long shot like a black man getting a crack at the world's heavyweight champion, but maybe he didn't have any other choice. Win or lose, a match against Strangler Lesko would put them all on easy street if it actually happened. He would need start-up capital and enough regular cash coming in to keep a training camp running. Where did a two-bit wrestling promoter go when he needed that kind of money? Not the bank, she thought. He didn't waltz into J. P. Morgan and invite the loan officer to squeeze Taft's biceps.

"I knew it," she said. "I knew from the moment I saw him again that Freddy was in over his head."

"You know what your problem is?" Carol Jean said. "You refuse to see the good in people. Even when they're trying to help you out."

"Does Mr. Taft know about this?" Moira asked.

"Of course he knows," Carol Jean said. "I mean, there's no telling what these men understand from one moment to the next. Their whole lives are a giant game of tag, all about who got who last, everybody keeping score in their heads all the time."

"Where is he now?" Moira asked. The whole time she'd been sitting in the parlor she hadn't heard the floorboards creak overhead.

"He doesn't sleep," Carol Jean said. "He walks. Ever since he got out of prison, he just walks and walks and walks."

"What do you mean he doesn't sleep?" Moira said.

Anger bloomed on Carol Jean's face. "It doesn't strike me as a particularly hard concept to grasp," she said. "He tosses and turns, he gets restless, he goes out. I don't pry, because, unlike you, I strive for optimism. I just thank my stars he's home at all and not locked up in some box somewhere."

Moira fought back the urge to snap at her—the oblivious sea captain whose ship had set a course for the edge of the earth. This thing they'd both spent so much time pining for. They weren't going to get it. Moira knew that now. Maybe it had taken hearing it from someone else's mouth to make her realize there was no going back to their old lives. They could only move forward. But with Pepper off on Fritz Mundt's Chicago adventure, Carol Jean was the closest thing Moira had to an ally at the hunting camp. So that she wouldn't tell her how silly it all sounded, she took a deep breath and held it, thinking carefully about what she would say next.

"I know what it's like, you know. To have to start over."

"Oh," Carol Jean said, like she didn't believe it. "What would you know about it?"

"My father died when I was fairly young," she said. "After that, I left home and went to St. Louis. I had nothing, I knew no one, maybe like you that first night you wandered into the Olympia Ballroom. But I made it. I made a little life for myself and then I met Pepper and I expect the rest would sound very familiar to you. For a while we had a lot. Now we don't have a thing."

As she talked, Carol Jean put her coffee cup down and tucked a strand of hair behind her ear. "Mine was a saloon owner," she said. "My daddy. Had a little corner bar down in Lexington. The kind that always kept a picture of John L. Sullivan in one of those little oval frames, like some long-lost member of the family? Well, you can imagine how he reacted when he found out about Garfield. The last time I talked to him, he blamed me for the death of my mother— said I killed her with a broken heart. Really, it was cancer, but I'm not sure he was thinking straight by that point. Thought it was some kind of divine message that he'd been right all along when Gar got sent away."

She was running again, so Moira got out of her way.

"We weren't married, of course, when he went to prison; but at first I didn't know how I would survive it," Carol Jean said. "They took him up to Dayton for the trial and I followed. Those nights alone in the hotel room, the not knowing and the loneliness. Those were probably my lowest points. And then of course the waiting while he served his time. I suppose the silver lining, if there was one, was that I proved capable of hanging around longer than the previous Mrs. Taft could manage."

"Three years is a long time," Moira said.

"Not for the man you love," Carol Jean said. "A blink of the eye."

"Still," Moira said. "I suppose anything seems preferable by comparison."

"Certainly you can't expect someone who's gone through that kind of hardship to come out unchanged," Carol Jean said. "But I'm hopeful things will get better. Maybe even go back to the way they were before."

"Changed how?"

"He's a harder man now," Carol Jean said. "Less interested. He barely rests, just wanders."

"What you said that first night at dinner," Moira said. "You indicated the papers got it wrong about Mr. Taft."

Carol Jean laughed, a booming slap of a laugh. "Complete lies, my dear, trumped-up nonsense. My Gar was no more a pimp than he was president of the United States."

"How can you be sure?" Moira asked. She found herself fascinated, in a strange way, by this woman. She seemed at once the boss of the house and also a fraud, every pose and facial expression studied, as if she had spent considerable time learning where to place her words, her arms, her breasts. Her energy bordered on manic, a look in her eyes that said if she ever stopped swimming, she would drown.

"I know my husband," Carol Jean said, leaning over to lay a hand across Moira's arm. "The truth is, the whole thing had nothing to do with prostitution or whatever else they said in court. It was wrestling, plain and simple. A group of promoters got together and decided not to let Garfield Taft win the world's heavyweight championship. They knew if they let that happen, a white man would never lay hands on it again. It was just a couple of months out from when he was supposed to wrestle Joe Stecher at Comiskey Park, you see. It took more than a year for Gar to get Stecher to sign the contract, and, well, the whole wrestling world was just terrified. So they had him arrested and Stecher went to Omaha and wrestled Stanislaw Lesko instead. They fought to a five-hour draw in front of thirty thousand people. Not as big a crowd as they would've drawn with Garfield on the bill, but still, the gate was almost two hundred thousand dollars. Can you imagine?"

"It sounds like quite a conspiracy."

"My dear," Carol Jean said. "When all you need is one Negro locked up in a cell somewhere, it's not like murdering Caesar. It's just a matter of which bagman leaves which bag in whose hotel room. Remember, there was a lot more money to be made in wrestling back then."

This brought Moira back to Eddy, who was of course one of the main reasons she'd walked up here in the first place. She asked Carol Jean about him again, if he was the kind of man who might leave a suitcase full of cash in some important man's hotel room. "My husband said he's a gangster," Moira said, trying not to feel like she was betraying a trust by saying it.

Carol Jean drank and chuckled. "A pitiful one, maybe. To nab a cherry assignment like this? He can't be anyone's favorite, whoever is the boss of him."

"It's so strange," Moira said. "All of it."

"Any stranger than anything else we've done?" Carol Jean said.

Moira pointed her coffee cup at the window. "These creatures. How long will they be in our midst?"

Carol Jean said the mountain roads would be too dangerous for the men to travel after dark. They'd stay the night to guard their treasure and leave in the morning.

"Wonderful," Moira said, and again Carol Jean sighed.

"Sweetheart," she said. "I'm going to tell you what Mr. Herman Cohn told me when I asked what to do the first time a customer at the Olympia Ballroom put his hand up my dress."

"Which was?"

"Hold your nose and hope the check clears."

⎯⎯•⎯⎯•⎯⎯

She intended to go straight back to the cabin, but after leaving Carol Jean to finish the dregs of the coffee, Moira circled around the far end of the lodge and crept up the hill toward the horse barn. It was even colder out than she had first thought, a stiff wind biting into her ankles, blowing up under the hem of her jacket. She wrapped herself tighter as she went, picking her way to the boarded-up gym where the men were supposed to spend their days training. In the shadows there she stopped to let her eyes adjust to the gloom, hoping to get a better look at what was happening. The doors to the horse barn were flung open and the truck was already backed up close, the sedan hunkering nearby with its motor still running. She counted six men working to unload wooden crates, the sound of their voices carrying in the dark, but the words washed out by the wind. She could no longer see Eddy up there with them and wondered if he'd gone off to settle some other business.

Before long she saw figures coming through the darkness toward her. At first she thought they were carrying shovels or axes, but as they got closer she saw each man had a shotgun propped against his hip. A surge of panic seized her, the urge to run, to scurry off and hide in the underbrush. She fought it down and immediately regretted it, wondering how many people got themselves killed for fear of looking foolish. By then it was too late. There were four of them, the lead man big and round-faced, his collar turned up to his ears. He was the only one not carrying a shotgun but instead had a large lamp, like something a miner might use, hanging from one fist. As his light fell on her, she could tell they were surprised to find she was a woman.

"Come out from there, now," the lead man said. In his voice she recognized the long, rounded vowels of Canada.

"What's the meaning of this?" Moira said, straining to be heard over the wind, trying to sound like she was the one being wronged. "I want to know what's going on here."

"I'm sorry, ma'am," the man with the lantern said. "I'm going to have to ask you to clear out of here."

Up close she could see he was too young to really be the one in charge. He was barely into his thirties, lips pressed tight against the cold. Under different circumstances he might have been handsome, and she wondered if he'd been chosen as lantern bearer precisely because he had a friendly, evenhanded way about him. She smiled at him.

"You can't come out here at this hour, make all this racket," she said, "and expect a girl to get her beauty rest, can you?"

One of the others, a dog-faced man wearing little round spectacles, prodded her with the barrel of his shotgun. "You bitch," he growled. "Do what the man says."

She felt the warm, watery feeling of having a gun pointed at her, but before she could move the lead man nudged the barrel away. "No sense in you being up here in this cold, ma'am," he told her in his easy voice. "Go on, now."

She looked over his shoulder to where a couple of men were still unloading the truck. The sedan belching white smoke into the sky. When she spoke again, it was with her father's calm.

"I apologize for being curious," she said, "but I won't abide by such rough talk. I'm a guest here of Fritz Mundt. Does he need to hear about this?"

The lead man's face turned so hard she knew she had misjudged him. She'd pushed it too far. He turned and, in a voice as deadly as a hot wire, told the dog-faced man and a couple of the others to escort her back to wherever she came from. As he strode back up the hill, he gave her a last look, pity plain on his face, as if he'd tried to help her but now she'd fouled it up. A nervous jitter quivered in her legs as the other men marched her down the road toward the cabins. She could still feel the sharp barrel of the shotgun burning against her ribs, even though the dog-faced man had only placed it there for a second.

"Naughty girl," he said to her now. "Trying to make me look bad in front of our young Mr. Templeton. That was a stupid thing to do."

When they got to the place where the road widened in front of the cabins, he used the shotgun to lift the back of her skirt, and she wheeled to slap it away. The men laughed and catcalled at her and the dog-faced man caught her by the wrist with a grip tight enough that she couldn't wrench free. His eyes were small and dumb, and she knew he was going to hurt her. Maybe he thought she was just some camp prostitute, or maybe he didn't care. As he backed her up, he tightened the squeeze on her wrist and a small whimpering sound escaped her lips.

On the porch of the cabin something moved, and they all turned their heads to look. Moira's first thought was of Pepper, a silly hope that he'd come back early from Chicago and was waiting for her. Her heart dropped when she saw it was just the old orange tomcat. It had been snoozing in front of the cabin's door, anticipating the bowl of food she might bring down from the lodge. Now it uncurled itself and slunk off the porch into the road, curious about the noise. When it saw Moira, the cat dipped its head and trotted toward them. All the men stood and gaped at it until the dog-faced man released his grip on her wrist, shouldered his shotgun, and fired.

Moira covered her face against the blast, and when she looked again the cat was down in the middle of the road. The dog-faced man stooped and hoisted it into the air by the stump of its tail, making sure to hold it at arm's length. It was gut shot, and ropes of blood and stringy entrails hung from its body. Half of one of its back legs was missing and thick gashes were ripped through its hindquarters by the heavy load of the shotgun. The cat was still alive, screaming and scratching, which made the dog-faced man laugh.

"Damn thing practically ran right up to me," he said, a grin full of brown, broken teeth slithering across his face.

One of the others whistled low. "That's some good shooting," he teased. "Bagged yourself a real trophy."

They all laughed, and Moira swallowed back a rush of bile. "Let it go," she said.

"I think I'll make a hat out of it," the dog-faced man said. "A nice fur hat."

"Let it go," she said again, louder, spinning and hitting the dog-faced man on top of the shoulder with her fist. It was a stupid, worthless blow, but the surprise of being hit by a woman made him drop the cat. The animal landed with a sickening flop, and as it tried to scurry off into the underbrush, she saw its one remaining hind leg wasn't working. It dragged itself a few feet with its front paws, leaving a trail of thick blood behind. The dog-faced man knocked Moira back a step with the flat of his shotgun, a snapping blow that felt like it had almost caved in her chest.

"What's it to you?" he said. "That old cat was half-dead already."

Tears welled in her eyes and she felt angry with herself for it. She'd seen the cat only a handful of times. She cleared her throat, determined not to give the bootleggers the satisfaction.

The sound of footsteps coming up the road made them all stop, readying their guns as Garfield Taft appeared out of the shadows. He was wearing his knee-length coat with wide fur lapels open over a white shirt buttoned to the collar with no tie. It was the first time Moira had seen him so close since the first afternoon she'd gone to see Carol Jean. His face was healing nicely and he looked even taller now than she'd thought during his match with Jack Sherry. The line of men moved aside for him as he passed, his steps long and confident. He didn't bother looking at them.

"What's all this?" he said, his voice a steady baritone, softer than she expected.

"It's none of your concern, nigger," the dog-faced man said. "You get on inside before you cause any trouble."

If the words aroused any anger in Taft, he didn't show it. "I wasn't speaking to you," he said, turning only his chin at the dog-faced man while keeping his eyes on Moira. This close she could see they were flecked with gold and green. "Are you all right?"

"These men shot that old tomcat," she said, as if that explained everything. "For no reason at all—just shot it."

Taft faced the bootleggers for the first time, studying each one of them in turn as he stepped between them and Moira. The dog-faced man lifted his gun slightly and grinned at them again. "What are you going to do about it, boy?" he asked. As his last word hung in the air it was unclear what the dog-faced man thought would happen next. Whatever it was, Moira guessed he probably didn't expect Taft to stroll over and shove him down on his ass in the dirt.

21

E ddy couldn't sleep, and so he lay awake on his small cot, trying to keep from thinking about California by making a map of the hunting camp in his head. For this kind of work, he imagined he was using a good, inky pen, and he drew from memory in thick, perfect strokes. Sketching out the distances from the lodge to the horse barn, from the horse barn to the rear gate. From there his thoughts followed the road up to the place where it disappeared about a half mile north of the camp. Marking out the terrain, the surrounding hills, and the place where a stream cut underneath a little wooden bridge.

On his drive back to the camp, he'd kept the papers Howard Livermore had given him wrapped in a handkerchief on the passenger seat. He tried his best to forget the man's wet cough and not to think about the germs that might at that moment be creeping from the pages to the upholstery, inching toward him as he drove. First thing, he snuck into the kitchen and stole a small cast-iron pot with a heavy lid. In his room he'd folded the papers inside and stowed it in the bottom drawer of his desk. He felt better about it now. He felt no tickle in the back of his throat. No sniffles coming on.

He'd missed dinner in the dining room and had the hired girl bring his food to him on a tray. She didn't like it but did as she was told. With Mundt and Van Dean gone, it had just been Mr. and Mrs. Taft at the table, she told him when he asked. The Van Dean woman stayed down in the guest cabins, and the girl had taken her down a sandwich.

"Running food all over," she said to him. "And me, with a certificate from the Silver Bow County Secretarial School."

She had a way of talking that set his teeth on edge. "What is this?" he'd said, using a fork to paw through some of the dry, colorless stuff on his plate. "Gruel?"

Afterward he'd gone out to meet the trucks and get the Canadians started unloading their shipment. As soon as he was able, he left them to their business. They were grimy, small-minded men and he doubted any of them had ever fired a shot in anger. Forty-five minutes ago he'd extinguished the lamp in his room and ever since he'd been lying in the dark, brooding over how he had wound up in this place. At some point he'd begun to wonder if O'Shea would send someone to kill him when this was all over and whether his little house in California ought to be more than just a backup plan.

That's when he started trying to still his mind with mapmaking. It was a trick he'd learned as a sharpshooter. By day he'd lie hidden for hours in front of some bush or along the wall of a gully, memorizing the zagging lines of the enemy's trenches, the ant-like movements of the men. At night he'd sit awake under the stars, mapping it in his head, looking for weak spots, trying to locate the most likely places for officers' quarters and where he might catch them unaware. It had a calming effect, the mapmaking, and came with the knowledge that he'd be well prepared for whatever happened. Now he'd almost finished sketching the hunting camp in his head and had just started to feel a peaceful, drowsy calm settling over him, when he was jarred awake by the unmistakable sound of a gunshot.

The report, a powerful slapping bang, rattled everything in the room. In his haste to grab his rifle from the corner, he toppled the coatrack and sent a glass paperweight to shatter on the floor. Cursing, he flung open a window, a gust of freezing wind slamming into his face. He dropped to one knee to rest the rifle against the sill and held his breath, straining his ears for roaring engines, scanning the perimeter for bursts of floodlights, shadows creeping through the underbrush with guns drawn. He saw nothing and he heard nothing, none of the chaos that would accompany an invading army of government agents. The hunting camp was still and quiet except for Moira Van Dean out in the road with the idiot Canadians.

He watched as one of the Canadians lifted something limp and wet off the ground, raising it to shoulder level. Before Eddy could make out what it was, the Van Dean woman rushed at him, flailing, and the man shoved her with the flat side of his shotgun, dropping the thing back into the dirt. Sighing, Eddy eased the rifle off safety with a flick of his thumb.

He hadn't fired a gun during his six months in Montana, but he trusted his aim would still be true from this distance, so long as the rifle was up to the task. It was a standard M1917 Enfield, an American knockoff of the original used by the British during the war, and Eddy hadn't yet had the chance to properly sight it in. The gun had been sporterized for civilian use, altered to take heavier .30-06 hunting cartridges. He'd bought it from an out-of-work miner, a foreigner who placed a classified ad in the newspaper and answered the door to his one-room shack bootless and trembling from hunger when Eddy came calling. He thought the man might actually break down in tears when he handed over the rifle, making him promise to take good care of it. Something about his accent reminded Eddy of the barber.

Eddy had never been what you might call a haunted man, but he thought a lot about the barber these days. If he had been able to keep himself from killing that man, he wouldn't have had to go away. Maybe O'Shea wouldn't have shuffled him to the side. Even as he thought it, though, he knew it wasn't true. He knew at some point O'Shea would've cut him out regardless. There was too much money in it now.

Maybe it was always meant to be that way. Maybe at some point, without even realizing it, Eddy had knocked his head against the upper limits of what was possible for him. At best he was a talented and methodical killer. At worst he was a babysitter, dispatched to the middle of nowhere to stand watch over things that didn't need watching, keeping tabs on O'Shea's least valuable possessions.

Now, as he rested the gun's open sights on the slim figure of Moira Van Dean, he thought about the way she'd stood up to Mundt during their first dinner at the hunting camp, needling him for a cut of the promoter's fees if a match against Lesko was signed. He had to admit he admired her for it a little bit. He was thinking it would be a shame to have to kill her over a dispute with the Canadians, when the figure of Garfield Taft appeared farther down the road wearing his ridiculous fur-lined jacket. Surrounded by the shorter men, he looked even more enormous than usual, and Eddy cursed under his breath. Words were exchanged with the Canadians, but he couldn't make them out. Taft approached the man Mrs. Van Dean had been fighting with and without any preamble sent him sprawling on the ground with one mighty shove.

Eddy didn't wait to see what happened next. He left the rifle on the floor under the window and grabbed his pistol, leaping over the upended coatrack as he ran for the door. He didn't stop to put on his coat, and the shock of sprinting out into the night was like plunging into an icy lake. He slipped once in the frost-covered grass as he charged down the hill, the wet spot soaking through his pants to the knee. By the time he got to the run of cabins, the ugly, dog-faced Canadian was up on his feet, holding Taft off with his shotgun. The rest of them stood with their own guns ready, watching the Van

Dean woman try to pull Taft away by the arm. For now, the big fellow was standing his ground. As he got closer Eddy saw that the thing in the road was the old cat Mrs. Van Dean had been feeding. It had been skulking around the property since Eddy had arrived, maybe an old barn cat or somebody's pet that had run away or been forgotten when the previous owners sold the place. Now it was suffering, nearly dead.

The dash down the hill left him out of breath and it took him a moment to get his bearings. "You cowards," Mrs. Van Dean screamed. "For no reason, you killed it. The least you can do is put it out of its misery."

The ugly Canadian's lips twitched. He acknowledged Eddy with a sideways glance and then looked at the cat, which was trying to drag itself along by its front paws. "I won't, either," he said, suddenly nervous, maybe because of Eddy, maybe because he'd pointed his gun at Taft without first figuring out if he really wanted to shoot the man. "I changed my mind. Let the damn thing go."

"Let it go?" Mrs. Van Dean said. "It could take hours to die like this. If you are any kind of man at all, you'll do the right thing and kill it now."

"I'll kill *you* in a minute if you don't stop that screeching," the Canadian said, shifting the barrel of his shotgun in her direction before settling it again on Taft.

For the life of him, Eddy couldn't remember the dog-faced Canadian's name as he stepped up and pressed his pistol to the man's temple. "I can't let you do that," he said.

The Canadian didn't even try to hide the look of hatred that filled his face. One of his partners, a small hatless man with a horseshoe hairline and a roll of fat underneath his chin, stepped forward and pointed his own gun at Eddy. Aside from a quick look that he hoped said *Don't be stupid*, Eddy paid him no mind but felt a slick of sweat bloom under his clothes. It was dangerous to have a gun held on you by a man who wasn't used to doing it. He hoped the little bald guy didn't shoot him out of pure nervousness.

"Where's Templeton?" Eddy said, talking only to the dog-faced man.

"How should I know?" the Canadian spat back. "Probably snug in his ruck with one of his books. What's that got to do with me? What's that got to do with this?"

"Listen," he said, pacing himself, nice and easy, his voice clear and strong. "Everybody out here has a job to do, and right now not a single one of you is doing it. It's time for you to take your men back up to the barn where you belong."

"That's rich," the Canadian said. "I'll be damned if I ever had a white man side with a Negro and a whore over me."

Eddy pushed the pistol a little harder into his head. "Right now there are only two sides," he said, "one that gets you paid and one that gets you shot. I'm on the side that pays you, but I'm giving serious thought to crossing over."

Slowly and with what Eddy imagined was secret relief, the Canadian lifted the barrel of his gun so it no longer pointed at Taft. He gave his bald partner a curt nod and that man raised his gun as well. The rest of them stood in the road not making a sound, waiting for a cue from Eddy. He let that feeling linger a moment before he lowered his pistol and walked over to where the tomcat was lying in the road. Its chest was heaving like a bellows with each panicked breath, and before he could think about it he pointed his gun and shot it, the report deafening in the quiet. The blast split the cat's body open. Innards flopping, its neck twisting unnaturally to one side. Eddy made the mistake of staring at it a second too long, and all at once his thoughts filled with the idea of rabies and squishy white maggots. He gagged, covering his mouth with the palm of his free hand, then turned away from the others, taking a few steps to let his stomach settle before swinging around.

"Get rid of it," he said to the dog-faced Canadian, hoping he didn't look as green as he felt. The Canadian sneered like he might say something smart, but then went to poke around in the brush until he found a long stick. He dragged the cat out of the road, leaving a smear of blood, and stomped back, refusing to meet anyone's eyes. "Now go on," Eddy said, waving his gun in the direction of the barn.

"We won't forget about you," the dog-faced man said to Taft and the Van Dean woman as his men started back up the road.

She laughed. "Now you're just trying to flatter us," she said, some of the pluck returning to her voice.

Eddy had half a mind to follow the Canadians up and order them to drive back to the border that night instead of waiting for the morning. He wouldn't want to have to explain to Mundt and O'Shea why one of their trucks got lost trying to make the trip in the dark, so he stood his ground until they were out of earshot.

"Don't mention it," he said to Taft and Mrs. Van Dean once the men were gone. "You're very welcome."

The woman squinted at him. "I wouldn't have thought you'd go weak at the knees at the sight of a little blood," she said. "And to think I was worried you might be dangerous."

"What I am is not your business," he said. His knee was freezing where he'd slipped, and it was possible his slacks were ruined. His hands felt dirty again, and in order to wash them he'd have to make a special trip down from his room to refill his bucket from the well. It would be worth it.

"I don't appreciate this," she said, as if announcing it to the world. "Being lied to, being led on."

He knew she meant the liquor, and for a split second his eyes strayed away from the group, up the hill to the horse barn. In a sudden flash Eddy understood what he was going to do. He realized the answer to all his troubles had been sitting right there, a hundred yards from his bedroom this whole time. His ticket out of Montana. His ticket out of everything. When he looked back at the woman, she was still staring at him, a queer look on her face like she could read his thoughts. He blinked his eyes and forced his face to go blank again.

"Let me share some advice with you, Mrs. Van Dean," he said. "The truth of our situation is that you're not bringing much to the table here. I came down tonight because I don't think my business partners would be very happy with any eventuality that called attention to this place or led to their star Negro getting killed for no reason. You? Those men can have you for all I care."

"Hey, now—" Taft said.

"And you," Eddy said, "if you want me to keep covering for you and our friend Dr. Paulson, I suggest you don't put me in a situation like this again."

Taft opened his mouth as if to say something but didn't. Eddy started up the hill, his arms and legs now feeling very heavy, like he wanted to curl up on his cot and sleep for a thousand years.

"What if those men come back for her?"

This was Taft's voice from behind him. He considered it and turned to face them. "That doesn't sound like my problem," he said.

He left them that way, climbing back up the hill to his room and changing out of his pants. He thought of going up to see if he could rouse Templeton, the big, spiritless man who was supposed to be in charge of the Canadians. He knew it wouldn't do any good, though, and anyway, the rage that had been seething in his chest had been replaced by a new feeling. For the first time in a long time he could see the future opening up in front of him. He had the urge to drive into town right then, call O'Shea on the telephone, get him out of bed and tell him exactly where he could stick this job. What had he called it that day back in Chicago? An important supervisory position? That was a laugh, and Eddy—sitting at his desk chair in the cold room in just his skivvies—nearly did laugh now at the thought of all of it.

He still wasn't totally sure why he'd agreed to set up that first meeting between Mundt, O'Shea and Stettler. To think about it now made him feel bewildered all over again. As he remembered it, his dealings with Mundt seemed to take on the quality of a runaway train. As if as soon as the wrestler opened his mouth there had been no stopping it, though Eddy's mind may have added that sense of things afterward. He should've told Mundt to take a hike that first night in the speakeasy, but he hadn't. Maybe he'd brokered the meeting as a show-off move meant to tell Mundt—and maybe prove to himself—that he could still get O'Shea in a room if he needed to. At first Mundt had been coy about exactly what proposition he had, but he made it clear it was something big. There was no shame in at least hearing him out, Eddy had told O'Shea, even though his friend was dubious that a retired meat tosser and small-time leg breaker could have anything that would interest him.

They met in O'Shea's office above the tailor's shop in River North. O'Shea brought in a couple of his new men, goons in outfits they'd bought downstairs, whom Eddy disliked with an intensity he knew could only be jealousy. Billy Stettler showed up alone, his strongman body stuffed inside a tight suit and his hair dyed a preposterous shade of midnight black, so dark it looked almost blue against his scalp. The rumor going around was that Stettler had been injecting himself with monkey hormones to increase his bulk. Eddy wasn't sure he could believe that. It seemed like the kind of story a schoolboy would make up. Where would you even get something like that? Bribe a zookeeper?

At least Stettler hadn't brought Stanislaw Lesko, a man Eddy

considered so brutishly stupid he lowered the collective intelligence of any room he entered. The fact that the world's heavyweight
champion wasn't there, either, meant Stettler wasn't interested in
what Mundt had to say, or that he was so interested he didn't want
Lesko to know about it yet. Eddy imagined Stettler leaving a bowl
of food on the floor when he left the house so the wrestler wouldn't
starve to death while he was out. He smiled at the image even
though he noticed that, despite being the one who set up the meeting, he'd been left to stand by the window while O'Shea and Stettler
took chairs around a small table with a coffeepot and a plate of
cookies.

Mundt showed up exactly on time, looking like his life had made
a complete rebound since Eddy had last seen him. He sported a
fresh manicure, and his mustache had been styled with wax that
smelled strongly of licorice. He came into the room shaking hands
and slapping backs—his eyes no longer glowing with drunkenness—
smiling as if they'd all come there to congratulate him on the birth
of a new baby.

It took a few agonizing minutes for everyone to get settled. While
they poured coffee and O'Shea offered to send out for sandwiches,
Eddy felt his mind getting wrapped tighter and tighter. Social gatherings had a way of winding him up, and these awkward moments of
small talk before the real business began were almost more than he
could bear. Finally Mundt settled into his chair. He thanked both
men for meeting with him and thanked Eddy for setting it up. He
said he knew they were busy, so he would do his best not to keep
them longer than he needed.

"We all have problems," Mundt said, "but I have a solution that I
think could make us all very rich men."

Eddy watched O'Shea and Stettler as Mundt talked, both of
them looking at him as if a traveling salesman had just promised to
show them the sharpest set of kitchen knives they'd ever seen. They

exchanged a glance, which Eddy read as saying, *We're already rich men.* Stettler had his legs crossed at the knee and his hands folded primly in his lap. O'Shea began tugging absentmindedly at his right earlobe. For the first time Eddy felt a small bell toll in his chest, because he knew this was a tic of his, something O'Shea did when he was trying not to look interested.

"Do tell," Stettler said with an exaggerated enthusiasm. "What problems do you mean?"

Mundt turned in his seat. "You," he said, pointing a sturdy finger, "have already put down a security deposit on a date at the Garden in New York at the end of the year, but have nobody the public would pay a buffalo nickel to see wrestle Stanislaw Lesko."

"We're going to get Joe Stecher," Stettler protested, though his face said he knew it was a lame reply.

Mundt ignored him, turning to O'Shea. "And you," he said. "I understand the police recently raided your brewery on Pacific Avenue. A half million dollars in losses, is that right? Not a crippler, maybe, but quite a setback. It certainly puts you a step behind our friends from the other side of town, does it not?"

O'Shea's round face had only grown more amused as Mundt talked. He turned to Stettler, the corners of his eyes crinkling. "Mr. Mundt reads the papers," he said. Then back to Mundt: "All right, sir, you have my ear. Supposing these terrible, debilitating ailments you speak of are real: What tonic do you propose?"

The tone in his voice was mocking, but Mundt didn't seem to notice. Eddy imagined he'd probably practiced this speech a dozen times at home in front of a mirror and now he was going to stick to his pitch no matter what happened. Mundt spread his hands like a magician about to perform his biggest trick.

"Montana," he said.

"Montana?" O'Shea said, the way you repeat something back when you're not sure you heard it right.

"It's a state," Mundt said. "It happens to be my home state. You know where it is?"

There was a dangerous second when everyone in the room appeared to be trying to figure out if he was putting them on. O'Shea shifted in his seat. Stettler sat as still as a cat about to pounce. Eddy felt the cold of the window behind him, pressing into his back. Earlier, he'd told Mundt he would be very angry if he'd gone through the trouble of setting up this meeting just so the wrestler could pour garbage in their ears.

When O'Shea spoke again, he went very slowly, willing to play along for the moment but not sure where any of this was leading. "Sure," he said. "Out west somewhere."

Mundt grinned, his face sweaty and glowing. "Exactly what I thought," he said. "Let me tell you a thing or two about Montana, the state where I was born, the state where I vacation each summer and where I continue to harbor many important contacts."

Eddy thought he might suffocate on pure embarrassment. He pushed himself up from the windowsill as if to call things off, but Mundt kept going. "It's the third-biggest state in the union, did you know that?" he said. "It goes Texas, California, then Montana."

"That's terrific," Stettler said.

"Isn't that something," O'Shea added, looking at Eddy like *Let's wrap this up.*

"Montana is six hundred thirty miles across, and yet the population is less than half the population of the city of Chicago," Mundt said. "It's cold and empty and mountainous as all get-out, and do you know how many Prohibition agents there are in the whole state?"

"Tell me," O'Shea said.

"Twelve," Mundt said. "A dozen federal officers trying to cover an area of land roughly three times the size of the state of Illinois. Hell, half the towns out there still have saloons up and running in broad daylight."

"Sounds like a great place to plan a party," O'Shea said. "What's it got to do with us?"

Mundt held one hand flat and said: "Montana is here." He lifted his other hand, put it on top. "Canada is here. You starting to get the picture?"

"Not really," O'Shea said. "I don't know anybody in Canada."

Now Mundt grinned back at him. "I do."

O'Shea inched forward in his seat, still doing his best to sound disinterested. "You're saying it'd be an easy place to import booze," he said.

"Not just to import," Mundt said. "To stockpile."

O'Shea snorted. "Okay," he said. "I'll bite. Why would I want to stockpile liquor a thousand miles away?"

Eddy took a step back and resumed his position against the window as Mundt started talking again. O'Shea had forgotten about him for the moment.

"Actually, it's more like fourteen hundred miles," Mundt said, "and I'll tell you exactly why."

Mundt said that in the time between when the federal government approved the Volstead Act and when it actually went into effect, nearly everybody had tucked some hooch away. The big social clubs in Chicago and New York filled storerooms with it. Saloon-keepers and café owners piled crates in their basements so they could have a bottle under the counter for their favorite customers. Everybody's grandma had a jug hidden somewhere, Mundt said. In Chicago, guys like O'Shea and John Torrio scrambled to get stills set up, and all over the country men who knew there was money to be made started bringing liquor in from Canada or Cuba or Mexico or wherever was closest.

"But eventually," Mundt said, "you're all going to run dry. Maybe not forever, but there's going to come a day when the great city of Chicago suffers a booze shortage."

"And?" O'Shea said.

"And that's our moment," Mundt said. "All we need is a couple of days' head start and, *boom*, just in the nick of time a dozen pallets of O'Shea liquor slide into town on some anonymous train car."

The phrase was not lost on Eddy: *O'Shea liquor.* He snorted and the noise seemed to startle everyone. "That's ludicrous," he said. "What are we even talking about here?"

"Yeah," said Stettler, dry as winter sun. "I admire your collection of state facts, Fritz, but I'm getting bored. What could be in Montana that would possibly be of any interest to me?"

The first-name basis and Stettler's tone were unmistakable. It occurred to Eddy that he and Mundt probably knew each other from the wrestling business. If Mundt had taken over for Abe Blomfeld after the old man died, Stettler probably viewed him as competition.

"What's there for you, Billy," Mundt said, "is the biggest forgotten drawing card in professional wrestling. The opponent who is going to pull your ass out of the fire and save you from losing your shirt trying to sell the sporting public Stan Lesko versus Joe Stecher for the fourth time."

Stettler obviously didn't care for his tone. "Who?" he asked.

Mundt was taking a sip of his coffee, and it took him a moment to answer. After he'd set his cup on his saucer, he said, "Garfield Taft."

At the mention of the name, Eddy felt the whole room deflate. Maybe Mundt had gotten them all going for a moment, but now he'd lost the momentum. With an exaggerated swing, Stettler uncrossed his legs and stood up. "I'm leaving," he said.

O'Shea held up his hand. "Sit down," he said.

Stettler didn't like that, but he sat. Eddy was surprised but then recalled that O'Shea had been fascinated with the Garfield Taft case when it was in the news a few years before. Each morning during the trial he insisted they nab a paper from the corner so he could sit at a little outdoor café and read it. As hard a man as he was, O'Shea could be like that, taken with show business and sporting stars, captivated by the stories and the big personalities. As he read aloud from the accounts of Taft's capture and subsequent trial, he would glance up at Eddy and say something like "How do you figure that, Jimmy? A Negro and all those white women. Sakes alive." Eddy, who usually had his nose buried in his own paper, would have to shrug and say he had no idea.

Now O'Shea regarded Mundt with a new curiosity. "If I recall correctly, Taft hailed from Ohio," he said. "What would he be doing way out in Montana?"

"He'll be there because that's where I'll put him," Mundt said, "to prepare for our shot at the world's heavyweight championship."

Stettler threw his hands up, flabbergasted, looking like a guy showing the size of the fish that got away. Mundt went on, launching into much of the same sob story he'd told Eddy when they'd run into each other at the speakeasy. Abe Blomfeld was dead, his wrestling outfit was failing and Mundt had exhausted his credit with what he called "all the normal channels." One day, out of the blue, Taft had come into the gym. He needed a place to stay and a promoter willing to give him a shot at a comeback. He was newly free from prison, eager to get back in the business and, in Mundt's professional opinion, still looked quite physically capable of doing it. Mundt reminded them that Taft had been undefeated when he'd been arrested, that there had been rumors that Joe Stecher was on the verge of granting him a championship opportunity.

"This is ridiculous," Stettler said. "They did right to lock him up the first time. You think we want another Jack Johnson on our hands?"

O'Shea ignored him. "It seems like a lot of trouble for one guy on a long-shot comeback," he said. "A long way to travel, even if it is your home state."

Mundt had worked a cigarette into the corner of his mouth and now he grimaced around it. "Taft's wife is white," he said, and everybody around the table momentarily lost control of their eyebrows. "I'm not sure his stint in prison taught him any manners. He struts around like he's still above the rules. At the moment I've got him in a rooming house in the second ward, but even there he's made trouble."

"I see," O'Shea said. "And you think he'll do better somewhere more isolated, is that it?" Eddy wanted to grab him by the shoulders and shake him. Was he sympathizing with Mundt, who was now nodding in such extravagant agreement that Eddy was worried his head might topple off his shoulders?

"I need to get him out of the city," Mundt said. "Someplace out of the way where we can work on getting him ready to return to the ring without distractions."

Stettler shook his head, one strand of black hair falling out of place across his forehead. He smoothed it back with his palm and said, "Lesko will never wrestle a Negro. Even if I wanted him to—which of course I do not—I couldn't convince him. He knows as well as any of us the public would never accept the idea of a black champion."

"You underestimate yourself, Billy," O'Shea said. Then, to Mundt: "You've piqued my curiosity, Mr. Mundt. Let's say such a place exists. What's in it for you?"

Mundt set his shoulders back. He needed an initial investment, he said. He needed a cash loan sizable enough to buy a good place and to keep a wrestling camp up and running for a few months. After that, he'd take care of the rest. His contacts in Canada would have no trouble supplying them, but they'd need to be paid, of course. Mundt would want his fair share of the profits from any resulting wrestling match, the mention of which still made Stettler frown. When it came time to sell off the liquor, Mundt would want a forty percent stake. That seemed reasonable, he said, a hopeful tone in his voice, like he was still trying to convince himself.

The furthest O'Shea was willing to go at that first meeting was to say he'd think about it. They all shook hands, with Stettler still furious, and he stormed out of the office after a short, hushed exchange with O'Shea. Mundt thanked Eddy for the legwork, and he spent the next five minutes working himself over with a dry handkerchief before he felt halfway clean again. The wrestler left aglow, having accomplished more than even he could realistically have anticipated.

When the two of them were finally alone, Eddy approached O'Shea at the sideboard and poured them both stiff drinks. "You can't be serious," Eddy said. "Even if you believe Mundt is on the level, it's totally impractical. A complete fantasy."

"Probably I'm not," O'Shea said in a lighthearted way that made Eddy think he was considering it. "But it's an interesting flight of fancy."

"What about Stettler?" Eddy asked. "Isn't the point of a wrestling camp to—"

"Jimmy," O'Shea cut him off. "Let me deal with Billy Stettler. You just keep your head down and keep plugging along. You're doing great work out there."

As he left the office, Eddy's last image of O'Shea was his friend leaning back against the sideboard, his nose hovering above the rim of his glass, one hand tugging on an ear.

Now, as he put his boots back on and crept between the shards of the broken glass paperweight, Eddy knew his fate had been sealed after that first meeting. Maybe even before that. Maybe O'Shea had always been looking for a way to get rid of him, and Fritz Mundt had merely given him an excuse. Picking up the pieces of glass with the tips of his fingers, he set them carefully in the bottom of the wastepaper basket. Mundt, he thought. O'Shea. This place. It felt like he had been through a lot for it to end here, in the middle of nowhere, chaperoning the idiot Canadians and trying to keep a man like Garfield Taft from killing himself.

Pulling open the bottom drawer of his desk, he stood for a long time looking down at the kitchen pot containing the papers he'd taken from Howard Livermore. There was another life in there, he thought. A different man living in a different place. He wanted to take the forms out and hold them. He wanted to burn the figures into his memory, parsing through the small pamphlet Livermore had given him with measurements and schematics, but he didn't dare open the lid. He didn't dare touch.

Instead, he got out his stationery and his pen and started writing a letter to John Torrio.

Part III

★

ONE FALL TO A FINISH

22

She slept in fits and when she woke he was still there, sitting in a chair with his forearms resting on the tiny table. Seeing him in the purple light of morning, the sheer bulk of him making the cabin seem full to bursting, Moira knew neither of them had been thinking quite straight the night before. Her ears had still been ringing from the gunfire, her mind buzzing from the encounter in the road when Taft followed her into the cabin and locked the door behind them. She hadn't expected him to do that, but she also couldn't very well send him back out into the night with those men. Instead, she had just gone to the table and lit a cigarette while Taft stood in the doorway looking at the meager clutter of their quarters. She could tell it amused him they were living this way while he and Carol Jean had their own room in the lodge.

"I hope you haven't gotten the wrong idea about me," she had said.

"I'm sorry?" he said, taking two steps inside to stand with his hands on the back of a chair. "You think I came inside hoping to look after more than just your safety, is that it?"

When he smiled she could see the scar tissue shining in his brows and a little triangular dent in the middle of his nose. They had not known each other long—maybe they still didn't know each other at all—but something seemed familiar about him. He was confident and easy in his manners, the kind of man who was used to getting what he wanted from women.

"Well," she said, "I'm sure I didn't mean to imply anything untoward."

"What *did* you mean to imply?"

"Fine," she said, "maybe I was being unpleasant. Maybe I think you resent it that my husband was hired to be your coach. Maybe I think you might like the idea of getting over on him by having it off with his wife."

He laughed, a clapping sound so loud in all the quiet that they both glanced out the window toward the lodge to see if anyone had heard.

"In that case, it wasn't me who had the wrong idea," he said. He pulled out the chair and sat. "I was out for my walk. It seemed like you were having trouble with those men, so I stopped to see about it. That's all."

She stayed on her feet, leaning on the opposite wall just to put some distance between them. "Who is Dr. Paulson?" she said.

"Who?"

"Outside," she said. "Mr. Eddy said you'd better shape up if you want him to continue covering for you with Dr. Paulson."

"Oh," Taft said. "Nobody. Just a doctor who's helping me with my comeback. It's not easy for a big fellow like me to try to get back into wrestling shape, you know. These old bones."

"There'll be more hell than a little over it if you stay in here tonight," she said.

"I should bid you good evening, then," he said.

She should've let him go. She should've seen him back out into the night, locked the door and been done with it, but she wasn't ready to be alone. She told him so, but said if he remained there, he wasn't to move from the chair. "I want that to be perfectly clear," she said.

He spread his hands. "Quiet as a church mouse," he said.

Eventually she'd gotten into bed and some time long after that must have drifted off, though only sparingly. Each time she woke he was still at the table, his chest and shoulders moving up and down with the slow, deliberate breaths of sleep. Now, though, as her eyes adjusted to the early gloom, she realized that his eyes were open and that he was looking right at her. In a panic she hauled the sagging blanket to her chin, pushing herself away until her back touched the cold cabin wall. He didn't move. Finally, she said his name.

"Mr. Taft," she said again when he didn't stir, louder this time, and still got no response.

From outside, somewhere up the hill, she heard the muffled sound of men's voices.

"Mr. Taft," she hissed at him.

This time his head lolled up and the light returned to his eyes. He looked startled at first to find himself in a strange place, but then the memory of the night before dawned on his face. He went to the window and peered out from behind the flimsy curtain, pressing his lips together in a way that let her know the bootleggers were still out there. When he'd seen enough, he crossed the room and filled the woodstove with kindling, then searched through his pockets for a match. Moira was cold and it was taking him too long, so she secured the blanket tightly around her shoulders and got up to retrieve a matchbox from one of the cabinet drawers. She tossed it to him, collecting her cigarettes from the table as he stooped to light the fire.

"I thought they'd be gone by now," he said, his voice casual, as if he found himself in these sorts of situations all the time.

He had his back to her, cupping his hands and blowing into the stove until the flames caught. Shaking the kettle to see if there was water, he set it on the stove to boil.

"I saw you watching me," she said. "When I woke up."

Now he turned. "I beg your pardon."

"Anyway," she said, feeling color rising in her face. "That's what it looked like."

He set the matches back on the table and went to stand in the same spot by the window. "I haven't been sleeping soundly," he said. "This morning it must've caught up with me. I dozed off in my chair, that's all."

"With your eyes open?" she said.

"If you say so," he said.

The light tone in his voice made her feel silly. Like this was all sort of a game to him. "Pretty lousy night watchman," she said.

When the coffee was done he poured a cup for each of them and she found herself watching his hands. They were blunt and thick, with fingers that bowed around wide, flat knuckles but narrowed to dainty tips. There was a delicacy in the way they moved, darting back and forth as he added scoops of sugar and then held his cup, looking comically tiny compared to the rest of him, between his thumb and forefinger. It was strange to think of the things those hands did to other men.

"You're looking at my finger," he said, splaying one hand in front of him like a woman trying on a wedding ring. "Leo Pardello broke it for me back in"—he thought a moment—"1915? Now it only bends this far." He crooked it to ninety degrees and showed her, smiling as he did.

How odd he was, she thought. How big and black and strange.

"That was in Italy," he said. "You ever been to Italy?"

She shook her head. "We were going to tour Ireland once, Pepper and I. When he was champion. We made it to Dublin and stayed in a hotel that was the converted manor of some lord. It was just about the grandest place I ever saw. But someone set off a bomb outside the arena downtown and they put us right back on the boat. He didn't even get to wrestle."

"Italy was my favorite," Taft said. "The food and the people? The women? It all seemed like a storybook to me. I even learned some of the language."

"You do speak very well," she said. "I mean, not like when they write about blacks in the papers."

"You means like this?" he said, bobbing his head and putting on a gibberish accent. "I thinks, Miss Moira, that you's a-cain't truss ev'rting you reads in dem papers."

She smiled and accepted a cup when he offered.

"My folks were schoolteachers," he said, the corners of his eyes crinkling when he thought about it. "My mother worked in the school library. The only black school in Cincinnati. My father taught science and arithmetic."

"I'm sorry," she said. "You must think I'm a terrible bigot."

"No," he said, "you seem better than most."

He was enjoying himself, so she decided to push a bit. "I've been talking with your wife," she said. "She insists you were sent to prison as an innocent man."

"You don't believe it?"

"I believe she loves you," Moira said. "That she'd say anything for you. I don't think you can do any wrong in her eyes."

His mouth was full of big, straight teeth. "Oh, I did plenty wrong," he said. "But as far as the law was concerned? I was just the big black demon who was going to take the title off Joe Stecher. Maybe I owned a house in the wrong neighborhood. Maybe I had the wrong color friends."

"And just for that they put you away for three years?" she said. "I can't imagine that's the whole story."

It took him a long moment to say anything else. "No," he said. "You can't imagine."

"She tells me you're different now, ever since."

He reset his shoulders, muscles moving underneath his soiled shirt. "It stays with you," he said. "That's a fact."

She was trying to think what to say next when they were interrupted by some fresh commotion up the hill, the sound of car doors opening. They got up and went to the window, Moira still wrapped in the blanket. She recognized the young, good-looking man and his dog-faced companion as they came out of the lodge with James Eddy walking between them. The two bootleggers had their collars turned up against the wind and shotguns draped over their arms. They looked like bird hunters, she thought, as they pulled themselves up into the cab of the truck. The other men piled into the sedan, their engines fired and then they all tottered up the road toward the crest of the hill.

Eddy stood there watching them go, hands in pockets, every now and then rocking back on his heels as if blowing in the breeze. There was sadness in him, Moira thought, and sadness always turned to rage in men like Eddy. She remembered the look that had come into his eye the night before as he glanced up the hill toward the horse barn. It was the same look a poker player gave his hole cards when he didn't want you to know he had a pair of aces hidden there. Whatever he was plotting, it was bigger than his business arrangement with Fritz Mundt and the bootleggers.

"How much liquor you think was on that truck?" she said.

"Hell if I know," Taft said. "Figure eighty to a hundred cases, that's—"

"Five thousand dollars," she finished for him.

"And a lot more than that sitting up there in that barn," he said.

She turned to him, but his gaze didn't register her presence. He was looking past, staring at something out the window.

"Shit," he said.

She followed his eyes, expecting to see the bootleggers coming back for something they'd forgotten, but instead it was Carol Jean cutting across the lawn in her nightgown.

"Shit," Taft said again.

He left her standing there, slamming the door hard behind him. Moira watched through the glass as he marched across the grass to meet his wife, big body moving gracefully with long steps, his chest bent slightly forward with purpose. Carol Jean said something to him as he got close, but Moira couldn't hear it. She could only see Carol Jean's mouth wide, her cheeks flushed. Taft put his hands up to meet her, and Carol Jean slapped him hard across the face.

● —— ●

For an hour after he left, Moira sat at the small table playing five-card poker against herself. The scene she'd witnessed between Carol Jean and Taft made her feel like she needed something to do with her hands. She was worried Carol Jean might come down to the cabin and have it out with her, but as the stillness of the hunting camp settled around her she realized it wasn't going to happen. When she got bored of poker she performed a hundred practice shuffles and a hundred one-handed cuts, then did the few magic tricks she could manage. Simple, card-up-the-sleeve stuff that all dealers knew.

As she sat there, the smallness of the cabin started to weigh on her. She thought of going for a walk but didn't want Carol Jean to see her and didn't want to be out in the woods by herself. She worried the bootleggers might still be skulking around somewhere. Even if they weren't, who knew what else was out in the trees off the main road? Until Pepper got back, she was stuck. The feeling of cabin fever began to remind her of the riverboat, when sometimes she got so sick of their stateroom or wandering the deck that she had to resist the urge to toss herself overboard from sheer boredom.

It was possible she had inherited this inability to sit still from either of her parents. Her father, obviously, had never been good with free time. Her mother told her that at one point she liked boats but grew to hate them soon after choosing to live on one. After Moira's father's disappearance and during their final weeks together, Moira's mother said many times that she believed boats had ruined her life.

She'd been working as a cook in an all-night diner in East St. Louis when she met Moira's father. Just a girl who had never been outside St. Clair County. He came in on an overnight stopover and waited for her at the counter until her shift ended so he could walk her home. They watched the sun rise over the city and a few hours later he was gone, shipped out again as the *Lady Luck* plowed upriver.

Ninety days later he was back, only to find that the woman whose touch he said he could still feel on his body but whose face he could barely remember was three months pregnant. This was the story her mother told, anyway, though even as a girl Moira wasn't sure she believed it. The light in her mother's eyes was strange when she talked about it, and Moira could never decide if the story was meant to be romantic, tragic or a warning about messing with a certain kind of boy. If it was the latter, Moira thought now with a wry smile, the message didn't take.

It had always been her opinion that her father had done right by her mother. At least as right as he could. He got her a job in the riverboat's kitchen and they were married just a month later with the ship's captain presiding. Five months after that, Moira was born, with the boat in dry dock and the crew scattered until the winter was over. Confined to a tiny one-bedroom apartment in East St. Louis, their relationship had already begun to sour. At least, that's how it seemed as far back as Moira could remember. As she got older, she realized her father was a man whose appetites were too big for him. He drank; he gambled to excess. He had been with half the women on the boat and had steady girls in many of the towns where the *Lady Luck* docked. Despite all this, people liked him. His easy smile and quick wit made him the kind of man women rolled their eyes over, slapping him playfully on the arm when he said something fresh.

"That's just Jack," they'd say to each other, sometimes close enough for Moira to hear. A few of them would just blush and shake their heads.

From the time she could push a broom, he arranged for her to have work on the boat. She swept out the grand dance hall and casino room, and the captain, an old man who looked like there was not a single hair anywhere on his body, let her keep the coins she occasionally found. Soon enough, she was promoted to ice duty, hauling buckets back and forth between the ship's massive cold rooms and its many bars. It was mindless and difficult work, but important, since one of the boat's main draws was the large, red-lettered banner hanging between the top and main decks blaring *Free Ice!* to each new town where the *Lady Luck* docked.

Later she worked the floor as a cocktail girl and, finally, at her father's urging, became an apprentice dealer in the casino. She started with the easy games—bunko, three-card poker and blackjack—but eventually worked her way up to faro and even dealt poker in the ship's exclusive private room. Whenever her father could slip away from his own duty—which was often, it seemed—he'd stand quietly behind her table and watch her, later delivering a full report of what she'd done right and wrong, appraising her mechanics, demeanor and posture behind the table.

"Never slouch," he told her once. "Players need to see the card turner as the most upstanding guy in the house."

The problem in the end was that her mother could never fall all the way out of love with him. Through all the fights and fleeting estrangements, she never stopped seeing him as the devilish and handsome young man who plucked her out of that greasy spoon in East St. Louis. Her mother's love was the suffocating kind. A couple of times Moira caught her snooping through her father's things while he was working, looking for clues to who he might be spending time with when his shift was over. Once she'd even tried to enlist Moira to spy on him, but Moira wanted no part of it. Most nights her mother riddled him with questions as soon as he came through the door of their stateroom, and when she got drunk those questions turned to shouts and shoves, the occasional slap. When she was sober there were whispered apologies, tearful apologies, apologies already loaded with the next night's suspicions.

Moira's father was her teacher and confidant and she wouldn't betray him, even to her mother. Of course, he really was a cheat, a drunkard and a cad, but that never mattered to her. She accepted it as part of him, as much as his tranquil table manner or his slow, affected way of talking. Then, when she was fifteen, he disappeared during an overnight run between Vicksburg and Lake Providence. He simply went off to his evening shift in the cardroom and never came back. In the morning the crew searched the boat from stem to stern and discovered one of their sad little lifeboats gone and a young, married cocktail girl also missing. The news just about broke what was left of her mother, as she screamed and thrashed and had to be restrained by two thick-shouldered engine-room workers. A day later they found the lifeboat empty and beached on a sandbar fifty yards from shore, and Moira began to suspect her mother had killed both of them. Probably shoved her father over the railing of the boiler deck in a drunken rage after catching the two of them in the act, then loosed the lifeboat afterward to make it look like they had eloped. Her mother could be clever like that.

Moira didn't wait long enough to find out for sure. Even if her mother hadn't done it, Moira couldn't stand the thought of living with her, just the two of them in their hot, overstuffed room. As soon as the *Lady Luck* docked at Lake Providence, she took what little money the family had saved in a tin on the shelf above the bed where now only her mother slept, then left. It was the last she ever heard of either of them until years later, when a bridge builder's engineering team churned what was left of her father's body up from the bottom of the river, identifying him by the gambler's charm bracelet still looped around one bony wrist.

Now, alone in the cabin with the smell of Garfield Taft still lingering in the air, she thought of her father's face. Not of the paunchy forty-year-old tippler he had become by the time he died, but as a younger man, rakish and handsome and as quick with a line as any man alive. She remembered something he told her during one of their Sunday trips to a gambling hall in St. Louis. She'd been too young to play then, so she spent the day standing at her father's shoulder and had been the only one who saw him slip an ace out of his shirtsleeve in order to take down a big pot just before they headed for home. She'd confronted him about it on the walk back to the boat, while he was still counting and re-counting the money and shuffling it from pocket to pocket like he was looking for a place he wouldn't lose it. She expected him to be angry with her for noticing his cheat, but instead he just laughed. Something like pride flashed across his face as he slipped a dollar bill into the pocket of her jacket and tucked her under his arm.

"One of the main rules to know," he said. "Only play fair when you've got the best hand."

23

Taft spent an hour locked in the upstairs bedroom hoping Carol Jean would cool down. It didn't work, and when he came down the front staircase carrying a pillow and blanket from their bed, she hurled a glass ashtray at him. It missed by a mile, sailing over his head to shatter high on the wooden archway between the foyer and the parlor. He shielded his eyes from the exploding shards of crystal and then, as a slow shower of ash began to fall around him like confetti, he set his things on the floor and held her down on the red velvet chair by the front window.

He tried to explain to her that nothing had happened between him and the Van Dean woman—that he'd only stayed in the cabin to keep her safe from the Canadians—but Carol Jean wouldn't listen. She smelled like sour mash and her thrashing eventually forced him to turn her loose. For some reason, when she was free she stayed seated in the deep, heavy chair, swearing and writhing as he went and retrieved the bedclothes from where he'd left them.

"I should've figured you'd take a run at that bony little cow," she hissed at him as he came back down. "I suppose I should be relieved it means you still like girls."

Hearing that, he put one boot on the side of the chair and, as gently as he could, tipped it over. Carol Jean went down on her backside, screaming with rage. She tried to chase him but couldn't get to her feet, pinned between the chair and the wall. Taft slammed the door behind him, hauling the blanket and pillow up to the old garage, where he used a rock to knock the padlock off its big swinging doors. He would have to do something about the boards Van Dean had nailed up on the smaller side entrance, too, but there would be time for that. Once inside, he saw that the smaller man had lied to him—that his racks of dumbbells and barbells were all still there. He was stiff from sleeping in the hard wooden chair in the tiny cabin, but felt wound up now.

Instead of lying down to try to rest, he took up some of the weights and worked his way through one of his normal warm-up routines. He went slow, concentrating on precise curls and smooth presses. At first it felt good, like his muscles were waking up from a long sleep, the exercises clearing his head and allowing his mind to wander. He raised sweat on his shoulders and brows and it only made him go harder, moving to heavier weights and liking the feeling of the pressure building up in his arms. After a few minutes he stopped and shook the tightness out of his torso, going outside to look out at the mountains and let the breeze dry his sweat.

Oh, you like girls, all right, he said to himself as he stood there. *You like every single wrong one you see.*

The first girl he'd ever kissed was white, back when his family was living in Madisonville, outside of Cincinnati. At sixteen Taft got a job working in the kitchen of a little neighborhood diner, the only job he ever had that wasn't wrestling. The diner served oily coffee and passable food, and its location up the street from city hall made it a favorite of local politicians and off-duty cops. Madisonville was one of the only places in the city where whites and blacks lived and worked together, so the diner's kitchen staff was all black, while the waitresses and most of the customers were white.

Waitresses were not supposed to come back into the kitchen to talk to the men working there, so of course they did it all the time. They were live-wire girls who held their hair back from their faces with paper hats and wore their aprons pulled tight over gray uniforms, white piping on the shoulders and sleeves. When the manager was at work they would flirt with the cooks, busboys and dishwashers through the small window that separated the dining room from the kitchen, and when he wasn't there, they'd come into the kitchen to chat while they smoked their cigarettes in a small alcove near the back door.

Taft didn't remember the name of the girl he kissed, just that she was one of the prettiest. Small and raven-haired, with bright blue eyes, the top of her head barely came to his shoulders, so he had to stoop way down to press his lips on hers. Clumsy, when he thought of it now, doing it in a rush in the alley out back, both of them on a smoke break and neither of them smoking. She knew of him from his wrestling, of course. In Cincinnati, white boys and black boys were not allowed to wrestle each other in competition, so they arranged special meet-ups and challenge matches whenever either group had a boy they thought was particularly tough. As the best in the city, Taft was the one the white boys wanted to wrestle most of all. The pretty waitress said her brother had been among his opponents, though Taft didn't remember him. Just some boy he'd beaten.

"No more of that now," he said after he kissed her. "You want to get me killed."

"You won't get in any trouble at all," she teased. "You're too special."

Then they kissed again.

He had gotten into trouble, though. He'd lost his job, and the diner's manager threatened to tell the authorities if Taft ever came back there. He wasn't sure he ever saw the dark-haired girl again. If he did, he didn't remember that, either. He did remember her words, though, as clearly as if she had just said them, even now when much of his memory was retreating to a dark place beyond his reach: *You're too special.*

As a boy, when Taft first became interested in physical culture, he'd tried to attend a few of the black sports clubs on the outskirts of Madisonville but found them too rough. Because he was already big for his age, the older men and boys there were always keen to try him in a fight. When he started coming home with black eyes and bloody noses, his parents, the kind of deeply religious folks other people rolled their eyes at behind their backs, forbade him to go back. Instead, his father pinched together as much money as he could and paid for him to join one of the downtown white clubs.

It wasn't easy, because blacks were barred from all of Cincinnati's better sporting associations. But the owner of the Chancery Athletic Club, an elderly white man named Adolph Fell, must have been intrigued after listening to Taft's father beg and plead and brag on the prowess of his son, because he demanded to see the boy in the flesh. So on a Saturday morning his father loaded him on a streetcar and shuttled him downtown to the club, as big and impressive a place as he had ever seen at that time, and ordered him through a series of jumps, sprints and weight-lifting feats for this strange old white man. Fell stood back the whole while against one of the gym's sweat-stained walls with his arms folded over a bare chest of scraggly gray hairs. It was unsettling, the first time in his life Taft felt like a show animal, paraded around, poked and jostled while Fell nodded and made small humming sounds as if cataloging every move in his mind.

Whatever Taft accomplished that day, the old man must have

been impressed, because with his father's money pocketed he said the boy could come in and do his work after hours, after the white members had gone home for the day. Taft was delighted. For him it was the perfect arrangement, as it allowed him to do his workouts in private, without having to worry about other guys testing him. Soon Adolph Fell himself began to take an interest in his progress, designing routines he said would maximize his unique physical gifts and helping him perfect the movements of each exercise.

It didn't dawn on Taft until much later that Fell was a homosexual. At the time he just thought of him as a peculiar old man. He never presented himself to Taft in any inappropriate way. There were no secret gropings or come-ons like you sometimes heard about in seedier gyms. Still, years later, when he finally realized what Fell was, it bothered him. Was the old man secretly lusting after him during those private sessions? Was that the reason Fell let him join the gym in the first place? Taft loved women, and as he grew older it was obvious that women loved him back, but he often wondered now if that early relationship with Adolph Fell had opened some tiny door inside him, one that made him consider possibilities that might otherwise have been unthinkable to him. He guessed now he would never know. He had been with all kinds of women, of course, but the two he'd pledged major parts of his life to were both white. He wondered now if Fell was somehow responsible for that, too.

His admittance into the Chancery Athletic Club was also the first time in his life he realized the rules didn't apply to him. He went places black men weren't supposed to go, did things they weren't supposed to do. He stayed in the best hotels, made extravagant requests of waiters and bandleaders, shot his mouth off to white men and did things with white women that would've gotten any other black man lynched. For him, though, it was allowed. At least for a while. And why not? He *was* special, wasn't he? He was, in his own opinion, the greatest natural wrestler who had ever lived. He had never been beaten and, had he not been arrested, he would've gone to Chicago and beat Joe Stecher for the world's heavyweight title. It would have been easy. Stecher was good, but he was no Frank Gotch. He was no Garfield Taft.

He had to laugh at himself a little bit, thinking this way. *Spilled milk,* his mother would have said, flashing the broad-minded but exasperated look she used when she thought her son was being ridiculous. Yet here he was, thinking that maybe he could still be champion.

I'm still ridiculous, Mama, he thought. *I'm the most ridiculous man alive.*

It had been a shock to him, once he was arrested, tried and sentenced to actual prison, to learn that he was not bigger than the rules after all. All of the special treatment he'd gotten as a famous wrestler had just been an illusion. In the only way that really counted, he was still just a black man, and if the whites decided they wanted to lock him up somewhere, they would. Simple as that. Even after the trial, in the days leading up to his sentencing, he half expected to be set free. As he lay awake at night in his holding cell in the county courthouse, he imagined he would be out and driving his race cars and eating at his favorite restaurants before he knew it. Sleeping in his big house with Carol Jean or Judith or whoever else he wanted. Thinking back on it, he wasn't sure what he thought might happen. Did he think old Adolph Fell was going to come around wearing one of his outlandish outfits and explain to the judge and jury that, no, no, this particular Negro had too much potential, was just too pretty to be treated like the rest? Did a lifetime spent being told nothing but yes, yes, yes make him believe his own specialness would trump it all? Maybe it did.

Well, that was all gone now, wasn't it?

He set the dumbbells down and went to the wrestling mat and did a series of push-ups and then, because he was still feeling good, some deep knee bends, hearing his joints creak and whimper under his weight. When that was over he did an exaggerated duck walk around the edge of the canvas, lunging forward with his front leg and trying to keep his torso as straight up and down as he could. Sweat dripped on the mat but he kept going, feeling the rush of it now after so much time off, so much doing nothing. He might not be special anymore, but he was still quick and strong. Carol Jean would come around, he told himself; she would sober up and see how stupid she had been to throw the ashtray at him and say those hurtful things. She would realize how silly it was to think he would have betrayed her with the Van Dean woman.

With his legs tiring, he stood up straight at the middle of the mat and was struck suddenly with a wave of dizziness that dropped him to one knee. The dirt floor spun around his head, the weight rack catapulting along with it, the whole garage twisting. He closed his eyes, feeling a tingling in the tips of his fingers. Shaking them out, he heard a strange fluttering sound whistling in his ears and he willed it to stop. He tried to concentrate on the physical things around him, the rough texture of the weight rack when he rested his hands there for balance, the coolness of the canvas under him, the smell of dirt and the faint tang of old motor oil.

He stayed down until he felt his balance come back to him and then stood slowly. Just as he got to his feet, a fit of coughing seized him and something came up in the back of his throat, a coppery taste, and he swallowed it down. His mouth was dry and he wished he'd thought to bring a bucket of water up from the pump. He'd have to go back to fetch one after a while. Maybe try again to talk some sense into Carol Jean.

He padded down to the far end of the wrestling mat, where he could see out the open doors. Pulling off his boots, he gathered his blanket around him, holding the pillow on his lap, still breathing a little heavy from the exercise. Being still now with just the view, the isolation of this place struck him all over again. He looked around the garage, knowing what he would do next was lie down on the wrestling mat and hope for sleep. Like a hobo curling up in a doorway. Like an animal looking for a place to die.

24

After two nights on a train, Fritz booked them adjoining rooms at the Blackstone, high enough up that Pepper could stand at his window staring down on Lake Michigan, the water looking like a sheet of metal in the chill. Chicago was battening down the hatches for winter, and everywhere they went people talked gloomily of snow and wind. They hoped things wouldn't be as bad as last year. The day of their appointment with Billy Stettler and Strangler Lesko, they ate a greasy hotel breakfast and then Fritz spent the rest of the morning locked in the bathroom. He emerged just in time to change for the meeting, looking green from nerves and breathing hard from the effort of squeezing into his good shirt. The big guy had been on edge the whole trip, and as he stood in front of the mirror patting his head and face with a bathroom towel, Pepper hoped he didn't pop an artery from the stress. They took a cab across the river, and as soon as it dropped them in front of Scott's River North tailor shop near the intersection of Chicago and State, Pepper understood what Fritz was nervous about. He hadn't counted on meeting Dion O'Shea again.

It was a tombstone of a building: a simple two-story brick structure with shuttered windows, its green-and-white-striped awning pulled out against looming rain clouds. He felt the itchy sensation of being watched as they approached the front door, wondering if it was just the hulking Catholic church that sat catty-corner from the store. Inside, they breathed the dusty smell of old cloth as they loitered in the showroom, waiting while the girl behind the counter helped a young man pick out a wedding suit. It turned out to be a process. When the man finally left and the bell above the door announced that Fritz and Pepper were alone in the store, the girl mumbled a few words into a wall-mounted telephone. She listened a moment and then hung up.

"You can go on up," she said. "Boots off."

They passed a glance but did as they were told, clomping up a short flight of stairs before stooping to unlace their shoes in the thick shag of the landing. They stood wiggling their toes while a million locks sprang open on the other side of a door and then a wide-shouldered goon with a hairline that swooped dangerously close to his eyebrows came out to pat them down. Pepper couldn't resist a grin, telling the guy all he was packing was five extra pounds of eggs, bacon, and flapjacks. The goon didn't react, just slid his hands around their bodies until he was satisfied and stood back to let them into the office with a bored stare that said they could stand out in the hallway all day for all he cared.

Compared to the cramped downstairs showroom, the office was airy and cool, dimly lit, the walls papered in a silver fleur-de-lis pattern. The goon who'd frisked them folded his hands over his crotch and stood to one side of the door. Another leaned against a sideboard while a pair of guys in shirtsleeves and shoulder holsters loomed behind where O'Shea sat in a high-backed chair. The gangster looked just as Pepper remembered, sitting with his legs crossed, his waxy, full moon face unchanged except for the roll of double chin that bubbled up from his collar. His gaze floated lazily from

Pepper to Fritz and back again, his expression reminding Pepper of a trophy animal, something that had been stuffed and put up on the wall. He didn't get up but offered them both a shake with a small, soft hand.

"The gang's nearly all here," he said in a voice too lively for his death-warmed-over face. He made a show of checking his wristwatch, a new one, army issue. Pepper felt something twisting inside him at seeing him again. He and Fritz sat, and when O'Shea offered them drinks, Fritz nodded his head like a man dying of thirst. Pepper didn't respond but took a glass when one of the goons handed it to him. Everybody lit cigarettes and Pepper dug out his pouch of chewing tobacco. O'Shea watched them out of hooded eyes. "So," he asked Pepper, sounding wholly unconcerned about getting a response. "How's the leg?"

Some guys just can't help themselves.

"The others," Fritz said. "They're coming?"

Annoyance trembled on O'Shea's face. "I just said that, didn't I?" Then, as if scolding himself for showing emotion, his face went slack again and he said: "What about our other project?"

"'Other project'?" Pepper said.

Fritz cleared his throat. "I had a telegram from Eddy this morning at the hotel," he said. "He tells me everything arrived as scheduled."

O'Shea held up a hand to stop Fritz from saying anything else and then pointed a finger at Pepper, a light playing in his eyes. "He doesn't know?" he said.

"Of course not," Fritz said. "You said tell no one."

"I always say tell no one," O'Shea said, "and yet everyone always seems to know my business."

Pepper was again about to ask what business, what other project, when it dawned on him that he was sitting in the private office of a bootlegger, drinking a bootlegger's booze, surrounded by a bootleg-ger's goons. He heard Moira's voice in his head, chiding him for being so slow on the uptake. "Hey," he said to O'Shea, "you're the one who brought it up. Why do that if I'm not supposed to know?"

O'Shea's jaw seemed to retreat into his face, as if he wasn't used to having his mistakes pointed out to him. They heard heavy foot-falls on the stairs and a moment later they twisted in their chairs as Billy Stettler and Stanislaw "Strangler" Lesko came into the room.

Stettler was a few years older than Pepper. He was as tall as Fritz and had the build of a body sculptor, with a thick shock of dyed black hair and the energy of a much smaller man. He wore a navy-blue suit and a peacock-blue shirt with a gleaming silk tie that split the difference.

"Our noble savages," he exclaimed. "Just in from the wild frontier and looking none the worse for wear. Well, not much worse."

He slapped Fritz on the shoulder, and Fritz dropped back into his chair as if it were a knockout blow. Pepper's eyes had already drifted behind Stettler, where the world's heavyweight champion was stand-ing in his stocking feet.

He knew at once they couldn't beat him.

Lesko was not so much tall or wide as all-around massive. His chest was thick and flat and his head was like a heavy piece of gran-ite, gray-brown hair razored flush to the sides. His face was kind and large-featured, with soft, almond-shaped eyes and a prominent nose. A thick scar cut a furrow through one eyebrow, but otherwise he looked like he'd never been in a fight in his life. He made a show of looking them over, uncurious, before sliding his hands into the pock-ets of his brown slacks. It was a simple, unpretentious move, but every dimension of the room seemed to have changed with him in it. This was a man, Pepper thought, and had to check the urge to stand up and shake his hand.

He only had a second to study Lesko before Stettler was in his face, buzzing forward as if he might hug him or punch him. He did neither, drawing back at the last moment, talking a mile a minute. "Long time no see, kid," he said. "I heard you became a sideshow freak. It made me sad when I heard that. You should've called me when Blomfeld cut you loose. I could've found a spot for you in my stable. Not for nothing, but when it came to scientific wrestling, you were just about the best I ever saw—present company excluded, of course. Too bad you weren't a hundred pounds heavier, am I right?" This time he did lean forward to punch him on the arm.

Pepper felt his whole body stiffen, a grimace screwing itself tightly to his face. "I did call you, Billy," he said, straining to keep his voice level.

"You did?" Stettler said, though of course he'd known that all along. "Oh."

There had once been a time when Pepper, Fritz and Stettler had all been at the same place in life, just some of the boys, knocking around trying to eke out a living. Pepper had been the best of them on the mat and had risen the highest. Now, though, only one of them owned a busy gym on Michigan Avenue. Only one of them managed the world's heavyweight champion. Pepper thought he saw a ripple of satisfaction pass through Stettler's body as he hummed across the room to shake hands with O'Shea, as if he'd already assessed them and judged them small-time.

He prodded the tobacco in his lip with the tip of his tongue. Something was making him feel light-headed, dizzy, but he couldn't tell if it was the chew or the company. Lesko lowered himself onto the edge of a filing cabinet and stared out a side window. He looked as if he were the only person in the room.

"Billy," Fritz said again, his voice shrill with anticipation. "You called us here. We're here."

Stettler settled into an armchair at O'Shea's elbow. "Indeed," he said, folding his hands across his knee. "I've had word out of Bellingham. Sounds like Alaskan Jack Sherry was no match for your man."

"Taft was impressive," Fritz said, nodding.

"He looked like shit," Pepper said, "but we'll have him ticking like a clock before we let him anywhere near Strangler Lesko, you can rest assured of that."

Lesko turned his face halfway from the window at the sound of his name. "I told Billy," he said like he was tired of repeating himself. "I won't wrestle a colored."

Fritz's voice sailed up another note. "Taft was considered the top contender for Joe Stecher's title a few years ago," he said. "Undefeated through twenty-five professional bouts. We all know Stecher was on the verge of agreeing to meet him in the ring when Taft was jailed. We believe this gives us cause to request a match with Lesko."

Stettler held a hand up, pleading for calm. "As you know," he said, "I was once of a similar mind as Stan. I don't relish the idea of going down in history as the first man to give a shot at the world's heavyweight wrestling title to a black."

"Billy's been talking to Jack Kearns about a fight with Dempsey," Lesko said.

This time Pepper laughed out loud. "Dempsey?" he said. "As in Jack?"

"We've been back and forth in the press," Stettler said. "I've offered to put up five thousand dollars of my own cash if Kearns will match it and agree to a mixed-rules fight. Dempsey doesn't even have to win to collect, he just has to last more than forty minutes in the ring with Stan."

"I'd like to lick that cornpone cocksucker," Lesko said. "The way he runs his yap."

His voice was bland Nebraska farm boy, deep and steady. Quiet,

Pepper noted. The best wrestler in the world was quiet. Some said Lesko was a better mat man than even Gotch. Though he was retired by the time Lesko won the title, there had been fleeting hopes for a bout between the two champions in 1916, before Gotch broke his ankle training for a comeback. A year later he was dead from blood poisoning.

"A boxer will never beat a wrestler in a match where both striking and grappling are allowed," he said. "That wouldn't be any kind of contest at all."

This seemed to please Lesko and he nodded slowly. Stettler scowled.

"Could be Kearns knows it, too," he said. "I'm starting to wonder if he's just using us for the publicity."

O'Shea pulled his chin up from his whiskey glass. "What are we doing here?" he said. "Shooting the shit?"

Stettler put a reassuring hand on his shoulder. "Dion is right," he said. "We're dealing with a limited window of opportunity to make this match. After the New Year we'll be spending most of 1922 touring France."

"They love me," Lesko said, "the French."

"As I said, at first I was inclined to tell you and your darkie to take a flying leap," Stettler said. "We had a rematch with Stecher lined up. Put a deposit down on the Garden and everything. Then, bang, Stecher tears up his knee in training for a vaudeville show. Some kind of song and dance number, you believe that? So you see our dilemma."

Fritz whistled low, letting them know he felt their pain.

"We pull out, we forfeit our deposit," Stettler said. "Besides, nobody wants to keep the world's title on the shelf until next year, least of all Stan."

"What kind of gate did you expect out of another match with Stecher?" Fritz asked.

"I'd hesitate to estimate," Stettler said, cagey as ever. "Their first bout was a hard-fought draw."

"Yes, but in their second and third, Lesko whipped him like a rented mule," Fritz said. "Ballpark it. Eighty thousand dollars?"

"That sounds about right." Stettler smirked.

"You wrestle Garfield Taft instead of Joe Stecher at Madison Square Garden in December and I guarantee we double that," Fritz said. "I guarantee we outdraw Gotch versus Hackenschmidt."

It was a bold statement. Stettler laced his fingers over his belly and contemplated it. "We have a block of rooms at the Plaza Hotel," he said, making it sound almost like a concession. "I'm sure we could find someplace with heat and hot water for Mr. Taft nearby."

"Fine, fine," Fritz said.

"Wait," Pepper said. "When exactly are we talking about here?"

"The date we have at the Garden is the week before Christmas," Stettler said. "Of course, we'd have to know all our stipulations would be met."

"You have our full cooperation," Fritz said.

Pepper shook his head. "It's too soon," he said. "Taft won't be ready."

Now that he'd gotten a look at Strangler Lesko up close, Pepper had his doubts that Taft could beat him on his best day, but just a few months to get ready would make it impossible. Taft was far too out of shape: Lesko, sitting there at the side of the room with a face as blank as a sheet of glass, would wipe the mat with him.

"We need more time," he said to Fritz.

Fritz waved him away. "Is this your official word?" he said to Stettler. "You'll grant Taft a shot at Lesko's title?"

Stettler said nothing. He held his chin in his hand and looked at O'Shea.

"He wouldn't be here if he wasn't going to do it," O'Shea said. "Would he?"

"Fritz," Pepper said.

"Point of fact, we're loath to do it," Stettler said. "Stan would rather not soil his hands and I personally think it sets a fairly dangerous precedent. I'm just not sure we have a choice at this point."

"Is anybody hearing me?" Pepper said. "Taft's been out of significant action too long to put a rush on it like this. You'll have to get somebody else. Earl Caddock. One of the Zbyszkos, maybe. If Lesko wins, we'll take him on whenever you get back from France."

"I didn't realize you were here to negotiate on behalf of Earl Caddock," Stettler said.

"Caddock hasn't been the same since the war," Pepper said. "Lesko whips him easy. We just need more time, that's all. If my name's going to be attached to this thing, I'm not happy to arrange a squash for you people. Give me until the spring to coach Taft up and I guarantee he hands Lesko his ass."

It wasn't true, but his blood was up now from being ignored. He glanced at Lesko, expecting some kind of reaction, but the world's champion hadn't budged. O'Shea's small, sly smile showed itself again as he placed his tumbler on a small side table. "Mr. Van Dean," he said. "I assure you Taft won't need long to prepare for this kind of match."

"What would you know about it?" Pepper said before it dawned on him. Moira's voice in his head again. He turned to Fritz. "Oh, for crying out loud. You told them we'd throw it?"

"You know we can't take the chance," Fritz said, looking angry with him. "None of us would ever hear the end of it if Taft should win."

Pepper was livid, partly from being lied to and partly from not figuring it out sooner. He glanced at O'Shea, whose level, unblinking stare seemed to go right through him. He imagined himself putting the gangster on the floor and beating him until his arms got tired and O'Shea's blood spattered on his shirt. Instead, he smoothed the wrinkles out of his pants. "'We'?" he said.

"Mr. Van Dean," Stettler said. "We're sure you understand, considering the circumstances and what's at stake here."

"Sure, I get it," Pepper said. "You'd have a hard time selling kinetic fitness brochures and Strangler Lesko signature hair tonic after losing to a jailbird with the wrong color of skin, is that about right?"

Lesko bristled. "For the record," he said, "this isn't my idea."

"What a relief," Pepper said, letting the champ get a full look at how unimpressed he was.

"My only stipulation," Lesko said, "is one fall only. Let's not drag this out any longer than we absolutely have to."

"It'll be huge," Fritz said, smiling now. "I've got people in the press who'll play it up as the match of the century. Taft will make the perfect villain."

"I have no doubt the papers will have a field day with it," Stettler said.

"Bullshit," Pepper said. "We don't agree to these terms."

"Sure you do," O'Shea said. "It's all you *can* do."

"It would be a mistake, sir," Pepper told him, "for you to think you can still tell me what to do."

His face was flushed and they all stopped what they were doing to look at him. Even Lesko folded his arms and regarded him as you might a man who'd climbed out on a ledge.

"Pepper," Fritz said. "This is the only way."

"The only way to what?" he said. "The only way to make fools of ourselves in front of the whole world? The only way to steal away another man's dream?"

Fritz looked as if every muscle in his body was cramping up. "One way or another, I'm leaving this room with a signed bout agreement for Garfield Taft to wrestle Stanislaw Lesko at Madison Square

Garden in December," he said. "I'll do it with your cooperation or without it, so I suppose the only thing you need to decide is whether you want your cut."

Fritz hadn't moved from his chair, but Pepper suddenly had the sense they were closer together, confiding, just the two of them. The look on his face said everything: He needed this. He was desperate for it. It was a familiar look, a kind of desperation that Pepper had seen in his own eyes more times than he cared to remember. He sat back, feeling like the bottom had dropped out of his stomach. He knew it had already been decided and nothing he could say would change that. He thought of Moira, probably sitting alone in their cabin at the hunting camp at that moment. What would they do if this job went belly-up? Looking around at O'Shea, Stettler and Lesko, he felt full of rage but swallowed it down, at least for the moment.

"Fine," he said. "Sign whatever papers you want. We're not done talking about this."

He felt very aware of his hands as he placed them on his knees.

O'Shea held up his empty glass until one of his mugs came and got it for a refill. He said: "Should I ring up the lawyers?"

Everyone stood up. Stettler and Lesko shook Fritz's hand and then turned to offer their hands to Pepper, too. He just let them hang there until the other men took them back.

"Who's going to tell Taft he's the world's biggest tackling dummy?" Pepper asked. "He's not liable to take it with a smile and a pat on the back."

"Yes," Stettler said. "About that . . ."

He had the sense they were all looking at him again as Fritz cleared his throat. "We feel it should be you to break the news."

"What?" Pepper said. "Why me?"

"He'll respect the situation more if it comes from you," Fritz said. "Brothers in arms and all that."

"Don't baby the poor fellow," Stettler scoffed. He turned to Pepper. "Why, we're relying on your technical expertise in the catch-as-catch-can style. We weren't lying about that part."

"I don't follow," Pepper said, this whole meeting reminding him what it felt like when that big millworker punched him in the face again and again.

"Before he went to prison, Taft had a reputation as a man who wouldn't do business," O'Shea said. "Word is, they asked him to lie down for Joe Stecher and he flatly refused. Our hope is that he learned a thing or two from his time away. If not, well . . ."

"We'll need you to cripple him," Stettler said.

Pepper sank back into his seat. He glanced at Fritz, who was still standing there with a drink in his hand. "I get it now," he said. "That line about how you needed a hard man to get Taft ready for Lesko's catch wrestling style. That was all hot air, wasn't it?"

"We're jumping to conclusions here," Fritz said. "We don't even know how Taft will react."

"You needed someone hard all right," Pepper said. "But you needed someone who would play ball, too, isn't that it? Well, you got the wrong guy. I won't do that."

Stettler had the bout agreement in his hand and he grinned as he passed it to Fritz. "A minute ago you said you wouldn't sign off on a fixed match," he said. "But here we are."

It was as if things clicked frozen for a moment, like they'd all been caught in the lens of a flash photograph. Stettler smiling as Fritz took the papers from his hand, O'Shea at his elbow, unreadable as ever, and Lesko staring into space like he couldn't be bothered with any of it any longer. Pepper closed his eyes and thought of Whip Windham leaning in his corner across the ring, a little smile on his lips that said he knew he was about to have the easiest night of his life. He felt the old stab of shame, the guilt weighing down his heart. Maybe it had never left him. He wanted to shout and scream and hurl his chair through the big window behind Lesko's head, but he didn't. He just sat there watching Fritz sign the papers, feeling his chest rise and fall under his shirt.

"Don't look so surprised, Mr. Van Dean," O'Shea said. "This is the sort of arrangement you're intimately familiar with, is it not?"

25

For three days and nights Moira stayed inside the cabin, coming out only to fill the water bucket or visit the outhouse. Since the morning she stood by the window and watched Taft carry a blanket and pillow out to the old garage, walking deliberately, head up, not looking back, she'd seen no sign of him, nor any trace of Carol Jean. A couple of times James Eddy came out to take his car into town, and the more she saw of him the more convinced she became that he was a man with a secret. The way he moved—constantly looking around like he was afraid someone would pop out of the bushes and catch him at something he wasn't supposed to be doing—made her almost want to laugh. Aside from Eddy, no one was talking or moving inside the camp, and the stillness was like something frozen inside her chest.

The cold afternoon of the fourth day she was boiling water for coffee when she heard the sound of an approaching motor. She went out onto the porch and after a few minutes saw a car crest the hill at the end of the long gravel drive. Fritz Mundt was behind the wheel, with Pepper bouncing along next to him in the passenger seat. Her heart leapt when she saw him, but the car didn't slow down as it passed. She raised her hand to wave and he waved back, his face looking almost completely healed now, but he made no move to tell

Fritz to stop as a cloud of grit enveloped her. Blinking, she watched them pile out in front of the lodge.

Carol Jean met them at the door, bracing herself in the entryway, looking brittle and hard in the failing light. Fritz hurried past, only nodding to her as he slipped into the house. When Pepper tried to follow, she blocked his way with her arm. Moira couldn't hear what they were saying, but Carol Jean clutched a half-empty highball glass in one hand. As her mouth curled into a sticky-sweet sneer Moira started up the hill toward them. Pepper looked back at her and then Carol Jean slammed the door, leaving him staring at the old, scarred wood for a second before he turned around.

At first Moira thought he would meet her halfway up the hill, but before she could get closer than forty yards, he took off toward the garage, his face clouding over and his steps quickening. He broke into a run and she dashed after him, calling his name, her breath torn away from her lips in ragged gusts of wind. Her heel snagged on something and she lost her shoe, sliding on the wet ground, wrenching an ankle as she righted herself. At the top of the rise he disappeared into the dark of the garage and she slowed, knowing she was too late. She heard a muffled yell and then the whole building shimmied as one of its sideboards cracked from the inside.

She began to run again and was out of breath when she reached the garage, mud splattered on the hem of her dress. The two men were standing at the far side of the room, Taft bracing Pepper against the wall, his long arms taut and shaking from the effort. They were both shouting at once and for a moment it seemed they were in a stalemate, but then Pepper kicked Taft on the inside of the leg, the sound like a gunshot, and they both went down in a heap.

She screamed at them to stop, but as Taft tried to scramble up, Pepper climbed onto his back, driving a fist into his face. He hit him again and again until Taft was able to get to his feet. Plucking Pepper off his back, Taft whipped him through the air, legs flailing, sending him crashing down onto the nearby wrestling mat. From the sickening thud he made, Moira thought he must be dead, but then Pepper rolled toward Taft, trying to snare one of his legs. Taft saw this and smashed a massive fist down on the side of Pepper's head, the blow producing a thick, whumping sound. She got between them, the two not having noticed her crossing the distance from the doorway to the wrestling mat.

Grabbing them both by their shirts, she yelled for them to stop, swearing at them in the thick, strange voice of someone else. She was close enough to smell the blood and sweat on them, but still they acted like they hadn't heard. They shouted and clawed at each other over the top of her head and then Pepper reared back and fired off a last punch. He was off balance and stumbled, missing his mark. His fist clipped Moira behind the ear and the next thing she knew she was sitting on the wrestling mat with her legs stretched out like a doll. As she fell she pulled the men down with her, faintly aware of the sound of ripping cloth, their weight coming down on top of her. She sprawled back, blinking up at the roof, seeing flashes of gold and white in the darkness.

"You son of a bitch," Pepper said, out of breath. He was reaching across her, still grabbing at Taft. "What did you do to my wife?"

Taft slapped his hand away, trying to get his wind. "Get off me," he gasped. "Enough."

Putting one hand to the back of her head, Moira found an egg-sized knot there. She tried to sit up but didn't have the strength. Her brain felt like it was trapped inside a beating kettledrum. Blood from Pepper's chin dripped onto her dress and across her bare neck, warm droplets in the cold air. She rolled over and vomited on the arm of his shirt.

He let go of Taft and looked down at her. "Jesus," he said.

Taft crawled away, dragging himself by the elbow, making it just a few feet before collapsing on the mat again. "You're crazy," he said.

His nose was bleeding, blood covering his mouth and chin. "You crazy bastard."

Moira covered her face with her arms. She smelled her own sick and the earth and mildew of the wrestling mat and felt a sudden lightness, like having nothing left inside her.

Pepper rested his hand on her shoulder. "How do you feel?" he asked. "Are you okay?"

"You'll be fired for this," Taft said. "I'll sue you. I'll sue Mundt, O'Shea. Everybody."

"You shut up," Pepper said to him, then to Moira: "Are you all right?"

"I didn't do a thing with her," Taft said, louder now, getting his breath. "I never touched her."

Pepper lunged for him again but Moira caught him by the belt. He pulled against her grip, but not hard enough to break it.

"That's not what your wife said." Pepper pointed in the direction of the lodge. "Why would she lie?"

"She's not lying," Taft said, "but she doesn't know, either. She's just trying to hurt me."

"For what?" Pepper said. "Why would she do that if you're so goddamned innocent?"

"She's just angry," Taft said, "and confused."

Moira rolled onto her back and looked at him, sitting now with his back propped against the wall of the garage.

"I don't understand," she said.

Taft readjusted himself against the wall, searching for a comfortable way to rest. The places where Pepper had hit him were starting to swell up under the leftovers of the black eye he'd gotten from Jack Sherry. Older wounds there, too, she thought, a lifetime of hurt passing across his eyes like a shadow moving over water. He shrugged, and she saw resignation take over.

"I don't go to bed with her anymore," Taft said. "Not for a while now." Moira let go of Pepper's belt. Taft didn't take his eyes off Pepper. "And the reason," he said, "I didn't go to bed with your wife is that I don't mess with women anymore. None of them."

There was a moment when they all just stared at each other.

"What are you saying?" Pepper said.

"I just don't," Taft said. "And I don't care what you think about it."

"Bullshit. Now I know you're lying."

"Believe what you want, midget," Taft said. "I'm telling you like it is."

A weird half smile crept onto his face as he looked out the open doors at the end of the garage, over the yellow fields, where a light snow had begun to fall. Moira watched him until the smile faded. She swallowed hard against a stinging dryness in her throat.

"He's telling the truth," she said. "At least about me, he's not lying."

Pepper blinked, regret ticking in the corner of his lips. "Well, goddamn it," he said. "I thought—"

"You thought what anyone would've thought," Taft said. "I can't blame you for it."

Pepper tried to take her hand, but she pulled it back. She avoided his eyes as she sat up, still feeling woozy. She had seen him beat men half to death in gutters and barrooms and on ballroom stages, but he'd never hit her. Now her ears rang with the knowledge that he was capable of doing it, even by accident. Her face was hot. She felt a weird guilt that Taft had been there to see it.

"Moira," Pepper said.

"We're not done talking about this," she said.

They heard footsteps crunching on the gravel path and then Fritz stood in the doorway in a crisp, clean suit. He had his thumbs hooked in the straps of his suspenders. "I thought we'd go into town for a celebration," he said, his smile turning to wood when he saw them all sitting on the mat slumped and bloody.

"Celebrate what?" Taft said with a little laugh. Like the idea of having something to be happy about was impossible to him. Like he could go to sleep if they would all just leave him alone.

"We got the match," Pepper said. "Against Strangler Lesko. At the Garden, just before Christmas."

Now Taft showed his bloody teeth, a real smile. "You're pulling my leg," he said.

"We kid you not," Fritz said.

Taft clapped his hands, his eyes focusing on something far away before he snapped back to reality. "How much?" he said.

"Thirty thousand," Fritz said. "I think this calls for something special, don't you? How about steaks, on me? If there's anything this state can do right, it's steaks."

"Thirty to show," Taft said. "How about a win bonus?"

Fritz and Pepper looked at each other, a single darting glance.

"No win bonus," Fritz said.

Taft squinted at him, then squinted at Pepper, adjusting his position against the wall again. The blood was drying on his face, hardening to a paste that cracked when he spoke. "But we got it," he said. "A square match, like you promised me?"

"You bet we do," Fritz said from the doorway. "Thirty grand."

"Minus my ten percent," Pepper added.

Taft ignored him. "What about you?" he said to Fritz. "What's your cut?"

Fritz unhooked his thumbs from his suspenders. "We've reached a financial agreement independent of yours."

"Meaning you get more than me," Taft said.

"I hardly see how that's anyone's concern," Fritz said, irritated. "Stettler and Lesko ultimately found themselves in a tight spot, with the arena deposit already put up and Joe Stecher out with an injury. You could say we're doing them a favor."

"A favor," Taft said, using the wall for support as he inched his way to his feet, going slow like a man rediscovering his own body. Once he was up, he pressed a hand to his side and grimaced. He pushed both fists into his lower back and stretched. "I want my money before the match," he said. "Otherwise I won't do it. I want it in cash, delivered to me personally when we get to New York, and I want Billy Stettler and you"—a tired wave in Fritz's direction—"to sit there while I count it."

"Fine," Fritz said. "Completely fine."

"Well, all right," Taft said. "Let's celebrate." His bottom lip was split and he touched it with a knuckle, shaking his head in wonder at the sting. He took a few uncertain steps and then found his legs, offering them a hand up. First Moira, then Pepper. "You hit pretty hard," he said, "for being so tiny."

Pepper dragged the back of his hand across his face and came away with a dull smear. "How about it?" he said to Moira. "You up for a night in town?"

He tried to slip his hand around her waist, but she shook him off and stumbled away, limping on one bare foot, a vague flash of pain in her ankle. She felt as though she couldn't be there another moment. She had to get out of that garage, away from these men. She wanted to go down to the cabin and crawl under the covers. For a second she caught herself wishing the old tomcat would come keep her warm, but then she remembered the cat was dead. She moved out the door into the low light of early evening, feeling like she was floating more than walking, hearing Pepper say her name.

She didn't stop to look back. The air seemed thinner as she started down the hill, as shrill on her skin as a woman's scream. Her adrenaline was ebbing and she swatted at snowflakes, ignoring Pepper when he called out to her again. She stopped to pick up her lost shoe, and as she did she heard Taft's voice, a low rumble compared to her husband's shouting.

"Just give her some time," he said. "She just needs time."

That made her want to turn and scream at all of them, but she didn't. She just kept walking. She didn't speak, either, when Pepper came down and changed out of his tattered clothes. He tried again to apologize, but she wouldn't give him the satisfaction, even though part of her wanted to let him take her in his arms. She just sat on the sagging bed and stared at the floor. In a few minutes Fritz and Taft came down the road in the car and sat, letting the motor run.

"I ought to stay," Pepper said to them when he went out onto the porch. "You all go on without me."

"Don't be ridiculous," Fritz said. "I'm sure this all will blow over in a jiffy."

She could tell from the pleading in his voice that Fritz didn't want to spend the evening alone with Taft. Pepper came back inside and held her hand. She let him but still wouldn't look at him. He told her how awful sorry he was but said that he had to go. It was part of his job, he said, and then added that if his two choices were to sit there and be ignored or go into town for a free meal, he'd take the meal. She might have laughed at that if he'd been talking to someone else. Instead she pulled her hand away.

He sighed as he stood up, exhausted, and after another minute of loitering—when she thought he might say something else—he left. She heard the grunting of the engine as Fritz set the clutch and they all sped off down the road. When her head felt better, she went to the window and looked out at the snow, the camp feeling even more desolate than before the men had returned.

26

Moira's ankle had swollen to twice its normal size by the time she knocked on the front door of the lodge. It had been just over an hour since Pepper, Taft and Fritz had gone into town and thirty minutes since she watched James Eddy leave the hunting camp and drive off in the same direction. She had no idea when any of them would return but was feeling rattled, every gambler's instinct in her body telling her it was time to move. Each step sent pain dancing up her side as she climbed the hill, and she was almost glad when Carol Jean jerked the door open and daggered her with her eyes. At least it meant she could just stand there for a minute.

Carol Jean propped one hand on the doorjamb like a model posing for an advertising sketch. "Well, look at you," she said. "I didn't know we were going to go on being so neighborly."

"I wanted to apologize," Moira said. "For the altercation that occurred this afternoon between our husbands."

Even as she said it she was aware of the way she put her words, deflecting blame away from Pepper. How many years had she been doing that? she wondered. Carol Jean must have read the look on her face and the awkward way Moira was standing, because the hard expression vanished and she reached a hand out to touch her.

"My goodness," she said. "You're injured."

A moment later Carol Jean was ushering her into the warm, bright parlor, where a bundle of logs cracked and spit in the fireplace. They moved awkwardly together, the dull ache pounding through Moira's leg, and she tried not to show how glad she was when Carol Jean finally pushed her gently into an armchair, sliding over a low ottoman so Moira could prop up her foot. She lifted the hem of her skirt so Carol Jean could unlace her boot, revealing the ankle fat and purple underneath.

"You just wait here," Carol Jean said. "I'll only be a minute."

As the click of her steps disappeared down the hallway, Moira sat and listened to the big, empty house settling around her. With all the men gone to town, the place felt enormous and abandoned, like something being reclaimed by the land. As she cast her eyes down at her lap she was surprised at the state of her own hands. Her wood chopping and back-and-forth trips hauling water from the well had raised blisters on her fingers, and her skin was red and cracked from the cold, dry air.

The sight of them reminded her of her mother. Years of splitting time between the riverboat's kitchens and laundries turned her mother's hands into sharp, callused claws, so that even as a child Moira shuddered and pulled away when her mother tried to touch her. As she got older, she was forced to spend free afternoons in the laundry, helping to wash, sort and fold the crew's silly, bright uniforms. The work burned and irritated her own hands, and on top of the pain she was horrified at the idea it was turning her into her mother.

Frequently, people forgot things in the pockets of their uniforms: coins and paper money, letters, pay stubs, scribbled notes. Her mother kept a stack of envelopes with her as she sorted, and each time she found a lost item she sealed it up in one and wrote the crew member's name on it, making sure each got his belongings back with his laundry bag. How Moira longed to peek at some of those letters, especially the ones written to crewmen on flowery, scented stationery. She knew there was something she wanted, maybe dreaded to see, in those letters. The only time Moira ever tried to reach for one, her mother slapped her hand away.

"Aren't you curious?" Moira asked.

"People need their secrets," her mother said. "Sometimes you have to let them have that much."

It was advice she never learned to take.

Moira didn't know if she'd closed her eyes as she sat waiting, but the next thing she knew, Carol Jean was back, squatting in front of the chair with a fat bandage rolled in one hand. Moira tried to tell her it wasn't necessary, but Carol Jean just told her to be still, her fingers feeling strange and cool on Moira's leg.

"I'd be a sorry excuse for a wrestler's wife," Carol Jean said, "if I didn't know how to wrap an ankle or splint a finger when I needed to."

"The other thing I wanted to make perfectly clear to you," Moira said, "is that nothing happened between Mr. Taft and myself."

Carol Jean started at the heel and gently but firmly wrapped the bandage up and around. "I know, honey," she said at last. "I believe you."

"You do?" Moira said. "I thought you put him out of the house."

"I did no such thing," Carol Jean said. "He's out there of his own accord, pouting. Waiting for me to apologize to him, probably. Maybe I owe him one, too, though he'll be waiting a long time if he thinks I'm going to crawl up there with my hat in my hand."

"Why?"

Another funny little Carol Jean smile. "You know why. You're married to one of them, same as me."

Carol Jean was a big woman with big hands, but she went about her work quick and deftly. Moira could feel the ankle throbbing under the thick material and for a moment it made her head spin.

"So," she said, closing her eyes and then opening them. "The match is all set."

"None of you thought it would happen, did you?" Carol Jean said. "But I always kept the faith."

Looking down on her, sitting childlike on the floor, Moira felt a pang of sadness for Carol Jean. This was her moment of victory, the triumphant cap on those years she waited for Taft to be released from prison. All the time she spent playing the doting wife after his first wife filed for divorce. She had been shuffled from Ohio to Chicago to the woods of Montana, and for what? For love, certainly, but also for this.

"You must know they'll never let him beat Lesko," Moira said. "They'll never let him win the world's heavyweight championship."

Carol Jean finished her wrap job with a little snap of the bandage and sat back on her heels. "Of course not," she said, eyes fierce. "I'm not a complete fool."

"I didn't say you were," Moira said. She thought back to a moment in the garage when Taft learned his contract didn't include a win bonus. Fritz and Pepper had moved the conversation along in a hurry when he asked about it. In her dazed state, Moira hadn't caught it, but now she recognized the careful steering of a lie. "But Mr. Taft doesn't know, does he?"

Carol Jean turned away as she stood, then set herself slowly on the adjacent seat. "Mr. Taft," she said, "is a man, and a wrestler besides. They'll believe almost anything so long as it gets them through the day."

"It seems cruel," Moira said. "Why let him go through all this thinking he'll get a square deal if you know the truth?"

Carol Jean nearly laughed. "Because he wouldn't have done it otherwise," she said. "His precious pride would've had us on the poor farm before long."

"Pepper will have to tell him eventually," Moira said. "What do you think he'll do when he finds out?"

"I have no earthly idea," Carol Jean said. "But I hope to God both of those fools are up to their tasks."

"Which are?"

"For your husband to convince him," Carol Jean said, "and for mine to make a better decision than he did the last time."

"I see," Moira said. "What was it you told me before? Hold your nose and hope the check clears, was that it?"

"Go ahead, make jokes," Carol Jean said. "You never saw what he was like before we found Mr. Mundt. He was a ghost, dragging us from one fleabag to another, moping around with this look in his eyes like some kind of neutered puppy. It's given him such a lift just being here, getting to wrestle again. Finally, the man I fell in love with is back in my life."

"Is he?" Moira said, meaning to leave it at that. But there was more she wanted to say, the words bubbling up in her with an intensity she no longer had the strength to fight down. "Because I'm not certain Mr. Taft will even make it to New York, or be well enough to wrestle the match."

"I beg your pardon?" Carol Jean said.

"The last time I came up here to see you, you said things had been different since he got out of prison. I asked how and you said Mr. Taft was disinterested. At first I thought you were speaking generally, but today he said some things to make me believe I hadn't caught your whole meaning. He said you haven't made love since he got out."

It was a push toward the truth, maybe a clumsy one, but one Moira felt she needed to make. She couldn't say exactly why, only that she wanted an answer to the mystery that Taft had become in her life. Carol Jean smiled in a way she first thought was patronizing, but then something cracked in it and it turned into the saddest smile she'd ever seen. Moira imagined she could go cascading down into it and never emerge.

"You remember I told you about the time I first met my husband?" Carol Jean said.

Moira said she did, and Carol Jean explained that at the time she first encountered Garfield Taft at the Olympia Ballroom in Cincinnati, she'd been living in a downtown flophouse owned by the club owner, Herman Cohn.

"He had trash apartments all over the city," she said. "The girls all lived there and he took the rent money out of our pay, which wasn't much to begin with, since we mostly worked for tips."

She said that after things became serious with Taft, he bought a rooming house in a nice part of town and installed her on the upper floor. It had an attached garage facing the alley, so he could park one of his cars there and come up through a back stairway without being seen. At first he started showing up weekly, and soon his visits became even more frequent.

"It gave me such a feeling," Carol Jean said, "this big, beautiful man spending all that money, going through all sorts of trouble, just to see me. I knew he was married, which naturally bothered me; but the way things turned out with Judith, I don't beat myself up much over it anymore."

"It sounds exciting," Moira said. She felt like the audience at a stage play, content to see what Carol Jean would talk herself into admitting.

"I suppose so," she said, "but everything gets boring if it goes on long enough."

It was lonely, Carol Jean explained, living hidden away in that big house. She had to walk six blocks to the nearest grocery and eight to find a liquor store. She teased Taft that she would need her own car and driver if she was going to go on being his kept woman. His travel schedule was hectic at the time, and even though he came to see her as often as he could, Carol Jean spent most of her time by herself. Taft said he didn't want her working, which left her nothing to do most days. Even though he gave her more money than she could spend, she didn't like the feeling of it. She had always been a girl who provided for herself, so suddenly depending on this man was difficult for her, no matter how much she loved him.

"Finally I let a friend move into one of the spare bedrooms," Carol Jean said. "I just had to do it for the company, you see. This girl, Liddy, from the Olympia, a little dark-haired stray, all arms and elbows the way some men like."

Even though Carol Jean was really doing her a favor, Liddy insisted on paying rent. They settled on a figure substantially less than the girl had been paying at one of Mr. Cohn's flophouses. It saved her a little bit of money and it felt good for Carol Jean to have some cash of her own coming in.

"I guess you could say I picked up a few things from old Mr. Cohn after all," she said.

Word got around how little she was charging, and before she knew it, she let another girl move in, then another. Eventually she had every bedroom filled with girls from the Olympia. It became like an all-the-time party, Carol Jean said, just a thrill a minute, with people coming and going from the club at all hours.

Moira asked what Mr. Taft thought of all that, and Carol Jean waved her away.

"I expect he enjoyed it," Carol Jean said. "All those girls fawning over him. Always someone to cook him breakfast and hear his stories from the road. It will come as no surprise to you that Garfield Taft likes a party as much as anyone."

"It does not," Moira said.

"Smart girl like you," Carol Jean said. "I bet you can guess what happened next."

Moira nodded. "The police," she said.

"They came down on the place with an army," Carol Jean said. "Busted down the door with a battering ram, arrested everybody. A black fellow in a house with all those white girls? A house that he owned? They weren't going to stand for it. Of course, in the papers they said girls had been whoring themselves out of that house."

"Had they?" Moira asked.

"Oh, how should I know?" Carol Jean said. "If they were, I wasn't going to stop them from earning a little extra on the side. We had the hottest after-hours spot in the city. All the gentlemen in town wanted to be there."

Moira sat back. Carol Jean had a sharp tongue and was a good deal smarter than Moira had first thought, but it must have been a lot of weight to carry around those years Taft spent in jail.

"It was you," she said. "You're the reason he got locked up."

"They charged him with being a pimp," Carol Jean said. "Can you imagine? The truth was he didn't care a thing about what the other girls in that house were doing. He only cared about me."

"So you waited for him," Moira said.

"Waited and waited," Carol Jean said, as if it was a feeling they both understood. "I thought the lonesomeness would crush me at first. It took ages to even find out where they'd taken him. I had no rights, you see, since we weren't married yet. But after Judith took off, I suppose I got excited about having him all to myself. It took about two weeks for her to pull up stakes and run, did you know that? I think she'd been waiting for her excuse to go long before he was arrested."

"It must have felt like a reprieve for you, in a way."

"Oh, it was all very romantic, the way I imagined it."

"He did marry you," Moira said. "That was what you wanted, wasn't it?"

She nodded. "Right there in the prison, as soon as they'd let us, after the judge granted Judith her divorce. It was a rush job, but they wouldn't even let me visit him unless we were married, so it had to be done. I had this purple chiffon dress I wore. I don't think either of us had quite realized how different things were going to be. Garfield thought when it was all over, when he'd served his time, he would be able to go back to doing anything he wanted. Instead we got this."

She lifted her arms to include the whole place: the room they were in, the half-finished lodge, the garage gym, the horse barn full of liquor, the woods and hills, the city at the base of the mountain with its mines forever spitting out smoke, the railways and roads. This enormous, empty state. This life.

"Just to be clear," Moira said. "Are you telling me there's nothing physically wrong with your husband?"

Carol Jean's eyes had floated away while she talked, but now they snapped back into focus. She was back to her woman-of-the-house act. Her every movement careful, as if planned out ahead of time. "Of course not," she said. "How could there be?"

Moira nodded. "Thank you for telling me that story," she said, because it felt like a necessary thing to say.

"You seem like the kind that can keep a secret," Carol Jean said. "Don't prove me wrong."

⬤━━━⬤

When Carol Jean finally announced she was turning in, Moira asked to sit there a bit longer to rest her leg. Carol Jean nodded, giving her hand a little squeeze before climbing the staircase.

As she went she kept her chin held high, everything else in her bearing telling Moira she'd be asleep as soon as her head touched the pillow.

Still, she waited an extra fifteen minutes, the quiet of the house roaring in her ears, before she slipped off her other shoe and crept up the stairs after her. Carol Jean had done a good, competent job wrapping her ankle, and Moira found she could move now with considerably less pain. The upstairs hallway was dark and the old wood groaned with every step, but she tiptoed as quietly as she could to the end of the hall where she knew James Eddy kept his room. The doorknob was smooth and cold in her hand, like a stone from a river bottom, and she applied just enough gentle, silent pressure to confirm it was locked.

Give Moira a half hour and a set of hairpins and she could jimmy most locks. A necessary skill, she'd found, when you followed the calling every modern woman dreamed of—from riverboat card girl to carnival shill. Up here in the hush of the hallway, though, there was no way. It would take too long and make too much noise, the sound of a thousand rats working their claws against the metal. Instead, she turned and snuck down the way she'd come, getting all the way to the bottom of the main stairs before a shape loomed out at her.

"May I ask exactly what you're doing?"

Moira caught her breath, putting a hand over her heart, before seeing it was just the hired girl, Eleanor, coming down the gloomy hall from the kitchen. "Goodness," Moira said. "I didn't know anyone else was still here."

"I could say the same to you," said Eleanor. She squinted at Moira for a long moment. "I heard you up there snooping around Mr. Eddy's door. You really think he'd leave his quarters unlocked?"

"I wasn't," Moira said, starting to protest, but stopped when she read the look on the girl's face. "Yes, I was. I think he's hiding something and I wanted to know what it was."

Eleanor snorted. "Hiding something?" she said. "Lady, a man like that doesn't know any other way to behave."

Moira noticed the crackle in her voice. "You know something about it," she said.

"I know everything," Eleanor said. "I'm the housekeeper."

Moira smiled, resting a hand on the glass globe at the bottom of the banister. "So?" she said. "Will you tell him?"

Eleanor tapped the toe of her shoe on the hardwood floor—click, click, click—as if trying to decide something. Moira thought she might give her a scolding, maybe want to go wake Carol Jean, but instead she just said, "Wait here," and disappeared down the rear hall again.

Moira eyed the door, wondering what would happen if she walked out and went back to the cabin, but in a moment the hired girl was back. She came from the kitchen waving a small bit of stationery in an outstretched hand.

Moira took it and held it up to the light, knowing before she saw the name at the bottom that Eddy had written it. The penmanship was tiny and exact, without so much as a smudge of ink or wavering line to suggest a trembling hand. The note was short and without pretension, just Eddy proposing terms for selling the load of liquor he and Fritz had squirreled away to a group of rival men. The longing and rage she had sensed in him were there, both in the hastily composed words and the sure, straight lines of the letters. There was no mistaking its meaning.

"Where did you get this?" she said.

"He gave it to me to put in the mail," said Eleanor. "Can you believe it?"

"You opened it?"

They kept their voices low in the quiet house, but now the hired girl straightened up, proud and unafraid. "Steamed it," she said, "and I'm glad I did. The things in that letter? They could put us all in danger."

"It was a daring move," Moira said. "Why risk it?"

Now Eleanor showed a sly grimace. "It was peculiar, him send-ing something like that. Mr. Eddy never sends anything besides bill payments. Plus, him always trying to tell me my business? Maybe I wanted to know a bit of his."

"You didn't worry what would happen if he found out?"

"Please," Eleanor said. "I traced a copy and sent that along in the original envelope. Not like whatever animals he's sending it to are going to know the difference."

Moira looked at her over the top of the letter and realized she'd misjudged the hired girl from the start. Eleanor's face had gone hard and callous—a woman who had grown up in a town full of two-bit operators and knew what it took to get by. Perhaps her frail body had the heart of a prizefighter beating inside it. Now she seemed to read Moira's expression, asking what she meant to accomplish handing over the letter.

"I'm sure you'll figure out a use for it," Eleanor said. "In a couple of months I'm getting out of this place. I'll find a job in an office making thirty dollars a week with weekends and holidays off. But it doesn't seem right, a wicked creature like that being allowed to go on, out into the world. Nothing good will ever come from a man like that."

Moira wasn't sure what to say, so she just nodded and tucked the letter into the pocket of her dress. She retrieved her shoes and let the hired girl walk her out, hearing the heavy door lock behind her as she went back out into the night. Coming down the steps from the porch, she cast her eyes down the road into town, as if she thought Eddy might come driving up at just that moment. Of course the road was deserted, looking forlorn in the dark. Keeping close to the house to avoid blundering off into the weeds, she crept around to the side and then to the unfinished section of the building. Bare wood striding up out of the foundation, like someone might show up any day to finish the job. Eddy's room was in a rear corner, with a single side window that looked down on the road and an exposed door that opened into the part of the structure left undone. Up the hill were the garage and the horse barn, and the other way she could see the main gate and the line of little guest cabins. Still no one moving anywhere.

The letter should've been the answer she was looking for, but somehow it only piqued her curiosity. She still wanted to see the whole picture. Hoping her ankle wouldn't fail her at exactly the wrong moment, she pulled herself up so she was standing on the lodge's foundation, then found another foothold about three feet up that looked like it was meant to be the base of a window. Then it was the top of a doorframe, bringing her knee up comically high to make the step and keeping her eyes down to make sure the hem of her dress didn't get caught on a loose nail. With another step, she was up inside the unfinished room on the second floor—easier than she expected—having used the exposed planks as a kind of ladder.

The rear door to Eddy's room was locked, just as the other had been, but out here she could have brought a brass band with her and not bothered Carol Jean. She let her hair down and, kneeling in front of the door, she went to work. After a few minutes of scraping and fumbling with the mechanism, the lock popped open.

Stepping into the room gave her a shot of adrenaline. Suddenly she felt wild-eyed and terrified. Eddy's quarters were sparsely furnished and spotless, just as she'd imagined they would be. Not even any smell to them, except the faint chemical punch of disinfectant. In one corner a rifle stood ugly and lurking, but aside from that you might not even know a man slept here. The cot was bare, as was the small desk. The glasses in the bar setup looked clean and new.

She didn't even know what she was looking for as she began

pulling open the cupboards of the credenza. Eddy's clothes were folded neatly in one of the drawers, a couple of jackets hanging from a coatrack to one side. She patted the pockets of the coats, finding nothing, before she ran her fingers around the inside edges of the drawer without disturbing the garments.

The floor creaked terribly as she moved across the room, but she forced herself to keep going. On the desk was a blotter calendar with several dates marked with a single horizontal line beneath the number of the day. She guessed these were the nights when the men brought in new shipments, and she quickly memorized them. She noted a load came in once every three weeks and that they were scheduled to keep arriving through the end of the year. The long middle drawer held only pens, and the wastepaper basket on the floor next to the chair looked as if it had never been used.

She was about to give up when she pulled open one of the desk's lower drawers and found a heavy kitchen pot sitting there. A small tickle worked its way down her back. The pot was the first out-of-place thing she'd found in the room. Carefully she lifted the stout lid and saw a small package inside, wrapped up in one of the white silk handkerchiefs Eddy always kept with him. The package was light, just a bundle of paper, but she took it out and replaced the lid before sliding the drawer closed again.

This was what she was looking for. It had to be, since it was the only thing there was to find. It was a reckless, stupid move to take something from a man as obviously paranoid as Eddy, but right then she didn't care. Holding the papers in one hand, she went back out the way she'd come, making sure the door was locked behind her.

Out in the open, a gale of wind brushed her back against the side of the lodge, threatening to rip the papers from her grasp. She huddled there until it passed, getting her breath, steadying herself, before creeping back to the place where she'd climbed up the network of boards and studs. One painful twinge in her ankle made her grit her teeth as she straddled the exposed wall. The way down was slower, more difficult than the way up. In the dark, she couldn't find the final foothold—dangling there, cursing, with her coat flapping in the breeze and one hand still clutching the package. Before she dropped the last four feet to the ground, she took a moment to close her eyes and prepare herself for how much it was going to hurt.

27

There was trouble at the restaurant. The steakhouse Fritz guided them to was a ramshackle little place at the center of Butte's tightening maze of streets, its front door set three steps below sidewalk level. Some of the other men there didn't appreciate Taft being seated in the dining room, and Pepper imagined a hundred eyes on them as they ate. He drank too many of the restaurant's bitter homemade beers, and by the time three guys cornered him inside the cramped restroom, he could feel the alcohol sloshing around in his stomach. He was tired and drunk, already beat up, and trying to decide which one of them to hit first when Fritz and Taft burst in with their napkins still tucked into their collars.

By the time they returned to the hunting camp, dawn lurked in the hills. Fritz dropped him in the road in front of the cabin, and as the car roared away Pepper found a little pile of his clothes waiting on the porch. He pounded on the door until his knuckles hurt, but eventually he scooped up the meager stack of his belongings and stumbled through the settling dust to the garage. Taft was sitting on the lowest row of the bleachers, pulling off his shoes when he came in.

"So we're going to be bunkmates," Taft said, nodding at the things he carried.

Aside from the brawl in the restroom, their evening in town hadn't been a complete disaster. Pepper was surprised to find Fritz and Taft were both good company. The food was decent and they spent most of the meal chatting about wrestling and high times back in Chicago. Their fight in the garage from earlier in the day was not forgotten exactly, but at least it had slipped into the background, letting them all carry on as men.

"I don't expect a long stay," Pepper said now. "Just until she gets her wits about her."

"If I had a nickel for every night I spent waiting on a woman to decide she still loved me," Taft said, taking his time folding his clothes and laying them flat, "I wouldn't have to worry about wrestling Strangler Lesko, I can tell you that."

Pepper set his load down on the edge of the wrestling mat and sat. "It'll blow over," he said. "We've been through worse spots than this."

Taft retrieved his blankets from a high shelf and padded over in his slacks and socks. Before stretching out, he tossed one of them to Pepper, saying it got cold out there at night.

"You know I was just trying to help her," he said to the rafters. "I promise you I never laid a hand on her."

At dinner he'd told Pepper the story about the bootleggers and James Eddy and the old tomcat Moira had adopted getting killed. "I guess I believe it," Pepper said, surprised to find it was true. "I won't apologize to you, but it's possible I had the wrong idea."

"It's possible?" Taft said. Without looking at him, Pepper could tell he was grinning.

He settled back on the mat, feeling Taft's presence big and heavy next to him. Through the garage's thin walls he could hear all the night sounds of the forest. Just as they'd arrived back at the camp that evening, a raccoon dashed out of the brush, its eyes glowing in the flare of their headlamps, and Fritz stomped on the brake, sending them all lurching forward in their seats. Pepper imagined the raccoon still out there, creeping though the weeds and falling snow. It made him fold his arms across his chest for warmth.

In the dark, Taft's voice seemed unnaturally loud. "You got anyone in New York?" he said. "Friends? People you trust?"

"There's a carnival owner there I'd like to kill," Pepper said. "Other than that, not really."

"I suppose I'll have to find a way to bet on myself," Taft said.

Pepper turned away, rolling onto his side, a hundred needles prickling the back of his skull. He knew he would have to tell Taft the truth about the match sooner or later. The train ride back from Chicago had not been pleasant. He and Fritz had gone back and forth the whole way about the fix and getting in bed with Stettler and O'Shea. In the end, Pepper had given up, telling himself it didn't matter, since Taft could never beat Strangler Lesko either way. After their fight in the garage, though, he wasn't so sure anymore. The thing that had surprised him the most was Taft's strength. Pepper had expected him to be fast for a heavyweight, but Taft's lanky body had turned to iron the moment they got their hands on each other. His punch was like getting kicked by a mule, and the effortlessness with which Taft threw him off made him feel sheepish and small.

"Listen," he said. "There's something we need to talk about."

"I already know," Taft said. "You don't think I can beat Strangler Lesko, but I promise you, I will. You'll see."

"Even if we could give him thirty rough minutes," he said, "it'd be nothing to hang our heads over."

Another rustling sound as Taft sat up. "What's that supposed to mean?" he said.

"Nothing," Pepper said. "Go to sleep."

He closed his eyes and must've drifted right off, because he never heard Taft lie back down on the mat.

Sometime later, he woke to Taft shaking him roughly by the shoulder. He rolled over, the rank surface of the wrestling mat scratching his face, and groaned. His body was full of hot poison, and as he rubbed the sleep out of his eyes, he tried to remember exactly how many beers he'd drunk at the restaurant. He could not.

"Van Dean," he heard Taft say. "Hey, Van Dean."

He rolled over, the glare of the sun like knives in his eyes, and saw Taft towering over him—a thousand feet tall if he was an inch—in his wrestling trunks and boots.

"Mark . . . set . . . go!" Taft said, and then he was gone, dashing out the door of the garage into the day.

It took a second for Pepper's wounded animal brain to catch up with what was happening, but then he cursed and jumped up. His first few steps were on the clumsy feet of a dead man, his head tossing like a ship, pulsing to the beating of his heart. He was wearing only his skivvies, but slipped into his boots and sprinted out the door without bothering to tie them.

Taft was already to the guest cabins, gliding along with those long strides. Pepper barely made it out of the garage before he had to stop and vomit, a watery rush clogged with chunks of steak. It filled his nose, and as he started running again he plugged each nostril and blew the other clear, turning his head to look at the cabin where Moira was surely still sleeping.

It was a cold morning, and once he was through the gate and on the road the breeze chilled his back and chest. Taft still loped along up ahead, and for a while it seemed like Pepper might be able to catch him. Soon, though, he had to stop and retch again, a string of frothy spit clinging to his chin. He tried to push on, but his tongue was an old dry sock in his mouth and he had to stop and walk to ease a cramp in one of his calves. If he thought he could find a stream to drink from, he might have gone off the trail to look for one, but instead kept moving down the hill as a light snow fell around him. He could smell booze in his sweat. Swallowing back the burning in his throat, he lifted his face to the sky, taking deep breaths to ease the light-headed, dizzy feeling.

He caught up with Taft at the base of the mountain, finding him on a flat rock at the side of the road. The big man's knees were tucked up around his chest, sweat making little clots in the dirt between his feet.

"I told you," Taft said, finding his breath. "I told you one day I'd beat you."

Pepper trotted over and stood with his hands on his hips. He stared at the ground for a long time, looking at his own shadow in the light dusting of snow.

"What kind of sorry son of a bitch preys on a decrepit man?" he said.

Taft stared off down the road as if waiting for something. "They stopped coming," he said. "It must've got too cold for them."

"Who?" Pepper said.

"Nobody," he said. "Just some boys. They used to come out here and wait for me on their bicycles. I would chase them."

Pepper didn't know what to say to that, so he closed his eyes and wiped the sweat from his face, his hands going up and down in a washing motion. Taft asked if he wanted to race back up the hill to the camp and Pepper showed him his middle finger. Instead, they walked, Taft flexing his one swollen hand.

"I think I damn near killed one of those old boys in that bathroom," he said. "Be lucky if I didn't break this."

Pepper had to admit, it showed tremendous courage for Taft to barge into that restroom along with Fritz. All it would have taken was one of those men to have a gun and for them to dig three holes somewhere deep in the woods. For a guy he'd had his own problem with earlier in the day? Pepper couldn't say for sure he would've done the same.

"I guess I owe you my thanks," he said. "I would've been in some trouble if you fellows hadn't come in when you did."

Just then a massive shadow passed across the road. They both looked up to see a huge, dark shape alight in a nearby tree. Its wings were brown with white tips, its beak hooked, the powerful neck of a gladiator. If they'd stood next to each other, the bird's head might've come to Pepper's hip.

"I'll be damned," he said. "Golden eagle."

Taft gave him a funny one-eyed squint. "You are a strange man, you know that? How come you know so much about this place?"

"I grew up near here," Pepper said. "When I was twelve years old I went into an orphanage in Idaho, up near the Canadian border. Stayed until I was seventeen."

Taft fixed him with a look out the corner of his eyes. "You serious?" he said; then, seeing he was: "Your parents died?"

Pepper felt his forehead with the back of his hand. The worst part of his hangover was lifting. He couldn't think of one reason why he should tell Taft about his past, things that he had never told anyone besides Moira . . . except that now Moira had him locked out of their cabin and when he thought about it—about the fight in the garage and then Taft and Fritz storming into the bathroom to save him—he felt a lurch of guilt and fear. He wondered if there might be a certain joy in telling Taft, a kind of daring in trusting this person no one else trusted. This person who right now was one of the only people in the world speaking to him.

"They didn't die," he said. "Maybe they're dead now, I don't know. I just ran off. Hopped a train, trying to make it to the coast. Seattle, San Francisco, someplace like that. It was stupid."

"You never made it?"

"No. A railroad bull pulled me off before I even got out of the state," Pepper said. "Beat the shit out of me."

Taft chuckled and Pepper thought to hell with it and told him the whole story. About how the cops didn't know what to do with him. How he refused to tell them his name, even after the sheriff took him in.

"I just didn't want them to send me back," Pepper said.

"Things were that bad for you growing up, huh?"

He felt the color rise in his face. "They weren't so rough," he said. "I just wanted something different."

He told him about the Handsome Academy, about Professor Willem Van Dien. "He's the one who taught me to wrestle," Pepper said. "He gave me my nickname. When I was old enough, I left. I needed a last name, so I took his. Once I turned pro, Abe Blomfeld changed the spelling. Americanized it, so crowds wouldn't boo me for being an immigrant. And here we are."

Pepper asked Taft if the hired girl had any ice at the hunting camp. If they could find some, it would help bring the swelling down in his hand. Taft shrugged and said not to worry about it.

"I'll be right as rain by match time," he said. "Lesko's got a surprise coming. A big one."

The look Taft gave him was enough to break his heart. He knew from watching his workouts with Fitch and Prichard and from the Jack Sherry bout that Taft didn't like to push himself. That could mean he had no heart, or it might just mean he was used to being the biggest, roughest guy in his own wrestling room. That happened to a lot of heavyweights, guys who had no one in their own clubs who could test them and therefore never found out what they could really do. Now, though, there was a new intensity in the big man's face. It was a look Pepper knew well. Here was a guy who thought his dream had come back to life. Taft started running again. Pepper tried to summon the urge to trot after him, but he felt too sick. He walked most of the rest of the way back to the hunting camp, turning the whole thing over in his mind.

He was still thinking about it when he rounded the final bend and found Taft leaning against the wood rail fence, his face dappled with sweat, his mouth curled into a funny, puzzled smile.

"So wait," Taft said. "What you said earlier. You're telling me that all this time you've been using a fake name?"

"It feels pretty real to me by now," Pepper said, "but it's not the one my mother gave me, if that's what you mean."

"But your real name?" Taft said, like it was a riddle he needed the answer to. "What is it?"

"Nothing you need to worry about, that's what," Pepper said.

"What about Mrs. Van Dean?" Taft said.

A stab to the chest, having to say her name. "Of course," he said. "Moira knows."

"It feels like a tease," Taft said, "you bringing it up and then refusing to say."

"You wouldn't be able to pronounce it anyway," Pepper said. "Believe me, if you had a name like mine, you'd go with Pepper Van Dean a hundred times out of a hundred."

Moira was sitting on the front porch of the cabin, a cigarette drooping ash held in her fingers. At first she didn't notice them, and Pepper went up and leaned against the railing before she had the chance to get up and go inside. He kept his distance, waiting as Taft went up the road toward the garage. Seeing her sent him rolling back into the depths of his hangover, his mind scratchy and dull, his lips cracked, something dark and oily boiling in his gut. Even his hair felt limp and damp on his head.

"You don't look well," she said.

"A little peaked, I guess," he said.

"Fritz came by. He said your night on the town had quite the dramatic ending."

Pepper could feel a fresh soreness on his temple where Taft had hit him during their fight, but his ribs were now completely healed and the rest of his face back to normal after his barroom fight in Oregon. "Moira," he said. "I was angry, but I know nothing happened between you and Taft. That's what he says, at least, and I guess I believe it."

She blew smoke. "And here I thought my word would be good enough," she said. "Regardless, I hope you don't think it gives you license to go out at night with your friends and behave stupidly. Do something to hurt yourself, or somebody else."

"We ran into some trouble," he said, "but it turned out all right." She shook her head in a way that told him how dumb that sounded and he pressed on. "Taft showed some sand. I'm starting to think I may have had him all wrong."

"I'd be inclined to give that more weight," she said, "if you weren't standing there in the snow in your boots and underclothes."

He looked down at his feet. What did he have without her? Nothing. They both knew it. "How long do you expect me to sleep out there in that garage?" he said.

"A good long while, I think," she said. "You know me, I just can't help myself when it comes to my emotions."

Nearly the same words he'd used with Fritz during their first dinner here. She jutted her chin at the garage, where Taft had disappeared into the dark yawn of the doorway. "So you're as thick as thieves now," she said. "Nothing like some rosy financial news to make the boys forget that just yesterday they tried to kill each other."

"The match is fixed," Pepper said.

"I know that," she said, and he realized she already had it all figured out. "Mrs. Taft knows it, too, and she doesn't seem to give a damn."

"What do you care what she thinks?" Pepper said.

"I guess I like her," she said. "At first I thought she was living in a fantasy, but now I'm starting to think she's the most realistic person in our whole bunch."

"I haven't told him yet," he said. "I'm not sure he's going to go along with it."

She watched him over the top of her cigarette. "You know as well as I do there's something the matter with him," she said. "She won't admit it and neither will he, but in his condition I doubt even he believes he could beat Lesko in a fair match."

"That doesn't make any sense," he said. "Why would he go through with it at all, then?"

Though as he said it, he remembered a moment at dinner the night before, when Taft's mind seemed to wander on him. When the waiter set the key lime pie he'd ordered for dessert down in front of him, Taft looked at it like it might jump up and bite him. It took him a moment to come back to them—a look on his face saying the needle was finding its place on the record again—and then he laughed it off. For a second, though, there'd been real fear in his eyes.

Moira stood up, grinding out her cigarette on the bottom of her shoe. "He's doing it for her, stupid," she said. "But I suppose that only makes sense when you know what it's like to love someone more than you love yourself."

He swallowed, but when he glanced up at her, she wasn't looking at him. She was staring up toward the lodge, where James Eddy had come out onto the porch and stood watching them. "I don't like that look on your face," Pepper said, finding his voice but hearing how small it sounded. "What are you thinking?"

"Nothing," she said. "It just suddenly seems like everyone has a fallback plan except us. What about you? Do you care what happens at the end of all this?"

"It's not like I had any choice, you know," he said. "Stettler, O'Shea and Fritz already had the whole thing settled before I even got there. You should have heard them when they were cutting the deal, Moira. They might've been talking about what to order for lunch."

She considered that for a long moment. The wind was in her hair and she was beautiful standing up there, just a few feet away from him, her blue eyes shining with something not quite tears. She let them settle on him and it made him feel like an even bigger fool for thinking she might have cheated on him with Taft, and mad at Mrs. Taft for feeding him lies. He wanted to run to her, grab her in his arms and tell her how sorry he was, but he felt rooted to the spot.

"That's not what I meant," she said, closing the door to the cabin behind her as she went.

•———•

During the next few weeks they started bringing in training partners. At first Fritz balked at the expense, but Pepper reminded him how important it was that everything looked aboveboard. The truth was, he wanted to bury himself in wrestling. He knew the only way to make himself feel better about training Taft for a fixed match was to scour himself clean with hard work. They got Clem Wallhead out of South Dakota, Frank Gundy from Iowa, and a big Swede named Lundin, who had once been European champion. Pepper insisted on handpicking each of them, making sure they were serious, hard men who all physically resembled Strangler Lesko—built as wide as they were tall, with cannonball shoulders and short, powerful limbs.

Wallhead—who might've been world's champion if he hadn't torn his Achilles tendon early in his career—was the quickest of the three and in the best shape. Gundy was the toughest, though off the mat he wore a pair of delicate wire-rimmed spectacles that made him look like a dandy. Lundin, though, was the prize. He had the full complement of size, strength and basic meanness to wrestle like Lesko. He had a headlock takeover that was almost as good as the world champion's and a grip you couldn't break with a sledgehammer.

There was a drill Pepper liked to run where he sent all three men at Taft one after another in ten-minute intervals with no breaks between. It was a trick he'd picked up in the orphanage, in which a boy who was preparing for a particularly tough match would battle against a ceaseless wave of other boys launched by Professor Van Dien as he paraded at the side of the mat with a whistle clenched in his teeth. It was a smothering feeling, with a fresh man coming at you all the time, on and on, with no rest and no water.

At first it looked like the drill would swallow Taft whole, but after a few days the wrestler started to emerge. Gradually he began winning some small victories. During the third week he surprised Wallhead with a clean double-leg tackle and, dumping him on his back with a satisfying whump, forced him into a pinning combination by cradling his leg and grinding a forearm across his face. Once, he got behind Gundy during a scramble, and for a second Pepper thought he was going to put a choke on the big man. He might've, too, but Gundy was saved by the bell at the end of ten minutes. When Pepper blew the whistle, Gundy rolled off the mat, red-faced, and Lundin charged in to clean up the arm-weary Taft. He couldn't yet get the best of the Swede, but Taft was trying, going longer and longer into the sessions before he had to call for a rest, go over to the door and ladle water out of the bucket. The others kept their own water bucket, but otherwise they appeared to have no issues training with a black man so long as the money was good.

Pepper would often take a turn with them on the mat, and being back out there with the other men made him feel as though the years were falling away. The wrestling cleared away his troublesome thoughts and his body was coming back to life a little bit at a time. He would have been pleased overall with the progress of the camp if Taft's strange spells weren't coming over him more and more. Even as his wind, timing and confidence improved, he seemed to be slipping further into some distant corner of his mind. Little things started to confuse him. When Pepper would call out for him to pick an ankle or attack his opponent's right leg, Taft would have to stop a second to think about it, hesitating, his eyes practically spinning like the reels of a slot machine, his hands pawing lightly at the air. Other times he would become aloof, quiet, and they would have to tell him things three or four times before he acknowledged them. He would go to the outhouse and not come back for half an hour.

Moira's words still buzzed in Pepper's ears. Every time he thought of the look on her face when she'd turned away and gone back inside their cabin, he felt a rush of shame so great that he forced himself to focus on something else. He kept telling himself he was there to do a job, to get Taft ready to make a good show of things against Lesko. He was there to get his money and get out, he thought, just like everyone else.

One bright afternoon Fritz came bearing gifts. He'd gotten Taft a new red sash to wear with his wrestling trunks and for Pepper a new pair of fancy black-and-white boots that would need some breaking in before he could wear them. It raised the spirits of all the men to have Fritz sitting in one corner of the garage, smoking cigars and swapping jokes. Once they even got him out there in his slacks and thin socks for a couple of one-minute rounds against Wallhead. Fritz showed off the surprising strength and cunning that had made him a decent attraction for Blomfeld, though soon enough his head had turned a shade of deep purple and he was leaning his hands on his knees. Wallhead got inside on him and tipped him over in a fireman's carry.

"That's enough for this old goat," Fritz said, chuckling from the pain as he limped off the mat.

Despite the increasing cold, the garage stayed hot and dank with sweat during training sessions, so they kept the big doors at the end of the building open. As the men all broke for lunch and Fritz pulled his shoes back on, Pepper caught his eye and motioned him outside.

"I'm starting to get worried here," he said, using a hand towel to mop the sweat off his face.

"Worried?" Fritz said. "I think we're making splendid progress."

"We're getting him in shape, sure," he said. "It's his focus that troubles me."

They both looked over their shoulders to where Taft was sitting on the edge of the mat with his boots off, massaging his feet and saying something to Wallhead, Gundy and Lundin. All the men laughed and then Taft saw Fritz and Pepper staring and smiled at them.

"He appears in high spirits to me," Fritz said. "When do you think you'll let him in on the arrangement?"

A new wave of guilt rippled through him. "Not yet," he said. "Nothing in the world is worse than an obvious fix. I say we let him go on training hard for a few more weeks. Can you imagine what the papers will say if we send him out there half-cocked, looking like a walking corpse?"

"Let me worry about the papers," Fritz said, picking a piece of tobacco off his tongue. He was still flushed from the workout, and for the first time in a long time Pepper saw the hardness of his gaze. The wind kicked up from the east, blowing a few straggling dead leaves across the snow, and together they turned their backs on it.

28

The snow started to become a problem the first week of November, coming down in sheets for three days and nights. When it finally let up they had to wade through mounds up to their knees to the outhouse and water pump, the air so cold that Taft could feel the ache in his bones no matter how many layers he piled on. He and Van Dean dug out big half-moons around the doors to the garage so they wouldn't be snowed in, and at night they kept a fire burning as close as they dared to the wrestling mat. Still they woke shivering and clawing at their limbs in the dark. The hired girl brought their meals from the lodge, tromping down in tall boots, balancing a tray and looking at them like this wasn't something she considered part of her job. They hunkered over their steaming plates and didn't speak until the food was gone.

Taft felt he was making a good show of it in training. He liked the new men Van Dean had brought in, and suspected even if they weren't being paid to be there they'd still work themselves to exhaustion for the sheer love of it. Their energy seemed to rub off on Van Dean, too, and he trained alongside them more often than not now, sweating and bleeding and laughing with the rest. The first couple of weeks were misery for Taft, but then all the old feelings started to come back, the sense of being tired and hollowed out from hard work. It was enough to let him forget his troubles for a few days, but soon the pain in his head returned, this time worse than before. The harder he worked, the more his condition declined. He ached all over at the end of each workout, often finding he couldn't remember much about what had happened. The gaps in his memory were getting wider, making him feel like he was running in sand, burying himself deeper and deeper the faster he tried to go.

His head and neck got so tender that he wanted to scream every time one of his training partners touched him. He was doubling his doses of Dr. Paulson's pain tonic now, drinking a full bottle before and another after training. It numbed the pain but also dulled his wits. He kept making the same mistakes over and over, and he knew Van Dean noticed every one. At one point he let the big Swede put him on his back three times with the same move, each thud to the mat sending a jolt of electricity through his entire body, and Van Dean got so mad he kicked an empty oil can. The sound of it was like a gun going off inside the garage. They all turned to watch as it rattled out the big doors at the far end of the building.

He started losing weight, and the lightness made him feel frail, like he had the bones of a bird. It was from the training, he told himself, and asked the hired girl if she would start bringing him double helpings at dinnertime.

"You think we have an endless supply of this stuff?" she said as she set his tray down on the old wooden bleachers, looking at him like he'd asked her to personally grow the vegetables and slaughter the animals.

"You wouldn't have any of it if it wasn't for me," Taft snapped. He swept his arm in a full circle. "All this, it's because of me."

The way the girl's face cracked, he knew he'd scared her, and instantly he felt sorry for it.

"And what a kingdom it is," Van Dean said. He was flat on his back on the wrestling mat, loosening his ankle by making small circles with the toes of one boot, his lip puffed full of tobacco. "Bring him what he wants, sweetheart."

With all the snow, Taft thought Van Dean might have no choice but to abandon their morning runs. Instead, he insisted they change directions, jogging up the hill to the crown of the mountain instead of down toward town. The snow up there was even deeper, covering the network of trails that snaked out of the hunting camp like frosting on a layer cake. The first couple of days they could barely make the trek, but after a week or so they got the snow tromped down enough that it was passable. It was cold and miserable and Taft probably should've thought of it as punishment, but he was starting to enjoy this time with Van Dean. These days, it was when he felt his best, striding along quick and surefooted, hopping over big rocks in places where they protruded from the snow. His wind was finally getting to where it needed to be, and after a few sessions of the uphill running, he began leaving Van Dean behind on the steepest stretches.

On one of those days the sun appeared from behind the gray steel of the clouds and lit the snow like a field of sparkling diamonds. It filled Taft with a giddy delight and he pushed himself hard on the final stretch of the run, reaching the top first and sitting down on a fallen log to catch his breath. He must have slipped away someplace while he sat there, because the next thing he knew, Van Dean was standing over him, saying words he couldn't quite hear. Repeating it, his voice growing louder and louder, the sun in the sky behind him making him an immense dark shape.

"What?" Taft finally said, shading his eyes with his hand.

"I said your nose is bleeding."

He felt the wetness on his lips with the tips of his fingers and then rubbed them together in front of his face. Sticky. He looked down and found a puddle of his blood thickening in the snow.

"You really dogged it today," Taft said. "How long have I been sitting here waiting on you?"

Van Dean sat down on the log, some of the old bark turning to dust underneath him. "You're going to have to level with me," he said. "What's wrong with you?"

"I'll race you," Taft said. "First one back to camp gets to sleep closest to the fire."

"Look at you, you're sick," Van Dean said. "Moira thinks so, too, but says not even your wife knows what it is. Either that, or she's covering for you."

"Leave Carol Jean out of this," Taft said. "It's got nothing to do with her."

"What, then?" Van Dean said.

Taft spat onto the ground, something inside him scraping bottom. "I didn't love her, you know," he said. "Not at first. She was just my little bit on the side. She's a goodhearted girl, but a little light in the practical skills department. She was twenty-six when I went away. Never in a million years did I think she'd stay, but she did. You know anybody you'd wait *three years* for?"

"Sure," Van Dean said. "For Moira, I'd do it standing on my head."

"How could I not fall for a person like that?" Taft said. "She deserves something for her trouble. Don't you think?"

"Tell me what's going on with you," Van Dean said.

Taft looked at his own blood. Everything was whirling inside him now, trying to force its way out. "You ever paint something?" he said finally. "I mean, like a room or anything?"

"Sure," Van Dean said. "The year I turned twelve they made us whitewash the dining hall at the orphanage. It was terrible."

"My daddy was the type that liked to put a fresh coat on the house every summer," Taft said. "The same color red, every goddamned time." He winced now thinking about it: paint on his skin, under his nails, the burn of the turpentine it took to get it out. "Our house was big for our neighborhood and Daddy was proud of that.

He'd get me up on this tall ladder to help him. After a few days star-ing at all that red, you'd lose track of what you'd done. You couldn't see where the last coat ended and where the new one started. Like, you'd get dizzy, kind of snow-blind. You understand what I mean?" Van Dean nodded. Taft could tell he did. "That's what it's like for me these days," he said. "I lose track. Have headaches, this ringing in my ears that never quite goes away. I get confused, lose time."

Van Dean asked how long it had been going on, but Taft just shrugged. *Button it up now,* he thought, *before you go spilling all the beans.* Van Dean said they could talk to Fritz and have him bring a doctor up from town. They could keep it quiet, he said.

"Nah, we couldn't, either." Taft said. He stood up, the conversa-tion over. "Come on, it's getting cold and those guys will be waiting for us."

———•———

The truth was, he couldn't say for sure when or how he'd gotten sick. Those years when he was at the height of his powers as a wrestler, there were a lot of girls. It could have been one of those friends Carol Jean let move into the house in Cincinnati. It could have even been Carol Jean. It could have been anyone, he told him-self, knowing it wasn't true. For one thing, his first wife Judith had never gotten sick, and neither had Carol Jean or any of the others. At least, none ever let on that they did. No, Taft knew deep down it was Fleetwood Wallace who had given him the bug, even though Fleet himself had never showed a single symptom, had never appeared to be anything besides the slipperiest, most self-satisfied motherfucker Taft had ever met in his life. Maybe it was Fleet's cool persistence, that air of always being in control, even in prison, that made Taft so sure it had to be him.

Of course, he had been too slow to realize that every single thing about Fleetwood Wallace was an act. He'd been too dense, too full of himself, to know that from the moment he'd walked into that cell in Foxwood, Fleet had played him for a fool. Oh, he practically groveled at Taft's feet those first few weeks, cowed by the presence of such a famous man. A colored man so dangerous that society had to lock him up just to teach him a lesson. Fleet had let him have the bottom bunk and let him roll cigarettes from the pouch of tobacco he kept wedged between his bedroll and the wall. He sat close and listened to Taft tell stories about his freewheeling days as a wrestler, about his cars and his women, smiling and laughing his strange high-pitched laugh, egging him on. Now Taft felt stupid for having been so blind.

Not even when three lifer convicts worked him over in a basement hallway with knuckle-dusters made from braided shoe leather and lengths of hose stuffed with sand did he guess it might all be part of Fleet's plan. He'd already been in the infirmary for two days when the three men who attacked him were brought in foaming bright red blood from purple lips and coughing up bits of their insides. Rat poison in their food, the blind old doctor told him. Two of them died; the third survived after an ambulance ride to the nearest hospital, where surgeons removed a full foot of his intestines. He came back to the prison in a wheelchair, with a canvas bag sewed onto him to catch his own shit. After that, life was hard for him.

As soon as he got back to the cell, still a little sore and limping from the beating, Taft knew Fleet had poisoned those men. There was no mistaking the cocky smile or the extra wiggle in his walk when he jumped up to catch him in a hug, telling how glad he was that he was okay.

The little man knew how to make a candle out of an old tin can, a scoop of kitchen lard and a piece of thread, and that night they sat up reading to each other after lights out. It wasn't until much later that Taft began to wonder if Fleet had paid those men to attack him just so he could poison them and earn his trust. It seemed impossible. What kind of mind even conceived of a plan like that? Even years later he didn't know whether to believe it.

There were times when, without warning, Fleet would go days without speaking to him. He'd lapse into a funk, curling up in his bunk, pouting over some careless word or perceived insult, until Taft practically begged him to say something, thinking he might burst from loneliness. When Fleet finally did speak to him again, he rationed out his kindnesses like there was a shortage on. Maybe that was the biggest trick of all, Taft reckoned now. Fleet didn't even have to lift a finger to draw Taft to him, he just had to sit back and let the time do its work.

Then again, maybe Fleet had needed Taft just as badly as Taft needed him. After all, wasn't the feeling of those walls bearing down just as smothering to Fleet? Hadn't he been stripped away from his life just the way Taft had? He had, but looking back on it he knew that Fleet had found ways to get by better than he ever could. Savvy to every trick a convict ever invented, he was friendly with all the prison cops, knew them by name and even looked a few of them in the eyes when he was feeling bold. Fleet taught Taft how to play backgammon using a set of child's marbles and a board drawn on a piece of paper. They passed long hours playing the game together during the periods when they were on speaking terms.

A year and a half into Taft's sentence, Fleet sank into his longest silence ever. Taft didn't remember how it started now, surely some thoughtless breach of manners that he had barely noticed but that Fleet took as a great offense. They went two months without talking and the isolation tore Taft in half. Each day he woke hoping that his friend would forget whatever it had been that had sent him into his brooding quiet, when he ignored all of Taft's efforts to win back his attention. He just stayed on his bunk reading books all day. Taft tried to do the same, but books didn't hold the same kind of magic for him as they did for some people. His parents made sure he'd been educated, but he'd never been an easy reader and could not trick his brain into the place where he stopped seeing the words and started imagining the story behind them.

He smuggled stale biscuits from the chow hall to leave as peace offerings, but each morning he found them hardening and untouched where he had set them on the tiny table. He tried different ways to apologize, starting at the top and working his way down to straight-up begging. As time passed he began to feel like he was appealing to a boulder. Day after day the only sound in their cell was the quiet *flick, flick, flick* of Fleet flipping the pages of the book he'd borrowed from the library. Finally, it had been getting on toward Christmas like it was now, Taft caught him alone in the dank hallway between the dining hall and the small, caged exercise area and slammed him roughly against the wall. Making fists out of the loose material under his armpits, Taft shook him, cracking his skull off the stones and screaming at him to say something. He felt tears brimming in his eyes, but Fleet's face did not change. He gave him a fearless stare that seemed to sap his strength, making him suddenly feel like a child, or a dog left barking at the locked back door, and Taft kissed him.

He pulled their faces together and worked his tongue into the little man's mouth. Fleet's lips parting, letting him do it. He smelled Fleet's sweat and the tobacco on his breath, churning with a mix of sickness and excitement. He still didn't know why he did it. He guessed the urge must've always been in him and now it came pouring through the hundred little cracks that Fleet and Foxwood Prison had pounded into his soul.

It lasted barely three seconds. "Let me go," Fleet said quietly when it was over. They were the first words he'd spoken since their falling-out and Taft did as he was told.

That night, as he lay awake on his hard sleeping pad in a panic over what he'd done, wondering if his friend would disown him, leave him to the other men in the prison who wanted to do him harm, the shadow of Fleetwood Wallace's head poked over the lip of the top bunk. His hoarse whisper filled the freezing cell and seemed to burst it open from the inside out. "Gar," he said. "Gar, you awake?" After that, he was on his knees beside the bunk, his hands on Taft's chest, fingers slipping between the buttons to touch his skin. Taft felt the same car-crash lurch in his gut, but he did nothing besides slide over toward the wall, making room for him to crawl up into the bed. For a long time they just lay there together, Fleet's back pushing warm against his chest. Then Taft worked his hands down Fleet's torso and undid his trousers. The little man bent forward, letting him do it, whispering things Taft couldn't hear. He wanted to shout at himself to stop, but instead he just leaned his back against the cold, frost-covered wall, pushing his hips forward, and did what he wanted to do.

In the daylight, they went on as they had before, going back to backgammon and telling jokes, Fleet explaining the story of the book he was reading, bargaining with the prison cops to get them the special things they wanted. He no longer gave Taft the silent treatment. After lights out, they stayed mostly in their own bunks except for certain nights when Fleet would appear at the side of his bed as he did that first time and Taft would make room for him. They carried on like that for another year or so—Taft doing what it took to keep Fleet happy, whatever it took to keep from being alone—until Fleet was transferred out of Foxwood to a lower-security place downstate. Taft never knew for sure if the transfer had simply been part of the normal shifting and reshuffling of the state's sprawling prisons or if Fleet had made it happen. They said good-bye as men, with a quick handshake while two bored guards leaned against the railing, waiting for Fleet to collect his things. After he was gone, Taft found a letter hidden in his bunk so full of sticky sweet declarations of love and oily apologies that he used Fleet's last tin can candle setup to burn it to ash. Days later, he got a new cellmate, a burglar with a round, soft body and pitch-black skin, whose name he could no longer remember.

He never saw or heard from Fleet again and didn't know now if he was dead or alive. A few weeks after his transfer, Taft was in the shower when he discovered the raw, burning sore on his privates. It filled him with such shame that he never said anything to the guards or prison doctors or anyone else, not that they would have done anything about it if he had. Even after it spread to his legs and back he kept quiet, just hoping it would go away, and eventually it did.

For a good long while he thought he was cured.

●──────●

In quiet moments, which were few, Taft kept pestering Van Dean about his real name. The two of them were still sleeping side by side on the wrestling mat in the garage, wrapped up in their old tattered blankets. He didn't know exactly why he couldn't let the thing with Van Dean's name go. Growing up in Madisonville, he'd known lots of guys with nicknames, funny-sounding handles they called out to each other in front yards and on street corners. Somehow, though, Van Dean seemed different. He never hid his feelings, never hesitated to get right up in your face and tell you what he thought. The fact that at the most basic level he was passing himself off as someone he wasn't nagged at Taft's thoughts.

Finally, after approximately the one millionth time he brought it up, Van Dean told him. It was late and the garage frigid, just the flickering light of their small fire. They were lying there talking, keeping their voices low like they were afraid a camp counselor might stroll by and catch them up after curfew. At first Taft thought he heard it wrong and asked Van Dean to repeat it. Then he tried to say it himself, and bungled it so badly that Van Dean insisted on writing it down. He tore the corner off a page from the little travel Bible Taft kept with him and scribbled the words on it with a nub of pencil. Taft took the paper and read it, sounding out the words.

"I guess that's about as close as it's going to get," Van Dean said, grimacing at his pronunciation. "Now you know more about me than almost anyone in the world."

Taft snorted. "I told you some things, too," he said. "Maybe we make this a keeping-it-between-us–type situation."

"What did Carol Jean say," Van Dean asked, "when you told her about your losing time, or whatever you call it?"

Taft stuck the piece of paper with Van Dean's name on it in his pants pocket. He hadn't said a word to him about Fleetwood Wallace and never would, so he assumed the little man was just asking about his condition.

"We haven't talked about it," Taft said. "She knows something is different. I suspect she thinks I've lost interest in her."

"I don't see how she couldn't know."

Taft thought about that. He settled back under his blanket and listened to the last of their fire crackling itself out. That day Carol Jean had come down and watched some of their training. Seeing her had put a lift in his step and he'd given those boys all they could handle for an hour or so. Afterward he had to sneak out to the outhouse and chug two bottles of Dr. Paulson's All-Purpose, but it still made him proud. He knew it would only be a short time now before she invited him back into her bed. He wondered if Van Dean's wife would do the same for him. He hoped so. He didn't like to think about him staying in the garage by himself. It was only going to get colder.

"You ever wonder where you'd be if you weren't here?" Taft asked in the settling dark. "If you'd done something different along the way?"

"You mean gone left somewhere instead of right?"

"That's it."

"No," Van Dean said. "I never have."

"Maybe if just one thing changed, something that seemed tiny and insignificant at the time, you'd be a whole different person," Taft said.

Nearby he could hear the chattering of some bird and he wondered what birds would still be doing out there in all that cold. Wouldn't they know to fly south before the winter came? He was about to ask about it when Van Dean spoke up.

"I'm not going to lie to you," he said. "At first I didn't think you could beat Strangler Lesko, but, anymore, I'm not so sure. You're big and you're quick and you've been doing a good job staying out of concession holds the past few weeks. I think it's possible you could outlast him."

Taft sat up on an elbow. "Did you just pay me a compliment?" he said.

"I'm asking you a question."

"Which is?"

"Do you believe you could beat him?" Van Dean said. "If we buckled down this last month and worked, really worked, could you go to New York and win the world's heavyweight championship?"

Taft started to laugh but then caught the seriousness in Van Dean's voice. There was something else buried in there, too. Was it hope? Was it fear? Taft couldn't tell. A couple of times during training he'd caught Van Dean and Mundt looking at him in ways he didn't like, but now he knew Van Dean was just as wrapped up in it all as he was. It felt like a betrayal, suddenly, not to admit to him how much pain he was in, about the doubts that dogged him.

Instead he said, "I know I can. I'm sure of it," and wondered if it sounded as false to Van Dean as it did to him.

Van Dean said nothing, just lay there breathing as if that wasn't the answer he was looking for. The quiet made Taft think of Adolph Fell and Fleetwood Wallace and how it must've made his parents feel when they read in the papers that he'd been operating a whorehouse out of a building he owned. They had never come to visit him in prison. He wrote them letters but heard nothing back. When he got out, he'd gone down to Madisonville to see them, found them living in the same house, a coat of red paint on it less than a year old.

He'd worn a nice suit and brought a chicken from one of the city's best butchers. He hadn't brought Carol Jean. His mother cooked the chicken in the same little stove he remembered from childhood and then they all sat around the table and had a nice meal, talking about everything except prison, his parents grinning and telling him they were sure he'd do fine, whatever he decided to make of himself now. Before he left, he hugged his father and kissed his mother on the cheek. As he climbed in the Rolls they both wished him well, the message delivered loud and clear: Don't come back.

It embarrassed him now to think that Van Dean might be treating him the same way, filling him with false confidence. Or maybe just now Van Dean had heard the lie in his voice and it had spoiled his belief in him. The little man was hard to read, lying there quiet, as if lost in his own thoughts.

"My first wrestling coach was an old queer," Taft said then, up into the empty air of the garage. "I ever tell you that?"

"You didn't," Van Dean said. "But now I have no idea what the hell you're talking about."

"I'm saying you should feel lucky you had a coach," Taft said. "A good person who put you on the right path. I never did."

"Is that what we're doing now?" Van Dean said. "Blaming what happened when we were kids because we're both lying here scared of our own shadows?"

Taft didn't understand what that meant. "I'm merely saying . . ." he said, but trailed off.

"Let me tell you a story about the man who taught me to wrestle," Van Dean said. "The good guy who, like you say, put me on the right path."

Taft heard the rustling of Van Dean's blankets, and even though it was too dark now to see, he imagined him sitting up on the mat. Van Dean started by telling him that on his first day of wrestling practice at the orphanage in Idaho, one of the older boys broke his arm on purpose and it took a while for him to heal up from it. After he did, the man Van Dean kept calling "Professor" took all the boys down to a wrestling tournament at one of the nearby towns. This was one of the main draws of being on the team, Van Dean said, since the boys weren't allowed to leave the orphanage grounds except for school trips chaperoned by one of the brothers.

"We whipped a bunch of boys from a local athletic club that day," Van Dean said. "Well, everybody but me. I pretty much got trounced by the first kid I wrestled."

"You lost?" Taft said. He'd never heard Van Dean willingly admit to losing a wrestling match.

"I lost a lot in those days," Van Dean said. "Mostly, though, the Professor was happy with the way we'd wrestled. A week or so later he called us all together and announced he was taking us out, like as a reward. The church from the next town over was hosting a big boxing smoker and he arranged to have all us boys attend for free. Well, that was just about the greatest news we ever heard. It seemed too good to be true, I guess. Like Christmas for a bunch of boys who never had Christmas. We all just about went crazy waiting for it.

"The morning of the smoker, we all rode over in the academy's wagons, with the Professor and a couple of the other brothers driving. A big convoy of us. The smoker was set up in a big pavilion tent behind this little brick church. I was just a greenhorn at the orphanage still—I'd been there less than a year—but, God, it thrilled me to be out in the world again. The smoker turned out to be one of the biggest annual events in the county. The backyard of the church was already full of people when we got there. We felt wild for it, like any bunch of boys would, but the Professor warned there'd be hell to pay if we weren't on our best behavior. There was set to be a bunch of different boxing bouts involving something like forty local men. Anybody could fight, really. Mostly it was big farmhands and fur trappers, street toughs and bullies. There was a men's division where the top prize was fifteen dollars and a few dozen eggs donated by some neighbor's farm. There was also a youth division and even a few women who were going to fight.

"After we found out about the women, we made sure we got seats right up front. It was a big, blue fall day and I remember thinking summer might still have a few good swings left in it before it got cold again. The church had a little refreshment table set up and I'd already had two cups of lemon punch by the time the Professor sat down next to me and put his arm around my shoulder. The second he did that, I knew something was wrong. I don't know how, but I did.

"He asks me, 'Did you bring your boots and tights?' and I'm just a kid, dumb, and I don't get what he's driving after, so I'm confused and I just look at him and say, 'No, Professor,' and he gets this little smile on his face. This mean look I'd never seen from him before. 'You better start limbering up,' he tells me, 'you're fighting today.'

"The weird thing I remember, when he told me that, I still had one of the little wax cups from the refreshment table in my hand, and I remember crushing it in my fist and throwing it on the ground. I remember exactly what that felt like. It turned out he'd signed me up for the smoker without telling me. I didn't need to be told why. It was punishment for my bad showing at the wrestling tournament. I don't know, maybe there was a lesson buried in it, too, and a test of my toughness in front of all those boys who were supposed to be my teammates."

Taft said: "What lesson?"

"Not to lose, I guess," Van Dean said. "Anyway, I was the youngest kid in the youth division. Smallest, too. I don't think the church people much liked the idea of me fighting, but the Professor talked them into it. He could be persuasive like that."

"What'd you do?" Taft asked. Despite Van Dean's grave tone, he felt a smile spreading across his face.

"What the hell *could* I do?" Van Dean said. "I got beat up. I got beat up bad. The next day I tried to run away again, but they caught me. They whipped me and put me on kitchen duty for six months. You ever scrub dishes for two hundred grubby orphan boys? I'd take a whipping from a couple of high school kids a hundred times before I did that again."

His voice sounded far away and deadly serious, but Taft couldn't stop himself from laughing. He had been lying on his side, listening to the story, but now he slumped onto his back. The sound of his laughter dry and wheezing. He still couldn't see anything, but felt Van Dean stretch out beside him on the mat. There was a pause in which he could tell Van Dean was trying to stifle it, but then he started laughing, too.

"Christ," Van Dean said. "What a terrible thing."

This set Taft into a new fit of giggles and Van Dean joined him. They twisted in their blankets, trying to catch their breath. It went on like that for a long time, the two of them laughing in the dark like fools.

On Thanksgiving, Fritz planned another evening out in town, but Pepper forbade Taft to go. He was finally starting to look in decent shape, and the last thing Pepper needed was Taft filling himself up on buttery restaurant food, too much drink and cigars with his training partners. Fritz didn't like it, but when Pepper asked him if he wanted a repeat of their trip to the steakhouse, he relented. Instead, early in the evening he loaded Eddy and the other wrestlers into one of his big touring sedans and drove them into town, leaving Pepper, Taft, Moira and Carol Jean alone at the hunting camp.

It was Moira's idea to have them all for dinner at the cabin. She even fixed it with the hired girl to add a chicken and some vegetables to the camp's weekly grocery order. She wanted to do mashed potatoes, but Pepper nixed it. Too starchy, he said, and starch thickened the blood. He and Taft were both still spending nights out in the old garage, but he and Moira were on more regular speaking terms again and he felt good about that. She cooked it all on the wood-burning stove, with pots and pans she'd stolen from the lodge, and Pepper even found a leaf for their table so they could all sit around it at the same time.

The Tafts came down dressed to the nines, as ever, and they ate early while the sun was still up. The food was delicious, like something cooked over a campfire. Carol Jean brought a bottle of wine and Moira served it in the cabin's small enamel coffee mugs, moving with no limp, her ankle looking slim and healed. Pepper felt glad of that, too.

"I'll be Lewis and you be Clark," Carol Jean said, offering her husband a toast. "Like a couple of frontiersmen riding the range."

Taft laughed. "I've never been camping," he said, like looking back on it he was trying to figure how that was possible.

"You've roughed it pretty good the last few weeks," Pepper said.

Taft nodded. "It is getting rank out in that old garage," he said. "These new men are good wrestlers, but together they put off an incredible funk."

"What's the first thing you'll do when you get the money?" Moira asked. "When this is all over."

Taft was slow to answer, but Carol Jean knew right away. "We'll buy our own home," she said. "Enough of this staying in hotel suites and living off other people's kindnesses. We'll get a house outside Cincinnati, maybe in Madisonville near Garfield's family. Something with a whole lot of bedrooms, isn't that right?"

She leaned over, bumping Taft with her shoulder. His eyes crinkled in a grin. "Of course," he said, then added: "I suppose I'd like to own a good, fast car again. Something where I could feel the wind in my face on a summer evening. How about you all?"

Pepper drummed his fingers on the rough wood of the table. He didn't like talking about money. It made him itchy and anxious. "I don't know," he said. "Whatever Moira wants, I guess."

She smiled. "I'd like a new bed," she said. "Sleeping on this old thing will make me a cripple before long."

They all looked for a moment at the cabin's drooping brass bed and the feeling in his chest deepened. The stove was going and it was warm in the little room, the windows fogged over. They were all flushed and had drunk just enough wine to be giddy. He hoped this would be the night she would let him sleep there again.

"That's it?" Taft said. "If you'll forgive me for saying so, Mrs. Van Dean, I thought you'd set your sights higher than that."

Some extra color appeared in her cheeks as she refilled their mugs. "What can I say?" she said. "I'm a simple girl."

They all had a good laugh at that.

When the plates were cleared, Pepper finally told them about his surprise. It had been burning a hole in his pocket throughout dinner, but he'd forced himself to wait, to gauge how things were going. Now he figured they were all in such good humor, it was worth a shot.

They gave him strange and suspicious looks as he dressed them in the leftover winter garb from a small chest by the cabin's front door. Moira had the quilted hunting jacket she'd taken when they first arrived at the camp, and they found one like it for Carol Jean. The women's boots were a little too big for them, and the only thing that would fit Taft was his long, fur-lined jacket, but Pepper said it would do as they marched up the hill toward the lodge.

"I don't like the look on your face," Taft said as they went. "I do hope this is a nice surprise."

Pepper just smiled and said Moira wasn't the only one who'd put in an order from town when they found out they'd be spending the evening together.

He'd set the skis out behind the lodge where they wouldn't be discovered, wedging them into the deep snowdrift that had piled up next to the porch. The skis were of good quality, handmade of laminated wood, with matching poles. Except for Taft—who'd surely need the longest anyone had—he'd made a guess on the lengths. Still, he had enough experience to know they would do.

"Where did you get these?" asked Moira, not sounding entirely happy.

"I bribed the hired girl," he said, still feeling a little proud of it.

"With what money?"

"Well," he said, "I told her to put a nice tip for herself on top of the tab."

"Fritz Mundt paid for this?" said Taft, and then he chuckled. "He's not going to like that."

Pepper said he doubted Fritz would even check the total on the monthly ledger, let alone look close enough to notice a hundred-dollar difference. Besides, he said, he was thinking of trying to return them after they'd had some fun.

"So be careful," he said. "Last thing we need is one of you going ass over teakettle."

"It'll be dark soon," Taft said. "I'm not sure this is my sort of pursuit. Not at all."

"A bit ago you were talking about feeling the wind in your face," Pepper said. "Why, the Nordic sports are some of the best for—"

"It does wonders for the constitution," Taft said. "I know, you've told me. Still . . ."

As they were talking, Carol Jean had pulled a pair of skis out of the snow and was working to tighten the straps around her boots. "Don't be such a nervous Nellie," she said to Taft. "The moon is full, it will be plenty bright. So long as we stay on the main road, we'll be fine."

"Absolutely right," Pepper said, laying out the rest of the skis. "Our biggest worry will be getting run over by a drunk Fritz Mundt."

"That still counts for me," Taft said.

They all fell at least once trying to get the skis fastened to their boots, and everyone but Pepper fell again while navigating the hill toward the main gate. By the time they got to the flat part of the road in front of the cabins, they had to stop so he could beat the snow off Taft's jacket with one gloved hand.

"So far so good," Pepper said.

"I really wish you'd told me you were planning this," Moira said. "A cooler head may have prevailed."

It was easy once you got the hang of it, he told her. Pepper and Taft took the lead as they shuffled through the gate. Darkness was coming on, but Carol Jean was right about the moon. It rose big and bright, casting everything in the soft purple shade of morning, the light reflecting off the snow enough for them to see their way. It had been years since Pepper had been on skis, but the fundamentals of it came back quickly enough. At first the motion was difficult and awkward, but soon he was kicking and gliding over the top of the fresh snow. There was one steep uphill grade just beyond the gate where they all had to stop and duck-walk up, but afterward the road was mostly a gentle downward slope all the way to town. The going was not difficult.

He gave Taft a bit of instruction to start off, telling him not to go too hard with his arms and poles, to let his legs do the work. The big man took to it easily enough, just as Pepper suspected he might, and then the two of them were slipping along side by side, hearing laughter from Moira and Carol Jean behind.

The sky was wide and full of stars, the sort of sky you never saw in the city. This was a mountain sky, and it took Pepper back to the early mornings he spent outdoors with Professor Van Dien. The skis and snowshoes the boys used at the orphanage were beat-up old clunkers that took a few tries before you got used to them. At first Pepper hated it, but there was an effortlessness once your body grew accustomed to the movements. Whisking across snow that would suck you in chest-deep if you fell or stepped off your skis, you didn't notice how hard you were working until you were flushed with sweat underneath your winter clothes and you had to stop to rest.

Now he and Taft raced along, as they would on any morning out for their runs. If the snow got much deeper, the skis would start to come in handy for more than recreation, Pepper thought. Taft's long strides made it difficult to keep pace with him once he really got cruising, but Pepper caught him at every bend in the road, chuckling at the way the big fellow teetered like a scarecrow as he negotiated the turns. A couple of times he fell, but Taft didn't complain. He seemed to be enjoying himself. On a long, flat stretch of road they stopped to wait for Carol Jean and Moira, realizing they'd left the women so far behind they were now out of sight. Pepper's skis and poles were starting to feel heavy from the exertion, but Taft was smiling as he rooted his poles in the snow and pushed back the silly knit stocking cap they'd found for him to wear.

"You weren't lying," he said. "Another month of exercise like this and Strangler Lesko won't know what hit him."

Seeing him like this, smiling and rosy in the cold, all of them happy for the first time in months, Pepper again felt the weight of the secret he'd kept from Taft since they returned from Chicago. He decided it would be better to give him the truth now, before he built himself up any more on the idea that he might be world heavyweight champion. Before he bargained too much on the promise that he could get his old life back.

"There's something I need to tell you."

Taft held up a gloved hand. "Let me stop you right there," he said. "I know I haven't done a good job staying out of the chokeholds. That Mr. Lundin is a rough customer, but I'm gaining on him. I'll be ready by Christmastime, you can believe that."

For a moment Pepper's resolve faltered, but he leaned on his poles, squeezing his gloved hands around them, feeling how cold his fingers had gotten now that they'd stopped to rest. "It's not that," he said. "Listen. To get the bout on paper we had to tell Billy Stettler you'd do business for Lesko. You have to take a dive."

Taft's smile fell apart piece by piece. He looked off into the trees, as if searching for something out in the dark, and when his eyes came back he'd blinked the sting away, replacing it with something harder but just as bright. "Yes," he said, almost to himself. "I suppose that's the truth. Who would be dumb enough to believe otherwise, right?"

"Lesko's scared of you," Pepper said. "They all are, and they won't take the chance of the world's heavyweight title falling into the hands of a black man. Not after the mess boxing had with Johnson."

Taft shuffled his feet, picking up one ski and shaking some snow off the top of it. "Lesko's supposed to be the toughest guy around," he said. "They say maybe the best wrestler ever, and he's scared of me?"

"I just need to know if you'll do it," Pepper said. "If you'll sign off on the arrangement."

Taft shook his head. "Do I have a choice?" he said. "Should I raise hell? Howl at the moon about all the lies Fritz Mundt told me the day since I first met him in Chicago?"

"If I go back to Fritz saying you balked, they'll call the whole thing off," he said. "Or worse."

"They can do what they want," Taft said. "You can all go to hell, as far as I care."

"You know it's not that easy," he said. "Even if they don't cancel the match, they'll have me injure you in training. Break your ankle or tear up a knee. Then they'll send you out there as a cripple and Lesko will clean your clock in under a minute."

"I'd like to see you try something like that," Taft said, but even as he did, Pepper could see the fire flickering out inside him. As if he'd just been waiting for them to find a way to cheat him and now was crushed at being proven right. The proud look that had been there just moments before dissolved, whatever small thing that had been pushing him forward finally snuffed out for good. It was like watching as a drowning man lost his grip on the piece of wreckage that had been keeping him afloat and it drifted out of reach.

"I'm not saying I'd do it," Pepper said. "I'm just saying we need to think carefully about what we do next."

"'We'?" Taft said, looking offended by the suggestion.

"You should've seen them at O'Shea's place in Chicago," he said. "Like a bunch of matinee villains twirling their mustaches."

"I'm not following you."

"It's possible," Pepper said, "that maybe I'm not as much in their pocket as you think."

"Are you saying, if I refused to go along with this plan, that you'd back my play?"

Pepper thought about that. Was that what he meant? He decided that it was. "We'd have to keep it between us," he said.

He could see Taft turning it over in his mind. A minute ago he'd been bursting at the seams to get to New York and wrestle Lesko, but now he seemed grim, unsure what to say. "What do you think would happen to us if we crossed those Chicago boys?" he said after a second.

"Kill us, probably," Pepper said. "But I did their bidding once before and it feels about the same."

"Is there more money in it?" Taft asked. "For taking the dive?"

"Is that all you care about?" he said. "The money?"

"Yes," Taft said, like that was a stupid question, "that's all I care about. Were you even listening back there? When our wives sat around the dinner table talking about the future?"

"But if you won," Pepper said, "they'd crawl back to you with their hats in their hands."

"Don't be a fool," Taft said. "It's Joe Stecher all over again, except this time they'd do worse than prison. They could murder me and say I fell out of bed. People would laugh about it over their morning papers."

"I think it'd be worth it just to see the looks on their faces," he said. "A second ago you were—"

"That was before," Taft snapped, hanging the last word out there loud and long, putting all his hurt into it. "Before I knew this whole thing has all been a joke on me."

"You're coming into this match in great shape," Pepper said, suddenly desperate to make him see. "If I had to guess, I'd wager Lesko isn't exactly killing himself in training, thinking he's going to have an easy night. That you're just going to go out there and lie down for him. We could do this. We could pull it off."

"You don't get it," Taft said. "Even when I win, I don't get to win. It's the story of my life: white folks messing with me."

He took one wide step, turning on his skis. He almost fell but didn't, and then was moving away, his shoulders hunched and his head down as he drove his legs in front of him. Pepper turned and went after him, the cold creeping under his jacket. A couple of times he called Taft's name but couldn't tell if the big man heard him. He was frustrated and angry and had to remind himself not to pull a shoulder out of joint from hacking at the ground with his poles.

They had gone a half mile back toward the hunting camp before they started worrying about the girls. Pepper was watching the snow for tracks but saw none. Moira and Carol Jean had been padding along in the grooves laid by Pepper's and Taft's skis, so it was hard to find signs of them. Taft pulled up short and pushed his stocking cap a little higher on his forehead.

"We should have found them by now," he said.

"Maybe they turned around," Pepper said, "went back to the cabin."

It felt strange to be talking to him about other things, as if their conversation farther up the road hadn't happened at all. For now, he put it out of his mind, telling himself there was still time to have everything out. The idea that Taft could want to beat Strangler Lesko one minute and then back down from it the next confused and upset him. He pushed it out of his mind as they kicked back up the road, hurrying now to make it back to the hunting camp.

Fresh snow began to fall as they sailed under the main gate. Up the hill the cabin was dark and quiet, but they skied right up the porch and called out for Moira and Carol Jean, just to make sure. Getting no answer, they turned back, Pepper starting to feel a bit of panic now that it was getting late, the temperature really dropping, small, hard snowflakes buzzing around him.

He and Taft were both huffing and puffing, Pepper's thighs burning, twenty minutes out of the camp again before they noticed the spot where a single line of tracks slipped off the road and onto a small game trail. The angle made it so they hadn't noticed it from the other direction, but now Pepper and Taft plunged down the trail, the going much tougher compared to the flat grade of the road. In another ten minutes they found them, coming up the trail single file, struggling through the snow in boots but no skis, both of them shivering and matted with snow. Carol Jean had fallen and broken a ski, she said, and they'd tried to turn back. Without their skis, though, they kept sinking up to their knees in the powder.

"What were you doing off the road in the first place?" Pepper said. His worry had turned to irritation now that they'd found them. He was worn-out and cold, ready for rest.

"You left us," Moira said. "We thought we'd try to catch you with a shortcut."

Snow clung to the strands of hair that stuck out of her hat. She strode past Pepper's offered hand, wading through the snow back up a short rise to the road.

"What about the skis?" Carol Jean asked.

"Don't worry about that," Taft said, taking her by the elbow. "We'll come down and get them tomorrow."

They struggled back to the road—moving slowly now, with

Pepper and Taft each carrying their skis slung over one shoulder—and hadn't gone far when headlights appeared behind them. It was Fritz and the others returning from town. There wasn't room in the car for all of them, but Carol Jean and Moira climbed in the back, collapsing onto the laps of Taft's training partners. The wrestlers didn't seem to mind.

"You all look like you've made a night of it," said Fritz from the driver's seat, eyeing the skis like he wanted to know where they came from.

Pepper thought of mentioning he could say the same of them, all the men except James Eddy looking drunk and stinking of cigars. The car moved slowly through the snow ahead of them and Pepper and Taft took a few minutes to get their skis back on before they started out again. There was no joy in it for them now, and they arrived back at the camp after everyone else had gone inside. His heart dropped as he tried the door to the dark cabin and found it locked. He thought about knocking but couldn't bring himself to do it with Taft standing there watching. Except when he turned around, Taft was already halfway up the hill. He was still on his skis, head down, arms pumping, a small, lonely figure slowly working his way back toward the garage.

30

The day before they left for New York, Fritz brought a group of reporters to the hunting camp to have a look at Taft. Everyone told him this was a terrible idea, but he wouldn't listen. Moira had noticed a change in him since they'd gotten the contracts signed for the match with Strangler Lesko. He was jollier now, but more like the hardheaded young man she remembered from their Chicago years: the hardscrabble miner's son who had come from nothing and had been so sure of his own talents. No one could tell him a thing. He informed them of his plan over a dinner he'd called at the lodge, and afterward he and Pepper argued about it behind the locked door of his office. Moira could hear the muffled sounds of their voices all the way from downstairs. When they emerged, both men were sweaty and red-faced but Fritz held on to a small smile that told her he wouldn't be swayed.

A cold morning a week later, she watched from the window of the cabin as they arrived: four husky men piling out of a car with typewriter boxes knocking against their knees. The wide-open wilderness seemed to unnerve the reporters and they clustered around the car, smoking and stretching, pulling their overcoats tighter against the wind. Fritz had driven them from the train station and he stood making dramatic gestures with his hands as he pointed out landmarks. All at once their eyes fell on the road. One of them said something and they all flipped out skinny notebooks. Half a minute later Taft and Pepper jogged through the main gate wearing undershirts and long pants. They didn't acknowledge the reporters, but Pepper turned his head and saw Moira in the window of the cabin. He waved to her as they trotted up the path toward the garage. Once they were gone, one of the reporters said something out the side of his mouth and they all laughed, turning away from the wind like a gaggle of nervous geese.

Moira had barely talked to Pepper since their Thanksgiving ski trip. At least once a day he walked up from the garage to knock on the door and ask to be let in. When he did, Moira would light a cigarette and sit down at the small table, concentrating on being very still. A couple of times she thought he was going to break the door down, and even more often she had to shush the tiny voice inside herself telling her to open it. The times they had been to dinner in the lodge they sat stiffly across from each other and made polite conversation, passing the potatoes and all that. When it was over, she went back to the cabin and he walked with Taft up to the garage.

Tonight, though, would be different. Fritz had called another dinner in the dining hall, this time so they could all put their best faces on for the reporters. They would eat and laugh and then Pepper would stay with her in the cabin. All one big happy family. The newspapermen would travel with them on the train to New York, Fritz said, and added with special emphasis that he hoped Taft would take the time to show them what kind of man he really was.

They would all grin and slap each other on the back and pretend everything was aces. They all had their marching orders to make Taft look like as dangerous an opponent for Stanislaw Lesko as possible, even though the truth was Taft would not win. It was as dishonest as anything Moira had done for Boyd Markham's traveling carnival. In one form or another she had been a swindler her entire life, but this scheme bothered her more than most. It stunk of desperation, the smell hanging on Taft and Fritz and even Pepper. It made her feel caught up in a whirlpool of things beyond her control. It had been that way for months and now she told herself it couldn't go on forever. She wouldn't allow it.

An hour later she put on her coat and wandered up the path to the garage, where she slipped through the open doorway and stood in the shadows against a back wall. On the mat, Taft was locked up with the big mustachioed foreigner called Lundin. They were both huffing and puffing, but it was clear even to her that Lundin was letting Taft push him around a bit. The reporters were there, hardly watching. They stood close to Pepper at the side of the mat, chuckling and scribbling the things he said in their notebooks.

"Van Dean," said a reporter with rectangular glasses perched on the tip of his nose. "What do you think the Negro's chances really are against Lesko?"

"Of killing him?" Pepper said. "I'd say about fifty-fifty."

The reporters laughed and glanced at each other out of the corners of their eyes. He had always been good at the talking part of it. He stood with his arms folded, lip pooching with tobacco, and Moira felt a tingle of pride knowing he was still a star to them. Quickly she swallowed it down, and just as she did, he looked over and saw her. His smiled flickered for a moment, and he shot her a sly wink.

"You can't be serious," a second reporter said. He had liver spots running around the crown of his head.

"Serious as smallpox," Pepper said. "Soon as we get to New York, I'm putting a big bet down on Taft. Any man that wants to turn a good buck will do the same."

The reporters shifted on their feet. The youngest, who was also the fattest, said: "Three years in the sneezer is a long time. Do you worry about ring rust?"

"I might," Pepper said, "if we had a tougher opponent. But Hackenschmidt is retired and Frank Gotch is dead."

The reporters laughed again. "Which part of Lesko's game do you think will give your man the most trouble?" asked the fourth.

"Slow-footedness," Pepper said. "Up here we're used to a slightly more challenging tempo. I suppose it might take Taft a few minutes to adjust to Lesko's snail's pace."

"What do you think of the champion's insistence on a single fall?" the first reporter asked. "He says he wants to spend as little time in the ring with the Negro as possible."

"It tells me he knows he'll be lucky to best Garfield Taft once," Pepper said, "let alone two out of three."

The reporters nodded in unison and scribbled on their pads. Out on the mat, Taft picked Lundin's ankle, and the big European toppled over in a heap. The noise momentarily distracted the men, and Moira could tell Pepper wanted to use the break to slip away to her. A reporter, though, caught his arm and whispered a question, hoping to get something exclusive. Before Pepper could free himself from having to answer, she walked back out into the weather.

●——●

That night she put on one of the dresses Fritz had bought her on their first day in camp and went up the hill. Eleanor had the dining room looking bright and clean, with a great roaring fire giving everything a cozy glow. Pepper and Taft had not yet arrived. To one side of the room, within easy reach of the bar setup, the reporters had Fritz surrounded. He was telling them fish tales, a grin plastered across his fleshy face. Every few minutes a burst of laughter floated up from the crowd. James Eddy was hovering at the edges of the circle, his handkerchief clutched in one hand. Each time she saw him, Moira expected Eddy to walk over to her and confront her about taking the papers from his room. Now, though, she saw nothing in his eyes, no suspicion or malice, just boredom as he watched Eleanor get things arranged. Taft's training partners were there, too, huddled at one end of the table, their own whiskey bottle set out between them like a hitching post.

Moira didn't see Carol Jean until she was clutching her elbow and taking up a post on the wall next to her. "I hate these things," Carol Jean said. "They drive me to drink."

"They drive everyone to drink from the looks at it," Moira said.

The men's voices were already too loud for the hour. Fritz's forehead was shining red and when he laughed—brow up, eyes pinched shut—it sounded like a lion roaring. A couple of the reporters were also sweaty and loose inside their jackets. She was about to ask Carol Jean where Mr. Taft was when she saw him gliding into the room picture-perfect in a windowpane suit and unadventurous dark tie. He showed off his brilliant smile when he noticed the two women standing together, and she had to admit he looked the part. Taft's chest was as wide and flat as a suit of armor and he moved with easy confidence, as though acutely aware of how small he made them all look. As he came over to them, she picked up a slack expression in his face.

Carol Jean fit her arm in his. "Garfield," she said. "You remember Mrs. Van Dean."

Moira was about to say of course they remembered each other when Taft reached out and took her hand, blinking a bit more than necessary: "I sure do," he said, giving her wrist a peck. "How do you do?"

As she took her hand back he nodded as if waiting for her to take the lead. It had been a couple weeks since she'd spoken to him. His eyes were deep and empty, his pupils crazy black holes, one of them a little bit larger than the other. A muscle twitched in his jaw and he touched his face with the tips of his fingers. She realized he had no idea who she was.

"Tell Mrs. Van Dean how well training has been going," Carol Jean said, "and what a wonderful job her husband, Mr. Van Dean, has been doing getting you prepared."

"Absolutely," Taft said. "It's going famously." The two of them wavering on their feet, moving together as dance partners.

"I'm sorry," Moira said. "I suddenly feel driven to drink."

She was pouring herself a stiff one when Fritz pressed his bulk against her. He'd wormed free of the reporters and made his way over without her noticing. "Where is he?" he hissed, trying to keep his voice down and failing at it. She glanced over at the throng of reporters, but they were distracted now by the giant bison head mounted on the opposite wall. One of them was dragging a chair over in an effort to climb up and pet the beast's mane.

"Not a clue," she said. "I haven't been keeping tabs recently."

"Find him," Fritz said. "I'm drowning here."

Moira scowled. "Send one of your lapdogs," she said. "They seem at loose ends."

The wrestlers had joined in the examination of the buffalo just as the youngest reporter climbed up on the chair. Reaching up to feel the animal's bulbous snout, he lost his balance and fell into their arms. Two of the wrestlers cradled him as easily as if he were a baby, swinging him back onto his feet, red-faced and laughing. Fritz leaned even closer to her.

"You're his *wife*, for Christ's sake," he said. "Go get him and bring him up here to do his goddamn job."

Moira pulled a quick curtsy. "Well, Freddy, since you put it so politely."

She had gotten to the foyer when she heard a great crash

and turned back to see the bison head rolling haphazardly on the floor, the reporters and wrestlers scattering away like ants in the rain.

⬤━⬤

Pepper was sitting on the edge of the wrestling mat, staring out the open doors, steadily adding to a great lake of tobacco spit between his feet. When he heard her footsteps he turned and grinned, grits of it speckling his teeth.

"My estranged wife," he announced, too loudly.

"Dear God," she said, stepping over the pool and sitting down next to him. "Tell me you're not already as drunk as the rest."

"I'm not drunk at all," he said. "But I'm looking forward to it."

"I just had the strangest encounter with Mr. Taft," she said. "He acted like he didn't know me at all."

She recounted it for him and he squinted at her. "He hasn't had a lot to say to me since I told him about the fix," he said. "He's angry. I guess we better get up there."

"In a minute," she said.

For weeks now she'd wanted to tell him about Eddy's letter and the real estate papers, which she'd stashed in one of the high cabinets in the cabin. There was no saying what he'd do with the information, though, once he had it. She worried he would be angry, that he would say something to Fritz or Eddy. She didn't want to add to the confusion or his trouble, so instead she said his name, and when he looked at her, she kissed him on the mouth.

"What's that for?" he said.

"Just so you remember that I'm on your side," she said.

Suspicion crept over his face. "I hope you're not planning something foolish," he said.

She sighed. "Unfortunately, my dear, I'm all out of tricks. Now, we have to get you to that party before Fritz comes down here and skins us both alive."

⎯⎯⎯⎯◆⎯⎯◆⎯⎯⎯⎯

They sat around the big table smoking as the hired girl brought out dessert. Somehow dinner had been a success. They had eaten cream of celery soup, asparagus with crumbles of blue cheese, venison with chunky brown gravy and Yorkshire pudding. Fritz and Pepper did well to keep the conversation moving as they ate, and even Taft managed a quick line or two when the reporters asked him questions. When he appeared stuck, Pepper would jump in, making cracks about Strangler Lesko until even the most skeptical writers were smiling and laughing along.

"I suppose there was a time when Lesko was genuinely tough," Pepper said as Eleanor put a trembling bowl of custard on the table in front of him, "but too many nights on silk sheets and room service breakfasts in the penthouse will make any man soft."

"You expect Lesko to be soft?" one of the reporters said, putting the question to Taft.

Taft had a spoonful of custard frozen in the air in front of him. He looked surprised by the question, suddenly confused. "Soft as an old piece of fruit," Pepper said.

"Gar lived in a penthouse for a time," Carol Jean said. "At the Zachary Hotel in Cincinnati."

Carol Jean's conversation strategy for the entire evening had been to bring any discussion back to Taft's glory days, using whatever details she had at hand. A few of the reporters were obviously taken with her, or at least with the green sequined dress that hugged her bust and the sapphire necklace that made her eyes sparkle like she had a secret to tell. Now, though, they appeared to be getting tired of her.

"How interesting," one of the reporters said. "The two of you lived there together?"

Carol Jean reddened. "Of course not," she said, "but it was an awfully grand place. Remember, honey?"

Taft nodded slightly. Carol Jean reached over and plucked his napkin from where he'd wadded it on the table and used it to dab a smear of custard from the corner of his lips. She did this without caring who saw, as if it were the most natural thing in the world.

"When you lived in the penthouse at the Zachary," she said again. "You remember that."

"Certainly," Taft said, sounding not all the way sure. "Those were good old times."

Moira saw the confusion in his face again as he set his spoon down, straightening it a bit to make sure it sat perfectly with everything else. He looked back at the reporters with deep, sorry eyes. A few of them were staring more intently at him now, sensing something was wrong. Carol Jean flashed a melodramatic smile, all teeth and lipstick, and put a hand across Taft's forearm.

"I remember the Zach from my time on the road," Pepper said. "Can't say I ever saw the penthouse, though. We smaller fellows don't need so much room to stretch our legs."

Taft looked at him like he'd just come into the room, and then glanced back to the sportswriters as if looking for a friendly face.

"You fellows," he said. "What brings you to our camp in the dead of winter?"

The reporters didn't know what to say to that.

"They're here to write their stories about you," Fritz said. "Before we depart."

Taft blinked at him. *Sure,* his look seemed to say, *of course.* All the sportswriters were sitting very still, like they were afraid the slightest movement, any reaching for a notepad, might prompt someone to shoo them away.

"I'm afraid Mr. Taft may have had quite a lot to drink," Carol Jean said, getting to her feet and trying to take him by the elbow. "We should bid you men good night."

"Wait a minute," one of the reporters said, though he seemed to have no idea how to follow it up. He looked at the others for help, but they were all just as confused. Fritz and Pepper got up and Moira pushed her chair back. Only Taft remained seated. He'd started eating his custard again, and Fritz came around the table to whisper a few words into his ear.

"You're right," Taft said. "I will feel better in the morning."

He stood, nodding to the sportswriters and to Pepper and to Moira. "Gentlemen and lady," he said. "I look forward to picking this up again tomorrow."

As they began to make their way out of the room, one of the sportswriters said, "What's going on here?" Nobody answered him.

Carol Jean and Taft huddled together, both of them tall and beautiful despite their feebleness. They could have been a young couple out for an evening stroll if not for Taft's cautious, delicate steps. Carol Jean had one hand in the small of his back and they got about halfway to the door before Taft stumbled and fell. The slow-moving, face-first fall of the unconscious. The kind that looks nothing like the movies. His shoulder toppled a tray of half-empty drinks from the side table. It flipped into the air and broken glass exploded across the floor a second before the weight of his body shook the whole room as it hit.

31

The spasms stopped by the time Pepper and Fritz got Taft to his room, but a white froth had crusted on his lips and he was mumbling things they couldn't make out. His eyes were open as they wrestled him out of his clothes and into the bed, but he didn't seem to understand what was happening to him. Carol Jean went to the dresser and leaned against it, hugging her arms to her chest as they got him situated. Fritz straightened him out in bed the best he could and Pepper was trying to use a towel to clean his face when Taft suddenly grabbed him by the wrist.

"I know you," he said. "What's your name?" There was a spooky insistence in his voice that made Pepper step back.

"I know you, too, sweetheart," he said, trying for a half grin. "I'm Pepper. You're Taft. Rest now; you'll feel better in the morning."

"He'll be fine," Fritz told Carol Jean. "The world always looks brighter after a good night's sleep."

Pepper thought she might slap him, but instead she buried her face in his shoulder and began to cry. Fritz gave Pepper a scared, helpless look before he wrapped one arm around her and patted her on the back. Pepper left them and went back down to the dining room, where he had to stay up for another hour drinking with the reporters just to make sure they all calmed down. After a few minutes

Fritz rejoined them, explaining that Taft had been running a fever the last few days and that he and Pepper hadn't said anything about it because they didn't want word to get back to Lesko's camp. He implored the sportswriters not to write anything about it in their stories, and in the end peeled off crisp fifty-dollar bills for each of them to keep them quiet. After they'd seen the last reporter safely off to bed, Pepper poured himself another drink and sat across from Fritz in the sunken lounge area of his upstairs office. "Tell me you didn't know about this," he said in what felt like his worst stage whisper.

"One more week," Fritz said. "That's all we need."

"Tell me you didn't know."

"Know what?" he said. "That Taft is sick? How could I have known? I'm a promoter, not a doctor. You want me to go around checking everyone's pulse, making them turn their head and cough before I agree to work with them?"

"That man's losing his mind," Pepper said. "I have a hard time believing you could be around him for so long without seeing it. So, what? You kept it from me? Did you keep it from O'Shea and Stettler just the same way? Because I imagine they won't be too pleased when they find out."

Fritz straightened his tie. "We did well to sell it to the reporters," he said. "If you don't think you're up for the same when we get to New York, you can back out now and we'll see how far you get without your cut."

"All that business about Taft's wife," Pepper said. "Needing to get them out of Chicago. That was all bullshit, wasn't it? You needed to hide him away, all right, but it was because you didn't want anyone knowing how bad off he really was. You couldn't take the chance your little partners would discover that this whole training camp was just a street corner shell game."

Massive muscles flexed in Fritz's jaw. His eyes went black and for a moment he was his old self again, Abe Blomfeld's enforcer, the leg breaker. In a blink, it passed. "Fine," he said. "Think whatever you like. Just get him to the ring."

After that, there was not a lot to say. When Pepper got back to the cabin, it was dark inside and Moira was in bed with the blankets pulled up to her neck. He hung his shirt on the back of a chair and started unbuckling his pants. "Do you mind?" he asked.

"Not a bit," she said in the dark. "Just don't think of trying anything fresh."

He slipped into bed wearing his underclothes, and when she pressed against him he discovered she was nude. She kissed him, sliding her hand up the inside of his thigh, and he breathed in the smoky smell of her hair. They made love in a tangle with the cold of the cabin all around them. He felt wrapped up in the warmth of her body, the wetness of her mouth, and when it was over they smoked cigarettes side by side and he told her how much he'd missed her. He told her about Taft's condition when he'd left the lodge and his conversation with Fritz. She was right, he said, it had been a bad idea coming here, but it was almost over. Soon they would be back on their feet. When he was done she ground out her cigarette on the windowsill and rolled over to kiss him behind the ear. She lay there clinging to him and he went to sleep feeling as happy as he had in weeks.

●━━●

The morning came too soon. He felt dizzy and light-headed from lack of sleep as the hunting camp came alive for its last few hours of operation. The reporters emerged as one from the lodge, bleary-eyed in their overcoats, a few of them using their typewriter cases as chairs as they waited by the car. Fritz seemed to have shaken off their argument from the night before and greeted Pepper with a grin and a rough clap on the shoulder. He even nodded congenially to Moira when they came up from the cabin, Pepper carrying their trunk. He wanted to ask Fritz how Taft was feeling, but didn't dare do it while the reporters were within earshot.

He got his answer soon enough. After Fritz sent the reporters ahead to the station in a car with James Eddy, they had to haul Taft out of bed and down the stairs. He was still in much the same state as the night before, mumbling and talking to himself, not acknowledging any of them. Carol Jean was wan and quiet. As little sleep as Pepper had gotten, she had obviously gotten less. He rode up front with Fritz, while Moira and Carol Jean squeezed into the back on either side of Taft. A couple of times, as they drove down the hill through the blinding snow, he glanced back to see Moira holding Carol Jean's hand atop Taft's knee.

Eddy was waiting for them at the curb in front of the station, his fingers squeezing the steering wheel like he wanted to snap it in half.

"What about this one?" Moira said, cutting her head in Eddy's direction as Pepper helped Fritz unload the bags from the trunk.

"I'm told he's to stay on at the camp," Fritz said. "One of their Canadian men will be joining him in order to help chaperone Mr. O'Shea's other interests there."

"*Chaperone*," Pepper said. "That's one word for it."

Fritz didn't smile at the joke, just walked over to the other car and rested his hand on top to have some final words with Eddy. As Eddy's car roared away, Pepper realized he'd never see the hunting camp again. The idea didn't bother him, though he couldn't help but notice how it fit the pattern of the rest of his life: the same place for a few nights, a few months, a few years, then gone, never to be back.

He'd packed hurriedly, stuffing his things into their trunk before it was time to go. Now he left it with a porter while he and Fritz helped get Taft to his private stateroom, hurrying him down the aisle as people stopped to stare. At least it would keep him away from the reporters until he came out of his spell, Pepper thought. They laid him out in the bed and tucked in the corners of the sheet so he wouldn't fall out. Carol Jean stood in the doorway with a handkerchief pressed to her lips, Moira still with her and still holding her hand. As they squeezed past her on their way out, she laid a hand on Pepper's shoulder as if to say thank you. It was an odd gesture, but he smiled at her in the most encouraging way he could.

"You don't look nearly worried enough about this," Pepper said as he and Fritz made their way back toward where the rest of the men were staying. Moira had remained behind to help Carol Jean get situated and, Pepper hoped, to keep an eye on Taft.

"It's all going to work out," Fritz said. "Trust me."

The reporters had gathered in Fritz's stateroom, wanting to know how Mr. Taft was feeling. The way the seats were set up in there, they all had to sit facing each other and Pepper watched Fritz squirm in his chair as he told them Taft was feeling much better. As the train lurched to a start, a couple of the reporters started in on an ambitious series of backgammon while Fritz and the others got a card game going. Despite their protestations, Pepper let himself out and walked to the room he would share with Moira at the other end of the car.

By the time she joined him, he'd eaten his way through the complimentary peanuts. The train had reached its cruising speed, clattering up over the continental divide and into the wide, flat belly of America. After she washed up using a damp towel from the room's small vanity setup, Moira sat with him on the bench seat. She said Carol Jean was trying to put a brave face on, but Moira could tell she was shaken. They would need to get Taft a doctor when they got to New York, she said. Probably one for Carol Jean, too.

"He'll snap out of it," Pepper said. "He's got to."

Eventually he dozed, and when he woke up, Moira was gone. Back to the Tafts' room, he guessed, to help keep an eye on the big fellow. After a while he got bored sitting by himself, staring out the window, and he drifted back to see Fritz and the reporters. He joined them at cards and discovered they were easy pickings. The few tricks he'd picked up from Moira were enough to unravel them in short order. One of the men even had a habit of biting his lower lip when he thought he had a hand.

There was an observation car on the train, and when Pepper got sick of deflecting the reporters' questions about how he thought they'd defeat Lesko and where Taft was hiding, he walked up there and ate dinner by himself. When he'd finished, he got a plate for Moira and carried it back to their room. At some point he slept again and woke in the bright light of morning to find the train stopped and the brick buildings of some midwestern city all around him. Moira had not returned, her plate of food untouched on the small table. He walked down to the Tafts' room and tapped lightly on the door but got no response.

He had never been good at this part: the downtime, the traveling. Being on the train, constantly moving, constantly vibrating and shifting into its turns, made him feel trapped, pent-up. He wanted to be back in the hills with Taft, running through the trees. The last thing he wanted to do was go back to Fritz's room and deal with the reporters, so he went out to stretch his legs.

Walking up and down the platform, he tried to determine which of the cars might belong to the Tafts, but couldn't tell for sure from the outside. Several had their blinds pulled down tight. He checked the station clock and was surprised how early it was. He put a plug of tobacco in his lip, and as he stood there listening to the train cough and chug, he felt the sudden urge to wander off. The idea of going back into the train to sit alone in their stateroom or to stare at the fat faces of the reporters for another forty-eight hours seemed like the last step before hell. If he could just find Moira, they could get lost in town for a few hours—whichever town this was—and once they were sure the train had left without them, they could figure something out.

It would probably be hours, maybe even a day, before anybody realized they were gone. By then they could be on to some new adventure, some new place where no one knew them at all. It was a crazy thought, just a passing fancy, but he reveled in it for a moment. He was looking for a bench to sit on when he caught sight of Fritz at the other end of the platform, standing in the middle of the flock of reporters, a fireplug of a cigar screwed into the corner of his mouth and swirls of blue smoke curling around him.

Their presence was turning a few heads among the other travelers. Even if they didn't know who Fritz was, they knew he was somebody and were stopping to have a look. Fritz was enjoying it, finally having his moment. He shook out the match he had in his hand and laughed at something one of the sportswriters was saying. Seeing Pepper, he tried to wave him over.

"There he is," Fritz called. "The invisible man!"

Pepper smiled back, waved and got back on the train.

From the observation deck, he watched the Great Lakes appear and recede into the gaping sprawl of the east. He and Moira had spent the last few years living in their apartment in the Hotel St. Agnes in Brooklyn while working for Markham & Markham, but he'd never really gotten used to it. The close quarters, the sheer crush of people always made him uneasy and it seemed only more pronounced after spending the last few months in the wide-open space of Montana. As the city sprawl took over the landscape, it washed away the initial feeling of calm he'd gotten from sitting in the observation deck and replaced it with heart-ticking apprehension. Late that night, when he was sure everyone would be asleep, he went back downstairs and let himself into their stateroom.

Moira was there, sleeping in the narrow bed. He tried to wake her to see how Taft was faring, but she shook him off without really coming back to reality. Instead he sat up late by himself, their schedules opposite now, and eventually he wandered back to the observation car to eat again. He slept very little and in the morning was quickly annoyed that the other men greeted his return to Fritz's stateroom with mock astonishment.

"We thought we'd lost you," one of the sportswriters said.

"We feared the worst," said another. "If you didn't turn up today, we were going to send out a search party."

The travel seemed to have given them their own language. There were inside jokes and meaningful glances that he didn't understand. Being cast as the outsider didn't bother him, but he wished the rest of them could shut up about it. Even Fritz had been allowed into their club, slapping his knees after what he thought was a particularly clever remark or cracking up midway through one of the sportswriters' jokes as if he already knew the punch line. Pepper had nearly had enough and was about to retreat back to the silence of the observation deck, when there was a quiet knock at the door and he opened it to find Moira and Carol Jean standing in the hallway.

Carol Jean was wearing a bathrobe, and if she'd slept at all during the last few days, she didn't look it. Her skin had turned ashen and he could see thin purple veins zigzagging through the dark circles under her eyes. Her whole body was quivering and he thought he felt some jittery, electric throb coming from her as the two women stepped inside, looking hesitant to come farther than a step or two. Moira was still wearing the clothes she'd slept in, and she squeezed his hand in a way that sent a shiver of alarm through his body.

In one hand, along with the key to her stateroom, Carol Jean was still clutching the handkerchief he remembered seeing the day they boarded the train. "Someone needs to come wake up Mr. Taft," she said.

The men all glanced at each other, but this time there was no secret, shared joke. Fritz stood up, looking for somewhere to set the mug of coffee he was holding.

"Someone needs to help me wake up Mr. Taft," Carol Jean repeated, her voice as thin as a reed, a catch in her throat making the words waver.

Pepper, Fritz and Moira walked as fast as they dared to the Tafts' compartment, with men eyeing them over the tops of newspapers and women glancing up from breakfast trays. As Fritz fit the key into the lock and pushed open the door, a strange and sour odor hit them. The stateroom was dark and messy, clothes and luggage strewn across the floor, and Pepper nearly tripped over a chair as he made the two steps to the bed.

He knew Taft was dead before Fritz pulled the chain on the bedside lamp. He was still exactly as they'd left him, the corners of the thin railroad blanket tucked under the mattress. His eyes were closed, his lips slightly parted. After a second to get his courage up, Pepper laid his fingers on Taft's forehead and found him cold to the touch. Fritz knelt and examined the label on a glass bottle lying on its side at the base of the bedside lamp.

"Dr. Paulson's All-Purpose Pain Remedy," he read aloud. He gave the lip of the bottle a sniff and recoiled: "Smells like laudanum. You think she's been sitting in here drinking laudanum?"

"I know *he* hasn't been drinking it," Pepper said. "Not for a few days. But Moira's been with her, on and off."

"You think Moira—" Fritz held out the bottle and Pepper shook his head.

"Jesus, no," he said.

He leaned back against the wall, suddenly exhausted. When he looked at Fritz squatting next to the bed, holding the empty bottle in one hand, Pepper imagined he felt the same.

"Go see if they have a doctor on the train," he said.

Fritz bit his lip. "Wait, now," he said, "let's think. Let's be smart about this."

"Freddy," Pepper said sharply, the sound of his real name bringing Fritz's eyes up from the floor. "Go see if they have a goddamn doctor on the train."

Part IV

★

THE GRANDDADDY
OF THEM ALL

32

The doctor was a little guy who really looked after his beard. He came from the rear of the train, following Fritz, flanked by a team of railroad employees all talking at once. Pepper watched them from his spot outside the locked door to Taft's stateroom. He'd let himself out not long after sending Fritz to find the doctor. He needed some air, unable to take it any longer in the stuffy compartment with the smell of death, Taft's body lying there left behind like something for the trash. Moira had taken Carol Jean back to their room. Anything to keep her away from the reporters while they figured this out, Fritz had said. As if there was something they could do.

"If you think he might be contagious," one of the railroad guys was saying as they approached, "then we really must ask you to keep him away from the other passengers. I'm sure you understand."

"We've got a sick man here, that's all," Fritz said, barely looking back. "Nothing to write the president over, though I assure you we will keep him under lock and key." He turned sideways to present the doctor to Pepper as if the man was about to crack some important secret code. "A doctor," he said, and then, with special emphasis: "For our sick friend."

"You work for the railroad?" Pepper asked.

"Certainly not," the doctor said. He looked sleepy, like they had gotten him out of bed. "I'm on my honeymoon."

"No kidding?" Fritz said, grinning at everyone and no one. "You didn't mention that."

"Not that you gave me the opportunity," the doctor said, "while you were pulling me from the arms of my new bride."

Pepper said, "Poor you."

"Please accept our apologies," Fritz said. "We've encountered a bit of a situation here."

Farther down, a stateroom door opened and a scruffy man in a nightshirt poked his head out. "What's all this?" he asked.

Fritz switched on the grin again. "Nothing at all, sir," he said.

"It's too early for this racket," the man said.

Pepper turned around. "Go back inside."

The man's head disappeared and the door clicked softly shut. The doctor was rolling up his shirtsleeves. "Shall we have a look?"

Fritz used his key and the three of them slipped inside, shutting the door behind them before the railroad employees could crowd in for a look. The room was still dark and the doctor had already set his bag down on the bedside table before he noticed that Taft wasn't breathing. It alarmed him. "This man is deceased," he said.

"Must've just passed," Fritz said. He already had a roll of bills in his hand and he passed them to the doctor, who, after a long moment to think about it, tucked the money into his pocket and bent to begin the examination.

He whipped the blanket back and took Taft's chin in his hand, rotating the head slowly from side to side, and then used two fingers to open the jaw a bit to peer inside his mouth. He unbuttoned Taft's shirt and inspected his chest and then motioned for Pepper and Fritz to help roll him onto his side to get a look at his back. The doctor made a few small grunting sounds as he worked. Pepper stepped back, looking at the floor as the doctor roughly jerked down Taft's pants. Pepper had seen his share of dead bodies, and it surprised him how unsettling it was to see Taft now regarded as just a thing. Here was a man who just a couple weeks ago could've folded the doctor up and put him in his pocket, a man about to wrestle for the world's heavyweight championship, reduced to a frog on a grammar school kid's examination tray. The doctor took a few more minutes to check Taft's body and then yanked his pants back up to his waist without fastening them.

"We want to know what happened to him," Pepper said.

The doctor stood straight and regarded them as fools. "This man is an obvious late-stage syphilitic," he said. "He should have sought medical care years ago. Left untreated . . ." He shrugged, the answer obvious.

Fritz was incredulous. "What are you talking about?"

"The scarring on the back is the giveaway," the doctor said. "There is some additional scarring on the legs and scrotum, likely from old pustules."

"Pustules," Fritz said.

"Sores," the doctor said.

"I think I'm going to be ill," Fritz said.

The doctor cocked an eyebrow. "This man was your friend?"

"He is," Pepper said. "Was."

"*Business acquaintance* would be more accurate," Fritz said.

"The three of you were staying in this room together?"

"Certainly not," Fritz said. "We have our own rooms a few cars down."

The doctor looked them both up and down. "Yes," he said. "Well, if either or both of you has had any contact with the deceased that you feel could put you at risk, I'd advise you to get yourselves checked immediately. The tests are quite accurate these days."

Pepper thought of the hours he'd spent on the wrestling mat with Taft. Close quarters, coming away drenched in sweat, tasting it, sleeping next to him in the garage at night. Then he realized what the doctor meant.

"I think it's time for you to go," he said.

The doctor paid him no mind, just turned and began patting down Taft's pockets.

"Stop that," Pepper said.

When the doctor withdrew his hands, all he'd found was a small scrap of thin, waxy paper. He held it under the lamp. "Who is Zdravko Milenkovic?" he said, slaughtering the pronunciation.

"I beg your pardon?" Fritz said. The doctor passed him the piece of paper and Fritz squinted at it in the low light. He turned it over, shrugged his big shoulders and passed it to Pepper, who didn't have to look at it.

"I don't know who that is," Pepper said. "Put it back in his pocket."

"I hardly see how it matters," the doctor said.

"Put it back," Pepper said, handing him the slip of paper.

The doctor hesitated, then slid the scrap back into Taft's left pocket. He cleared his throat. "So," he said.

Fritz peeled a few more bills off his roll and passed them over. "We appreciate your discretion," he said.

"I'm sure you do," the doctor said, collecting his things. "When we arrive in New York, you'll want Public Health to dispose of the remains."

With that, he let himself out and they were left alone with Taft's body again. Fritz sank onto the room's bench seat and rested his hands on his knees. He was pale, his face slack with the expression of a man who was tired of getting kicked while he was down. "What are we going to do?" he said to the floor. Then, to Pepper: "What are we going to do?"

"Look me in the eye right now and tell me you didn't know he was dying," Pepper said. "Or at least suspect it."

Fritz sighed. "We need to focus here, if you don't mind."

"All that stuff about wanting a coach who could teach Taft the catch-as-catch-can style," Pepper said. "About wanting me because you knew I would work him hard and I was tough enough to stand up to him. You wanted me because you knew I wouldn't ask too many questions. You knew I'd go along with it because I was desperate to get back in the wrestling business. Hell, we'd already fixed one match together; why not another one?"

"You believe whatever you like," Fritz said. "I'm through arguing with you."

"Moira was right," Pepper said. "From the beginning this was all a goddamned scam."

Fritz threw his hands up. "What," he said sharply, "do we do now?"

Pepper almost laughed. "Nothing," he said. "We're fucked."

Fritz glanced around, his mind reaching out for something it couldn't quite catch. "We have to keep this quiet," he said. "Maybe we can get Stettler and O'Shea to give us the money up front. Some of it, anyway. We do that, I'll split it with you fifty-fifty. Maybe we can get out of town. Go someplace they won't look for us."

"Listen to yourself," Pepper said. "You're bringing a six-foot-four, two-hundred-forty-pound dead man into New York City. You're going to keep that quiet?"

Fritz punched the wall. It was like a pistol shot in the room and his fist left a dent in the faux wallpaper. "Help me think," he said. "We've got to figure out our play."

"I know our play," Pepper said.

He opened the stateroom door. A few of the railroad employees were still loitering around outside. When the door popped open they jumped back, trying to make it appear as though they hadn't been pressing their ears to the wall.

"Gents," Pepper said. "We've got a dead man in here. No foul play suspected, but we're going to need you to alert the authorities when we arrive in the city."

◆——◆

The railroad people sealed Taft's stateroom, and Pepper and Fritz went back to Fritz's compartment, where the reporters already had their typewriters out. They gave a version of what had happened, saying that Taft had passed away of a sudden illness. The sportswriters riddled them with questions, and this time they honestly didn't know many of the answers. As soon as the train stopped again, the reporters would all get off to call their stories in to the papers in New York. News of Taft's death would be everywhere by the time they arrived.

Fritz wouldn't speak to him and Pepper didn't care. The truth was, he already knew what Fritz would do next. There was only one move left. Once they got to New York and he had a chance to meet with Stettler and O'Shea, they would all realize it. After that, there would be plenty of talking.

Moira and Carol Jean were sitting together on the bench seat when Pepper got back to their room. The light was eerie with the shades pulled shut. There was a flask lying on its side on the table, and because he didn't know what else to do, he picked it up, found it empty, and set it back down. Moira was saying something very quietly in her ear, and then Carol Jean looked up at him with a sadness so arresting that he had to look away.

"How could I not have known?" she said, her voice too loud, as if accusing him of something. "All those months he wouldn't take me to bed, I thought it was just prison. I thought he would snap out of it."

Pepper didn't know if he believed her. It was hard to tell sometimes if this woman was just acting out some part she imagined for herself. Just as he knew there were things Taft had refused to tell him, he wondered if Carol Jean was the same way. Maybe she sensed something was the matter with her husband but would just never admit it. As if saying it out loud would spoil the careful way she'd arranged things in her head. Right then, maybe it didn't matter. He tried to make his voice easy when he spoke again.

"None of us knew," he said. "He hid it from us all."

The train shimmied, the floor pulsing under their feet. On other cars, people were repacking their things, laughing, preparing to arrive in New York. In here, though, there was a stillness that made him want to split the seams in his clothes. It felt like ice creeping toward his heart. He wished the walls would fall away and he could be out in the open air again. Back in the mountains, where a sweetness hung in the breeze, tickling his lungs no matter how warm the afternoon got. He was thinking of something else to say when Carol Jean suddenly grew hard, shrinking away, with a disgusted look in her eyes.

"You men," she said. "It's shameful the way you keep each other's secrets. I was his wife. His *wife*, and no one thought to tell me what was happening to him."

It made him angry, but he tried not to let it show in his face. He thought of all the cold nights he'd spent with Taft in the garage. The talks they'd shared with the fire flickering and the smoke gusting out the big doors at the end of the building. There had been times when it seemed as if Taft was on the verge of admitting things to him but had stopped short. He supposed by then there was nothing to be done, but he still wished Taft had trusted him enough to say something. He didn't like the idea of him carrying around this secret. It must have been a tremendous burden.

Moira held Carol Jean's hand so tightly, both their knuckles went white. "You've suffered a great loss," she said. "We just can't imagine."

Carol Jean's eyes grew wild and she looked around like she didn't know where she was. A few strands of her hair had come loose from their tie, reminding Pepper of an animal, of a bag lady on the street. "Where will I go?" she said. "How will I live?"

Moira smiled, a look he'd seen her use to calm men who'd lost their fortunes at the poker table. "You'll come with us to New York, of course," she said. "They already have a room for you at the Plaza Hotel. You'll stay with us there and we'll all figure it out as we go."

"They'll cancel the event now," Carol Jean said. "They must. Do you think Mr. Mundt would loan me some money? To help me get on my feet, I mean?"

"You could ask him," Pepper said. "But I doubt it."

His anger had wilted and now he felt heavy and sad for her all over again. It seemed as though her mind couldn't stay focused on one thing. She was jumping from trouble to trouble, like she couldn't decide where to start. It was hard to watch. He unbuttoned his jacket and was going to sit down, but Moira looked at him in a way that said, *Don't you dare.* He left them like that, sitting side by side on the seat. He went back into the hallway and headed for the observation deck again, a little guilty at the delight he felt to be free.

———•———

When they arrived in New York, he sent Moira and Carol Jean ahead to the hotel, while he and Fritz stayed behind to deal with Public Health. It seemed to take forever even though there really wasn't much to be done. A couple of cops came on the train and asked some questions while Pepper and Fritz signed their names to the necessary forms. Then a team of white-jacketed men who never introduced themselves came and took Taft away on a stretcher, covering him with a sheet so that he looked like some massive piece of cargo. One of the cops asked about next of kin and Pepper gave them Carol Jean's name. He hoped that Moira was able to keep her away from the reporters and, if not, that they were going easy on her.

It was well after dark by the time their cab let them off in front of the Plaza. Despite the cold, the sidewalks were busy with couples out for a stroll in the park. A few of the great horse-drawn tour wagons were still running, and Pepper saw smiling, rosy-faced people bundled up in blankets riding in them, waving to the folks on the sidewalk as they clip-clopped past.

Fritz went straight through the crowd into the lobby, his head down, not looking around. They stood in line at the front desk, got their room keys and took the stairs up, parting ways in the upstairs hall without saying a word. Moira was already there when he let himself into their room. She was under the covers of the big hotel bed but was still awake, the bedside lamp the only light burning.

He asked her how Carol Jean was doing and Moira just shook her head. He stretched out next to her and she switched off the light. He closed his eyes and wondered how long it would be before they came for him. He knew Fritz would go straight up to talk with Stettler and Lesko. O'Shea, too, if he was in town.

"What are you going to tell them?" Moira said in the dark. Her voice sounded thin and hollow. Of course, she'd figured it out, too.

"I don't know," he said. "But I'm looking forward to watching them squirm."

He hadn't expected to like Taft, but in the end he had. Now that the man was dead, he was sorry for it, but also felt as though it brought a kind of clarity to things. For the first time in a long time, he felt like he was ahead of the game. He knew with absolute certainty what would happen when they came. He knew what he would say to them and what the looks on their faces would be when he said it. He was looking forward to it.

The knock came after one in the morning and he cracked the door to find Fritz standing in the hallway, looking grim and bloodshot in a vest and shirtsleeves. They climbed the stairs up to the penthouse level, the entire hotel sleeping around them, the railing creaking under their weight. Fritz leaned on it especially hard, it seemed to Pepper, like a man twice his age.

"I thought you'd be happier to see me," he said as they went out into the top-floor hallway. "Considering I'm about drag your ass out of the fire."

"We'll see about that," Fritz said.

It was the biggest hotel room Pepper had ever seen, and it was terribly bright for the time of night. Stettler, Lesko and O'Shea were all there, all of them looking tired and edgy. Stettler offered him a drink.

"Make it a double," Pepper said, grinning at Lesko as they all gathered in a sitting area surrounded by doors to other, unseen rooms.

Of the three, O'Shea seemed to be the one most saddened by Taft's death. The circumstances of the illness were especially troubling to him.

"You wouldn't know it to look at him," O'Shea complained. "He was such a big fellow. Stout."

"No," Pepper said, trying and failing to catch Fritz's eye. "Who could've known?"

Fritz was the one who laid it out for him. Tickets for the match had already sold out and they were up against it, having paid the building fee and sold advertising inside the arena and done weeks of press and promotion. Taft's death was tragic, he said, but at this point they couldn't afford a cancellation. It would ruin them all from a promotional standpoint, not to mention the financial hit.

They'd talked about it at length and kept coming back to the same conclusion.

"With consideration to public interest and the press coverage we're expecting, there's only one attraction that won't result in heavy refunds and won't make us a laughingstock in the papers," Fritz said. "We want you to step in for Taft and wrestle Lesko for the world's heavyweight championship."

Pepper took a slow drink of scotch and savored the feeling, waiting for the silence to get a little uncomfortable before he answered.

"I know you do," he finally said.

"And?" Fritz said.

"And," he said, "if you think for one minute that I'm going to go out there in front of ten thousand people and lie down for this sorry sack of shit, you can all go fuck yourselves. I threw a match once for you bastards and it damn near ruined my life. I won't do it again. Any deal you had with Taft died with him. The real tragedy in all of this is that he was never going to get a level chance to go out and whip Lesko in front of the whole world. If I owe that man's memory anything, as imperfect as he was, it certainly won't be served by me taking a dive. That's never going to happen, so just forget it. Do I make myself clear?"

This outburst did not have the effect he had planned. He expected them to get mad, maybe just throw him out right then and there. Instead, Stettler and O'Shea looked amused, while Fritz stared at a spot on the carpet a few inches in front of his own feet. Pepper wasn't sure Lesko moved at all.

"He's a presumptuous little fellow," O'Shea said. "I admire his fire."

Stettler smiled what looked like his most patient smile. "I think you may have jumped to an unfortunate conclusion here, Pepper," he said. "The truth is, we talked it over and we all agree that we'd like you to win."

33

The three of them sat across from him, looking pleased with themselves. Only Lesko's expression hadn't changed. The heavyweight champion just folded his arms, unfolded them, and then stood up to fix himself a drink. Pepper followed him with his eyes, feeling a flash of irritation at the thought they might be having him on. He hadn't figured on this.

"Are you serious?" he said.

"Think of it," Fritz said. "The former lightweight champion of the world, outweighed by nearly one hundred pounds, comes out of retirement and wins the heavyweight title. It's the perfect underdog story."

Pepper reminded himself to go slowly, to think. He nodded at Lesko. "What about you?" he said. "Are you ready to sign off on the perfect underdog story?"

Lesko's eyes focused on the wall behind his head. "Whatever Billy says," he said. "So long as my money's right."

Pepper wished he'd woken Moira when Fritz had come to get him, wished she was with him now. He'd thought he had their scheme figured out, but now they'd re-schemed it on him. He sneered at Lesko. "Whatever Billy says," he repeated. Then back to Stettler: "I don't get it. No one would willingly give up the world's heavyweight championship. It's like a license to print your own money. What's the angle here?"

"We've already got a capacity crowd paid in the hopes of seeing Taft get a beating from Lesko," Stettler said. "With you in the mix, it'll be the exact opposite. People will want to see if you can *win*. When you do, they'll go absolutely nuts for it. We'll make a mint on the rematch."

"Whoa, hold on," Pepper said. "Don't I have to sign off on the first one before we start talking about the rematch?"

Fritz tried out a little laugh. "Don't be rash," he said. "We're talking about big money here."

"If you won't do it, somebody else will," Stettler shrugged. "We've already rented the Newcastle Ballroom next month in Philadelphia. No matter what you decide, Lesko loses the title this weekend and wins it back then."

Pepper put his hands up. "You're going to have to back up and explain what's going on," he said. "Remember, I'm just a dumb wrestler. I'm over my head with all you geniuses."

The three promoters passed a glance as slowly as if it were a flask of liquor, and Lesko found something interesting to look at in the bottom of his drink.

"Tell him," O'Shea said finally.

A queasy feeling crept into his belly. "Tell me what?" he said.

"Listen," Stettler said, his seat groaning as he shifted. "What we're talking about here is a whole new kind of wrestling show. Fritz, Stan and me, we're putting together a team of talented men who can travel the country together performing nightly"—he searched the ceiling for the right word—"*exhibitions*, from town to town. No more one-off bouts that take months to put together. Our men would each work a whole program of bouts together. Two wrestlers—say, you and Lesko—could perform in Philadelphia one night, New York the next, New Jersey the night after that."

"Like a traveling carnival troupe," Fritz added. They all looked at Pepper as if he were a man on a high wire. Waiting to see if he would make it to the next platform, or if he might teeter off and fall. "What do you say?"

"I say it's the stupidest thing I ever heard," he said. "When you say exhibitions, you mean fixes, right? You mean business matches." As he said it, the enormity of what they were suggesting spread out in front of him. Here he was sitting in a room with four of the most powerful men in wrestling and they were talking about turning the whole sport into a sideshow. He could scarcely believe it. He looked at Fritz but saw no shame in his big cow eyes, his bald head bobbing right along with Stettler. "That's ludicrous," he said. "Fans will smell the fix a mile off. They won't stand for it."

"Some people might be wise to it," Stettler said, "but they won't care. These working stiffs just want an excuse to get out of the house for an evening. We'll give them the whole shebang—the drama, the excitement—it'll be like moving pictures come to life."

"What about the other promoters?" Pepper said. "They'll make a mockery of you in the papers."

"Dinosaurs," Stettler said. "With O'Shea backing us, we own the papers. Same with the politicians. You won't see any of our boys dragged through the mud or brought up on fraud charges, that's a promise. Plus, we have Lesko. If anybody gets frisky and refuses to do business, he'll whip them on the square. Inside of a year or two we'll be the only game in town. Anybody who doesn't go along will be out. Mark my words."

"You can't be serious," Pepper said. "You'll kill us. You'll sink the whole thing."

Stettler snorted. "Do you have any idea what's happened to the wrestling business since you've been away?" he said. "While you spent the last five years traveling around with your little carnival act, the rest of us have been trying to save it. The whole thing is in the toilet. Nobody cares about it anymore."

"Because Gotch retired," Pepper said. "People loved Gotch. It happens. Business slacks off for a bit, but it always comes back up."

"This time there's no coming back," Stettler said.

"Nobody wants to watch two guys pulling on each other for a three-hour match," Fritz said. "They want to drink some suds, see a slam-bang show, and still get home at a reasonable hour."

"Bullshit," Pepper said. "Scientific wrestling is a huge drawing card."

"We're living in a new era," Stettler said. "The sooner you make peace with it, the easier it'll be on you."

"You said yourself we've already got a sellout for tomorrow night," Pepper said. "You'll probably draw close to two hundred thousand dollars at the gate."

"Maybe," Stettler said, "but only because it's a curiosity. Lesko versus Taft was a freak-show act from the beginning. People wanted to see something unique, and that's exactly what we'll give them with our new show. It'll be better than the real thing. It'll be *bigger* than the real thing. Hell, it'll be bigger than baseball."

Stettler seemed to swell as he became the center of attention, and now he was practically bursting with pride. His eyes were bright, and it occurred to Pepper that he really was a hell of a promoter. Still, he waved them away. "Fuck that," he said. "I'm not doing it."

Their heads dipped. This was starting to become a very tiresome experience for them, he could tell. It was late and none of them looked like they'd slept.

"You will so do it," Fritz said.

"You'll do it for the money," Stettler said. "If you join up with us you stand to make upwards of fifty thousand dollars a year. That's a damn spot better than the twenty-five dollars a week you were making as a carnival freak. You'll do it because your other option is to sit there and make your little jokes while the rest of us drag this business out of the past and put it back in the big theaters. Deep down, the last thing you want is to be left out of that, am I right?"

"Besides," O'Shea said, "let's not act like you haven't done this before. You're getting a better deal from us than you got last time."

Their eyes were hard, but there was something fragile in them, too. It was more than just fatigue. It was desperation. They needed him to do this. They had to get him to take this deal or their whole plan would go under. They would be out the building deposit and end up refunding thousands to people who'd already bought tickets. For maybe the first time in his life, the men in charge needed him more than he needed them, and he savored for a moment the feeling of being the thorn in the lion's paw. He was going to let them dangle for as long as he could before he told them to go fuck themselves. Really, what could they do? Kill him? He supposed they could try. He could roll the dice, walk out of this room, and let them come for him if that's what they decided. First they'd have to catch him.

He was considering all this when Lesko spoke, his low rumbling voice flat and forceful in the quiet room. "He'll do it," he said, "but not for the money. That's not why."

Pepper crooked an eyebrow and beckoned for him to get on with it. "Oh?" he said. This, at least, was interesting.

"Make no mistake, you will do it," Lesko said. "From the moment you walked in here with that stupid, self-satisfied grin on your face there wasn't a chance in the world you were going to turn this offer down."

Pepper crossed his legs, ankle on knee. "How can you be so sure?" he said.

"You know how many men I've met just like you?" Lesko said. "How many Wild West cowboys with more guts than brains have tried to test me? A hundred. Hell, a thousand. I know that somewhere in the back of that pea brain of yours there's a fantasy that you can beat me. You're gonna walk out that door and leave your chance lying on the table? No way."

He was right, but Pepper didn't want to give him the satisfaction. He said: "We won't learn a thing if the fix is on."

Lesko shook his head, dismissive. "It'll be enough," he said. "I'll give you a taste of what I could do to you and you'll know straightaway. Never in a million years, little man, would you have a chance against me on the level. A million fucking years."

Pepper's shirt suddenly felt tight across his back and he willed himself to relax. He wondered if they'd put Lesko up to this, if this had been their plan all along: to have the promoters show a little leg and then get the champion to swoop in to close the deal. He fought hard not to let his expression crack when he spoke again. "I'm going to go real slow now, so that even the big ox can understand," he said. "I'm not wrestling a business match. I won't do it. Not for you, not for anybody. Call me old-fashioned, but I liked it better when the two guys in the ring got to decide who won and who lost. You remember that, you assholes? The two guys out there sweating and bleeding and pouring their guts out? You want me in on this thing, there's only one way to do it."

The only thing that moved in the room were Lesko's eyes as he looked at Stettler. "I can beat him, Billy," he said. "That's not a problem."

"Absolutely not," Stettler said. "Aside from the gate, Mr. O'Shea and I have substantial gambling interests at stake here. Sending you out there for a prick-measuring contest puts all of that at risk."

A coaster stuck to the bottom of O'Shea's drink as he lifted it from the table. He plucked it off with a little pop, a lazy grin uncoiling on his face. "Don't do anything on my account," he said. "If the principals insist on a legitimate confrontation, well, it might be worth it to me just to watch."

Stettler stared at him as if he couldn't believe it. He said the gangster's name, but O'Shea didn't look at him, just continued fiddling with the coaster as he set it back on the table. Stettler turned back to Lesko, who hadn't budged. Finally he fluttered both his hands in the air, a womanly gesture. "Sure," he said. "Why not just chuck months of planning at the last moment. It looks like I'm outvoted again. Congratulations, Mr. Van Dean, you've just inherited the beating of a lifetime."

"I want a hundred thousand dollars," Pepper said. "I want it in cash before the match, and that's just for the weekend. We'll talk about Philadelphia after."

"Fifty," said Stettler. "Don't push it."

"Fine," Pepper said. "If I find out you're trying to fuck me, you'll be sorry. If I even think I smell a double cross, your little partnership won't make it out of New York in one piece."

O'Shea grinned. "I've always enjoyed you," he said. "Never a dull moment."

They had the contracts already drawn up and laid out on the small table in the adjoining dining room. Pepper watched over their shoulders and Stettler and Fritz changed the terms of his compensation from the thirty thousand they'd previously promised Taft to fifty thousand. O'Shea produced a pen from his jacket and Pepper signed, then stood back while the heavyweight champion applied his own wide, looping signature.

"You," Pepper said, as Lesko turned away, going back to the sideboard and discarding his empty glass. "You've got yours coming."

Lesko didn't look back as he walked out of the room, closing the door to a connecting suite quietly behind him. Pepper stared at the door until Stettler broke the spell by saying someone would have to alert the press.

34

The grand ballroom on the ground floor of the Plaza Hotel filled up early for the press conference. Fritz and Stettler had gotten the story of Pepper stepping in for Taft out to their contacts in the press, and for two days the papers had been going crazy with it. This would be the first and only time reporters would get the opportunity to see Pepper and Lesko before Saturday's match, and no one wanted to miss the chance. At least, that's how it looked to Pepper as he stood on the side of the stage, eyeing the crowd through the curtain.

The wrestlers had come down from their rooms on different staircases and would enter the press conference from opposite sides of the stage. It was just Pepper and Moira standing there now, holding hands in the dark. Somewhere in the deep recesses across the way, he knew Fritz, Lesko and Stettler were watching him. It gave him a tickling feeling, but he made sure not to fidget. He was barely breathing. His mind was racing with other things, trying to plan his moves a step at a time, trying to make sure he had it all straight in his head. The longer they stood there, the thicker the silence felt, the more he could feel their eyes boring into him. It was like a weight on top of him, pushing him into the floor through the soles of his shoes.

Just to be saying something, he asked how Carol Jean was holding up. Moira said she hadn't seen her that morning. Carol Jean hadn't answered the door when she'd gone down to check on her. Since Taft's death she'd barely left her hotel room, agreeing only to see Moira. Now Moira said she didn't know if she'd finally gone out to get some air of if she just wasn't coming to the door.

The two of them were murmuring to each other, barely moving their lips like a couple of ventriloquists practicing their act. It felt queer to him, the two of them standing there, trying to be quiet, waiting for him to go onstage. Like old times.

"She'll turn up," he said. "Probably just went on a walk to clear her head."

"I wish I was that confident," Moira said. "She hasn't been well. Not that I blame her."

At precisely four o'clock Stettler and Fritz walked onto the stage to address the crowd, ignoring questions shouted at them by the reporters long enough for each to make some brief introductory remarks. Both men agreed that Garfield Taft's death from a sudden illness was tragic but were pleased to be able to offer the sporting people of New York a spectacle just as, if not more, compelling. Stettler even made a point to say they were indebted to Mr. Van Dean for taking the bout on short notice and without proper time to prepare himself for Lesko and his scientific wrestling arsenal.

"A gargantuan task," Stettler said, "for a lightweight competitor with an outsized heart."

This drew some guffaws from the crowd, and those chuckles bubbled into a wave of laughter as the promoters introduced the wrestlers. As the challenger, Pepper came onstage first, smiling and waving, dressed in three thick winter overcoats and carrying a milk crate in one hand. Under his shirt he'd stuffed two pillows from the bed in his room, giving him the outlandish look of a lumpy heavyweight. Holding his arms away from his sides, he strutted to the center of the stage in an exaggerated cowboy walk. Some of the reporters applauded politely as Lesko entered from the other side, looking staid by comparison in a brown suit, cream-colored shirt and gold tie. He came to center for the face-off, his mouth tight, his eyes betraying nothing as Pepper made a show of setting down his milk crate and climbing carefully on top of it.

Standing on top of the crate, Pepper was almost a full head taller than Lesko. From there, he squatted low into an embellished wrestling pose, facing the heavyweight champion eye to eye, giving him a grin. Lesko looked bored and simply held up one massive fist.

They had to hold the pose for an uncomfortably long time while the reporters got their cameras into the position and squeezed off a series of loud, popping photographs. Neither man looked away, and Pepper felt a single trickle of sweat roll down his ribs underneath his thick outfit. He searched Lesko's eyes for some reaction to their earlier conversation, but saw none.

Once the photographers had gotten what they wanted, the two men took their seats. The first question came from the back, a reporter asking Lesko what he thought of Pepper as a new opponent. The champion answered in a low monotone, his voice without emotion as he recited an obviously rehearsed response. "Van Dean was a great champion in his day," Lesko said, "but he's never been in the ring with someone like me."

The reporters began to scribble, but Pepper interrupted. "Not true," he said, hearing his voice echo in the big room. "Mr. Lesko overlooks my carnival experience. I've wrestled plenty of bears."

The reporters smiled into their notebooks and kept writing. One of them asked Stettler about Lesko's insistence that he would wrestle Taft only in a one-fall match and whether the same held true now with Van Dean in as a substitute. Stettler nodded, but Pepper held up a finger before the promoter could open his mouth.

"I'll take this one, Billy," he said. "If the winner of this bout is to walk out of Madison Square Garden with the world's heavyweight title, it's only fair he should take two out of three falls."

"Let's not be hasty," Stettler said. "Strangler Lesko has trained for a one-fall match and we're dealing with a replacement opponent here. One fall makes the most sense."

"Two out of three falls," Pepper repeated. "The paying customer has already been dealt a blow with Mr. Taft's unfortunate passing. Let's give folks their money's worth. Plus, I don't want any of these vultures in the press saying my win was a fluke."

"Wouldn't three falls favor the bigger man?" one of the reporters asked.

"Not at all," Pepper said. "Lesko had vastly underestimated Mr. Taft from the start and now he's underestimating me. I believe his conditioning is suspect. I believe his wind is suspect. Over the course of three falls, he won't be able to contend with my pace."

"I have no issue wrestling three falls," Lesko said, a note of annoyance finally creeping into his voice. "I'm in the best shape of my life."

"Indeed," Pepper said, "and that shape is round."

He could feel his momentum building, the old feeling of performing in front of a crowd. It'd been months since he'd felt it and just now realized how much he missed it.

"You think you'll fare better against Lesko than Taft might have?" a reporter asked.

"No," Pepper said, "but I'm still pretty sure I'll win."

Now they all looked at him like he'd lost his mind. It was exactly what he wanted. "So you think Taft would've bested Lesko?" another asked.

"I think Garfield Taft was the greatest natural wrestler I've ever had the pleasure to be around," Pepper said. "Meanwhile, I think Lesko is the kind of man who pretends people won't notice how fat he's getting so long as he just keeps hiking up his trunks over his belly."

The long table in front of Lesko screeched across the floor as he tried to stand up. Stettler kept him in his chair, one hand resting lightly on his shoulder.

"I don't have to stay here and take this kind of talk," Lesko said. "We'll all see on Saturday."

"Mr. Van Dean is certainly very confident," Stettler said, smiling half to the reporters, half to Pepper. Underneath the grin he'd begun to look a little stiff in his fancy suit. "His boundless optimism is one of the things we admire most about him."

They spent the next half hour answering questions. The sportswriters pitched mostly slow balls and Lesko responded in his bored drone while Pepper cracked his jokes. The crowd wanted to know what would happen if Pepper managed to beat Lesko—he saw a few incredulous shakes of the head when the topic came up—and Stettler told them about Philadelphia. Immediate rematch clause, he said. Normal stuff for the world's heavyweight champion. And if Pepper lost? somebody asked.

"If I lose, you fellows will never see me again," he said. "I'll go right back into retirement. If I can't beat a fat buffalo like Lesko, I don't deserve any more of your time."

At that Lesko grunted, announcing he was finished with this folly. He shook off Stettler's hand and stood up, upsetting his chair. He'd turned to storm off the stage when the double doors at one side of the ballroom flew open and the reporters all turned, a booming new voice ringing through the crowd.

"What about this woman?" the voice demanded. "What will be done to assuage her terrible grief?"

Pepper's chin sagged down against his chest. He knew that voice without having to look, but after slowly squeezing all of the air from his lungs he glanced up to confirm it.

Boyd Markham was pushing his way through the sea of reporters, a fire-engine-red carnation pinned to the lapel of his best ringmaster's suit. His silver mane of hair was oiled to a high shine and slicked back on his great lion's head. He was flanked by two dour men in black suits, guys Pepper had never seen before, both of them wearing a dusty, stone-faced look that said they could only be lawyers or undertakers. The sportswriters moved back to let them pass, and as they came to the front, Markham opened his arms like he wanted to take the whole room into an embrace. Something tightened like a screw at the base of Pepper's skull. It took him a moment to realize that Carol Jean was standing with him, her hair pinned up over a chaste black gown. She was staring, unblinking, at her own toes.

"What's the meaning of this?" Stettler sputtered, but his voice was lost in the din.

"Will these fat cats stand idly by as this poor woman goes uncompensated after the terrible loss of her husband?" Markham said, sounding like a preacher who had waited a long time to get his pulpit. "A man stolen from her in the prime of both their lives?"

Pepper looked over at Moira. She had moved forward and now stood squeezing a handkerchief at the fringe of the curtain.

Many of the reporters looked confused and were whispering to each other, while others were just struggling to keep up with their shorthand. Pepper thought he saw the ringmaster flash a quick smile his way before his face flattened back into pious sincerity. One of the sportswriters who'd come to the hunting camp in Montana had also worked his way to the front.

"What makes you think the Negro's whore deserves a dime?" he called.

Markham didn't look at the man or acknowledge him in any way. Instead he dug a meaty claw into the inside pocket of his jacket and came out with a sheaf of paper folded into thirds. "I hold in my hand a service contract signed both by myself and Mr. Pepper Van Dean," Markham said, leveling a finger in his direction. "It clearly elucidates that I am owed a fifty-percent stake of any earnings he collects through professional wrestling or any other like athletic endeavor."

"You unbelievable fuck," Pepper said, putting his fists on the table and rising from his chair.

He felt Fritz's hand on him and sank back into his seat. The reporters were now in an out-and-out frenzy, trying to yell questions all at once. Markham rolled on as if they were flies buzzing around his head.

"Having been contacted by the recently widowed Mrs. Taft," he said, "my legal analysts and I request an audience with the promoters of this weekend's farce. We demand satisfaction on her behalf. Might I suggest we retire to better-sequestered environs to discuss these rather delicate matters?"

At the center of the stage Stettler stood gripping the lectern. He'd been joined by a couple of O'Shea's goons, their heads pressed together as they conferred. All at once O'Shea's men broke off from the stage, hopping down to usher Markham and Carol Jean out a side door while several of the reporters tried to follow.

"Gentlemen," Stettler said, holding up his hands for quiet. "We thank you for attending this event today. Our apologies for the unplanned outburst. We assure you it will be sorted out in short order and we look forward to seeing all of you ringside on Saturday night. It should be an interesting endeavor, to say the least."

As soon as he turned away from the crowd the smile died on his face. He crossed the stage to Pepper in two quick steps. "My suite," he hissed. *"Now."*

❖

Boyd Markham had helped himself to a drink and a small bowl of mixed nuts by the time they got to Stettler's suite. Only Fritz came over to greet them as one of O'Shea's goons let them inside. Carol Jean sat in an armchair, making a point of not looking at anyone. Stettler, Lesko and O'Shea skulked around in the far corner.

Around the table, Markham's lawyers had been joined by another group of men Pepper had never seen before. He assumed they must be lawyers who belonged to O'Shea and Stettler. They were engrossed by a series of papers they had set out in front of them.

During the long walk up, a hard rock had formed between his shoulder blades. Moira climbed the stairs in front of him and he tried to focus on the backs of her shoes to keep everything from going red. When they got to the landing at the top, she turned and whispered to him that no matter what happened inside the suite, he needed to keep calm. Her eyes were bright and wet, but her gaze was steady. She was in full cardsharp mode now, he knew, watching everything with a calculated stillness that came just before the biggest bet of the evening.

He nodded to her and said that he would go easy, but as soon as they were inside, his rage bubbled up again and he tried to get ahold of Markham.

"I should have known you'd come back begging for scraps," he said. Fritz and Stettler held him back.

Markham reared away, a stricken look on his face, nuts and salt spilling onto the carpet. "A fool never appreciates when his disgraces are his own making," he remarked, as if repeating a prayer to himself.

Even after Fritz and Stettler turned him loose, Moira held on to his arm to make sure he was settled. "I don't know where you ran across this skunk," she said to Carol Jean, "but I know he's not looking after your best interests."

Carol Jean looked every bit the petulant child. "I just want what I'm owed," she said.

"You're owed nothing," Fritz said. "You'll get nothing."

"We'll see about that," Markham said.

He was right, and knowing it made Pepper want to go after him all over again. For an icy half hour they all sat in the hotel suite while the lawyers went over the papers, then another fifteen minutes while Stettler and Fritz followed the men in suits into a back bedroom, where he could hear their muffled voices going back and forth behind the door. The entire time Markham sat perched on a high-backed barstool like a great toad, leering at Pepper and refilling his drink each time he drained it. Lesko also watched him, nothing knowable in his flat eyes. Only Carol Jean seemed to have no interest in Pepper, Moira or in anything else in the room. She merely sat still, occasionally dabbing at the corners of her eyes with a handkerchief.

"We could have done this another way," Moira said to her. "You could have just come to me. We could have worked out a deal between the two of us."

"A deal?" she said, finally showing them the full fury in her eyes. "Would you say a deal between us would work out better or worse for me than the one these men had with my husband?"

Every muscle in Pepper's body tensed. Mixed in with his confusion and anger, he couldn't stop himself from feeling sorry for her. He didn't know exactly what Markham had promised Carol Jean, but he thought he understood a bit of what she was going through. He recognized the proud set of her shoulders, her boiling glare not quite covering up the pain beneath. He remembered what that was like. He knew how easy it could be to let yourself be taken in by the carnival barker's smooth talk, especially when you had nothing else left to believe in. Markham had told her he could win the day for her. He'd told her he could get her a bit of money, enough to start over, and had done it well enough that she believed him. Sitting there, Carol Jean thought the terms they'd struck were legitimate, even though everyone else in the hotel suite knew Markham was just a swindler. She was just his new mark.

"I know this has been hard for you . . ." he said.

"Don't pretend to know a thing about me," Carol Jean said. "Three years I waited for that man. Visiting him in that awful place.

I took his name. I lost my family. When he got out, I suffered his moods, his peculiar behaviors, his rages and spells. I stayed when he told me we were broke. I stayed after he stopped sleeping with me. I followed him to the middle of nowhere and gave him the prime years of my life, and now he's gone and all of it means nothing. What would you do?"

His response was cut off by the sound of the bedroom door opening. Stettler and Fritz exited, followed by their troop of lawyers. Everyone stood as Stettler came to the center of the room like a world leader about to give a great speech. His ridiculous dyed hair tumbled into his eyes and he swept it away with the back of his hand. "I regret to report," he said, "that Mr. Markham's contract appears genuine. It's a strongly worded agreement, to say the least."

"So," Pepper said, rising from his seat. "What's that mean?"

"It means," one of Markham's lawyers said, "you owe our client restitution for damages and reimbursement for the losses he incurred after you left him in the lurch some months ago."

"Restitution?" Pepper said, the word jabbing him like a bone in something he was eating.

"This is ridiculous," Moira said. "It was *Markham* that abandoned *us*, not the other way around."

"I'm afraid it's your word against his on that aspect," the lawyer said, "and the contract makes it quite clear. Mr. Van Dean's no-compete clause bars him from performing with another outfit in any similar endeavor, athletic or theatrical, for up to two years. On top of that, there's the matter of Mr. Markham's losses at the box office after your departure, plus advance-advertising monies spent publicizing appearances with the Markham & Markham Overland Carnival that Mr. Van Dean failed to make. Plus the transport of Mr. and Mrs. Van Dean's belongings back to New York, at considerable expense, plus the deposit and rent money Mr. Markham spent keeping rooms for you at the Hotel St. Agnes—"

"Enough," Pepper said. He could not contain himself any longer. He stormed past the lawyer and into the bedroom. The contract was laid out on a small side table and he went and stood over it, doing his best to look like he was seeing it for the first time.

"Well," Fritz said from behind him. "Is it your signature?"

Of course it was, but could he tell them that? Could he explain what life had been like for them those years ago? How desperate they'd been when they lost the house? That they had no way to make a living? Could he explain to them that back then he would've signed anything Markham put in front of him if it meant a little money in his pocket? No, he couldn't, and he wouldn't. It would mean nothing to them. These were not men who dealt in real life. They dealt in contracts, in fine print and stipulations. When he turned to face them they were all standing in the doorway, the lawyers huddled in the background. Carol Jean and Moira had not left the sitting area, as if they both already knew the outcome.

"You sons of bitches," he said, to all of them. "How much will we owe?"

"There will have to be a legal proceeding," one of Markham's lawyers said. "Ultimately, it will be up to a judge. But, given the circumstances, we feel justified in petitioning for approximately eighty-five percent of your earnings from the wrestling match, plus a share of the wages you incurred working for Mr. Mundt and Mr. Stettler in recent months."

Pepper ignored him, closing in on Markham again. The carnival barker looked like he wanted to suck his fat face all the way into his neck to get away, but he stood his ground.

"This is you all over," Pepper said. "You show up after all this time, shouting accusations and waving your papers. You never saw a headline you didn't want to steal, did you?"

"I'm sure I don't know what you mean," Markham said.

"This woman," Pepper said, pointing at Carol Jean. "Hasn't she been through enough? You've got the contract and she means nothing to you. But you couldn't resist playing yourself off as the hero, could you? What is she? Your insurance policy? Make a big stink in the papers so O'Shea can't sic his goons on you? Sing a song looking for sympathy so I won't try to drag this out?"

From the way Markham's grin flickered across his face, Pepper knew he was right. "Drag it out?" Markham said, again sounding like they were two friends just shooting the breeze. "Pepper, we're just talking about the worst thing that could happen here. Really, there's no need for judges or courtrooms or a messy altercation in the press. As I was saying, I'm certain we can come to terms on a one-time lump-sum payment to settle this matter before the end of the weekend."

"Yeah?" Pepper said. "This ought to be good. How much?"

Markham made a show of collecting himself, rocking back on his heels and standing up straight. "Seventy-five percent," he said.

"I'll tell you what's going to happen," Pepper said. "I'm going to murder you. I'm going to kill you and I'm going to drag your fat body out where no one will ever—"

"Mr. Van Dean"—this was one of the lawyers again—"I assure you, sir, your threats of physical violence—witnessed here by each of us—are not helping your case."

"You and I both know that contract is very real," Markham added.

Pepper said it seemed like they had very different definitions of what that word meant. He said if Markham felt, by some twisted bastardization of the truth, that he and Moira somehow owed him more than the five years of their lives they'd already given him, he was free to file suit in court. They would meet his challenge with everything they had, he said, and if Markham was that kind of man, they would let a judge decide what everyone was owed.

"Seventy-five percent, eighty-five, whatever," Pepper said. "But it'll be slow going, and you won't get a dime from me until the agents show up to take it straight out of my hands."

As he was talking, they all stood around looking at him. Moira had gone to stand by the suite's main door, looking as white as death. Near the end of his speech, Markham's other lawyer came and leaned one shoulder against the wall behind the carnival barker. He had his hands in the pockets of his slacks and a smug look on his face that made Pepper want to squeeze his neck until his eyeballs popped out.

"Frankly," the lawyer said. "If that's the route you want to take, we may ask for all of it."

35

As soon as they got back to their room, Moira sank onto the love seat and tried to massage the ache out of her jaw. She felt shaky and ill, as if she hadn't eaten, even though she and Pepper had wolfed down a big room service lunch just before the press conference. The fact that she'd been expecting something like this all along had done little to prepare her for the moment Boyd Markham came through the crowd with Carol Jean at his heels. After her encounter with them in the promoter's suite, she wasn't sure if she wanted to slap Carol Jean's face or lend her a hanky.

She didn't have any time to dwell on it, as Fritz and Billy Stettler barged into the room before she and Pepper could get settled. Both men were still wearing their press conference suits, but Fritz looked shrunken and tired inside his. Stettler moved around the room with the hectic buzz of a drug user. He was a strange-looking fellow, with artificially colored hair and the puffed-up body of a man who had nothing better to do than exercise.

"We'll have to get our own account of it in tomorrow's papers," Stettler was saying, moving to one side of the room to examine a painting hanging over the bed.

"This changes nothing, of course," Fritz said. He'd lingered behind in the doorway, propping one hand on a little table like he was afraid he might keel over. "We still have our agreements, which everyone must continue to honor. Forge ahead and let the courts sort it out later, that's what I say."

"Or just pay Markham out from your end and be done with it," Stettler said to Pepper, who was sitting on the opposite corner of the bed, hands on knees.

Fritz looked surprised by Stettler's suggestion, but then he nodded. "That's right," he said. "I hate to sound callous, but this situation has very little to do with any of us."

"Far be it from you to sound callous, Freddy," Moira said.

"What I want to know," Pepper said, half quiet like he was talking to himself, "is how he managed to get in her ear."

They all suddenly turned to Moira, and the surprise of it made her sit up straight. Up to that point the men had all but ignored her, as if she had no real part to play in their drama. Now, as their eyes all fell on her, she was angry. Did they think she was Carol Jean's keeper? In addition to consoling the poor woman, was she supposed to have her on a leash? Guard her against salesmen, bill collectors and the odd carnival owner who might come out of the woodwork trying to bilk her?

"I'm sure I don't know," she said, and it seemed to satisfy them, even though as she said it the pieces were falling into place in her mind. That morning, when Carol Jean hadn't answered her knock, Moira had just assumed she must have wandered down to the restaurant. Late the night before she'd stopped by to find her in unexpectedly high spirits. She'd put on fresh clothes and was drifting around, inspecting the furnishings, offering to pour drinks, just as she would have done on any late night at the hunting camp. There was still sadness in her eyes, but at least she was back among the world of the living. When Moira commented on it, Carol Jean flashed a funny, embarrassed smile and said she knew things were going to work out. In the moment Moira took it for good news. Now she wondered if her instincts were slipping.

Stettler had walked over to where Pepper was sitting. "You sure about all this?" he said. "It's not too late to go back to the original plan. We do that? It makes everybody a lot happier. Maybe we can work something out, find a way to get you paid off the books in a way that fat fuck can't touch."

A look of hope passed across Pepper's face. "You would do that?"

Stettler grinned and Moira nearly laughed to see how straight and white his teeth looked. Like a row of marble gravestones in his mouth. "Sure we would, Pepper," he said, her husband's name ringing artificial in his voice. "We'd do practically anything if we thought it would get you on board with us long-term. Wouldn't we, Fritzie?"

"By all means," Fritz said, though he hadn't moved from his spot.

Pepper shook his head, chasing away a pleasant dream. "You heard Markham," he said. "The non-compete runs two years. You could pay me under the table that long?"

Stettler shrugged, turning his palms at his sides as if to say, *Why not?*

Moira stood up. She put her hand on Pepper's shoulder. "It won't work," she said. "If Boyd Markham thinks he's owed that money, he won't rest until he gets it. Lawyers, Pinkertons—he knows just as many unsavories as your man O'Shea, I assure you. You really want people like that constantly sniffing around your new scam?"

Stettler looked annoyed, like she wasn't supposed to know about their plans, but Moira didn't care. Pepper had told her of Stettler's idea to fix the wrestling business the morning after they'd arrived in the city. He'd also informed her, in a matter-of-fact way, that he'd cut a side deal with Stanislaw Lesko to have their match be on the level. At the time, she'd done her best to smile at him and say she thought it was the right move, though she worried for him. It had been so long since he'd been in a real wrestling ring, and Lesko was so much bigger. But if Markham's contract was genuine and things were spoiled anyway, she was glad he would get his chance and was happy to see how dismayed it made the other men. It made her skin crawl to think of them getting duped into a long-term deal with Stettler, Mundt and O'Shea. Like a return to the carnival circuit, with more comfortable beds.

"Maybe our best bet is to get through the weekend," Fritz said, "and sort the rest out later."

Pepper shook his head again. His voice was suddenly grave, almost apologetic. A tone she seldom heard him use. "I know you fellows don't like it," he said, "but I'm going to wrestle Stan Lesko in a square match on Saturday night. It's what Lesko and I both want. If Boyd Markham has got me over a barrel and there's nothing we can do to change that, then so be it."

Stettler was nearing the end of his rope. "You'd wrestle Lesko nearly for free?" he said.

"This time," Pepper said. "After I'm the world's heavyweight champion, perhaps we can restructure our agreement."

The promoter's smile returned—those huge teeth—as if he'd just remembered he was talking with a crazy man. "That sounds like our cue to leave," he said.

⚬——⚬

Moira was worried Pepper would stay up all night, pacing a gully into the rug at the foot of the bed, but after they'd shared a meal of dry, flaky roast beef sandwiches and oily au jus— terrible, considering the price—he crashed into one of his dead-to-the-world sleeps on top of the bedspread, his shoes still on. She sat smoking in a lounger on the opposite side of the room, hoping he was dreaming about revenge.

He looked small and vulnerable on the big hotel bed, his ankles pressed together and his knees tucked almost to his waist. His hands occasionally fretted around his face, but otherwise he was at peace, his breathing barely audible as the hotel slammed and gurgled around them. Public spaces like this never settled all the way down, no matter what the hour. Doors crashed open and shut, pipes groaned in the walls. People shouted merrily to each other in the halls: old friends parting at the end of the night, traveling salesmen announcing they'd see each other at breakfast. A thousand strangers meeting to spend a single night under the same roof and in the morning scattering out into the world.

His face lost its edge as he slept, the nervous lines of his forehead going slack, his lips relaxing into a pout. It was the face of the man she had married, the one who was still out to make the whole world say uncle. She imagined this was what he must have looked like as a boy, before first his father and then the orphanage pounded him into something harsher. One of the things she loved about him was that he was never afraid, but sometimes she enjoyed watching him rest. The way he slept was part of how he lived, fighting and scratching against everything, as hard and as long as he could until he finally collapsed, exhausted and a million miles deep.

When her cigarette was finished she gathered what she needed and quietly left the room. It was late in the evening, but not so late that a man like Dion O'Shea wouldn't still be up. Even so, there was a moment of quiet surprise inside when she rapped on the door to O'Shea's suite, trying to make her knocks sound even and confident. The scowling thug who answered had eyebrows that nearly grew up into his widow's peak. He looked like he was about to close the door in her face when O'Shea himself appeared at his shoulder and insisted that she come in at once.

He'd been with the rest in Stettler's room earlier that day, but this was her first time seeing the gangster up close. He was of unremarkable proportions, dressed neatly in a brown suit and a maroon polka-dot bow tie. His wispy hair was combed to one side and his round, sagging face reminded her of a frog. Brushing aside thoughts of how badly she'd missed the signs of Carol Jean's betrayal with Markham, she hoped O'Shea would be as easy to read as his friend James Eddy.

She made herself appear cool as she walked in and declined his offer of a drink. The way his hands fussed at his sides when she said no made her think he wanted one himself, but he left the bottle on the side table. He brought her into the suite's small sitting area, where the chairs were sturdier and done of finer woodwork than the stuff in their room. The man who'd answered the door sat a good distance behind her in a leather armchair, where she could hear the material squeaking under his weight. Having an audience gave the meeting a weird, staged feel, but she pretended not to mind. The important thing was to sell it, she knew, and so she needed to be calm and matter-of-fact. Just a person doing a favor for a man who she hoped could be her friend.

When she set the papers facedown on the table it was with the sure, captivating poise of her father. Since she'd come in, O'Shea had been chattering nonstop, saying how interesting it was to be working with her husband again, a note of irony flashing in his voice. He told her he was starting to know the Van Dean family as people who showed up at all hours when they had something important to say. He liked that, he said, he really did. As they were getting settled in their chairs he asked her if she was excited for the match.

"I've always been a man of sport," he said. "A good fight, a fine wrestling match—there's just something exhilarating about it, don't you agree?"

She smiled at him, batted her eyes a little bit and said, "No, sir. I daresay I'm less excited for it than almost anything in my life."

He grinned in response, and she could tell he liked her, maybe thought she was pretty. He said he was sorry to hear about the death of Garfield Taft. He had always been intrigued by the Negro and had been hoping to see him give Stanislaw Lesko a test, even if Billy Stettler insisted that Lesko emerge the winner in the end. O'Shea said Stettler was angry now that Pepper had refused to take part in the fix and had foiled his plans to place bets on the match, but— leaning forward as if sharing a secret—O'Shea said he honestly didn't mind. In fact, he was interested in seeing her husband take on Lesko in a square match.

She nodded, encouraged by his openness. She hadn't expected him to play it that way, but it was a good thing.

"And now this Markham fellow," he said, rattling on, almost like he'd been waiting for someone he could tell about it, "a great, fat slob of a man, eh? I hope he doesn't make too much trouble for you all."

She took a deep breath, knowing it was time. Telling herself that every nickel poker table and backroom betting circle she'd ever taken part in had been leading her to this moment. The time for being scared had passed. She was here now, sitting with him, with the papers on the table. Second thoughts would only undermine her play. She was a gambler and it was time to gamble.

"That's precisely why I'm here," she said. "I've come across a piece of information I feel might be helpful to you."

O'Shea's eyes darted to the man behind her, as quick as a wrestler's hand feint. He was on his guard now, though you couldn't tell it from the friendly way he said: "Information?"

"While we were still in Montana," she said, "I discovered something that could mean your other venture there is in danger."

"Danger?" he said. "Other venture?"

Jesus, she hoped he wasn't going to keep talking like that. "Yes," she said. "I have reason to think the man you left behind there to guard your interests actually intends to do you harm."

O'Shea fiddled with his ear. "What is this about?" he said. "It's too late at night to listen to nonsense. If you mean Jimmy Eddy, you should know you're talking about a man I've known my whole life."

"Be that as it may," she said, "I believe Mr. Eddy intends to rob you and sell off the liquor you have stockpiled there for his own profit."

O'Shea laughed, a strange slapping laugh that ended with him wheezing and coughing into his fist. The man behind her laughed, too, and when O'Shea had recovered there was a small, hard light in his eyes that hadn't been there before. "That's a very serious thing to say," he said. "You shouldn't say things like that to a man like me unless you are very, very sure you're right."

"I'm sure," she said, hearing her own voice clear and self-assured, watching him as it sank in. O'Shea's eyes fell on the documents and suddenly she could feel the texture of the paper under her fingertips.

"What have you got there?" he said.

"I'm not going to show you," she said. "Not without your assurance that it's worth something to you."

She flinched when he moved, thinking he was going to snatch the papers from her grasp. Instead, he just crossed his legs. "I see," he said, like somebody had explained a joke to him. "Mrs. Van Dean is here to shake us down, Francis."

The leather groaned as the third man shifted in his seat, though all he said was, "Yeah?"

Another little bubble of panic inside her. "No," she said, too fast. "It's not that at all. It's just that in light of recent events, the reemergence of Mr. Markham, I've realized a few things about my situation."

"Realized what?" O'Shea said. "That your husband isn't the world's greatest future planner?"

She closed her eyes, reset herself and opened them. "All that booze sitting in that barn," she said, "what do you suppose that's worth? A hundred thousand dollars? More? If I can show you that it's in jeopardy, I'll want two things from you."

O'Shea sighed. "It's not in any jeopardy," he said. "In fact, I just assigned another man out there to help keep watch on it."

She remembered Fritz mentioning the same thing the day they left Montana. Quickly, her mind spun back through the night she'd encountered the Canadian bootleggers in the road. What could she say that would throw O'Shea off his game? She decided to play a bluff. "Ah," she said, "you must mean our young Mr. Templeton. Do you think he's up to the challenge, if Mr. Eddy is really planning to betray you?"

At the mention of Templeton's name, O'Shea dropped his shoulders, tugging on his ear again. It was twice he'd done that, and now he didn't seem so sure of himself. He was trying to figure out how she'd known that. "Show me," he said, nodding at the papers.

"Not yet," she said. "Not until you agree to my terms. I came here as a person with needs. I think the information I have to trade is of considerable value. If it turns out you agree with me, I want twenty thousand dollars."

He repeated the sum back to her as if he couldn't believe it. "Why don't I just take those papers and give you nothing?"

"You could absolutely do that," she said. "But you said yourself you're a man of sport, and that wouldn't be very sporting."

He didn't find any humor in that. "Fine," he said. "If what you've got there is enough to make me believe one of my closest associates has turned on me, I'll pay you. If not, then I'm going to have Francis break one of your legs. How does that sound?"

Her mouth was very dry, the backs of her teeth rough against the tip of her tongue. She flipped over the first half of the papers and slid the pile across the small table. It was the receipt showing that Eddy had put down a deposit on a property outside of Los Angeles. O'Shea reached for them quickly, their fingers briefly touching, and then his face darkened as he scanned through the documents.

"Now," she said. "What would James Eddy want with a house in California? Does that make sense to you?"

"What?" he said, distracted. "This is nothing. This doesn't prove anything."

"With all due respect, sir," Moira said, "I spent the last few months living in Montana like some kind of lumberjack, while you've been getting your information at some remove. Mostly, I assume, from James Eddy. I know Eddy was angry you sent him there, I know he hates the Canadian men who bring the liquor across the border, and I know you have a shipment being brought in tomorrow. You tell me who knows more about what's going on there."

Mentioning the next shipment of booze tore his attention away from the papers. One of the dates she'd noticed marked on the desk calendar in Eddy's room was the next night. Some color was starting to show in O'Shea's face.

"How do you know all this?" he said.

"I'd rather not say," she said. "Just know my information is valid."

"What else have you got there?"

She shook her head, just one little nod. "Do you agree to my terms?"

"Jesus," he said, aggravated now. "Will it mean something to you if I say I do? I could easily be lying."

"You won't be."

"How could you know that?"

"A man in your position understands the value of his word," she said. "If you didn't, you wouldn't be here right now. You'd probably already be dead."

She could see her words had an effect on him. "Fine," he said. "I accept. But if what you have there isn't very, very convincing I can guarantee with equal certainty you won't walk out of this room."

She slid the letter she'd gotten from Eleanor across the table facedown. Her last hole card. O'Shea turned it over and read it. Then he picked it up off the table and read it again. A small, almost imperceptible tremor in his hands. When he spoke it was to his man. "Francis," he said. "Telephone Canada. Tell them I need to speak with them right away."

Moira turned in her seat so she could see Francis. He was looking at his watch. "Is there time?" he said. "I know we have a couple hours on them, but—"

"Go!" said O'Shea, slapping his free hand on the table.

As Francis hurried from the room, O'Shea settled back into his seat, the documents lying askew on the table in front of him. "I hope you're not wasting my time," he said to her. "Jimmy is my oldest friend."

"I know," she said. "That's probably why he thinks he'll get away with it."

He sighed. "You're making me angry," he said. "I think you should go."

"What about the money?" she said.

"Mrs. Van Dean," he said carefully. "I'm not an unreasonable man, but it's late, I'm tired, and now I'm not going to sleep. When I say you should go, you must know that's really the best course of action for you."

She'd brought along her handbag and picked it off the floor as she stood up. "Wait," he said, his voice not quite as icy. "You said you wanted two things. What else is there?"

She turned to face him. "Five years ago my husband lost the world's lightweight title to a man named Whip Windham," she said. "He wrestled the match with a broken leg and then never wrestled professionally again. I'd like you to tell me what you know about it."

O'Shea looked exhausted, but he had enough left in him to offer a sad little lift of the eyebrows. "What do *you* know about it?" he said.

It gave her a sick and slippery feeling, but she sat down again and told him the story as she knew it. That a promoter or someone had paid Fritz Mundt to injure Pepper during training before the match against Windham. That Pepper had wrestled with a spiral fracture in his leg and still put up a good fight before he was finally pinned and beaten. After that Pepper's leg had never quite been right again and no promoter would give him a shot at a comeback.

When she was finished, O'Shea sat eyeing her in a way she didn't like.

"And you know this how?" he asked.

"Everyone knows it," she said. "No one would come out and say it, but there were whispers."

"Whispers?" O'Shea said.

"That's right," she said. "Whispers that Fritz Mundt got paid five thousand dollars to break his leg with a toehold during a workout."

O'Shea held up a finger. "Aha," he said. "See what you said there? He got paid five thousand dollars. Nobody said who paid him."

She felt like a pit was opening on the path in front of her, but that she was powerless to do anything but press forward. "It was Blomfeld," she said, "or it was you. Who else could it be?"

O'Shea sat forward, folding his hands on the table. "Would it surprise you to learn," he said, "that once upon a time a certain former lightweight wrestling champion of the world found himself unable to pay some substantial debts he'd accrued to some very serious people? And that as a way to be forgiven for those debts, he was offered the simple solution of losing his title to a heavy underdog, in a time and place chosen by his creditors?"

"That's a lie," she said, feeling the pit growing in size and herself now stumbling toward it. "We had no debts when Pepper was champion. We had everything we could ever want."

He pressed on: "Would it further surprise you to learn that this former lightweight wrestling champion of the world, a hardheaded little fool if there ever was one, categorically refused to take part in such a solution, as easy as it would have been?"

"Of course not," she said. "Pepper would never lose a wrestling match on purpose, no matter what the stakes."

"That he relented only when these people, these very serious people, threatened to do some very serious things to his equally hardheaded and infuriating little wife?"

She swallowed, searching for a retort.

"That even then," O'Shea said, "the champion refused on principle to take part in a fixed match, but offered to take on this man Windham under tremendously disadvantageous circumstances? That the champion's creditors agreed to go along only because the circumstances made any other outcome impossible and the champion agreed to foot the bill for services rendered?"

"You're saying it was Pepper's idea to have Fritz break his leg?"

O'Shea nodded. "And your husband paid him out after collecting on a substantial wager he'd made against himself beforehand. How do you think the people in charge felt about that? The creditors, I mean. The serious people."

"Well, it's nonsense to begin with," she said. "But if it did happen, I suppose they would be happy they got what they wanted."

"Happy?" O'Shea said. "My dear, it scared the shit out of us. A man who would *pay* to have that done, to *himself*? We couldn't believe it. A man like that is capable of anything. A man like that is totally impossible to control."

"It's ridiculous," she said. "Why would he need to take out a loan from a bunch of gangsters when we had more money than we could spend?"

"That sounds like a topic you'll have to take up with the former lightweight wrestling champion of the world," he said. "All I can tell you is, there were *whispers* that his wife liked to gamble."

The door opened and the man called Francis stuck his head in. "I've got them for you," he said.

O'Shea nodded and made a solemn little stack out of the papers Moira had brought with her. She thought he might say something else to her, but suddenly he didn't seem to want to look at her anymore. He looked only at the papers. "I'll be right there," he said as he stood up.

3G

More than once as he sat cross-legged in the failing light of the day, his back pressed against the sticky trunk of a wide pine, Eddy asked himself what he was doing. The place he'd found to hide was seventy-five yards uphill from the hunting camp, at the fringe of a thick grove of ponderosa between the lodge and the horse barn. He sat half obscured by a tangle of fallen logs, invisible to anyone coming or going on the road. It was a good spot, and ever since he'd found it while hiking the hills around the camp weeks earlier, he hadn't been able to get it out of his mind.

Snow was coming down, and it might have been beautiful if it weren't so cold. From this position everything looked just as he'd mapped it out. He'd brought along two blankets: one of them folded under his ass, the other laid out on the ground as if for a picnic. Still, the chill crept through the folds of wool, into his legs and up his spine.

He had almost decided to call the whole thing off when he'd finally heard back from John Torrio. The Italian's note arrived a couple of weeks earlier, scrawled in a child's hand on a piece of cheap card stock. The tone of the short, crude message didn't exactly convey an outpouring of enthusiasm, but Torrio said if what Eddy was proposing was on the level, he would send some men to Montana to check it out. Eddy had driven into town to meet with them the night before and found them to be nearly as awful as the Canadians. Just a bunch of amateurs hiding their fear inside cheap suits and loud talking. They didn't want any part of the shooting, naturally, but said if Eddy had liquor to sell, they were buying. The sight of them almost convinced him to change his mind once and for all. Then they'd opened a big, double-locking attaché case and showed him the money.

That morning he'd slipped out of his room before dawn and strangled Wes Templeton in his bed. There was no going back now.

Eddy's original plan had been much cleaner, with more maneuvering and less cowboys-and-Indians stuff. He would simply wait for the Canadians to deliver the booze, suffer through a few final hours with them before they headed back across the border and then carry out the rest of the plan at his leisure. O'Shea had fouled it all up with his bright idea to send Templeton to Montana. Templeton, who packed as many trunks and bags as a woman, one of his satchels full of nothing but books. Templeton, who liked to sit by the window in the parlor reading and making inane comments about passages he found amusing. Sometimes reading them aloud and then looking at Eddy over the tops of his glasses like Eddy was supposed to have something smart to say back. The man's very presence there had been an insult, to his intelligence and to his pride.

Now Templeton was dead and he was on to plan B.

It gave him a quivering feeling to change things at the last minute, but now that Templeton was gone, most of Eddy's original planning was spoiled. He couldn't very well let the Canadians drive all the way to the hunting camp and unload the booze as normal—especially if they ran late, like they were doing now, and had to spend the night again. They would expect to see Templeton there, and every question they asked about his absence would compound the likelihood that Eddy would slip up and tip them off somehow. Luckily he had this location as a fallback. Proper preparation, he liked to call it. If there had to be violence, it was going to be violence on his terms, in a situation that he controlled.

Before his meeting with the Italians he'd made a couple of calls to verify the legitimacy of the Frank & Livermore real estate company. A week earlier, he'd bought himself a ticket on an overnight train to the coast. In Portland, Oregon, he planned to buy a car to drive south to Los Angeles and had spent a couple of evenings memorizing a road map he bought at a local filling station.

He could feel the promise of California glowing in his chest like a hot lump of coal. He had no idea what he would do when he got there—and the prospect of having no plan made him feel frayed around the edges—but he kept reminding himself that he didn't have to stay if it turned out Los Angeles wasn't right for him. There were plenty of out-of-the-way places a man like him could find work. O'Shea fancied himself a king of sorts, but the truth was he didn't have much reach outside of the midwest and a few friends in New York. Since the day he had returned from Howard Livermore's rooming house, he had not disturbed the papers from their hiding place in the bottom drawer of his desk. He thought of them often but was still too worried about the possibility of germs to take them out and hold them in his hands. When this was over, he would have to risk it, heading back to the lodge to retrieve them along with the last of his things.

One of Eddy's main worries had been the hired girl. He thought she might make a stink when he let her go the same day the rest of them left for the wrestling match. Closing up shop, he'd told her, and when he gave her a cash bonus to thank her for her service, the only question she asked was whether she could take some of the housewares to sell in town. Eddy told her that was fine.

He'd brought along a sandwich wrapped in wax paper, but it had taken him longer than he'd planned to bury Templeton, so he was saving it for after. Templeton was a big man and it had been a job just getting him down the stairs and out the back door. The ground was frozen so solid that he had to spend an hour going after it with an old, dull axe before he could make any headway with his shovel. The grave he dug was slim and shallow but far enough into the trees that it probably wouldn't be discovered. Even if someone happened across it, he'd have to know what he was looking for to notice it. It was hard work and Eddy had thought of quitting, but he wanted to leave no trace of Templeton. Anything to muddy the waters for the men O'Shea would send looking for him. He liked to think Dion would come himself. His old friend hadn't given him much attention these past few years, but by the end of the day Eddy expected to have his full, undivided.

This was what he was thinking about, tucked away in his nest, when he heard the low rumble of engines coming up the road. Crawling forward on his stomach, he pressed the butt of the rifle to his shoulder and closed his eyes, taking a slow, deep breath to steady his hands. When he opened them and sat staring over his sights at the empty road, two things occurred to him. First, no matter how this day turned out, it would be a relief to finally be done with it all— done with Montana, the isolation of the hunting camp and all the ridiculous men he was supposed to watch over there. He was looking forward to putting it behind him.

Second, he was starving.

Knowing there was no one out there to catch them, the Canadians came over the hill with headlights blazing. There would be six of them: two riding in the covered flatbed truck full of crates, and four behind in a touring sedan. The magazine in his rifle held six shells, and he had an extra lying on the ground at his side, but their numbers meant he couldn't afford to miss. If he had to stop to reload while any of the Canadians were still alive and possessing working limbs, there was a high probability he could lose them in the woods.

The convoy slowed to a stop just after the truck and sedan

lumbered across the small wooden bridge that stood over a low, iced-over stream. This was a surprise. The truck was still about fifty yards from where Eddy planned for it to be. He'd thought the Canadians would pull all the way up to the horse barn to unload their cargo as normal. Instead they just sat there, headlamps blaring, both machines idling. What were they doing? Did they sense something was different about the camp, the lodge standing dark and still? Had they been spooked when they saw no one had come out to meet them?

Eddy could feel something ticking in his mind like a stopwatch. From this angle, he could see the driver of the truck but not the man riding in the passenger seat. He didn't have a shot. *Drive on,* he whispered to himself. *Drive on like you always do.* Finally, after a minute of no movement at all, the driver of the truck leaned out the window and yelled something to the men in the car, his words garbled on the breeze. The four of them got out and scrambled forward, holding long guns at their waists, their heads scanning side to side as if looking for enemies.

Eddy relaxed his finger on the trigger. As quickly as he could, he reviewed his options. He could abort his plan and slip away through the woods, but he could not go back to the hunting camp for his train ticket or his proof of deposit on the property in California. At least, not while the Canadians were there, and with him and Templeton both suddenly gone without explanation, there was no telling how long they would stay. He didn't like the idea of hiking through the cold all the way to town, especially with no money and no prospects. Plus, the Italians were there now, waiting at their rooming house for him to drive in and give them the all clear.

No, he could still make this work. He just needed to take good shots. His finger touched the cold metal of the trigger again. The Canadians were moving up the road carefully, but they were clearly men with no formal training. They were grouped too tightly together and walked standing at full height, like a family of prairie dogs on alert. When they got to the front of the truck they paused in the ghostly glow of the headlamps, and Eddy dropped them where they stood.

Shot. Lever, lever, shot. Lever, lever, shot. Lever, lever, shot.

In the war he'd met British riflemen who could crank out thirty shots from their Enfields in under a minute. Eddy was not quite that fast, but killing the first four men took less than twelve seconds, and before the last body hit the ground he was sighting in on the men inside the truck. He could see only the driver, who was in a panic, terrified by the sudden booming reports of the rifle and the sight of his escorts falling dead. Eddy knew the man couldn't see him, not in the dark with the hill and trees behind him. The way the reports had deflected off the flat rear side of the lodge, he probably didn't even know which direction the shots had come from. The truck lurched as the driver cranked it into reverse, but he only managed to crash into the sedan, pushing it back against one side of the narrow bridge, boxing him in.

Just as Eddy loosed his fifth shot, the truck jumped forward and stalled. Sparks flew from the roof as his bullet ricocheted high of its target. He cursed under his breath, and as the driver opened the door to clamber out he shot again. The driver was moving, so this shot was also not quite as true as the first four. The bullet caught him in the throat and rocked his head back against the metal of the truck cab before he fell, one hand clawing at the black blood flooding from the wound. The other hand struggling to pull a pistol from his belt. Eddy left him that way and ejected the rifle's magazine, fitting the extra in its place as he tried to sight in on the last man, the passenger, who would still be in the cab of the truck. The man must've crawled across the seat and pulled the driver's door shut and was now out of sight. Eddy cursed. He'd expected that in his terror he would also try to run, but now the man was hunkered down on the floorboards of the truck, maybe with a gun in his hands, maybe not.

After another minute of watching, Eddy started down the hill in a crouch. He didn't like leaving his nest but saw no other way to finish the job. Keeping his eyes on the truck and holding the rifle at chest level, he quickly but carefully covered the distance to the wash at the side of the road. The truck driver was still trying to die with his revolver in his hand, his elbow propped against the ground and the barrel pointing straight into the sky. When Eddy got close enough, he threw the rifle over his back, pulled out his own pistol and shot the man in the head.

He was stiff from sitting so long in the cold, but the climb down the hill had at least got the blood moving in his legs. Crouching behind the front wheel of the sedan, he called for the man in the cab of the truck to throw down his weapon. His ears rang from the boom of the shots, making his voice sound strange and hollow. He was irritated with himself for not bringing cotton to plug them. He got no reply from the man in the truck, and as he sat there in the buzzing silence he started to feel a tickle at the back of his neck. What had he forgotten? What had he missed? What did the Canadians know tonight as they approached the camp? Nothing, he told himself, it was all going perfectly. It was all going exactly as he'd drawn it up.

Odds were the man still in the truck only had a handgun. Anyway, if he had a rifle or a shotgun, it would be clumsy and awkward at such close range. That might give Eddy the advantage. His biggest worry at the moment was time. Eddy didn't want to hang around out in the open any longer than he had to after all that shooting, all that racket. Chances were that no one was around for miles, but chance was something Eddy liked to avoid. Just in case some farmer or hunting party had heard the noise and decided to come investigate, he planned to be long gone before they arrived.

Quickly he made a checklist in his mind of the things he still needed to do: He'd have to move fast to hike back up to his nest to collect his blankets, then back to the road to pick up the dead men's guns. Earlier he'd planned to load the bodies into the sedan and run it off the road, but now decided against it.

He needed to move.

To hell with it, he thought. He took the Enfield off his back and leaned it against the side of the sedan. Creeping forward, moving deliberately over the frozen turf, he rapped the butt of his pistol against the truck's passenger-side door. Still he got no response. His pistol ready in his right hand, he used his left to reach up and yank the door handle. To his surprise, it opened easily. As it did, he swung around to face the cab, bringing his gun up and clearing it over the top of the seats.

The truck was empty.

Eddy dropped back to his crouch and turned to look up and down the road. Was it possible the man in the truck had slipped out and run into the woods while he was on the move? No, he was sure no one had gotten out of the truck; he'd kept his eyes on it the whole way. Still, the Canadians always sent six men. Why had they changed their methods for this trip?

He sat there in the stillness until his anxiety had subsided. Nothing but the breeze moved through the trees around him, and there was no sound but his own breathing and the ringing in his ears. Five men, he thought, feeling a small wave of pride at the number. It was the most he'd killed since Amiens. For a man who knew his way around a rifle, there was simply no substitute for a hidden position in the high ground.

He had only fired one shell from his pistol, but he reminded himself to reload it when he got back to the lodge. It was still a couple hours before the Italians were expecting him, and even if they were nothing more than small-timers, he'd rather greet them with a fully loaded weapon, just to be safe.

He was about to make the hike back up to his nest when a queer sensation came over him. Something wasn't right. He'd overseen the Canadians bringing shipments in for nearly a year and they had never used fewer than six men, never stopped the truck near the bridge and sent armed men up the hill to check things out. They had never deviated from the plan. Eddy didn't believe in coincidence, and even if he did, it would be a lot to swallow that this load of all loads was the one where the Canadians changed their methods.

Unless.

Suddenly thinking of snipers, he scanned the hills above him for movement or the glint of metal against rock. Impossible, he decided. As if to prove it to himself, he stood up, pistol hanging at his side, and stepped away from the truck and into the open. Nothing happened, just a wind stiff enough to make him suck his chin into his chest to avoid losing his hat. Still, the feeling that something was wrong nagged at him. He looked at the sedan, sitting in the road like a giant insect from dinosaur times. Going back to the driver's side of the truck, he switched off the motor and pocketed the keys. Resting his hand on the hood, he listened to the engine tick and stared for a minute at the empty cab. There had never been a second man up there.

Five men, not six. It made no sense. Turning on his heel, he walked to the back of the truck, running his fingers along the rough canvas tarp that held the load. He squatted, his knees creaking, and undid the knot that held the tarp to the truck's rear bumper. As he did, an eerie feeling rose up the back of his skull until it felt like a hot water bottle sitting underneath his hat.

When he threw back the tarp, the first thing he noticed was the empty bottles, that this truck hauled nothing more than a dummy load of open crates and rattling glass.

Then he saw the Canadian. It was the sour-smelling, dog-faced man he'd threatened that night in the road with Mrs. Van Dean. The crates were stacked around the outside of the flatbed to create a hidden dead space in the middle, and he was crouched there, wearing a winter hat, a blanket wrapped around his shoulders. His eyes were full of fear, but the mouth of the pistol he held in one outstretched hand yawned wide and bottomless.

Eddy dove to one side, and the dog-faced man's first shot hit him in the elbow. Even in his astonishment, he noticed that it didn't really hurt any worse than a blow from a nightstick, though the force of it spun him in midair and sent his own gun clattering into the underbrush. He landed on his back on the cold ground, his hat tumbling off. As he rolled toward the driver's side of the truck, his mind whirring, he knew at once that the Italians must've betrayed him. They were the only ones who knew his plan. They must've settled with O'Shea for more money than he'd offered them. For that, he would find them and kill them all.

He rolled onto his stomach and, folding his tattered arm across his chest, began to crawl. Blood filled his shirtsleeve and his legs kicked involuntarily against the earth. Eddy had seen enough people shot to know his body was going into shock. He needed to move fast. The truck driver still held a pistol in one dead hand, and if Eddy could get to it before the dog-faced man got to him, he would be all right. He could shoot the man down, clear the road and make his escape. He could still get out of this, if he didn't bleed to death first. Once he got back to the lodge, he would have to tourniquet the wound, maybe rig up a splint. Did he have any spare shirts? Had the hired girl taken his dry cleaning before he dismissed her? He suddenly didn't know. No matter, he could get some new clothes before he got to where he was going.

He cursed himself for having trusted those dagos in the first place. That was the problem with working with amateurs, he thought: You couldn't count on them. Maybe it was not worth it to try to hunt them down. Maybe he would just let them go, get out of town, get to California and get settled in his new place. He would have to stash the load of liquor someplace where it would be safe until he could come back for it.

He heard the sounds of the dog-faced man scrambling out of the bed of the truck, but it seemed to be coming from a long way off. He was almost to the truck driver, pulling himself along the ground with his one working arm. Who would buy the liquor now? Best leave that part of the planning for later, when he had a chance to sit down and work it all out. This was all starting to feel very complicated.

A faint, acrid smell filled his nostrils as he reached the truck driver's body, and it reminded him of blood and dirt and the stink of Chicago. He discovered he barely had the strength to wrest the gun from the dead man's hand, but he finally got it free. California would be warm and full of people. It would be a place where a man could sit and not have to worry about his mind running away with him. A place where a guy could get a decent cup of coffee and drink it at a table on the street. Read a newspaper and watch the world go by. What was it Livermore had said? California was for new beginnings? A second chapter? Something like that.

He was still trying to remember the exact words when he rolled over to find the dog-faced man standing over him, pointing the pistol at his face. The man must've been waiting there for a little while, a few seconds at least, watching him crawl along the ground. He was standing to one side, keeping out of the blood trail Eddy had left behind him in the snow. The sky at his back was nearly black and something had changed in his face. Eddy tried to raise the truck driver's gun but realized it had fallen out of his hand onto the ground. As the dog-faced man took a step closer, Eddy saw what was different about him. The man didn't look scared anymore.

37

For fifteen minutes, Pepper stood in his dank dressing room, staring up at a row of high, narrow windows. The room was just a concrete box with a couple of chairs, a rubdown table, and a rough wooden bench. His one remaining suit hung inside a crude locker. The windows were frosted glass and opened with a single pane that pulled inward. One of them stood slightly ajar, and outside he could see snow falling in the alley between Twenty-seventh and Madison. He was trying to decide, if he dragged a chair over and stood on it, whether he could squeeze through one of the slender openings and escape.

Behind him, Moira sat with her legs crossed at the knees, staring at her fingernails with the cold poker face she used to try to hide her fear. She'd been distant since Boyd Markham had returned, and Pepper knew he'd let her down. She'd been right about all of this, of course. Now, underneath her pretend boredom and the nerves of tonight, she was still waiting for him to apologize. He promised himself he would, just as soon as they were clear of all this mess.

"You're going to kill him," she said when she looked up. "You'll be the world's heavyweight champion and then we'll charge them a mint for the rematch."

"I know," he said, though it sounded like a lie.

It was always like this just before a match. No matter how much training he'd done or how prepared he'd convinced himself he was, suddenly the idea of walking out into a ballroom full of people and fighting another man in his underclothes filled him with unspeakable terror. As bell time drew nearer, every fiber of muscle in his body would be screaming to run. Just bolt, chuck it all, get out of there and never look back. It would be cowardly, yes, but shame was no match for what might happen to him if he actually went through with it and tried to wrestle Strangler Lesko.

He knew it would be deserted in the alley behind the arena, and he wanted to grab Moira and whisper to her that they could just go. If they made it through the window and out to the street in either direction, there would be cabs. He could hail one and take it to the train station. They would make an odd pair walking through Grand Central Terminal, Moira in her evening gown and him wearing only his purple cape, wrestling tights and boots, but he didn't care. *Let people stare,* he thought. *Anything to get out of here.*

His every instinct begged him to make a break for it, knowing he would do no such thing. His body hummed like a tuning fork. Skin prickling in the cool air, his fingers worrying the rough cut of the stitches at the hem of the cape. It was foolhardy to still be there, with Stettler, O'Shea, Markham and maybe even Fritz all scheming against them. He hadn't fully realized the ramifications of Markham's return until they'd met with the lawyers. It was too late to change course now. There was nothing to do but go through with it. He could hear the slow grinding of what looked like an old schoolhouse clock, but beyond the metal door were the sounds of the crowd filling up the arena above. It was all as it should've been, he told himself, all normal. If you didn't feel out of your mind with nerves just before a match, you'd already lost.

When the door to his dressing room cracked open and Fritz

stuck his head in, Pepper was almost glad to see him. Anything for a distraction.

"We'd like a word," Fritz said. He was not smiling.

"Now?"

Fritz stood aside to let Billy Stettler into the room before he locked the door behind them. Both were wearing their best suits and Stettler had his blue-black hair plastered hard to one side. He was patting his forehead with a houndstooth handkerchief, grinning at Pepper as he propped himself up on the high padded rubdown table.

"The granddaddy of them all," he said, spreading his arms to indicate he meant the Garden itself. "How do you like it?"

"It could use a coat of paint," Pepper said. "The dressing rooms are bigger at the Coliseum."

Stettler's smile was wax on his face as he picked an imaginary piece of lint off his shirt cuff and blew it into the air. "You're really starting to become one of the more tiresome people I've ever met, you know that?" he said.

Fritz had pulled off his jacket to drape it on a chair. "You say the word right now, we can go across the hall and square things with Lesko," he said. "We can start promoting Philadelphia tonight. It could be a new life for all of us."

"Once we walk out that door, you're on your own," Stettler added.

"We've been on our own this whole time," Moira said.

Stettler paid her the scarcest glance. "What I'm saying is, as of right now? This moment? We can all still be friends. But you tell us to go fuck ourselves now and it'll be the last time. We'll walk over there and tell Stan to take you apart limb by limb. I still think it seems like a fairly easy choice."

Pepper flashed back to the athletic tent, the exhibition of holds he performed nightly with Gun Boat Walters before the challenge matches began. The two of them working together to make it look good for the audience—the big man going easy with his weight, leaning into his throws and tackles so they would look effortless. In a way, working a fixed match with Lesko wouldn't be so different, he thought. He'd been a carnival huckster for so long, maybe there was no point in trying to make a stand now. Maybe it would be better if he just went along, shook hands with Stettler and Fritz, and let Lesko go out there and lie down for him.

He wondered suddenly where Taft was: if his body was still lying on a slab somewhere in some anonymous government building. If nobody claimed him, would they take him out to a potter's field and dump him in some unmarked grave? A small stab of guilt needled him when he thought of how Taft had gone through the motions for weeks in training, even though he must have been in tremendous pain and even after the last flicker of hope in him had been stomped out.

Pepper thought of Taft's words the night of their ski trip: *They're scared of me?* and when he looked at Stettler, he knew it was true. The stress was starting to show in the hollows beneath his eyes. Everything about him seemed pulled tight, like he was about to burst. Fritz, too, looked like a man who was down to his last roll of the dice. He almost laughed now to realize how right Taft had been. They were terrified. They knew Stanislaw Lesko was out of shape. They knew if the match was on the level, Pepper had a real chance to win. If he did, and refused to back their scheme, they had nothing. They would lose all control of the wrestling business. Their plan would be as dead as Pepper's career had been the night he lost the lightweight title to Whip Windham.

"Where's Markham?" Pepper said.

"Is that really what you're worried about right now?" Fritz said.

"I'm not worried about anything," Pepper snapped. "I just want to see him."

It turned out the carnival barker was just outside. He came into the dressing room glowing with confidence, giddy with the knowledge he'd schemed his way to victory. He shook all their hands brightly and even gave Moira a polite little bow. He'd gotten a fresh haircut and a manicure, maybe already living it up on credit from his future windfall. Carol Jean was not with him.

"The agreement was that I would get my money before the match," Pepper said, once they all were settled in the room.

"That's right," said Stettler, annoyed, but pulling his checkbook out of the inside pocket of his suit jacket.

"I want you to just make the check directly to Mr. Markham," Pepper said. Even Moira stopped staring at her fingers to look at him. "He's got me dead to rights and we all know it. I'm not going to fight him on this."

Markham seemed to grow an extra inch on hearing that. Pepper turned to face him. "This is why you came back, right?" he said. "This is why you tricked that poor woman. For money? Fine, fuck you, take it. But I want you to know that this is the only dime you'll ever get from us. You'll take this and then we'll never see you again. If you ever come sniffing around us again, I'll kill you with my bare hands."

As Pepper got close to him, Markham stepped back, tripping over a chair that was pushed against a wall. He tumbled to the floor, going down flat on his back, the wind knocked out of him, his lungs making the sound of water being dumped from a bucket all at once. Pepper turned away from him.

"I don't want to see him here when I get back," he said to Fritz and Stettler, and for once they all seemed to be on the same team.

"I think we can handle that," Fritz said.

As they helped Markham off the floor and guided him into the hall, Pepper did some warm-up exercises, bending at the waist to stretch his back and legs. He made big circles with his arms until he felt the heat in his shoulders and then stretched each one across his chest, the stress slowly working its way out of his muscles. His right leg clicked as he did a few deep knee bends, but he could live with it. He'd be fine, he told himself. He'd be great.

Stettler came back in and folded his arms across his chest. "Well?" he said.

Pepper was bouncing from foot to foot in front of the full-length mirror, but now he stopped. "You hear that?" he said. The clock on the wall groaned as the minute hand crawled one more tick toward the top of the hour. Underneath it was the murmuring sound of the crowd filing into the theater. "There's a crowd full of hardworking people up there who paid to see a fight. I think tonight your man Lesko and I will give them one they'll remember for quite a while."

Stettler started to speak, but stopped when a man Pepper had never seen before stepped into the room wearing the dark uniform of one of the Garden's ushers. He had the longest gray whiskers Pepper had ever seen. The man didn't smile or move or even seem to look at them at all. "Time to go," he said.

Pepper hugged Moira, the knowledge that she would be watching him cranking the vise a little tighter on his heart, but also making him feel buoyant, like his feet were barely touching the floor. She kissed him on the cheek.

"This is your moment," she said.

"I know," he said.

"The next time I see you, you'll be world's heavyweight champion," she said.

"I know," he said, pausing in the doorway to slap himself twice in the face as hard as he could.

The usher led him into the corridor, the way crowded with the debris of the arena. They passed a pair of old dressing tables sporting cracked mirrors and dead bulbs, heaps of discarded pipes, racks of empty seats and piles of costume clothing. He let the usher walk in front of him, turning sharply around a corner and going up a short flight of steps. The overhead lights here were old and shoddy, giving parts of the walk a weird, quivering feeling. The only other person they passed was a bored-looking cigarette girl leaning in a doorway, smoking, an empty display tray strapped cross the flat belly of her sequined suit. She raised her eyebrows at them, unimpressed, and Pepper stared right through her.

The man in the uniform pulled back a curtain and Pepper stopped to bounce on his toes once more. Beyond the curtain was the white-hot cone of a spotlight, and beyond that, darkness. He could hear the strange hush of the arena. It was like standing at the edge of a high cliff, knowing he was about to jump. He nodded to himself, slapped the man in the uniform on the shoulder to say thanks, and stepped through. After that, all he could feel was the blinding glow of the spot, the heat of the crowd and concrete under his boots.

38

Lesko made him wait.

It was an old trick, something Pepper liked to do himself when he was champion. Lingering an extra few minutes in the dressing room while his opponent stood alone in the ring, listening to the jeers from the crowd. The sweat from his pre-match warm-up cooling on his skin. The enormity of the moment putting all its weight on him. As calm as he might look on the outside, any man about to wrestle for a world's title was a hurricane of emotion inside. Most could barely keep a lid on it. For some, just the waiting was enough to break them. It didn't always work, but it was worth a shot.

If Lesko thought it would do the trick on Pepper, he was a fool. All it accomplished was to give him time to test out the ring, pacing back and forth across the mat, pretending to be oblivious of the thousands of men watching him. The ropes were nice and tight and covered in sleeves of new white canvas. That was good: Tight ropes would make it more difficult for Lesko to bully him against them or trap him in a corner. For the bigger man, it would have been better to keep the ropes loose. The footing was a different story. The mat was rough enough to discourage prolonged ground grappling, and the padding underneath was deep and soft. This would favor Lesko, mitigating Pepper's speed and allowing the heavyweight champion to dig in and get his hips into his throws and tackles. On a mat like this it would be best not to let the big guy get ahold of him, he decided as he took a couple of experimental shots across the ring to gauge the surface.

He couldn't feel the heat from the lights but was already sweating. The referee kept his distance, leaning in a far corner with his elbows propped on the top rope. Pepper didn't recognize the man, but while his white shirt and black slacks looked brand-new, his recently polished boots were worn and soft. As Pepper circled around the ring to where he was standing, he saw that one of the man's ears was hard and cauliflowered.

"Hey," Pepper said, smiling in a way he hoped would make the fans at ringside think he wasn't nervous. "What's the best steak you ever had?"

The referee's head jerked up as if he'd been interrupted from a nap. "What?" he said.

Pepper repeated the question, and the referee gaped at him for a moment. "Fillipelli's," he said finally, "in Chicago."

He smirked as he circled back to his corner, knowing Stettler and Lesko had the referee in their pocket. He'd have to watch out for the man.

A blooming spotlight and a sudden rush of fans toward the rail alerted him to the champion's arrival. Lesko moved steadily up the aisle in a simple black cape and matching singlet, his eyes never straying from the ring. Like Pepper, he came alone, pausing in his corner to whip off the cape and send it sailing casually over the top rope. His body looked a bit harder than Pepper might have hoped for, but he still had a small roll of flab around his belly. His shoulders were hairy cannonballs, a bit sloped but powerful, and his thinning hair was plastered down on his skull. His face betrayed nothing as he squatted in his corner and tugged at the ropes to stretch his back.

The public address announcer was all pomade and talcum powder as he bounded into the ring to introduce the participants. Though no one had ever bothered to have Pepper step on a scale, he was announced at 155 pounds and hailing from Brooklyn, New York. When the fix was still on, Stettler no doubt hoped playing him as a hometown hero would make him even more popular with the fans in the theater. The ring announcer said Lesko hailed from Nekoosa, Wisconsin, and entered the ring at 242 rough-and-ready pounds. He made the part about the "undisputed heavyweight champion of the world" sound like it was about eleven words long. If Pepper had to guess, he'd put Lesko closer to two sixty.

The referee called them to the center so he could check their boots for loads and their hair for chemicals. He rubbed them down to make sure they weren't greased and demanded they turn their hands over to show their fingernails were properly trimmed. Pepper kept his chin tucked into his chest, not looking up from Lesko's knees but feeling the bigger man's eyes burrowing into him as they faced off to receive their final instructions.

"Any questions from the champion?" the referee asked. Lesko gave the smallest possible shake of his head.

The ref turned to Pepper. "From the challenger?"

Now Pepper looked the champion in the eye. "Two trains leave Kansas City," he said. "If the westbound train proceeds twenty miles per hour slower than the eastbound train—"

Lesko spun on his heel and stalked back to his corner without hearing the rest. Pepper shrugged at the ref and then retreated to his own side.

This moment seemed like the longest of the night as the houselights dimmed and the referee conferred briefly with the timekeeper. Lesko was still staring at him, but Pepper kept his eyes fixed on an empty spot in the middle of the canvas, his arms idly swinging at his waist. He knew that by now Moira had made her way out of the dressing room and had found her seat in the crowd. He didn't waste time trying to find her face in the darkness, but knowing she was out there made him feel quick and strong.

When the referee came back to center, clapped his hands and shouted, "Wrestle!" it was like someone had pulled a bathtub stopper deep in his chest. The nervousness and anxiety he'd felt backstage drained away, leaving him light and nimble. From somewhere a thousand miles away he sensed the crowd rising to its feet, and Strangler Lesko charged out of his corner with such fury that all he had to do was stand his ground and let him come. When Lesko got within range, Pepper kicked him savagely in the shin and stepped out of the way, allowing the big man's momentum to carry him crashing into the empty corner.

Lesko spun around, a wild look of pain and confusion twisting his features as the referee caught Pepper by the arm. "What the fuck was that?" he said. "No kicking. I'll disqualify you."

The second time Lesko came at him he was more wary. The kick—while a silly, childish gesture—had been enough to make him think twice about rushing Pepper full bore. At the center of the ring, they locked up, and for the first time Pepper felt Lesko's power. It was like trying to budge a hunk of granite, sinewy muscles flexing beneath the downy hair of his chest and shoulders. Lesko had the expert strength of the lifelong athlete, and was solid through his legs and midsection in a way you couldn't get from sit-ups and free weights. It was force built from years of moving other men—of lifting and throwing them, tying them up on the mat so they couldn't move or breathe.

Luckily, Lesko's hands were a beat slow, and before he could get a good grip Pepper wrenched free and threw a hard, slapping punch into one of his floating ribs. It landed flush and the champion grunted, eyes clouding again with anger.

"What's your problem?" the ref yelled, but before anyone could do anything, Pepper stepped behind Lesko and stomped down hard on his Achilles tendon.

The blow sent him down on one knee, a sound escaping his lips like all the air was rushing out of his body. The boos were thick as the referee pushed Pepper into a corner on the other side of the ring. "This is your last warning," he said, his face red, spittle collecting on his lips as he shouted to be heard above the crowd. "I'll give this match to Lesko."

"You won't do shit," Pepper said, "unless you want a riot on your hands."

It took Lesko a minute to compose himself, standing in a neutral corner, rolling his shoulders and shaking out his arms as he glared across the ring. When they locked up once again in a collar-and-elbow, the champion was just as Pepper wanted him, furious and thoughtless. Spitting a curse into his ear, he sucked Pepper forward into a vise-grip bear hug. It was the setup for his signature hip throw, the one he had used to defeat most of his opponents, the one Pepper had scouted and spent countless hours drilling with Taft in Montana.

Pepper knew it was coming: he'd been waiting for it. He knew if Lesko's mind was clouded with rage, he'd go back to his bread-and-butter attacks. It would be instinct for him to retreat to what he knew best, the animal memory of his muscles reverting to the move he'd spent years perfecting. But Pepper and Taft had worked out a counter. When the champion caught him in his favorite move, Taft would drop his weight and step between Lesko's legs for an inside trip tackle. He would kick one of Lesko's feet out from under him and send the champion sprawling to the mat on his ass. It was a risky move, but once they pulled it off, Lesko would be demoralized—hurting from the kick to the shin and the punch to the ribs and now knowing his best move was useless in the match.

Except when Lesko locked him up, Pepper felt powerless to drop his weight. The man was too strong, his grip too tight. He inched his way forward and went for the trip, but when he attempted to kick Lesko's foot off the mat, the impact sent a shiver of pain shooting through his own leg. The bone he'd broken years earlier glowed like a white-hot wire and he cried out in pain.

His stomach flip-flopped as Lesko lifted him off the canvas and tossed him head over heels. For a moment he was weightless, plucked from the earth and heaved through the air like a small dog ousted from its owner's lap. He landed flat on his back, the air crushed from his lungs. It felt as though he were drowning, and he opened his mouth for air just as Lesko's weight collapsed on top of him. The champion cradled his head and legs and the referee slapped the mat hard with an open palm.

His chest was screaming and his head throbbed with each beat of his heart as he limped back to his corner for the second fall, his leg feeling numb and dead. As the crowd trumpeted Lesko's victory in the first Pepper squatted on the mat and pretended to retie his boots. Really, he untied them and then set about tying them again as slowly as he could, making a mental check of every part of his body. Gripping his leg with both hands, he slid his palms from knee to ankle, finally deciding the leg was not broken.

He steadied his breathing. This was fine, he told himself, it would pass. He would work through it. He could stall Lesko until the feeling returned and then he'd be as good as new. Jesus, though, that man was strong. And big. Lesko's arms were longer than he'd anticipated, his movement around the ring catlike for such a hulk. Pepper would have to be careful. He couldn't afford to make another mistake. That was okay. That was what he'd been trained to do since he was a boy in the orphanage—to wrestle match after match without making an error. He reminded himself that he was the technically superior athlete. There was more science to his game. He just needed time to let his leg recover, and once Lesko's wind failed him, Pepper would make his move.

When he looked up, the referee was waiting for him.

———

E xactly as he expected, Lesko started the second fall with more urgency, and for the first few minutes Pepper would not let the champion lay a hand on him. With Lesko controlling the center, he bounced just in and out of his reach, periodically stomping his foot on the mat to try to knock some feeling back into it. As Lesko lurched forward, Pepper slapped his hands away and backed off. A couple of times when it looked like Lesko had finally trapped him in one of the corners, Pepper slipped to the side to avoid him. This drew some catcalls from the crowd, but still he refused all of Lesko's efforts to tie up.

The champion's face remained impassive, but Pepper knew his patience would wear thin. After a few minutes he saw sweat beading on Lesko's brow, frustrated by Pepper's agility and his refusal to wrestle with him. "Come on," Lesko said a couple of times after failing to corral him with ponderous lunges. "Come on."

Soon the big man started to slow down. The adrenaline had drained off during the first fall and his wind was beginning to falter. After spending his training preparing for just a single fall in a rigged match against Taft, he was in no condition to keep up. Seeing that, Pepper increased his tempo, dodging to the right when Lesko advanced left, going left when the champion went right. A couple of times his leg seized up on him, pain piercing up his side, but he managed to stay out of Lesko's long reach. When the champion got irritated and shot straight in for a tackle, Pepper sprawled out of it easily, hopping away as Lesko came up from the mat with clenched teeth.

A wadded-up program bounced across the canvas and disappeared underneath the ropes on the far side of the ring. The crowd wanted action and now even the referee was getting anxious, clapping his hands together and reminding them they weren't there for a footrace.

Pepper could see the fatigue building in Lesko's posture. He was starting to get sloppy with his attacks, his normally fearsome blend of power and technique deserting him as the frustration continued to mount. He began telegraphing his shots, reaching high with his right hand before stepping in to go low on the left side. Each time, he came up empty as Pepper slunk out of the way. The muscles in Lesko's jaw fluttered as he tried to walk Pepper into a corner, fidgeting, his fingers twiddling like a man who couldn't figure out the final answer to his morning crossword.

For nearly twenty more minutes Pepper was a ghost floating just out of the champion's reach. When Lesko grabbed for him, he slapped his hands away. When he lunged, Pepper slid to one side, dancing and circling, smiling all the while. He wouldn't be suckered in and he wouldn't be trapped, just moving, evading and waiting, waiting, waiting. Eventually the feeling in his leg began to return. The tingling in his toes faded and he felt whole again, the nerves no longer on fire, his bones no longer numb and clumsy.

When Lesko's frustration finally got the better of him, Pepper saw it first in his eyes. The champion's last desperate dive at his legs came from too far away, nearly the opposite side of the ring. It was slow and careless and he circled deftly away from it. As Lesko spun to follow, Pepper finally darted in, scooping up one of the big man's legs at the knee. Lesko grunted in surprise. The ankle that now bore his weight was the one Pepper had stomped on during the first fall, and it buckled under the strain. Lesko crashed to the canvas in a heap, landing hard on one hip.

The impact shook the ring, but it was lost in an explosion of cheers. Lesko was not used to fighting from his back, and Pepper could feel the panic in him as soon as he hit the mat. He kicked and thrashed, trying to scramble free, but Pepper would not let him go. With Lesko up on his hip to avoid a pin, he put his knee into the champion's ribs and leaned with all his weight. Lesko grimaced, and as he did Pepper seized him by the wrist and rolled for a straight armlock. Rearing back with the full power of his torso, he felt Lesko's elbow stretch and then lock as it began to bend the wrong way.

Pepper thought Lesko would concede the fall, but somehow the champion struggled to his feet. He stood tall and dropped Pepper headfirst onto the canvas, the impact rattling his vision once, then twice. Still he held tight to the arm, each impact only strengthening the lock. He pulled harder, popping his hips forward and arching his back as a gasp and a shudder escaped Lesko's lips. Something cracked in his arm, the sound like a piece of driftwood breaking over someone's knee, and the champion sank to the mat, swatting the canvas with his free hand to concede the fall.

The referee separated them and Lesko sat back on his heels, his right arm folded protectively across his belly. His look was a mixture of pain, resignation and anger. Pepper stood over him and, putting one foot on Lesko's shoulder, toppled him backward onto his ass. The crowd roared, and as Pepper walked back to his corner, he raised his arms, the first man ever to win a concession from Stanislaw "Strangler" Lesko.

◆━━━◆

The referee asked Lesko if he wanted an intermission before the final fall, but the champion shook his head. Getting his hands on Pepper did not seem to be the kind of pleasure he was willing to put off another fifteen minutes. Pepper bent at the waist and stretched, every joint in his body hurting now, his muscles aching the way they did just before they started to cramp on him. Just a little bit further, he told himself, almost there.

He expected a stern lecture from the referee before the final restart, but instead the man just stood in the center of the ring and looked at him with flat, dispassionate eyes.

"Fillipelli's is a fine place for small-timers," Pepper shouted at him. "But you ought to try the Broken Spoke on the South Side. Really, you'll thank me for it."

The ref just shook his head in wonder. Pepper glanced across the ring at Lesko, who was bouncing and sucking in big breaths. He winked, and when Lesko grinned back, there were flecks of blood on his teeth.

A moment later they were off.

They faced off in the middle of the ring with five feet between them, Lesko looking more cautious this time. The champion circled left and so did Pepper, keeping his distance. Slowly, Lesko began trying to walk him down, cutting off the ring, taking little bites out of the space between them with every pass. But he was exhausted now, his arm certainly injured, and his feet dragging on the canvas with each step, as if there were cinder blocks tied to his boots. For the first few minutes Pepper managed to escape his grasp, edging away each time it looked like the champion had him trapped. The crowd was openly jeering both of them now, and Pepper could tell it bothered Lesko. His face betrayed nothing, his jaw still set in the same hard line as when they'd started, but his eyes were clouded with frustration and fatigue. Once Lesko had decided Pepper wasn't going to attack—that he was just going to stall and continue to run until the referee declared a draw—his hands dropped a bit and his shoulders went slack.

As he did, Pepper saw a drop of sweat roll out of Lesko's hairline and across his forehead. An inch at a time, it ran the length of his nose and settled at the tip, and when the champion reached to brush it away, Pepper finally charged him. He shot in on a tackle, quick and perfect, slipping under Lesko's defenses and locking his hands around his hips. Lesko grunted in surprise and he tried to sprawl out, but Pepper had him. As he planted his weight and tried to hoist Lesko off his feet, something snapped in his leg again. The side of his body went numb from armpit to ankle and his momentum faltered. Lesko powered out of his grip and, putting a hand on the back of Pepper's neck, drove him face-first into the canvas.

Before Pepper could get off his hands and knees, Lesko circled behind him and climbed on his back, looping his legs around him like a baby monkey riding its mother. The crowd gasped. This was not a position you came back from, especially against Lesko, who had earned his nickname with one of the deadliest choke attacks in wrestling history. As Lesko wrapped a thick arm across his face, Pepper tucked his chin into his chest, hiding his neck and taking the full force of the champion's squeeze on his jaw.

It fucking hurt.

"You wanted it this way," Lesko whispered to him, his breath hot in Pepper's ear. "Just remember that."

Even though he'd done some damage to Lesko with the armlock during the second fall, it still felt like someone was trying to fold a steel bar across his face. It was not unheard-of for Lesko to break a man's jaw if he couldn't get the choke sunk in around the throat, and Pepper hoped the champion didn't have that kind of strength left. The referee hovered over them, hands at his waist, ready to dive in and separate them as soon as Pepper tapped the mat to concede.

The whole arena seemed to be thinking the same thought: It wouldn't be long now.

Lesko put his meaty left hand across Pepper's forehead and yanked his head back, trying to gain the few inches he needed to sink the chokehold under his chin. There was no real use fighting it, but Pepper held out as long as he could before his head rocked back, his jaw popped up and Lesko's grip slid into place. He could feel the heaving of the champion's chest against his back as he put everything he had into the squeeze. The crowd was on its feet again, cheering for the climax of the match. From his position facedown on the mat, Pepper could see men in the front row gathering up their hats, tucking them under their arms and clapping expectantly while Lesko cinched the hold tighter and tighter.

The cheering reached its crescendo and plateaued. The moment stretched, and stretched.

And stretched.

Lesko's victory was at hand, but still it didn't come, and as the crowd waited, the applause wavered and the cheering died away. Suddenly it got very quiet. The referee took a step forward as if to call a halt to the match, but Pepper stopped him in his tracks with an outstretched hand. Slowly he raised his index finger, the referee regarding it as if it might be a poisonous snake. The finger waggled back and forth reproachfully, and some in the crowd began to laugh.

Lesko struggled to redouble his grip, and Pepper felt the pressure wall up across his throat. Each time Lesko locked the hold in tight, he felt himself start to fade, his vision collapsing in on itself, and he shifted his weight just a bit to either side. He moved into the pressure of Lesko's grip, finding just enough space to breathe and to keep the blood trickling into his brain. When the champion corrected his grip, Pepper moved with him.

Lesko's breathing grew ragged in his ear and the referee took another cautious step forward. Again Pepper stopped him with a raised finger, this time seeing the ref's eyes go wide when he noticed that Pepper was smiling at him.

The two wrestlers stayed like that for what felt like a very long time, Lesko putting everything he had into the chokehold and Pepper holding his hand out to let everyone know he was not troubled by it at all. Finally, the champion's grip began to weaken. It started with a barely perceptible quiver in the arm across his throat. The quiver slowly became a shake, and as Lesko struggled to retain the grip, Pepper felt his own breathing start to get easier. The hand Lesko still had clamped across his forehead was damp with sweat and he knew the grip was becoming pliable.

He was just waiting for his moment now. The instant Lesko's grip broke, Pepper would spin into him. He would step out of the champion's grapevine and get to the side for a pinning combination. Lesko would be too tired to stop him, his arms useless and full of blood from trying to apply the choke. The referee would count him out and Pepper would become the world's heavyweight champion. He would stand in the ring while the referee raised his hand, Lesko hanging his head, barely even able to stay on his feet. He would take the title and then Stettler, Fritz and O'Shea would be powerless over him. If they wanted a rematch, he would make them beg for it, and he would show up in Philadelphia and whip Lesko again.

The sensation of victory was already rising inside him as he made to spring out of the champion's grasp. The years were falling away: the time he'd spent blackballed from the business, the nights doing the hangman's drop, their time in Montana—it was all worth it now. He wanted to see Moira's face when he came backstage with the heavyweight title. Whatever distance had developed between them would be gone. They could start anew, leaving everything behind them. They would have money; they could go anywhere and do anything. The world would be wide-open to them. They would have everything they wanted and nothing they didn't.

This is what he was thinking when Lesko's forearm closed again around his throat. The champion's last gasp, some final energy reserve he'd found deep inside himself. It felt more powerful than before, but Pepper knew what to do. He turned into the grip, just as he'd done each time leading up to this moment. Lifting his arm again to tell the referee he was okay. He was fine.

He would survive this.

39

He was quiet for a long time after he woke up. He didn't ask what happened or touch the fresh bruising around his neck. It made Moira sad and tired to look at it, that part of his body that always seemed to be sore or raw, like it might never heal. When he saw the lights of the dressing room and the doctor leaning over him, he knew. Blinking, he sat up, legs hanging over the side of the rubdown table. She got out of her chair and stood by him, putting her hand on his knee.

"I lost," he said.

"You did," she said, just glad to see him moving. Glad to hear him speak.

They'd brought him in on a stretcher, four orderlies in white smocks who'd hoisted him up onto the rubdown table and left once the doctor was there, checking to make sure his breathing and heart rate were normal. It had taken the referee a few moments longer than it should have to realize he was out. Lesko had held the choke too long and Pepper had been unconscious for almost five minutes.

After the doctor was gone, a warm teardrop landed on her knuckle and beaded there. He made no sound as he wept. His shoulders didn't shake. He didn't lurch and snort trying to catch his breath. There was no bubbling mucus, or splotchy red spots on his cheeks. He just sat there watching her hand on his knee, looking perfectly normal, looking like her husband, with tears falling from his eyes. She'd seen a lot of wrestlers break down in backstage areas, dressing rooms and rings in front of a thousand people. They all cried when it was over and they'd lost. Every one of them. All of them except Pepper.

When proud, tough men suffered a loss in life, what they needed most was stillness. This she knew well. It was like a death. They needed to sit alone, not talking, until the numb pain faded and they made peace with whatever dark knowledge had been passed to them. They needed to brood, to wallow in it, until their wounds were licked clean and their strength came back. Then, and only after an appropriate while, if they couldn't budge themselves, you had to give them a kick in the ass.

So, even though there were countless things she wanted to ask him—as much about the future as the past—she sat quietly with him and patted his knee as the clock ground and clicked on the wall behind them. After a bit he reached up and touched the side of his head, saying that it ached. He'd mostly got himself together by the time Stettler and Fritz let themselves into the dressing room. Moira cursed herself for not locking the door after the doctor left.

"You had to be the big man," Stettler said. "Well, this is where it gets you."

Pepper didn't respond, which scared her far more than the tears.

"Lesko asked us to pass along his regards," Fritz said. "Said you almost had him out there."

Pepper snuck his head up, a little look around. "He didn't come himself," he said finally.

"Well," Fritz said, "he's left already. Places to go and all that."

"We want you out of the Plaza by eleven a.m. tomorrow," Stettler said. "We're not paying for you to spend another night there."

Moira took her hand from Pepper's knee. "We'll stay on as long as we like and you'll foot the bill," she said. "He needs to recuperate."

"Another thing you should've thought about," Stettler said, "before you kicked dirt in our eyes."

Moira slapped him across the face. Stettler's head jerked to one side and his raven's hair fluttered into a mess of bent wire. Before she could draw her hand away, he caught her arm in his fist.

"This man just took a fall from Strangler Lesko," she said, putting her face as close to Stettler as she dared. "He just gave you the match people will be talking about for the next year. He almost won the world's heavyweight title from a man who outweighed him by more than a hundred pounds. Putting him up in a hotel until he feels well enough to travel would be the only halfway human thing to do."

"He looks fine to me," Stettler said, glancing at Pepper, who'd gotten up from his spot on the rubdown table and was being held back by one of Fritz's giant paws.

Stettler was mashing the bones of Moira's wrist and Fritz said, "Please," standing in the middle of the room a like traffic cop. "It's all done now. There's no sense in any of this."

The door opened again and Dion O'Shea stuck his face inside. He looked slightly alarmed at what he saw, but not as alarmed as Stettler, who dropped Moira's wrist and backed away. O'Shea came in accompanied by the big, dangerous-looking man called Francis.

"We were just hashing out some final details," said Stettler, rearranging the cut of his suit jacket.

"Yes," said O'Shea. "I'm sure that's all it was."

Pepper still hadn't said a word—was just standing on the other side of the dressing room, looking exhausted, but like he was trying his best to keep up with what was going on. When O'Shea saw him, he pushed past the rest to shake his hand, lustily pumping his arm as he grinned and slapped him on the back.

"Well met," O'Shea said. "Just extraordinary. I thought you were going to give me a heart attack out there."

"Yeah?" Pepper said.

O'Shea was beaming, seemingly oblivious that anything could be the matter. "I mean it," he said. "One of the best scientific wrestling matches I've ever been privileged to see."

Pepper nodded, but Moira could see his mind working back over the match, his face falling as he remembered each failure all over again. She wanted to go to him but felt trapped on the other side of the room by Stettler and Fritz. Perhaps the men were feeling it, too, after O'Shea's sudden arrival.

"Dion," Fritz said. "What are you doing here? We thought you'd gone back to the hotel."

Annoyance flashed on O'Shea's face, a grimness returning to him as if the work bell had just called him back to the real world. "You two fellows can leave now," he said. "But hold the car for me. I'll get a ride back with you, if that's quite all right."

Like cattle being urged through a chute, Fritz and Stettler pawed around a moment before Francis pushed the door open and ushered them into the hall. Moira felt cheered to see them go but still dejected over the things she might never get to say to Stettler. She also wondered if she owed Fritz an apology. Even though he showed up out of the blue to sucker them into this mess, she knew she'd misjudged him during the last several years. She blamed him for things that were not his fault. When the door swung closed she noticed for the first time that Francis was carrying a small satchel in one hand. The sight of it, swinging low and close to his body like something he didn't want people to see, chased away thoughts of anything else.

The satchel went on the seat of a chair by the door after O'Shea took it from Francis's hand. He fumbled with it for a moment, trying to get the latch to spring, and then stepped back to let Moira peer inside. Her knees and back tightened when she saw the low stacks of cash.

"You were right," he said. He didn't look happy about it. "We've had a near miss thanks to you."

"I don't understand," Pepper said. He'd come over to huddle with them around the bag of money. "What is this?"

"It's twenty thousand dollars," O'Shea said. "Kind of steep for reward money, if you ask me, but I'll share the loss with Mr. Mundt." He looked at Francis. "Remind me to tell him about that."

"And Mr. Eddy?" she said, keeping herself steady.

O'Shea grimaced. "I'd known that guy my whole life," he said. "Things hadn't been right between us for a while. I guess he turned out to be the jealous type. Still, I didn't think he'd take it this far."

"What are you talking about?" Pepper said. He was starting to look manic, wild.

"I have to run," O'Shea said. "But I'm sure you'll work it out between the two of you."

"Wait," she said. "Why are you doing this?"

O'Shea shrugged at her, spreading his hands as if apologizing. "Like you said," he said. "We made a deal, and I like to think I honor my commitments."

He was an ugly man, sweaty and weirdly complected, in a way that reminded her of some shiny upholstery. He shook Pepper's hand again, telling him what a fine match it had been. One of the greats, he said. Pepper just stood there staring at the bag of money, nodding and thanking him very much.

When it was just the two of them again, of course he wouldn't let up until she told him the whole story. He leaned back against the rubdown table while she talked, a look of alarm spreading across his face. When she was finished they both gazed at the floor a moment before Pepper whooped and grabbed her up in a hug. He lifted her off her feet and spun around once before setting her down, as if remembering how much pain he was in. But he was smiling. The news had given him a burst of energy and she hoped it held out for a while.

"Jesus, Moira," he said. "That was really stupid, putting in with O'Shea like that. Brave as hell, but stupid."

She kissed him lightly on the cheek. "I guess I'll take that as a compliment," she said.

●——————●

While he went to take his shower, she loaded half the money into his small travel bag and let herself out into the bowels of Madison Square Garden. She found Carol Jean in another cramped dressing room not far away, alone and still sitting there after most of the others had left.

"Can I help you?" Carol Jean said, in a way that told Moira she still thought she'd won.

She was all in black again, a dress just slightly too revealing for a grieving widow. Her arms came up instinctively as Moira stepped inside and thrust the bag at her, eyes going as big and wide as fried eggs when she saw the bundles of cash inside. She blinked, her indignation losing a lot of its steam. She said, "What's this?"

"Ten thousand dollars," Moira said. "God knows you earned it. It might not last you forever, but it's enough for a running start."

"What?" Carol Jean said, as if she had suggested they go into business together on a candy store. "No. No, I can't accept this."

Moira told her she wouldn't try to understand what she was going through. She hadn't known Mr. Taft for very long before he died, but she thought he was a decent man and knew he would want her to have that money. Carol Jean held the bag against her chest, suddenly looking every bit the old spinster. Her face fell as Moira talked, her eyes ticking up to the clock as if realizing she'd been had. But by the time Moira finished explaining it, a new stubbornness was fixed there.

"I'm waiting for Mr. Markham," she said. "He promised me a lift back to the hotel."

"I think most everyone has already gone," Moira said, trying to keep her voice light. "We're the last ones left. The stragglers."

"I'm sure that's not true," Carol Jean said. "There's still so much to figure out. With the lawyers and the like."

Her voice was big and empty in the hard little room. It was difficult to know if she believed what she was saying.

"Well, either way," Moira said, "I hope that money helps to get you wherever you're going."

"What's left for me anywhere, I wonder?" Carol Jean said, looking at her with those impossible green eyes.

Moira didn't know what to say to that. Carol Jean was so young to have seen so much sadness, but seemed somehow too old to start over again. She didn't have a home to go to, or any other place that might offer her anything. Moira wished she could tell her to just run. To get out of this place, set herself up in a new town, and not tell a soul where she was. If she couldn't bring herself to pretend none of this had happened, at least she could put as much distance as possible between herself and people like Boyd Markham.

"I wish you'd come back to the hotel with us," she said. "At least for tonight. If we all shared a cab we could leave one heck of a tip."

"Thank you, no," Carol Jean said. "I think I'll sit here a while longer. I'm sure Mr. Markham will be along. He promised me a lift."

As she spoke, Carol Jean sank back into her rickety folding chair, the bag resting on her lap. Moira wished they had more time together, but she wanted to be back in Pepper's dressing room when he got out of his shower. She couldn't think of anything else to say that wouldn't sound cruel, so she just touched her lightly on the arm one more time before letting herself out. The last she saw of Carol Jean, she was still sitting with her eyes fixed on the near wall, her jaw set proud and false, as though she might never move from the spot.

40

The Fourth of July blossomed into a hard shine. As the sun vaulted over the mountains and across the great blue sky they napped together on the creaking bed in the rental cabin. Moira woke with her hair wilted from the heat, and for an hour they played cards in the feeble breeze of the front porch. After the second time she took every toothpick and bottle cap he had to his name, he announced he wasn't going to play with her anymore. Late afternoon, a clap of rain rushed through, battering down the dust, and with the yellow light of evening filtering through the pines she turned in her chair and asked him what was fast becoming the defining question of their new lives.

"What on earth about dinner, do you suppose?"

Pepper tore himself away from his thoughts and smiled, because they both knew the answer. While she went in to fetch her hat he brought the car around and then they drove the half hour down the mountain into Flagstaff. Their new car was a Cole the color of sandpaper, a few years old but still nice. It was the first car they'd owned since he was lightweight champion, and he drove it as he always had, with a recklessness that made them both squeal with delight. The dirt road unrolled in front of them like a long, dark ribbon, gales of wind filling her ears as he pushed down the accelerator on the straightaways. They sailed over rolling hills and around bends, flying up off their seats on the bigger bumps. At the base of the hill they sped past a field of freckled cattle and Pepper goosed the horn, sending a few of them scurrying a step or two before they forgot their surprise and went back to nosing the ground with big felt snouts.

Their regular place was open despite the holiday, just as she knew it would be. The restaurant sat a block off Flagstaff's main drag: a tumbledown building of rough wood siding with an actual hitching post out front. As it was the only place cooking, they had to wait for a table and Pepper spelled his name three times for the poor man keeping the list. He was giving his real name a try, just in case Markham or the New York newspaper reporters were still out trying to find them. Moira thought it was cute, but told him if he expected her to call him Zdravko, he had another thing coming.

They'd been staying in the little cabin close to four months and ate at the restaurant most nights. Flagstaff was built into the strange belt of land where the desert met the mountains, and the feeling of the place reminded her a bit of Montana. If anything, it was even more deserted here, since the town was just a few thousand people. But it was neighborly, the locals all acting like they were just getting started on something together. The state highway expansion was all they could talk about, but for now the only way in or out of town were the single-lane dirt tracks that jutted out in all four directions. Moira had picked this place precisely for its smallness, and because she thought the mountains would give Pepper some comfort as he found his bearings. Already, though, the aimless, isolated feeling was starting to wear on her.

They stood in the restaurant's small entryway and watched a group of diners as rough as any she'd ever seen eat sitting down. Gaunt men with dirty fingers guarding their plates like junkyard dogs. Ranchers in overalls treating their wives to a night on the

town. A couple of cowboys wearing fuzzy chaps. The place served
meat from the nearby ranches, with sides of root vegetables and not
much else. She was sick to death of beef and said as much to Pepper
as they finally took a two-top in the very middle of the room. He
answered by squinting at his menu for a long time and asking the
waiter what he thought about the chicken.

"Big enough to ride," the waiter beamed. He was a heavy man,
with wool pants hitched up almost to his nipples.

Moira stubbed out her cigarette and said in that case she'd better
double down on drinks. She didn't bother to tell the waiter what
kind. All they had was tequila. When the man was gone, Pepper
smiled in a way that reminded her how handsome he could be when
he tried.

"Let's make a night of it," he said, reaching across the table to
squeeze her hand.

He'd been squeezing her hand a lot lately, his way of telling her
he was slowly coming out of his mood. There was another look
tucked in behind his smile, a hopefulness that made her want to look
away. She knew what it was and didn't want to think about it.

They'd lingered for a week in New York after the match. The
night they returned from Madison Square Garden, Moira snuck
Pepper in a side entrance of the hotel so the after-hours crowd gathered in the lobby wouldn't see him. As they climbed the steps she
could hear them hooting and laughing at each other—some of them
already headed out to catch late trains, but most just blowing off
steam. Turning the front desk area into their own personal party. In
the morning she went down there herself and used some of O'Shea's
cash to upgrade to a suite. After that, Pepper locked himself away in
the bedroom and for three days only came out to eat and use the
bathroom.

Bored and left to her own devices, Moira started clipping out
newspaper stories. The New York reporters were going wild for him.

Lesko may have won their match, but there were just as many articles about Pepper filling the inside pages. One of her favorites had a headline reading "Pint-sized Pepper Pushes Champ to Brink" and even included a small sketch portrait of him between the columns.

She kept them all tucked inside an envelope at the bottom of their old trunk, half for safekeeping, half so he wouldn't find them if he suddenly emerged from the bedroom and commandeered a paper. She suspected the loss would never fully let him be, but hoped the sting would fade in time. She imagined one day it would be a thing he thought of infrequently, like when a man spotted his old bowling trophies in a forgotten corner of the garage. Maybe then she would take the clippings out and let him see all the wonderful purple things the sportswriters had written about him. Until then, she knew he would read each flowery compliment as a slap in the face.

Once it was clear that he was hiding out somewhere, the sportswriters were rabid to find him. They wanted more words from the great man. They wanted to know how it felt, what he thought and what he would do now. Moira wondered what they'd think if they could see him nearly comatose from the pain and depression, not eating, not even letting her open the bedroom curtains. It had been like this after the loss to Windham, too, but this time was worse. At least after losing the lightweight title he had his own righteous anger to fire him back up. This time he'd lost a square match with no strings attached, and she knew it was going to take longer for him to make sense of it.

On the fifth day she answered a knock at the door to find Stanislaw Lesko standing there, looking as massive as if someone had rolled a boulder into the hallway. He stood a little cockeyed, as if one of his legs was troubling him, and had one arm riding in a sling. It was early evening and Pepper was already asleep, dead to the world in the other room.

"I'd like to have a word with the mister," Lesko said, all custom tailoring and expensive hair tonic. His eyes were glassy, and she wondered if he'd been drinking.

Moira told him the mister wasn't feeling up to accepting visitors at the moment. "Why are you here?" she said. "I thought you'd skipped town with the rest."

"I do what I like," he said, not sounding angry or boastful. Merely stating facts. "I had some business to look after in the city and I wanted to see a show."

"High times for you," she said, and could see the world's heavyweight champion wasn't used to this sort of reception.

"He gave it to me pretty good out there," Lesko said, his tone suggesting she might invite him in for a place to sit. She did not, and he moved his feet around in the hallway carpet. Small feet, she noticed, packed tight inside soft leather shoes.

"I wrestled with Gotch once," he said, after what felt like a long time. "Only in training, you understand, exhibition stuff. I was very green back then, but I could tell it was true what everybody said. He had a special way about him. Sometimes he didn't seem like a man at all."

Moira looked up the hall, where a porter was bringing a tray out of one of the other suites. The man was tall and barrel-chested, and his elegant stride reminded her all over again that Taft was dead. Lesko cleared his throat, looking uncomfortable, as if it were difficult for him to be there, saying these things.

"Being in the ring with your husband," he said, "it brought me back to that feeling. Maybe for only the second time in my life."

Moira asked if that was the extent of the message he wanted her to pass along, and Lesko scowled. "I don't know, damn it," he said. "I wanted to tell him it was quite a battle, that's all."

"I know," she said. "I watched it. He should've won. He almost had you in the third."

"Well," he said, "I suppose I may have been undertrained." He turned as if to go but then didn't. He lingered. "I take it you know all about Billy's new show?"

"I know that it's a fake, if that's what you mean," she said.

A short clapping sound as he coughed into his fist. "*Fake's* not completely the word I would use," he said. "But, look, if I'm really going to let Billy and Fritz turn me into the world's biggest ballet dancer, I could do a lot worse than to have Mr. Van Dean as a partner. We could have some fun, he and I. We could make a lot of money."

She told him they'd already made a lot of money and no one seemed much better off for it. She thanked him for coming and made to close the door when he spoke again, announcing to the hallway: "I heard you slapped him," he said. "Billy, I mean."

It didn't sound like a threat, but she stood her ground just in case. "Not as hard as he deserved," she said.

Lesko allowed a brief smile to pass over his face. "I would've liked to see that," he said.

After shutting the door she stood holding on to the handle for a few seconds so it wouldn't make a sound when she carefully let go. The next night she got Pepper out of the crush and cold of the city. He needed space and quiet, she knew, so his body could heal and his thoughts could run themselves dry. As soon as their late train rattled out of New York, his mood lifted. He still spent most of the ride brooding, staring at nothing, but smiled at her jokes about the train staff. When a kid recognized him in the dining car, Pepper even signed a napkin for him.

At first they just drifted, spending Christmas in Baltimore and New Year's in Washington, D.C., after taking a week to see the sights. She enjoyed it, being the only one in charge for once, deciding where to go and what to do. On a chilly January day in Charlotte they bought the new car from a wide little pug of a salesman who pumped their hands like he was trying to draw water as soon as he saw the cash. They drove west slowly, taking their time, with a little less than nine thousand dollars stowed in a hard-shell suitcase on the backseat, buried under the shopping bags and tailor's boxes full of things they bought to restart their lives.

They arrived in Flagstaff in early March and rented the cabin outside of town. It was a tidy little place hemmed in by trees, a short hike from a mountain lake. You could stand on the bank and watch trout dart around in water as clear as glass. The first night Pepper pried up the floorboards in the bedroom and hid the money in the dead space down there.

Now it felt as if they'd been in Arizona the exact wrong amount of time—too long for a vacation, too short to put down roots. They had no appointments, weren't needed anywhere. One day became the next, the two of them creeping around the cabin, not sure what to do with themselves after breakfast and coffee. In moments she was able to pretend it was all just some weird, spur-of-the-moment holiday. It had been years since they'd gone anywhere by themselves, and it was a nice, romantic idea—just the two of them alone with their car and box full of cash. It really was quite a lot of money. It should've been enough to last them a few years, maybe more if they pinched their pennies. Of course, she had to keep reminding herself, this was them she was thinking about.

When the waiter came back with their plates, Pepper tucked his napkin into his collar and Moira pulled a chalky chicken breast around her plate. Before either of them could take their first bites, they were interrupted by a sharp bark of laughter from another table. A group of men had built a pyramid out of empty highball glasses and now one of them was out of his chair, holding the hem of the tablecloth like a magician about to whip it free. The waiter rushed over to stop them and one of the men stuck out a foot, sending him sprawling on his face. They all began chanting the name of the guy with the tablecloth in his hands, scooting their own chairs back in anticipation.

"Hey," Pepper said, just loud enough to be heard over the noise.

They turned to look at him and the smiles died on their faces. They were all big men, round guys with the doughy bodies of salesmen, but they saw his eyes, his ears, the way his hands gripped the side of the table as if he was ready to launch himself at them like a cannonball. Their expressions became those of children caught at some naughtiness. The man who was standing let go of the tablecloth and lowered back into his seat. A couple of the others mumbled things and held up their hands to say they wanted no trouble as the waiter picked himself up, red with anger, and began loading the empty glasses onto a tray.

Moira forked some chicken into her mouth. "This isn't bad," she said.

Pepper smiled at her, and a moment later he was eating and laughing with his mouth full like nothing had happened. Nothing *had* happened, she reminded herself. Still, she felt like a gavel had dropped in her mind, a verdict rendered. He had spoken just one word, barely moved, but she suddenly felt slapped in the face by a truth that had been traveling with them since they left New York. They were not normal people. They would not take the money and squirrel it away for a rainy day. They would not live simply in a cabin by the lake, making babies and strolling through the trees. It was not in them.

●—●

A week later she woke in the dark of early morning to find him gone, his side of the bed cold to the touch. She sat up in her nightgown, rubbing sleep from her eyes, and went out to look for him. He was not at the kitchen table or in the front porch rocker, where he sometimes sat when he couldn't sleep. The outhouse stood empty, its door swinging in the breeze. She was about to pull her boots on and hike up to the lake when he emerged from the woods, shirtless and grinning from a run.

It gave her a charge to see him moving again, and for a few days she rode it like a hot streak at cards. In the mornings they sat out on the porch and let the sun restore them, watching tiny lizards chase each other across rocks at the edge of the woods. They made love in the afternoons with the windows flung open and took evening dips in the lake, shouting from the cold, Moira feeling the occasional fish brush against her legs.

Then one evening she caught him doing tackling drills in the backyard, wearing the ridiculous two-tone wrestling shoes Fritz had given him before they left Montana. Leaving little S curves in the dirt with his back foot as he glided across the open space, his brow furrowed and his mouth tight. Looking good and quick and full of life. He didn't notice her standing in the window and she backed away, sinking into one of their two kitchen chairs.

He tried to laugh it off when he came in, saying he was just staying fit, knocking the cobwebs out of his muscles after so much time doing nothing. She knew better. Wrestling was back in his blood after the match with Lesko. It was still part of him, and he couldn't ignore it any more than a horse could ignore the urge to run. He announced he was going to the lake for a soak, and she smoked three cigarettes in fifteen minutes before going after him.

As she hiked, she wondered if it had been a mistake to tell Pepper about Lesko's visit. At first she had no intention of sharing it with him, but in those first days he just seemed so low. Finally she came out with it, hoping it might help him spring back to life. She recounted it as they rode the train south from Baltimore, Christmas wreaths hanging in all the windows. She left out the part about Lesko offering him a job, and Pepper listened to her as if he didn't quite believe any of it. When she was done, he settled back into his seat looking content for the first time since after their match, and for a while she believed she'd done the right thing.

She reached the lake and found him sunk to his chin, twenty feet from shore, his arms making little circles just beneath the surface. His boots and tights were piled on a rock and she sat next to them to pull off her own shoes. The gravel of the bank was cool under her bare feet and she stayed there a moment, listening to the cackling and knocking of unseen birds.

"I thought I'd be better at this," she said, keeping her hands folded on her knees, but saying it loud enough that her voice wasn't lost in all the wilderness.

"Better at what?" he said, treading water, tipping his head back a little to keep his mouth above the surface.

"I'm not sure," she said. "Doing nothing? Sitting watching the sunset like a couple of old codgers?"

He showed her the grin she loved. "Is that what we're doing?" he said. "Rattling around like a couple of beans in a tin can?"

She got up and stood with her feet in the shallows. Sand and green moss twisting around her toes. "I know what you're up to," she said.

He took two strokes to a place his feet could touch and crept out of the water, pulling on his tights so he could stand beside her. His skin cold against her arm. "There's got to be another promoter that would take me on," he said. "Curly or Pfeffer, somebody. There's no shortage of guys who want to do Lesko and Stettler harm."

It occurred to her that, since she'd kept the news clippings from him, he didn't even know how right he was. He was more famous now than he'd ever been as champion. All it would take would be for them to drive into town and give some local reporter the scoop of a lifetime. In a couple of days—a week, maybe—the big promoters from New York and Chicago would come calling.

"Is that what you want?" she said. "Is that what *we* want?"

The breeze rippled the water against their legs. Freezing but nice. "You saw me against Lesko," he said. "I was right there."

She tried to smile back at him but didn't quite make it. She'd watched the match from a balcony seat, a handkerchief crushed in one hand. During the bout, the whole arena roiled and churned like some great animal, and once an usher had to come down the aisle to tell her to please sit down, though she had no memory of getting out of her chair.

It was electric joy to watch him wrestle again after all those years. Running hard and heavy each step of the way with the world's heavyweight champion. She was still bursting with pride over it, but she'd also seen enough to know she never wanted to see him wrestle again. Despite the things Lesko had said and the glowing accounts in the papers, Moira knew Pepper wasn't the same man he was as champion. No one in the world had watched him compete more than she had. She knew his every move by heart. She understood the easy grace with which he moved around the ring. His bottomless strength and wind. The man she saw in New York that night was good, but he wasn't Pepper. She could tell his leg had never quite come back after Fritz broke it. He was just a step slower, a second more tentative. He was okay for busting up railroad toughs and fieldworkers in nickel challenge matches, but he wasn't young or quick enough to compete with the best professionals anymore. If he went back, even to carnival wrestling or the crooked stuff Fritz and Stettler were pitching now, eventually some rough, headstrong kid would come along and hurt him.

It broke her heart to tell him all that now, but she did, and when she was done she kissed him. They pulled apart and he was quiet for a long time.

"You talked to O'Shea," he said finally, "and I bet you made him tell you everything."

"I did," she said.

At first she couldn't believe the things the gangster had told her about her gambling debts, but in time she knew it was true. It was she who had broken them. She was a good gambler, one of the best, but nobody won all the time. Those days when Pepper was champion were such a whirlwind, there was nobody keeping track of the ledger. At some point she supposed she'd fallen into the same trap as all the wrestlers, imagining they would all stay young forever and the money would just flow and flow. She wasn't furious with herself over it anymore, or furious with Pepper for keeping it from her for so long. Now she just felt sorry. For who, she'd couldn't decide.

"All that money you lost," he said, "I never asked you to stop playing."

"No," she said. "But maybe you should have."

She felt a tear sprout at the corner of her eye and she touched her face to stop it. He saw it and slipped an arm around her waist, pulling her close. "Hey," he said. "It doesn't mean a thing to me. It never did. All I'm asking for is the same treatment. If I've got one shot left, I'm just saying we should think about it."

It wasn't the same thing, and she told him so, but she knew she couldn't stop him. If this was what he wanted to do, no one could keep him from it. The wind kicked up another notch, whipping her dress against her legs. "I'll think about it," she said. "So long as you promise me you'll think about it, too. I mean, really think."

He nodded, squinting one eye at her, looking boyish and sad and annoyed with the breeze all at once. "In any case," he said, "I don't think we're going to figure it all out standing here in the cold. You know what I'm thinking of? That little speakeasy we found right when we got here. That little shack on the edge of town. You know?"

She said she did.

"I bet that place is open," he said. "I bet they've got a card game going, too."

"It's possible," she said.

"How about we take a ride into town?" he said. "See what's happening."

"Would that be smart?" she said.

"It would be fun," he said.

Standing hip to hip, they turned and were about to walk up out of the water when they heard a low growl coming out of the north. Lifting their faces, they watched as an airplane skirted over the tree line on the opposite side of the lake, dipping its wings slightly as it righted its course along the water. The sight of it stopped her breathing and she took Pepper's cold, callused hand in hers. The plane's body was painted sunny yellow, and it flew so low it seemed to shake the ground with the great slapping of its propeller. She shaded her eyes and as it got closer she saw the sleek, slippery mole head of the pilot slung low in the cockpit. As the plane zoomed over top of them, trees quaking and water trembling, the pilot turned, fixing the gaze of his figure-eight goggles down at them. There was an awkward moment, like they were all surprised to see each other there, before Pepper raised his hand and waved.

On Wrestling

Discerning wrestling fans likely noticed early on that this book plays fast and loose with parts of the sport's history. Certainly, the novel shouldn't be read as a strict historical account. Just as the principal characters and events are fictional, certain details of wrestling's place during the early twentieth century had to be fudged a bit. For example, in the real world it seems unlikely that by 1921 Pepper Van Dean would be quite so naïve about a group of wrestling promoters conspiring to fix a world title bout. However, given modern professional wrestling's on-again, off-again relationship with the truth, I hope *Champion of the World* can be forgiven for taking a few liberties.

Readers interested in exploring nonfiction accounts of wrestling's murky past should peruse Scott M. Beekman's *Ringside: A History of Professional Wrestling in America* or Mark S. Hewitt's wonderfully detailed *Catch Wrestling: A Wild and Wooly Look at the Early Days of Pro Wrestling in America*. Marcus Griffin's 1937 book *Fall Guys: The Barnums of Bounce* is also required reading, providing a fascinating look at the grapplers of the time. In addition, Jonathan Snowden's fine

Shooters: The Toughest Men in Professional Wrestling offers character studies of America's toughest wrestlers, from Frank Gotch to modern stars like Brock Lesnar and Kurt Angle.

Even the most scholarly tomes, though, leave ample gray areas. The truth is, nobody knows for sure exactly when wrestling crossed the line from legitimate athletic contest to scripted performance. Certainly, wrestling's early American practitioners were exceedingly skilled, exceedingly ruthless men who wouldn't take that kind of transformation lightly. For much of the eighteenth and nineteenth centuries their reputations were as fearsome, authentic men of sport. Many of our early presidents—including George Washington and Abraham Lincoln—were avid wrestlers, and some credit victory in a high-profile 1831 match with helping launch Lincoln's political career. Later, Theodore Roosevelt and other proponents of "muscular Christianity" backed it as healthy exercise in the face of increasingly sedentary lifestyles.

As America's modern sporting culture took shape during the Industrial Revolution, wrestling shifted from a largely rural, working-class pursuit to a nationwide powerhouse appealing to middle- and upper-class consumers. The rise of sports-minded national publications like the *Spirit of the Times* and the *Police Gazette* helped establish wrestlers as popular stars from coast to coast. Constant barnstorming tours made the sport immensely profitable and helped expand regional grappling styles like New England's collar-and-elbow, the brutal rough-and-tumble style of the Wild West, European Greco-Roman and British catch-as-catch-can (usually shortened to *catch wrestling* today).

Wrestling was a popular leisure activity in the Union army camps of the Civil War, and the gatherings served as a melting pot for grappling techniques. There, American wrestlers from far-flung towns mingled with each other and with European imports, who brought their own disparate styles with them across the Atlantic. By the late

1800s, mixed-style bouts were common and the marathon push-and-pull sessions of the collar-and-elbow and Greco-Roman styles began to wane in popularity. With its faster pace and more visceral appeal, catch wrestling took the lead, borrowing the most effective techniques from other Western forms and incorporating aspects of Asian martial arts as well.

Most likely, a certain amount of chicanery was always afoot. Owing to its carnival roots and a tradition of showmanship dating back to ancient Rome, the wrestling business was perpetually flush with con men. In an era of limited media and lax government oversight, the truth was frequently stretched in the name of making a buck. The barnstorming tours and circus troupes wrestlers used to make their money were rife with fixed matches. By 1905 the *Police Gazette* trumpeted that the outcomes of "90 percent" of professional wrestling bouts were predetermined, though at the time that may have been hyperbole, written in the magazine's notoriously over-the-top style.

If wrestling had indeed morphed into such a widespread (and public) swindle so early on, it's hard to understand why sportswriters continued to report on it with more or less straight faces for at least another twenty years. A glance at newspaper wrestling results in the late 1910s reveals the appearance of cartoonish characters like the Masked Marvel, but staid written accounts differentiating some matches as "obvious fixes" and others as "on the level"—not to mention the fact that wrestlers could be arrested on fraud charges for participating in faked bouts—imply that at least an expectation of legitimacy persisted well into the 1920s.

Few wrestling writers question the rise of Frank Gotch as anything but authentic. It was Gotch's mentor, Martin "Farmer" Burns, who popularized the hangman's drop carnival trick performed by Pepper during the early part of this book. Popular legend says Burns was so incensed about a loss via chokehold early in his career that he embarked on a vigorous physical fitness regimen focused on strengthening his neck muscles. The 165-pound Iowa native eventually sported a 20-inch neck and began performing the hangman's drop while on carnival tours across the United States. Burns could reportedly withstand a six-foot drop from a platform with a noose around his neck, hang for three minutes and whistle "Yankee Doodle" before finally returning to earth.

Also renowned as a wrestling coach, Burns plucked Gotch out of obscurity after defeating the young heavyweight in a challenge match in 1899. Under Burns's tutelage, Gotch came quickly to national prominence, winning the American heavyweight championship from Tom Jenkins in Bellingham, Washington, in 1904 and the world title from Estonian strongman Georg Hackenschmidt in 1908 at Dexter Park Pavilion in Chicago. Known for his brutal catch wrestling style, Gotch capitalized on his celebrity as world champion better than perhaps any wrestler before him. He launched a number of successful exhibition tours at home and overseas, sold workout brochures and wrestling manuals and starred onstage in "All About a Bout," a play that ended nightly with a worked match between Gotch and his manager, Emil Klank.

Newspapers portrayed Gotch as a patriotic American hero in the wake of his victory over Hackenschmidt, and that image only intensified after African-American fighter Jack Johnson won the world heavyweight boxing championship near the end of 1908. Long cast as villain in the press, Johnson's title reign touched off significant turmoil nationwide. White Americans turned away from boxing and the sport's temporary decline helped lift the fortunes of both wrestling and football. There were even some public calls for Gotch to don gloves and fight Johnson. The wrestler steadfastly ignored those cries, though he did help get Jim Jeffries in shape for his 1910 loss to Johnson in the "Fight of the Century."

Like boxing, the elite levels of wrestling remained strictly segregated for much of the early 1900s. Nineteenth-century Greco-Roman champion William Muldoon—perhaps America's first true wrestling star—was close friends with boxing titlist John L. Sullivan, and both men steadfastly adhered to each sport's long-standing "color bar." So did Gotch, though reports indicate he took on African-American grappler Silas Archer during a barnstorming tour of Alaska early in his career. It should be noted that on that trip Gotch wrestled under an assumed name.

From 1908 to 1911, Gotch set about expeditiously expunging the heavyweight ranks of all its top (white) talent. His dominance was so thorough and credible challengers so scarce that promoters began to fear wrestling's popularity was in decline. In late 1910, Gotch announced he wanted a rematch with Hackenschmidt, who had complained loudly in the European press that Gotch had greased himself with oil during their first bout. The rematch—held at Chicago's Comiskey Park in front of thirty thousand spectators on September 4, 1911—is largely considered the end of professional wrestling's early golden age.

In that bout, Gotch defeated Hackenschmidt via straight falls after less than thirty minutes of disastrous action. On the heels of a massive promotional buildup, Hackenschmidt's performance was so poor that it spawned numerous match-fixing accusations. Later the European champion said he entered the ring hobbled by a knee injury and unable to give his best. There were also rumors that Gotch paid one of Hackenschmidt's training partners to cripple him during a pre-match workout, but those stories have been largely discounted by wrestling historians.

In any case, the public had seemingly had its fill of wrestling. When Gotch retired in 1913, the sport slipped into disarray as a gaggle of different promoters rushed to prop up lesser champions in his place. It took nearly a decade for wrestling to find its legs, and by the time it did, the action in the ring had become almost completely scripted. Gotch periodically appeared in comeback matches, but nothing major materialized before his sudden death in 1917 at age thirty-nine. The official cause was uremic poisoning, but speculation persists that he had syphilis.

New York impresario Jack Curley established himself as the most successful post-Gotch wrestling promoter. Forging business relationships with the best midwestern talent, he made Joe Stecher, Earl Caddock, and Ed "Strangler" Lewis the top draws at Madison Square Garden as they traded the title back and forth during the years surrounding World War I. It's theorized that Stecher's victory over Lewis in 1916 was wrestling's last wholly on-the-level championship bout. Soon, though, Lewis fell out with Curley, won the title back from Stecher and took it with him when he joined up with promoters Billy Sandow and Joe "Toots" Mondt.

Lewis, Sandow and Mondt were known as the Gold Dust Trio and, though the business was likely already mostly rigged, are regarded as the architects of modern professional wrestling. Together they implemented many staples of today's histrionic business, including its wild "slam-bang" style, frequently controversial outcomes and wrestlers working a series of matches with increasingly dire stakes. Under the new system, championships weren't awarded to the best, most skilled wrestlers but to the men capable of generating the most revenue. Still, promoters kept on hand a number of able catch wrestlers—called "shooters"—to sort out athletes who balked at doing their bidding in the ring. In April 1925, wrestler Stanislaus Zbyszko conspired with Curley to steal the heavyweight title away from the Gold Dust Trio, and with it control of much of the industry. By the 1930s the hard-nosed, no-frills professional wrestling popular at the turn of the century was gone for good, replaced by the scripted theatrics and ballyhoo of the modern hustle. Along with a cadre of promoters east of the Mississippi, Curley instituted the territory system that would serve as wrestling's organizational structure until cable television and Vince McMahon's powerful World Wrestling Federation usurped it during the 1980s.

Legitimate wrestling became the domain of amateurs, though the art of catch-as-catch-can survived and has even experienced a renaissance during the last few decades. Today, submission wrestling tournaments are common, but still appeal only to small, niche audiences. The best modern analogue to early American wrestling—and the wrestling that occurs in this book—could be mixed martial arts fighting. Catch wrestling practitioners like Josh Barnett, Frank and Ken Shamrock and Kazushi Sakuraba all became MMA stars during the 1990s and early 2000s. Many of these contemporary grapplers trace their lineage back to the wrestling legends of the late nineteenth century.

On Bootlegging

Montana bootleggers were smuggling alcohol across the border from Canada as early as the 1870s, when they began bringing whiskey into the northern town of Fort Benton via steamboat to trade with local Native American tribes. Understaffed border agencies and Canadian Mounties had trouble monitoring the comings and goings in the rugged, isolated terrain, so for decades liquor, opium and illegal immigrants (mostly Chinese laborers) trafficked across the border more or less unchecked. The illicit trade went both ways, as western U.S. states and Canadian provinces each experimented with various ways to regulate alcohol during the early 1900s. In addition, Canadian farmers often found it less expensive to buy cars and field equipment in America and then brave the region's remote roads to secretly drive them back across the border.

Statewide prohibition took effect in Montana at the beginning of 1919, after most neighboring states had already gone dry. Rural counties overwhelmingly approved the move in a 1916 vote, while its three most urban counties (Deer Lodge, Lewis and Clark and Silver Bow) all voted against. At the time of the alcohol ban, the state's largest city of Butte—near where much of this novel is set—had a population around 60,000 and was known as a hardscrabble, "wide-open" town that boasted some 250 taverns. The county government there collected more than a quarter million dollars annually from license fees and property taxes for drinking establishments.

Montana women had earned the right to vote in 1914, and the state's well-organized wing of the Women's Christian Temperance Union (WCTU) was instrumental in the passage of statewide sanctions. Just as it did nationwide, Prohibition ushered in a decade of sweeping social change in Montana. Before Prohibition, saloons were regarded as the domain of men, while women did their drinking at home. The new laws changed that, as law-abiding bars were shuttered and more clandestine spaces took their place. Moonshining was common, and Montana's speakeasies, blind pigs and nightclubs welcomed women and ethnic groups that had previously been shunned. Women took to bootlegging alongside male counterparts and on their own. For some Montana women, Prohibition served as an introduction to the working world, providing a crash course in how to successfully run a business.

In urbanized settings like Butte, saloons played an important multifaceted role prior to Prohibition. For a city populated largely by immigrant mine workers, the neighborhood tavern often doubled as the bank, post office and employment agency. In Butte's many Irish, Slavic, German and Italian enclaves, the saloon was the place to hear news from home, and many stocked foreign language newspapers. Bars in poor neighborhoods often kept a pot of stew or soup bubbling, so men gathered there not only to have a drink after work but to get a hot meal.

Likewise, drinking provided the bedrock of many social activities for Butte's wealthy elite. The city's exclusive Silver Bow Club, founded by copper king William A. Clark in 1882, charged its members a $50 entrance fee and $60 in annual dues. The club's four-story location, built in 1905, featured opulent furnishings, a cigar lounge and a full-service kitchen, but most members went there for the bar. Considering the local tavern's central place in society, it's no surprise that cities like Butte did everything they could to sidestep new alcohol regulations. Some of the city's saloons closed or were converted into "soft drink parlors," but many merely changed their names and continued selling booze on the sly. The uptown Crown Bar, for example, became the Crown Cigar Store and kept right on serving.

As the need for liquor grew and in-state stockpiles dwindled, Canadian border towns like Lethbridge, Moose Jaw, Medicine Hat and Govenlock became the sites of large export houses. American rumrunners ferried loads of liquor over the border by car and truck, traveling roads that were little more than glorified horse trails, often at high speeds, in all weather, sometimes at night. Hijackings were common and occasionally deadly, especially for independent bootleggers operating without the protection of larger crime syndicates. Locals cooked liquor to supplement family incomes and a handful small-town businessmen—like C. W. "Shorty" Young of Havre— ruled their communities as homegrown organized crime kings.

By the time the whole country went dry in 1920, many Montanans already believed the laws were unenforceable. The state was just too big and too wild to adequately police. Federal Prohibition agents joined the battle with state authorities, and some Montana counties hired Pinkertons or Burns International Detective Agency operatives to help corral bootleggers. Yet still the illegal liquor flowed, while the state government reported significant revenue losses in 1921 and 1922.

Shorty Young's Havre gang eventually grew into nationwide suppliers. At one point they bragged that they'd ferried liquor to every state except Maine—where there were too many toll roads. They imported alcohol from Canada as well as illegal merchants all over the American west and stockpiled it in perhaps dozens of locations around northern Montana. Their stash spots included abandoned coal mines, remote cabins, dilapidated barns, the basements of schoolhouses and secret rooms in businesses they owned in town. They commandeered ranchlands and hid their vehicles inside hollowed-out haystacks, and Havre's daily newspaper reported they even used the airplane of a local war veteran to fly the stuff in and out of state. Young himself owned both a hotel and a secret brewery, which produced beer he adorned with phony Canadian labels.

In 1923, federal Prohibition agent Addison K. Lusk wrote Montana governor Joseph Dixon about the problems he faced enforcing the alcohol ban in the state. Lusk commanded a force of around a dozen men, and the 550-mile border between Montana and Canada featured only two customs stations. Two major rail lines ran into Canada, and Lusk wrote that railroad workers showed little interest in trying to sniff out alcohol shipments. The same may have been true of many city police forces, where officers sometimes sympathized with local bootleggers over federal interlopers. Corruption and payoffs were common among both state and federal officers, and newspapers reported that bootleggers serving time in the Silver Bow county jail paid off jailers to let them run the place like a social club, complete with liquor, food service and jazz records.

By the mid-1920s the previously powerful state chapters of the WCTU and Anti-Saloon League began to lose steam. Membership declined, along with fund-raising efforts and lobbying power. In 1926, voters repealed the statewide prohibition law—in Butte, seventy-three percent voted for repeal—and in 1928 voted down an effort to reinstate it. By the early 1930s, federal prohibition enjoyed next to no support in Montana. A poll by the *Literary Digest* reported that eighty percent of state residents favored repeal. When Congress passed the Twenty-first Amendment to undo the Eighteenth in December of 1933, most Montanans likely responded with sighs of relief.

Concerning Montana history during the 1920s and the Butte/Silver Bow area specifically, Montana State University professor Mary Murphy and University of Montana professor emeritus David Emmons remain the authoritative sources. Murphy's book *Mining Cultures: Men, Women, and Leisure in Butte, 1914–41* is indispensable and provided many of the details for this note. Emmons's books *The Butte Irish: Class and Ethnicity in an American Mining Town, 1875–1925* and *Beyond the Pale: The Irish in the West, 1845–1910* both provide fascinating expanded reading. In addition, Gary A. Wilson's book *Honky-Tonk Town: Havre's Bootlegging Days* gives rollicking insight into the wild, lawless times of Prohibition in northern Montana.

ACKNOWLEDGMENTS

So many people worked minor miracles to see *Champion of the World* into print. From the start, Nat Sobel and Judith Weber showed the book tremendous care and support. Their notes were invaluable. They were right about everything. The rest of the staff at Sobel Weber Associates were equally wonderful at shepherding a nervous first-time author through the chute and into the performance ring.

Any writer who lands with Sara Minnich at G. P. Putnam's Sons has already hit the jackpot. She's everything you want in an editor—smart, perceptive, kind, patient. I need a lot of help in all those departments. I'm indebted to her and Ivan Held for giving a quirky little book about wrestling a chance. The Putnam copyeditors saved me from a scatter-gun blast of mistakes. Any bullet holes still visible in the walls are mine alone.

Todd Robinson and his fine noir journal, *Thuglit,* published my short story "The Rightful King of Wrestling," which first caught the attention of Nat and Judith. Todd published the story when he said he would and paid me right on time. He'd probably bristle at the notion, but he's all class. Support his work.

There's no better crew of writers, readers and critics in Missoula, Montana (or anywhere else, I'd wager), than Sarah Aswell, Dan Brooks, Erika Fredrickson, Ben Fowlkes and Jason McMackin.

They all suffered through early drafts of the manuscript and the finished novel wouldn't exist without their input. You'll be hearing more from each of them, I promise you.

Kate Gadbow read an early version of the book and her critique made it instantly better. Her positivity gave me the courage to start querying agents.

Courtney Ellis read and read and read. She talked me off the ledge about a hundred times. She was brilliant, insightful, and she believed.

TURN THE PAGE FOR AN EXCERPT

After losing his memory from a traumatic brain injury, army veteran Matthew Rose must journey to Montana to settle his late father's affairs, even though he can't recall that part of his past. But when Matthew sees a house go up in flames, it sparks a memory of a different fire, an unsolved crime from long ago. As Mathew searches for answers, what he finds will connect the old fire and the new, a series of long-unsolved mysteries, and a ruthless act of murder.

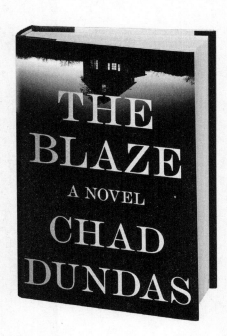

THE BLAZE

A NOVEL

CHAD DUNDAS

ONE

The first thing Matthew Rose remembered was pitching forward in the back of an army Humvee and puking beef stew between his boots. The chalky Dinty Moore broth had a chemical tang on the way back up—chunks of stringy meat mixed with the subtle flavor of plastic bag. It took a couple of good heaves to get it all out. He pressed the top of his helmet against the seat in front of him and dotted tears on the backs of his tactical gloves. When he was able, he sat up, and found the other three soldiers in the Humvee all staring at him like a puppy who had just shit on the rug. Their faces said it wasn't the first time. He must've been throwing up a lot lately.

They were all pocket-eyed and filthy, weighed down by ballistic plates and the ammunition strapped to their chest rigs. It was so hot—so ungodly hot—that it took him a few heartbeats to realize he didn't recognize any of them. Panic gripped him. A rolling wave of pain surged from behind his molars and crashed like a sucker punch on his frontal lobe. A soldier in the front passenger seat hissed his name like it was the worst curse word he could think of. *"Rose!"* he said. "Tell me you didn't just yack all over my new vehicle." Tracks of sweat ran out of the soldier's sideburns. His blunt little mustache looked like it had been grown as a joke. He had staff sergeant's stripes on his chest and a name tape that read POTTS. Matthew didn't think he'd ever seen the guy before.

There was so much about this moment he wouldn't learn until later: that he was twenty-six years old and moving with the rest of his fire team down a narrow strip of blacktop on the crumbling edge of eastern Baghdad. That he'd just been promoted to sergeant and was supposed to be Potts's second-in-command. That Potts felt protective of the Humvee because the last one had just blown up in an IED attack; a member of their team killed. That it was July and their unit had just one month left on a twelve-month deployment. They were all counting the days until they went home, paranoid and half crazed from lack of sleep. But Matthew didn't know any of that. Not yet.

He tried to say "sorry," but the word caught in the burning clot of his throat and came out as a wet cough. The soldier across the backseat from him reached over the deck of gear and clapped him on the shoulder. "Holy shit, dude," he said, "you okay?"

The guy's name tape said RICKERT. His freckles and cow-brown eyes made Matthew think of farmland, of rolling wheat fields and the domes of grain silos. From the casual way he touched him, Matthew guessed they were friends. It made him want to grab Rickert's hand and hold it. He wanted to tell him that he didn't remember who he was or what they were doing. He wanted to yell for help, but as he opened his mouth to try to explain he registered something else about how they were all looking at him. The other men in the Humvee were just as terrified as he was. Their eyes begged him to shut the fuck up. Whatever was wrong with him, they didn't want to hear about it. Not at that moment. What they wanted to hear was that he had his shit together. He was fine. He had their backs. He covered his mouth with a fist and belched. "I'm good," he said.

He *was* good, he thought. This feeling would pass. He would be fine. Just as he thought this, the Humvee lurched to a stop, sending them all rocking forward in their seats. Through the bulletproof windshield, he saw a slender bridge standing over a sluggish river. Beyond that, dark catacomb buildings rode the low crest of a ridge. At the mouth of the bridge a dead cow lay rotting in the middle of the road, blocking their way. Its hide was slick brown, almost black, a dark stain spreading out on the pavement beneath it.

"Fuck," the driver said. He wore mirrored sunglasses, his lip fat with chew. "Not again."

Rickert leaned into the center console to take a look. "The same exact spot?" he asked. "Do these motherfuckers think we're that stupid?"

"I told you," the driver said. "This is how it happens. One guy gets killed and the bad luck spreads like a fucking virus."

"Both of you shut up," Potts said. "Rollo, back it up. Now."

The Humvee lumbered into reverse, pushing Matthew back. Behind them he saw another vehicle riding their rear bumper, two more Humvees behind that. Potts spoke into the handset of a dash-mounted radio as the whine of the engine filled the cab. The convoy retreated three hundred yards and stopped again, the guy called Rollo easing the brakes this time. Matthew sat stock-still, his thoughts moving as if underwater. Every synapse firing a beat too slow. He worried anything he might do would give away how confused and dizzy he felt. Before he could steady himself, the other soldiers in the Humvee cracked their doors and bailed out into the road.

A layer of dust coated him as he followed them out. He sucked a breath, taking in the stench of decaying concrete, sweat, and burning oil. As he rounded the back of the vehicle, the world began to reorient itself around him. A few things were obvious: The desert. The war. Road signs printed in Arabic. Clockwork dials spun in his head, tumblers dropping into place. He knew who he was—Matthew Rose, sergeant insignia patched on his uniform in the same place Potts wore his. *What else?* he thought. *What else?*

Other soldiers appeared from the rear Humvees and pushed into the open land beyond the road. They had their rifles up, moving with the steady precision of training and muscle memory. He felt a jolt of relief to see Rickert waiting for him, but when the guy's fingers latched around his wrist, they squeezed hard enough to pinch bone. "You think you can fucking stick with me this time?" Rickert asked, pulling him close, shouting over the noise. Matthew nodded, not knowing why. "Good," Rickert said. "Come on."

They followed the others into the sand. Matthew pressed the butt of his rifle to his shoulder and felt strangely comforted at the way it fit. The horizon was empty besides the jigsaw face of the buildings. Nothing moved in there. They looked abandoned. Rickert dropped to one knee and Matthew copied him. The sun was a red marble in the sky, the air thick and damp. "What do we do now?" he asked, swallowing down the raw sting lingering at the back of his throat.

Rickert's eyes shifted across his rifle sights, making clear this was a stupid question. "We wait for EOD to see if there's a bomb stuck up that dead cow's ass," he said.

Matthew glanced back at the road, where Rollo and Potts leaned against the hood of the Humvee. Potts scribbling on a metal clipboard.

"What are they doing?" he asked.

Now Rickert's whole head turned. "They're filling out the fucking UXO," he said. "Jesus, Matt, are you sure you're all right?"

Before he could answer, a crackling sound erupted from inside the buildings, followed by the *thunk, thunk, thunk* of slugs punching into the Humvees. Rickert's rifle bounded as he returned fire. Matthew's mind snapped into the hyperawareness of being shot at. His finger closed around the trigger of his own gun, but before he could fire, a strange, high-pitched cry made him turn again. Rollo was down in the dirt, clutching his leg with both hands. Potts squatted behind him, trying to drag the man to cover, his face twisted from the effort.

Rickert and Matthew sprinted back to the road and each slipped an arm under Rollo's shoulders. They dragged him behind the front wheel of the Humvee, where he sprawled on the ground, gripping his knee and saying *"Fuck-fuck-fuck-I-told-you-fuck-fuck-fuck"* as blood flooded from a quarter-sized hole in his pants. Rickert ripped the Velcro strap off a prepackaged tourniquet and slipped it around the leg. The fabric band made a crunching sound as it ratcheted tight. Potts shouted into his radio. Crouching down next to Rickert, Matthew felt light-headed and useless until Rollo reached up and grabbed his hand. The sudden touch startled him. Rollo had pulled off his sunglasses and Matthew saw he was just a kid. Eighteen, nineteen, maybe. Face pale and grubby. "I'm sorry, Matt," he said, tears brimming in the wells of his eyes. "Fuck, I'm sorry. I didn't mean to get shot."

He tried to smile. "You didn't do anything wrong," he said. Not knowing if it was true.

The medic appeared and shooed them back. As he worked on Rollo, Matthew glanced up over the hood of the Humvee and saw a man making his way across the floodplain toward them. The man was a hundred yards out, balancing in the loose sand with a long, awkward-looking stick in his hands. When he got to a low series of boulders near the riverbank, he crouched down and fumbled to get the stick up on one shoulder. Matthew shaded his eyes and squinted, making out the bulbous, diamond-shaped head of a rocket-propelled grenade.

"Down!" he yelled, pulling Rickert onto the concrete just as the RPG made a hollow *whompf* and fired.

He covered his head with his arms and waited a single, long second for the grenade to hit them, but it never did. The man missed his shot. The grenade streaked between the bumpers of the Humvees and slammed into an embankment behind them, flinging a plume of dirt into the air. The explosion was a loud, flat sound, more like a slap than a boom. Matthew and Rickert stayed down as debris pinged against the hoods of the vehicles.

"Well," Matthew said, his lips against the chunky blacktop. "This is pleasant."

The words came in a sarcastic monotone his brain hadn't authorized, his voice muffled by his arms and the ringing in his ears. When he lifted his head to take a peek, Rickert was grinning at him. The skin around his eyes was so crusted with grit and sweat that it mapped every crease in his face. Stretched out side by side on their bellies, they might have been two kids at sleep-away camp. "I can't fucking wait to go home," he said. "See Ali and the baby."

"Yeah," Matthew said, though he didn't feel it. "Me neither."

"You going to get back with that girl?" Rickert asked, resting his cheek on his bicep.

Matthew thought: *What girl?* He said: "I don't know. Maybe."

"You should," Rickert said. "I mean it, Matt. No bullshit."

He gave a slight nod, not knowing what to say.

Rickert pushed him himself up and stood. "Come on, my man," he said, offering a hand. "Let's get the fuck out of here."

TWO

An eleven-foot grizzly guarded the bottom of the stairs leading to the airport terminal. The taxidermist had done a good job stuffing it, posing the bear mid-roar—its yellow teeth flashing, paws swiping the air as if warding off a cloud of bees. Somebody had wrapped the beast up in Christmas lights and perched a red-and-white Santa hat between its fuzzy ears. As Matthew came down the steps carrying his duffel and messenger bag, the blinking lights made it hard to tear his eyes away. He thought at any moment the bear might cock one fuzzy hip at him and wave hello.

The digital wall clock said 6:15 p.m. A sparse crowd loitered in the arrival bay, waiting for passengers on the Saturday-evening connecting flight from Denver. He searched their faces with his eyes but walked right past Georgie Porter before she reached out and pulled him into an awkward hug. It felt like being grabbed by the person next to you at a football game when the home team scores a touchdown.

"I'm so sorry," she said, her breath hot on his shoulder. "Shit, Matthew, I'm so sorry."

"Thanks," he said, "for doing this. I didn't know who else to call."

The first thing he noticed was how tall she was—almost as tall as him. She had fine features and big dark eyes and wore a puffy purple parka over jeans and knee-high Sorel boots. Just a fringe of brown hair stuck from under her navy watch cap. From the snow-flakes still melting on top of the hat he guessed she hadn't been wait-ing long. *So,* he thought, *this is you.*

She stepped back and held him by the elbows. "You look differ-ent," she said.

"I am different," he said without thinking. "I have a brain injury."

Her grin flickered but she steadied it. "I meant your hair," she said, tugging softly at a loose curl. "It's longer than I remember."

He tucked the strand behind his ear. "Oh," he said, "yeah. I guess I kind of let it go."

She led him through the terminal, asking easy stuff like: "How was your flight?"

"Just a six-hour party in the sky," he said. "Plus, an hour layover in Denver. On this last connection the guy next to me took his shoes off? I think he was smuggling onions in there."

A little scar dimpled on her chin as she smiled at him. It felt like a physical thing in his chest. He reminded himself: *Be normal. Make small talk.*

The truth was, this had been Matthew's first day of commercial travel since getting out of the army. Back in August, the military had issued him a new uniform for his trip home—a full kit of cammies still stiff and creased from the bag, the dome of the patrol hat not yet wilted and crusted with sweat. At every stop, people came up to shake his hand and thank him for his service. Their faces were eager, all trying to do a nice thing for him, but none taking the time to notice how damaged he was. They couldn't tell his head was pound-ing and the itchy new uniform made him want to squirm out of his own skin. Today's trip had been the opposite. It had been sunny and seventy-seven degrees when his mom dropped him at the airport that morning in Fort Myers. Nobody had looked twice at him all day. In his civilian clothes he moved easily through security and boarding gates. Just a regular guy flying home for Christmas. No reason to notice him in the rush of holiday travelers.

Now here he was: on the ground in Montana, in the town where he'd spent the first twenty-three years of the life he no longer remembered. They whooshed out through the airport's automatic doors and a gust of wind cut him to the bone. It was dark and hard little snowflakes blew by his face. He zipped his jacket to his chin and clamped a hand on his hat to keep it from flying off. Georgie laughed. "Kind of different than Florida?" she asked.

"Little bit," he said.

Before the trip, he'd gone online to buy himself some warm clothes. He'd picked out a billed farmer's hat, a red-and-black-plaid parka, jeans, and sturdy boots. Now he realized they weren't good enough. The cold hung on him like a chain around his neck as they walked across the parking lot. Georgie's truck was an old Chevy S-10, painted the distinctive mint green of an old Forest Service vehicle. Matthew could still see where they'd scraped the words PARK RANGER off the side doors. Inside, the plastic seats leaked chunky orange stuffing, but the engine fired up when she cranked the key.

"So," she said, "I'm just going to ask. How are you doing, really?"

The way she looked at him across the bench seat he knew "fine" wasn't going to cut it. "Honestly?" he said. "I walk around feeling doomed most of the time."

"Jesus," she said, "that's awful."

"What can you do?" he said. "The doctors say it's normal to experience a certain amount of paranoia after a severe cranial trauma."

She handed the woman in the parking booth a few bucks and turned onto the highway. "And your mom?" she asked. "How's she handling it?"

"My mom," he said, "is different than I imagined."

"In what way?"

A few times during his last days in the army, after his memory had been scrubbed clean, he'd tried to dream his mother up from scratch. He pictured a woman in a garden somewhere, her hands in the dirt, skin brown and creased from the sun. Once he got to Florida, he realized the only thing he got right was the suntan. His mom worked in PR for the public school system. She played golf on weekends and drank too much at book club.

For four months he'd been staying in her big house outside Naples—Matthew, his mom and stepdad all getting to know each other again. He relearned his mom's shampoo-and-skin-cream smell, the rich, fluttery sound of her laugh. One of his first nights back, she cooked his favorite dinner—beef stroganoff—and the taste of the mushrooms made him retch. He couldn't finish it. As he scraped his plate into the garbage disposal he could feel them staring at him from the table. This stranger who now lived in their house.

"I'm sorry," his mom had said. "I thought you liked it."

"I did, too," he'd said.

He told the story to Georgie, hoping it explained what he meant. "She wants to help but doesn't know how—and I honestly don't know what I need from her. I try to ask her things about the past, what things were like while I was growing up, but she mostly sticks to the broad strokes. I get the feeling the past isn't her favorite subject."

"I don't blame her," she said. "Toward the end of their marriage, your dad wasn't an easy guy to live with."

"To hear her tell it," he said, "neither was I."

The truck rounded a bend and the lights of town filled up the belly of a wide valley. Drawing himself up, he scanned the landscape for anything familiar. He'd already gone online to learn what he could about his hometown and had the basics in his head: Population: 67,000. Elevation: 3,200 feet. Date of incorporation: 1885. The city's Wikipedia page showed pictures of a university clock tower, a packed football stadium, the pillars of city hall. They were all taken in sunny weather—chamber-of-commerce stills that made the place look homey and inviting. None of it helped him get a feel for what it was like to actually be here. Winter had leached the color out of everything, the blacktop and sky now the same color slate. He saw the glowing moon-base of a grocery-store parking lot and the hulking silhouette of a hospital. In the distance, mountains loomed like tall white ships. There was nothing he recognized.

The third time she glanced at him in the glow of the dashboard light he said: "What?"

"What do you mean, what?" she asked. "You don't think this is a little weird?"

"No, I get it," he said. "You pick your ex-boyfriend up from the airport—a guy you've known your whole life—and he says he doesn't remember you at all. Does that about cover it?"

She scrunched her nose. "I don't like the word 'ex-boyfriend,'" she said. "More like ex-*best* friend. And you skipped the part where you don't speak to me for eight years, join the army, go off to war—"

"Get blown up."

"Get blown up," she repeated, cutting him an apologetic glance, "and then e-mail me out of the blue trying to reconnect. So, yeah, it's pretty weird. You really don't remember anything? You don't remember me? Us?"

"I know the basics," he said. "Now."

"You know what I told you," she said. "What your mom told you. It's not the same as really remembering it."

That stung him. "Ouch," he said. "I guess we're going to dive straight into it, huh?"

Her eyes darted back to the road. "You don't want to talk about it," she said. A statement, not a question.

"It's not that," he said. "It's just not really a drive-in-from-the-airport kind of conversation."

They drove in silence until she asked: "How long are you around?"

"Two weeks," he said. "I fly out Christmas Day. Look, don't get me wrong, I definitely want to talk. You're one of the only people who might be able to help me get back what I've lost. I just might need to ease into it a little bit."

That seemed to satisfy her. She asked where he was staying and when he told her the name of his motel she made a face like she'd just noticed a bad smell. "Why that place?"

"It was the cheapest I could find with a swimming pool."

"A swimming pool? What for?"

"For swimming," he said. "I've been doing it a lot in Florida. It keeps my head on straight."

"Huh," she said. "Well, that's a switch."

"What do you mean?" he asked, smiling to keep things light.

"I haven't seen you swim since you were fourteen years old," she said. "It was a big deal when you quit the team. Your parents saved up for private lessons, a youth aquatic club membership, all that. You won the city meet for your age group in eighth grade, made varsity on the relay team as a freshman in high school. People thought you might get a scholarship, but you quit before sophomore year. Said your parents pressured you into it and—" She caught herself and stopped. "Sorry."

"Don't be," he said. "I'm still getting used to playing so much catch-up. It's like every social interaction is a test set up for me to fail."

He had one hand propped on his knee. She reached across the gearshift and squeezed it. A few blocks later, the sign for the Hollywood Motel appeared on the left. Its neon-orange sun and twinkling palm tree were out of place in the middle of the Rockies. She pulled the truck in front of the main office and he looked at the C-shaped layout of the place. Two floors of rooms all facing the parking lot. Most of the cars parked there were clunkers, holes rusting in some of the bodies. He guessed most of the other people staying there weren't passing through. Still, there it was: at one end of the complex, a large square enclosure with big windows fogged over in the cold. The pool. Just seeing it eased the tension between his shoulder blades.

"You didn't have to come back here, you know," she said. "You could have handled all the executor stuff from Florida."

"I know," he said. "I wanted to come."

"My mom said when you left, you told everyone you were done with this place forever."

He let a breath out slow. "You want to know how I found out my dad was dead?"

"I don't know," she said. "Do I?"

"I'd been calling him on the phone," he said. "Ever since I got back from Iraq. I had an old number for him in my phone. I didn't even know if it was still good, but I probably called it two dozen times. I left a bunch of messages. My mom said it was a waste of time. She didn't like seeing me get my hopes up. She said my dad was a deadbeat, that it had been years since he and I wanted anything to do with each other. So, eventually I gave up. Then, on the day I went to see the neurologist and got my diagnosis, I tried him again—just to give him the news, you know?—and a cop answered."

"Oh," she said. "Shit."

"Yeah," he said. "It was a woman's voice, which confused me at first, because nobody had said anything about my dad having a girl-friend or whatever. Then she asked me, 'Are you any relation to David Michael Rose?' and just from the tone in her voice I knew he was dead. Nobody else would say it like that besides a cop."

"You mean he had just done it?" she asked.

"The landlords found his body that morning. The cop told me

he'd shot himself in his rental house by the lake. That's how she said it—*the lake*—like I was supposed to know where that was."

"That's the fucking worst," she said.

"Sort of," he said. "I mean—yeah, it was—but my mom said it had been at least a few years since he and I last talked. I don't remember my dad at all, so it's hard for me to feel sad about it, to be honest. The point is, now he's dead, and I might never remember him. I missed my chance. I don't want to miss anything else like that. Something about talking to that cop made me realize, all the people I want to remember, the life I want to figure out, it's here. It's not in Florida. So here I am."

She smiled a sad smile at him. "You want me to wait until you get checked in?"

"I can manage," he said.

"Tomorrow is my day off," she said. "If you feel like it, you should give me a call."

"Can you do evening?" he asked. "I have to go to my dad's in the morning. Load up all his earthly possessions so we can get the probate started."

"Jesus," she said again.

"Your mom is going to help me with the legal stuff. Maybe with my other thing, too."

"Laurie Porter will set you straight," she said, making it sound like an advertising slogan. "No case too big or too small."

They shared a half hug across the seat and he watched her drive away before shouldering through the door into the motel office.

Nice 'n Easy
■ German ■
Grammar

ISABEL WILLSHAW

PASSPORT BOOKS
a division of *NTC Publishing Group*
Lincolnwood, Illinois USA

Also available

Nice 'n Easy French Grammar
Nice 'n Easy Spanish Grammar

1991 Printing

This edition first published in 1985 by Passport Books,
a division of NTC Publishing Group,
4255 West Touhy Avenue,
Lincolnwood (Chicago), Illinois 60646-1975 U.S.A.
Originally published by Pan Books Ltd, © I. Willshaw
1983.
Manufactured in the United States of America.

1 2 3 4 5 6 7 8 9 ML 9 8 7 6 5

Contents

Nice 'n Easy
■ German ■
Grammar

Nice 'n Easy
■ German ■
Grammar

Introduction

You may have decided to buy this German grammar because you have been studying German for some time but have never really understood the system behind it. Perhaps you fell behind in the grammar when you missed a few classes. Perhaps you used a textbook that didn't give grammar explanations. Perhaps you already own a German grammar but can't make head or tail of it.

This book is designed to make German grammar accessible and understandable to people who do not want a thick reference book. It aims at keeping the explanations as clear and simple as possible and concentrates on those items of grammar essential to everyday conversation. It is also aimed at the person who enjoys coming to grips with the grammar of a foreign language and who may have already learned one or several foreign languages.

However, the most important idea behind this grammar book is this: grammar is your *tool* and *not* your *master*. Grammar is merely the structure, the system of the language. Although it is important, it is not an end in itself. Living people do not talk or read or write grammar. So keep things in perspective. It is far more important to get your message across and make a few grammar mistakes than to keep quiet because you are afraid of making mistakes. People want to hear *what* you have to say. *How* you say it is definitely less important to them. Anyway, don't you occasionally make mistakes in your own language?

I am not trying to say that German grammar is simple. Wherever possible I have tried to reduce the complexities and point out the minimum you should know. The *Learn by Heart* sections should help you deal with very common situations without your having to remember all the rules.

How to use this book

This book is not a course book. It is a reference book which can be used together with a course book. It is small enough to take on a visit to Germany. Because it is compact and deliberately focuses on certain high-priority areas of grammar, it is not an all-embracing, exhaustive reference work. It does not claim to cover all the subtleties and fine points of German grammar.

The book is arranged according to grammar topics, listed on the Contents page. The Index contains references to non-technical terms as well as grammar points. There is a Glossary of grammatical terms for quick reference on page 167.

Bear in mind that not all grammar points are equally important. This grammar has been designed primarily for people who want to communicate with confidence in German.

Each grammar topic is subdivided and contains information under various headings:

INTRODUCTION. This gives you a general introduction to the grammar point, and often indicates the sort of situations you will find it particularly helpful in.

EXPLANATION. This gives you some extra information about the grammar point, helps you to be aware of traps and to use it correctly.

WHEN TO USE. This tells you in some detail the types of situation where the grammar point is appropriate.

HOW TO USE. This gets down to the 'nitty gritty', the hard-core information about the grammar point.

LEARN BY HEART. This is a very important section because it gives you the chance to practice what you have just learned. Once you have digested the information about the grammar point there are exercises in which you write down a missing part of the German sentence. The English translation is given alongside and the correct answer is at the bottom of the same page. This enables you to check your answer immediately. Then you can cover up one side or the other to help you learn the sentences by heart. If possible, write out the German sentences on a separate piece of paper. All the *Learn by Heart* examples have been carefully chosen because you will either encounter them or want to say them yourself when in Germany.

Help yourself

Your attitude towards language learning

Many of us have learned or tried to learn a foreign language at school or college. For some it was a wonderful experience, but for many it was a great disappointment. It is easy to blame others – textbook writers, teachers, poor facilities and so on, but very often the learner's own attitude contributes to the sense of disillusionment too. It takes native speakers 15 to 20 years to learn all the subtleties of a language. How can you possibly expect to attain this standard under very different circumstances?

1. Aiming for perfection is unrealistic – so lower your expectations.

2. All foreign language learning is an experiment. In order to improve you *have* to make mistakes because it is only through your mistakes that you will learn.

3. Nobody will think you are stupid if you try. They may very well think that you are stupid or extremely boring if you are always silent, afraid to make a mistake.

4. Try to develop a sensitivity to other people speaking the language. If you are not quite sure how to say something, try it out and ask others for help. Listen and digest what they say – this is the best way of refining your own ability in a foreign language.

So don't aim for native-speaker perfection right away, but do aim at improving your personal performance at your own pace. This means keeping your eyes and ears open, and asking questions, looking up things which puzzle you. Remind yourself why you are learning German – your motivation is the most important single factor in insuring your progress.

If your attitude towards language learning is positive and realistic, you will go a long way and make a lot of friends. Let your motto be 'I'll give it a try.' The Germans say 'Fragen kostet nichts' – it costs nothing to ask. So give it a try, have fun with your German grammar – and you'll succeed!

About you and German grammar

Help yourself learn by using what you know already. As a speaker of English, you already have a great deal of useful knowledge which will help you to learn German vocabulary and grammar.

English and German used to be one language, and many of the features of the two present-day languages are still closely related.

1. VOCABULARY

If you look at words like **Mann** (man), **Freund** (friend), **Sohn** (son), **Tochter** (daughter), **Brot** (bread), **Butter** (butter), **Milch** (milk) etc. you can see how closely many of the simple everyday words are linked. In addition, there are many more sophisticated, Latin-based words that the two languages have in common: **Professor, Akademie, Museum, Universität, Revolution, Opposition, Koalition** etc.

2. GRAMMAR

It will help you to understand German grammar if you consider that English used to have a grammar system which was very similar to that of present-day German. English used to have lots of different endings, but we gradually got rid of most of them. In English, we now use word order instead of endings to show, for example, whether a noun is the subject or object of a verb.

But we still have some traces of the old system:
We form the plural by adding -s or -es or -en etc. to nouns.
We still use he/him, I/me, who/whom to show subject/object.
We still have verb endings: I sit/he sits/you sit.
We also have lots of strong verbs: sing, sang, sung; write, wrote, written etc.
If you keep this in mind, you will perhaps accept more readily that although German may seem to be a 'difficult' language, it is in fact based on the same system as our own language.

Verbs

INTRODUCTION

Verbs are words like 'do', 'eat', 'drink', 'sit', 'stand'. They are often action words but they can also be words like 'be', 'stay', 'lie', 'wait' etc. which describe a state of affairs with no movement, a position etc. Every sentence, no matter how short, contains a verb. The verb is the hub of the sentence – the rest of the sentence is formed around it. When you look up a German verb in a dictionary, you will find various pieces of information:

1. The form of the verb you see in the dictionary will end in **-en**.
      spielen (to play)   **machen** (to do) etc.
We call this the *infinitive*, which in English always has 'to' in front of it, and in German always ends in **-en**. If you take away the **-en** ending you are left with the *stem* of the verb. It is to the stem that you add various verb endings.

2. Sometimes the dictionary will say 't.v.' or 'i.v.' (transitive verb or intransitive verb). 'Transitive' means that the verb can take a direct object (see p.84 if you do not understand this term). So words like 'eat', 'drink' etc. are transitive because you can eat or drink *something*. But words like 'go' and 'lie' are intransitive because you can't go or lie something.

EXPLANATION

In order to use a verb, you have to know:
1. what type of verb it is;
2. what person or thing is performing the action;
3. what tense the verb is in;
4. where the verb is placed in that particular sentence.

1. Types of verbs

There are several types of verbs in German:
a) weak verbs or regular verbs   (see p.26)
b) strong verbs or irregular verbs   (see p.27)
c) separable verbs   (see p.28)
d) modal verbs   (see p.34)
e) reflexive verbs   (see p.39)

2. The person or thing performing the action
This could be:

Singular		*Plural*	
ich	I	**wir**	we
du	(informal) you	**ihr**	(informal) you
Sie	(formal) you	**Sie**	(formal) you
er	he, it	**sie**	they
sie	she, it		
es	it		

der Mann, das Restaurant
or any other singular noun

Susanne or any other
person

man ('one' = person not specified)

die Männer, die Bücher or
any other plural noun

Susanne und Manfred or
any other people

Sometimes grammar books refer to the 1st, 2nd and 3rd persons.

1st person	=	I, we
2nd person	=	you
3rd person	=	he, she it, one, they + all nouns and names of people, places etc.

3. Tenses
Tenses are the forms of the verb which tell us when the action is/will be/was/taking place. The most important tenses are: the present; the imperfect (= the continuous past); the perfect (= the past); the pluperfect (= the past, one step further back than the perfect); the future. Each tense is formed differently. Some are variations of the stem + endings. Others are formed by combining the main verb with a second verb. We will also look at other forms, such as commands, the subjunctive etc.

4. Position of the verb in a sentence
In a simple sentence you will find the verb in the second position if the sentence is a statement (see p.51). However, in more complicated sentences where there are two or more verbs, the rules are different. See: modal verbs (p.34); conjunctions (p.73); and sentence structure (p.56).

Present tense

INTRODUCTION

In English we can say either, 'I read the newspaper' (implying habitual action), or 'I am reading the newspaper' (at this moment). These are both present tense forms but have different meanings. In German, this difference does not exist. There is only one present tense to cover both meanings. So for both of the above statements you would say, '**Ich lese die Zeitung**'. This is one of the relatively few examples of German being simpler than English!

WHEN TO USE

You use the present tense in German:

a) To talk about what habitually happens.
   Ich lese jeden Morgen die Zeitung. I read the newspaper every morning.

b) To talk about what is happening now.
   Ich lese gerade die Zeitung. I'm reading the newspaper right now.

c) To talk about what is going to happen in the near future.
   Ich komme nächste Woche nach I'm coming home next week.
   Hause.

HOW TO USE

1. Weak Verbs (= regular verbs)

Take **-en** off the infinitive and add these endings to the stem:

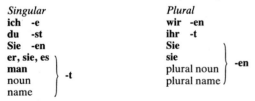

Singular		*Plural*	
ich	-e	wir	-en
du	-st	ihr	-t
Sie	-en	Sie	
er, sie, es		sie	
man	-t	plural noun	-en
noun		plural name	
name			

N.B. For details about the use of **du/ihr** see p.103.

Take, for example, the verb **spielen** (to play). You say:

ich spiel*e*		**wir spiel***en*
du spiel*st*		**ihr spiel***t*
Sie spiel*en*		**Sie spiel***en*
er, sie, es		**sie**
man		**die Frauen**
der Mann } **spiel***t*		**Anna und Maria** } **spiel***en*
Manfred		

If the stem ends in **-t** or **-d**, e.g. **baden** (to take a bath) or **arbeiten** (to work), you will have to add an extra **e** to the **er/sie/es** form in order to be able to say it. Otherwise you will sound as if you have a terrible stammer!

Er bad*et*   **Sie arbeit***et*

2. Strong verbs (= irregular verbs)

Take **-en** off the infinitive and add the same endings to the stem as for weak verbs. *But* sometimes there will be a change in the stem for the **du** and **er/sie/es** forms. How can you tell whether there is a change? In a dictionary you might see: **fahren** (¨), or you will find the **du** (2nd person singular) form and the **er/sie/es** (3rd person singular) forms written out for you: **du fährst, er fährt**.

The change usually involves a radical change in vowel sound.

infinitive	*present tense stem changes*	
schlafen	**du schläfst**	**er schläft**
lesen	**du liest**	**er liest**
essen	**du ißt**	**er ißt**

Now check with your list of strong verbs (p.163) and write out the **du** and **er/sie/es** forms of the following very common verbs: **nehmen, sprechen, sehen, helfen, tragen, treffen, werfen, geben.** When you have written them down, practice saying them aloud. Make sure you pronounce the umlaut (¨) clearly if there is one, as well as the difference between **e, i,** and **ie, ei.** Write down the English meaning of the verb at the same time.

3. Present tense summary

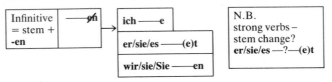

4. *Sein*

The only verb which doesn't fit into either pattern is **sein** (to be) (see p.165). The present tense is:

ich bin	**wir sind**
du bist	**ihr seid**
er/sie/es ist	**sie/Sie sind**

PRACTICE/LEARN BY HEART

Talking about your daily routine. Fill in the blanks with the correct form of the verb. They are all in the present tense.

1. **Wir .... um acht Uhr.** — We have breakfast at 8 o'clock.
2. **Ich .... die Kinder um Viertel vor neun zur Schule.** — At a quarter to nine I drive the children to school.
3. **Dann .... ich die Zeitung.** — Then I read the newspaper.
4. **Dann .... ich zur Arbeit.** — Then I go to work.
5. **Abends .... wir Musik.** — In the evening we listen to music.
6. **Wir .... Freunde.** — We visit friends.

ANSWERS

1. frühstücken. 2. fahre. 3. lese. 4. gehe. 5. hören. 6. besuchen.

Imperfect tense

INTRODUCTION

The imperfect tense (called *Präteritum* in German grammar books) is used for description, for narrative and for continuous action in the past. You are most likely to encounter it when reading newspapers and stories.

WHEN TO USE

In practice you will often find yourself using the imperfect tense of:

sein (to be) **ich/er/sie/es war** (was) **wir/Sie/sie waren** (were)
haben (to have) **ich/er/sie/es hatte** (had) **wir/Sie/sie hatten** (had)

because that's how you say where you have been, what was wrong with you, whether you enjoyed yourself etc. You will hear and read other verbs in the imperfect tense, but they are quite easy to recognize. By all means spend some time learning these, but you may find it more profitable to concentrate on other, higher priority areas of German grammar. As long as you can use **sein** and **haben** and can make intelligent guesses about the other verbs, you will get along very well.

HOW TO USE
1. Weak verbs

Take off the **-en** ending from the infinitive, add **-te** for the singular and **-ten** for the plural and **Sie** forms:

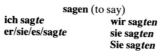

	sagen (to say)
ich sag*te*	wir sag*ten*
er/sie/es/sag*te*	sie sag*ten*
	Sie sag*ten*

In other words:

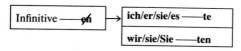

Infinitive ——**en** →	ich/er/sie/es ——te
	wir/sie/Sie ——ten

2. Strong verbs

A complete list of strong verbs appears on pages 163–164. Take off the -en ending of the infinitive. There is always a significant change in the stem. There is no ending for the singular, but in the plural -en is added to the changed stem.

schlafen (to sleep)
ich/er/sie/es schlief   **wir/sie/Sie schliefen**

fahren (to travel)
ich/er/sie/es fuhr   **wir/sie/Sie fuhren**

In other words:

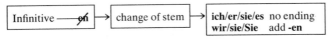

PRACTICE

Now do the same for: **sehen, lesen, essen, ziehen, trinken, finden, geben.** (Answers at the bottom of the page.)

Perfect tense

INTRODUCTION

'Perfect' is another word for 'completed'. You use the perfect tense in German when you talk about completed action in the past. We do this in two ways in English:
1. Simple past tense: I *ate* an apple.
                        He *waved* goodbye.
2. Past tense with 'have' + ——ed or ——en:
                        I *have fixed* the doorhandle.
                        He's *replaced* the fuse.
                        Have you *eaten* your breakfast?

ANSWERS

sah/sahen, las/lasen, aß/aßen, zog/zogen, trank/tranken, fand/fanden, gab/gaben.

The examples under 2. are much closer to the present time, but in both 1. and 2. the action is complete.

You use the perfect for both of these in German, and you will need to use it whenever you are talking about the past.

HOW TO USE

To form the perfect tense, you use the present tense of **haben (ich habe, er hat, Sie haben** etc.) + the *past participle* of the verb. The past participle is the '—ed' or '—en' form you find in English '(have) replace*d*', 'eat*en*' etc.

To form a past participle in German:
Take the **-en** ending off the infinitive.
Add **ge-** to the beginning of most verbs.
Add **-t** or **-et** ending to weak verbs. (This is parallel to adding '-ed' to English regular verbs.) Add **-en** ending to strong verbs (parallel to '-en' in English irregular verbs).

The past participle for strong verbs often has a radical change of stem, so check with the verb list on p.163 until you have learned them. Very often you can guess them because they are similar to the English forms:

singen	**gesungen**	sing	sung
trinken	**getrunken**	drink	drunk

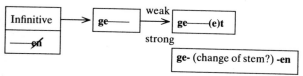

Examples:
1. Weak verbs.
fragen (ask) → **gefragt**   **machen** (make) → **gemacht**
arbeiten (work) → **gearbeitet**   **antworten** (answer) → **geantwortet**
2. Strong verbs.
essen (eat) → **gegessen**   **fallen** (fall) → **gefallen**
stehlen (steal) → **gestohlen**   **brechen** (break) → **gebrochen**
Sometimes you think that a mouthful like **gearbeitet** can't be right, but it is.

PRACTICE

Write down the meaning and the past participle for each of these verbs:
hören, tragen, nehmen, baden, sehen, helfen, sagen, ziehen, kosten.

Perfect tense word order

The form of **haben** goes in the usual 2nd position in statements and 1st position in questions and the past participle goes at the very end of the sentence. Everything else you want to say is sandwiched in the middle.

ich	habe	rest of sentence	ge——(e)t.
er/sie/es	hat		
wir/sie/Sie	haben		ge——?——en.

Look at these examples:

Es	hat	den ganzen Tag	geregnet.	It rained all day.
Er	hat	mir den Weg zum Bahnhof	gezeigt.	He showed me the way to the train station.
Wir	haben	mit dem Beamten	gesprochen.	We talked to the official.

Negative

In these sentences **nicht** usually goes just before the past participle.

Er	hat	das Auto	nicht	genommen.	He didn't take the car.
Ich	habe	meinen Schirm	nicht	gefunden.	I didn't find my umbrella.

ANSWERS

to hear, gehört; to carry, getragen; to take, genommen; to take a bath, gebadet; to see, gesehen; to help, geholfen; to say, gesagt; to pull, gezogen; to cost, gekostet.

PRACTICE/LEARN BY HEART

Tell somebody what you did yesterday.

1. **Ich habe Pommes frites**	I had (ate) some French fries.
2. **Ich ... eine Tasse Kaffee**	I had (drank) a cup of coffee.
3. **Ich ... ein Buch**	I read a book.
4. **Ich ... das Essen**	I cooked the meal.
5. **Ich ... mit meinem Chef**	I talked to my boss.
6. **Ich ... einen Brief**	I wrote a letter.
7. **Ich ... einen Freund**	I met a friend.

Verbs that do not add *ge-*

1. Some verbs do not add **ge-** to the beginning of the past participle because they already have a prefix and they are not separable. If a verb begins with **be- emp- ent- er- ge- ver- zer-** you form the past participle by taking the **-en** ending off the infinitive and adding **-(e)t** for weak verbs and **-en** for strong verbs, together with a possible stem change. Here are some examples:

Weak verbs	*Strong verbs*
bestellen → bestellt	**bekommen → bekommen**
empören → empört	**empfehlen → empfohlen**
enttäuschen → enttäuscht	**entscheiden → entschieden**
gehören → gehört	**gefallen → gefallen**
vermieten → vermietet	**verstehen → verstanden**

The meanings of the above verbs follow in parentheses but are mixed up. Can you match them up correctly? (Please, rent, hire, anger, recommend, order, decide, understand, belong, get, disappoint)

2. Verbs ending in **-ieren** do not add **ge-** either. They are always weak, so add **-t** in the past participle:

diskutieren → diskutiert   **operieren → operiert**

ANSWERS

1. gegessen. 2. habe ... getrunken. 3. habe ... gelesen. 4. habe ... gekocht. 5. habe ... gesprochen. 6. habe ... geschrieben. 7. habe ... getroffen.

REVIEW PRACTICE
Write down the past participle of these verbs:
arbeiten, essen, lesen, trinken, kochen, besuchen, telefonieren, schreiben, treffen, fragen, tanzen, verstehen.

Verbs that take *sein*

INTRODUCTION
There is a small group of strong verbs that take **sein** (to be) instead of **haben** when they form the perfect tense. This is a nuisance, but since they are very common verbs you should learn them. If you know French, compare them with the verbs which take 'être'. The past participle is formed in exactly the same way as with **haben** and the word order is also unchanged. However, with the negative, **nicht** comes nearer to the beginning of the sentence than with **haben**.

HOW TO USE

Ich	bin			
Er/sie/es	ist	(nicht)	rest of sentence	ge—?—en.
Wir/sie/Sie	sind			

Examples:

Sie	ist	neulich		gestorben.	She died recently.
Wir	sind	nicht	zu Fuß	gelaufen.	We didn't go on foot.
Sind	Sie	in Spanien		gewesen?	Have you been to Spain?
Sind	Sie	mit dem Auto		gekommen?	Did you come by car?

ANSWERS
gearbeitet, gegessen, gelesen, getrunken, gekocht, besucht, telefoniert, geschrieben, getroffen, gefragt, getanzt, verstanden.

The German verbs which take **sein** instead of **haben** are:

1. verbs of motion
laufen, kommen, gehen, fahren, fallen, fliegen, schwimmen, reisen, ein/steigen, aus/steigen, um/steigen, an/kommen, ab/fahren, zusammen/stoßen, auf/stehen etc.

2. others
bleiben, sein, werden, sterben.
In a dictionary or word list you will recognize them like this:
laufen (infinitive), **er läuft** (present), **lief** (imperfect), **ist gelaufen** (perfect).
Notice that they are all strong verbs, so they take the **-en** ending and often change stem. Spend some time getting familiar with these verbs, since they are very useful in everyday German. In particular practice:

bleiben	**ich bin** ..... **geblieben**	I stayed
sein	**ich bin** ..... **gewesen**	I was/have been
werden	**ich bin** ..... **geworden**	I have become

LEARN BY HEART
Look up the past participle of the verb to the left of each sentence. Then say what you and your family did last weekend.

1. **fahren**	**Wir ... ans Meer**	We went to the seaside.
2. **bleiben**	**Wir ... zu Hause**	We stayed at home.
3. **laufen**	**Wir ... im Wald**	We walked in the forest.
4. **gehen**	**Wir ... einkaufen**	We went shopping.
5. **kommen**	**Wir ... sehr spät nach Hause**	We got home very late.

To sum up:
Checklist for using the perfect tense.
1. Start with the infinitive.
2. Be sure that you want to use the perfect tense.
3. Is it a weak or a strong verb?
4. Does the past participle take **ge-** at the beginning?
5. If it is a strong verb, is there a stem change in the past participle?

ANSWERS
1. sind ... gefahren. 2. sind ... geblieben. 3. sind ... gelaufen. 4. sind ... gegangen. 5. sind ... gekommen.

6. Does it take **haben** or **sein**?
7. Is it a separable verb?
8. Remember the word order in the sentence.

You want to say: 'I visited my mother yesterday'.
1. To visit = **besuchen**.
2. It is perfect tense.
3. **Besuchen** is a weak verb.
4. Verbs with **be-** prefix do not take **ge-**.
5. ——
6. Takes **haben**.
7. Not separable.
8. **Haben** in 2nd position, past participle at end.
So you say: **Ich *habe* meine Mutter gestern *besucht*.**

You want to say: 'I walked into town this morning'.
1. To walk = **laufen**.
2. It is perfect tense.
3. **Laufen** is a strong verb.
4. Does take **ge-**.
5. No stem change.
6. Takes **sein**.
7. Not separable.
8. **Sein** in 2nd position, past participle at end.
So you say: **Ich *bin* heute morgen in die Stadt *gelaufen*.**

Pluperfect tense

INTRODUCTION
The pluperfect tense (had done/seen/been etc.) is one stage further back in time than the perfect or imperfect. It is a direct translation of the English 'had done', 'had gone', etc.

HOW TO USE
The formation of the pluperfect is very similar to the perfect. Instead of the present tense of **haben** or **sein** + past participle, you use the imperfect tense of **haben** (**hatte/hatten**) or **sein** (**war/waren**) + past participle:

Ich/er/sie	war/hatte	rest of sentence	ge——(e)t (weak)
Wir/sie/Sie	waren/hatten		ge—(?)—en (strong)

For the small group of verbs which take **sein** see p.23.

You often find the pluperfect used after **nachdem** (after), **bevor** (before), **als** (when).

Future tense

INTRODUCTION
The simplest and most popular way of talking about the future is to use the present tense together with a future time reference, like 'tomorrow', 'next year' etc.

Ich fahre nächste Woche nach München.	I'm going to Munich next week.
In zwei Monaten sind wir wieder zurück.	We'll be back in two months' time.
Wann sind Sie wieder da?	When will you be back?

There is also a real future tense, which is given here mainly for your reference.

HOW TO USE
To form the future tense, use the present tense of the verb **werden** + the infinitive of the verb. **Werden** is being used as an auxiliary verb, which means that its role is to help form the future tense.

Ich	werde		
Du	wirst		
Er/sie/es	wird	rest of sentence	infinitive of main verb
Wir	werden		
Ihr	werdet		
Sie/sie	werden		

The main verb, the one in the infinitive form, goes at the end of the sentence, the present tense of **werden** goes in the normal verb position – 2nd position for statements, 1st position for questions – and the rest of the sentence is sandwiched in the middle.

Examples:

Es	wird		regnen.	It's going to rain.
Es	wird	heute nachmittag	regnen.	It will rain this afternoon.
Ich	werde	in Berlin Musik	studieren.	I'm going to study music in Berlin.

Important:
Do not confuse 1. the future tense using **werden** with 2. expressions with **wollen** (to want or intend to do something):

Er wird Deutsch studieren. He will study German.
Er will Deutsch studieren. He wants to study German.

There's a world of difference between the two! It's a very tempting mistake for English speakers to make, so be on your guard.

Weak verbs

Weak verbs are regular verbs. If a verb in a dictionary has no distinguishing marks, you can assume that it is weak. All verbs ending in **-ieren** are weak.

Weak verbs follow the rules for all the tenses, so you don't have to worry about stem changes etc.

Strong verbs

INTRODUCTION

Strong verbs are irregular verbs. This means that they act differently from weak or regular verbs. They may have different endings and the stem may change. You can recognize a strong verb in a dictionary because it will have 'ir.' (irregular) after it or there may be an indication of stem change in parentheses after the verb: **halten (ä, ie, a)**, to stop.

Next to adjective endings, strong verbs will be the most complicated feature of German grammar you will have to try to master. Please don't try to learn all the strong verbs in one day or you will lose all hope. A useful strategy is to learn three or four every day. The good thing about strong verbs (although you may not think so) is that they are very common, so that when you are in Germany you will constantly hear them in use – and this will help you learn the correct forms. You won't be able to avoid using them yourself, so it's in your own interest to try and learn them. You will!

Once source of comfort is that you have already mastered one system of strong verbs. English also has strong verbs. You may not have thought about this before, but look at these examples:

find	I have fo*und*	stem change just like German strong verbs.
eat	I have eat*en*	'-en' ending.
write	I have wr*itten*	stem change + '-en' ending.

Use your knowledge of English to help you learn German strong verbs. You are not starting from scratch!

HOW TO USE

The tenses in which strong verbs most often change are:
1. Present tense: **du/er/sie/es** forms often have a stem change.

| **halten (ä)** to stop | **du hältst** | **er hält** |
| **lesen (ie)** to read | **du liest** | **er liest** |

2. Imperfect tense: all strong verbs have a stem change throughout; the singular takes no ending, the plural adds **-en**.

halten (ie)	**der Bus hielt**	**sie hielten**
lesen (a)	**ich las**	**wir lasen**

3. Perfect tense: there is often a stem change in the past participle and the past participle ends in **-en**.

halten (a)	**Der Bus hat gehalten.**
riechen (o) to smell	**Es hat nach Fisch gerochen.**

Sometimes you may suspect a verb is strong and you may want to use it in the perfect tense. If you don't have a dictionary handy, try inventing a 'Germanized' version of the English past participle – and watch the other person's reaction. If it's right, you'll feel very pleased with yourself. If it's wrong, he may still guess your meaning and be able to tell you the correct version.

Separable verbs

INTRODUCTION
Certain verbs in German split into two parts. We have a similar pattern in English. We say: I'll *go up* the stairs.

I'll *look* it *up* in the dictionary.

Have you *made* your mind *up*?

Take your shoes and socks *off*.

EXPLANATION
You can often recognize German separable verbs in a word list because there is a slash mark (/) between the two parts that separate. The first part of the verb is the prefix and the second part is the real stem of the verb.

These are the most common prefixes you will come across:

ab	**ein**	**nach**	**zu**
an	**fern**	**vor**	**zurück**
auf	**mit**	**weg**	**zusammen**

Verbs which begin with **durch, um, über, wieder** are sometimes separable but not always. See p.32 for details.

You can *hear* when a verb is separable because the prefix is stressed.

You say **éinsteigen** and not **einstéigen**. This is in contrast to other verbs with inseparable prefixes, which take the stress on the main stem of the verb.

HOW TO USE
Separable verbs can be either strong or weak and can take either **haben** or **sein** in the perfect or pluperfect tense and they follow the usual rules for verbs of that type.

1. Present tense
1. Take off the **-en** ending from the infinitive. 2. Split the prefix from main stem. 3. The prefix goes at the end of the sentence. 4. The stem adds the present tense ending. If it's a strong verb, there may be a change of stem. The stem stands in the usual verb position in the sentence.

Infinitive splits	stem+present tense endings		prefix
—/——en	Ich ——e	rest of sentence	—.
	Er/sie/es ——(e)t		
	Wir/sie/Sie ——en		

You want to say: 'The train is arriving at half past five tomorrow'. To arrive is **ankommen (an/kommen)**; **der Zug** takes **-t** ending.
Der Zug *kommt* **morgen um halb sechs** *an*.

You want to ask: 'Do you close as early as 12 o'clock?' To close is **zumachen (zu/machen)**; **Sie** takes **-en** ending. In a question, the verb goes in the first position.
Machen **Sie schon um 12 Uhr** *zu*?

You want to say: 'The concert begins in a quarter of an hour's time'. To begin is **anfangen (an/fangen)**; **das Konzert** takes **-t** ending. **Anfangen** is a strong verb with stem change a→ä.
Das Konzert *fängt* **in einer Viertelstunde** *an*.

2. Imperfect tense

1. Take off the **-en** ending from the infinitive. 2. Split the prefix from the main stem. 3. The prefix goes at the end of the sentence. 4. The stem adds **-te** or **-ten** if it is a weak verb. Strong verbs have a stem change + no ending in the singular, add **-en** in the plural. The stem stands in the usual verb position in the sentence.

			1	2	3	4
Infinitive splits	strong	Ich/er/sie/es	stem change, no ending		rest of sentence	prefix
		Wir/sie/Sie	stem change, + -en			
—/— ~~en~~	weak	Ich/er/sie/es		——te		
		Wir/sie/Sie		——ten		

You want to say: 'He was just closing the window'. To close is **zumachen (zu/machen)**; **machen** is a weak verb, so the **er** form takes **-te** ending.
Er *machte* gerade das Fenster *zu*.

You want to say: 'The conference took place in the Adelphi Hotel'. To take place is **stattfinden (statt/finden)**; **finden** is a strong verb with a stem change from **i→a**, **die Konferenz** is singular, so the verb has no ending.
Die Konferenz *fand* im Hotel Adelphi *statt*.

3. Perfect tense
HOW TO USE
To form the past participle:
1. Remove the **-en** ending from the infinitive.
2. Split the prefix and the main verb.
3. Insert **-ge-** between the prefix and the main verb.
4. Add **-(e)t** ending for weak verbs.
Add **-en** ending for strong verbs, plus a possible stem change.

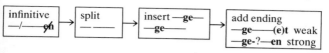

Most separable verbs take **haben**, but some take **sein** (see p.23). The past participle as usual goes at the end of the sentence.
Example:

Wir *haben* viele Leute *kennengelernt*.	We got to know a lot of people.
Sie *haben* noch nicht *aufgemacht*.	They haven't opened yet.
Wann *haben* Sie damit *angefangen*?	When did you start it?
Wir *sind* pünktlich *angekommen*.	We arrived on time.

PRACTICE

Consult your dictionary or verb list and write down a) the past participle and b) whether the following verbs take **haben** or **sein**:
abschleppen (to tow away); **aufhören** (to stop); **zumachen** (to close); **anziehen** (to put on clothes); **anrufen** (to phone); **aussteigen** (to get out of a vehicle); **ankommen** (to arrive).

LEARN BY HEART

Choose the correct verb from this list, put it into the perfect tense, then complete the following questions which you might find useful when you want some information:

zumachen einkaufen anrufen   ankommen abfahren

1. ... **Frau Schmidt schon** .....?	Has Frau Schmidt phoned?
2. ... **der Zug schon** .....?	Has the train already left?
3. ... **Sie schon** .....?	Have you already been shopping?
4. ... **der Laden schon** .....?	Has the store already closed?
5. ... **der Zug aus Braunschweig** .....?	Has the train from Braunschweig arrived?

ANSWERS

1. Practice

abgeschleppt, aufgehört, zugemacht, angezogen, angerufen + haben
ausgestiegen, angekommen + sein

2. Learn by heart

1. Hat ... angerufen. 2. Ist ... abgefahren. 3. Haben ... eingekauft.
4. Hat ... zugemacht. 5. Ist ... angekommen.

4. Pluperfect tense

The pluperfect tense follows exactly the same pattern as the perfect tense, except that instead of the present tense of **haben** and **sein**, you use the imperfect.

ich/er/sie/es	hatte / war
wir/sie/Sie	hatten / waren

5. After modal verbs and *werden* (future tense)

Modal verbs (see p.34 for details) or forms of **werden** stand in the usual main verb position while separable verbs go at the end of the sentence and are in the infinitive form, so they do not split.

1	2	3	4
Ich	werde/möchte/ etc.		—/——en. infinitive of separable verb
Er/sie/es	wird/möchte/	rest of sentence	
Wir/sie/Sie	werden/möchten		

Ich *möchte* meine Familie *anrufen*. I'd like to phone my family.
Wann *werden* Sie in Frankfurt ankommen? When will you arrive in Frankfurt?

EXPLANATION

Unfortunately the prefixes **um- durch- über-** and **wieder-** sometimes indicate a separable verb and sometimes not. There is no easy way to tell which one is separable – you have to keep your eyes and ears open. Separable verbs are stressed on the prefix, whereas verbs which don't separate are stressed on the stem. Here are a few common examples:

separable	*not separable*
úm/ziehen to move (to a new location)	**umgéhen** (to avoid)
dúrch/fahren (to travel through)	**durchdénken** (to think something through)
wiéder/sehen (to see again)	**wiederhólen** (to repeat)

LEARN BY HEART

You are talking to a friend who is going to Berlin. Using the verbs from the list at the bottom, write down what you would say in German.

1. What time did you get up today?
Wann ... Sie heute .....?
2. When does your train leave?
Wann ... Ihr Zug?
3. When are you coming back?
Wann ... Sie .....?
4. What time do you arrive in Berlin?
Um wieviel Uhr ... Sie in Berlin .....?
5. Who's picking you up at the station?
Wer ... Sie vom Bahnhof .....?
6. When will you phone me?
Wann ... Sie mich .....?

abholen, abfahren, anrufen, aufstehen, zurückkommen, ankommen

Separable verbs are used a lot in everyday conversation. Here are a few farewell messages you might hear. The English translations have been mixed up. Can you match the correct English sentence with the German one?

1. **Geben Sie nicht zuviel Geld aus!**   A. Come back soon!
2. **Kommen Sie gut an!**   B. Phone us next week!
3. **Kommen Sie bald wieder!**   C. I hope you arrive safely.
4. **Ruhen Sie sich gut aus!**   D. Don't spend too much money!
5. **Rufen Sie uns nächste Woche an!**   E. Have a good rest!

Notice that in the imperative (or, command) form, the verb goes in the first position and the prefix goes at the end of the sentence.

ANSWERS
1st exercise
1. sind ... aufgestanden; 2. fährt ... ab; 3. kommen ... zurück; 4. kommen ... an; 5. holt ... ab; 6. rufen ... an.
2nd exercise
1. D; 2. C; 3. A; 4. E; 5. B.

Modal verbs

INTRODUCTION

When dealing with other people it's important to be polite and appreciative. Modal verbs ('can', 'should', 'have to', etc.) help you, for example, to make polite requests or offer help to someone, and are especially effective when combined with **bitte**, **danke** or **entschuldigen Sie** (excuse me). They provide you with a much more sophisticated way of giving orders than simply using the imperative. Look at the difference between 'Bring me another piece of bread' (imperative) and 'Could you please bring me another piece of bread?'. 'Could' is a modal verb and it turns the order into a request.

It's worth taking the trouble to learn and practice these verbs because you can combine them with hundreds of other verbs to make lots of different sentences. They will be invaluable to you in stores, banks, going to the theater – whenever you are in contact with German people.

EXPLANATION

The nice thing about modal verbs is that there are only two forms for each tense. To form the singular of the present tense, take off the **-en** from the infinitive. There may be a change of stem and there is no ending. The plural form of the present tense is exactly the same as the infinitive:

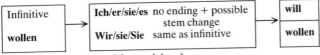

Infinitive	**Ich/er/sie/es** no ending + possible stem change		**will**
wollen	**Wir/sie/Sie** same as infinitive		**wollen**

Here is a complete list of the modal verbs:

	müssen must	dürfen may	können can	könnte could	wollen want to	sollen shall	mögen would like to
ich er sie es }	muß	darf	kann	könnte	will	soll	möchte
wir sie Sie }	müssen	dürfen	können	könnten	wollen	sollen	möchten

HOW TO USE

Modal verbs cannot stand on their own because the meaning of the sentence would be incomplete. They are always used with a second verb. When using the present tense, the modal verb stands in the usual verb position (see p.51) and the second verb goes at the end of the sentence and is in the infinitive form:

Ich/er/sie/es	muß		
Wir/sie/Sie	müssen	rest of sentence	infinitive of 2nd verb

Look at these examples:

Ich *muß* jetzt nach Hause *gehen*.	I have to go home now.
Wir *möchten* jetzt *bestellen*.	We'd like to order now.
Kann ich mit einem Scheck bezahlen?	Can I pay by check?

You will soon get into the habit of putting the second verb at the end – very often German people will finish the sentence for you! People will still understand you if you put the second verb in the middle of the sentence but you will sound very American because the rhythm is wrong.

LEARN BY HEART

1. Here are some very polite expressions which will help you to get what you want without offending other people:

Ich möchte zahlen/ein Zimmer bestellen/Plätze reservieren.	I'd like to pay/book a room/reserve seats.
Darf ich hier rauchen/parken?	May I smoke/park here?
Muß ich lange warten?	Do I have to wait long?
Könnten Sie mir bitte helfen?	Could you please help me?
Könnten Sie mir bitte sagen/zeigen …?	Could you please tell/show me …?
Könnten Sie das bitte wiederholen/ buchstabieren?	Could you please repeat/spell that?
Könnten Sie etwas lauter/leiser/ langsamer sprechen?	Could you please speak a bit louder/softer/more slowly?

2. Offers of help:

Kann ich Ihnen helfen?	Can I help you?
Soll ich Sie um sieben Uhr wecken?	Would you like me to wake you at seven o'clock?

3. Suggestions:

Wollen wir in die Stadt fahren?	Shall we go into town?
Wir könnten ins Theater gehen.	We could go to the theater.
Möchten Sie das Museum sehen?	Would you like to see the museum?
Ich kann den Film wirklich empfehlen.	I can really recommend the movie.

EXPLANATION

Some notes about individual modal verbs:

1. *wollen* = to want to

N.B. **Ich will** does not mean 'I will' (future). See future tense, p.25.

Wollen + nicht indicates unwillingness to do something and can be strong enough to mean outright refusal to do something.

Das will ich doch nicht machen.

I don't want to do it/I'm not going to do it.

The imperfect tense of **wollen** is:

ich/er/sie/es	**wollte** = wanted
wir/sie/Sie	**wollten** = wanted

2. *Möchte/möchten* = would like (to)

There is no verb **möchten**. These forms are a part of the verb **mögen** = to like, but they are used just like modal verbs. It is important to recognize the difference in tone between saying:

Ich will ein Stück Kuchen.	I want a piece of cake. (a bit rude)
Ich möchte ein Stück Kuchen.	I'd like a piece of cake. (much more polite)

Try not to confuse **ich möchte** (I would like) and **ich wollte** (I wanted).

3. *Können* = to be able to

kann/können = can	**könnte/könnten** = could

4. *Müssen/dürfen*

Ich muß = I must, I have to

Ich darf = I may, I am allowed to.

But contrary to what you might expect,

Ich muß nicht = I don't have to (literally 'I don't must').

Sie müssen nicht vorher anrufen. You don't have to phone in advance.

Sie können eine Flasche Wein bringen, Sie müssen aber nicht.	You can bring a bottle of wine, but you don't have to.

If you want to say 'should not', use **dürfen + nicht** or **kein**:

Sie dürfen nicht hineingehen.	You should not go in.
Ich darf kein Fett essen.	I should not eat any fat.

5. *Sollen*

This is a rather strange verb. It is tempting to translate it by 'shall', but there's more to it than that. Look at these examples:

Ich soll morgen um 10 Uhr am Flughafen sein.	I am to be/ am supposed to be/ am expected to be at the airport at 10 o'clock tomorrow.
Es soll in Südfrankreich sehr warm sein.	It's supposed to be/ They say it's very warm in the South of France.
Um wieviel Uhr soll ich kommen?	When shall I/ am I to/ would you like me to come?
Soll ich Ihnen einen Tee machen?	Shall I/ would you like me to make you a cup of tea?

In other words, you can sometimes use 'shall' to translate **sollen** but you must be clear that underlying **sollen** is often the idea that a third person has to give his consent or that the information is dependent on a third person. There is often an idea of duty or obligation to someone other than the speaker.

Similarly in the imperfect tense, **sollte/sollten** can mean 'should', but also means 'ought to, was expected to, was supposed to'.

LEARN BY HEART

You have been invited out to dinner with friends. Choose the correct verb to give you some useful expressions.

1. **Sollte/Könnte ich bitte das Salz haben?**	Could I have the salt, please?
2. **Kann/Möchte ich Ihnen helfen?**	Can I help you?
3. **Muß/Darf ich rauchen?**	May I smoke?
4. **Möchte/Könnte ich ein Glas Wasser bekommen?**	Could I have a glass of water?

5. **Ich muß/darf keine Milchprodukte essen.** I'm not allowed to eat any dairy products.

6. **Ich muß/darf leider jetzt gehen.** I'm afraid I'll have to go now.

7. **Könnten/Sollten Sie mir bitte sagen, wo die Toilette ist?** Could you please tell me where the rest room is?

MODAL VERBS IN THE PAST

Although there is a perfect tense for modal verbs, it is much more common to use them in the imperfect. To form the imperfect, take **-en** from the infinitive and add **-te** or **-ten**. There is often a change of stem too. People often get confused using the imperfect of modal verbs because they use umlauts incorrectly. In the imperfect tense of modal verbs *there are no umlauts.*

wollen	ich wollte/Sie wollten	wanted to
müssen	ich mußte/Sie mußten	had to
können	ich konnte/Sie konnten	was/were able to
sollen	ich sollte/Sie sollten	ought to/should/was expected to
dürfen	ich durfte/Sie durften	was/were allowed to

The word order is the same as for the present tense.

Ich *mußte gehen.*	I had to go.
Wir *konnten* nicht *sehen.*	We couldn't see.
Er *sollte* jetzt da *sein.*	He ought to be there by now.

Perfect tense

Use **ich habe** etc. as for any perfect tense, but instead of using a past participle the modal verb stays in the infinitive form and comes after the other verb at the very end of the sentence.

Present tense: **Das kann ich machen.**   I can do it.
Perfect tense: **Das** *habe* ich *machen können.*   I was able to do it.
That's when the real fun starts, piling up all the verbs at the end of the sentence!

ANSWERS

1. Könnte; 2. Kann; 3. Darf; 4. Könnte; 5. darf; 6. muß; 7. Könnten.

Note:

Ich wollte = I wanted to **Ich konnte** = I was able to	**Ich möchte** = I would like to **Ich könnte** = I could
Imperfect (no Umlaut)	Subjunctive (Umlaut)

Reflexive verbs

INTRODUCTION

Reflexive verbs are verbs which seem to 'come back on themselves'. They are used to describe actions or feelings which are important to the speaker personally. The nearest thing we have in English is the use of 'myself', 'yourself' etc. with a verb:

I addressed myself to the problem.
Can you let yourself in?
Make yourself at home, etc.

I addressed myself

The circular movement revolving around the verb emphasizes the personal nature of the verb.

HOW TO USE

In order to use reflexive verbs in German you use the verb in the usual way, taking into consideration tense, type of verb etc., but in addition you add an extra reflexive pronoun which is the equivalent of 'myself', 'yourself' etc. The reflexive pronoun usually goes in the 3rd position in the sentence, sticking very close to the verb. The German reflexive pronouns are:

ich → mich	wir → uns
du → dich	ihr → euch
er/sie/es → sich	sie/Sie → sich

How can you tell that a verb is reflexive? In the infinitive you see: **sich irren** or **s. irren**.

1. Present tense

ich irre mich	I am mistaken	**wir irren uns**	we are mistaken
du irrst dich	you are mistaken	**ihr irrt euch**	you are mistaken
er irrt sich	he is mistaken	**sie irren sich**	they are mistaken
sie irrt sich	she is mistaken	**Sie irren sich**	you are mistaken

Question
Irren Sie sich?   Are you mistaken?

2. Imperfect tense

The word order is exactly the same as for the present tense. The reflexive pronouns are exactly the same. The verb takes imperfect tense endings and stem changes.

3. Perfect tense

1	2	3	4	5
personal pronoun	haben/sein	reflexive pronoun	rest of sentence	past participle
Ich	**habe**	**mich**		**geirrt.**
Er	**hat**	**sich**	**nicht**	**geirrt.**

Question

Haben	**Sie**	**sich**		**geirrt?**

Here are some common reflexive verbs:

sich aus/ruhen	to have a good rest	**sich setzen**	to sit down
sich ärgern	to get angry	**sich beeilen**	to hurry up
sich erinnern	to remember	**sich waschen**	to wash oneself

HOW TO USE

In the examples so far, the reflexive pronoun has been accusative (see p.85): **mich**, **sich** etc.

There is a second type of reflexive verb with which the reflexive pronoun is dative (see p.89): **mir**, **dir**, **sich** etc. Look at these examples:

Ich habe *mir* die Zähne geputzt.   I brushed my teeth.

Ich kann *mir* im Moment kein Auto leisten.	I can't afford a car at the moment.
Er wollte *sich* die Nachrichten ansehen.	He wanted to have a look at the news.

In all these examples the reflexive pronoun means either: 'your', 'my' etc.; as in 'I brushed *my* teeth' (i.e. to myself); or 'to/for myself, yourself' etc., as in 'to have a look (for himself) at the news'.

The dative pronouns for reflexive verbs are:

mir	**uns**
dir	**euch**
sich	**sich**

so the only difference occurs with the **mir** and **dir** forms. All the rest are the same as for the accusative. Still, the difference is important because it involves a different idea of relationships.

Some common verbs of this type are:

sich etwas leisten	to afford something
sich etwas ansehen/anschauen	to have a look at something
sich etwas kaufen	to buy oneself something
sich etwas überlegen	to think something over
sich die Haare waschen	to wash one's hair

LEARN BY HEART
Here are some sentences which are useful for personal conversations. Choose the correct reflexive pronoun to insert in each blank.

1. **Ich habe … geirrt.**	I've made a mistake.
2. **Es tut mir leid, ich kann … nicht erinnern.**	I'm sorry, I can't remember.
3. **Er hat … so geärgert!**	He was so angry!
4. **Guten Tag, ich möchte … anmelden.**	Good morning, I'd like to register.
5. **Ich muß … die Haare waschen.**	I'll have to wash my hair.
6. **Interessieren Sie … für Musik?**	Are you interested in music?
7. **Wir freuen … auf Ihren Besuch.**	We look forward to your visit.
8. **Bitte setzen Sie …**	Please sit down.
9. **Das muß ich … noch überlegen.**	I'll have to think it over.

ANSWERS
1. mich; 2. mich; 3. sich; 4. mich; 5. mir; 6. sich; 7. uns; 8. sich; 9. mir.

Imperative

INTRODUCTION
There are several forms for giving commands, depending on how friendly, polite etc. your relations are with the other person.

HOW TO USE
The straightforward imperative form (i.e. command form) in German is the same as the present tense but the verb goes into the 1st position:

$\overset{1}{\text{Gehen}}$ $\overset{2}{\text{Sie!}}$	Go!
$\overset{1}{\text{Kommen}}$ $\overset{2}{\text{Sie}}$ $\overset{3}{\text{hierher.}}$	Come here!
$\overset{1}{\text{Trinken}}$ $\overset{2}{\text{Sie}}$ Ihren $\overset{3}{\text{Kaffee}}$ aus.	Drink your coffee!

But you won't get very far if you order people around like that. In order not to offend people you often have to cushion your command:

1. With words like **bitte**.

Gehen Sie bitte durch.	Please go straight through.
Kommen Sie bitte ins Vorder-zimmer.	Please come into the front room.
Hören Sie bitte.	Please listen.
Gucken Sie mal.	Have a look here.

2. Or you could be even less abrasive and use modal verbs (see p.34):

Könnten Sie bitte leiser sprechen? Could you please speak more softly?

Your command is phrased as a polite request, the other person is made to feel he is doing you a favor.

Wollen wir ins Kino gehen? Shall we/ let's go to the movies?

3. The infinitive (see p.168) is used especially for instructions on packages and labels as well as public signs and loudspeaker announcements:

Hier öffnen	Open here
Hier schneiden	Cut here
Bitte weitergehen	Move along, please
Bitte sofort einsteigen	Please get into (vehicle) at once
Türen schließen	Close the doors

Here are a few more – can you guess what they mean?
1. **Nicht stören!**
2. **Geld einwerfen!**
3. **Bitte zurücktreten!**
4. **Karten hier entwerten!**
5. **Zimmerschlüssel abgeben!**
6. **Rauchen einstellen!**

Sein

The imperative form of **sein** is: **Seien Sie**. You can use it if you want to bend over backwards not to offend someone when asking him or her to do something:

Seien Sie bitte so nett.   Would you be so kind?

Negative commands

To the foreigner the most important commands often take the form of regulations or signs telling you something is forbidden. The vocabulary is also often difficult to figure out. Here are a few examples:

Kein Zutritt	No entry, no access
Kein Durchgang	No way through
Kein Trinkwasser	Not drinking water
Keine Durchfahrt	No through road

Das Rauchen/Das Spielen auf dem Rasen/Das Autowaschen etc. { **ist untersagt** / **ist nicht gestattet** / **ist verboten** / **ist streng verboten** / **ist nicht erlaubt** } Smoking/Playing on the grass/Washing your car is forbidden!

Sie dürfen hier nicht parken/zelten/ kochen/waschen/ etc.   You're not allowed to park/camp/ cook/wash here.

ANSWERS
1. Do not disturb. 2. Insert money. 3. Please step back. 4. Stamp tickets here. 5. Hand in your room key. 6. Put out your cigarette.

LEARN BY HEART

Here are a few imperatives which you might find useful in social situations:

Try to fill in the correct form of the verb. Choose four of the six verbs below.

1. ..... **Sie bitte herein.**   Please come in.

2. ..... **Sie bitte Platz.**   Do sit down.

3. **Entschuldigen Sie, das Rauchen**   Excuse me, you're not allowed
   ist hier nicht .....   to smoke here.

4. ..... **wir heute abend in die Stadt** Shall we go into town tonight?
   fahren?

nehmen   gestattet   verboten   kommen   wollen   könnten

Subjunctive

INTRODUCTION

This grammar is not really the place to go into all the details of the German subjunctive, but many of you have heard of the term and may be a bit confused about it. I have tried to reduce the subjunctive to what is really useful for everyday use.

ANSWERS

1. Kommen. 2. Nehmen. 3. gestattet. 4. Wollen.

EXPLANATION

Up until now in this book, we have been looking at verbs in very concrete, real settings. The subjunctive is a form of the verb which introduces a certain distance from reality, sometimes an element of doubt or wishful thinking. It is used for example:

1. When reporting what someone else has said.

Er sagte, sie *wäre* zum Flughafen gefahren. — He said she'd gone to the airport.

Because you are relying on what he said, you can't be absolutely sure that she really did go to the airport. So 'had gone' is subjunctive: **wäre gefahren**.

2. When translating the English 'if'.

Confusingly, the German word for 'if' is **wenn**. The word 'if' introduces an element of unreality or wishful thinking into the sentence:

Wenn ich ein reicher Mann *wäre* ... If I were a rich man ...

But I'm not and probably never will be. The English word 'were' in this sentence is a leftover form of the old English subjunctive and expresses the uncertainty caused by 'if'.

3. When translating the English 'would/could'.

a) Making polite requests:

***Könnten* Sie mir bitte ... zeigen?**	Could you please show me ...?
***Würden* Sie bitte so nett sein ...?**	Would you be so kind as to ...?
***Würden* Sie bitte die Tür zumachen?**	Would you please close the door?

b) Reacting very politely to other people:

Das *wäre* nett.	That would be nice.

c) Making suggestions:

Wir *könnten* nach Mexiko fahren.	We could go to Mexico.
An Ihrer Stelle *würde* ich ...	If I were you I would ...

d) Expressing wishes:

Ich *würde* gern mal nach Australien fahren.	I'd love to go to Australia.

4. Some everyday expressions which make conversation and dealings in banks, stores etc. pleasant and civilized.

Könnten Sie das bitte einpacken?	Could you wrap it up, please?
Könnte ich das bitte anprobieren?	Could I try this on, please?
Das **müßte** reichen/ gehen.	That ought to be enough/ be OK.
Das **wäre** nett.	That would be fine/ nice.
Danke, das **wäre** es.	Thank you, that's all for now.
Ich **hätte** gern + noun	I'd like ...
Ich **würde** gern + infinitive	I'd like to ...

HOW TO USE

Infinitive	Subjunctive			
haben **sein** **können**	ich/er/sie/es	**hätte** **wäre** **könnte**	wir/sie/Sie	**hätten** **wären** **könnten**

Please note the umlaut throughout. In fact in these examples above, the subjunctive form is exactly the same as the imperfect tense except for the umlaut. To translate 'would', you generally use **würde/würden** + infinitive.

Ich **würde** meine Stelle **kündigen**.	I'd hand in my resignation.
Er **würde** nach Amerika **fahren**.	He'd go to America.
Würden Sie so freundlich **sein**?	Would you be so kind?

Putting it all together

Here are a few examples of the subjunctive which you might find useful:

1. In conversation:

Wenn ich die Zeit **hätte**, **würde** ich gern mehr Deutsch **lernen**.	If I had the time, I would love to learn more German.
Wenn ich die Wahl **hätte**, **würde** ich zu Hause **bleiben**.	If I had the choice, I would stay at home.
Wenn ich so jung **wäre**, **würde** ich eine Weltreise **unternehmen**.	If I were as young as that, I'd go on a trip around the world.

2. In business letters:

Ich *wäre* Ihnen sehr dankbar, wenn Sie mir Ihre Broschüre zuschicken *könnten*.	I would be very grateful if you could send me your brochure.

There is more to the subjunctive than this, and if you are interested in taking it further, it is better to consult a more specialized grammar book.

Passive

INTRODUCTION

You use the passive when you don't want to be specific about who was/is performing the action.

EXPLANATION

If I say: 'John kicked the ball over the fence', I am being quite specific about who performed the action. But if I say: 'The ball was kicked over the fence', I leave the identity of the kicker open. The form 'was kicked' is passive. So the passive is really a different way of describing the same event. The emphasis is on the action itself and is deflected away from the person performing the action.

This can often be very useful if you want to highlight the action or keep the identity of the doer vague. The Germans are very fond of using the passive and you will hear and see it a lot more than in English. You do not have to learn it yourself, because there is a simpler alternative using **man** (one, people in general), see p.102. However, it is certainly useful to be able to recognize the passive.

HOW TO USE

1. Present tense

Use the present tense of **werden** (p.25) which goes to the usual verb position (see p.51) + the past participle (p.19) of the main verb which goes to the end of the sentence. The rest of the sentence is sandwiched in the middle.

1	2	3	4
Ich	**werde**		**ge——(e)t.** weak
Er/sie/es	**wird**	rest of sentence	
Wir/sie/Sie	**werden**		**ge—(?)—en.** strong

Sie *werden erwartet.* — You're expected./They're expecting you. ('They' not specified.)

Nein danke, ich *werde abgeholt.* — No thanks, I'm getting a ride./I'm being met. (You don't want to be specific about who is meeting you.)

Das Haus *wird* gerade *gebaut.* — The house is (in the process of) being built.

2. Imperfect tense

Use the imperfect tense of **werden** (**wurde/wurden**) + the past participle:

Ich/er/sie/es	**wurde***	rest of sentence	**ge——(e)t.** weak
Wir/sie/Sie	**wurden***		**ge—(?)—en.** strong

*N.B. no Umlaut!

Er *wurde* gestern *operiert.* — He was operated on yesterday.

Wir *wurden* vom Bahnhof *abgeholt.* — We were picked up from the station.

Die Kirche *wurde* im 16. Jahrhundert *gebaut.* — The church was built in the 16th century.

There are two important points which often confuse people:

1. **Werden** *does not have an umlaut* in the passive. Many people think it does because they confuse **wurde/wurden** with **würde/würden** (=would), see p.46.

2. Many people ask: what's the difference between
Das Geschäft *ist* geschlossen and
Das Geschäft *wird* geschlossen?

You can say both, but they mean different things. If you use **sein** with a past participle, you are describing a state of affairs. The shop is closed. It's a description of the shop, just as you could say the shop is big or small or expensive. The word **geschlossen** is being used here just as any other adjective. If you use **werden** with the past participle, you are describing the act of closing the shop. **Das Geschäft wird geschlossen** means that the shop is being closed. In your mind's eye you can see the action taking place.

Ihr Wagen ist repariert.	Your car is repaired, i.e. it is OK now, it is in a repaired state.
Ihr Wagen wird repariert.	Your car is being repaired, i.e. the repairing is going on now.

This problem is difficult for English speakers because we use 'to be' to form our own passive.

3. Perfect tense
This looks quite complicated, but you can survive without learning it. Use the present tense of **sein** (to be) + past participle of main verb + **worden.**

1	2	3	4	5
Ich	bin		ge——(e)t	
Er/sie/es	ist	rest of sentence	ge——(?)——en	worden.
Wir/sie/Sie	sind			

1	2	3	4	5	
Ihr Auto	**ist**	**gestern**	**repariert**	**worden.**	Your car was repaired yesterday.
Mein Bruder	**ist**	**in der Klinik**	**operiert**	**worden.**	My brother was operated on in the clinic.
Meine Handtasche	**ist**		**gestohlen**	**worden.**	My purse has been stolen.

In most cases you can use the imperfect just as well as the perfect for actions in the past.

EXPLANATION
A word of warning: many people confuse **worden** (which is used only in the perfect tense of the passive) with **geworden** (which is *not* used in the passive). **Geworden** is the past participle of **werden** (to become).

Sentence structure

INTRODUCTION

If you can master German word order and sentence structure you will sound much more German than someone who gets all the endings right but still sticks to English word order. German is a very logical language and the rules about word order are very straightforward. They may seem a lot to take in at one time, but persevere and you will astonish yourself! Train your ear to listen to how German people structure their sentences and try to copy them. Train yourself to predict what is coming at the end of the sentence. This will help you to think ahead and will stop you from being preoccupied with English word order – which won't be of much help to you.

EXPLANATION

I am going to distinguish between two types of sentences: simple sentences and complex sentences.

1. Simple sentences

In simple sentences (i.e. sentences containing only one verb) which are statements (i.e. not questions or commands) the most important rule is that the main verb always stands in the 2nd position. This does not mean that it is the 2nd word in the sentence because the 1st position may be occupied by a phrase consisting of several words.

1	2	3
Die Tür	**ist**	**auf.**

The door is open.

Die Tür is a unit forming in this example the subject of the verb. The verb **ist** is in 2nd position, i.e. the 2nd unit in the sentence. Here are some more examples:

1	2	3	
Wir	**fliegen**	**morgen nach Hause.**	We're flying home tomorrow.
Meine Tante	**besucht**	**uns nächste Woche.**	My aunt is visiting us next week.

In these examples the first unit is the subject (i.e. performs the action), the second unit is the verb and the rest of the sentence (expressions of time or place etc.) comes afterwards.

This is the usual sentence structure which we have in English. We nearly always begin a sentence with the subject, followed by the verb, followed by the object. Most other phrases get attached to the end of this core sentence, and expressions of time may go before or after the subject-verb-object core.

Yesterday | I went to see my friend in Cleveland. |
| I went to see my friend in Cleveland | yesterday.

German sentence structure is much more flexible. You can begin a sentence with almost anything you like: the subject, the object, an expression of time or place, the dative and many other expressions. Take a sentence like:

Ich fahre nächste Woche mit   I'm going to America next week
   meiner Tante nach Amerika.   with my aunt.

You can say:

1	2	3	4	5
Ich	fahre	nächste Woche	mit meiner Tante	nach Amerika.
Nächste Woche	fahre	ich	mit meiner Tante	nach Amerika.
Nach Amerika	fahre	ich	nächste Woche	mit meiner Tante.
Mit meiner Tante	fahre	ich	nächste Woche	nach Amerika.

Another example:

Der Mann	hat	mein Auto	genommen.
Mein Auto	hat	der Mann	genommen.

N.B. the main verb is *always* in the 2nd position.

How can you start a sentence with virtually any type of word and still avoid total confusion? How can you tell who performed the action and who was on the receiving end of it? The answer lies:

1. With the verb. The second position is an anchor point around which the rest of the sentence floats. The verb ending can already tell you a lot about who performed the action.

2. With the well-defined system of endings for words which accompany nouns (**der/die/das**, **ein/kein/mein** etc. see pp.94, 97). This is where the time and trouble spent in learning the nominative, accusative etc. endings is repaid in full, because it enables you to tell whether the car took the man or the man took the car.

Mein Auto hat der Mann genommen.

It's tempting to assume that **Mein Auto** is the subject, but look at **der Mann**. **Der** words only take **der** in the nominative, so **der Mann** must be the subject. Of course, common sense tells you that it must be that way, but you'd be surprised how often people get it wrong.

Although I said earlier that the rest of the sentence seems to float around the verb in the 2nd position, the parts which float do not just appear in any position whatsoever. Within the floating structure there are strict rules of word order:

1. Expressions of time (=*when*) must come before expressions of manner (=*how*), which must come before expressions of place (=*where*).

2. Pronouns must come before nouns.

3. If there are two nouns together, the nominative must come before the dative, which must come before the accusative.

4. If there are two pronouns together, the nominative must come before the accusative, which must come before the dative.

German sentence structure:

1	2	3
Nominative Accusative Dative Time Manner Place etc.	verb	rest of sentence. Rules: 1) time 2) manner 3) place 1) pronouns 2) nouns two nouns: 1) Nom 2) Dat 3) Acc two pronouns: 1) Nom 2) Acc 3) Dat

Here are some examples of simple statements with other tenses and verb constructions:

1. Perfect tense

1	2	3	4
	haben/sein	rest of sentence	past participle
Mein Onkel **In dem Lokal**	**ist** **haben**	**neulich** **wir Steaks**	**gestorben.** **gegessen.**

2. Modal verbs / **werden** (future tense) / **würde/würden** (=would)

1	2	3	4
	modal/ **werden**	rest of sentence	infinitive of 2nd verb
Ich	**möchte**	**meine Schwester**	**anrufen.**
Nächste Woche	**werde**	**ich meinen Geburtstag**	**feiern.**
Das	**würde**	**ich so gern**	**machen.**

3. Passive
a) Present and imperfect tenses

1	2	3	4
	werden	rest of sentence	past participle of 2nd verb
Nach dem Krieg	**wurde**	**Deutschland**	**geteilt.**
Die Wohnung	**wird**	**einmal in der Woche**	**geputzt.**

b) Perfect tense

1	2	3	4	5
Meine Schuhe **Wir**	**sind** **sind**	**schon** **um sieben Uhr**	**geputzt** **geweckt**	**worden.** **worden.**

4. Separable verbs
a) Present and imperfect tenses

1	2	3	4
Er Ich	bat kaufe	mir sein Auto immer bei Horten (=name of store)	an. ein.

b) Perfect and pluperfect tenses

1	2	3	4
Sein Auto Er	hat war	er mir schon	angeboten. wegegangen.

5. Simple questions and commands
To form simple questions or commands, you put the verb in the 1st position and the subject usually (but not always*) goes in the 2nd position.

1	2	3
Fahren	Sie	bitte etwas langsamer!
Geben	Sie	mir bitte den Schlüssel!
Fahren	Sie	immer so schnell?
Haben	Sie	gut geschlafen?
*Hat	Ihnen	das Essen geschmeckt?
Ist	das Haus	schon geputzt worden?
Möchten	Sie	in den Garten gehen?
Haben	Sie	viele Leute kennengelernt?

Questions using question words (when? where? etc.)

1	2	3	4
question word	verb	subject *(usually)	rest of sentence

There is no room left for maneuvering in the 1st position because it is occupied by the question word, so the subject or other word from the 1st position is shunted further down.

1	2	3	4
Wie lange **Wann** ***Wie**	**haben** **sind** **hat**	**Sie** **Sie** **Ihnen**	**Deutsch studiert?** **nach Deutschland gekommen?** **das Essen geschmeckt?**

*The questions marked with an asterisk are examples of the subject (**das Essen**) not occupying its expected position. The reason for this is the rule on page 53 which says that pronouns (**Ihnen**) must come before nouns (**das Essen**) when both follow the verb.

2. Complex sentences

In a complex sentence (i.e. a sentence with more than one main verb), each section of the sentence focuses on a particular verb. We call these sections *clauses*. In the following examples the beginning and end of a clause is shown by a slash mark (/) and the verb on which it focuses is written in italics.

/He *told* me/ that he *would phone* at eight o'clock/.

/I *am* not sure/ whether it *is going* to rain today/.

/He *kissed* her goodbye,/ then *walked away* quickly/ and *was lost* in the crowd/.

In German the beginnings and endings of clauses are always clearly marked by commas. The commas must be there and are part of the grammatical structure of the sentence. There are several types of complex sentences because there are several sets of rules about word order, depending on the construction used.

1. Verb stays in the usual position (2nd for statements, 1st for questions/commands).

a) After **und** (and), **aber** (but), **oder** (or), **sondern** ('but' after negative statement), **denn** (because).

                1   2

Bleiben Sie hier, oder kommen Sie lieber mit?

Are you staying here or do you want to come along too?

Wir können entweder bei uns zu Hause essen, oder¹ wir können² zu den Italienern gehen.
We can either eat at home or go out to the Italian restaurant.

Wir waren heute am Strand, aber¹ es war² eigentlich zu kalt zum Schwimmen.
We went to the beach today but it was really too cold to swim.

N.B. **und**, **aber** etc. are connecting words *between* clauses. They do not occupy a word-order position in the clause that follows.

Er kommt nicht? Das kann ich schon verstehen, *denn*¹ er wohnt² sehr weit von hier.
He's not coming? I can well understand that because he lives a long way away from here.

b) In the shortened form of indirect speech and expression of opinions. (N.B. no word for 'that'.)

Ich finde,	das	ist sehr nett von ihm.	I think it's very nice of him.
Ich meine,	er	ist schon weg.	I imagine he's already gone.
Ich glaube,	er	kommt nicht.	I think he's not coming.

2. Verb stays in the 2nd position, but there is no room in the 1st position because it is occupied already by words like **dann** (then) and **also** (so). This forces all other parts of the sentence to go after the verb. The subject therefore normally occupies the 3rd position.

Wir sind zu Karstadt gegangen, dann¹ waren² wir³ bei Hertie, dann¹ sind² wir³ in die Konditorei gegangen. Dort haben wir ein Stück Kuchen gegessen, dann¹ wollten² wir³ ins Kino gehen. Das Kino war zu, also¹ sind² wir³ nach Hause gefahren. Ich hatte meinen Schlüssel vergessen, also mußten² wir³ draußen warten.

We went to Karstadt*, then we were in Hertie*, then we went to the pastry shop. We had a piece of cake there, then we wanted to go to the movies. The theater was closed, so we went home. I had forgotten my keys, so we had to wait outside.

You can either start a completely new sentence with **dann/also** or you can add a comma at the end of the previous clause and continue in the same sentence.

3. The verb is moved from its 2nd position to the very end of the clause.

This word order occurs:

a) After **daß** (that), **weil** (because), **obwohl** (although), **damit** (so that), **wenn** (if) etc. They are all words which introduce clauses that can not stand on their own – these are known as subordinate clauses.

N.B. this overrides any other word order rules which affect the sentence.

1	2	3	4
	verb		

Modal verbs move from the 2nd position to come after the 2nd verb infinitive.

1	2	3	4	5
	modal verb		infinitive	

For separable verbs: the stem moves from the 2nd position and joins up with the prefix at the end of the sentence:

1	2	3	4
	stem		prefix+stem.

In the perfect tense, **haben/sein** move from the 2nd position to come after the past participle:

1	2	3	4	5
	haben/sein		past participle	

*Department stores in Germany.

Wir freuen uns, *daß* Sie gekommen *sind.*	We are pleased that you came.
Uns hat keiner gesagt, *daß* das Autowaschen hier verboten *ist.*	Nobody told us that you're not allowed to wash your car here.
Ich bin etwas später gekommen, *weil* ich mich zuerst anmelden *mußte.*	I arrived a bit late because I had to register first.
Ich möchte nicht, *daß* Sie zuviel Geld *ausgeben.*	I don't want you to spend too much money.
Wir haben ihn nicht gesehen, *weil* er um die Ecke gewartet *hat.*	We didn't see him because he was waiting around the corner.
Er kommt heute nicht mit, *weil* sein Geld alle *ist.*	He's not coming with us today because he's run out of money.

Notice the comma which comes before **daß/weil/wenn** etc. This is an essential point of German grammar indicating the end of one clause and the beginning of the next. It is *not* a piece of decoration to be put in or left out at will.

b) In relative clauses (with 'who'/'which'/'that')

Wo ist das Buch, *das* Sie in der Hand *hatten?*	Where's the book (which) you had in your hand?
Das war der längste Film, *den* ich je gesehen *habe.*	That was the longest film (which) I've ever seen.
Ich habe gestern mit dem Mann gesprochen, *der* unser Auto repariert *hat.*	I spoke yesterday to the man who repaired our car.

c) In indirect questions (e.g. 'I don't know where he is'. The direct question is: 'Where is he?' The indirect question is contained within the sentence and is introduced by a question word).

Könnten Sie mir bitte sagen, *wo* die Toiletten *sind?*	Could you please tell me where the rest rooms are?
Wissen Sie zufällig, *wann* dieser Zug in Basel *ankommt?*	Do you happen to know when this train arrives in Basel?
Ich habe keine Ahnung, *wer* die Hauptrolle im Film gespielt *hat.*	I've no idea who played the lead in the film.
Ich weiß nicht, *ob* das *stimmt.*	I don't know if that's right.

d) After **als** ('when' in the past), **nachdem** (after), **wenn** ('when' in the present and future), **bevor** (before), **seit** (since), **während** (while), **bis** (until). These are all expressions of time. They follow the same word order pattern as a), b) and c) but the time clause can come either at the beginning of the sentence or later on in the sentence. Notice what happens to the word order in the other clause:

Time clause at beginning of sentence	Other clause: verb in 1st position
Als wir wegfahren wollten, Just as we were about to depart, it	$\overset{1}{\text{hat}}$ $\overset{2}{\text{es}}$ gegossen. poured down.
Bevor Sie sich entscheiden, Before you make up your mind, you	$\overset{1}{\text{sollten}}$ $\overset{2}{\text{Sie}}$ unbedingt die Broschüre lesen. ought to read the brochure.

Other clause first: normal word order	Time clause follows
Ich habe viel gelesen, I read a lot	**als ich zwanzig war.** when I was twenty.
Wir haben schnell ein Bier getrunken, We had a quick beer	**bevor wir zum Bahnhof gegangen sind.** before we went to the train station.

Now look at each of the above examples in a), b), c) and d) very carefully and note down: 1. what type of verb it contains and 2. what tense the verb is in. Check again with the explanation at the beginning of each section and see if you can figure out why the word order is the way it is.

4. The verb in one clause is in the infinitive form.
a) After **um … zu** (in order to)
The infinitive goes at the end of its clause. Separable verbs insert **-zu-** between the prefix and the main stem:

First clause	Second clause			
	um	rest of clause	**zu**	infinitive
Wir sind etwas früher gekommen,	**um**	**Ihnen**	**zu**	**helfen.**
Ich brauche etwas,	**um**	**die Dose**		**aufzumachen.**

b) After certain verbs which are followed by **zu**, e.g. **vergessen** (to forget), **versuchen** (to try), **auf/hören** (to stop), **an/fangen** (to start), **empfehlen** (to recommend) etc.

Ich habe vergessen, ihn zu fragen.	I forgot to ask him.
Er hat mir empfohlen, den Intercity-Zug zu nehmen.	He recommended I take the Intercity train.

LEARN BY HEART
In the sentences below the verbs have been taken out of position. Rewrite the German sentences with the verbs in the correct position. The verbs are underneath the sentence, and they are in the wrong order.

1. **Ich Sie nicht, weil es zu spät.**
   angerufen, war, habe
   I didn't phone you because it was too late.

2. **Ich, wo wir ihn.**
   kennengelernt, habe, haben, vergessen
   I've forgotten where we met him.

3. **Sie Lust, jetzt in die Stadt zu?**
   haben, fahren
   Do you feel like going into town now?

4. **Ich nicht, ob die anderen schon zu Hause.**
   sind, weiß
   I don't know whether the others are already home.

5. **Ich mein Studium, weil ich kein Geld.**
   aufgeben, hatte, mußte

   I had to give up my studies because I had no money.

6. **Ich mit meinem Bruder ins Krankenhaus, dann wir mindestens eine Stunde.**
   gewartet, bin, haben, gegangen

   I went with my brother to the hospital and then we waited for at least an hour.

ANSWERS

1. Ich *habe* Sie nicht *angerufen*, weil es zu spät *war*. 2. Ich *habe vergessen*, wo wir ihn *kennengelernt haben*. 3. *Haben* Sie Lust, jetzt in die Stadt zu *fahren*? 4. Ich *weiß* nicht, ob die anderen schon zu Hause *sind*. 5. Ich *mußte* mein Studium *aufgeben*, weil ich kein Geld *hatte*. 6. Ich *bin* mit meinem Bruder ins Krankenhaus *gegangen*, dann *haben* wir mindestens eine Stunde *gewartet*.

Questions

INTRODUCTION

You will find yourself having to answer many questions in Germany and you will want to ask many questions yourself. Questions in German are quite straightforward. There are several types:

HOW TO USE

1. Simple questions expecting a 'yes/no' answer.

To form this type of question you simply reverse the word order of a normal statement so that the verb stands in the first position and the subject of the verb goes into the second position.

Statement	Question	
Er hat lange gewartet.	**Hat er lange gewartet?**	Did he wait long?
Er wohnt in Paris.	**Wohnt er in Paris?**	Does he live in Paris?
Sie kommen aus Berlin.	**Kommen Sie aus Berlin?**	Do you come from Berlin?

Notice that there is no German word for 'do/does/did' – it is absorbed into the verb.

Of course not all statements begin with the subject of the sentence. You might have a statement like:

Gestern hat er seine Mutter besucht.   He visited his mother yesterday.

To make this into a question, the verb has to go in the first position, the subject goes into the second position, so **gestern** is moved further down the question:

```
1       2        3
Hat er gestern seine Mutter besucht?  or  Hat er seine Mutter gestern
                                              besucht?
                                          1       2           3
```

2. Use of **nicht wahr?** (isn't it/aren't you? etc.)
If you are expecting the answer 'yes', you can save yourself the trouble of forming a question. Instead you express a normal statement, then tack on **nicht wahr?** at the end. The result is a question you expect the other person to agree with. **Nicht wahr?** means 'isn't that so?'.

Das Essen schmeckt gut, nicht wahr?	The food's good, isn't it?
Sie sind Fräulein Schmidt, nicht wahr?	You're Fräulein Schmidt, aren't you?
Sie wohnen in Kiel, nicht wahr?	You live in Kiel, don't you?
Der Bus fährt um acht Uhr, nicht wahr?	The bus leaves at 8 o'clock, doesn't it?

3. Use of question words (who? when? where? etc.)
The word order when using question words is:

1	2	3	4
question word	verb	subject (usually)	rest of question
Was	**haben**	**Sie**	**heute gemacht?**
Wann	**wollen**	**wir**	**essen?**

Sometimes the subject can not come in the third position because there is another rule of word order which says that in the part of the sentence which comes after the verb, pronouns must come before nouns (see p.53). So, if the subject is a noun and there is another pronoun after the verb, the subject gets moved further down the line:

1	2	3	4
Wie	**hat**	**Ihnen** (pronoun)	**das Essen geschmeckt?** (subject)

The most common question words are:
Wann? = when?

Wann fahren wir?	When are we leaving?

Wieviel? = how much/how many?

Wieviel Zigaretten haben Sie noch?	How many cigarettes do you have left?

Wo? = where?

Wo sind hier die Toiletten?	Where are the nearest rest rooms?

Wohin? = where to?

Wohin fahren Sie?	Where are you going (to)?

Woher? = where from?

Woher kommen Sie?	Where do you come from?

Wer? = who?

Wer? changes its ending depending on whether it is nominative, accusative, dative or genitive. It takes the same endings as **der** (see p.94).

Nom.	**wer?**	who?
Acc.	**wen?**	whom?
Dat.	**wem?**	(to/with etc.) whom?
Gen.	**wessen?**	whose?

Wer ist jetzt an der Reihe?	Who is next?
Für wen ist der Brief?	Who is the letter for? (for whom?)
Wem gehört der Koffer?	Who does the case belong to? (to whom?)

Note:
1. Many English people confuse **wer?** (=who) and **wo?** (=where). Try to get this clear in your own mind – it is the other way around from what you might expect.
2. Make sure you pronounce **wen?** (=whom?) with a long **e** (sounds like English 'vein') and **wenn?** (=when?) with a short **e** (sounds like the 'e' in English 'when'). Otherwise nobody will understand you.

Wie? = how?

Wie geht es Ihnen?	How are you?
Wie sagt man das auf Deutsch?	How do you say that in German?
Wie alt sind Ihre Kinder?	How old are your children?

Welcher/welche/welches? = which?
Welcher is an adjective (see p.112 Situation type 4).

Welches Zimmer haben Sie?	Which room do you have?
In welchem Zimmer sind Sie?	Which room are you in?
Welche Größe nehmen Sie?	Which size do you take?

Warum? = why?

Warum haben Sie das gemacht?	Why did you do it?

Was? = what?

Was ist das?	What's this?
Was kostet das?	How much is this? (What does it cost?)

PRACTICE/LEARN BY HEART

A. Questions you might hear:

Wie ist Ihr Name?	What is your name?
Woher kommen Sie?	Where do you come from?
Was sind Sie von Beruf?	What do you do for a living?
Was kann ich für Sie tun?	What can I do for you?
Was möchten Sie?	What would you like?
Haben Sie gut geschlafen?	Did you sleep well?
Hat Ihnen das Essen geschmeckt?	Did you enjoy your meal?

B. Questions you might want to ask:

Was kostet das Zimmer?	How much is the room?
Kann ich hier telefonieren?	Can I make a phone call here?
Sprechen Sie Englisch?	Do you speak English?
Wo ist hier eine Bank?	Where is there a bank around here?
Wann fährt der Zug nach Basel?	When does the train for Basel leave?
Wie heißen Sie?	What is your name?
Könnten Sie mir bitte helfen?	Could you please help me?
Wie sagt man 'spaniel' auf Deutsch?	How do you say 'spaniel' in German?
Was ist das?	What's this?

HOW TO USE

You can also form question words with prepositions. You add **wo-** to the beginning of the preposition. If the preposition begins with a vowel, you add **wor-**.

Worüber sprechen Sie?	What are you talking about?
Wofür ist das?	What is this for?
Wovon hängt das Ergebnis ab?	What does the result depend on?

Was für? = what kind of?

Was für eine Stadt ist das?	What kind of a town is this?
Was für Leute sind das?	What sort of people are they?

Negatives

INTRODUCTION

There is an art to saying no. It can be embarrassing not knowing how to say 'no' in a foreign language.

HOW TO USE

1. No

The simple word for 'no' is **nein**. But it is not always appropriate on its own. If somebody says to you:

Möchten Sie eine Tasse Kaffee?   Would you like a cup of coffee?

it would be very rude to decline with **Nein**, so here are some helpful expressions to soften your refusal.

If somebody offers you something you don't want, say

Nein danke or		
Danke or	} =	No, thank you.
(Nein) Vielen Dank		

If they insist and you still want to decline:

Nein danke + give a reason (e.g. **Ich muß fahren./Ich habe keinen Hunger** etc.)

Nein, wirklich nicht!	No, thank you, I really don't want to.
Das ist sehr nett von Ihnen, aber + reason	That's very kind of you, but …
Es tut mir leid, aber + reason	I'm sorry but …

You can express regret by using:

Es tut mir leid.	I'm sorry.
Leider …	Unfortunately . . .
Wir haben leider keine Zimmer frei.	I'm afraid we have no rooms.
Das Hotel ist leider ausgebucht.	I'm afraid the hotel is completely booked.
Es tut mir leid, aber ich kann nicht.	I'm sorry but I can't.

It can be awkward trying to refuse an invitation. It's clearly better to give some kind of reason so that the other person doesn't feel offended. On the other hand, you are not obliged to tell them all the details of your private life or the real reason why you want to refuse. The polite but firm way to refuse an invitation is to say:

Nein danke, ich bin schon verabredet.	No, thank you, I'm already committed elsewhere.

or

Es tut mir leid, ich habe schon etwas vor.	I'm sorry but I'm busy then.

You don't need to go into any more detail.

2. Not + verb. Use *nicht*.

Ich weiß es nicht.	I don't know.
Ich habe das Haus nicht gefunden.	I didn't find the house.
Bitte rauchen Sie nicht.	Please don't smoke.

Notice that there is no word for 'don't/didn't'. That is the English way of making the negative and it is unnecessary in German.

Nicht likes to stay close behind the verb in 2nd position, but if there is a subject (nominative), object (accusative) or indirect object (dative) after the verb, **nicht** is moved further down the sentence. Look at the following examples:

a) **Nicht** stays close behind the verb in 2nd position:

Ich bin nicht müde.	I'm not tired.
Ich habe nicht sehr gut geschlafen.	I didn't sleep very well.

b) **Nicht** is moved further down the sentence:

Er hat mir die Fotos nicht gezeigt.	He didn't show me the photos.
Geht es Ihrem Mann nicht gut?	Is your husband not well?
Gefällt Ihnen die Bluse nicht?	Don't you like the blouse?

You can also add **nicht-** as a prefix to nouns, like 'non-' in English.
der Nichtraucher non-smoking (car in a train etc.)

3. 'No not … any/ not … a' + noun. Use *kein*.
EXPLANATION
Kein is a sort of negative article. An exact equivalent does not exist in English, and English people find it tricky to use. The most important thing is to study the examples carefully and try to learn them by heart. Above all, if you catch yourself saying **nicht ein** for 'not a' – STOP! It is not German. **Nicht ein** can not exist in German – it must be replaced by **kein**.

HOW TO USE
Like the definite article (**der/die/das**) and the indefinite article (**ein/ eine/ein**), **kein** also takes endings which depend on:
1. whether the noun it accompanies is singular or plural;
2. which **der/die/das** group the noun belongs to;
3. what role the noun plays in the sentence (=case).

The endings are exactly the same as the endings for **ein** (see p.97).

	der group	**die** group	**das** group	plural
Nom.	no ending	-e	no ending	-e
Acc.	-en	-e	no ending	-e
Dat.	-em	-er	-em	-en

Examples:

Es gibt hier keine Luft.	There's no air in here./There isn't any air in here.
Wir haben heute keine Tomaten.	We don't have any tomatoes today./We have no tomatoes today.
Ich habe keine Ahnung.	I have no idea.
Er spricht kein Deutsch.	He doesn't speak any German.
Ich habe kein deutsches Geld.	I don't have any German money./I have no German money.

LEARN BY HEART

Go back over the examples with **nicht** and **kein** then decide how to put these sentences into German. Remember, if you find yourself writing **nicht ein** or **nicht** + noun, STOP AND THINK AGAIN!

1. I can't speak German.
2. I'm not hungry.
3. I don't understand.
4. I'm sorry, I don't know.
5. I can't pick you up at the train station.
6. I don't have any time.
7. I'm sorry, that's not possible.
8. Aren't you tired?
9. There's no beer in the refrigerator.
10. Don't you eat any meat?

4. Nobody / not ... anybody = *niemand*

Ich sehe niemand.	I can't see anyone.
Hier ist niemand.	There isn't anybody here.

5. Nothing / not ... anything = *nichts*

English people often have difficulty connecting 'nothing' with 'not ... anything'. It's tempting to look up the word 'anything' in the dictionary and add **nicht** to it, but that's not German. The way to say 'not ... anything' is **nichts**. And **nichts** is a very different word from **nicht** (='not'+verb).

Ich verstehe nicht.	I don't understand.
Ich verstehe nichts.	I don't understand anything.
Ich weiß nicht.	I don't know.
Ich weiß nichts.	I don't know anything.
Ich habe noch nichts gegessen.	I haven't had anything to eat yet.
Danke, ich möchte nichts trinken.	No thank you, I don't want anything to drink.

6. Nowhere / not ... anywhere = *nirgends* or *nirgendwo*

Er ist nirgends zu finden.	He can't be found anywhere.
Ich habe ihn nirgends gesehen.	I haven't seen it/him anywhere.

ANSWERS

1. Ich spreche kein Deutsch. 2. Ich habe keinen Hunger. 3. Ich verstehe nicht. 4. Es tut mir leid, ich weiß es nicht. 5. Ich kann Sie nicht vom Bahnhof abholen. 6. Ich habe keine Zeit. 7. Es tut mir leid, das geht nicht. 8. Sind Sie nicht müde? 9. Es gibt kein Bier im Kühlschrank. 10. Essen Sie kein Fleisch?

7. Never/not ... ever = *nie* or *niemals* or *noch nie*

Ich fahre nie ohne Gürtel.	I never drive without my seat belt fastened.
Ich habe nie Tee mit Milch getrunken.	I've never drunk tea with milk.
Ich war noch nie in meinem Leben betrunken.	I've never been drunk in my life.
Wir waren noch nie in der Schweiz.	We've never been to Switzerland.

8. Not ... yet = *noch nicht* + verb/ *noch kein* + noun

Ich kann mich noch nicht entscheiden.	I can't make up my mind yet.

9. Neither ... nor = *weder ... noch*

Weder ich noch meine Freundin wird da sein.	Neither I nor my friend will be able to come.

Conjunctions

INTRODUCTION

'Conjunction' means 'joining together'. Conjunctions are words which join two parts of a sentence together (e.g. 'and', 'but', 'so' etc.). If you say, 'The dress is red and blue', the word 'and' is a conjunction joining the two colors. You can also use conjunctions to join clauses (longer sections of a sentence which contain a verb). You can alter the tone of your sentence by choosing different conjunctions:

Clause 1	Conjunction	Clause 2
We went to the beach	and but because although when	it was raining.

HOW TO USE

The most important thing to know about German conjunctions is that when they join two clauses together they often affect word order.

1. Simple conjunctions

These do not affect word order:
Und (and), **aber** (but), **oder** (or), **denn** (for, because) etc.

klein *aber* fein	small but fine
mit *oder* ohne Sahne	with or without cream
Wir sind in die Wirtschaft gegangen *und* haben ein Bier getrunken.	We went into the tavern and had a beer.
Wir haben einen Picknick gemacht, *aber* es war sehr kalt.	We had a picnic but it was very cold.

2. Conjunctions that affect word order

a) Inversion of subject and verb. When you use these conjunctions, the subject and the verb exchange positions so that the verb goes into the 1st position and the subject goes into the 2nd position. **Also** (so – N.B. **also** never means the English 'also'); **dann** (then); **sonst** (otherwise); **deshalb** (therefore, for that reason) etc.

Ich muß jetzt gehen, *sonst* **komme ich zu spät.**	I'll have to go now. Otherwise I'll be late.
Ich möchte ein Paar Schuhe kaufen, *deshalb* **will ich morgen früh in die Stadt fahren.**	I'd like to buy a pair of shoes, which is why I want to go to town early tomorrow morning.
Wir haben Tee getrunken, *dann* **sind wir spazieren gegangen.**	We had some tea, then we went for a walk.

b) The verb is placed at the end of its clause.
Time – **nachdem** (after); **bevor** (before); **seit/seitdem** (since); **als** (when); **wenn** (when); **bis** (until); **während** (while) etc.
N.B. use **als** for 'when' in the past and **wenn** for 'when' in the present and future.
Reason – **da** (since); **weil** (because).
Objection – **obwohl** (although); **trotzdem** (in spite of that) etc.
If – **wenn** (if); **falls** (if, in case).
Purpose – **damit** (so that); **so ... daß** (so that)
daß (that)
ob (whether).

Sie müssen warten, *bis* **der Zug hält.**	You have to wait until the train stops.
Stimmt es wirklich, *daß* **er sehr krank** *ist*?	Is it really true that he is very ill?
Wissen Sie, *ob* **Herr Schweik jetzt zurück** *ist*?	Do you know whether Herr Schweik is back now?
Man muß lange warten, *wenn* **man ein Paket aufgeben** *will*.	You have to wait a long time if you want to send a package.
Kinder dürfen hier nicht schwimmen, *weil* **das Wasser sehr tief** *ist*.	Children are not allowed to swim here because the water is very deep.

Notice that there is always a comma before the conjunction if it introduces a new clause. In English, we often don't bother with a comma but in German it must be there to indicate the end of one clause and the beginning of another.

Nouns

General Information

INTRODUCTION
Nouns in German are always written with a capital letter.

Every noun belongs to one of three groups:

masculine	*feminine*	*neuter*
der	**die**	**das**

The terms masculine, feminine and neuter are a bit misleading because you find objects such as 'table' (**der Tisch**) belonging to the **der** group, and 'bus stop' (**die Haltestelle**) belonging to the **die** group. How can you tell which group a noun belongs to? Even Germans don't know every one. In a dictionary you will often see m. (for **der** group), f. (for **die** group) or n. (for **das** group). But you can't always go around with your nose in a dictionary so here are some rules which will help you.

EXPLANATION
The following nouns are usually in the **der** group:
– Nouns ending in **-er** which describe a person's job: **der Verkäufer** (salesman); **der Kellner** (waiter) etc.
– Nouns referring to a male person: **der Mann** (man); **der Onkel** (uncle); **der Vater** (father); **der Junge** (boy); **der Polizist** (policeman) etc.

The following nouns are usually in the **die** group:
– Nouns ending in **-in**, which is the female ending for a person's job: **die Studentin** (female student); **die Verkäuferin** (saleslady); **die Reiseleiterin** (female tour guide) etc.
– Nouns referring to a female person: **die Mutter** (mother); **die Frau** (woman); **die Tante** (aunt) etc.

– Nouns ending in **-ung**: **die Quittung** (receipt); **die Rechnung** (bill); **die Zeitung** (newspaper); **die Abteilung** (department); **die Heizung** (heating); **die Bedienung** (service); **die Übernachtung** (overnight stay); **die Verpflegung** (board, meals) etc.
– Nouns ending in **-heit**: **die Krankheit** (illness) etc.
– Nouns ending in **-keit**: **die Staatsangehörigkeit** (nationality) etc.
– Nouns ending in **-e**: **die Sprache** (language); **die Speisekarte** (menu); **die Steckdose** (electric socket); **die Stunde** (hour) etc.
– Nouns ending in **-schaft**: **die Botschaft** (embassy) etc.
– Nouns ending in **-tät**: **die Spezialität** (specialty); **die Elektrizität** (electricity) etc.
– Abstract ideas: **die Jugend** (youth); **die Ruhe** (peace, tranquility) etc.
– Nouns ending in **-bahn**: **die Autobahn** (super highway); **die Straßenbahn** (streetcar) etc.
– Nouns ending in **-tion** or **-sion**: **die Koalition** (coalition); **die Situation**; **die Rezeption**; **die Konfession** (religion) etc.

The following nouns are usually in the **das** group:
– Foreign words imported, e.g. from English or French: **das Restaurant**; **das Taxi**; **das Büro** (office); **das Hotel**; **das Parfüm** etc.
– Nouns ending in **-chen**: **das Mädchen** (girl); **das Brötchen** (bread roll); **das Würstchen** (small sausage) etc.
– Nouns ending in **-lein**: **das Fräulein** (girl) etc.
– Latin words: **das Studium** (period of study), **das Museum** etc.

Does it matter if you make a mistake with these groups? Yes and no. No, if you only want to get simple messages across. Provided your pronunciation is clear enough people will understand you even if you get the **der/die/das** wrong. Yes, if you want to speak reasonably correct German. It is important to know which group a noun belongs to because this affects many other grammar items, such as pronouns (p.99) and adjective endings (p.110). It also helps to avoid misunderstandings. But remember the golden rule: it's more important to say *something* even if it's wrong than to say nothing because you can't remember whether it should be **der**, **die** or **das**. Germans will appreciate the *effort*!

LEARN BY HEART
Whenever you meet a new noun, look it up in the dictionary and write down which group it belongs to. Try to learn the nouns which crop up again and again.

Here are some nouns you will need when looking for accommodations in Germany. Sort them out into three groups (**der/die/das**) and write the English meaning next to them:
1. **Campingplatz**. 2. **Hotel**. 3. **Gasthaus**. 4. **Frühstück**. 5. **Jugendherberge**. 6. **Empfang**. 7. **Formular**. 8. **Übernachtung**. 9. **Zimmer**. 10. **Parkplatz**.

Now try to learn them by heart.

Here are the names of some well-known German newspapers and magazines. Fill in the **der/die/das** and write down the English meaning:
1. **Spiegel**. 2. **Bildzeitung**. 3. **Welt**. 4. **Abendblatt**. 5. **Zeit**.

Plural forms

INTRODUCTION
Just as in English we say 'one man' but 'two men' and 'one guitar' but 'two guitars', so in German the plural form of a noun is often different from the singular form. In addition, **der/die/das** changes to **die** for all three groups.

EXPLANATION
These are the main types of changes together with the way they are shown in dictionaries:

ANSWERS
1st exercise
1. der (campsite). 2. das (hotel). 3. das (guest house). 4. das (breakfast). 5. die (youth hostel). 6. der (Reception). 7. das (form). 8. die (overnight stay). 9. das (room). 10. der (car park).
2nd exercise
1. der (mirror). 2. die (picture newspaper). 3. die (world). 4. das (evening paper). 5. die (time).

Dictionary

– Add **-n** or **-en** or **-nen**:
   Frau → Frauen   **Frau** *f.* (**-en**)
   Freundin → Freundinnen   **Freundin** *f.* (**-nen**)

– Change a vowel sound by adding an umlaut (**ä, ö, ü**):
   Garten → Gärten   **Garten** *m.* (**¨**)
   Apfel → Äpfel   **Apfel** *m.* (**¨**)

– Don't change anything at all:
   Kellner → Kellner   **Kellner** *m.* (**–**)
   Schlüssel → Schlüssel   **Schlüssel** *m.* (**–**)

– Add **-er**, usually with an umlaut (**ä, ö, ü**):
   Haus → Häuser   **Haus** *n.* (**¨ er**)
   Glas → Gläser   **Glas** *n.* (**¨ er**)

– Add **-e**, often with an umlaut (**ä, ö, ü**):
   Fahrplan → Fahrpläne   **Fahrplan** *m.* (**¨ e**)
   Tag → Tage   **Tag** *m.* (**-e**)

– Add **-s**:
   Bar → Bars   **Bar** *f.* (**-s**)
   Ticket → Tickets   **Ticket** *n.* (**-s**)

How do you know how to form the plural of a new noun? Unfortunately there's no easy answer. Most **die** group nouns form the plural by adding **-n** or **-en**. Some **das** group nouns (foreign words) add **-s**. Does it really matter? Only up to a point. Try to learn the plural form of new nouns when you look up the **der/die/das** information and make a special effort to memorize the nouns you keep coming across. It really is a question of memorizing and practice.

SURVIVAL

If you don't know the plural:
1. Stop and consult your phrase book, or
2. Try **-en** or **-er** on the end of the noun and see how the other person reacts. If they still don't understand, say the singular, e.g. **ein Kind** and then say **Wie sagt man, zwei was?** (How do you say two of them?).

N.B. Certain words which are singular in English are always plural in German:

a headache	**Kopfschmerzen**
a toothache	**Zahnschmerzen**
pain	**Schmerzen**
hair	**Haare**
furniture	**Möbel**

Others are plural in English but always singular in German:

clothes	**die Kleidung**
trousers	**die Hose**
eye glasses	**die Brille**
scissors	**die Schere**

LEARN BY HEART

Here are some nouns you might need when talking about your family or going out shopping. Use your dictionary to find the plural forms and write them down, together with the English meaning.

1. **Mann**	4. **Kind**	7. **Taxi**	10. **Bus**
2. **Apfel**	5. **Mantel**	8. **Tomate**	11. **Kartoffel**
3. **Kaufhaus**	6. **Glas**	9. **Fahrkarte**	12. **Geschäft**

Now cover them up and learn by heart.

Here are some signs you will nearly always see in the plural. Can you match the English words with the German?

1. **Zigaretten**	4. **Liköre**	7. **Lebensmittel**
2. **Damen**	5. **Herren**	8. **Toiletten**
3. **Möbel**	6. **Streichhölzer**	9. **Spirituosen**

liqueurs/ matches/ toilets/ liquors/ Ladies/ furniture/ Gentlemen/ food/ cigarettes/

ANSWERS

1. Männer (men) 2. Äpfel (apples) 3. Kaufhäuser (department stores) 4. Kinder (children) 5. Mäntel (coats) 6. Gläser (drinking glasses) 7. Taxis (taxis) 8. Tomaten (tomatoes) 9. Fahrkarten (tickets) 10. Busse (buses) 11. Kartoffeln (potatoes) 12. Geschäfte (stores)

1. cigarettes 2. Ladies 3. furniture 4. liqueurs 5. Gentlemen 6. matches 7. food 8. Toilets 9. liquors

Cases

INTRODUCTION

In English, nouns are quite simple. Usually the only thing you have to bother about is adding -s for the plural. But in German, nouns have four different *cases*.

Case refers to the role of a particular noun or pronoun in a particular sentence. You may never have thought about nouns or pronouns as having different roles unless you have studied grammar.

If you take a sentence like: '*John* wanted *me* to give *him* an *apple*', you can see that there are several nouns or pronouns in this sentence. If we try to replace 'John' with a pronoun we could say: '*Him* wanted to give me an apple', or '*He* wanted to give me an apple'. But one of these is wrong. Similarly we don't say: 'John wanted *I* to give *he* an apple'. Why not?

The reason these versions are wrong is that 'I' and 'he' can only play a certain role in a sentence. We say that 'I' or 'he' must be the *subject* of the sentence, in other words the person *doing* the action. Similarly 'me' or 'him' cannot be the subject of the sentence. They are on the *receiving* end of the action (or the verb). We say that 'him' or 'me' must be the *object* of the sentence. In English, the subject usually comes before the verb and the object comes after it.

Furthermore, we make a difference between different kinds of objects, the *direct object* and the *indirect object*.

What John said was: 'Give me the apple'. Here we have two objects: 'me' and 'the apple'. Which one does John want? – 'the apple'. We call this the *direct object*. We call 'me' the *indirect object* because John really means: 'Give (to) me the apple'.

When looking at German grammar, these three different roles, subject, direct object and indirect object are called *cases*.
The *subject* corresponds to the *nominative case*;
the *direct object* corresponds to the *accusative case*;
the *indirect object* corresponds to the *dative case*;
and there is one more: the *genitive case*, which is used for *possession*, e.g. 'my brother's house' etc.

In English we only notice the different cases when using pronouns such as I/me or he/him. But in German you notice the cases with nouns as well. The fact that a noun is in for example the dative or the accusative case will affect the endings of words that accompany nouns:
– **der/die/das** (definite article, see p.94);
– **ein/kein** (indefinite article, see p.97);
– **mein/Ihr/sein/ihr** etc. (possessive adjectives, see p.120);
– adjectives, see p.110
as well as the words that replace nouns:
– pronouns, see p.99.

N.B. usually the noun itself does not change. You use the form you find in the dictionary. However, there are a few common nouns which add **-n** or **-en** in all cases except the nominative singular:

der Student (-en)	student
der Bauer (-n)	farmer
der Junge (-n)	boy
der Name (-n)	name
der Herr (-n)	gentleman

HOW TO USE

To find out more, look up nominative, accusative, dative and genitive, where each case is explained in full. If you want to see an overall picture of German case endings, check with the section on patterns (p.161).

Nominative case

INTRODUCTION

Nominative describes the role of a particular noun or pronoun in a particular sentence.

WHEN TO USE

Nouns are in the nominative case:

1. when they are *doing* the action, i.e. when they are the *subject* of the verb. Look at these examples. The noun in the nominative case is in italics.

Das Telefon klingelt.	The phone is ringing.
Peter raucht eine Zigarette.	Peter's having a cigarette.
Die Deutschen essen viel Schweinefleisch.	The Germans eat a lot of pork.
Da drüben liegt *meine Tasche*.	My purse is over there.
Gestern ist *meine Schwester* gekommen.	My sister arrived yesterday.
Wo wohnt *Ihre Mutter*?	Where does your mother live?

From these examples it is clear that the noun in the nominative case is not automatically at the beginning of the sentence as it usually is in English, so it is sometimes a bit tricky to work out who did what to whom! The clue is to look for the signs:

a) verb ending – tells you whether the subject is singular or plural and which person (he/you/they etc);
b) the **der/die/das** form or **ein/kein/mein/Ihr** form also gives information about singular/plural and case;
c) use your common sense! The cigarette didn't smoke Peter.

2. After verbs like **sein** (to be) and **werden** (to become) where the person before and after the verb are one and the same, e.g. **Mein Bruder ist Ingenieur**. **Mein Bruder** and **Ingenieur** are one and the same person so both are in the nominative case.

EXPLANATION

If a noun is in the nominative case, you use the form you find in the dictionary for either singular or plural. The accompanying words look like this:

NOMINATIVE ENDINGS

Singular			Plural
der group (*no ending*)	**die** group (*-e ending*)	**das** group (*no ending*)	all groups (*-e ending*)
der	die	das	**die** the
ein	eine	ein	— a/an
kein	keine	kein	**keine** no/not...any
mein	meine	mein	**meine** my
Ihr	Ihre	Ihr	**Ihre** your

Try to teach yourself: can you spot the *pattern* of endings?

PRONOUNS

Pronouns are used to replace nouns and therefore can also be in the nominative case. If a pronoun is performing the action, it is the subject of the verb and looks like this:

Singular			Plural		
ich	(I)		**wir**	(we)	
er	(he/it)	to replace **der** words			
sie	(she/it)	to replace **die** words	**sie**	(they)	to replace
es	(it)	to replace **das** words			**die** plural
Sie	(you)		**Sie**	(you)	

PRACTICE/LEARN BY HEART

In order to ask about other people's families etc., you need the nominative case and a few basic verbs such as: **sein** (to be), **haben** (to have), **arbeiten** (to work), **wohnen** (to live), **kommen** (to come), **gehen** (to go). Can you underline the nominative words in these statements and questions?

1. **Das ist mein Mann.**   This is my husband.
2. **Er ist Beamter.**   He is a civil servant.
3. **Wir wohnen in San Francisco.**   We live in San Francisco.
4. **Wir haben drei Kinder.**   We have three children.
5. **Was sind Sie von Beruf?**   What do you do (for a living)?

Now fill in the blanks with facts about yourself. Then learn the questions and information by heart.

1. ...... **ist** (your name).   *My name is* (your name).
2. ... **bin** (your job).   *I am a* (your job).
3. ... **komme aus** (your town).   *I live in* (your town).
4. .... **arbeitet in** (town).   *My husband/wife etc. works in* (town).

ANSWERS
1st exercise
1. Das, mein Mann 2. Er, Beamter 3. Wir 4. Wir 5. Sie
2nd exercise
1. Mein Name 2. Ich 3. Ich 4. Mein Mann/Meine Frau

Accusative case

INTRODUCTION
Accusative describes the role of a particular noun or pronoun in a particular sentence.

EXPLANATION
Nouns and the words which either accompany them (adjectives, **der/die/das** or **ein/kein/mein** etc.) or replace them (pronouns) are in the accusative case when they are the *direct object* of the verb, i.e. on the *receiving* end of the action.

Look at these examples:

Ich möchte *ein kaltes Bier.*	I'd like a cold beer.
***Den Mann* kann ich nicht leiden.**	I can't stand that man.
Das verstehe ich nicht.	I don't understand that.
Rufen Sie *mich* bitte an.	Please give me a call.
Kochen Sie *Kaffee*?	Are you making coffee?

All the *italicized* words are in the accusative case. In English the word order is quite rigid: 1. subject 2. verb 3. direct object; but as you can see, in German the accusative can be found almost anywhere in the sentence. This can be a bit confusing.

The key is to look for the signs of the accusative:
1. Endings of **der/die/das**, **ein/kein/mein** etc.
2. Verb ending – tells you who is performing the action, and whether the subject is singular or plural. This helps you to narrow down the possibilities.
3. The meaning of the sentence as a whole – does it make sense?

HOW TO USE
If a noun is in the accusative case, you use the form you find in the dictionary for the singular or plural. The accompanying words look like this:

ACCUSATIVE ENDINGS

	Singular		Plural
der group (**-n/-en** *ending*)	**die** group (**-e** *ending*)	**das** group (*no ending*)	all groups (**-e** *ending*)
den	die	das	die
einen	eine	ein	—
keinen	keine	kein	keine
meinen	meine	mein	meine
Ihren	Ihre	Ihr	Ihre

For the details about adjectives, see p.110.

As you can see, the accusative affects the **der** group much more than any other, and the sign to look for is the ending **-n**.

Pronouns in the accusative go like this:

	Singular			Plural	
mich	(me)		**uns**	(us)	
ihn	(him/it)	to replace **den** words			
sie	(her/it)	to replace **die** words	**sie**	(them)	to replace **die** plural
es	(it)	to replace **das** words	**Sie**	(you)	
Sie	(you)				
sich	(yourself)		**sich**	(yourself)	

WHEN TO USE

1. With the direct object.

2. There are certain prepositions (see p.127) which always take the accusative case. The most common are: **für, durch** and **ohne**.
   Das ist für *meinen* Sohn.   That's for my son.
   Gehen Sie durch *den* Park.   Go through the park.

3. The prepositions **in/an/auf** with verbs of movement always take the accusative case.

Ich gehe heute abend _ins_ Theater. (in das→ins)	I'm going to the theater this evening.
Wir fahren morgen _in die_ Stadt.	We're going into town tomorrow.
Gehen wir _an den_ Strand?	Are we going to the beach?
Er fährt morgen _auf eine_ Konferenz.	He's going to a conference tomorrow.

4. The expression **es gibt** (there is/there are) is always followed by the accusative case.

Es gibt _keinen_ Aschenbecher.	There's no ashtray.
Gibt es hier in der Nähe _eine_ Bank?	Is there a bank around here?

5. Expressions of time.

einen Moment	just a moment
diese Woche	this week
nächstes Jahr	next year
Er war _eine_ Woche krank.	He was sick for a week.
Ich bleibe _einen_ Monat.	I'm staying for a month.

HOW TO USE

Once you have decided that a noun or pronoun is in the accusative case:

1. Decide whether your noun is singular or plural.
2. Decide which group it belongs to.
3. Choose the right ending for your accompanying word or replacement pronoun.

If you want to say 'I'd like an ice cream', you know 'ice cream' is the direct object, therefore accusative case.

1. **Eis** is singular.
2. **Eis** belongs to the **das** group.
3. Therefore you say: **Ich möchte _ein Eis._**

If you want to say, 'I'm looking for a present for my boyfriend', you know 'present' is the direct object, therefore accusative case. 'My boyfriend' is accusative after **für** (see p.127).

1. Both **Geschenk** and **Freund** are singular.
2. **Geschenk** belongs to the **das** group, **Freund** to the **der** group.
3. Therefore you say: **Ich suche _ein Geschenk_ für _meinen Freund._**

Now go back and look at all the examples once again to make sure you understand.

Here are some important phrases if you stay in a German hotel. Look at the English translation then fill in the correct form of the missing words. They are all accusative.

1. **Haben Sie ... Zimmer frei?** — Do you have a room?
2. **Ich möchte ... Doppelzimmer für zwei ...** — I'd like a double room for two nights.
3. **Kann ich hier ... Reisescheck einlösen?** — Can I cash a traveler's check here?
4. **Können Sie bitte ... Hundertmarkschein wechseln?** — Can you please change a 100 Mark note?
5. **Gibt es hier ... Telefon?** — Is there a telephone here?
6. **Gibt es hier ... Toilette?** — Is there a washroom here?
7. **Gibt es hier ... Reinigung?** — Is there a dry cleaning service here?
8. **Gibt es hier ... Parkplatz?** — Is there a parking lot here?
9. **Ich verstehe ... nicht.** — I don't understand you.
10. **Gibt es Post für ...?** — Is there any mail for me?
11. **Das ist für ...** — That's for you.
12. **Könnten Sie ... bitte um 8 Uhr wecken?** — Could you please give me a call at 8 o'clock?
13. **Ich möchte ... Zeitung.** — I'd like a newspaper.
14. **Ich möchte ... Kännchen Kaffee.** — I'd like a pot of coffee.
15. **Ich möchte ... Aschenbecher.** — I'd like an ashtray.
16. **... Augenblick bitte.** — Just a minute please.
17. **Ich hole ... Gepäck.** — I'll get my luggage.
18. **Ich hole ... Koffer.** — I'll get my suitcase.
19. **Ich hole ... Tasche.** — I'll get my purse.
20. **Ich hole ... Auto.** — I'll get my car.

ANSWERS
1. ein 2. ein, Nächte 3. einen 4. einen 5. ein 6. eine 7. eine 8. einen 9. Sie 10. mich 11. Sie 12. mich 13. eine 14. ein 15. einen 16. einen 17. mein 18. meinen 19. meine 20. mein

Dative case

INTRODUCTION
Although we virtually possess no dative case in English, it is extremely important in German, particularly in many common conversational situations such as inquiring after someone's well-being, whether they are enjoying their meal, what they like and dislike etc.

EXPLANATION
Nouns and the words which accompany them (**der/die/das**, **ein/kein/mein** etc., adjectives) or replace them (pronouns) are in the dative case when they are the *indirect object* of the verb. In English we tend to use 'to'/'for' to indicate the indirect object, but the Germans prefer to use endings to express the dative.

First let us be quite sure what we mean by indirect object. If we take a sentence like 'I bought myself a beautiful coat yesterday', we can break down the sentence as follows:

Subject of verb = I
Verb = bought
Object of verb = a beautiful coat

But what about 'myself'? I didn't hand over money and buy myself. I bought a beautiful coat *for* myself. This is what we mean by the indirect object as distinct from the direct object – 'a beautiful coat'.

Here are some more examples. The dative is italicized.
Zeigen Sie *mir* bitte auf der Karte. Please show *me* on the map (show to me).

Er hat *uns* die Zeitung gebracht. He brought *us* the newspaper (i.e. brought to us).

The most common verbs you will find with an indirect object are: **geben** (to give), **bringen** (to bring), **zeigen** (to show), **kaufen** (to buy), **schicken** (to send), **sagen** (to say, tell).

HOW TO USE

How do you recognize the dative in German? The word order in the sentence won't help you very much, so you will have to recognize the endings which express the dative, which are:

for **der/das** group words	**-m** (think of him)
for **die** group words	**-r** (think of her)
for all plural words	**-n**

Look at the patterns:

DATIVE ENDINGS

Singular			Plural
der group (-m ending)	**die** group (-r ending)	**das** group (-m ending)	all groups (-n ending) + noun, which adds -n/-en
dem	der	dem	den
einem	einer	einem	—
keinem	keiner	keinem	keinen
meinem	meiner	meinem	meinen
Ihrem	Ihrer	Ihrem	Ihren

The pronouns in the dative are:

Singular		Plural	
mir (me)		**uns** (us)	
ihm (him/it)	to replace **dem** words		
ihr (her/it)	to replace **der** words	**ihnen** (them)	to replace **den**
ihm (it)	to replace **dem** words		plural
Ihnen (you)		**Ihnen** (you)	
sich (yourself)		**sich** (yourself)	

As you can see, every group is affected by the dative, so try to learn the patterns above. Does it matter? Yes and no. You can get away with swallowing in the right places and bluffing. I suggest you at least try to remember **mir** and **Ihnen** because they occur very frequently and are much more noticeable than the others if you get them wrong. For those who would like to sound correct, try learning our examples by heart, but don't get too preoccupied with being correct – it takes the Germans years to learn it at school!

EXPLANATION

1. The dative case is also used with other types of phrases which mean 'to like something' 'to belong' (to).

Es gefällt *mir.*	I like it (people, things, places).
Es schmeckt *mir.*	I like it (food, drink). Literally: 'it tastes good to me'.
Schmeckt *Ihnen* **der Wein?**	Do you like the wine?
Das gehört *mir.*	That belongs to me.

2. Some very common expressions which must be learned by heart:

Guten Tag, wie geht es *Ihnen?*	Hello, how are you?
Danke, es geht *mir* **gut.**	I'm very well thank you.
Und wie geht es *Ihrem Mann/ Ihrer Frau?*	And how's your husband/wife?
Mir **ist schlecht.**	I'm not feeling very well.
Oh, das tut *mir* **leid.**	Oh, I'm sorry.
Ist *Ihnen* **zu warm/kalt?**	Are you too hot/cold?
Mir **ist warm/kalt.**	I'm too hot/cold.
Das ist *mir* **egal.**	I don't care.

3. With a few verbs which in English do not take an indirect object: **helfen** (to help), **danken** (to thank), **glauben** (to believe).

Wir glauben *ihm* **nicht.**	We don't believe him.
Kann ich *Ihnen* **helfen?**	Can I help you?
Ich danke *Ihnen.*	Thank you.

4. When describing some personal activities where in English we would use 'my/your/his' etc.

Ich will *mir* **die Zähne putzen.**	I want to brush my teeth.
Ich lasse *mir* **die Haare schneiden.**	I'm going to have my hair cut.

5. After many prepositions (see p.127). The most common are **bei, zu, mit, von, nach.**

Wir haben *mit den Kindern* **gespielt.**	We played with the children.
Ich wohne *bei meinen Eltern.*	I live with my parents.
Nach den **neuesten Nachrichten.**	According to the latest news.

6. After the prepositions **an/in/auf** with a verb describing position (see p.127).

Ich wohne *in der* Dahlemstraße.   I live in Dahlemstraße.
Die Zeitung liegt *auf dem* Tisch.   The newspaper is on the table.

HOW TO USE

Having decided that the word you want to use is dative,
1. Decide whether your noun is singular or plural.
2. Decide which group it belongs to (**der/die/das**).
3. Choose the right ending for your accompanying word or replacement pronoun.

You want to say: 'Give him the book'.
1. 'Him' is singular.
2. 'Him' is a pronoun replacing a **dem** word.
3. Therefore you say: **Geben Sie *ihm* das Buch.**

You want to say: 'How's your brother today?'
1. **Bruder** is singular.
2. **Bruder** is a **der** group word.
3. Therefore you say: **Wie geht es *Ihrem* Bruder?**

PRACTICE/LEARN BY HEART

Here are some very useful phrases for personal conversations. Try to fill in the blanks. They are all dative and are in our examples above.

1. **Kann ich ... helfen?**   Can I help you?
2. **... ist schlecht.**   I feel sick.
3. **Wie geht es ...?**   How are you?
4. **Wie geht es ... Frau?**   How's your wife?
5. **Die Bluse gefällt ...**   I like the blouse.
6. **Schmeckt ... der Wein?**   Do you like the wine?
7. **Oh, das tut ... leid.**   Oh, I am sorry.

ANSWERS
1. Ihnen 2. Mir 3. Ihnen 4. Ihrer 5. mir 6. Ihnen 7. mir

Genitive case

INTRODUCTION
Genitive means possessive, and the genitive case is a way of showing who owns what. It translates the English 's or 'of', e.g. 'My brother's car', 'the top of the hill' etc.

HOW TO USE
This is what the genitive looks like:

der group	die group	das group	plural
des + -s or -es on noun eines + -(e)s keines + -(e)s meines + -(e)s	der einer keiner meiner	des + -s or -es on noun eines + -(e)s keines + -(e)s meines + -(e)s	der — keiner meiner

Notice that, for **der/das** group words, **-s** or **-es** is added on to the noun. For **die** group and plural words, there is no extra ending for the noun.

In addition to showing possession the genitive case is also used after some prepositions and other expressions: **während** (during); **wegen** (because of); **trotz** (in spite of); **aufgrund** (because of); **im Laufe** (in the course of/during); **in der Nähe** (near).

Examples:

Ist das das Haus Ihr*er* Eltern?	Is this your parents' house?
Das ist Onkel Fritz, der Bruder mein*er* Mutter.	This is uncle Fritz, my mother's brother.
Das können wir während *des* Essens besprechen.	We can talk about that over lunch.
Wir hören im Laufe *des Tages* von ihm.	We'll hear from him in the course of the day.
Das ist der Wagen *meines* Freund*es*.	This is my friend's car.
Man sieht den Gipfel *des* Berges nicht.	You can't see the summit of the mountain.
Angebot *des* Monat*s*	Special offer of the month
Auto *des* Jahr*es*	Car of the year

With people's names you add **s**:
Petras **Bruder**   **Hermann**s **Schwester** etc.

To sum up: the sign of the genitive for **der/das** words is an **-s** + **-s** or **-es** ending on the noun, and for **die** words and plural ones it is **-r** + no special ending for the noun.

The definite article

INTRODUCTION

'The' is a relatively minor piece of English grammar because it has only one form, but in German the words for 'the' are extremely important. There are several forms for the word 'the'. Every noun (see p.75) belongs to one of three groups. If you look up a noun in a dictionary, you will probably find something like: m. (masculine) or f. (feminine) or n. (neuter) after it to tell you which group it belongs to.

der group   (m. in dictionary)
die group   (f. in dictionary)
das group   (n. in dictionary)

Der/die/das etc. are used whenever we use 'the' in English, and they nearly always are followed by a noun. Before you decide which form of **der/die/das** to use you have to know a few things about the accompanying noun:
1. whether it is singular or plural;
2. which **der/die/das** group it belongs to;
3. what role it plays in this particular sentence (i.e. case, see p.80).

EXPLANATION

Look at the pattern:

	Singular			Plural for all 3 groups
	der group	**die** group	**das** group	
Nom.	**der**	**die**	**das**	**die**
Acc.	**den**	**die**	**das**	**die**
Dat.	**dem**	**der**	**dem**	**den**
Gen.	**des**	**der**	**des**	**der**

This looks like a lot, but you will help yourself if you concentrate on two ideas:

1. Reduce your learning to the minimum by remembering: nominative and accusative are the same for all groups except the **der** (masculine singular) group, where **der** changes to **den** in the accusative.

And for the dative remember:
-**m** ending for **der/das** groups
-**r** ending for **die** group
-**n** ending for all plurals

2. These endings set the pattern for many other endings. If you learn them thoroughly now, you will find other grammar points much easier to cope with.

HOW TO USE

In order to decide which form of **der/die/das** is the correct one, you have to follow three steps:
1. Decide whether the accompanying noun is singular or plural;
2. If it is singular, which group does it belong to?
3. What role does it play in this sentence? (which case?)

For example, you want to say: 'The car is in the garage'.
1. Both nouns are singular.
2. **Das Auto; die Garage**.
3. **Auto** is nominative because it is the subject of the verb. **Garage** is dative after **in** + dative for position (see p.128).
Das Auto ist in der Garage.

You want to ask: 'Where are the toilets?'
1. 'Toilets' is a plural noun.
2. Does not apply here.
3. **Toiletten** is nominative because it is the subject of the verb.
Wo sind die Toiletten?

WHEN TO USE

Der/die/das is used just the same as 'the' in English, for example:
Wo ist das Telefon?   Where's the telephone?
Wo ist die Tür?   Where is the door?
Wann kommt der nächste Bus?   When's the next bus?

Der/die/das is sometimes used differently from the English 'the':

1. With people's names. You will often hear German people refer to friends and relatives as: **der Peter**, **die Monika**, **der Schmidt** etc. This is colloquial and only acceptable when you are on very friendly terms.

2. Die meisten = most

Die meisten Engländer trinken Tee mit Milch.	Most English people drink tea with milk.

3. With prices, **der/die/das** = per

Zwanzig Pfennig das Stück.	Twenty Pfennigs apiece.
Zehn Mark das Kilo.	Ten Marks per kilo.

4. The names of some countries:

die Schweiz	Switzerland
die BRD (die Bundesrepublik Deutschland)	The Federal Republic of Germany
die DDR (die Deutsche Demokratische Republik)	The German Democratic Republic
die Sowjetunion	The Soviet Union
die USA/die Vereinigten Staaten	The USA/The United States
die Türkei	Turkey
die Niederlande	The Netherlands

LEARN BY HEART

Nobody expects you to know the **der/die/das** group for every noun in the German language but you will help yourself a great deal if you try to learn the common ones.

Here are some places you may need to find at any German train station or airport. It will help you to be able to ask where to find them:

1. **Entschuldigen Sie bitte, wo ist …** Excuse me, where is the
   Restaurant? restaurant?
2. **Entschuldigen Sie bitte, wo ist …** Excuse me, where is the
   Auskunft? information desk?
3. **Entschuldigen Sie bitte, wo ist …** Excuse me, where is the taxi
   Taxistand? stand?
4. **Entschuldigen Sie bitte, wo ist …** Excuse me, where is the
   Wechselstube? exchange booth?
5. **Entschuldigen Sie bitte, wo sind …** Excuse me, where are the
   Toiletten? washrooms?

ANSWERS

1. das 2. die 3. der 4. die 5. die

The indefinite article

INTRODUCTION

The indefinite article ('a', 'an') is used when you are not referring to any specific object already mentioned. In German, you use the word **ein** or one of its forms. **Ein** always accompanies a noun, and therefore it has endings which change depending on the **der/die/das** group the noun belongs to and also the role the noun is playing in that particular sentence (i.e. case). 'A'/'an' is a very straightforward little word in English, but in German **ein** has a whole system of endings.

EXPLANATION

Look at these examples:

Ich möchte *eine* **Tasse Kaffee.**	I'd like *a* cup of coffee.
Haben Sie *einen* **Bleistift?**	Have you got *a* pencil?
Gibt es hier in der Nähe *eine* **Bushaltestelle?**	Is there *a* bus stop near here?

Warning! If you have a negative sentence involving 'not a'/'not an', you must never say **nicht ein**. Instead you must always use **kein** or one of its forms. This is a very important German grammar point (see p.70).

HOW TO USE

	der group	**die** group	**das** group
Nom.	ein	eine	ein
Acc.	einen	eine	ein
Dat.	einem	einer	einem
Gen.	eines	einer	eines

This pattern is important because it is the model for **kein** and the possessive adjectives (**mein**, **ihr** etc.) (see p.120; see also p.161 an overview of endings).

Checklist for using **ein**:
1. Decide which group the accompanying noun belongs to (**der/die/das**).
2. Decide which role the noun is playing in the particular sentence.

You want to say: 'I have a son and a daughter'.
1. **Der Sohn, die Tochter**.
2. Both nouns are accusative because they are the direct object of the verb.
So you say: **Ich habe *einen* Sohn und *eine* Tochter.**

You want to say: 'I am staying with a family in Berlin'.
1. **Die Familie**
2. 'Family' is dative after **bei** (see p.131).
So you say: **Ich wohne bei *einer* Familie in Berlin.**

PRACTICE/LEARN BY HEART
Using the checklist above, fill in the correct form of **ein**:

1. **Was kostet ein– Kilo?**   How much is a kilo?
2. **Das ist ein– schöne Wohnung.**   This is a lovely apartment.
3. **Haben Sie ein– Zimmmer frei?**   Have you got a room?
4. **Ich möchte ein– Schachtel Zigaretten.**   I'd like a pack of cigarettes.
5. **Wir haben ein– guten Film gesehen.**   We saw a good movie.

WHEN TO USE
There are a few situations when English 'a/an' is different from German:

1. With people's jobs, leave out **ein** in German:
Sie ist Sekretärin.   She's *a* secretary.
Ich bin Ingenieur.   I'm *an* engineer.

2. In expressions of time, use **pro** (=per)
einmal *pro* Woche   once *a* week
zweimal *pro* Tag   twice *a* day

3. Expressions like 'half a', 'such a', 'what a':
ein *halbes* Pfund Edamer   half *a* pound of Edam cheese
So ein netter Junge!   what *a* nice boy!
so eine nette Überraschung! what *a* nice surprise!

4. 'A lot of' = **viel**
Er hat viel Geld.   He has a lot of money.

ANSWERS
1. ein 2. eine 3. ein 4. eine 5. einen

Pronouns

INTRODUCTION

Pronouns make our language neater and more compact. Once we have mentioned 'the lady who lives down the street with her husband and ten cats', we don't want to repeat all this each time we talk about the lady, so we use *she* and *her* to replace the long description. In other words, once we have established who or what we are talking about, we use pronouns as a quick reference.

EXPLANATION

Pronouns refer to people and things and they often replace nouns. Therefore they also have cases, depending on their function in the sentence. If you are not quite sure what cases are, see p.80. The endings of verbs also change depending on the noun or pronoun performing the action.

Personal pronouns

1. Refer to people:

Nom.	**ich** (I)	**Sie** (you)	**wir** (we)
Acc.	**mich** (me)	**Sie** (you)	**uns** (us)
Dat.	**mir** (me)	**Ihnen** (you)	**uns** (us)

2. Refer to people and things and replace nouns:

Replace	**der** group	**die** group	**das** group	*Plural* all groups
Nom.	**er** (he/it)	**sie** (she/it)	**es** (it)	**sie** (they)
Acc.	**ihn** (him/it)	**sie** (her/it)	**es** (it)	**sie** (them)
Dat.	**ihm** (him/it)	**ihr** (her/it)	**ihm** (it)	**ihnen** (them)

It looks like a lot, but can you see any patterns to help you? Look at p.161 for an overall picture of ending patterns.

Notes

1. **Sie** is the polite form of *you*. Always use it unless you are on extremely friendly terms. For the informal **du** etc., see p.103. As in English, **Sie** is both singular and plural. The verb always ends in **-en**. **Sie** and **Ihnen** (meaning 'you') are always written with a capital letter.

Sometimes it's difficult to figure out in a conversation whether **Sie/sie** means *you/she/it/they*. Then it's important to listen for the verb ending. If it's **-t**, **Sie/sie** means *she* or *it* and you have to recall whether a thing or a person (female) has been mentioned. If it's **-en**, **sie** means *you* or *they/them*. If it's *they/them*, there must have been a noun somewhere along the line. If you've lost track, ask **wer?** (who?) or **was?** (what?).

2. **It** in English always refers to things. But in German, things belong to all three groups of nouns (**der/die/das**). So if you were talking about a thing in the **der** group, you would replace it by **er/ihn/ihm** depending on the case.

Wo ist der Tisch? Ich sehe *ihn*   **Wo ist meine Bluse? Ich finde *sie***
nicht.   **nicht.**

So don't be tempted to say **es** for *it* every time. It's just as likely to be a variation of **er** or **sie**.

3. Notice that **ich** (I) is written with a small letter when it's not the first word in a sentence.

HOW TO USE

When using pronouns, follow these three steps:
1. Decide whether the noun or pronoun is singular or plural.
2. Decide which group it belongs to: **der – er, die – sie, das – es**.
3. Decide which case it is in.

You want to say: '*He* (my brother) is very happy there'.
1. *He* is singular.
2. *He* is replacing a **der** group word, **Bruder**, brother.
3. *He* is nominative, because it is the subject of *is*.
So you say: ***Er* ist sehr glücklich dort.**

You want to say: 'Could you help *us* please?'
1. *You* could be singular or plural, *us* is plural.
2. *You* and *us* are not replacing nouns.
3. *You* is nominative (performing the action), *us* is dative after **helfen**.
So you say: **Könnten *Sie uns* bitte helfen?**

PRACTICE

Now try this exercise. Fill in the blanks and replace the italicized phrases by pronouns.

1. ... bin mit *der Kamera* sehr zufrieden.

I'm very pleased with the camera.

2. ... fahre mit *meinem Freund* in die Stadt.

I'm going into town with my friend.

3. *Mein Bruder* hat den *roten Wagen* gekauft.

My brother bought the red car.

4. *Die Leute* sind von überallher.

The people have come from all over the place.

5. ... können *das Zelt* da drüben aufstellen.

We can put the tent up over there.

LEARN BY HEART

Here are some useful expressions with personal pronouns to express how people feel, what they want etc.

Ich habe Hunger/Durst.	I'm hungry/thirsty.
Mir ist kalt/warm.	I'm cold/hot.
Wir frieren/schwitzen.	We're freezing/boiling hot.
Ich muß auf die Toilette.	I have to go to the bathroom.
Es tut *mir* weh.	It hurts.
Ich habe Kopfschmerzen.	I've got a headache.
Ihm/ihr ist schlecht.	He/she is feeling sick.
Er ist ganz blaß.	He's very pale.
Es geht *ihm/ihr* gut.	He/she's fine.
Sind *Sie* müde/krank/nervös?	Are you tired/ill/nervous?
Haben *Sie* Schmerzen?	Are you in pain?
Wie geht es *Ihnen*?	How are you?

ANSWERS
1. Ich, ihr 2. Ich, ihm 3. Er, ihn 4. Sie 5. Wir, es

man

INTRODUCTION

man is an impersonal pronoun. You will come across it particularly when reading or being given instructions, asking for suggestions or help, talking about official regulations or making very general statements or questions.

EXPLANATION

man is a very useful little word. It can be used to translate the English words: 'one', 'people', 'someone', 'you' (impersonal), 'they' (not specific). It also offers a convenient way of avoiding the passive (see p.47) in German. It can be used whenever you don't want to be specific about a person or people.

Look at these examples:

Man trinkt viel Tee in England.	They drink a lot of tea in England.
Hier muß man immer lange warten.	You always have to wait a long time here.
Hier kann man überall gut essen.	You can get a good meal everywhere here.
Man spricht Englisch.	English spoken (sign in store).
Hier darf man nicht rauchen.	Smoking not permitted.
Wie sagt man das auf deutsch?	How do you say that in German?
Man hat mir gesagt …	I was told …/Someone said to me …

HOW TO USE

man is a pronoun and therefore it has cases:

Nom.	**man**
Acc.	**einen**
Dat.	**einem**

In practice, you will probably only need to use **man**. Man takes the same verb ending as **er/sie/es** which is **-t**.

Man verdient gut hier. The pay is good here. (One earns well here.)

Warning: Don't get **man** (one/you/people etc.) mixed up with **Mann** (husband/man).

LEARN BY HEART

Here are some questions you might want to use:

1. **Wo wirft man das Geld ein?** Where do you (does one) insert the money?

2. **Wo kann man Geld wechseln?** Where can you (can one) change money?

3. **Was kann man da machen?** What can you do there?

4. **Was kann man in der Stadt unternehmen?** What can you do in the town?

5. **Wie kommt man am besten dahin?** What's the best way to get there?

6. **Wie kommt man am besten zur Autobahn?** What's the best way to get to the expressway?

7. **Wie spricht man das aus?** How do you (does one) pronounce that?

8. **Kann man das reparieren?** Can it be repaired?

9. **Braucht man ein Visum/eine Karte?** Do you (does one) need a visa/ticket?

du / ihr

INTRODUCTION

One of the most important things about learning a foreign language is to develop an awareness of when certain words are appropriate – and when they are not. This is as important to good communication as vocabulary and grammar. English-speaking people in particular should be careful when they use the familiar forms **du** ('you', singular) and **ihr** ('you', plural) – using them at the wrong time could create terrible misunderstandings, even lose you a business contract, for example.

WHEN TO USE

It is perfectly OK to use **du/ihr** when talking to children or animals. However, do not use **du/ihr** with adults:

1. If you are a child/teenager/student etc. and they are much older – even if *they* call you **du**.

2. Unless you are a member of a group of e.g. students, fellow golfers etc. who are all pals together, and everybody uses **du** to each other.

3. Unless your German friend/business contact etc. suggests you both call each other **du**. This will quite often be accompanied by a formal drinking to the new intimate relationship. The suggestion might be made like this:

Wollen wir uns nicht duzen?   Shall we call each other *du*?

Duzen means 'to say **du** to someone', or to be on first-name terms.

The reason that **du/ihr** present problems for English speakers is that in English we have only one word 'you' to cover all degrees of formality. We express formality or informality, keep our distance or get friendly quickly by using titles and names in different ways. Have you ever felt slightly affronted when someone has called you by your first name and you weren't quite ready to get on such friendly terms? Something similar happens if you use **du** to a German acquaintance. They will probably feel a bit insulted, and certainly embarrassed.

With **du** you use first names. Once you are on **du** terms with somebody, you have established a familiar relationship. It is virtually impossible to go back on the decision to say **du** to someone, even if you decide that you don't like them very much after all or don't want to be on such familiar terms. That is why the Germans are a bit wary at first of offering **du** to new acquaintances. It does not mean that they are being unfriendly.

Therefore, for most people most of the time, the safest thing is always to use **Sie + Herr/Frau/Fräulein + last name** to all adults unless any of the conditions 1–3 above apply.

HOW TO USE

1. Verbs.

The **du** form of the verb ends in **-st**, the **ihr** form ends in **-t**.

Present tense

For weak verbs add **-st**   add **-t**

du machst, du frühstückst etc.   **ihr macht, ihr frühstückt**

For strong verbs there is often a stem change in the **du** form, but not in the **ihr** form.

schlafen	du schläfst	ihr schlaft
lesen	du liest	ihr lest
nehmen	du nimmst	ihr nehmt

For modal verbs add **-st** to the **ich/er/sie/es** form to make the **du** form, add **-t** to the infinitive stem to make the **ihr** form.

wollen	**du willst**	**ihr wollt**
können	**du kannst**	**ihr könnt**

Imperative

For the **du** imperative take off the **-st** ending from the **du** form of the present tense. Strong verbs which take an umlaut in the present tense lose it in the imperative. The **ihr** imperative is the same as the **ihr** form of the present tense.

schlafen	**schlaf**	**schlaft**
nehmen	**nimm**	**nehmt**

Schlaf gut!	Sleep well!
Sei still!	Keep still!
Komm her!	Come here!

Imperfect tense

For the **du** form, add **-st** and for the **ihr** form, add **-t** to the usual imperfect stem.

Weak verbs:

du machtest, du fragtest etc.   **ihr machtet, ihr fragtet** etc.

Strong verbs:

du aßt (from **essen**), **du nahmst**   **ihr aßt, ihr nahmt** etc.
   (from **nehmen**) etc.

Modal verbs:

du mußtest (from **müssen**),   **ihr mußtet, ihr wolltet** etc.
   du wolltest (from **wollen**) etc.

Perfect tense

Use **du hast/ihr habt;** } + past participle in the usual way (see p.18)
du bist/ihr seid.

Pluperfect tense

Use **du hattest, du warst/ihr hattet, ihr wart** + past participle in the usual way (see p.24).

Future

Use **du wirst/ihr werdet** + infinitive (see p.25).

Passive

Use **du wirst/ihr werdet** + past participle for the present tense. Use **du wurdest/ihr wurdet** + past participle for the imperfect tense (see p.47).

2. Personal pronouns

Nom.	du	ihr
Acc.	dich	euch
Dat.	dir	euch

N.B. in letter writing, **du** and **ihr** are written with a capital letter.

Here are some examples of **du/ihr** to give you a feeling for how to use them.

Hast du die Tür zugemacht?	Have you closed the door?
Kannst du dich erinnern?	Can you remember?
Mach dir keine Sorgen.	Don't worry.
Ich gebe dir den Schlüssel.	I'll give you the key.
Wolltest du auch mitfahren?	Did you want to go too?
Setz dich.	Sit down.
Was wollt ihr jetzt machen?	What do you want to do now?
Was habt ihr vor?	What are you intending to do?
Können wir heute zu euch kommen?	Can we come to your place today?
Wie geht es euch?	How are you?
Wie gefällt euch die Wohnung?	How do you like the apartment?
Bitte setzt euch.	Please sit down.
Bitte kommt herein.	Please come in.

3. Possessive adjectives

dein   euer

They follow the same pattern of endings as **ein/mein** etc. (see p.97).

Relative pronouns

INTRODUCTION

We use relative pronouns ('who', 'which' etc.) to refer to specific people or things we have already mentioned in a previous part of the sentence. In English, we use 'who' (or 'whom') for people and 'which' or 'that' for things. Sometimes we omit the relative pronoun altogether, but nevertheless it is still assumed or understood to be there. Look at these examples: 'This is the girl *who* helped me'; 'Do you have any pills *that* are effective against migraine?'; 'The man I want to see is away today' (*whom* is omitted); 'That's the drink I tried yesterday' (*which* is omitted).

EXPLANATION

Relative pronouns act as a bridge between one clause and another. They refer back to an object or person in the previous clause and they also play an important grammatical role in their own clause.

In German the relative pronouns are:

	for **der** words	for **die** words	for **das** words	for plural words
Nom.	der	die	das	die
Acc.	den	die	das	die
Dat.	dem	der	dem	denen
Gen.	dessen	deren	dessen	deren

As you can see there is a very close connection between relative pronouns and the **der/die/das** form of the words they refer to. There is no separate form for 'who' and 'which'.

HOW TO USE

Like all pronouns, relative pronouns have different endings depending on:

1. whether the noun they refer back to is singular or plural;
2. which **der/die/das** group it belongs to;
3. which role the relative pronoun is playing in its own clause (i.e. case).

Examples:

Der Film, *der* heute im Fernsehen läuft, ist sehr gut. The movie *that* is on TV today is very good.

1. **Film** is singular.
2. **Film** is a **der** word.
3. 'That' is in the nominative case in its part of the sentence because it is the subject of **läuft**.

Der Wagen, *den* ich gemietet habe, ist kaputt. The car I have rented has broken down.

1. **Wagen** is singular.
2. **Wagen** is a **der** word.
3. 'Which' (understood) is in the accusative case in its part of the sentence because it is the object of **ich habe gemietet**.

You can also use relative pronouns with prepositions ('with', 'from' etc.).

Das ist die Frau, von *der* ich die Tasche gekauft habe.	That's the lady I bought the purse from (from *whom* I bought the purse).

1. **Frau** is singular.
2. **Frau** is a **die** word.
3. 'Whom' (understood) is dative after **von**.

Das sind die Leute, mit *denen* ich zusammen arbeite.	Those are the people I work with (with *whom* I work).

1. **Leute** is plural.
2. Not relevant because **Leute** is plural.
3. 'Whom' (understood) is dative after **mit**.

You probably think of **der/die/das** only as meaning 'the', so this role as 'who'/'which' takes a little getting used to. Study the examples carefully to make sure you follow what is going on.

Notes:
1. Notice the comma which comes before the relative pronoun. It looks strange to us but is absolutely essential in German because it marks the boundaries of the clauses. You don't take a breath or make any pause to interrupt the flow of the sentence when you are speaking.
2. You *never* leave out the relative pronoun in German.
3. The relative pronoun sends the verb in its clause to the end. Here are some more examples:

Wie heißt der Mann, *der* gegenüber von uns wohnt?	What's the name of the man who lives across from us?
Haben Sie noch das Kleid, *das* ich gestern anprobiert habe?	Have you still got the dress I tried on yesterday?

LEARN BY HEART
Fill in the correct relative pronoun.

1. **Das ist die Stadt, in ... ich gewohnt habe.**	That's the town where (in which) I lived.
2. **Ist das der Mantel, ... Sie suchen?**	Is this the coat (that) you are looking for?

3. **Ist das der Brief, … gestern gekommen ist?**

Is that the letter which arrived yesterday?

4. **Das sind die Leute, mit … ich nach Paris gefahren bin.**

Those are the people I went to Paris with (with whom).

5. **Kennen Sie den Mann, mit … ich gesprochen habe?**

Do you know the man I spoke to (with whom I spoke)?

ANSWERS
1. der 2. den 3. der 4. denen 5. dem

Adjectives

INTRODUCTION

Adjectives describe nouns. They make our language more picturesque, they fill out bald statements consisting of nouns and verbs:

The cat sat on the mat.

The *large*, *fluffy*, *Persian* cat sat on the *beautiful red* and *green* mat.

I want a coat.

I want a *short*, *navy blue* coat with *red* trim. Not too *expensive* but *stylish* and *attractive*.

You can't learn German adjectives in a day – so don't try! But don't give up either. Persevere, and one day you will be able to use German adjectives with confidence (and correctly, 90% of the time – which is better than many native German speakers).

HOW TO USE

Because adjectives accompany nouns, they are directly affected by:

1. whether the noun is singular or plural;
2. which **der/die/das** group the noun belongs to;
3. what case the noun is in;
4. whether the noun is accompanied by **der/die/das** or **ein/kein/mein** or nothing at all.

Basically there are four different situations affecting adjective endings. This sounds like a lot to learn, but it does have a certain logic and the important thing is to recognize the basic patterns.

Situation Type One

Adjective standing on its own, without a noun or after the verb **sein** (to be) or **werden** (to become):

schön!	lovely!
toll!	great!
Das ist schön!	That's lovely!
Die Bluse ist schön.	The blouse is beautiful.
Das Wetter wird schön.	The weather's getting nice.
Die Kleider sind schön.	The dresses are beautiful.

You use the adjective just as it appears in the dictionary, without any endings.

Situation Type Two
Der/die/das + adjective + noun:

	der group	**die** group	**das** group
Nom.	der rote Pullover	die grüne Bluse	das blaue Kleid
Acc.	den roten Pullover	die grüne Bluse	das blaue Kleid
Dat.	dem roten Pullover	der grünen Bluse	dem blauen Kleid
Gen.	des roten Pullovers	der grünen Bluse	des blauen Kleides
	Plural		
Nom.	die weißen Schuhe		
Acc.	die weißen Schuhe		
Dat.	den weißen Schuhen		
Gen.	der weißen Schuhe		

Here are some common phrases with the accusative in this situation. They are all expressions of time:

Ich war *die ganze Woche* krank.	I was ill all week.
Er wartet schon *den ganzen Tag.*	He's been waiting all day.
Das Hotel ist *das ganze Jahr* geöffnet.	The hotel is open all year.

The dative is often used to describe where things are, so here are some common examples in this situation:

Auf der rechten Seite	On the right hand side
Im zweiten Stock	On the second floor.
In der ersten Etage	On the first floor.
Im blauen Koffer	In the blue case.
In der großen Halle	In the main hall.

Situation Type Three
Ein/kein/mein/Ihr + adjective + noun:

	der group	**die** group	**das** group
Nom.	ein gut**er** Rotwein	eine warm**e** Mahlzeit	ein kalt**es** Bier
Acc.	einen gut**en** Rotwein	eine warm**e** Mahlzeit	ein kalt**es** Bier
Dat.	einem gut**en** Rotwein	einer warm**en** Mahlzeit	einem kalt**en** Bier
Gen.	eines gut**en** Rotwein**s**	einer warm**en** Mahlzeit	eines kalt**en** Bier**s**

	Plural
Nom.	keine neu**en** Kartoffeln
Acc.	keine neu**en** Kartoffeln
Dat.	keinen neu**en** Kartoffeln
Gen.	keiner neu**en** Kartoffeln

Try to acquire a 'feel' for the rhythm of these groups and concentrate on learning the nominative and accusative forms. If you can remember **ein guter Wein** (**der** words) and **ein kaltes Bier** (**das** words), you are well on your way to sorting them out. Nearly all the others take **-n**.

Situation Type Four

Adjective + noun, no **der/die/das** or **ein/kein/mein/Ihr**. Here the adjective takes on the endings which you would normally put on **der/die/das** except in the genitive. The adjective has to take on this job because otherwise you wouldn't know what role the noun was playing in the sentence.

	der words	**die** words	**das** words
Nom.	gut**er** Wein	schön**e** Landschaft	deutsch**es** Geld
Acc.	gut**en** Wein	schön**e** Landschaft	deutsch**es** Geld
Dat.	gut**em** Wein	schön**er** Landschaft	deutsch**em** Geld
Gen.	gut**en** Weins	schön**er** Landschaft	deutsch**en** Geldes

	Plural
Nom.	nett**e** Leute
Acc.	nett**e** Leute
Dat.	nett**en** Leuten
Gen.	nett**er** Leute

Here are some examples of this use of adjectives that you would find on labels:

reine Baumwolle	pure cotton

In brochures:

ruhige Lage	quiet situation
fließendes Wasser	running water

At the market:

frische Eier	fresh eggs

And talking to people:

Guten Tag	Hello
Guten Abend	Good evening
Gute Fahrt	Have a good trip
Gute Reise	Bon voyage!
Guten Appetit	Enjoy your meal
Gute Besserung	Get well soon

This is the sort of thought process you have to go through when using adjectives: You want to say: 'I don't have any German money.'
Geld is
1. singular;
2. a **das** word;
3. accusative;
4. the situation is type three.
So you say: **Ich habe kein deutsches Geld.**

You want to say: 'Where are my black shoes?'
Schuhe is
1. plural;
2. **der/die/das** group not relevant;
3. nominative;
4. the situation is type three.
So you say: **Wo sind meine schwarzen Schuhe?**

You want to say: 'I'd like a good red wine'.
Rotwein is
1. singular;
2. a **der** word;
3. accusative;
4. the situation is type three.
So you say: **Ich möchte einen guten Rotwein.**

You want to say: 'Do you know the old man over there?'
Mann is
1. singular;
2. a **der** word;
3. accusative;
4. the situation is type two.
So you say: **Kennen Sie den alten Mann da drüben?**

You want to say: 'I hope you have nice weather'.
Wetter is
1. singular;
2. a **das** word
3. accusative;
4. the situation is type four.
So you say: **Ich wünsche Ihnen schönes Wetter.**

PRACTICE/LEARN BY HEART
Go through the steps above then choose the right answer:

Situation Type One (= adjective alone or after **sein** or **werden**)
You are describing your favorite restaurant:

1. **Es ist**…	It's very cozy.
2. **Das Essen ist**…	The food is good.
3. **Die Kellner sind**…	The waiters are nice.
4. **Es**…	It's not expensive.
5. **Das Bier**…	The beer is cold.
6. **Die Weinkarte**…	The wine list is very good.

gut/kalt/nett/teuer/ganz/gemütlich/sehr gut

Situation Type Two (= der/die/das + adjective + noun)
You are in a store deciding which clothes you would like to buy:

1. **Ich nehme**…	I'll take the green pants.
2. **Ich nehme**…	I'll take the white blouse.
3. **Ich nehme**…	I'll take the black jacket.
4. **Ich nehme**…	I'll take the blue shoes.
5. **Ich nehme**…	I'll take the red dress.
6. **Ich nehme**…	I'll take the gray sweater.

Hose/Pullover/Kleid/Bluse/Schuhe/Jacke
den/die/die/die/das/die
grüne/grauen/rote/blauen/schwarze/weiße

Situation Type Three (= **ein/eine** etc. + adjective + noun)
You are trying to decide what to order in a restaurant:

1. **Ich möchte**...	I'd like a hot soup.
2. **Ich möchte**...	I'd like a light beer.
3. **Ich möchte**...	I'd like a black coffee.
4. **Ich möchte**...	I'd like a dry white wine.

ein/einen/einen/eine
herben/helles/warme/schwarzen
Kaffee/Bier/Weißwein/Suppe

Situation Type Four (= adjective + noun)
You have gone to the market and are asking if things are available:

1. **Haben Sie**...	Do you have fresh milk?
2. **Haben Sie**...	Do you have German butter?
3. **Haben Sie**...	Do you have new potatoes?
4. **Haben Sie**...	Do you have firm tomatoes?
5. **Haben Sie**...	Do you have inexpensive lettuce?
6. **Haben Sie**...	Do you have red apples?

Äpfel/Tomaten/Salat/Butter/Milch/Kartoffeln
frische/neue/billigen/rote/feste/deutsche

ANSWERS
Situation One
1. ganz gemütlich 2. gut 3. nett 4. ist nicht teuer 5. ist kalt
6. ist sehr gut
Situation Two
1. die grüne Hose 2. die weiße Bluse 3. die schwarze Jacke
4. die blauen Schuhe 5. das rote Kleid 6. den grauen Pullover
Situation Three
1. eine warme Suppe 2. ein helles Bier 3. einen schwarzen Kaffee
4. einen herben Weißwein
Situation Four
1. frische Milch 2. deutsche Butter 3. neue Kartoffeln 4. feste Tomaten
5. billigen Salat 6. rote Äpfel

Adjective Endings at a glance.

X = noun

1. Situation Type One = adjective alone or after **sein** or **werden**.
No endings.
2. Situation Type Two = **der/die/das** + adjective + noun

	der group	**die** group	**das** group	plural
Nom.	der ... e X	die ... e X	das ... e X	die ... en Xe
Acc.	den ... en X	die ... e X	das ... e X	die ... en Xe
Dat.	dem ... en X	der ... en X	dem ... en X	den ... en Xen
Gen.	des ... en Xes	der ... en X	des ... en Xes	der ... en Xe

3. Situation Type Three = **ein/kein/mein/Ihr** etc. + adjective + noun

	der group	**die** group	**das** group	plural
Nom.	ein ... er X	eine ... e X	ein ... es X	meine ... en Xe
Acc.	einen ... en X	eine ... e X	ein ... es X	meine ... en Xe
Dat.	einem ... en X	einer ... en X	einem ... en X	meinen ... en Xen
Gen.	eines .. en X(e)s	einer ... en X	eines ... en X(e)s	meiner ... en Xe

4. Situation Type Four = adjective + noun

	der group	**die** group	**das** group	plural
Nom.	...er X	...e X	...es X	...e Xe
Acc.	...en X	...e X	...es X	...e Xe
Dat.	...em X	...er X	...em X	...en Xen
Gen.	...en X(e)s	...er X	...en X(e)s	...er Xe

Comparison

HOW TO USE

When you compare things in English you say: 'My house is bigg*er than* yours'; 'His car goes fast*er than* ours'; 'Could you speak *more slowly*'. You add '-er' to the adjective if it is short or you put 'more' in front if it is long, and you put 'than' in between the two things you are comparing.

German is very similar but it is simpler because you add **-er** to all adjectives and adverbs, no matter how long they are. For 'than' you say **als**.

Mein Haus ist größ*er* als Ihres.	My house is bigger than yours.
Sein Auto fährt *schneller als* unseres.	His car is faster than ours.
Könnten Sie bitte langsam*er* sprechen?	Could you please speak more slowly?

When you want to compare three or more things in English you say for example:

big, bigg*er*, bigg*est*   **groß, größer, größte**
small, small*er*, small*est*   **klein, kleiner, kleinste**

and as you can see the same thing happens in German:
add **-er**, **-(e)ste**.

Ich bin der jüng*ste*.	I am the youngest.
Unser Ält*ester* arbeitet bei der Bank.	Our oldest son works in the bank.

Some points to remember:

1. Almost all German adjectives and adverbs follow the rules above. But there are some very common adjectives which add an umlaut (¨), so make a note of these:

alt	**älter**	**älteste**	(old, older, oldest)
jung	**jünger**	**jüngste**	(young, younger, youngest)
kalt	**kälter**	**kälteste**	(cold, colder, coldest)
warm	**wärmer**	**wärmste**	(warm/hot, hotter, hottest)
lang	**länger**	**längste**	(long, longer, longest)
kurz	**kürzer**	**kürzeste**	(short, shorter, shortest)

2. Adverbs have no endings, but many of the comparative words are adjectives and must follow the rules about adjective endings.
For example, you want to say: 'I'll take the bigger dress'.
Here you add first the comparative ending **-er** to **groß→größer**, then you go through all the steps on page 113.
Kleid is

1. singular;
2. a **das** word;
3. accusative;
4. the situation is type two.

So you say: **Ich nehme *das größere Kleid* bitte.**

You want to say: 'We're looking for a smaller apartment'.
Add the comparative ending: **klein→kleiner**.
Wohnung is
1. singular;
2. a **die** word;
3. accusative;
4. the situation type is three.
So you say: **Wir suchen *eine kleinere Wohnung*.**

3. We have one or two exceptions in English to the rules. We don't say *good, gooder, goodest*. Neither do the Germans. Here are the few exceptions:

gut, besser, beste	good, better, best
viel, mehr, meiste	a lot, more, most
hoch, höher, höchste	high, higher, highest

4. To compare two things (as.. as) use **so... wie**:

Unsere Wohnung ist ungefähr *so groß wie* diese.	Our apartment is about as big as this one.
Er ist ungefähr *so alt wie* meine Schwester.	He's about as old as my sister.
Mein Auto ist *nicht so schön wie* Ihres.	My car's not as nice as yours.

Adverbs

INTRODUCTION

Adverbs are words which accompany and describe verbs (here, there, loudly, softly etc.). You can say: 'She drives the car'. If you add an adverb, you can say how/when etc. she drives the car:
'She drives the car /badly/well/often/always/sometimes'.

EXPLANATION

To form adverbs in English, you often add '-ly' to the adjective.

beautiful	beautiful*ly*
neat	neat*ly*

German adverbs have no such distinguishing mark. The adjective and the adverb are usually the same word.

Sie ist sehr *schön.*	She/it is very beautiful.
Das ist sehr *schön* gemacht.	That is beautifully done.

But their use is different. The adjective describes a noun or pronoun, the adverb describes a verb.

You can use adverbs to describe:

1. *How* things are done.
Langsam (slowly), **schnell** (quickly), **schön** (beautifully), **fest** (firmly), **gut** (well), **schlecht** (badly) etc.

2. *When* things are done.
Oft (often), **schon** (already), **manchmal** (sometimes), **sofort** (immediately), **nie** (never), **heute** (today), **immer** (always) etc.

3. *Where* things are done.
Hier (here), **da drüben** (over there), **oben** (up there), **unten** (underneath), **rechts** (to the right), **links** (to the left) etc.

You can also add comparative endings to adverbs, in the same way as you can to adjectives. Add **-er** ending for 'more'.

Bitte sprechen Sie lauter.	Please speak louder.
Bitte sprechen Sie langsamer.	Please speak more slowly.

Use **am** + **-sten** ending for 'most'.

Am schönsten ist es hier abends.	It's at its most beautiful here in the evenings.
Am besten kommen Sie heute nachmittag vorbei.	The best thing for you to do is to come around this afternoon.

Possessive adjectives

INTRODUCTION
Possessive adjectives (my, your, his etc.) tell you who owns what, who is related to whom, and are very useful for example when talking about your family and friends or reporting lost property etc. Like all adjectives, they describe nouns, and their endings are affected by the noun they accompany. They follow the same pattern of endings as **ein** (see p.97).

EXPLANATION
The possessive adjectives are:

mein = my	**unser** = our
dein = your (familiar singular)	**euer** = your (familiar plural)
sein = his/its	**ihr** = their
ihr = her/its	**Ihr** = your (formal)

HOW TO USE
The endings are:

	der group	**die** group	**das** group	plural
Nom.	no ending	-e	no ending	-e
Acc.	-en	-e	no ending	-e
Dat.	-em	-er	-em	-en
Gen.	-es	-er	-es	-er

Notes.
1. **sein**/(his)/**ihr** (her)
People who speak languages like Spanish and French, where the words for 'his' and 'her' are exactly the same, get confused with **sein** (his) and **ihr** (her). If you find this difficult try the next exercise.

PRACTICE

You are talking about Manfred and Barbara who are very careless and have lost various items. Look up the following nouns in your dictionary and find out which **der/die/das** group they belong to. They are all accusative. Then fill in the blanks with a word for 'his' or 'her'. Use each word only once.

Nouns:

Fotoapparat/Portemonnaie/Rasierapparat/Koffer/Fahrkarte
his/her: **seinen/seinen/sein/ihre/ihren/ihre**

1. **Manfred hat... Rasierapparat verloren.**	Manfred has lost his razor.
2. **Barbara hat... Handtasche verloren.**	Barbara has lost her purse.
3. **Manfred hat... verloren.**	Manfred has lost his suitcase.
4. **Barbara hat... verloren.**	Barbara has lost her camera.
5. **Manfred hat... verloren.**	Manfred has lost his wallet.
6. **Barbara hat... verloren.**	Barbara has lost her ticket.

2. **ihr** (her)/**ihr** (their)/ **Ihr** (your)

It is often very difficult to distinguish these three meanings when people are speaking because they all sound the same. You really have to be alert! If you didn't follow the conversation, don't pretend you did. Ask **wessen?** (=whose?) and get some clarification as to the person's or people's identity. You will probably be told the person's name and then you will be able to follow the conversation.

LEARN BY HEART

Here are some expressions I hope you won't need! Fill in the correct form of **mein**.

1. **Wo ist... Tasche?**	Where is my purse?
2. **Es tut mir leid, ich habe ... Fahrkarte verloren.**	I'm sorry, I've lost my ticket.
3. **Ich habe ... Portemonnaie zu Hause vergessen.**	I've left my wallet at home.
4. **Ich habe ... Fotoapparat verloren.**	I've lost my camera.
5. **... Auto ist weg!**	My car's gone!
6. **Ich habe ... Uhr vergessen.**	I've forgotten my watch.

And some expressions for dealing with officialdom:

1. **Ist das Ihr Vorname?**	Is that your first name?
2. **Ich habe meinen Paß vergessen.**	I've forgotten my passport.
3. **Wo sind Ihre Papiere?**	Where are your papers?
4. **Ihre Adresse bitte.**	Your address please.
5. **Und Ihre Telefonnummer?**	And your telephone number?

ANSWERS

1st exercise
1. seinen 2. ihre 3 seinen Koffer 4. ihren Fotoapparat
5. sein Portemonnaie 6. ihre Fahrkarte

2nd exercise
1. meine 2. meine 3. mein 4. meinen 5. Mein 6. meine

Some and *any*

INTRODUCTION
'Some' and 'any' require a bit of careful thought before using them in German.

HOW TO USE
Some
1. 'Some' as an adjective = **manche** + plural noun.

Manche Leute glauben ...   Some people think ...

But leave out the word 'some' entirely when dealing with quantities:

Möchten Sie Brot? Tee?   Would you like some bread?/some tea?

2. 'Some' as a pronoun = **welcher/welche/welches**. Use the same endings as for **der/die/das**.

Brauchen Sie Kartoffeln? Nein, ich habe noch welche.	Do you need potatoes? No, I've still got some.
Im Kühlschrank sind noch welche.	There are some in the refrigerator.
Möchten Sie welches?	Would you like some of it? (**das** word)
Möchten Sie welchen?	Would you like some of it? (**der** word)

3. Sometimes = **manchmal**.

Manchmal gibt es Schweinefleisch mit Pommesfrites.   Sometimes there is pork with French fries on the menu.

4. Someone/anyone = **jemand**.

Ist da jemand?	Is someone/anyone there?
Hat jemand angerufen?	Has someone/anyone phoned?
Haben Sie jemand getroffen?	Did you meet someone/anyone?

5. Something = **etwas** or **irgendetwas** (shortened forms: '**was**, **irgend'was**).

Suchen Sie etwas Bestimmtes?	Are you looking for something in particular?
Etwas stimmt nicht.	There's something wrong.
Ich wollte Ihnen etwas sagen.	I wanted to tell you something.

6. Somehow = **irgendwie**.

Er kommt irgendwie nach Hause.	He'll get home somehow.
Ich habe irgendwie das Gefühl ...	Somehow I've got a feeling that ...

7. Somewhere = **irgendwo**.

Irgendwo auf dem Land.	Somewhere in the country.

8. Sometime = **irgendwann**.

There is a difference in emphasis between words beginning with **irgend-** and the other words for 'some'. **Irgend-** conveys the idea that you don't know, and possibly don't care, who, what, where etc. **Welche, manche, etwas, jemand** etc. are much more definite – you do have a good idea who or what or where you mean.

Any

'Any' has several different uses:

1. When asking whether something is available, leave out the word 'any' in German.

Haben Sie Brot?	Do you have any bread?
Gibt es hier Toiletten?	Are there any washrooms here?
Haben Sie Kinderschuhe?	Do you have any children's shoes?

2. With a negative. Use **kein**, **nichts** etc. (see p. 71.)

Ich habe kein Brot.	I don't have any bread.
Ich kann mich an nichts erinnern.	I can't remember anything.

3. 'Any' can be vague and indefinite and is very close to 'some'.

Kann ich irgendwo parken?	Is there anywhere (somewhere) I can park?
Wissen Sie etwas über ihn?	Do you know anything (something) about him?

4. 'Any' can be positive, and mean 'all', 'every' etc.

Er kann jeden Tag kommen.	He'll be coming any day now.
Sie können jederzeit zu uns kommen.	Come and see us any time you like.

5. Any time = **jederzeit**.

6. Anybody

jemand	anybody/somebody
Ist da jemand?	Is anybody/somebody there?
niemand	not … anyone, nobody
jeder	everybody
Jeder kann mitmachen.	Anybody (everybody) can join in.

7. Anywhere

irgendwo	anywhere/somewhere
überall	anywhere/everywhere
Sie können überall parken.	You can park anywhere you like.

8. Anything and everything

etwas, irgendetwas	anything/something (not definite)
Ach, kaufen Sie irgendetwas.	Oh, just buy anything. (I don't care.)
nichts	nothing/not … anything (see p. 71.)
Ich habe nichts gekauft.	I didn't buy anything.
alles	anything/everything
Hier können Sie alles finden.	You can find anything you're looking for here.
Sie können alles bestellen.	You can order anything you like.

9. Anyhow

irgendwie	anyhow/somehow
auf jeden Fall/sowieso	anyhow/anyway
Das wollte ich sowieso machen.	I wanted to do that anyway.
Wir gehen sowieso ins Theater.	We're going to the theater anyway.
Auf jeden Fall wollte ich Ihnen alles erklären.	Anyway, I wanted to explain everything to you.

Prepositions

INTRODUCTION

Prepositions are the little words like 'to', 'for', 'with', etc. which we use to indicate, for example, where, how and when an action is taking place. Although they are very small words, mistakes with prepositions can lead to very big misunderstandings, so you should treat them with the respect they deserve. If you can understand the concept behind the preposition you will have an insight into the German person's way of thinking. Where it is helpful, I have included diagrams to illustrate these concepts.

EXPLANATION

Most German prepositions can take the prefixes **wo-** or **da-**. **Wo-** means 'what'/'which' and **da-** means 'it'/'that'. You can use **wo-** with a preposition to make a question. If the preposition begins with a vowel, you insert an extra **-r-**.

auf	on
worauf?	on what?
darauf	on that/it
sprechen über	to talk about
Worüber sprechen Sie?	What are you talking about?
Wir sprachen gerade darüber.	We were just talking about that.

Some prepositions are shortened when they are used with **der/die/das**. For example, **an dem** is shortened to **am**; **bei dem** is shortened to **beim**; **an das** is shortened to **ans** etc.

There are two problems facing us when dealing with German prepositions:
1. Some are followed by the accusative case (see p. 84) and others by the dative case (see p.88) and others by both – so how do we know which takes which?
2. Very often you cannot translate English prepositions directly into their apparent German counterparts. For example, there are at least six different ways of translating 'to'!

1. Prepositions that always take the accusative:

bis	**durch**	**entlang**	**für**	**gegen**	**ohne**	**pro**	**um**
until	through	along	for	against	without	per	about/around

2. Prepositions that always take the dative:

ab	**aus**	**außer**	**bei**	**gegenüber**	**mit**	**nach**	**seit**	**von**	**zu**
from	from	except	at	across from	with	to/after	for/since	from	to

3. Prepositions that always take the genitive:

aufgrund	**in der Nähe**	**trotz**	**während**	**wegen**
because of	near	in spite of	during	because of

4. Prepositions that take both the accusative and the dative:

an	**auf**	**hinter**	**in**	**neben**	**über**	**unter**	**vor**	**zwischen**
at/	at/on/	behind	in/	near	over/	under/	before/	between
to	to		into		across	among	ago	

Why do some prepositions take both the accusative and dative? If you take a closer look you will see that all of the prepositions in this group are connected with a *place*. The Germans say that there are two ways of talking about a place:

1. Movement from one place to another. The action starts in one place and finishes in another place. To express this idea of movement from A to B,

A   B

you use verbs of motion, such as **kommen**, **gehen**, **fliegen** (to fly), **einsteigen** (to get into), **stellen** (to put) etc. + one of the prepositions in list number 4 + the accusative.

2. Position in one place, i.e. no movement. To express this idea of no movement, you use verbs which describe stationary activities, such as **sein**, **liegen**, **essen**, **trinken**, **stehen** (to stand) etc. + one of the prepositions in list number 4 + the dative.

Let us look at some examples:

In + accusative = in/into/to

Ich fahre in die Stadt.	I'm going into town.
Gehen Sie ins Bett?	Are you going to bed?
Stellen Sie den Wein in den Kühlschrank.	Put the wine in the refrigerator.

In + dative = in/inside

Er arbeitet in einer Fabrik.	He works in a factory.
Bleiben Sie im Auto.	Stay in the car.
Wir essen im Restaurant.	We'll eat in the restaurant.

In + accusative means you are going into a building/space etc. from a starting point outside. **In** + dative means you are already in the building/space etc. and are staying there.

Warning. We say in English: 'Let's go *to* the movies/the theater' etc. It's very tempting to say **zum Kino/zum Theater** etc. But if you say this your German friends will think that for some reason you are not intending to go into the movie house and see the film or into the theater and watch the play. You seem to want to go to the door and then go away again! The German says **ins Kino** and **ins Theater**.

An + accusative = to

Wir gehen an den Strand.	We're going to the beach.
Gehen Sie nicht ans Fenster!	Don't go to the window!
Ich schreibe einen Brief an meine Schwester.	I'm writing a letter to my sister.

(Yes, a letter also goes from A to B, even though you don't think of **schreiben** as a verb of movement.)

Bitte hängen Sie das Bild an die Wand.	Please hang the picture on the wall. (on = onto)

An + dative = at/on

Wir haben am Strand gelegen.	We lay on the beach.
Wir saßen noch am Tisch.	We were still sitting at the table.
Ich bin am Bahnhof.	I'm at the train station.
Der Zeitungskiosk ist an der Ecke.	The newspaper stand is on the corner.

REMINDER

For movement from A→B, use accusative.

For stationary position, $\boxed{A}$, use dative.

Auf + accusative = on/onto/to

Stellen Sie die Flasche auf den Tisch.	Put the bottle on the table.
Legen Sie bitte die Zeitung aufs Regal.	Put the newspaper on the shelf, please.
Setzen Sie sich bitte auf den Stuhl.	Sit down on the chair, please.
Ich gehe auf eine Party.	I'm going to a party.
Ich muß auf die Toilette.	I have to go to the bathroom.

Auf + dative = on/at

Das Buch liegt auf meinem Schreibtisch.	The book is on my desk.
Die Katze ist auf dem Dach.	The cat's on the roof.
Er ist auf der Toilette.	He's in the bathroom.
Sie ist auf einer Konferenz.	She's at a conference.

REMINDER ONCE AGAIN:

Movement from A→B	= accusative.
Position in one place A	= dative.

Über + accusative = over/across

Wir fahren über die Grenze.	We're going over the border.
Gehen Sie über die Kreuzung.	Go across the intersection.

Über + dative = over/above

Die Leselampe ist über Ihrem Sitz.	The reading lamp is above your seat.

Do you get the idea? This basic difference between movement from A to B (accusative) and position/no movement (dative) applies to all the prepositions in this group.

LEARN BY HEART

You have rented your home to some Germans. Here are some instructions and information which you have left for them. Fill in the blanks with a preposition and the appropriate form of **der**, **die**, **das**.

1. **Der Fernseher ist ...**
   Wohnzimmer ... ... Ecke.
   The TV is in the living room in the corner.
2. **Die Schlüssel für die Garage**
   liegen ... ... Fernseher.
   The keys for the garage are on the TV.
3. **Milch und Eier sind ...**
   Kühlschrank.
   There are milk and eggs in the refrigerator.
4. **Bitte tun Sie den Abfall ... Eimer.** Please put trash in the trash can.
5. **Das Fremdenverkehrsamt ist**
   ... ... Taft Street.
   The tourist office is on Taft Street.

Now explain to a German visitor how to get to the nearest supermarket:

1. **Fahren Sie ... die Kreuzung.**
   Go across the intersection.
2. **Dann biegen Sie nach rechts**
   ... ... State Street.
   Then turn right onto State Street.
3. **Und der Supermarkt ist ... ...**
   Ecke.
   And the supermarket is on the corner.

bei + dative
Warning! **bei** never, never, never means the English 'by'!
Use **bei dem** shortened to **beim** for **der/das** words, **bei der** for **die** words.

1. = 'near'
bei der Tankstelle   near the gas station
Das Hotel liegt ganz nah beim   The hotel is right next to the
Bahnhof.   station.

_____

ANSWERS
1st exercise
1. im, in der 2. auf dem 3. im 4. in den 5. in den 6. in der
2nd exercise
1. über 2. in die 3. an der

2. = 'during'/'at'

Wir sprechen beim Essen darüber.

We'll talk about that at lunch.

3. = 'given'/'if there is …' + weather conditions

Bei Gewitter findet das Konzert im Auditorium statt.

If there is a thunderstorm, the concert will take place in the auditorium.

4. = 'at'/'in'/'at the house of'/'at so and so's place' (like French *chez*). Use **bei** + where you live, where you work or shop etc., i.e. with the name of the person or company or store and *not* with a word for a building.

Sie können bei uns wohnen/ schlafen.

You can stay with us.

Er wohnt bei seinen Eltern/bei seiner Schwiegermutter/bei Neuraths.

He's staying with his parents/ his mother-in-law/the Neuraths.

bei Schmidt

c/o Schmidt (on letters, also when answering the phone at Schmidt's house. This tells the caller they have the right number and that you are not one of the Schmidts)

Er kauft immer bei Horten ein.

He always shops at Horten (= name of store).

Er arbeitet bei BASF/bei Mercedes etc.

He works at BASF/Mercedes etc.

beim Friseur.

at the hairdresser's.

Notice you can't say: '**Ich bin beim Supermarkt** or name of any building. With a building you must use **in**. You say: **Ich kaufe bei Safeway ein** (name of company) but: **Ich kaufe im Supermarkt ein** (building). This is a point which English-speaking people often make mistakes with.

seit + dative = 'since'/'for'
Seit answers the question **Wie lange?** (how long?).
Be very careful when using **seit**. You use the German present tense to express English 'have been doing' and the imperfect tense to express 'had been doing'. English-speaking people find this difficult to grasp, but if you look at it from the German point of view it makes sense: they argue that you are/were still doing the action, so the verb should be present or imperfect.

1. = 'for' + length of time

Ich warte schon seit einer halben Stunde.	I've been waiting for half an hour .
Er wohnt seit drei Jahren in Duisburg.	He's been living in Duisburg for three years.
Er wohnte seit einem Jahr im Haus.	He had been living in the house for a year.

2. = 'since' + specific point in time

Seit meiner Rückkehr bin ich sehr beschäftigt.	I've been very busy since my return.
Er wartet schon seit elf Uhr.	He's been waiting since 11 o'clock.
Ich bin seit gestern wieder hier.	I've been back since yesterday.

ENGLISH PREPOSITIONS

Some English prepositions can be translated directly into German and their use is quite straightforward. Other English prepositions have several different translations in German. The most complicated ones are discussed here in greater detail.

At

1. Saying where you are/live etc.

There is no one word for 'at' in German. Look at these examples:

Ich wohne Friedrichstraße 19.	I live at 19 Friedrichstraße.
Ich bin *beim* Zahnarzt.	I'm at the dentist's office.
Ich bin *im* Hotel.	I'm at the hotel.
Ich bin *am* Flughafen.	I'm at the airport.
Ich bin *zu* Hause.	I'm at home.
Ich bin *auf* einer Party.	I'm at a party.

Six different ways of saying 'at', all of them meaning 'at a place'! A German person has a very clear picture in his mind as to which word for 'at' is right in each situation. He sees a lot of difference between 'at the airport' and 'at the dentist's office'. In order to appreciate this we have to look a little more closely and try to envisage how the German person thinks in this situation. Sometimes it's very difficult for foreigners to understand, so I have listed the most common expressions you are likely to need. If you don't see the logic behind them, forget about any explanation and learn the expressions by heart because you will need them.

1. **Ich wohne Friedrichstraße 19.**
When you give an address, you don't use any word for 'at'.

2. **bei** = at a person's place/on someone's premises. **Bei** is always followed by the dative, and you use it with a person or the name of a store or company. You never use **bei** with a word for a building.

Ich bin beim Friseur.	I'm at the hairdresser's.
Wir schlafen bei meinem Freund.	We are staying at my friend's place.
Ich bin jetzt bei Horten.	I'm at Horten just now (name of store).

3. **in** + dative = inside a space/building etc. It is used with verbs of position.

Ich bin im Restaurant.	I'm at the restaurant
im Theater	at the theater
im Kino	at the movies
im Hotel	at the hotel
im Krankenhaus	at the hospital
Wir sind in der Buchhandlung.	We're at the bookstore
Wir treffen uns in der Fotoabteilung.	We'll meet in the photography department
in der Oper	at the opera

4. **An** + dative = at a place, usually referring more to being very near the building or space rather than being right inside. It is used with verbs of position.

Die Kinder spielen am Strand.	The children are playing at the beach.
Ich bin jetzt am Flughafen.	I'm at the airport now.
am Bahnhof	at the train station
am Fenster	at the window
Ich warte an der Rezeption.	I'm waiting at the reception desk.
Er ist an der Theke.	He's at the counter/bar.
An der Kreuzung fahren Sie nach rechts.	At the intersection, turn to the right.
an der Ampel	at the traffic light

5. **Zu Hause**
This is a special expression which you just have to learn. It doesn't belong to any group.

Wir sind jetzt zu Hause.	We're at home now.

6. **auf** + dative

This is used with a small number of nouns. The best thing is to learn them by heart because there is no real explanation for why this particular group of nouns takes **auf**.

auf einer Konferenz	at a conference
auf der Messe	at the trade fair
auf der Toilette	in the bathroom
auf einer Party	at a party
auf der Bank	at the bank
auf der Post	at the Post Office

In addition to all these ways of saying 'at a place', there are some other ways of saying 'at':

7. **vor** + dative = in front of.

Das Auto steht vor der Tür.   The car's at the door.

8. For 'at' + expressions of time use **um**:

um Viertel vor acht	at a quarter to eight
um Mitternacht	at midnight
um sechzehn Uhr dreißig	at 16:30 (4:30 p.m.)

By

Never translate 'by' with the German word **bei**.

1. **von** = action done by someone. Use the dative after **von**.

Das Buch wurde von Agatha Christie geschrieben.   The book was written by Agatha Christie.

2. **mit** + dative = 'by' + means of transportation.

Wir sind mit dem Zug gekommen. We came by train.

mit dem Auto	by car
mit dem Bus	by bus
mit der U-Bahn	by subway

3. For 'by' + time reference use **um, vor, bis**:

Wir müssen bis zwanzig Uhr zurück sein.   We must be back by 8 p.m.

Wir wollen um vier Uhr in der Stadt sein.   We want to be in town by four o'clock.

Das müssen wir vor morgen fertig haben.   We have to have it ready by tomorrow.

4. **mit** + dative

Kann ich mit Scheck bezahlen?	Can I pay by check?
Das ist mit der Hand geschrieben.	It's written by hand.
Das schicke ich mit der nächsten Post.	I'll send it by the next mail.

5. **aus**

aus Versehen	by mistake

Near

There is no single translation of our preposition 'near'. The best way to translate 'near' is to use one of the following expressions:

1. **in der Nähe von** + dative = in the vicinity of/ near:

Wir wohnen in der Nähe vom Bahnhof.	We are staying near the train station.
Das Hotel liegt in der Nähe vom Flughafen.	The hotel is near the airport.

You can also use **in der Nähe** with the genitive:

Wir wohnen in der Nähe der Clark Street.	We are staying near Clark Street.

Notice the use of **der** with the street name.

2. **nicht weit von** + dative = not far from.

Wir wohnen nicht weit von der Stadtmitte.	We are staying near the center of town.
Das ist nicht weit von meinem Hotel.	That's near my hotel.

3. **neben** + dative/accusative = near/next to.

Neben can only be used with places which are very close to each other. Use the dative when describing position and the accusative when there is movement towards one of the places.

Die Toiletten sind neben der Treppe.	The rest rooms are next to the stairway.
Stellen Sie bitte den Koffer neben den Wagen.	Please put the suitcase next to the car.

4. **bei** + dative = near/at/around.

Bei der Tankstelle biegen Sie nach links.	Near the gas station, make a left turn.
Ich wohne beim Flughafen.	I live near the airport.

To

1. Saying where you are going to.

There is no one word for 'to' in German. Look at these examples:

Wir fahren morgen nach Berlin.	We're going to Berlin tomorrow.
Ich gehe jetzt ins Büro.	I'm going to the office now.
Fahren Sie zum Flughafen?	Are you going to the airport?
Wollen wir an den Strand gehen?	Shall we go to the beach?
Wir sind auf eine Party eingeladen.	We're invited to a party.

Five different ways of saying 'to', all of them meaning movement towards a place!

A German person has a very clear picture in his mind about which word for 'to' is right in each situation. He sees a lot of difference between 'to the office' and 'to the airport'.

1. **nach** + name of a city or country = to.
Don't use **nach** with countries which begin with the definite article (**der/die/das**) – use **in** + accusative for them (see point no. 2).

Wann fahren Sie nach Schweden?	When are you going to Sweden?
Ich fahre übermorgen nach Denver.	I'm going to Denver the day after tomorrow.

nach Chicago, nach Seattle, nach Bonn, nach Deutschland etc.

2. **in** + accusative.
Use this when 'to' really means 'into'. You are going into a different building/space etc. It is also used for the few countries which begin with **der/die/das**:

Wir fahren in die Schweiz/in die Türkei/in die Bundesrepublik/ in die DDR/.	We're going to Switzerland/ Turkey/The Federal Republic of Germany/The German Democratic Republic/.
Gehen wir ins Kino/ins Konzert/ins Hotel/ins Theater/ins Freibad.	Let's go to the movies/to the concert/to the hotel/to the theater/to the swimming pool.
Ich gehe jetzt ins Bett.	I'm going to bed now.
Fahren Sie in die Stadt?	Are you going into town?

3. zu + dative

Zu focuses more on traveling to your destination than the actual going inside. If you say **Ich fahre zum Flughafen**, you mean you are driving to the airport and you might go into the building as well. If you say **Ich fahre in den Flughafen**, you mean you are driving your vehicle right into the airport building (which might have disastrous results!).

Zum Flughafen bitte!	To the airport, please! (Taxi)
Fahren Sie zum Bahnhof?	Are you going to the train station?
Fährt dieser Bus zum Zoo/zum Theater/zum Hallenbad/?	Does this bus go to the zoo/the theater/the indoor swimming pool/?
Wie weit ist es zur nächsten Haltestelle?	How far is it to the next bus stop?
Gehen Sie bitte zum Schalter drei/ zur Kasse.	Please go to counter number three/ to the cash register.
Ich gehe jetzt zum Bäcker/zu Hertie.	I'm going to the bakery now/to Hertie (name of store).
Ich gehe jetzt zu meinem Freund.	I'm going to my boyfriend's place.
Wie weit ist es zur Schillerstraße?	How far is it to Schillerstraße?

Notice that in German you use **die** etc. with street names.

4. an + accusative.

An implies going very near a building/space etc. rather than going right inside it. When you say **Wir fahren ans Meer**, you mean 'we're going to the seashore' (i.e. the edge of the sea) rather than plunging into the sea in your car.

Kommen Sie bitte ans Fenster.	Come to the window, please.
Der Kellner kommt an Ihren Tisch.	The waiter comes to your table.
Wollen wir an den Strand heute?	Shall we go to the beach today?
Wir fahren ans Meer.	We're going to the seashore.

5. auf + accusative.

This is used with a small number of nouns. The best thing is to learn them by heart because there is no real explanation as to why this particular group of nouns takes **auf**.

Ich gehe auf eine Konferenz.	I'm going to a conference.
Ich gehe auf die Messe/auf die Bank/auf die Post/auf die Toilette/aufs Klo.	I'm going to the trade fair/to the bank/to the Post Office/to the washroom/to the john.
Ich gehe auf eine Party.	I'm going to a party.

In addition to these various ways of saying 'to a place', there are some more expressions with 'to':

6. **Vor** + time
zehn Minuten vor acht   ten minutes to eight
viertel vor neun   a quarter to nine

7. **von ... bis** = from ... to.
Das Museum ist von zehn bis   The museum is open from 10 a.m.
   fünfzehn Uhr geöffnet   to 3 p.m.

Numbers

INTRODUCTION

Numbers are quite easy to handle as long as you can see them written down, but unfortunately for much of the time you will find yourself having to understand and give numbers in conversation. Think of all the information you hear which contains numbers – times, prices, sizes, dates, addresses, quantities and so on. If you don't have a thorough knowledge of spoken numbers you could end up paying DM15 instead of DM5 or missing the train because it left at 6:30 not 7:30. The possibilities are endless!

You will also need numbers when giving or asking for personal information such as birthdays, telephone numbers, addresses etc.

Since numbers perform such a key role in so many situations, it's worth taking the time to learn and practice them aloud for yourself.

HOW TO USE

The German number system is similar to our own and is very logical, so try to see the parallels which exist between English and German – they will help you to learn.

There are two kinds of numbers:
1. *Cardinal numbers*, e.g. one, two, three etc. They describe quantity, how many.
2. *Ordinal numbers*, e.g. first, second, third etc. They describe the order of things in a system.

Cardinal Numbers

0–19 **(null bis neunzehn)**

0	**null**	7	**sieben**
1	**eins**	8	**acht**
2	**zwei**	9	**neun**
3	**drei**	10	**zehn**
4	**vier**	11	**elf**
5	**fünf**	12	**zwölf**
6	**sechs**	13	**dreizehn**

14	vierzehn	17	siebzehn
15	fünfzehn	18	achtzehn
16	sechszehn	19	neunzehn

From 0–19 the German numbers are parallel to English. From 13–19 (**dreizehn bis neunzehn**) the **-zehn** ending is the same as our *-teen* ending in 'thir*teen*' etc. Be sure to say the **-zehn** ending very clearly, so you don't get **neunzehn** (19) confused with **neunzig** (90). Most people learning German mumble because they're not quite sure, but this is a case where mumbling can get you into trouble. Here it's essential to be *absolutely sure*. If you're not sure, write down the number and show it to the other person.

20–99	(zwanzig bis neunundneunzig)		
20	zwanzig	40	vierzig
21	einundzwanzig	41	einundvierzig
22	zweiundzwanzig	50	fünfzig
23	dreiundzwanzig	51	einundfünfzig
24	vierundzwanzig	60	sechszig
25	fünfundzwanzig	61	einundsechszig
26	sechsundzwanzig	70	siebzig
27	siebenundzwanzig	71	einundsiebzig
28	achtundzwanzig	80	achtzig
29	neunundzwanzig	81	einundachtzig
30	dreißig	90	neunzig
31	einunddreißig	99	neunundneunzig

From 20–99 there are three points to notice:
1. **Sieben** gets slightly shortened in **siebzehn/siebzig**.
2. Our *-ty* ending in *forty* etc. is matched by the German **-zig** in **vierzig** etc. (but note: **dreißig**). Make sure you say the **-zig/ßig** ending clearly.
3. Instead of saying *twenty-one*, Germans say *one-and-twenty*. Think of 'four and twenty blackbirds' and you'll be on the right track.

Warning! Numbers need a lot of practice, especially writing down numbers spoken aloud. Some people find it helps to write down numbers between 20 and 99 from right to left because this is the order in which the Germans say them.

PRACTICE

Write down the following numbers as numerals:

1. **Neununddreißig**
2. **dreiundvierzig**
3. **fünfundfünfzig**
4. **fünfundvierzig**
5. **einundzwanzig**
6. **fünfzehn**
7. **vierundfünfzig**
8. **sechsundsiebzig**

HOW TO USE

Over 100

100	**hundert**
101	**hunderteins**
102	**hundertzwei**
103	**hundertdrei**
120	**hundertzwanzig**
136	**hundertsechsunddreißig**
147	**hundertsiebenundvierzig**
179	**hundertneunundsiebzig**
200	**zweihundert**
265	**zweihundertfünfundsechszig**
300	**dreihundert**
400	**vierhundert**
500	**fünfhundert**
600	**sechshundert**
700	**siebenhundert**
1,000	**tausend**
1,100	**tausendeinhundert**
2,000	**zweitausend**
5,000	**fünftausend**
10,000	**zehntausend**
100,000	**hunderttausend**
1,000,000	**eine Million**

Although these words look long, this is only because all the numbers are written together. 121 is just as much of a mouthful to say in English as it is in German. While in English we say 'one hundred and twenty-one', the Germans say 'one hundred one and twenty': **einhunderteinundzwanzig**. The 'and' is in a different place, but it takes just as long to say.

ANSWERS

1. 39; 2. 43; 3. 55; 4. 45; 5. 21; 6. 15; 7. 54; 8. 76

Some useful abbreviations with numbers:
Mio. = **Million**
Mrd. = **Milliarde** (1 billion)
Nr. = **Nummer**
ca. = **circa/zirka** (approx.)

Some words which often accompany numbers:
ungefähr, **rund**, **zirka** (**ca.**) all mean 'about, approximately'.

über	more than
weniger als	less than, fewer than
knapp	just under
knapp hundert Gramm	just under 100 grams (98 or so)
knapp sechszig Leute	just under 60 people (58 or 59)

English decimal points are replaced by commas in German:

> 5,2 **fünf komma zwei**
> 0,4 **null komma vier**
> 0,18 **null komma eins acht**

Percent = **Prozent**

> 6,2% **sechs komma zwei Prozent**
> 8,9% **acht komma neun Prozent**

The comma used in English to represent thousands is replaced in German by a space:

> 10 000 **zehntausend**
> 21 456 **einundzwanzigtausendvierhundertsechsundfünfzig**

Fractions

die Hälfte	half
ein Drittel	a third
ein Viertel	a quarter
ein Fünftel	a fifth
ein Sechstel	a sixth etc.

Note: These are all **das** words except for **die Hälfte.**

anderthalb	one and a half
zweieinhalb	two and a half
dreieinhalb	three and a half
viereinhalb	four and a half etc.

Once, twice, three times etc.

einmal	once
zweimal	twice
dreimal	three times
viermal	four times
hundertmal	a hundred times
x-mal ⎫	
-zigmal ⎭	hundreds (lots) of times

Ich habe ihm -zigmal gesagt, er sollte das Rauchen aufgeben.   I've told him time and time again to give up smoking.

PRACTICE

Here is Frau Lange telling you about herself. Write in all the numbers in the English translation.

1. **Ich bin achtundvierzig Jahre alt.**   I am ... years old.

2. **Meine Telefonnummer ist sechzig, neunzehn, neunundzwanzig.**   My telephone number is ...

3. **Ich wohne Hardenbergstraße dreiundvierzig.**   I live at ... Hardenbergstraße.

4. **Ich habe zwei Söhne und eine Tochter.**   I have ... sons and a daughter.

5. **Michael ist achtzehn Jahre alt und Günther ist einundzwanzig.**   Michael is ... and Günther is ... years old.

6. **Meine Tochter Anna ist vierundzwanzig Jahre alt.**   My daughter Anna is ... years old.

7. **Ich trage Kleidergröße vierzig und Schuhgröße neununddreißig.**   I take size ... in clothes and shoe size ...

8. **Ich wiege dreiundfünfzig Kilo und bin ein Meter sechzig groß.**   I weigh ... kilos and am ... tall.

9. **Ich verdiene zweitausend dreihundert Mark im Monat.**   I earn ... Marks a month.

Now try to give the same information about yourself and your family.

ANSWERS

1. 48; 2. 60 19 29; 3. 43; 4. 2; 5. 18, 21; 6. 24; 7. 40, 39; 8. 53, 1 meter 60 cms; 9. 2,300.

Ordinal Numbers

INTRODUCTION
You can expect to use or hear ordinal numbers with dates, directions (floors or stories in a building, which street, room etc.), asking for tickets (1st, 2nd class), on a guided tour (which king, which century etc.) and so on.

EXPLANATION
It is important to remember that ordinal numbers are adjectives and follow the rules governing adjective endings (see p. 110). So you must know whether the noun they accompany is:
1. singular/plural;
2. **der/die/das**;
3. nominative/accusative/dative/genitive;
4. situation type 1/2/3/4.

You will usually find ordinal numbers in situation type 2 (with **der/die/das**).

HOW TO USE
Most ordinal numbers are formed quite simply from the cardinal numbers (see p. 139). The rule is: for numbers from 1–19 add **-te** to the cardinal number; from 20 upward add **-ste** to the cardinal number.

However, there are one or two exceptions. Just as in English, *one* does not become *oneth*, so in German you have:

erste	first
zweite	second
dritte	third

Numbers involving **sieben** are shortened: **sieb** + ending.

1st	**erste**
2nd	**zweite**
3rd	**dritte**
4th	**vierte**
5th	**fünfte**
6th	**sechste**
7th	**siebte**
8th	**achte**
9th	**neunte**
10th	**zehnte**

11th	**elfte**
12th	**zwölfte**
13th	**dreizehnte**
14th	**vierzehnte**
20th	**zwanzigste**
21st	**einundzwanzigste**
22nd	**zweiundzwanzigste**
30th	**dreißigste**
99th	**neunundneunzigste**
100th	**hundertste**

LEARN BY HEART

Here are some examples you will see, hear or use yourself.

(In a guided tour)

written form	spoken form	English
Heinrich VIII.	**Heinrich der Achte.**	Henry the Eighth.
Das Schloß wurde von Ludwig II erbaut.	**Das Schloß wurde von Ludwig dem Zweiten erbaut.**	The castle was built by Ludwig the Second.

(In a hotel or store)

Ihr Zimmer ist im 5. Stock/ in der 5. Etage.	**Ihr Zimmer ist im fünften Stock/ in der fünften Etage.**	Your room is on the fifth floor.
Die Schuhabteilung ist im 3. Stock.	**Die Schuhabteilung ist im dritten Stock.**	The shoe department is on the third floor.

(Tickets)

Einmal 2. Klasse bitte.	**Einmal zweite Klasse bitte.**	One second class ticket please.

(Dates)

Wir kommen vom 28. April–15 Mai.	**Wir kommen vom achtundzwanzigsten April bis zum fünfzehnten Mai.**	We're coming from the 28th of April to the 15th of May.

Notice that when you write the short form **1. Stock** etc. you must put a period after the number. There is no short ending to correspond with our 1*st*, 2*nd* etc.

Dates

EXPLANATION
There are four things you need to know before you can say or understand dates in German:
1. days of the week (see p.151);
2. months (see p.152);
3. ordinal numbers (see p.144);
4. years.

HOW TO USE
1. To say today's date, use **sein** (to be) + **der** + **-e** ending. When using ordinal numbers, remember that they are adjectives and take endings. If you want to say: 'Today's the 15th of June', the date is nominative after the verb **sein** (see p.82). So you say: **Heute ist der fünfzehnte Juni.**

2. For dates in letters, with signatures etc. use **den** + **-en** ending (= accusative). There are several ways of writing the date but they are all spoken the same way:

written: **den 27. April 1982**
       den 27.04.82
spoken: **den siebenundzwanzigsten April neunzehnhundertzweiundachtzig.**

Sometimes instead of **April** you will also hear **vierten** (= 4th month): **den siebenundzwanzigsten vierten**. There is no word for *of* as in 'the fifth *of* June'. Remember always to put a period after the number.

3. The way to say *on* a certain date is **am** + **-en** ending (=dative).

am zweiten Januar	on the second of January
am sechsten Mai	on the sixth of May

The way to say *from* one date *to* another is **vom** + **-en** ending, **bis zum** + **-en** ending.

Ich möchte ein Zimmer vom zehnten August bis zum ersten September.	I'd like a room from the 10th of August to the 1st of September.
Ich bin vom vierten siebten bis zum zwanzigsten siebten im Urlaub.	I'm on vacation from the 4th to the 20th of July.

4. Years

1926 = **neunzehnhundertsechsundzwanzig**

1955 = **neunzehnhundertfünfundfünfzig**

It's quite easy. Split the year into two parts and say **hundert** in the middle.

Important: when talking about years in dates, don't add *in*. In English we say: 'I was born *in* 1953'. In German it is: **Ich bin 1953 geboren.**

PRACTICE/LEARN BY HEART

Now write down some information about yourself, using days, months and years in full, e.g. when your birthday is; when you're going on vacation; when you started learning German etc.

Time

INTRODUCTION

Time is one area where you can't get away with bluffing. You have to make sure you have understood exactly what the other person has said, so if you are in any doubt ask them to repeat it, write it down, or even say it in English:

Könnten Sie das bitte { wiederholen? aufschreiben? auf Englisch sagen? }   Could you please { repeat that? write it down? say it in English? }

And if you still don't understand, say so!

Es tut mir leid, ich verstehe nicht.   Sorry, I don't understand.

HOW TO USE

You need to be able to use and understand:

1. The everyday expressions of time used in conversation.

Question: **Wie spät ist es?** **Wieviel Uhr ist es?** }   What time is it?

Answer: **Es ist …**   It's …

Uhr = o'clock

Zehn Uhr   10 o'clock

Acht Uhr   8 o'clock

Viertel vor = a quarter to

Viertel vor eins   A quarter to one

Viertel nach = a quarter after

Viertel nach sieben   A quarter after seven

Notice that **Viertel** has a capital letter because it is a noun.

halb = half. Warning! **halb** needs special attention. Always stop and think when someone says **halb**:

Es ist halb *elf*.   It is half past *ten*.   10:30

Germans say it is 'half way towards eleven o'clock', while in English we think of it as being half way after ten o'clock. We are both correct, but express the idea differently.

Here are some more examples:

Es ist halb neun.	It is half past eight.	8:30
Es ist halb zwei.	It is half past one.	1:30

Now you try:
1. **Es ist halb eins.** ....
2. **Es ist halb elf.** ....
3. **Es ist halb acht.** ....
4. **Es ist halb zwölf.** ....

Other times

Vor = before   **nach** = after, past

Es ist zwanzig Minuten vor neun.	It is twenty to nine.
Es ist elf Minuten vor zehn.	It is eleven minutes to ten.
Es ist zehn Minuten nach acht.	It is ten after eight.
Es ist dreizehn Minuten nach drei.	It is thirteen minutes after three.

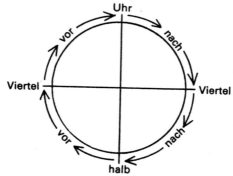

Question:	**Um wieviel Uhr?** ⎱	When?
	Wann? ⎰	
Answer:	**Um** + time	at ...
	um zwanzig vor zehn	at twenty to ten
	um halb sechs	at half past five
	um Viertel nach zwölf	at a quarter after twelve

ANSWERS
1. 12.30   2. 10.30   3. 7.30   4. 11.30

PRACTICE

Fill in the time:

1. **Ich komme um zwanzig vor acht.**   I'll be there at ...
2. **Ich komme um halb zehn.**   I'll be there at ...
3. **Ich komme um zehn nach sieben.**   I'll be there at ...
4. **Ich komme um Viertel vor zwei.**   I'll be there at ...
5. **Ich komme um halb eins.**   I'll be there at ...
6. **Ich komme um neun Minuten vor elf.**   I'll be there at ...

If you use this system it is sometimes not clear whether **acht Uhr** means 8 o'clock in the morning or in the evening. In this case you will need to use the '24-hour clock', which is used in stations and airports, and timetables. (The 'speaking-clock' is used for opening and closing times, performances, etc.).

24-hour clock	written	English
zwanzig Uhr	20.00 Uhr	8:00 p.m.
neun Uhr	9.00 Uhr	9:00 a.m.
siebzehn Uhr zehn	17.10 Uhr	5:10 p.m.
neunzehn Uhr dreißig	19.30 Uhr	7:30 p.m.
vierzehn Uhr fünfundvierzig	14.45 Uhr	2:45 p.m.
vierzehn Uhr fünfzig	14.50 Uhr	2:50 p.m.
sechszehn Uhr fünfundzwanzig	16.25 Uhr	4:25 p.m.

Now cover up the spoken forms and practice saying the time aloud.

Today, tomorrow, yesterday

If today (**heute**) is the 25th of January, the 24th was **gestern** and the 26th is **morgen**.

Jan 23.	**vorgestern**	the day before yesterday
Jan 24.	**gestern**	yesterday
Jan 25.	**heute**	today
Jan 26.	**morgen**	tomorrow
Jan 27.	**übermorgen**	the day after tomorrow

ANSWERS

1. twenty to eight 2. half past nine 3. ten after seven 4. a quarter to two 5. half past twelve 6. nine minutes to eleven

You can combine these expressions with the parts of the day to specify times:

morgen abend	tomorrow evening
heute morgen	this morning
gestern nachmittag	yesterday afternoon
vorgestern abend	the evening before yesterday
heute mittag	today at lunchtime

Although **morgen** means both 'tomorrow' and 'morning', it is nearly always clear which is meant. You never say **morgen morgen**. 'Tomorrow morning' is expressed by the phrase **morgen früh**.

PRACTICE

Someone is suggesting times when you could meet. Write down the English equivalent.

1. **morgen früh um acht Uhr**
2. **morgen nachmittag um Viertel nach zwei**
3. **übermorgen um zwanzig Uhr fünfundvierzig**
4. **heute abend um halb sieben**
5. **morgen abend um zwanzig vor zehn**
6. **heute nachmittag um drei**

Days of the week

The difficult ones to remember are **Dienstag** and **Donnerstag**, so give them some extra attention.

Day	Abbreviation	English
Sonntag	So.	Sunday
Montag	Mo.	Monday
Dienstag	Di.	Tuesday
Mittwoch	Mi.	Wednesday
Donnerstag	Do.	Thursday
Freitag	Fr.	Friday
Samstag (Sonnabend) }	Sa.	Saturday

ANSWERS

1. 8:00 a.m. tomorrow morning 2. 2:15 tomorrow afternoon 3. 8:45 p.m. the day after tomorrow 4. half past six this evening 5. 9:40 p.m. tomorrow evening 6. 3:00 p.m. this afternoon

Months
Januar, Februar, März, April, Mai, Juni, Juli, August, September, Oktober, November, Dezember.

Sometimes, especially on the phone, it is not clear whether someone has said **Juni** or **Juli**, so you pronounce them: **Juni** ('yoonee' to rhyme with 'see'), **Juli** ('yooly' to rhyme with 'sky').

im Juni   in June

Wordbuilding

INTRODUCTION

If you like playing with words or you want to have a clearer insight into the system behind German word formation, it is worth spending some time reading this section. It will help you:

1. To decode the seemingly endless long words in German. If you regard these as a challenge, you will really enjoy breaking them down and figuring out their meaning. You will discover that you have unlocked a very powerful door.

2. To make up your own German words. You'll never be stuck for words again! Try taking an English word, add a suitable prefix or ending, and make it sound German. More often than not, people will understand you. They may even marvel at your sophisticated vocabulary!

EXPLANATION

The first group of words we look at are *nouns*.

1. You can put two nouns together:

Zehnmarkschein	a ten Mark note
Gepäckannahme	luggage registration/baggage room
Wetterbericht	weather report
Studentenausweis	student ID card

In English we put two nouns together as well, but we still write them as separate words. The only difference with German is that the words are all written together in one word. If you write two nouns together in German, the last noun determines which **der/die/das** group the whole word belongs to: **Stadtzentrum = die Stadt + das Zentrum**, so **das Stadtzentrum**.

So, be bold! If you find yourself writing **Winter Sport** in German, – write them as one word! **Wintersport**. It looks so much more German.

2. You can connect a verb and a noun:

Wartezimmer	waiting room
Kochtopf	cooking pot

3. You can connect an adjective and a noun:

Großstadt	big town
Rotwein	red wine
Weißwein	white wine

4. There are all sorts of prefixes you can tack onto the beginning of nouns. Here are some of the most useful:

Haupt- (= main)	**Hauptbahnhof**	main train station
	Hauptsaison	high season
	Haupteingang	main entrance
Neben- (= less important)	**Nebenstraße**	side street
	Nebensaison	low season
Sonder- (= special)	**Sonderangebot**	special offer
	Sonderfahrt	special trip
Lieblings- (= favorite)	**Lieblingskuchen**	favorite cake
	Lieblingsfarbe	favorite color
	Lieblingsessen	favorite food
Außen- (= outside)	**Außenpolitik**	foreign policy
	Außentemperatur	temperature outside
	Außenminister	Foreign Minister
Innen- (= inside)	**Innenpolitik**	domestic policy
	Innenraum	inside space
	Innenminister	Minister for Home Affairs
Nord- (= North)	**Norddeutschland**	North Germany
Süd- (= South)	**Südwestengland**	Southwest England etc.
West- (= West)		
Ost- (= East)		
Gesamt- (= total)	**Gesamtbetrag**	total amount
	Gesamtzahl	total number
	Gesamtpreis	total price
Höchst- (= maximum)	**Höchstpreis**	maximum price
	Höchstgeschwindigkeit	maximum speed limit
	Höchsttemperatur	maximum temperature
Mindest- (= minimum)	**Mindestpreis**	lowest price
	Mindestalter	minimum age

Not- (= emergency)	**Notstand**	state of emergency
	Notfall	emergency case
	Notarzt	emergency doctor
Fern- (= long	**Fernseher**	television
distance)	**Fernsprecher**	telephone
	Ferngespräch	long distance call

You will have noticed that German seems to specialize in very long words like: **Lebensmittelabteilung, Geschirrspülmaschine, Frühstücksteller, Anmeldeformular** etc. This all looks very intimidating at first, but once you know the simple rules it becomes much clearer.

Next time you see a long word, remember that it can be broken down into smaller units. Take **Lebensmittelabteilung**. **Abteilung** = department, **Leben** = life, **Mittel** = means. So it's the 'department for the means of life', which is the grocery department.
Geschirrspülmaschine. **Geschirr** = crockery, **spülen** = to wash, rinse, **Maschine** = machine. So it's a dishwasher.
Frühstücksteller. **Teller** = plate, **früh** = early, **Stück** = bit, piece, **Früstück** = breakfast. So it's a breakfast plate.
Anmeldeformular. **Anmelden** = to register, **Formular** = a form. So it's a registration form.
Here are a few more for you to try.
1. **Staubsauger**   4. **Fernsehapparat**   6. **Rasierklinge**
2. **Mittagessen**   5. **Autobahngaststätte**
3. **Zimmervermittlung**
So you see it can be fun! Next time you see a long German word, don't cringe. Regard it as a challenge and see if you can crack the code. And remember – you can have a try at making your own long words too.

Adjectives can also be put together:

hellblau	light blue
dunkelrot	dark red
schwarzweiß	black and white (photos etc.)

ANSWERS
1. vacuum cleaner 2. lunch 3. hotel reservations office 4. television
5. restaurant on a superhighway 6. razor blade

Verbs

Here are some very common prefixes for verbs:

ab-	= away
abmachen	undo
abnehmen	take away, lose weight
auf-	= up
aufsteigen	climb up
aufstellen	put up, (e.g. tent etc.)
auf-	= open
aufmachen	to open
aufdrehen	to unscrew
aufschließen	to open
aus-	= movement out
ausgehen	to go out
aussteigen	to get out of vehicle
durch-	= through
durchgehen, durchfahren	to go through
ein-	= movement in
einlaufen	to shrink
einwerfen	to mail (literally 'throw in')
einsteigen	to get in (vehicle)
her-	= towards the speaker and away from somewhere else
herbringen	to bring over here
herholen	to bring from somewhere else etc.
hin-	= away from you and towards something else
hinlaufen	to go towards something
hinlegen	to put something down over there
hinhängen	to hang something up over there
mit-	= with
mitfahren	to get a ride
mitnehmen	to take away with you etc.
vorbei-	= past
vorbeigehen, vorbeifahren	to go past
weg-	= away
wegwerfen	to throw away
weggehen	to go away
weiter-	= farther on – direction

weitergehen, weiterfahren	to keep going
weiter-	= continue doing something
weitermachen	to continue doing
wieder-	= again
wiedersehen	to see again
wiederholen	to repeat
wiederhören	to hear again
wieder-	= back
wiederkommen	to come back
wiedergeben	to give back
zurück-	= back
zurückfahren	to go back
zurückkommen	to come back
zurückrufen	to call back (phone etc.)
zu-	= closed
zumachen	to close
zudrehen	to screw shut

Word endings

1. Nouns

-in for female jobs, nationality:

Reiseleiterin	female tour guide
Studentin	female student
Engländerin	lady from England

-er for male jobs, nationality:

Bäcker	baker
Politiker	politician
Amerikaner	man from America
Berliner	man from Berlin etc.

-chen and **-lein** for a small version of something:

Brot	bread
Brötchen	bread roll
Paket	package, pack
Päkchen	small package
Buch	book
Büchlein	booklet

-ei for stores, places of work, etc.

Bäckerei	bakery
Metzgerei	butcher shop
Molkerei	dairy

(added to an adjective) **-heit**:

Sicherheit	safety
Schönheit	beauty

(added to an adjective) **-keit**:

Möglichkeit	possibility

(added to an adjective) **-igkeit**:

Müdigkeit	fatigue
Arbeitslosigkeit	unemployment
Geschwindigkeit	speed

(derived from a verb) **-ung**:

Mitteilung	message
Anmeldung	reception desk
Rechnung	bill
Störung	fault, disturbance

2. Adjectives

Noun + **-lich**:

freundlich	friendly
wissenschaftlich	scientific
jährlich	annual

Noun + **-ig** (similar to '-y' in English):

salzig	salty
durstig	thirsty
giftig	poisonous

Noun + **isch** for nationality:

österreichisch	Austrian
griechisch	Greek
europäisch	European

Noun + **-los** (similar to '-less' in English):

arbeitslos unemployed (literally 'without work')

hoffnungslos hopeless

problemlos without problem

Verb + **-bar** (similar to '-able' in English):

machbar feasible

waschbar washable

eßbar edible

un- + adj. (negative)

ungenießbar inedible

unmöglich impossible

ungesund unhealthy

3. Verbs

If you're stuck for a verb in German, take the English word, add **-ieren**, and give it a strong German pronunciation. More often than not, people will understand you or tell you the real German word for it.

studieren study

spezialisieren specialize

organisieren organize

telefonieren telephone

diskutieren discuss

profitieren profit

diktieren dictate

kritisieren criticize

PRACTICE

Here are some signs which you will come across in German streets, train stations, on buses etc., which might have baffled you up to now. See if you can figure them out.

1. KEINE DURCHFAHRT
2. BAHNHOFSMISSION
3. NICHTRAUCHER
4. STADTRUNDFAHRT
5. REISEZUGAUSKUNFT
6. ABFAHRT DER FERNZÜGE
7. EINBAHNSTRASSE
8. NOTAUSSTIEG
9. SPEISEWAGEN
10. SCHLIESSFÄCHER
11. MIETWAGEN
12. NICHT EINSTEIGEN
13. HALTESTELLE
14. VERKEHRSAMT

Next time you are in Germany, make your own list of signs. You'll be surprised how much more you understand about your surroundings.

ANSWERS
1. Dead-end Street 2. Traveler's Aid Station 3. Non-Smoking 4. City Tour 5. Train Information 6. Departures, long-distance trains 7. One-way Street 8. Emergency Exit 9. Dining Car 10. Luggage Lockers 11. Car Rental 12. Do not get on 13. Bus Stop 14. Tourist Office

Grammar patterns

The following is an overview of German grammar endings to help you see the patterns.

1. masculine

	the	who?	he/him it	a	your	no	endings
Nom.	der	wer?	er	ein	Ihr	kein	-r or none
Acc.	den	wen?	ihn	einen	Ihren	keinen	-n
Dat.	dem	wem?	ihm	einem	Ihrem	keinem	-m

2. feminine

	the	she/her it	a	your	no	endings
Nom.	die	sie	eine	Ihre	keine	-e
Acc.	die	sie	eine	Ihre	keine	-e
Dat.	der	ihr	einer	Ihrer	keiner	-r

3. neuter

	the	it	a	your	no	endings
Nom.	das	es	ein	Ihr	kein	-s or none
Acc.	das	es	ein	Ihr	kein	-s or none
Dat.	dem	ihm	einem	Ihrem	keinem	-m

4. plural

	the	they/them	your	no	endings
Nom.	die	sie	Ihre	keine	**-e**
Acc.	die	sie	Ihre	keine	**-e**
Dat.	den	ihnen	Ihren	keinen	**-n**

The sign of the nominative is -**r** or -**e** or no ending.
The sign of the accusative is -**n** for **der** words, -**e** for **die** words, no ending for **das** words.
The sign of the dative is -**m** for **der/das** words, -**r** for **die** words, -**n** for plural.

Can you see that the pattern of endings is the same for the words in each group? Learn the pattern, then you won't have to remember every single ending separately.

Verbs
Minimum endings to learn which will help you in most tenses.

ich	-**e**	**wir/sie/Sie**	-**en**
er/sie/es	-**t**		

Appendix

Strong verbs

Infinitive	English	Present	Imperfect	Perfect
bekommen	to get	bekommt	bekam	hat bekommen
bieten	to offer	bietet	bot	hat geboten
bitten	to ask	bittet	bat	hat gebeten
bleiben	to stay	bleibt	blieb	ist geblieben
brechen	to break	bricht	brach	hat gebrochen
empfehlen	to recommend	empfiehlt	empfahl	hat empfohlen
essen	to eat	ißt	aß	hat gegessen
fahren	to drive	fährt	fuhr	ist gefahren
fallen	to fall	fällt	fiel	ist gefallen
finden	to find	findet	fand	hat gefunden
fliegen	to fly	fliegt	flog	ist geflogen
geben	to give	gibt	gab	hat gegeben
gefallen	to please	gefällt	gefiel	hat gefallen
gewinnen	to win	gewinnt	gewann	hat gewonnen
halten	to stop	hält	hielt	hat gehalten
heißen	to call	heißt	hieß	hat geheißen
helfen	to help	hilft	half	hat geholfen
kommen	to come	kommt	kam	ist gekommen
lassen	to let	läßt	ließ	hat gelassen
laufen	to run	läuft	lief	ist gelaufen
leihen	to lend	leiht	lieh	hat geliehen
lesen	to read	liest	las	hat gelesen
liegen	to lie	liegt	lag	hat gelegen

Infinitive	English	Present	Imperfect	Perfect
nehmen	to take	nimmt	nahm	hat genommen
riechen	to smell	riecht	roch	hat gerochen
rufen	to call	ruft	rief	hat gerufen
scheinen	to shine	scheint	schien	hat geschienen
schlafen	to sleep	schläft	schlief	hat geschlafen
schneiden	to cut	schneidet	schnitt	hat geschnitten
schreiben	to write	schreibt	schrieb	hat geschrieben
schwimmen	to swim	schwimmt	schwamm	ist geschwommen
sehen	to see	sieht	sah	hat gesehen
singen	to sing	singt	sang	hat gesungen
sitzen	to sit	sitzt	saß	hat gesessen
sprechen	to speak	spricht	sprach	hat gesprochen
stehlen	to steal	stiehlt	stahl	hat gestohlen
steigen	to climb	steigt	stieg	ist gestiegen
sterben	to die	stirbt	starb	ist gestorben
tragen	to carry	trägt	trug	hat getragen
treffen	to meet	trifft	traf	hat getroffen
trinken	to drink	trinkt	trank	hat getrunken
vergessen	to forget	vergißt	vergaß	hat vergessen
vergleichen	to compare	vergleicht	verglich	hat verglichen
verlieren	to lose	verliert	verlor	hat verloren
waschen	to wash	wäscht	wusch	hat gewaschen
werfen	to throw	wirft	warf	hat geworfen
ziehen	to pull	zieht	zog	hat gezogen

Special verbs – *sein, haben, werden*

Sein (to be)
In many languages the verb 'to be' is different from all the rest. **Sein** has irregular forms:

Present tense	ich bin	wir sind
	du bist	ihr seid
	er ist	sie sind
Imperative	sei (du)	seid (ihr)
	seien Sie	
Imperfect	ich war	wir waren
Perfect	ich bin gewesen	
Pluperfect	ich war gewesen	
Subjunctive	ich wäre	wir wären

Haben (to have)
Haben is more regular than **sein**:

Present tense	ich habe	wir haben
	du hast	ihr habt
	er hat	sie haben
Imperative	hab (du)	habt (ihr)
	haben Sie	
Imperfect	ich hatte	wir hatten
Perfect	ich habe gehabt	
Pluperfect	ich hatte gehabt	
Subjunctive	ich hätte	wir hätten

Werden

Present tense	ich werde	wir werden
	du wirst	ihr werdet
	er wird	sie werden
Imperfect	ich wurde	wir wurden
Perfect	ich bin geworden	
Pluperfect	ich war geworden	
Subjunctive	ich würde	wir würden

Werden has four very different uses.
1. = to become, followed by a noun or adjective.

2. to form the passive (see p.47).
Werden here has no meaning of its own. Its function is merely to help form the passive. Notice that there are no umlauts.

3. to form the future tense (see p.25).
Again, **werden** is purely an auxiliary verb, helping another verb to form the future tense.

4. = would (see p.45).
Use **würde/würden** + the infinitive of the second verb, which goes at the end of the sentence.

Glossary of grammar terms

ACCUSATIVE The accusative case describes the role that a noun or pronoun is playing in a particular sentence. Nouns and pronouns are in the accusative case if they are on the receiving end of the verb (=direct object) and also after certain other words and expressions. (See p.84.)

ADJECTIVE An adjective describes a noun. Words like 'pretty', 'big', 'thick', 'thin', 'easy' etc. are adjectives. (See p.110.)

ADVERB An adverb is a word that describes a verb or action. 'Slowly', 'well', 'beautifully', 'often', 'sometimes' etc. are adverbs. (See p.119.)

AUXILIARY VERBS These are verbs that help other verbs form a particular tense. For example, you use **haben** to help form the perfect tense (see p.18) and **werden** to help form the passive. (See p.47.)

CLAUSE A clause is a part of a sentence that contains a verb. If it can stand on its own, it is called a main clause. If it can not stand on its own, it is called a subordinate clause.

'I went to bed'	is a main clause.
'When I went to bed'	is a subordinate clause.

CONJUNCTION This is a word like 'and', 'but', 'so' etc. which joins two parts of a sentence together. (See p.73.)

DATIVE The dative case describes the role of a noun or pronoun in a particular sentence. The dative is used when you want to say 'to/from a person' (=indirect object) and also after certain words and expressions. (See p.88.)

DEFINITE ARTICLE = 'the'. (See p.94.)

DIRECT OBJECT A noun or pronoun is the direct object of a verb if it is on the receiving end of the action. Normally, the direct object comes after the verb in English, e.g. 'I ate an apple' – *an apple* is the direct object.

FUTURE TENSE describes actions that have not yet taken place. (See p.25.)

GENITIVE = possessive. You use the genitive case to translate English apostrophe 's or 'of'. (See p.92.)

IMPERATIVE = commands, orders. (See p.42.)

IMPERFECT TENSE is used for descriptive passages and incomplete action in the past. (See p.17.)

INDEFINITE ARTICLE = 'a'/'an'. (See p.97.)

INDIRECT OBJECT A noun or pronoun is an indirect object when it is not directly on the receiving end of the verb, e.g. 'I gave *her* a bunch of flowers' – *her* = *to her* and is an indirect object. (See p.88.)

INFINITIVE is the reference form of the verb that you find in word lists and dictionaries. The English infinitive always has 'to' in front of it – 'to do', 'to see' etc.

NOMINATIVE A noun or pronoun is nominative if it is the subject of the verb, i.e. if it is performing the action. (See p.81.)

NOUN Words for people, places and things are nouns. 'Pen', 'book', 'man', 'church', 'Berlin' etc. are all nouns. (See p.75.)

OBJECT See DIRECT OBJECT and INDIRECT OBJECT.

PASSIVE This is a special form of the verb that concentrates on the action being performed, rather than on the person performing the action, e.g. 'He *has been injured*'; 'The ball *was lost*.' (See p.47.)

PAST PARTICIPLE In English, this is the '-ed' or '-en' form of the verb, e.g. 'talked', 'eaten', 'drunk' etc. (See p.19.)

PERFECT TENSE This form of the verb describes an action that happened in the past. (See p.18.)

PERSON = 'I', 'you', 'he', 'she', 'it'. (See p.13.)

PLUPERFECT TENSE This form of the verb describes an action that happened a stage further back in the past than the perfect or imperfect tense. (See p.24.)

POSSESSIVE ADJECTIVE = 'my', 'your', 'his', 'her' etc. (See p.120.)

PREPOSITIONS are words like 'to', 'for', 'with' etc. (See p.126.)

PRONOUN e.g. 'I', 'you', 'he', 'she', 'it' etc. A pronoun is a word that refers to a person or thing. It is often used in place of a noun. (See p.99.)

SUBJECT A noun or pronoun is the subject of the verb when it is initiating the action, e.g. '*He* played football' – *He* is the subject of the verb 'played'. In English, the subject usually comes before the verb. (See p.81.)

SUBJUNCTIVE This is a special form of the verb used to describe actions that are in some way tentative, unreal, uncertain. The English words 'would', 'could' are usually reliable indicators for using the subjunctive. (See p.44.)

SUBORDINATE CLAUSE See CLAUSE.

TENSE Tense is the form of the verb that indicates *when* the action took/takes/will take place. (See p.13.)

VERB Words like 'eat', 'do', 'sit', 'stay' etc. that describe actions, states, position etc. are verbs. The verb is the focal point of every sentence. (See p.12.)

Index

FOREIGN LANGUAGE BOOKS

Multilingual
The Insult Dictionary:
  How to Give 'Em Hell in 5 Nasty
  Languages
The Lover's Dictionary:
  How to be Amorous in 5 Delectable
  Languages
Multilingual Phrase Book
Let's Drive Europe Phrasebook
CD-ROM "Languages of the World":
  Multilingual Dictionary Database

Spanish
Vox Spanish and English Dictionaries
The Spanish Businessmate
Nice 'n Easy Spanish Grammar
Spanish Verbs and Essentials of Grammar
Getting Started in Spanish
Spanish à la Cartoon
Guide to Spanish Idioms
Guide to Correspondence in Spanish
The Hispanic Way

French
NTC's New College French and English
  Dictionary
French Verbs and Essentials of Grammar
Getting Started in French
Guide to French Idioms
Guide to Correspondence in French
The French Businessmate
French à la Cartoon
Nice 'n Easy French Grammar
NTC's Dictionary of *Faux Amis*
NTC's Dictionary of Canadian French
Au courant: Expressions for Communicating
  in Everyday French

German
Schöffler-Weis German and English
  Dictionary
Klett German and English Dictionary
Getting Started in German
German Verbs and Essentials of Grammar
Guide to German Idioms
The German Businessmate
Nice 'n Easy German Grammar
German à la Cartoon
NTC's Dictionary of German False Cognates

Italian
Zanichelli New College Italian and English
  Dictionary
Getting Started in Italian
Italian Verbs and Essentials of Grammar

Greek
NTC's New College Greek and English
  Dictionary

Latin
Essentials of Latin Grammar

Hebrew
Everyday Hebrew

Chinese
Easy Chinese Phrasebook and Dictionary

Korean
Korean in Plain English

Swedish
Swedish Verbs and Essentials of Grammar

Russian
Complete Handbook of Russian Verbs
Essentials of Russian Grammar
Business Russian
Basic Structure Practice in Russian

Japanese
Easy Kana Workbook
Easy Hiragana
Easy Katakana
Japanese in Plain English
Everyday Japanese
Japanese for Children
Japanese Cultural Encounters
Nissan's Business Japanese

"Just Enough" Phrase Books
Chinese, Dutch, French, German, Greek,
  Italian, Japanese, Portuguese, Russian,
  Scandinavian, Serbo-Croat, Spanish

Audio and Video Language Programs
Just Listen 'n Learn Spanish, French,
  German, Italian, and Greek
Just Listen 'n Learn...Spanish,
  French, German PLUS
Conversational...Spanish, French, German,
  Italian, Russian, Greek, Japanese, Thai,
  Portuguese in 7 Days
Practice & Improve Your...Spanish,
  French, Italian, and German
Practice & Improve Your...Spanish,
  French, Italian, and German PLUS
VideoPassport French
VideoPassport Spanish
How to Pronounce...Spanish, French,
  German, Italian, Russian, Japanese
  Correctly

PASSPORT BOOKS
a division of *NTC Publishing Group*
4255 West Touhy Avenue
Lincolnwood, Illinois 60646-1975